Forgotten Dreams

By

Georgia Wright

First Edition

First Printing: February 14, 2012

ISBN: 978-0-9825279-1-7

Dedication

To my precious, loving husband,
who helped me learn how to enjoy
one of God's most intimate gifts.

And to 'Anne Wright,'
the first published book author in our family,
who inspired me and gave me courage.

And to our loving Creator,
who gave us the gift of sex.

"To him who is able to do more
than all we ask or imagine …
to him be the glory!"

About Intimate Press

Intimate Press is a publisher of Christian-oriented books with sexual themes, such as *Grandma's Sex Handbook*, or sexual issues, such as Christian novels that include moral lessons interwoven with Christian stories that involve sexual aspects of character and relationship development, presented in a tasteful manner.

Intimate Press novels are intended to celebrate sex within marriage from a Christian perspective, and thereby give readers stories to expand their knowledge and stimulate their imaginations for their own lives, marriages, and sexual activities. The inclusion of sexuality in a Christian inspirational romance is based on the principles described in *Grandma's Sex Handbook*, especially the principle that sexual fantasy is different from lust. The Publisher's Foreword addresses this issue in more detail.

Intimate Press novels' characters are always fictitious, but some story elements and places cited may be based on real events and places. "Based on" means they are not exactly as described in the novel. Our novels also substitute "xx-xx-xx" for words and phrases that are spoken harshly or in a derogatory manner.

Warning: Intimate Press novels include sexually explicit language and mature themes and are intended only for mature readers.

Publisher's Foreword

Publishing a novel that combines Christianity and sexually explicit descriptions in a novel is unusual enough to require some explanation. While Thomas Hardy's *Jude the Obscure* may have been the first work of Christian fiction to be attacked for including sexual themes (in addition to being attacked for other themes), it was not sexually explicit. Nevertheless, it was considered outrageous by many, and was so fiercely condemned that Hardy decided not to write any more novels.

Why then, publish a novel mixing Christianity and sexuality? Because novels are an excellent way to educate people, and not many people spend their evenings contemplating the Greek influence on St. Augustine's treatises on marriage. People like stories, and though many are intended for entertainment only, there's no reason that stories can't be informative and sometimes thought-provoking, in addition to being entertaining. Due to the dual-nature of the content, Intimate Press novels have two purposes: If read by non-Christians who are interested only because of the sexual aspects of the stories, they may learn more about Christianity than they otherwise would; When read by Christians, they may gain ideas that can help them improve their own or their spouse's sexual satisfaction, or they may learn ways to cope with serious sexual problems.

As counter-intuitive as it might seem, we believe sexually explicit Christian novels will be worthwhile if there are some people who can benefit from them without harming anyone else. Intimate Press, therefore, strives to provide stories that have the potential to benefit at least some people, without harming anyone else.

In 1923, the reverend Herbert Gray wrote in the introduction to his explicit *Men, Women, and God,*

> "In the following pages, I propose to write simply and plainly about the social, personal, and bodily relations of men and women, and about the ways in which their common life may attain to happiness, harmony, and efficiency... I do it all on the basis of one assumption, namely, that a God of love in designing our human nature cannot have put into it anything

which is incapable of a pure and happy exercise; and in particular that in making the sex interest so central, permanent, and powerful in human beings He must have had some great and beautiful purpose... And yet even as I write the word 'sexual' I cannot but remember that the mere word will for many good people produce a sensation of distaste. Partly because they have a sincere passion for purity, and partly because this whole subject has been defiled for them by the excesses and indecencies of mankind, they doubt whether it can be right or useful to think about it at all. They regard the facts of sex with a mixture of fear, perplexity, and shame, and take themselves to task if still some curiosity about them lingers in their minds. Therefore before I go any further I would like to ask such people to realize that they are denying my initial assumption. They have not yet come to believe that there is any divine and holy purpose enshrined in the sexual side of life, although God is responsible for its place in our humanity; and I would beg them forthwith to think this matter out."

Likewise, the reverend Oscar Lowry wrote in *A Virtuous Woman*, published by Zondervan in 1938, that "some earnest Christians may feel that it is presumptuous and altogether out of place for a minister of the gospel to be dealing with sex life in the plain manner in which it is handled in the following pages." But he then asks "why should a minister of the gospel seek to be more nice than God, or modest than Jesus Christ and the Apostles who used the plainest possible language when dealing with the various phases of sex life." He concludes that in order to declare the *whole* counsel of God (Acts 20), the declarations must include the topic of sex, and thus he was compelled to pen his rather explicit book.

Perhaps the most common objection to a sexually explicit novel from a Christian perspective would be based on the issue of lust. We believe this issue is resolved in *Grandma's Sex Handbook*, which presents a strong case that sexual fantasy is not the same thing as lust. Until we published that book, it seemed almost universally thought that any sexual thoughts other than those for a person's spouse constituted the sin of lust, and therefore all literature that prompted fantasy sexual thoughts were harmful. Now recognizing the distinction between fantasy and lust, however, we believe it is acceptable for a Christian work of fiction to explicitly describe physical interactions between a loving husband and wife. For Christians, any sexual arousal that may be prompted by such fantasy will be fulfilled within their marriage, and happily so.

We believe that God gave us both imagination and sexual desire, and that the two can be perfectly compatible and help us grow into maturity in Christ. Most people enjoy good stories that are well-told, because they are entertaining, thought-provoking, and more. While many people may simply want to enjoy stories, people also usually learn something from them, and Intimate Press stories purposefully strive to provide satisfaction on all counts. We hope you enjoy this story, and that it entertains you, causes you to think, and helps you grow in your Christian faith and in your marriage.

We welcome your feedback, even if it's negative, as long as it is constructive and given in a kindly spirit. You may provide feedback at www.IntimatePress.com.

Editor's Note

Though my task was to polish, it was impossible to edit without getting involved in the story, and I love this story. The characters are well-written, the plot is interesting, and I love the way Georgia included so many details without getting the storytelling bogged down in them, and the interesting way she combined romance with drama.

Yeah, I'm a guy, but I've long been a big fan of Grace Livingston Hill's books, and this story has some similar characteristics, though the GLH books I've read were never sexually explicit, and always presented the Gospel of Christ explicitly. Maybe it was just the ones I happened to read (she wrote well over a hundred from 1877 to 1949), but the GLH books I've read focused on young women, and I like the fact that *Forgotten Dreams* features a woman in her fifties. Maybe that's because I'm in my fifties.

I was embarrassed to edit *Grandma's Sex Handbook*, but was even more embarrassed while editing this novel. However, as Anne Wright said in her family's handbook, "God invented sex. He's not surprised by it, and he's not embarrassed by it." That seems consistent with the large amount of rather explicit sex in the Bible (e.g. Ezekiel 23:20), so I've been trying to adapt myself to God's perspective, rather than expecting him adapt to my previous perspectives.

As a result, it now seems reasonable to me that this story, including the sexually explicit elements, could help some people. I'm sure others will disagree, but if this adult-oriented approach to story-telling challenges you to think about your faith, and the proper role of sex in literature or in your life, good! The apostle Paul complimented the Christians in Berea for questioning what he said, and for examining the Scriptures for themselves to see if what Paul said was true.

I hope you come to agree that this novel is worthwhile, but more importantly, I hope you come to agree based on good reason.

John Lambert

Author's Preface

I've always been a voracious reader, and I've wanted to be a writer most of my life. Though I'd made many attempts to start novels over the years, I faltered in every case, and never even figured out what my problem was, let alone overcame it.

Then I heard about *Grandma's Sex Handbook*, a project by my extended family to compile our collective wisdom about sex for newlyweds, headed by my cousin "Anne," and I got to read early drafts of many chapters. The chapter on Fantasy vs. Lust really surprised me, and either my Grandmother didn't pass that part down to me, or I forgot it completely in the fog of getting married. When I read the detailed explanation though, I was amazed, and it really stirred me to think about it, especially in light of my recent reading activity.

Now, I enjoy reading just about every kind of novel except horror stories, but I'll stick with one genre for a year or so, get tired of that, and switch to another. As it happened, when I read the draft Fantasy vs. Lust chapter, I had been reading mostly romance novels lately. Romance novels, if you don't know, can have a level of sensuality from zero to constant, detailed sex. And I admit, though I've thrown away some of the books where a plot barely existed to provide a setting for sex, I've also secretly enjoyed some pretty spicy scenes in otherwise well-told stories. I had also worried that it wasn't a very Christian thing to do.

So after reading about the distinction between fantasy and lust, I reasoned that reading the sexual scenes in some novels was okay, as long as it didn't prompt me to want to actually cheat on my husband, since it was just imaginary fantasy. Something still bothered me, though, and then it hit me: The vast majority of the explicit sex scenes in romance novels are between unmarried couples, and they were frequently just one-night stands, or even between total strangers. Why weren't there any explicit scenes between happily married couples? I came up with an answer to that, too. Because there weren't any Christians writing explicit romance novels. But should there be?

Might God want a Christian to write a sexually explicit novel? And even if so, who would publish such a daring thing?

I asked Cousin Anne about her plans to get GSH published, and she put me in contact with John Lambert, a friend of hers who generously helped me learn about self-publishing and print-on-demand. Armed with the knowledge that I could upload a word-processing file and have the manuscript become available as a print-on-demand book for free, I started toying with the idea of trying to write again.

Based on my track record to that date, I had little reason to have any confidence in being able to complete a manuscript, but I felt compelled to try anyway. And to my astonishment, I kept writing and writing. I liked my characters. I liked my story. Somehow, the word-count kept growing. Once I got to the point in the story where my protagonist was about to get married, I had written over 70,000 words, and I was starting to get excited. I had never gotten so far, and somehow, it just felt like I was going to be able to finish this story. Whether anyone else thought it was any good was, well, another story. I know a lot of authors have written stories they think are wonderful, but no one else does. I still didn't know if I'd end up in that camp.

By this time, John's wife Carla had decided to create Intimate Press and publish *Grandma's Sex Handbook*. So, I timidly asked John if he would review what I had so far and give me his opinion. He agreed, and I waited anxiously for his first comments. I guess he liked it pretty well, because he offered me a hundred bucks to finish the story just so he could read the rest. Even if he was teasing, that was very encouraging, and he said Carla liked it as much as he did.

Although the first part John read related a character's explicit sexual thoughts, it didn't include any fictitious sexual acts yet. I actually hoped to avoid those, but the story just seemed to write itself, and it included substantial detail about the initial sexual activity of the main couple, including the middle-aged, just-remarried wife's first-ever orgasm. (For those who think that's too far-fetched, I assure you that while I hope it's uncommon, that aspect of the story accurately reflected the circumstances of a good friend of mine.) Now I was worried about what John and Carla would think of the additional material.

So, I talked to John, and he read what I had so far. Much to my relief, though he thought the additional material was pushing the envelope, he thought it was justifiable as integral to the character and plot development, and for its potential educational value. And at his suggestion, I made a few revisions that improved some important plot issues and eliminated some logical inconsistencies.

And to my delight, Carla decided she'd be willing to publish my story as the first-ever novel by Intimate Press! That was thrilling news, to be sure, but it also dawned on me what a great responsibility we were undertaking. A novel teaches people whatever it talks about, and teachers will be judged by God with greater strictness, according to James 3:1. With that in mind, we reviewed and revised the manuscript to try to ensure that it's Godly in addition to being interesting.

Though I'm sure there will be Christians who believe it's impossible to please God and discuss sex in fictional narrative, I obviously disagree. I hope this book is in line with the goal of Intimate Press that non-Christians who read it for the story will see a more abundant life than they know, and will be drawn to our wonderful Savior, and that it will help Christians who read it to enhance every aspect of their relationship with their spouse.

Having read some of the early reader comments about Cousin Anne's *Grandma's Sex Handbook*, I hope this book encourages readers in an entertaining way as much as her book does in a factual way.

In Jesus' Name,

Georgia Wright

Chapter One

Susan's hands trembled slightly as she poured the coffee from the mixer into a tall paper cup. She set the cup down with one hand as she reached for a Coffy Corner branded lid, struggling to remember which size lid went with this size cup and huffed in exasperation.

Why do they have to be so close in size they're hard to tell apart, she whined to herself as she made her best guess and tried to get the one on top of the stack loose from the rest. Relieved to discover she picked the right size, she risked a glance to see if her manager had appeared and noticed how long it had taken her. He hadn't. Then she remembered the one-way glass that allowed him to watch without being seen and sighed involuntarily.

Graying hair, long divorced, recently laid-off from her job after nineteen years, with one child in his grave and the other estranged from her, today was her second day on this below-minimum-wage job. Plus tips. *Like tips will pay the mortgage,* she thought as she gathered the napkins and other items.

She turned around and smiled at the nameless customer as she put his coffee on the counter in front of him and started to ring up the order. She hadn't remembered to smile, she just did it naturally. At least that was one thing her manager wasn't likely to find fault with.

She was alone behind the bar and it was supposed to be the slowest time of day, but there were three people lined up by the time she gave the customer's change to him and started to ask the next customer for her order.

Out of the corner of her eye she noticed Andy, the early-to-mid-twenties manager, coming out of the office toward her. Judging from his pace, he was not happy. Again.

He said nothing to Susan as he took the order from the next person in line, but she couldn't help but notice that whenever he was facing away from the customers his Coffy Corner branded smile snapped into a scowl. She had learned in the first few hours yesterday that this was the way he acted when he was offended by her lack of proficiency and he was planning to berate her as soon as there were no customers close enough to hear. Until then, if she had to ask him a question, she could count on him to snap at her. Very quietly, of course.

She started to give the last customer in line his coffee but was jostled as Andy awkwardly grabbed it with one hand and an insulated sleeve with his other hand.

"Oops. Mustn't forget the protective jacket, mustn't we?" Andy snapped the sleeve open and slid it into place as smoothly as if he had done it thousands of times. He gave an exaggerated smile to the customer, and the moment the customer turned away, Andy turned toward Susan with the already too familiar scowl.

"How many times must I tell you," he said through almost clenched teeth, "you must put a Coffy Corner branded jacket on every cup, with the logo facing the customer."

Susan could feel her face flushing. "Including this time? That would be twice."

"Don't get smart with me, Ms. Taggart. Just because you're old doesn't mean you don't have to learn as fast as anyone else..."

Just because I'm old?! Susan's mind shifted to wait-out-the-pointless-lecture mode. *Does this boy have a clue about age discrimination? Has he had any management training at all? Why would an owner put in a manager with so little..."*

"Are you paying attention to me?!" Andy said too loudly. He was now red in the face and veins were standing out.

What are the odds of a twenty-year-old having a stroke? Susan wondered, as she pointed behind Andy.

Andy turned to find a distinguished-looking gentleman waiting to be served. Caught off guard, without his "customer face" on, he stammered as Susan stepped around him.

With a silent sigh of relief, however temporary it might be, she smiled to the customer, "Good afternoon, sir, may I take your order?"

He didn't respond right away, yet wasn't staring at the menu board. He was also smiling, and was looking carefully first at Susan, then at Andy, then back at Susan. Susan found something about his face reassuring, and it helped calm her nerves. Andy, however, recovered his normal composure, such as it was, and stepped forward a bit.

"Would you like more time to study the menu, sir? Or would you like a recommendation?" Andy then remembered to smile. Such as it was.

Despite Andy's subtle effort to take control, the customer

continued to look at Susan, and his smile widened as he finally spoke. "Do you have any Kenyan coffee?"

"Yes, sir, we…" Susan began.

"Oh, yes," Andy interjected, "we have the finest Kenyan coffee, with beans hand-picked by experts, which we roast in our patented…" Andy continued the recitation of the wonders of his chain store's superior prowess with steaming flavor out of beans.

The gentleman's smile partially dissipated as he looked away from Susan. "Young man…" he said and waited.

Andy paused and looked at the man, not knowing quite what to expect.

"If I have a choice between ordering from you or ordering from a beautiful woman, I'd prefer to order from the lady." He turned toward Susan and his warm smile grew wider again.

Beautiful woman? Susan blushed and turned enough to take in however Andy would react.

It took an awkward moment for the gentle rebuke to register with Andy, and then he turned abruptly, pausing to stage-whisper to Susan. "He's a new customer, try not to mess this up!" And with that he stalked off back to his office.

Susan turned back to the stranger. "Thank you. For the compliment, I mean." *You have the most interesting eyes.* "So, would you like a Kenyan Roast?"

"Yes, I'd like to try that. I've heard of Kenyan coffee and am curious to find out if it tastes much different from other coffees."

"Very well, sir, what size?"

"How about ten ounces?"

Susan's mind whirled trying to remember if she had heard the number of ounces associated with their different sizes. *I know the little weasel is watching, and there's no way I want to have to ask him what size…"*

"Whatever your smallest size is will do, ma'am, since I'm experimenting with something new."

Is he a mind reader, too? "Okay, and what would you like in it?"

"Oh, just the coffee. No cream, no sugar, nothing else." His smile grew wider again. "I actually want to taste the coffee."

Susan laughed, and so did he.

"Yes, I see how those would defeat your experiment, unless you want to compare Kenyan cream as well." *How long has it been since anyone made me laugh?*

They chatted idly about his recently acquired hobby of

comparing coffee from different countries as she prepared his order.

She finally put his coffee on the counter, with insulation sleeve logo facing him and smiled at him. *Kind, considerate, handsome. What a nice afternoon treat.* "That will be..." she rang up the order on the register, "four dollars and thirty eight cents."

He already had his wallet out and was peering into it.

No wedding ring, she noticed.

He looked up with a thoughtful expression. "Do you have change for a fifty?"

"Oh, sure. No problem."

He handed her a fifty and she started to make change when her smile faded sharply. *Suave, debonair... could this "nice" guy be a con man, passing counterfeit fifties? Andy never mentioned if we have a bill checker.*

With no other recourse that she could think of to check the authenticity of his money, she slowly handed him his change.

He accepted it with a nod and a thank you. And then... leaned over enough to drop the entire handful of money into the tip jar.

Susan's eyebrows went up as he gave her one last smile, picked up his coffee, took a sip, thought about it, nodded with a smile, and started away from the counter.

Susan's mind raced. *Lord, did he mean to do that? He had to mean to. Hardly anyone even seems to notice the tip jar. It's partly hidden by the cookie display. A forty-five dollar tip for a five dollar coffee?! If the bill was counterfeit... what would be the point of using a counterfeit bill if you give all the change back as a tip? A free coffee?*

"Sir...? Sir...!"

He paused and turned enough to look at her. "Just to brighten your day," he said and started to walk toward a table again.

"Sir, that's too generous... that's... I don't know what to say."

He stopped again, turned and then walked back to her. *What is that look? Sympathy? Does he think I'm poor? Well, I guess I am, but that...*

"Ma'am, I just thought you were having a hard day, and I thought a big tip might let me see more of that beautiful smile of yours. I certainly didn't mean to offend you."

Beautiful smile? "You gave me a... what..." *forty-five divided by five... times a hundred...* "a nine-hundred percent tip because you like my smile?!"

"Well, let's see..." he began as he gazed up and to the left in concentrated thought.

Just then Andy came storming back from his office. "What's the matter sir, did she get your order wrong?"

The stranger's smile disappeared completely as he turned toward the manager.

"Did she…" Andy started to continue, but was cut off.

The stranger straightened up and seemed to gain an inch or two in height, and looked very stern as he thrust a finger back toward the office door and said in a commanding voice, "Get out."

Andy stopped so quickly he almost toppled and was turning around before he even regained his balance. He literally ran the few steps back to the doorway without a word or a glance back.

Susan took in the whole scene with astonishment. *Who is this guy? A cop? A general? Definitely not a crook, anyway.* The stranger seemed to deflate, closed his eyes, and put his hand to his forehead and rubbed it.

"I'm sorry. I'm very sorry. I hope I haven't made things worse for you."

Worse? It can't get much worse. And why should you care? "Don't worry about it. This is just a temporary job anyway. Until I can find something that pays better."

He lowered his hand and looked at her again, and now he looked weary.

Looks like he has his own problems. "I was working for Nolan's car dealership until they closed a couple of months ago. Everyone got let go."

He looked into her eyes again. "That must have been tough."

Susan nodded. *Compassion. Not just chatter.*

Susan glanced at another customer walking in, and back to the stranger. The stranger glanced at the new customer and back to Susan.

He raised his cup in a casual toast, and started to return to the seating area. He paused again to tell Susan with a wink, "Next time I'll just give you an average tip."

She laughed, "Yeah, okay." *'Yeah, okay…?' The best I could come up with was 'yeah, okay?!'*

"Yes sir, may I help you?"

It was much busier than Susan would have liked since she had an extracurricular activity of trying to keep tabs on the man who took a seat by the corner table closest to the front window. He had nursed his coffee for quite a while, reading and looking out the window. He must have carried the book in his pocket, since she hadn't seen him carrying one. Then he'd left without her seeing him leave and she was surprised at how empty that made her feel.

Then Brenda came in to lead for the going-home crowd, and Susan's job was basically to help her and try to learn as much as she could. Andy came and went, whenever the line got more than two people long, but he said very little to Susan and avoided looking at her. None of the work was hard, but there were too many little things coming way too fast to absorb it all.

Susan got off at 7:00 PM, and felt completely worn out. She wasn't used to being on her feet all day, let alone struggling to learn so many details so fast. After hanging up her smock and getting her purse and jacket, she waved goodnight to Brenda as she walked through the main room toward the front door. *What a day. I was so good as a processing clerk. Now it feels like I'm back in high school again. As a freshman.*

She opened the door and laughed. *A fifty-six year old high school freshman!*

Susan stepped to the side of door and leaned against the outside wall between the Coffy Corner and the Chinese restaurant next door, took a deep breath and exhaled slowly while looking up at the sky. *Wednesday evening... Daylight Savings Time. Still plenty of time to eat out and walk home. But it'll be cheaper to...*

A cab had been parked almost right in front of the Coffy Corner, and it caught Susan's attention now as the back door opened up and a man exited, putting away a cell phone. He left the cab door wide open.

"Hi," he said with a sheepish grin.

Susan looked at him with a mixture of surprise and concern and couldn't think of what to say.

"I, uh, hope this doesn't make me look like a stalker... I left, I went home, actually, and, uh, actually, I couldn't stop thinking about you."

Wow. He likes me.

"So, I came back. I planned to come in and ask you to dinner, but after making a fool out of myself in front of your boss and possibly endangering your job, I thought it'd be better to wait outside."

Well, I could sure use a free meal. But are you a stalker? A self-deprecating, congenial, considerate big-tipping stalker? Susan laughed, and he brightened up considerably. "How long have you been waiting?" She glanced at the cab. *Did you just get here in the nick of time?*

His gaze went up and to his left. "Um…" his gaze came back to her, to her eyes. "About six hours."

"Six hours?!" *Why would you wait six hours?!*

He looked sheepish again and looked down, around, anywhere but her eyes, and talked fast. "Well, I don't know your name, well, actually I know your last name from when your boss was fussing at you, but that's not enough to find a person, and I don't have your phone number, or address, and I couldn't be completely certain you'd be coming back to work here if that kid fired you or you got fed up with him, so I didn't want to take a chance of missing you. When I got back here, I made sure you were still here, and then I just sort of camped out."

She looked at the cab and back at him. "You hired a cab for six hours just to sit and wait?!"

"Oh, no! He's only been here about twenty minutes."

She cocked her head. *You waited six hours and then called a cab? How did you know when I'd get off? Lord, is this guy safe?*

"Well, he was here earlier, too. Twice, in fact."

Now she looked more puzzled, and he continued to rush his explanation.

"In case you got off work at five. Or six."

Wow. A Knight gallant or Don Quixote? Either way… you really seem to like me. Why? I don't know anything about you. "I don't…"

"Oh!" He put out his hand. "My name is Charles Parker. And I'm between jobs at the moment, but I assure you I'm a reputable man. You can call my pastor or someone if you'd like a personal reference."

Your pastor? He does seem to have something of your Spirit, Lord… Susan slowly reached out and took his hand. "How do you do, Mr. Parker, my name is Susan Taggart." *Still though, there are wolves in sheep's clothing…*

His face lit up as they shook hands.

And you're out of work, eh? Yet leaving forty-five dollar tips and hiring cabs to nowhere? Are you that desperate for a dinner date? "Well, I still have my job, Mr. Parker, so if you're out of work, maybe I should pay for dinner." *No! Why did I say that?! I can't…*

Charles laughed merrily. "Well, I have enough savings to last awhile, Susan, even including food. May I call you Susan? And please call me Charles!"

Susan paused, then bowed slightly. "Very well, Charles. Were you serious about dinner? I'm beginning to get a little hungry." *I could eat a horse as long as I get off my feet first.*

"Oh, yes, absolutely!" He fetched a list out of a pocket, and talked rapid-fire. "I have a long list of possibilities, depending on what you're in the mood for. Almost any type of food, fancy or laid back. Dancing afterward, too, if you'd like to, but I imagine after working on your feet all day, you'd rather eat in a casual place where we can take our shoes off and save the dancing for another night. What would you like?"

Dancing? I'm going to disappoint you there... "Uh, you know a restaurant where we could take our shoes off?"

"Several." He ushered her toward the cab's open door, and he followed her in. "What would you like to eat? What kind of dinner music would you like?"

Less than an hour later, Susan and Charles were finishing hot dogs barefoot in the grass in a back corner of the Chilhowee Park amphitheater, listening to a classical concert.

She leaned back, relaxing and drinking in the music. *An unexpected event, with an unexpected man, at the end of an... unusual day. Well, not quite at the end.*

She sat up a bit, getting uneasy. *Just what might your expectations be for the end of our date, Charles Parker? Our date? Yeah, last minute or not, this is a date alright. And I didn't even have time to worry about it ahead of time.*

Susan cast a discreet glance at Charles' crotch. *No noticeable bulge. But a man I hardly know will be taking me home. Am I really safe with him, Lord? He's much stronger than I am, and in the coffee shop he showed a temper, and a lack of control. Still, he mentioned having a pastor. Even a nominal Christian wouldn't try to force himself on me, right?*

Unconvinced by her attempt to assure herself, Susan shivered despite her jacket. Early May in Knoxville, Tennessee was having typically warm days and cool evenings.

"Not much of a crowd," Charles observed. "Suits me, though," he said while looking at Susan again.

"Too early in the season. Too chilly," Susan replied.

"Hmm. I was thinking of ice cream for dessert," he suggested, nodding toward the refreshment stand, "but I guess it's too cool for that."

"Oh, it's never too cold for ice cream."

"Are you serious?!" He jumped up. "All right, girl, what flavor are you tonight?"

What flavor am I? "What flavor am I? What do you..."

"Hmm. You look like chocolate to me. Do you feel like chocolate to you?"

She furrowed her brow. "You mean do I feel like having chocolate?"

"Yes, of course! I'm sure they'll have vanilla, too, maybe strawberry, but probably not much more. It's not Baskin Robbins, you know. So, out of this enormous selection, what are your taste buds salivating for?"

What flavor am I? Is that just a cutesy way to ask what flavor I want, or is he being devious trying to dig deeper? "Chocolate."

"Chocolate! We have a winner!" Charles whipped out his cell phone and pretended to make a call. "Nat, sell vanilla, buy chocolate! Corner the market, Susan is a chocolate girl!" He dropped the phone back into a pocket and ran off to the refreshment stand, still barefoot.

Susan is a chocolate girl? Is this guy stable? Is he more dangerous than I thought? What have I gotten myself into... A wave of concern crossed Susan's mind and she closed her eyes.

Stephanie, where are you? What are you into now? Jesus, please look after my daughter. Please protect her. Protect her? It feels kind of useless to ask you to protect her, she's already been into so much evil, so many boys, STDs, and who knows what else. Please keep her as safe as you can, God. I don't know why you haven't kept her safer than you already have, but please keep her safe from now on. Please touch her heart, help her find forgiveness, help her find your love, real love.

When Susan finished praying a few minutes later and opened her eyes, Charles was quietly sitting beside her again. *Oh no, he picked now to be The Quiet Man,* she thought as she brushed away tears. *Some date. He'll think I'm a basket case.*

He gave her an ice cream and ventured, "If you're worried I'll want to have sex on the first date, I won't."

She turned toward him again. *So you're willing to wait all the way until a second date?* "Oh, you thought... No, I... I'm concerned about my daughter. I didn't hear you come back. I didn't mean to look like..." she turned toward the concert again, "...I don't know what."

"Susan, are you a Christian?"

Well, you're direct, aren't you? Don't want to waste time on a goody-two-shoes? Or since you apparently go to Church, maybe you're only interested in a Christian woman. Well, win or lose, here goes... She looked at his eyes so she could carefully measure subtle aspects of his reaction. "Yes, Charles, I am. I..."

Charles whooped and pumped a fist into the air very unsubtly. "I knew it! Well, I couldn't be absolutely sure without asking you, of course, but I thought you were!"

You're glad I'm a Christian! So maybe you're a real Christian and not just a Church-goer who thinks he's a Christian? Is that part of why you like me?

He beamed and turned to sit cross-legged facing her. "I became a Christian about a year ago. I wasted most of my life, but thank God he didn't give up on me."

Susan blinked, and a smile crept onto her face. *Now that sounds like the real thing. Is that why... I'm so attracted to you?*

"He changed me, Susan. Radically, completely. I don't mean I just started going to Church, that doesn't mean much by itself."

She nodded in agreement. *Exactly...*

"I mean he changed my heart... he filled me, with himself."

Oh, praise God, you're a real Christian, all right...

"I don't know how to describe it! But, well, when I saw you in the Coffy Corner, there was something about you that was different. I thought, I hoped, that maybe you were a Christian, too."

Oh, my! Her smile grew into a shy grin and she looked down.

"Something about your face, your smile, your eyes."

My eyes. You were going great with the face and smile. Why did you have to mention my eyes?

"You were obviously having a hard time, but despite that, you seemed... Well, I guess you seemed to have God's Spirit shining through you."

Wow... that's... a surprise. Oops, he's waiting for me to say something now. "Well, that's... very nice. I didn't become a Christian until I was forty-five, but ever since I've loved God with all my heart, and I guess every real Christian hopes their faith is real enough for others to see, somehow." *And you're a young Christian. Is that why you're so excitable?*

Charles nodded. "That should be inevitable, I think, that the closer we get to God, the more like him we become, the more obvious it should be to other people."

Susan smiled, and studied his face. He also seemed to be studying hers. *Handsome, considerate, and an eligible Christian.*

She sighed inwardly. *Why are my eyes such a big deal to me?*

Just a silly romantic notion. Totally unrealistic. It's unfair to expect a guy to see it… yet I can't let it go!

She sighed and looked back at the symphony as they finished a number. On impulse, she started putting her shoes back on.

Without a word, Charles did likewise. "Shall I get a cab to take us home now?"

"Take us home…" She gave her head a quick shake to get her thoughts on track. "Yes, if you don't mind, I would like to get home. It's been a long day."

He nodded, using his cell phone to call a cab.

When he hung up, she said, "I hope I haven't… I hope I… well, I'm not sure how to say it. I haven't been on a date in… oh, my. I'm embarrassed. I haven't been on a date in decades."

Charles stood, offered her a hand up, and they started walking toward the parking area. "I noticed in the store that you aren't wearing a wedding ring. If you haven't been dating lately it must mean you've just recently become single?"

"Oh, no, I've been single for… over fifteen years, I think."

He stopped and stared at her. "And you haven't had a date in that time?"

Susan blushed. *Why should that surprise you? I'm old, my hair makes me look even older, I don't wear much makeup…* "No, no dates. I… I haven't been looking, for anyone, to date, I mean…"

"You must have been fighting the men off left and right. Or perhaps you only recently took off your ring?" He looked genuinely puzzled.

She looked into his eyes. *You don't look like you're teasing, but you can't be serious.*

"I don't even want to take my eyes off you."

"What?" Susan tilted her head. *Except for God, my entire life has been a failure. My body is a worn-out rag. How can you want to look at me?* Her eyes started to water.

He took her hands in his, and struggled for words. "Susan… your smile makes my heart beat faster… I love being in your presence, I love being near you. I've been married twice before, but that was before I was a Christian. I've never felt this way about anyone before. I didn't know it was possible."

Charles continued to talk, but Susan's mind lost track of what he was saying. Her head was swimming, and she was trying not to cry as her mind played over and over, *'Your smile makes my heart beat faster.'*

He dropped her hands and started digging into a jacket pocket, and she lowered her gaze to his feet.

She put her hand on her purse just to have something to do. *I'm a mess. How can he like me?*

He retrieved a pocket-sized package of tissues and pulled one out and offered it to her.

Do you think of everything? She took the tissue and wiped at her tears, then blew her nose. "I don't know what to say. I don't even know what to think! This is so unexpected."

"I understand. I think. I didn't expect anything like this either, honestly. I apologize if I've been too bold... I get that way sometimes. And this whole being-a-Christian business has had me dealing with a lot of emotions I'm not used to. I'm sorry if I came on too strong, or too fast."

Susan nodded slowly and looked up. She started walking again, and he walked beside her. "I'm sorry, too. I don't know why I started crying, but, your... attention... isn't something I'm used to." *And I don't know if I can get used to it. I don't know if I want to get used to it.* "And I don't want to lead you on, Charles. I don't know if there's room in my life for a man. Any man."

He didn't reply right away and she glanced at him. *He looks lost in thought. What are you thinking now? Tell me something!*

They walked on in silence for a minute or two, with Susan fretting every step. They saw their cab pull up and walked over to it. He took a position to open the door, but waited. She knew he was looking at her, but she kept her eyes glued to the door.

"I hope you at least have room in your heart for a new friend."

She finally looked up at him. "Are you mad at me?" *How badly have I disappointed you?*

"No." He opened the door for her. "I've gotten mad at just about everyone I've ever known at one time or another. But I suspect you may be the exception."

What does that mean...? she pondered as she got in and slid over. *'Your smile makes my heart beat faster,' you said. Has no one else ever made your heart beat faster? Have I ever caused anyone else's heart to beat faster? Just by looking at me, that is. Does he really like me that much? Is that a good thing? For me? For him?*

"Where to?" the cabbie asked, and Charles looked at Susan expectantly.

"Oh, uh, 124 Whitehurst Street, please."

Charles smiled. "So you're not afraid to let me know where you live? Have I at least convinced you I'm not a stalker?"

"Not necessarily. You could just be a very polite, big-tipping stalker." She looked over for a moment and smiled at him, then looked back out the front window of the cab. *His face lit up when I smiled at him. And all I did was smile.*

She looked at him again and they gazed at each other. *Why does gray hair on men look so much better than gray hair on women? And your hair is complemented so well by those gorgeous dark gray eyes... Eyes! Back to eyes again!*

Susan looked out her passenger window and they drove on in silence for a while. *When was the last time I had sex with Marty? Almost twenty years ago. For twenty years I've gotten along fine without a man... no, I've gotten along far better without a man. Married for fourteen years. It started out okay, but it didn't take long to become... more trouble than it was worth? That might be sacrilegious, but it seems accurate. The last ten years with Marty were certainly miserable.*

Her thoughts drifted back to the man beside her in the cab. *The Quiet Man again. I don't want John Wayne or Sean Thornton. I want what I've always wanted...* She kept looking out the window and was startled by the recollection of an old dream that had been a constant in her youth... *A romantic stranger swept into the ballroom and ignored the other finely dressed ladies and takes her hand. They begin to dance and he looks deep into her eyes... and he notices. He's the one man in all the world who truly notices her eyes. He describes them, and like a magic spell all the other people disappear... he lifts her into his arms and carries her up the curving staircase... to his bedroom. He knows her secret, and he owns her, body and soul.*

"...again?"

Susan flinched, and realized Charles had been saying something finally. Then she realized the cab had stopped... in her own driveway.

"Are you okay?" he asked.

"Yes, I'm sorry. I was just lost in thought." She gathered her jacket and purse and put her hand on the door handle.

"May I see you again?" he asked.

She paused for a moment, then looked at him. "Just as friends?"

It was his turn to pause. "On any terms you choose."

Wow. That's a powerful statement. Much more than I deserve. More than anyone deserves, I think. "Then I would like to see you again, as a friend. I don't know if we could ever be more than that, but I know I need more time. I'm completely out of practice with having a male as a... friend." *Come to think of it, maybe I've never had a true friend who was a male.*

He nodded. "Could I come by your shop tomorrow and get your phone number?"

The thought of him in the coffee shop was a pleasant one. "Oh, please do." She opened the cab door. *Sorry, buster, if you were expecting a kiss, that's not on the menu.*

"I'll be looking forward to it!"

She saw him smiling again from the corner of her eye as she started getting out. *Ask him.*

Susan stood up but didn't move. *I can't ask him! He won't know and it will ruin the evening. It may ruin the friendship.*

Something inside was compelling her, but her mind was fighting it. *Ask him.*

She sat back down on the edge of the back seat, still facing out.

He leaned toward her. "Is something wrong, Susan? Do you want me to walk you to your door?"

She shook her head, eyes watering again. *I can't! It will break my heart to hear his answer!*

She wanted to get up, to run into the safety of her home, but the question held her in place. *Ask him!*

"Charles?"

"Yes, what is it? What's wrong?"

"You said earlier that you liked my eyes."

"Yes, I like them very much."

"What color are they?" She scrunched them shut and set her jaw as she waited for a crushing blow.

"Dark brown, with a delicious tinge of green around the outside edge." His voice was calm, warm, deep.

Susan stopped breathing. She felt like she was going to throw up. Or faint. Or both.

She didn't move. He waited patiently for her.

She finally inhaled quietly, then began breathing heavily, while making a conscious effort to appear normal.

"Thank you for dinner and the concert, Charles. I'll look forward to seeing you tomorrow." And with that she stood, closed the door, and walked to her house. It was a just a small ranch house, but it was the home she grew up in.

She noticed the cab was not leaving yet as she removed her keys with a shaky hand and let herself in. She closed the door behind her and looked through the spaces in the lace curtains without touching them to see the cab back out of her driveway and disappear down the street. She sank to her knees and sobbed.

"Oh, God! Oh, God... he knows my secret! He knows! He knows my secret! The littlest bit of dark green right around the edges! No one's ever noticed that before, no one! But he saw it! He saw part of me no one else has ever seen!

Long years of anguish poured out of her soul as she wept, going over and over the last few minutes in the cab.

Susan finally slipped into bed in her usual night bra and panties and reached over and turned off her bed-side lamp. She took a deep breath and exhaled slowly, relaxing her body as the air left her lungs. And she remembered the handsome stranger who came to her rescue in the coffee shop.

'A beautiful woman' he said. The first words he ever spoke about me. 'A beautiful woman.' 'Lady,' he said.

Her mind followed the events of the day, focusing on the little comments he had made. *'I couldn't stop thinking about you.'*

'What flavor are you?' Was that his sense of humor? Expressed in silly verbal twists? 'Susan is a chocolate girl.' Hmm, don't know if I like that or not. '...there was something about you that was different...' oo, definitely like that. 'Something about your face...' 'you seemed to have God's Spirit shining through you.'

She turned and pulled her extra pillow into her chest and cuddled it, picturing Charles talking softly at the concert. *'Something about your smile...' How many times did he say something about my smile? And how he responded to my smile! Just a simple smile... he lit up every time I smiled at him. 'Something about your eyes!'*

She moaned without realizing it. *'Dark brown, with a delicious...' delicious! '... tinge of green around the outside edge!'*

Her mind floated to filling out job applications, school forms, health records, and getting her first driving license: *eyes, brown. Eyes, Brown. Eyes, BROWN. Marty... my life-altering Marty Mistake... 'That top matches your brown eyes...' the only thing he ever said about my eyes. One of his few attempts to compliment me.*

Now in her mind Marty was yelling again, cursing, threatening, before she left for work. She was going to be late. And she would never see Marty again.

'I'm sorry, Mrs. Towns,' she remembered the banker saying, *'but Mr. Towns is on that account with you. We had to let him withdraw the money.' And the credit cards... I was on the hook for those, too.*

The lawyer... who first suggested the lawyer?

'We're going to have to close the store...' after nineteen years? How am I going to pay the mortgage? Four hundred dollars a month... My home... why did I let Marty talk me into mortgaging the house? My parents' house, my home. My children's home. All my memories...

Chapter Two

Susan awoke with a start when her alarm went off. She leaned over, turned it off, and flopped back with a groan.

Delicious tinge of green, she recalled. Her body was still tired, unrefreshed, but she smiled nevertheless. *Charles noticed my eyes... it's amazing enough that he noticed me at all, but he even noticed the very little bit of green in my eyes. Just like the Prince Charming in my dream... Lord, could that be... a real sign from you...? Oh, shoot, Lord, now I kind of feel like Gideon with his fleece. One sign wasn't enough... he had to ask for a second one. Yeah, but that dream was from before I was a Christian. Still, though, you knew me before I was formed in my mother's womb, so you could have given me that dream even way back then. But did you? Or was that just a silly fantasy? The fact is, though, that no other man ever noticed before... and last night I was ready to tell him I didn't ever want to see him again if he hadn't known that secret...*

She sighed. *I don't have to get up this early since I don't start my shift until eleven again today, so I could get some more sleep... No, this is just temporary! I've got to stay ready for early morning job interviews, and a good paying nine-to-five type job again.*

Well, I'm awake. It won't hurt to lay here a little longer and think about Charles some more. Lay here? Lie here? Forget that... what about... oh, yes, "I noticed you're not wearing a wedding ring." That's right, you gorgeous hunk, I'm available... to the right man. Am I, though? Do I want to risk marriage again, with all its headaches?

Susan rolled over and realized her bladder needed attention. "Oh, well," she said to herself and pulled back the covers. *No one else to be concerned about waking up accidently.*

She made the familiar trek and snapped the light on, a self-defense mechanism she had acquired the hard way. *No one else to leave the toilet seat up...*

She recalled the first time she went into the bathroom in the middle of the night, pulled down her panties and sat down on the toilet... and fell in! She shrieked with the shock, and Marty's only reaction was to get angry that she woke him up!

She unrolled some paper, wadded it up and started to wipe herself. "*I don't even want to take my eyes off you.*" Ha! *You want to see me naked, too, then! Well... that would be normal, I guess.* If we *got married. Married?! Yikes... I met the man yesterday morning, for crying out loud. How can I be thinking about marriage? Well, he seems to really be taken with me... but why...? Because of my smile? And he noticed God's spirit in me? Well that's a first, too.*

She stood up and flushed, and stepped over to the sink to look in the mirror. *Too many wrinkles... and I wonder how the way he looks at me now would change after a few years of marriage?*

She struck a few poses. *I wonder how it would change when he looks at me without clothes on?*

Susan hefted her C-cup breasts, still in the night bra. *Saggy. But this is loose, that's why I sleep in it.*

She took the bra off, hung it on the doorknob, and looked at her breasts in the mirror again. *I've always been careful to wear supportive bras... doesn't look like it helped much. Well, I guess it could have been worse. Yikes! I wonder how much worse it could still get? What do you think, Mr. Parker?*

She turned profile and sucked in her stomach, though she only had a little paunch. *Will this keep your eyes glued to me?*

"*On any terms you choose,*" she remembered. *That's not what he meant!*

"*You must have been fighting men off left and right.*" *What?!* Susan covered her breasts instinctively with her hands, then laughed at her reaction. She started to walk back toward the bed, but instead took a step back to see more of her body in the mirror. "*...fighting men off left and right...*" "*...fighting men off...*"

How do I really look to other people? "*...a beautiful woman...*" *Am I attractive?*

She tried to judge her appearance objectively, but with difficultly. *Maybe my gray hair isn't as bad as I thought. I keep it clean, trimmed, and brushed. It's only the color that's off. Maybe it only bothers me because it's not what I grew up with. I like a gray color on some things, like some cars, like... Charles' hair! His hair looks great.*

She turned her head back and forth. *Maybe he could find my hair attractive.* "*I've never felt this way about anyone before.*"

Susan's cheeks grew pinker. "*Your smile makes my heart beat faster.*" She smiled at the remembrance. "*I love being in your presence...*"

She turned the light off, picked up her bra, and walked back to her bedside table, folding it as she went. *What would it be like to be married to you, Charles?* She put it in the top drawer and walked over to her chest of drawers.

Would you ever yell at me like you yelled at Andy? She took out a clean bra and pair of panties. *Like Marty always yelled at me?*

She walked back to the bathroom, put the toilet lid down, put the clothes on top, and turned on the water for a shower. *He waited six hours for me. Six hours. Everything I've seen of him so far... well, so far is only part of one day. Still, other than yelling at Andy... to defend me... he's shown nothing but patience.*

She closed the bathroom door to keep the steam in. *And he's considerate. No, he's exceptionally considerate. That could just be while he's in dating or seduction-mode... no, he's not like that. It seemed to be his natural state, at least now that God changed him... no telling what he was like before.*

She tested the water. Still too cold. *"God changed me, Susan, radically, completely... he changed my heart... he filled me with himself."*

She closed her eyes. *"God changed me, Susan."*

Slowly, Susan sank to her knees and bowed at the edge of the tub. "Lord, thank you for changing Charles. Thank you for making him your son. Please change Stephanie. Please draw her to you, and make her your daughter." *And me? God, do you want to change me some more? I don't know how much I can handle. I... I still hurt... from Marty. How many times did I ask you to change Marty? To make him stop drinking? That was before I was a Christian, but even after that, I thought you might want to bring him back to me someday, as a changed man. Am I supposed to give up on him? Did you bring Charles to me instead of Marty?*

"Oh, God, help me... I don't even know how you can help me... but I know you do. So however I need help, please help me, too."

She opened her eyes, and put a hand in the water. *Perfect.*

She stood up, closed the curtain, and reached in to pull the knob to make the water come out of the showerhead. She waited a few seconds to let the hot water flush out the old, cold water between the tub and the showerhead, and stepped into the tub.

She got wet and started shampooing her hair first, as usual, and in her mind she replayed the scene where Charles came to her rescue with Andy. She remembered how she had been tickled when Andy almost stumbled when he turned around so quickly to flee, and now she felt guilty. "God, please help Andy. He's a lousy manager. I don't know if he's not cut out for it, or if he just needs to learn, but whatever it is, he's in over his head right now. Please help him."

Susan finished rinsing her hair and lathered up some soap in her washcloth, then began washing from the face down. *"...tinge of green..."* "Oh, Charles, you know my secret. You know!"

Her washing slowed down unconsciously as she washed her breasts. "I had given up, Lord. I didn't think anyone would ever know. I didn't think anyone would ever share that with me." Then she remembered another part of the daydream she had repeated since childhood. *"The stranger who discovers my secret will own me, body and soul."*

She sucked in her breath. *Oh, Charles, do you own me? Can I give myself to you? Has God already given me to you? Or you to me? Is the decision already made? Heavenly Father, is this for real? Was yesterday a divine appointment you brought to pass? Can I even handle being married again? Am I crazy for getting carried away?*

She had worked the washcloth down to her pubic area and began washing it thoroughly as usual, without thinking about it. *"Dark brown, with a delicious tinge of green around the outside edge." "... there's something about your eyes..."*

Susan suddenly dropped the cloth as she realized she was massaging herself between her legs. "Oh, God, I'm sorry! Oh, God..."

Ashamed of herself, she hurriedly started rinsing off, skipping her legs entirely. *If the stubble causes any itching, that's just tough.*

As quickly as she could, she dried off, blew-dry her hair, and got dressed, trying to put the shower incident behind her.

She went in to eat some cereal for breakfast and realized it was three hours before she had to be at work. At just over a mile, it only took forty-five minutes to walk at the most. Fifteen minutes for breakfast left her with two hours to fill.

Looks like some Bible study and a trip to the grocery store are in order for this morning. A lesson on lust, or debauchery, perhaps?

She shook her head. *I repented. Now move on.*

She got a paper pad and started jotting down grocery items. A moment later she realized she was planning meals to include Charles, and she put the pencil down with a snap and huffed.

"Okay, so maybe I'll invite him over for dinner. What's wrong with that?" The incident in the shower played through her mind. "Okay, God, I said I was sorry. I didn't even mean to, and I won't do it again." She paused. "Is that okay?

Her mind replayed the moment when she had glanced at his crotch to see if might have an obvious erection, which he didn't, but her memory dwelled on the sight. She jumped up and paced. "Well, that's... that's disgusting... that's..." *Disappointing? What?! No way! But still, if he found me as attractive as he said, then why didn't... Oh, this is terrible. I've got to get my mind clean!*

Susan pulled her Bible across the table to her usual chair, sat down, opened it up randomly, and tried to focus on the page. *I wonder if his cock is bigger than Marty's?*

Argh! She jumped up again. She paced. Seemingly against her will, she started remembering countless sexual interludes with Marty, but Charles' face, and other imagined parts, frequently replaced Marty's in her mind.

"Oh, God, what's wrong with me?! This isn't like me! This isn't who I am! It isn't who I want to be!" Still pacing, she shook her fist in front of her and closed her eyes. "Satan, if this is your work, you can just back off. I love God with all my heart. I belong to him, and him only... God, protect me from Satan's snares! Protect me, guard my heart! Keep my thoughts pure!" *Guard my heart. Heart... in the armor in Ephesians, that's the breastplate of... righteousness. Okay, how do I put on the breastplate of righteousness?*

She sat back down and started reading the first verse her eyes fell on.

> *I am a wall, and my breasts are like*
> *towers. Thus I have become in his eyes*
> *like someone bringing contentment.*

"What...?! That's... that's...!" She flipped a thick handful of pages and read:

> *But if they cannot control themselves,*
> *they should marry, for it is better to marry*
> *than to burn with passion.*

"What?!" She flipped her Bible shut and looked up. "I've been controlling myself my whole life! All right, most of it. All right, I've been trying my best, most of the time. That's all I'm asking for! Help me control myself. I don't want to think about sex! That's what I want help with!"

She folded her arms tightly across her chest, then unfolded them to rip the grocery list off the pad. She got up, picked up her pen, purse, canvas grocery bag and looked up again. "I'm going to the store. You can come if you want to." And with that, she marched out of the house fuming.

I'm supposed to bring contentment in his eyes? What about my eyes? I like my peace and quiet! I'm supposed to become a pin cushion again for another man? For his "contentment?" "They should marry?" That's if *they can't control themselves. Well, I can jolly well control myself, even if he can't.*

A Ready-Ride cab drove past her, with its distinctive white and green pattern. *"Dark brown with a delicious tinge of green..."* Arrgh!

Susan turned a corner and was relieved to see no cabs at all. *"Have I at least convinced you I'm not a stalker?"* "No!" she shouted to the world. "And no soup for you, Charles Parker!" alluding to one of her favorite *Seinfeld* episodes.

She focused on her list as she continued her walk, and got to the grocery store. She picked out a small cart and turned right, into the fresh vegetable and fruit section, as usual. She picked up several items and crossed them off her list. She got to the bananas and looked for the right shade of yellow and paused.

Susan's mind pictured a banana slowly entering her mouth, which changed into Marty poking his tool into her face instead. He put his hands on her head and pumped her head back and forth. Oh, how she hated that! Then Charles was standing naked before her with an erection and she was on her knees before him. He just waited. And waited.

She turned away without bananas and crossed them off her list. *What else has lots of potassium?* she wondered.

She had no more wild sexual thoughts as she finished her shopping and her anger faded. By the time she checked out and started the walk home, she felt mostly tired. She stopped to sit on a bench with a pretty oak tree creating a canopy overhead.

I don't mind walking to work since it's as close to home as it is, but I wish my old station wagon was working so I could at least get groceries in it. And go to Church in it...

She sighed, and her shoulders relaxed. *I've been acting crazy. Kind of like Charles was last night. No... more like when I first got involved with boys. Or am I even crazier than I was then? Well, I've got a lot more sexual experience than when I was in high school and college.*

She winced at some the fleeting memories of teenage angst and pre-Christian efforts at love and sex.

She laughed to herself. *Well, I haven't had much experience lately. No sex in... how long? Marty left me... nineteen years ago, and we hadn't had sex for several months before that, after I found out he was cheating on me. So, twenty years. Twenty years of no sex. I don't guess I've missed it very much. Doesn't seem like it was ever all that great. Well, maybe a few times.*

Susan picked up her bag and purse and started walking again, more slowly than before.

God? If it's all the same to you, I think I'd rather not get married again.

She walked along for a while not thinking of anything in particular, and then she pictured Charles in the shop. *"Any terms you choose."*

Her mind stayed on Charles as she walked. He raised his gaze and their eyes met. His eyes warmed her soul. And she knew he was seeing the tiniest trace of green around the edges of her dark brown eyes. The trace that no one else had ever looked closely enough to notice. And then... he smiled. His smile chased all the gloom and clouds away and filled the room with cheer and freshness. Where did he get such a magic smile? She knew. He had told her. It was her own smile. She could turn him on... with her smile.

She got back to her house and starting putting the groceries away. *"Could I stop by your shop tomorrow, Susan?"* *"Oh, please do, Charles."*

Her smile came creeping back to its normal place. *Please do. Charles. Charles Parker. If I smile again for you, will you smile again for me? Will you take my hands in yours again? I could use a good friend. A true friend. Someone to seriously pray with me for Stephanie.*

Susan walked to work and got there thirty minutes early. Andy wouldn't let her clock in early, because she was scheduled for another eight-hour day, and he didn't want her to leave early or work more than eight hours. He didn't want her hanging around the dining area either, so she went for walk until she found a bench to sit on.

She started at eleven o'clock and worked through the lunch crowd expecting every person entering to be Charles. The afternoon wore on, and Andy wore on her nerves.

Charles hadn't said what time he was going to come by, but she expected early rather than late. He was out of work, right? And he was eager to see her again. Wasn't he?

She dropped a decanter and it splashed scalding hot coffee on her calf. Andy only expressed concern for the dent in the decanter. If there was going to be a cue for a knight in shining smile... but

Charles was still not there.

She worked through the going-home crowd, distracted by a variety of notions both reasonable and wild as to why Charles had not yet arrived.

When she finally clocked out at seven PM, she got her share of tips from the day before. That big tip of Charles' got split four ways. Today's tips were meager.

Susan walked very slowly out of the store, and then got excited about the idea of seeing a waiting taxi. There wasn't one.

She waited around on the sidewalk a few minutes, but her feet were already very tired and she still had to walk home. The coffee burn still hurt, and she limped the entire way.

When she got home, she sat down on her front porch steps to rest before facing going into the house alone.

She looked up and down the street. No cabs to bring an apologetic suitor. Which took her back to random ideas of car accidents, heart attacks, and instant Alzheimer's. But she was just too tired to get worked up over any of them.

You see, God? This is what I was talking about. I can't take this. Please, just let me keep my house and have some peace and quiet.

And Stephanie! Of course, and Stephanie. If you can do anything for her, please do. I don't care if she ever loves me again, if you just help her love you. Yeah, I know that doesn't make sense. I don't much care. Just... do something good for her, please.

Finished with her prayer for the moment, Susan stood up, got out her keys and unlocked the door. She took one last forlorn look up and down the street before going in and closing the door. She turned the lock and the click seemed much louder than usual.

Walking into the living room, she sat down in the dark. The thought passed her mind that she should eat, but she didn't have enough enthusiasm for it to bother getting up.

A tear formed in one eye, then the other. She dabbed at them. They were replaced.

It started getting dark outside, and still she sat quietly in the living room. She sighed and finally got up to eat. As she limped toward the combined kitchen and dining room, a car's lights swept across the front of her house and her living room window, causing her to turn. It had turned into her driveway.

It must be him. Who else could it be? A policeman coming to tell me he's in the hospital? Or that Stephanie's dead? Her mind flashed back to the soldiers who came to tell her that her only son

24

Steve was dead, and she felt weak. Killed in Afghanistan… in a lousy training exercise.

She walked to the front door, turning on lights as she went. She opened it and saw Charles getting out of a small sports car of some kind. *Well, you're out of the running for most considerate man of the… whatever.*

He was walking slowly. Too slowly. His shoulders were sagging, his head was down. *He's not here just to apologize… something's wrong. Stephanie? No, he couldn't have gotten news about Stephanie before me.*

He stopped a few feet from the steps and raised his head.

You've been crying. Suddenly she felt selfish for all her whining.

"What's wrong, Charles?"

"I'm sorry. I… I, uh… Can we talk…? I could really use a good friend right now."

"Yes, of course. Please come in."

Without thinking, she took him toward her dining room.

"I'm sorry I didn't come by the store today… oh, how was your day today? Were things any better? Worse?"

She thought about the burning sensation on her leg. "Let's talk about that later. Right now I think you need to unload whatever's bothering you."

She ushered him to a chair while she got two glasses from her cupboard.

"I got a call from my son this morning. My oldest son… I have two sons, William and Robert… no girls. Well, two daughters-in-law."

Susan poured a glass of apple juice for each of them.

"I know I was a bad father, and they don't want much to do with me, but… I think William must actually hate me."

She paused before putting the glasses on the table and sitting across from him. "Why do you think that?"

He sighed heavily and looked away. "I never had much time for them when they were growing up… and it seemed like most of the times I did talk to them I was mad at them and yelled at them. I knew it was bad, but I could never stop myself. Of course, that was before I was a Christian… that's one of the ways God changed me."

How many times did our kids hear Marty yelling at me? At least he didn't always yell at the kids. Charles… are you crying?

He started looking around, and Susan got up and got a box of tissues for him. "Maybe it's not as bad as you think." *Did Marty ever cry?... I don't remember him ever crying.*

"He's moving, Susan. And he doesn't even want me to know where they're moving to. He doesn't even want me to know his phone number. He doesn't want me to spend time with my grandchildren. Can you imagine what a rotten father I was to make my son hate me that much?!" He wiped his eyes and blew his nose.

Susan fetched a wastebasket for him. *I guess it is that bad. I sure know something about having a child who hates me. I'm sorry, Charles, but I have no idea what to suggest.* She put the basket down and returned to her seat. "What did your son say when he called?"

"That's when he told me he's moving, and that he won't tell me where. And he won't let Julie tell me... that's his wife. He knows I've been trying to use her to reconcile with him."

He looked down. "Just three weeks ago, I sold my house, and I moved down here last week in hopes that I could at least spend time with my grandchildren... maybe make up a little for how I loused up with my boys. I rented an apartment, a twelve-month lease, figuring I'd live there while I looked for a house near William."

"After he called this morning and dropped his bomb, I went over to his office to plead with him. They told me his last day there was over two weeks ago. I asked if he had put in a two-week notice, and they didn't want tell me, but I talked them into it. He had."

Susan gasped at the realization.

"I had told him my plans, through Julie. He knew. He let me sell my house, move down here, and sign a lease, just to be near them, and he knew they wouldn't be here."

"Wow." *No wonder you're upset.*

He dipped his head more so she couldn't see his face. "I went out to my car and cried awhile, then went over to their house. There was a moving truck. One of the big ones, that would hold everything, so they could be going anywhere."

He lifted his head to take a long drink, and his face was covered with tears. "He wouldn't talk to me, and wouldn't let me in. Julie came outside to talk to me, just once, to say good-bye. I didn't even get to say good-bye to the children."

He put his head on his hands and sobbed.

All the compassion I've seen in you. Did it come too late? Is that what happens when we're not smart enough to become Christians when we're young? Is it too late for Stephanie to forgive me, too? Or to... to understand... why I divorced Marty?

Susan folded her hands and closed her eyes. "Father, I don't know what you can do for Charles and William, but I ask you to do something. At least help them to not hurt so much."

Charles nodded, then blew his nose.

"Thank you," he said quietly.

Susan smiled, and Charles inhaled deeply, slowly, and as he let it out he gazed at her and some of his pain seemed to fade.

He used another tissue on his eyes. "After I left, I was so upset, I just drove around and cried out to God. I poured my heart out, and I lost track of time. I didn't realize how late it was until it started getting dark... then I realized how close I was to your house, and I thought, I hoped... it wasn't too late to see you."

Should I share how much it hurt not to see you all day? "I'm glad you decided to come by." *I don't know how much sleep I would have gotten if you hadn't.*

She glanced over at the kitchen clock.

"Oh, what time is it?" Charles asked, and then spotted the clock. "Oh, my, I didn't realize it was this late." He started to get up. "I should be getting home. What time do you work tomorrow?"

"I'm supposed to be there at five to help Andy open. But I'm only scheduled for five hours. I'll get off at ten."

He threw away his tissue and pulled out a couple of extras. "Oh, I'm sorry. I've kept you up too late."

"It's okay. I wasn't ready to go to bed yet, anyway." *Unless it was to cry myself to sleep.*

Susan saw him to the door and he apologized a few more times as he left. This time she pulled the curtain back to watch his car leave her house, and she sighed heavily.

She felt too drained to have an appetite, and decided to go on to bed without eating. She walked back through the house dragging her feet, turning off lights, and as soon as the last one was off, she headed toward her bedroom with just the light coming through the front windows from the streetlights. She undressed as she went, tossed her clothes in the hamper, put on her night bra, and fell into the bed.

As she tried to drift off to sleep, the throbbing in her calf became more noticeable. She tried to focus her thoughts about what she could put on it, and somehow that led to remembering that she needed to set the alarm.

She got back up with difficulty, set her alarm clock, and smoothed some aloe vera lotion on her leg.

She flopped onto her bed on top of the covers and didn't move. *Oh, God, please let this night be better than the day.*

Chapter Three

"Uuuuuh." Susan let the alarm continue for a while before finally reaching over to turn it off.

She pushed her legs over the side and slowly sat up without opening her eyes. *Four AM. Have to be there at five. Thirty-five minutes to walk if I walk fast. Forty to be safe. That leaves twenty minutes to be walking out of the house. That means I have to leave at... four-twenty.* "Uuuuuh."

She staggered to the bathroom and started the water running for a quick shower. *No time to shave my legs. Have to skip the hair. Shoot. Gray and dirty to boot. Boot, shoot... fruit. Fruit?* She tapped on the side of the tub.

Where did that come from? Is my mind falling apart? What kind of disease would do that? She pulled the shower knob and got in. *The dreaded fruit-mind disease...*

"Aaah!" *Cold!* She shook her head and her thinking started to clear up. Her hands worked rapidly without thinking. *Got to hurry if I'm going to eat something before I go. Can't be sure I'll have time at work. Oh... don't have to have cereal. I can fix something to eat while I walk. What am I going to wear? Have to draw attention away from my dirty hair. No earrings. Emerald pendant... No, don't want to complement my eyes and draw his eyes up there... oh, shoot! Charles is going to be looking at my smile no matter what I do. So he's going to see my hair no matter what I do! Well, dummy, of course he's going to see my hair. Well... matching emerald pendant, earrings, and ring, then. Might as well 'go down fighting.'*

She turned the water off and grabbed a towel. *What am I saying? I'm not trying to seduce him! I'm not trying to... win his heart. Am I? No... dating and marriage are too much trouble... too much pain. Lord, I don't want to get married again! Is it just a natural feminine trait to try to impress a man who shows romantic interest? Can you help me overcome that?*

Susan threw the towel over the curtain rod, brushed her teeth, then rushed to her chest of drawers and started putting on basics. *Does part of me... want... something? Am I just flattered that a good-looking man is attracted to me?*

Up to her jeans and bra, all she had left to pick was a top to set off the pendant. *Maybe he won't make it into the store this morning. Yeah, I'll have a chance to get home before I see him again. Will... will he come over here again? My phone number... he still doesn't have it!* "Shoot!" *I don't have time for this!*

She snatched a top off a padded hanger, put it on, and looked in the mirror on the back of her closet door. *My lowest neckline...! Good Lord! Oh... my smock! It'll cover it up anyway. Good! He won't think I want him to look at my boobs and get ideas...*

Her socks and shoes were next, and she put on eyeliner, some green eye shadow, and some concealer before rushing into the kitchen and looking at the clock. *Twelve after? Can that be right? Must be a record. How long does cereal take? Can't chance it.*

Susan made a quick baloney sandwich, gathered her purse and jacket and headed out the door, locking it behind her.

She skipped down the two steps from her porch onto her walkway, headed toward the driveway to the sidewalk and noticed a car parked by the curb. She slowed her pace down to a crawl. *What is... is that the car Charles was in last night...? Why would...?*

The driver's door opened, and a bleary-eyed Charles got out and waved.

There's that shy grin again. Wow. Does he know how... attractive that is? "What are you doing here?"

"Well, I know you walked to work yesterday, so I thought you might walk all the time. And I thought you might have a hard time getting up this morning, and if you were running a little late, you might need a ride."

It's a quarter after four in the morning. Is he safe? Well of course he is... I'm pretty sure. I should be sure, shouldn't I? He's not faking being a Christian is he? He's just standing there waiting for me to say something. Or do something.

Susan smiled a bit awkwardly and walked closer. "I'm sorry, you just caught me off guard."

"I didn't mean to impose. If you'd rather walk, so you can pray or whatever, please don't feel obligated just because I'm here." Then Charles chuckled.

She stopped beside the car. "What're you laughing about?"

"I was going to say I'll just go on home, if you'd rather walk, but do you know where my apartment is?"

"No, where?"

"It's in the apartment complex above your coffee shop."

"Oh."

He laughed again. "So even if you want to walk, I'm still going to be driving right there."

"Oh! Well, I guess it would be a little silly not to take you up on your offer, then. Thank you."

Charles opened the passenger door for her, and as she got in with him looking down at her, a sway in her semi-exposed breasts caught her attention. *Oh, no! Why didn't I close my jacket before I came outside? Should I explain my rush to pick a top? Apologize? He'll think I'm a slut.*

Once he was back behind the wheel and they were buckled up, he started the engine, and started driving. "You look *very* nice."

"Thank you," she said after hesitating and fidgeting with her purse. *"Very," huh? I didn't notice you staring... are you complimenting how much skin I'm showing? My overall outfit? Did you get a good look down my blouse? Or...*

"So, you walk back and forth to work, when you don't have a chauffeur. Are you trying to save the environment, force yourself to exercise, or what?"

"I have a car, but it's broken. It's in my garage, but I can't afford to get it fixed right now."

"Oh, what's wrong with it?"

"It won't start. It was getting worse and worse, and I took it to a shop and they told me it was the transmission. They said it'd cost about twelve hundred dollars to fix."

"The transmission? Exactly how was it behaving?"

"Well, I'd turn the key and it'd make a grinding noise. Or just a clicking noise... Now it doesn't do anything at all."

"Hmm. Who told you it was the transmission?"

Susan blushed. "Well, the place I used to work was out of business, so I took it to the dealership where I bought it. They sold it to me as-is, so there wasn't a warranty."

"Hmm."

"Anyway, I wouldn't be able to afford it no matter how much it was. The Coffy Corner isn't going to pay many bills."

"Ah, I guess not."

They drove on in silence for a moment, and Susan cast a glance at her "chauffeur." *He had to have less sleep than I did. Yet he got up and came over, just on the chance that I might get up late and need a ride.* "How much sleep did you get?"

"None... I was afraid I wouldn't be able to wake up... even after

I got to your house, I was afraid you'd come outside and find me asleep in the car and not know what to think. I brought some coffee, listened to the radio, got out and walked around periodically."

"You shouldn't have done that. I would have been okay."

"Well, I had kept you up late."

I probably got to sleep earlier than I would have if you hadn't come by to tell me why you didn't come by the Coffy Corner.

Charles started slowing down to turn into the building's below-ground parking deck. "Listen, I'm going to go upstairs and crash. Since you get off at ten, you take my keys and parking pass and take my car home when you get off. It's an automatic transmission, and as easy as can be to drive. I can take a taxi over later after I get up."

"Oh, no, I'll just walk home. I'll be fine."

"You're going to be working on your feet for hours. I'm going to be off mine."

Susan remembered how tired her feet were the day before, and could still feel some sting on her calf. "But I don't want you to have to pay for a cab, that would…"

"You're right, I give up."

Shoot. I didn't think you'd give up that easily.

He pulled into a parking spot, turned off the ignition, and held out the keys for her. "You're right. I won't take a cab, I'll walk." He gave her a big smile. "I'll be fresh and can use the exercise."

Susan stared at the keys. *I walk or he walks. I'm tired, he won't be.* She snatched the keys. "Sold."

He handed her the parking pass also, they got out, and he showed her where the elevator was and they rode up to the lobby where she got out. "If you don't mind, I'm going to go on upstairs. I don't think I'm going to last much longer."

"Oh, sure, go ahead. And Charles, thank you very much for the loan of your car," she said with a smile.

Charles just looked at her for a long moment, and a big smile grew across his own face. "Thank you for the smile," he said as the doors closed.

Susan sighed contentedly and looked at the keys. *If you're trying to impress me… it's working.*

She quickly ate her sandwich in the lobby and then looked up and down the sidewalk for suspicious characters before letting the lobby door close behind her. *What time is it? Driving got me here early…*

She got out her cell phone and looked at the time. *I've still got twenty-five minutes. I won't even be able to get in yet.*

She stopped in her tracks when she spotted someone coming from around the corner. *Oh, it's Andy!*

"Good morning, Andy, you're here early."

Andy looked surprised and paused. "Oh, good morning," he said with relief. "For a moment there I thought you might be a mugger... Anyway, I always get here early to get things started." He unlocked the door and went in first, but held the door for Susan.

"Thank you, Andy," she said as she walked past him into the darkened shop.

He paused, then closed and locked the door.

Susan turned to face him again, and he turned back toward her. *Uh-oh. I don't think you'll try anything, but...* She pulled her jacket closed in front.

"We keep it locked until opening. You'd be surprised how many people would come in otherwise."

"Oh." *Well why are you acting nervous?*

Andy fidgeted. "Listen, I want you to just tell me straight up. Are you here to replace me?"

Susan cocked her head. "What?"

"Is Mr. Burton going to make you the manager as soon as you get trained?"

"What... you thought... no. Why would you think that?"

"Well, he's never hired anyone so old before."

There you go again with the 'old.'

"And you don't have to work Sundays."

At least now I know what's bothering you. Now how can I reassure you? "Well, Andy, he didn't say anything to me about replacing you, or even me being co-manager or a manager of any kind, and it seems like he would have if that's what he had in mind. As for Sundays, I told him I won't work on Sundays... He told me I'd have to, and I turned down the job. I guess he's had a hard time finding people for the low pay he offers, because he hired me even with no-Sundays."

She shifted her weight to one leg. "And it might make you feel better to know I told him I only wanted this job until I can find something like what I've been doing for the last... few years. And Mr. Burton seemed okay with that. And I haven't spoken to him since."

Andy still looked skeptical. "Yeah, but that's what you'd say if he was planning to give you my job."

"No, I'm a Christian, and I wouldn't lie about it. If he had asked me to take over eventually and keep it confidential, I would have just told you I can't talk about it."

"Huh. Well, I guess I'll find out eventually," he said as he walked past her and started getting to work.

Susan pitched in but had to ask a lot of questions... Andy wasn't volunteering any information about the first-of-the-morning tasks. *Lord, I can't think of any way to convince him I'm not out to take his job away from him. Can you please do that?*

Susan finished her short shift and walked back into the parking deck to Charles' sports car. She got behind the wheel, settled into the seat, and turned on the interior lights to look the car over. *Mmm, the leather smells good.*

She turned on the radio and heard singing as if she were in the middle of an auditorium. *Christian praise & worship!*

She glanced at the display to see which station it was. *89.1, my favorite! That speaks volumes about Charles. "Speaking" of "volume..."*

Susan cranked up the volume till it hurt and it was crystal clear even at that level. *Wow.* She backed off a smidgen for a moment, then finally lowered it to a comfortable setting.

It took her a few minutes to get the seat and outside mirrors adjusted to her satisfaction.

She started the engine. *Can't even hear it over the music...* She turned it down to make sure the engine was running, and could barely hear it even when she pressed on the gas.

Didn't notice how quiet this car is this morning... she mused as she raised the volume again and drove out of the parking garage and turned onto the street.

Wow, it really handles well... She glanced at the dashboard clock. *Ten fifteen. Charles will probably sleep for hours still. I wonder if he'd mind if I find a "long" way home...? If he did, he probably wouldn't have loaned me his car at all. Hmm...*

Susan turned left and a few blocks later turned onto an I-40 on-ramp and pressed the gas pedal harder. *Whoa! That's some kind of acceleration!*

She eased off as the car reached the merge area and put the turn signal on. *Traffic's light.*

Once she got comfortable with the flow of traffic, she shifted a lane to the left and sped up. *Wow, this car feels smoother at sixty-five than my car does at...* She laughed out loud. *At any speed!*

She was slowing approaching a car ahead in her lane and looked around to see that the next lane to the left had no cars at all, so she shifted over again. And slowly kept speeding up.

After a few minutes, she noticed something seemed wrong, and instinctively looked around. *Did everyone slow down for some reason? Is there...?* She glanced down at the speedometer. *Ninety? No way! Ninety?*

She eased off the pedal with her mouth hanging open and saw the speed slowly decrease back to sixty-five. *I don't believe it! Ninety miles per hour feels so smooth it's almost like sitting still! That was amazing! That was...*

Flashing blue lights in Susan's rear-view mirror caught her attention. *Oh, no! I didn't mean to! I... ohhh!*

Susan walked into her house, locked the door behind her, went into the kitchen, and put the speeding ticket on the dining room table. She sat down and kicked her shoes off. *Two hundred dollars! A week's pay at the Coffy Corner, or more. Ohhhh, why did I go joy-riding?! How foolish! What if I had wrecked it?! At least the officer believed me that a friend loaned me the car... and he didn't see me at the top speed. Don't know how much more the ticket would have cost if he had. Ohhhh, Lord, I'm sorry!*

She stood up. *What should I eat? No, forget food, I need sleep. Wait! When will Charles come over? What if I'm still asleep? Do I go to sleep with the door unlocked, or make him wait outside until I wake up? Or try to stay awake until he gets here?*

No way I can stay awake much longer. After he was nice enough to loan me his car, there's no way I'm going to leave him locked out for who knows how long. I'll leave the door unlocked and take a nap on the sofa...

Susan unlocked the front door, laid down on the sofa, and immediately fell fast asleep.

Chapter Four

Mmm. Charles sitting on my coffee table, watching me sleep. I like that. And he's smiling... because he likes my smile... '...that beautiful smile of yours...' No, it's because I'm naked and he likes looking at me while I'm naked. I'm glad he likes to look at me. But I wonder why he's not touching me? Because he has self-control...? Is... hey! Why doesn't he have a bulge? Being naked ought to get him aroused! Maybe if I take his pants off. Wait, then he'll want sex, and the drapes are open. Why are we in the living room...?

Susan lifted her hand and tried to reach out. *Wait... I'm facing the back of the sofa... how could... am I dreaming...?*

"Ohh..." she moaned as she felt the stiffness in her body and stretched, then felt her bladder wanting attention. "Uhhh."

She opened her eyes and looked around, her senses and memory flooding back, including that the front door was unlocked. "Charles?"

Oh, my, I sure hope I wasn't talking in my sleep! "Charles...? Charrlles...?!"

She put her feet on the floor and struggled to sit up. *Where are my shoes?*

She got up and headed toward her bathroom while looking around to make sure Charles wasn't there and spotted her shoes under the dining room table. She passed by the family bathroom off the hallway and went to her private bathroom out of habit, then gave her bladder the relief it needed.

When she came out of the bathroom, she glanced at her bedside clock. *Four-forty. I expected him to be here before now. If he got to sleep by five this morning and slept eight hours, he would've been up by one o'clock this afternoon. Even if he slept ten hours, he'd have been up by three, and that was almost two hours ago!*

She walked to the kitchen and made herself a sandwich, then ate it while she walked out to check the mail. She pulled the mail out of the mailbox absent-mindedly and looked as far as she could down the street in the direction of the coffee shop. There were no cars coming and no familiar form hiking toward her, so she went back inside.

Finishing the last bite of her sandwich as she reentered the house, she closed the door and started to lock it, but caught herself and left it unlocked. She started going through the mail, which was all junk except a letter from her mortgage company. She opened that letter and read it with some trepidation.

Thirty days overdue. A month's wages will barely cover a mortgage payment and food. But I'll be running at least a month behind on the mortgage, and might fall even further behind, and that's if I stay healthy. I need to keep my phone service so Stephanie can call me. I've got to keep the water turned on to use the toilet and shower. Maybe I could do without electricity... I'd have to stop using the refrigerator... wouldn't have hot water... oh, how I hate cold showers. Lord, should I stop tithing until I get a good paying job again? No, that's out. Maybe I should quit the coffee shop so I can job-hunt full time. I still have some unemployment benefits available, and that's as much as I make at the coffee shop... maybe more... while it lasts.

She went back into the kitchen, threw away the junk mail and put the bill in her bill box with the other outstanding bills. *If I get just two more months behind they can start to foreclose if they want to. They said to call back after I'm three months behind and then they'd try to work out something, but that article I read said they don't have to, and often don't. My current income won't give them much incentive to be patient.*

Slowly, Susan walked through her beloved home, remembering her childhood there... it had seemed like such a large house back then. She came to the first bedroom, Steve's room, and quickly moved on. Those memories were still too painful.

She looked in Stephanie's room, her own childhood bedroom, and remembered the first time she had sex there one afternoon after school while both her parents were at work. *Joel Matthews... I thought you were the hottest thing on two legs. Well, I got you... for a little while. You sure didn't know anything about being gentle, though. Six months of after-school sex until you graduated, then two months of summer sex, and then you went off to college and never called me again. You never even found out I was pregnant. Would you have cared?*

Then I moved out for college... kept thinking I was in love... kept having sex. Oh, God... I thought I was being good, only having sex with boys I thought I'd end up marrying... but when I got pregnant again I wasn't even sure who the father was that time. She sighed and stepped back into the hallway and leaned on the wall.

How dumb was I? After all that, I still got involved with Marty. When he got me pregnant with Steve, I was so determined not to have another abortion... I pressured him into marrying me. The Marty Mistake.

She walked the few steps to her bedroom door, originally her parents' room. Noting she'd left that morning without making up the covers, she started straightening them out. *They were so good... and so good together... how did I mess up so badly?*

Susan remembered the many times Marty had his way with her even when she tried to tell him no, the times he forced her, even hit her, and once tied her to the bed. And none of that was as bad as the harsh words he struck her with.

All the fights... I cried, he yelled, and I yelled back. None of it made any difference when he wanted sex. Whenever he wanted it, he took it. And that still didn't keep him from cheating on me.

Tears were welling in her eyes as she walked to the door. *God, I don't want to get married again! I don't want another man in my house, in my life, in me! I don't want to share my life.*

She sank to the floor and her mind drifted back to the tiny mobile home she and Marty moved into after they got married. Stephanie was born a year after Steve, and Susan's mother died three years after that from cancer. And it was almost three years after her mom died that she got the awful call that her father had been killed by a drunk driver.

A short time later she and her little family moved back into her childhood home. *I never did get used to having sex in Mom & Dad's room. Marty didn't have a clue... and didn't want one. He never worried about waking up the kids, either.*

She got up and walked back toward the kitchen, pausing at the door of the family bathroom... her bathroom when she was young. That was where she thought she must be dying the first time she started her period. *I knew I'd bleed some down there, but there was so much blood! I thought sure something was broken and I'd bleed to death... I tried to prepare Stephanie better than I had been, but with Marty gone, she was so angry at me all the time...*

She closed her eyes and tears rolled down her cheeks unimpeded. *God, what's going to happen to my house? Who'll live in it if I lose it? Are they good people? Will it be better for them than it was for me?*

"Hello?!"

Charles' voice pulled her out of her reflections, and she brushed away the tears as she rushed the few steps to the end of the hallway. "Charles!" she said with a huge spontaneous smile.

Charles' face lit up when he saw her, but then his smile faded as he noticed she had been crying. "Are you okay, Susan?"

She nodded and shrugged as if it were nothing. "I was just reminiscing. I'm fine, really."

He looked relieved and smiled again. "Oh, good!" He straightened up and inhaled deeply while he gazed at her as if for the first time. "Gee, it's so nice to see you again!"

Susan laughed, "After *all* this time?"

He just stood there, studying her. "And I love your laugh."

Then he looked down, sheepishly. "And it did seem like a long time. I got up around noon, and I had a terrible time waiting to come see you."

"Oh, well, why didn't you come sooner, then?"

"I sure wanted to, but I figured you'd need some sleep when you got home, and I had no idea how long you'd be asleep... Then a little while ago it dawned on me that you might try to stay up until I got here, and was afraid that if you still hadn't gotten any sleep, you'd be ready to pass out on your feet by now..."

All his concerns were for me. I... I want to hug you, Charles Parker. Outwardly, Susan just nodded with understanding and continued to smile.

"I didn't know what to do. I didn't want to wake you up, and I didn't want to keep you waiting. Once I got here, I tried the door, figuring if you had it unlocked, that must mean it'd be okay to let myself in..."

"Oh, yes, that's exactly why I left it unlocked."

He paused before continuing, "Well, I must say you look wonderful. That is, I mean, you don't look sleepy. I mean... I don't mean that you don't look beautiful when you're sleepy... I mean..."

She laughed again, and his relief was obvious. "I did indeed get some sleep, and..." *I was going nuts waiting for you.* "...I feel quite well rested."

"And what time do you work tomorrow?"

"Eleven to three."

Charles looked elated. "Well, then, would you perhaps be interested in a Friday night out on the town?"

Susan's countenance took on a more considerate aspect. "Well, what did you have in mind?"

"The Star of Knoxville."

"The... oh, the big boat?"

"Yes, the big paddle-wheeler. Tonight they have dinner and dancing for a two-hour cruise on the river!"

Susan looked doubtful.

"What's wrong? You don't like that idea? The waves shouldn't rock enough to make anyone sea-sick. But..."

"No, no, it's not that..."

"What is it? Please don't be afraid to tell me."

"It's just that I... don't really know how to dance." *It'd be terrible, and you'll lose all interest in me.*

Charles looked thrilled, closed the distance between them, and took her hands in his. "Oh, please, may I teach you?"

She looked down at their hands and felt her entire body grow warmer while her mind panicked at the idea of trying to learn to dance.

"I'd love to," he continued. "We can start with the waltz, and when you get comfortable with that, I can teach you some swing-steps. What do you say?"

She looked into his eyes. *Charles, I can't learn to dance. I'm too... I'm not...*

"Please?"

Oh, God, how do I tell him no without disappointing him? What can...

"Do you object to dancing on moral grounds?"

"Oh, no, Charles... it's just... I don't think I can learn to dance..."

It was Charles' turn to laugh. "Oh, Susan, I promise you can learn! And I would be so honored to be the one to teach you! Please give me a chance! I promise you won't regret it! Please?"

"Oh, Charles... if you really want to, I'll give it a try, but I'm really afraid I'll disappoint you."

"I could never be disappointed with you in my arms." He let go of her hands abruptly, and stepped back, blushing. "I mean, dancing, I mean. I didn't mean to... I'm not trying to overstep..."

"It's okay! I understand. It was a nice thing to say, and you didn't mean anything more than dancing." She pictured him holding her close, his right arm around her waist and his hand on the small of her back, while his other hand rested on the back of her neck, cradling her head as she leaned back to let her lips...

"... before we go?" Charles asked...

She gave her head a shake. "I'm sorry, what did you say?"

"I asked if you needed to eat before we go. The ship leaves port at seven, and dinner will start around seven-thirty. It's about five now, so... what's wrong?"

"I'm sorry, I ate just a little while ago..."

"Okay, may I make myself a sandwich?"

Susan nodded with surprise. "Uh, sure..." she managed and they headed toward the kitchen.

'May I make myself a sandwich?' Not, 'Please make me a sandwich?'

Charles opened the refrigerator and peered around.

Okay, so get ready for all the 'where's this, where's that' questions...

He pulled out baloney and mayo, closed the fridge, and found the breadbox. Next he found the silverware drawer, withdrew a knife, and started making the sandwich.

He's not... helpless, she thought in amazement. She looked at Charles and then in the direction of her bedroom. *You're not Marty, are you, Charles Parker?*

She cast an involuntary look at his crotch, caught herself with reproach and instantly shifted her view to his head and shoulders before realizing he had nothing to drink with the sandwich.

Susan stepped forward toward the coffee maker. "Would you like some coffee?"

Just at that moment, Charles turned to put the meat and mayo back in the fridge and they started to collide. They both altered courses, and Susan's breasts brushed against Charles' back. The touch seemed electric to her.

"No thanks, I think I've had enough coffee for today," he said without pause or change in tone.

She put a hand on the counter. *Did you feel what I felt?*

He looked over the fridge door. "Do you mind if I have one of your sodas?"

"Uh... they're caffeine-free diet Cokes."

"Yeah, that's why I want one! Thanks!"

He took one to the table while he started eating, took out his cell phone, and started texting.

I guess you didn't feel... what I felt when I brushed against you. Either that, or you're really good at hiding your... at hiding when...

"So, how did you like my car?" He asked.

"Oh." She refocused her thoughts as she joined him at the table. "Oh, it was wonderful! I've never driven a car like that." *Should I tell him about taking it on the highway? About the ticket? Will the ticket affect his driving record? No... just mine, I'm pretty sure.*

He swallowed another bite as he nodded, finished his text message, and put the phone on the table. "I sure love that car. And I keep it in mint condition." He took another bite.

Oh, God, thank you for not letting me wreck it! "I can understand why you like it so much."

It's an awfully expensive car, though. "I was wondering... with you being out of work, do you think you'll have to sell it?"

Charles shook his head. "No... I've thought about selling it since I became a Christian, but it just doesn't make sense to me. I mean, a sports car doesn't fit my image of what a Christian should drive... but this car is retaining its resell value. It's actually gone up in value the last couple of years. If I sold it, I'd have to buy another car to get around. And if I bought a cheap car, it would lose value... eventually most of its value. So this car's a good investment. And like I said, I've got some savings."

He took another bite.

Hmm. That makes sense... might as well keep it until he needs the money for food, I guess. She nodded, "I never thought about it that way. That makes good sense."

"Want to drive it to the pier?"

Susan blushed as she tried to summon the courage to tell him about taking his car on the highway without asking and getting a speeding ticket. *Ohhh... I really don't want to do this... what will you think of me? I took a liberty you didn't offer. You just said I could drive it home...!*

He paused and cocked his head as he watched her.

"I, uh... have a confession to make." She lowered her face then raised it back. *No, for better or worse, I want to see his reaction. See if it hurts his feelings for me.*

"On the way home... driving your car was so nice... I took it out on the highway for a few miles."

He smiled.

What kind of a smile is that? A half-smirk?

"How did it go?"

I can't tell what he's thinking! "Well, uh... it... I'm not used to it, and I didn't realize how fast I was going..."

She couldn't take it anymore and looked away. "I got a speeding ticket in your car, Charles."

She quickly looked back at him, studying his face. *He looks so somber now. Is he mad?*

Her voice was shaky, "I'm soo sorry. Will you forgive me?"

Charles' serious expression broke into merry laughter and he reached out and moved the ticket from its resting spot on his left to right in front of her.

Susan looked at him hopefully as he began to laugh, and then cringed with embarrassment as she saw the ticket and realized he'd already seen it. Then she slapped his hand. "Oh, you! You already knew and you let me torture myself…!"

Charles leaned forward with a conspiratorial gleam in his eye. "That car will fly, won't it?"

"I honestly had no idea cars could be like that."

Charles sighed. "That whole car isn't worth one of your smiles."

Susan raised her eyebrows. *Charles! Are you…? How do you come up with lines like that?* She drew in a deep breath and looked down. "That's… very kind of you to say."

"I…" his voice trailed off. A moment later he snatched his cell phone off the table top. "Say… I still don't have your phone number…! Would you give me the tremendous privilege of possessing that connection to your life?"

Connection to my life? You make it sound like a momentous occasion. "Well… I don't know. How do I know you won't abuse the privilege by actually calling me?"

He laughed again, then turned a little more serious. "You may put any conditions you like on me regarding your phone number, and I'll honor them."

You're serious. Just what kind of a man are you? And just how did you come into my life?

She gave him the number and he entered it into his cell phone, then he looked at her expectantly, waiting…

"No restrictions," she offered, remembering how he poured out his heart at this very table regarding the strife with his children.

"None?"

"Nope. None." *I don't know why you seem to like me so much, but yes, I'd be happy for you to call me anytime you want.*

"Oh!" Susan exclaimed. "What should I wear on the boat?"

"Dressy, but less formal than an evening gown," he replied.

A gown? I haven't had a gown since the high school prom… there I go with the high school thing again…

"I'll need to stop by my apartment to change out of my jeans," he said, "but we've got plenty of time. And you're definitely driving…

I need to teach you how to stay within the speed limits," he teased.

She ignored the jab. "Should I wear heels?" *I've only got a pair of black ones, but they'll go well with a lot of things.*

"Do you usually wear high heels?"

She shook her head, "No, not really." *When would I? I never do anything...*

"Then you definitely shouldn't wear them tonight. You need something solid while you're first learning."

She smiled. *Good, that gives me a lot more options!*

Susan pulled Charles' car into a parking spot at Bicentennial Park.

"Leave your purse here in the car, if you don't have to have it," Charles suggested. "I can carry any small items you need in my pockets, like tissues, lipstick, or whatever."

"You'd be willing to carry my lipstick for me?"

"Sure. Why not?"

Susan tried to picture Marty making such an offer and knew it would never have happened. She considered the contents. "Okay, I'll leave it. And I won't take anything if you're buying."

"Oh, I insist!"

Susan started to get out, but Charles reached out and put a restraining hand on her right arm, then got out and raced around to open the door for her.

"My, aren't you the gentleman?" She held out her left hand daintily and he held it as she got out. Charles whistled, and Susan posed before releasing his hand.

"I don't know who else will be here, but you will definitely be the belle of the ball," he said with studious admiration.

Susan was wearing a dark green long-sleeve dress she had bought years ago for formal Church occasions, with matching flats and all her fake-emerald jewelry. The dress was old, but in good condition, and she thought it flattered her figure while remaining conservative.

Charles was wearing a typical dark suit with a shiny dark blue tie and shiny black shoes.

They walked along pointing out sights to each other. "Oh, look, you can rent all kinds of watercraft, too!" he said, nodding to the signs.

Susan, however, had happened to glance down. *Such large shoes... I didn't notice that before. I wonder... is it true about men with large feet being 'well-endowed?' Susan! That's... think about something else.*

"Look, there's the Star of Knoxville!" Charles said, pointing past the truss footbridge.

"Yes," Susan replied, relieved at the distraction. "Oh, and somewhere right around here is where James White built Fort White... or White Fort, I think. That was the very beginning of Knoxville, back in the late seventeen hundreds."

Charles looked at her admiringly again. "So, you're a history buff, too?"

"Well, I grew up here. We studied that kind of thing." She looked up at him. "The Tennessee river, and the State, for that matter, are named after a Cherokee Indian village."

"Wow, you really paid attention to that stuff."

They started over the footbridge and Susan slipped her hand into his and walked just a little bit closer. *Is this okay? Am I being too forward?*

Charles looked straight ahead for a moment, but then looked down at his date before looking forward again.

He looks... proud? Proud of me? Proud to be with me?

Susan felt him swinging their arms just a little bit more, and she looked at him again. He was grinning, ear-to-ear. And her heart was beating just a little bit faster.

"I guess we could have parked down here," Susan observed.

"I'm glad we had the extra walk," he said, still hand-in-hand.

As they neared the entrance for the paddleboat, she noticed a large sign, quickly took it in, and pulled Charles to a stop. "Uh-oh. It says you have to have reservations," she said with distress.

Charles pulled on her hand. "Taken care of."

"The cruise and the dinner is only forty dollars?"

"Just thirty-nine fifty per person."

They kept walking toward the entrance and Susan's mind was whirling. She pulled him to a stop again.

"When did you make reservations? Before you even came over to my house? What if I'd been too tired?"

"No, I texted my... requests... while I was eating a sandwich at your place," he explained.

"Oh."

They started walking again.

"That's very up-to-date of them," she mused.

"Mm, yeah."

They made their way on board, and an announcement was made over a speaker-system. "Ladies and gentlemen, tonight's departure will be delayed for a half-hour, and dinner will be delayed until eight. In the meantime we'll be serving complementary h'orderves and cocktails. The cruise will remain a two-hour cruise, so we'll be returning at approximately nine-thirty instead of nine."

Charles looked at Susan. "That okay with you?"

"Oh, sure!"

They walked idly around the boat, and music started playing softly over the speakers.

"Oh, here's something we don't know about each other," he said as they leaned on a rail, looking out over the river. "Do you drink alcohol?"

Oh, no, another chance to spoil things. Well, here's goes... "Yes. That is, I like to drink wine, sometimes." She studied him to gauge his reaction. "But it's not important to me," she offered, "if you don't approve."

"Oh, no, I see no problem with it. Morally speaking. I mean, not counting alcoholics, obviously."

She nodded. *Whew! Wait... why am I so concerned about meeting his approval? Maybe this date isn't such a good idea...*

"I used to drink a lot of beer. Quite a lot. I quit when I decided I didn't like the beer gut I had back then."

"*You* had a beer gut?!" Susan looked at his physique. "There's sure no sign of it now!" *Should I have said that? Is he self-conscious about it? Does it make me sound too interested in his body?*

He smiled. "Well, thanks. I lost about forty pounds after I quit drinking. A few years after that I started trying to exercise, really for the first time in my life. I've been inconsistent with it, but I keep getting back to it over and over."

Charles stepped aside to let Susan go up the steps first to the upper deck.

"After I became a Christian, I wondered about alcohol, but it seems very clear that the Bible says it's okay as long as you don't drink too much," he said.

"Oh, I agree. Paul even told Timothy that he should drink wine," Susan added.

"Yeah, and would Jesus have turned water into wine if he thought it was wrong for people to drink it?"

"Ah, that's a good point, too."

Charles stopped and Susan looked at him.

"That song has three beats... good for waltzing. Shall we try your first lesson?" he asked.

Susan looked around nervously. "No one else is dancing yet..."

"True, but it's not crowded yet, either. If you'd rather wait till everyone else is dancing, that's okay with me."

Oh, Lord, have mercy... I should probably put it off as long as possible...

When Susan didn't answer right away, Charles stepped forward and took her in his arms. "Trust me."

She looked up into his eyes as he put his right hand on the center of her back and a shiver went through her. *Right over my bra strap, huh? If I was a cat, I'd purr. But maybe that...*

"Too cold?"

She shook her head, "No, I'm fine."

He placed her left hand on his right bicep. "You just rest your left arm on my right, like this."

Then he clasped her right hand with his left hand and raised those arms out to their sides, elbows bent and relaxed. "Comfy?"

She nodded, but glanced around again.

"Don't look around. We're the only people on earth." He spoke softly, his mouth close to her ear. "This is the way we hold each other for all the basic waltz steps."

The way we hold each other... Mmm.

"We don't have to do anything more fancy than this."

She looked up again and smiled. "Won't we have to move our feet?"

"We can," he chuckled, "but I was referring to how we hold each other. Now, don't worry about speed. The secret is to learn the steps very slowly. Once you're comfortable with the steps, you can always speed up later."

"*If* I get comfortable with the steps."

"Oh, you'll get comfortable with it," he assured her. "When I start, I'll move forward with my left foot, and you'll feel my body start to move. When you feel me start to move, you move your right foot back one step. Don't worry about anything else right now. Just the first step. You move your right foot back one step, nothing else."

Susan took a deep breath. "You move, I step back with my right foot."

"That's it," he said calmly. "Let's try that. Just that, nothing more. I'll start on the count of three. One, Two... Three," and he stepped forward while Susan stepped back.

Then they just stood there, with the entire right side of his body touching the left side of hers.

"You're prefect... I mean, that was perfect. Well, actually, I mean both."

She smiled at him, and he smiled in response.

"Next, I step forward with my right foot and you step back with your left foot." He looked at her. "Make sense?"

She took another deep breath. "I think so."

"I'll move on three. One, Two... Three," and they both stepped together.

Susan looked up happily. "So far, so good?"

"*Very* good. And that was the hardest part."

Susan warmed inside. *'Very' good, he said.*

Charles let go of her and stepped back. "Now this time, I'm going to take my first two steps forward, but on my second step, I'm going to put my right foot off to my right side."

He demonstrated alone and stopped with his feet wide apart. "I know this looks funny, but that's because this is only the first two steps of a three-step dance. Once you know how to do all three steps, we'll do them without pausing after the second step, and then it won't look funny at all."

She nodded. "Okay."

He turned around and stood next to Susan's left side, facing the same direction as her. "Now look at my feet, and I'll demonstrate your first two steps."

"When I move forward, you step back with your right. Then when you step back with your left, you move it off to your left side, like this." He stepped back with his right foot, then brought his left foot back, off to the left side, stopping with a larger than normal gap between his feet.

"Now let's try that together, both doing your steps."

They practiced it twice.

"Think you've got that?"

She nodded again, "Feels weird with my feet apart like that."

"That's just temporary, trust me."

I'm starting to, Mr. Parker. I'm starting to.

Charles turned around and placed his right hand behind her back again and took up her right hand. Susan put her left hand on his upper right arm.

"Like this?"

"Yes, I certainly do," he responded.

Susan laughed and stepped back. "You silly boy, you know that's not what I meant!"

He lowered his voice. "I know what you meant. And I know what I meant."

"Easy, tiger." *Actually, I really, really like your compliments.*

He stepped forward and took her in his arms again, and again she placed her left hand on his right bicep. "That's absolutely perfect," he said.

Sure feels natural.

"Okay, now I'm going to take my two steps, one after the other, and end up with my feet apart. You'll also take two steps, one right after the other, without stopping, and you'll end up with your feet apart. I'm moving forward, you're moving backward, and *we* are moving together."

Mmm.

"You'll move your right foot back first, then your left foot… Ready to try?"

"Yes. Ready to try."

"On three. One, two… three."

Susan took a step back with her right foot and then immediately moved her left foot back and apart. Charles had moved just as expected, and they both stood face-to-face with their feet spread apart.

Susan blushed, but Charles didn't seem to notice.

"Don't move yet. Feels a little awkward, right?"

"Yes…"

"And what would feel normal at this point? To bring your feet together. To do that, you could move either one of your feet. However, since your last step was with your left foot, if you had kept going, you would have moved your right foot next. So, now move your right foot next to your left foot."

"Now?"

"Yep, any time you're ready."

She moved her right foot next to her left foot and at the same time, Charles moved his left foot next to his right foot.

"Now just stand here for a moment, and notice that our bodies are in the same position we started out in."

"Oh, yeah…"

"Okay, now I'm going to count one, two, three and we're going to take a step with each count. What's your first step?"

"I go backward with my right foot."

"Right. What's your second step?"

48

"I go back and wide with my left foot."

"And what is your third step?"

"I bring my right foot over next to my left foot."

"Exactly." He took a step back and took her left hand lightly in his right hand and held her at arm's length. "Okay, do it this time without me holding you, so you won't worry about where my feet are."

She took a deep breath and let it out.

"I'll count one, two, three, and you take your three steps. Ready?"

"Ready to *try*."

He smiled. "One."

She stepped back with her right foot.

"Two."

She stepped back and wide with her left foot.

"Three."

She brought her right foot over next to her left foot. She looked down at her feet, then up at Charles, smiling.

Charles smiled with his eyes. "You sure you never had lessons before?"

Susan giggled, then frowned. "The music stopped."

They paused and another song started.

Charles nodded with satisfaction. That's another three-count. Let's do it again. Ready?"

"Ready, sir!"

"One... Two... Three!" he called out as Susan took her three steps perfectly.

Charles stepped back into position with one arm around her and holding her hand with the other. "Same thing again. Ready?"

"Uhh..."

Slower this time, he called out, "One." They stepped. "Two." They stepped again. "Three." They stepped again.

"Again! One... Two... Three."

"Again. One... Two... Three."

They kept holding each other as he looked into her eyes. "Remember you said you didn't think you could learn to dance?"

She nodded.

"You just waltzed."

I... waltzed?! Susan beamed. *You're so patient, so gentle. You explain things so clearly.* "I... never imagined... I'd have such a good teacher."

"And I never imagined I'd have such a beautiful student."

Susan took another deep breath. *Is this what a real man is like?*

"Okay, now you may have noticed, I'm always walking forward, and you've only been walking backwards."

"Well, I didn't, but now that you've called my attention to it…"

"Well, that's obviously unfair, and we'll end up in the river in no time, so there's a way to even things up. First we take those three steps with you going backward, then we take three steps with you going forward. Your three steps going forward are the same as mine when I go forward. So we alternate."

Charles let go again and demonstrated her forward-moving steps for her, then helped her pace through them, and finally led her through the steps while they held each other.

Once Susan was comfortable with that, he stepped her slowly through her backward steps again, then a little faster.

Finally he stepped her through the complete waltz-box of six steps in a row, and she took three steps back followed immediately by three steps forward.

"Again," he barely whispered as soon as the box was complete.

"Again," he said right before the last step, and they just kept going until the song ended.

As the music faded away, they stepped apart, and Charles applauded and bowed. Two couples who had been watching joined in the applause.

Susan laughed and curtsied. *I did it! I danced a waltz! Me!*

"I knew you could do it," Charles said as he took her hand again.

"That was so much fun!" Susan said as the music started again. "Is that the right kind of music?"

Charles nodded. "Yes, when you listen, you can kind of hear a three-count in your head… one, two, three, one, two, three. Hear it?"

Susan smiled, put his arm around her, and smiled mischievously. "Again."

A few minutes later, it took only a simple explanation or two and Charles had shown her how they could take four steps in a straight line to "promenade" and add some variety to their box-steps.

The sound system kept playing waltz music, and they kept dancing as the ship left the dock and until dinner was announced. The recorded music was replaced by a live band as they found a table by the window looking out on the river on the lower deck.

"They have two main courses on this cruise, ribs or chicken. What are you hungry for?" Charles asked.

Hmm, chicken is probably more lady-like… but Charles is so easy-going, I'll be he wouldn't care in the least. No, I bet he'd like me to get whatever I actually want. He asked what I'm hungry for...

"Ribs!" she said with conviction.

"And red wine?"

"That sounds delightful."

The waiter came and Charles ordered ribs for both of them, and he asked for plenty of paper napkins.

When the waiter returned a few moments later with their meals, Charles took off his jacket, hung it on the back of his chair, and rolled up his sleeves. Susan pushed her sleeves up to her elbows, and they dug in, laughing and smiling.

They each drank one glass of wine and started on a second.

"Dessert?" he asked after dinner was cleared away and he had put his jacket back on.

It was dark outside now, and the interior lights were dim. Susan was nodding her head to the beat of the music. "That's a three-count, isn't it?"

He smiled. "Yes it is. Would you care t..."

Susan jumped up and pulled Charles onto the dance floor. "Dessert after we dance some more." She remembered all the steps and she held him closer than she had before.

After waltzing several dances, Susan said, "Waltzing is a lot of fun, but you know what? I wish they'd play a slow-dance number."

"Perhaps they will," Charles replied.

A moment later he promenaded them closer to the band. When they were as close as they could get to the band leader, Charles caught his attention and asked, "Hey, do you fellows take requests?"

"Yes, sir, if we know the song you want."

"Anything that would be good to slow-dance to," Charles said.

The band leader nodded thoughtfully. "We got something that will work for that."

Charles thanked him and waltzed Susan back into the middle of the dance floor.

A moment later the waltz ended and all the dancers politely applauded before the band began the next song.

"Oh, that's definitely a good one for slow-dancing," Susan remarked.

"So it is," Charles replied.

She put both her arms around his waist and held him tightly. "May I have this dance, Charles?"

"You may have anything I have to give."

"Ooo, you could get into trouble with promises like that," she said with her head against his shoulder. *Oh, God... it feels so good to be held... by someone who... who really likes me.*

He lowered his head to hers, and with one arm around her waist and the other around her shoulders, they slowly swayed in time with the music.

Mmm... Susan sighed with more contentment than she could ever remember. *Is that...? It is... he's aroused! He... he likes me that way, too. I was beginning to wonder. That could be very dangerous... but the truth is, I like the fact that a man finds me that attractive.*

For the next few minutes her attention was riveted to the pressure she felt brushing against her from the prominence in his pants. *Oh, my, that feels so... stimulating. It's getting me warm all over. But will this change your behavior? Will this make you less patient now? Will you try to force yourself on me when we get home? Hmm... that is, if I don't encourage you to keep going. No...! We've just met. I am not going to make the same mistakes I made in high school and college.*

She looked up, and he looked into her eyes. *Moment of truth, Charles Parker... what are you like when you're aroused and have some alcohol in you?*

"Susan?"

"Yes?"

"We've known each other only three days."

What? Oh, no! What're you getting at?! Are you...

"I've loved you from the first morning we met."

Susan stopped dancing but her mind began to spin. *You... do...?* Her eyes started watering.

You love me...? From that moment in the coffee shop? When you saw my smile? Oh, Lord Jesus... I think... I love Charles, too... Is that possible?

He moved his left hand from behind her shoulder to stroke her hair, then her cheek. He tilted his head toward her lips, and she kissed him willingly, deeply.

Oh, Charles, oh, yes! I want this... I want you! I want all of you!

They stopped kissing, and she looked at him again. "Charles, what's wrong? You look worried!"

"I'm very worried. You said... you don't have room in your life for another man... that you only want to be friends... and I promised not to pressure you..."

Susan gently put her fingers on his lips to silence him. "It's okay,

Charles. Let's try to take things slowly, but... I'm ready for this. I mean, I think I'm ready for more than... I mean, I'm ready for kissing... if you are." *I'm still kind of scared... but I don't care. My... desire for you... is getting stronger than my fear now. Oh, God, I... desire... Charles...*

She started crying freely. "I've never met anyone like you before. I don't know what to expect from you. Every time you say something, you surprise me. Every time you do something. And every time I'm amazed."

"Oh, Susan, I love you so!"

She nodded as her tears soaked into his jacket. "I've think you've shown me more real love in three days than anyone else has shown me in my whole life, except my parents."

He kissed her head and whispered, "I can't help it. I've never known anyone like you, ever. You... you... you're like a part of me that's been missing my whole life, and now that you're in my arms, I don't ever want to let you go!"

"Oh, Charles... I want you..." *with all my heart,* "but... at the same time it scares me that I want you. In fact, the more I want you, the more it scares me." She pulled back enough to look into his eyes again. "Something's still telling me that you're too good to be true. I don't deserve you, and I can't understand why you love me..."

She buried her face in his shoulder again. "Maybe I'm afraid you'll stop loving me after you really get to know me."

Charles lifted her chin. "Susan... you're burned into my heart. I feel like you're part of me... like you were always supposed to be."

Oohhh! Charles...

She kissed him again and then they just held each other for a while before she finally led him off the dance floor and back to their table. *Lord, I want to be patient, and follow your will... but I've gotten very hungry for a dessert that isn't on the menu, so you'd better help me control myself...*

Susan didn't notice that the song the band had been playing on and on ended as they walked off.

After a strawberry cheesecake dessert and quite a few more waltzes, it took a lot longer to walk from the Star of Knoxville to the car than it had taken to walk from the car to the ship. Susan and Charles stopped several times to kiss, hug, and coo in the moonlight.

Charles drove, as they planned for him to drop her off at her house before going home to his own apartment.

Should I invite him in when we get home? That could be dangerous... he had a serious erection every time we hugged. She looked as inconspicuously as she could at his lap. *And... the way his pants are poking up, he still does. If he comes in the house, I don't know if I can keep my hands off of him.*

She sighed quietly. *I'm disgusted with myself for being aroused, but it's better to face the truth and deal with it than ignore it and end up doing something I'll regret. It wouldn't take much, and my ovaries will be in control... and I was worried about him taking advantage of me...*

"You're awfully quiet over there. What are you thinking?"

Oh, there's no way I'm telling you what I was thinking! "Oh, how wonderful this evening was..." *That's not truthful. Let's see...* "And... I was thinking, if you don't mind, I'd rather you didn't come inside when you drop me off." *Well, part of me wants you inside.*

He nodded. "Okay. We danced an awful lot tonight, and you're not used to it."

Oh, thank you, God, he doesn't sound angry. Or even disappointed. Guess I wish he was at least a little disappointed...

He laughed, "Well, I'm not used to it either. I haven't been dancing in years."

"Oh? You sure didn't seem out of practice."

He dipped his head in a slight bow. "Except for the couple of times I stepped on your feet?"

It was her turn to laugh, "At least my feet won't be bruised. When we got going a few times there, I seemed to walk on your feet as much as mine."

"Oh? I didn't notice." They glanced at each other and laughed again. "Okay, I did barely notice, but I surely didn't care."

I danced. I waltzed... in your arms. A dream come true... except for the staircase and bedroom part. No, this was better than my dream. This was real. Susan gazed dreamily at Charles. *You're real.*

Soon they pulled into the driveway and Charles shifted the transmission into park. Susan unbuckled, picked up her purse, found the door handle, and then turned to look at him. They leaned toward each other and kissed. Susan leaned toward him more and put her right hand on his left shoulder. Charles tried to reach around her to embrace her, but his left hand only reached to her side, putting the heel of his palm firmly against her breast.

Susan inhaled sharply through her nose. "Mmmm." *Oh, that*

feels so warm... so good. I can't stand it.

She broke off the kiss and pulled away, opening the door, but not taking her eyes off him. "I..." *I love you!* "I'd... uh... can we see each other tomorrow?"

"Yes, what time?"

"Uh, why don't you call me in the morning?" Susan suggested.

"Okay, what time do you want me to call?"

She pondered a moment. "Nine?"

"Nine it is, then."

Susan nodded, got out, closed the door, and walked toward her front door. She paused once to look back longingly, and she looked over her shoulder twice on the short walk. She unlocked her front door and looked again as she waved.

She entered, locked the door, pulled the curtain aside from the window beside the door and waved again. Charles waved back and only then did he back out of the driveway and slowly drive away.

Susan squeezed her thighs together in frustration. "Oh, God! I can't believe how much I want to have sex! After all these years! I've never even dated since I became a Christian, and I want to be holy, but I'm going to need a lot more help!"

An unwelcome option crossed her mind. "Oh, Lord, should Charles and I not see each other anymore? Should we..."

Her mind then flashed back to when she had cried out to God and found a verse in her Bible: *'But if they cannot control themselves, they should marry...'* *They should...marry?*

She caught her breath as tears formed once again. "Oh, God! Should we...? May we...?" *Marry him? Oh, God...*

She spun around. "Oh, yes, God, YES! I'm ready! I'm ready to share my life again... as long as it's with Charles!"

Susan skipped through her living room and dining room, and then down the hall to her bedroom. "I want him, Lord! I want him in my house! I want him in my living room, in my kitchen, at my table, in my hallway... Oh, yes! I want him in my bed, God! Oh, wow, I really, *really* want him in my bed! I don't care if he leaves the toilet seat up! I don't care if we have a toilet seat! I want him in my life..." *Is it okay to say it, Lord? Is it okay to think it?* "Lord, God, I want him inside me. I want to feel him inside my body... I... oh, my!"

Suddenly the tingling feeling that had been slowing building between her legs was magnified and she quickly sat down on the edge of the bed and squeezed her thighs together. "Oh, Lord..."

Her breathing became rapid and shallow, and the tighter she

squeezed her thighs, the more intense her arousal became. "Oh, God, what is this? I don't want this without Charles! This should only happen after we're married!" *This... Did I ever feel this way when I was married to Marty? Have I ever felt like this...?* "Oh, Lord, what should I do? How do I calm down?"

A cold shower? That ought to help, she thought, and started walking to the bathroom. She took one step and the sensation between her thighs became more intense. *Uh, maybe if I keep my legs apart.*

She walked bowlegged to the bathroom. When she finally made it, she turned on the water with only enough hot water to keep it from being freezing, pulled the curtain shut, and reached through to pull the shower knob. Then she quickly pulled her dress off and started to take off her bra when she remembered Charles' hand against her right breast. "Unngh." The intensity of the memory caused her to shake. *I'll leave the bra on until I calm down.*

She started to get in still wearing her panties too, but decided at the last moment to take them off, then stared in surprise. *They're soaked! Did I get so excited I peed? I would have felt... Oh! Oh, my! I guess post-menopausal dryness won't be a problem.*

Stepping into the cold water was a shock and it immediately started suppressing her libido. "Oo, oo, oo, oo, oo!" She turned on a little more warm water. *Not too much. Don't want to defeat the purpose. Might as well go ahead and wash my hair while I'm at it. Oh, darn it! I didn't wash it this morning... I should have washed it before Charles came over!*

Susan took off her now soaking-wet bra, gently squeezed the water out, and hung it over the curtain rod. After washing her hair, she lathered up her washcloth and started to wash as normal, then paused. *Should I wash my breasts and vaginal area, or skip them? I don't want to stink... but I don't want to get all worked up again, either. Hmm. One pass with the cloth will have to do.*

Dare I shave my legs? They really need it... Susan lathered a leg and started shaving, being wary lest it get her aroused again, and being very gentle on the spot burned by the hot coffee, but she finished without incident.

She got out and dried off, with just a few pats of the towel on her more sensitive areas, then wrapped it around her head.

Susan started to walk back into her bedroom but stopped in the doorway, imagining Charles there... his arms wide, welcoming her to come to him. *Lord, I do want him. I want him in my house the rest of my life… oh!*

The mortgage due and inadequate income came rushing back into focus. Slowly, she walked to the foot of her bed and knelt in prayer.

Father… I don't know what the future holds, and that scares me. If I can't stay in my house… well, I want to marry Charles either way, I guess, but I just can't seem to imagine where we could be as happy. I don't even know where Stephanie is, and she wouldn't want us living with her even if she has a place with enough room… which I doubt. And it doesn't seem likely Charles' kids would want us around. Where could we go?

She laid her head down on the mattress and smoothed a hand over the cover. *Can I at least keep my parent's old bed?*

A sudden thought caused Susan to gasp. *Stephanie! If I have to move, how will you be able to find me?! Oh, no! God, help me! How can Stephanie and I find each other again if I lose the phone number that goes with the house?! Oh! As long as we don't move too far away, I should be able to transfer the number to a new place…! Oh, thank you, God. And please, please, please, don't let her forget our old phone number! Oh, thank you God for telephones. Thank you for loving Stephanie, and me, and Charles. Thank you for…*

A minute or two later, Susan realized she had almost fallen asleep at the foot of the bed. *Why am I so tired? Short night last night, short nap this afternoon… and lots and lots of dancing. And I got very aroused, and very excited…* She roused herself enough to put on some fresh panties and her night bra, dry her hair, and finally climb between the covers before quickly fading into sleep.

"I could never be disappointed with you in my arms," she remembered him saying as she drifted to sleep. *Oh, Charles…*

A few moments later she was dreaming again… *The ballroom is so beautiful… who's that coming this way? Marty? Oh, no, I… oh, Charles… I'm so glad it's you! Yes, I'd love to dance with you! We're all alone now. You see my eyes… you see the green that no one else has seen, you see everything there is to see in me… in my soul. I'm part of you now… hold me tight, don't let me go! The room is swirling; I feel like I'm falling. But now I'm in your arms, and you're carrying me up the stairs… to… whose house is this? Whose bedroom? Whose bed are we in? Did you lock the door so the kids can't interrupt us? Do you want to come inside me? I'm ready. Oh, I'm so ready…*

Chapter Five

...flying... wind blowing on my face, rushing though my hair... at the front of the Titanic, leaning out, but I feel safe because Charles has his arm firmly around my waist... I have a ring on my finger again... but it's the first time I'm really happy... with a man... I'm looking into your eyes, Charles... I want to see you... I want feel you...

Susan laid on her side hugging her extra pillow. She felt the pillow with one hand, then reached across the bed, feeling nothing else but her cover.

Charles? "Charles?"

In a few moments, her dreams vanished as she became fully awake. She took a deep breath as she opened her eyes and noticed the strong sunlight coming in through her window, then gasped. *What time is it?!*

She quickly turned and looked at her bedside clock. *Seven thirty-three... and I have to be at work at... uh... eleven today.*

She relaxed and settled down into her pillow. *Guess I forgot to set the alarm last night. Last night! What a night! I danced! With Charles!*

The circumstances that led to her chilled shower also came back to mind. *What was that verse...? "If they can't control themselves, they should marry?"*

Her mind leapt back to their parting kiss in the car, and his hand on her breast. *Did you do that on purpose Charles? I don't know, but you sure did get my motor running... We're going to need to be more careful until we're married, Mr. Parker. Parker? Susan Parker... ooo, I like that! In fact I like that much better than Susan Taggart or Susan Towns. Well, Charles hasn't proposed yet...Will you, Charles? You said that now that I've been in your arms you don't ever want to let me go... Did you mean it? Doesn't that mean you want to marry me? Surely it does... but when will you ask me? How long will we need to date before you ask me to marry you? Am I ready for that question...? I was ready last night, but I was all emotional...*

Susan closed her eyes again. *Mrs. Susan Parker... mmm... that sounds perrrrfect.*

A moment later she rose up on her elbows in panic. *Call! What time did we say... Nine? Yes, nine.*

She looked at her clock again and sighed as her shoulder muscles relaxed. *Seven thirty-five. How am I going to wait until nine?! I could call you... ohh, shoot, I gave you my phone number, but I didn't get yours!*

Throwing back the cover, she got up and went to the commode. *Don't need a shower this morning since I had one right before bed. Set a speed record yesterday morning, now I need to set a record for how long it takes me to get going. Well, Bible study and prayer will be a good way to fill the time. Maybe he'll just come over at nine instead of calling first!*

Susan finished in the bathroom and got dressed, choosing dark brown slacks with matching flats and a loose fitting top with buttons half way down. The top was light-brown, made of a coarse-weave, and accented with cream-colored lacey patches. She made up her bed and ate breakfast, trying unsuccessfully not to think about how very long it was until nine o'clock.

By nine, Susan was seated at her kitchen table trying to keep focused on a Bible passage while idly toying with her cell phone with one hand. Promptly at nine, her cell phone rang and she flipped it open to answer. "Aha!"

"Aha?" replied the now familiar voice.

"I gave you my phone number, but you didn't give me yours. But now that you've called me, I have your number in my call-history! So... aha!"

"Well, I'm just glad you want my number. Did you get a good night's sleep?"

"Oh, yes, wonderful," she enthused. "And you? Any permanent damage to your feet?"

"I had a little trouble getting to sleep... but not because of my feet! And I slept well once I got to sleep," Charles added, "so my feet and I are ready again anytime you are!"

Susan's words rushed out. "Would you like to come over now? Have you had breakfast? I'd be happy to fix something for you..."

"Well, I've already eaten. I've been awake for a long time."

I wish you had called me earlier then!

"And... I was wondering, would you mind if I took a look at your car... to see if I can fix it?"

"Oh, you know something about cars?"

Charles chuckled. "A little bit. And I'm pretty sure it's not as bad as that dealership told you. Transmissions don't prevent engines from starting."

But I can't afford anything to get it fixed! My house has to come first, and I can't even get caught up on those payments!

"You're hesitant?" Charles asked.

"I... it's just... I really can't afford any expenses to fix it. Oh, I don't mean... I'm not trying to... what I mean is, I don't want you putting your money into it either!" *I may not be earning much, but it's more than you are right now.* "Besides, it may not even be worth fixing."

"Uh-huh... uh-huh. Well, I don't have much else to do, so I'd at least like to take a look at it, if you don't mind."

"Well, if you promise not to be disappointed if you can't do anything with it." Susan said. *That was the wrong thing to say. The big guy needs to feel useful, especially since he's out of work.*

"Well, a second opinion would be very much appreciated," Susan added, "if it's not too much of an imposition." *I guess it's safe to let him tinker with it. Besides, it already doesn't work, so he can't make it any worse.*

"Okay, great! Charles' voice sounded much happier. "How about if I swing by about ten-thirty, and you can take my car to work and back. Then I can look your car over while you're at work."

We won't get to visit before I go to work?! "Oh... okay... and thank you..." *That will keep you busy while I'm working, but couldn't you come over now instead?*

"And what about after you get off work? May I take you out to dinner tonight?"

Now you're talking! Oh, wait... "I'd love to, Charles, but you need to watch your spending. How about if I cook for us tonight?"

"Okay, beautiful lady, that'd be great!"

Beautiful lady?! That sounded corny, but I loved it anyway. You must be the only guy in the world who thinks so, but you're the only one whose opinion I care about.

"Oh, and Susan, do you work tomorrow morning?"

"Oh, no, I don't work on Sundays at all."

"Well, um, I've only been in town a little while, and I haven't found a good Church, yet... and I was wondering... if you'd mind if I visited your Church?"

Oh, wow! That's... that's... "That would be wonderful, Charles! I'd love that! *Worshipping God next to the man I love... the man I hope to marry... what could be better than that?!*

"Oh, great! Thank you! I, uh... I'll really be looking forward to that."

"Oh, me, too!" *He sounds relieved. Does he get as nervous about seeing me as I get about seeing him? Uh-oh. Should I tell him about my Church duty? Mm... maybe I could wait about that...*

There was a brief silence before Charles carried on. "Well, then, I'll see you in an hour or so, and then dinner tonight!"

"Okay, Charles, I'll see you then!"

A few goodbye's later, they finally hung up. *Now what am I going to do? Another hour to wait... oh, phooey, I should have asked you to come over now. We'll only be able to talk a few minutes before I have to go to work.*

Susan pouted before bouncing up and getting a dust cloth and spray. *This will keep me busy and help me make a better impression. If he's the kind of guy who notices things like dust... or the lack thereof.*

Susan saved dusting the living room for last, so she could be looking out the picture window at ten-thirty. Despite dusting slowly, she was on her second round, dusting small keep-sakes this time, as ten-thirty turned into ten-thirty-five and beyond. Worried thoughts had started intruding when she finally spotted Charles' sports car pulling into her driveway, magnifying the relief and joy she now felt.

She watched and waited impatiently as Charles got out, then unhurriedly went around to the trunk of his car and opened it.

Susan was now bouncing on her toes. *Ooo, what are you doing? Come in!*

Charles removed something from the car and shut the trunk and as he came around its corner, she saw that it was two cases. *Hmm. Both the wrong shape for brief cases... oh, something for working on cars, perhaps?*

He looked in the window and smiled, and Susan waved excitedly before remembering she was standing there holding a dust cloth. *Oh, no...* she thought as she ran toward the kitchen, grabbing the can of dust spray and putting them back in their cabinet.

Just then the doorbell rang. "Oh, no!" *I forgot the door's locked!* She ran back to the front door, unlocked it and threw it open.

Susan stood in the doorway beaming at Charles and gave a breathless sigh. "Finally...! I'm *so* glad to see you again!"

Charles stood there with his cases on the porch by his feet, and he didn't move as he gazed at her from head to toe before centering his attention on her face. His eyebrows slowly went up.

"Well, aren't you going to come inside?"

He still didn't move, or speak.

Susan laughed merrily and tilted her head. "I promise I won't step on your feet...!"

This time she waited as she could see he was struggling for words.

"You... look... stunning."

Oh, wow! You've done it again! Susan instinctively blushed and bowed her head slightly. She spoke more softly, "Thank you, Charles. I... I'm glad you think so."

Perking up again, she pulled one side of her shirt tail out to the side as she curtsied slightly and waved an arm to usher him in. "Now please grace my humble abode by actually coming inside," she said with her eyes twinkling.

Charles finally bent his knees and picked up his cases without taking his eyes off Susan. Then he just stood in the foyer, still lost in her eyes. "I, uh..."

"What's in your cases?"

Charles blinked, then looked down as he hefted the cases. "Oh, yeah, these. Tools. These are tools."

Susan laughed again, and Charles seemed all the more dumbstruck. *Me Jane, you Tarzan, you have tools.* "For the car?" she offered, trying to help him recover his senses.

"Uh, yeah, for the car."

She nodded, "Okay... well, it's in the garage, right through the kitchen."

He didn't turn to look, so Susan pointed, and that finally prompted him to look away from her.

"Oh, right, the car!" He put the cases down again and got his keys and parking pass out of his pocket. "You'll... you'll need these."

She accepted them and waved a hand toward the kitchen. "Well, there's plenty of food for you to fix yourself a lunch, but I'll want to go to the grocery store this afternoon to get some more things for supper... This will be the first time I've cooked for you, and I want to make something special."

"Special? Anything you make will be special."

"Charles...! You might want to reserve that opinion until you've eaten some of my cooking first."

"Oh, may I have your car keys?"

Susan laughed again while getting her purse and giving him the keys. "I guess these would help, wouldn't they?"

He nodded seriously. "Oh, and a house key, in case I need to leave?"

Her smile dimmed a bit. *Leave...?* "There's one on the keychain with the car keys... Will you be here when I get back?" she asked hopefully.

"Oh, yes. Definitely."

Her smile returned to its previous intensity.

"It's just in case." Charles said. "I wouldn't want to leave it unlocked. Well, I could just lock myself out, and then walk down to the coffee shop."

"Well, there's no need for that. You have both keys..."

He jingled the keys while nodding, gazing at her once again.

"It... this... was my parents' house. I inherited it... a long time ago."

Charles looked at her seriously. "I'll treat it with the utmost respect."

"Thank you," she said while fidgeting. "Well... I guess I'd better get to work," she said taking a step closer.

Charles barely managed a nod.

Well...? You don't look like you're quite yourself... but... I really would like a good-bye kiss...

Charles didn't move.

Well... Susan closed the gap and planted a kiss on Charles' lips.

Two loud thuds surprised her and she jumped back a step. Charles had dropped both cases.

Susan laughed and started toward the door, then paused. "Charles... are you going to be okay?"

"Yeah. Yes. Sure, of course," he replied taking a step toward her.

"Well, I've got to go. Help yourself to anything in the kitchen..." she said on her way out, "and I'll see you this afternoon! Call me if you need me!"

She pulled the door shut behind her, and a minute later, she was driving away in his car.

Susan got off work promptly at three and drove straight home, happily wondering what Charles was up to. As she got close to her house, she could see him relaxing on the front porch with the door wide open. She felt festive as she parked his car and hopped out.

"Hi, Charles!"

"Hi, Susan!"

She bounced over to the porch and sat down, and he offered her a glass of iced tea as he took a sip of his own.

"Thanks!" she said and tasted it. "Mmm. Delicious...!"

"Good day at work?"

"Pretty good. But I could hardly wait to get home!"

"I've been a little excited myself," he said with a mischievous grin.

"Oh? And why are you looking like the cat that ate the canary?"

"I'll tell you over dinner."

"Oooh... trying to test my patience?" she asked. "I can go ahead and tell you I don't have much."

"Well, about our dinner plans..." he looked directly at her now. "I really am looking forward to trying your cooking... but if trying to help me save money was your primary reason... I've come up with a different plan, if you think you'd like it."

"Oh, so we'll postpone the home-cooked meal? What did you have in mind?"

"I heard about a nice restaurant about a half-hour drive up the highway, looking out over Lake Douglas."

"Oh, that sounds beautiful! Douglas Lake is a reservoir they made when they dammed up the French Broad River."

"Oh, so you've been there?" he asked with a slight drop in enthusiasm.

"No, I never have..."

Charles brightened up again.

"Isn't that sad?" she said. "I've lived here all my life, and I've never been to Douglas Lake."

"Well... would you like to go tonight? Perhaps we could eat here tomorrow night?"

You have 'hope' written all over your face! "I'd love to, if you're sure you can afford it." *I can't say no to you, Charles, and it does sound nice... even though I was really looking forward to a quiet night at home with you.*

The reason for Susan's cold shower the night before popped back into her head. *Hmm, perhaps it's too dangerous to stay home tonight, anyway. Oops... what did he just say?* "I'm sorry, Charles, my mind drifted. What did you say?"

"I said I thought you might like to drive on the highway again. It's far enough to really feel the drive, but not so far that we'll get tired of driving."

Susan giggled. "Are you sure you don't mind? Obviously you

enjoy driving it too, or you wouldn't have bought it in the first place."

"Ah, but I have an ulterior motive… I'd do anything to keep a smile on your face!"

"Oh, well…" *You're really good at that, Charles Parker!* "In that case, I accept!" *And I wish you'd lean over and kiss me! Well, once we get inside the house. That kiss this morning only whet my appetite…*

"Great. I just need to make a call to confirm reservations. Oh… what time would you like to eat?"

"How about six?"

"How about if we have a snack soon and have dinner at eight?"

"Okay, but why do you want to have dinner so late when we don't have anything else to do?"

Charles smiled again. "Well… dinner at eight would give us several hours out on the lake, and by dinner time it would be dark enough to appreciate the lights around the lake."

You sure do have a busy, complex mind. "What did you mean by 'out on the lake'?"

"They rent boats."

Uh… "You mean those little paddle boats, or fishing boats…?"

"Well, they might have those, if you prefer. But no, I was thinking a power boat… a cabin cruiser, to be precise."

"Oh! I've never been on a boat like that. That sounds fun!"

Charles started to dial his phone. "Okay, then, I'll…"

"But Charles," Susan interrupted, "won't that be expensive? You still don't have a job…"

He leaned over enough to pat her knee, twice. "Please don't worry about that. I want to enjoy this afternoon with you, and at least for today, I don't want either of us worrying about money."

Susan missed most of his last comments. The moment his hand touched her knee, her sense of touch erupted and she felt an almost electric sensation over her entire body. *Oh, dear Father, I… I could just melt right now. I… am I flushing? I haven't had a hot flash in… how long? A year…? I… I don't even dare look at him, I'm afraid I'd drag him into the house and climb all over him.*

"Susan…? Are you okay?"

"Uh, yeah," she said meekly, "I, uh, think I might be having a hot flash or something." *I wish you hadn't asked. This is embarrassing.*

"Can I get you anything?"

"No… no, you go ahead and call in the reservation," she said as she stood up, "and I'll go make us a snack to take with us."

He jumped up. "I'll walk you in, you look a little weak."

I was trying to get away from you for a few minutes... She straightened up. "That's okay, I'm feeling better already, and I need to go to the bathroom. You go ahead and make your call."

"Are you sure?"

"Yes, absolutely. Thanks."

She left him on the porch and went back to the master bathroom. *Well, I really can stand to empty my bladder, so it wasn't exactly a lie.*

As she pulled her panties down, she noticed they were damp. *Oh, no... it's not as bad as last night, but this is troublesome. Am I getting incontinent? Am I going to have to start wearing panty liners again?*

She pulled her pants and panties all the way off and started to throw the panties into the hamper, then paused, wondering about the moisture. *Ew, I don't want to do this...*

She lifted her panties close to her nose and sniffed. *Oh, that doesn't smell like pee, that smells like sex.*

Once again she started to toss the panties and stopped herself. *I didn't shut the bedroom door! I can't get clean panties without... ooooh, rats!*

She finished with the toilet and sullenly put her panties back on, then her pants. *That's gross! They feel cold and wet!*

Susan quickly closed and locked the bedroom door and got some clean panties, then went back in the bathroom to swap them and wash her hands thoroughly. *Definitely dangerous to get too physical... at least, for me. I wonder how Charles is handling it? Maybe it's just my hormones being out of whack from the tail-end of menopause.*

Chapter Six

Forty-five minutes later Susan was blissfully driving Charles' car south from I-40 on highway 92.

"That's it..." Charles said as they approached the bridge over the dammed up river. "Douglas Lake."

"Left turn ahead," announced the GPS.

"This car is so much fun to drive!"

"Once we get in the boat, most of the lake probably won't have speed limits... so you can go as fast as you want when there aren't many other boats around, and you won't have to worry about another ticket!"

She slapped at his arm playfully. "That was totally the car's fault."

She cast him a hopeful glance. "Do you mean I'll get to drive the boat, too?"

"If you'd like to, sure!"

"Oh, yeah! How fast will it go?"

"That depends on whether it's got a semi-displacement or full-displacement hull, the size and type of engine, the..." Charles looked at Susan and noticed a playful frown. "I don't know... but we'll find out!" he concluded.

They pulled onto Boat Dock Road and quickly found a parking spot. Susan grabbed her beach bag with her purse, sunglasses, a book, a windbreaker for each of them, and other items.

"That's probably where we check out the boat," Charles remarked. "See if you can spot someplace to get some chips and soft drinks or something."

A few minutes later Sam was walking them down to the dock, carrying a pair of life jackets. "You folks sure made a good choice. The *River Rider* is only a year old, and it's one of the nicest boats on the lake. A Sea Ray, of course. Biggest an' best pleasure boat company there is, and their headquarters is right there in Knoxv'lle. There're local boat owners who rent this when they want to spend a weekend on something bigger or nicer than their own."

That sounds expensive, Susan worried.

"That's it on the right side of the dock, forth one up."

Susan counted boats. "Forth from this end?!"

"Yes, ma'am."

She looked at Charles, who was nonchalantly looking all around the lake as they walked. *It's the biggest boat around here... oh, I guess you didn't know that before, but still... you must have known the price. Well, maybe it's not as expensive as it looks.*

The *River Rider's* stern was backed up to the dock, and as they got close enough to see into the boat, Susan's jaw dropped.

"Charles! This is... this is luxurious! It looks like something out of... some fancy magazine or something!"

Charles looked it over and smiled at her. "Like it?"

"Like it? I'm afraid to touch it!"

Sam stepped onto the wakeboard from the dock, opened a gate panel in the transom and stepped through into the cockpit, leaving it open for Charles and Susan as he put the life jackets on one of the seats. "This's the main deck, with a stateroom below, and a fully equipped galley and head. All folks like you need to bring on board is yourselves, food, clothes, things like that."

Charles stepped down to the wakeboard. "Take my hand, Susan."

She stepped on and walked into the space between the curved white leather seats, followed by Charles.

Sam looked them over. "Water's still a little cold for skiing, but I guess you folks weren't planning on that anyhow."

He turned to Charles and handed him the keys. "You've got your boater safety card, so I won't go over a bunch'a stuff you already know. Things like the light switches are all labeled, an' she's got a GPS and tracking system we can follow from the marina, and the radio is tuned to us. If you run into any problems or have any questions, just key it up and we'll hear ya, and find ya, if need be."

"Thanks, Sam, but I think we'll be fine," Charles assured him, as he put in the key, turned it just enough to enable electrical systems, found and turned on the switch for the ventilation system.

Susan put her beach bag down while observing the rich detail of all the features and trim of the cockpit.

"Okay, and you said up at the marina you're plannin' ta be back about sundown?"

"Right. We have dinner reservations at The Point Marina Restaurant."

Sam nodded and took his leave. "Awright then, if we don't see her headin' back awhile after dark sets in, we'll give ya a call on the radio to check on ya."

"We'll be fine. Thanks again!" Charles called out. He turned to Susan and smiled, "Well, it's all ours for the rest of the day."

Susan was watching Sam walk away and took a step to stand next to Charles so she could speak to him without Sam hearing.

"Charles, how much did this boat cost to rent?"

Charles looked at her carefully before asking her to sit down on one of the cockpit seats and he sat down beside her.

Uh-oh. If I have to sit down for this, it must be bad... how much is it, as much as a car payment? Maybe a house payment?

"Susan, tell me something... have you ever been on a boat like this?

Are you avoiding the question, or just taking a roundabout way to get to it? She shook her head. "No, not even close. I've only been on a paddle boat when I was a little girl and a row boat once when I was in college."

"You live in a modest house, the same one you were raised in. You have a modest car, and can't afford to take it to the repair shop."

Susan cocked her head. *If you're trying to make me feel better about you spending a fortune on a boat trip, it ain't working.*

"Do you think it's wrong for a man who adores a woman to want to give her something special, something she's never had before? Something she could never do for herself?"

Special would be okay, but I didn't ask for a ride in a fancy boat! You're out of work, and you need to save your money!

Charles paused before continuing, "Or something she probably wouldn't do for herself even if she could?"

That's because it's too big of a waste of money...

"What if I gave you flowers on your birthday?"

"That would be nice, of course." *And reasonably priced.*

"What if I gave you flowers once a month?

Wow, every month? "Well... that would be okay, I guess."

"Suppose we had known each other since we were teenagers, and I had given you flowers every month. Say forty years... times twelve months, that's four hundred and eighty months... let's round it off to five hundred."

Where are you going with this?

"Let's say that each bouquet cost fifty dollars in today's dollars... that would be..."

Five hundred times fifty is... Susan gasped.

"Twenty-five thousand dollars," Charles concluded.

Susan looked stunned, and looked away. *Twenty-five thousand dollars… for flowers…*

"Flowers wither and die, but if they were given in love, the memory of the love they represent lives on… and those memories magnify their worth."

A lifetime… of flowers…? Marty never gave me flowers… not even once.

"Renting this boat for an afternoon didn't cost nearly that much… but even if it did, it wouldn't make up for forty missing years."

Forty missing years… with me? Forty years… of you and me? Susan blinked and her mind swirled. *'Dark brown, with a delicious tinge of green around the outside edge,' you said. You. You're the one who discovered my secret. You're the one in my dreams. Oh, Lord…* "Why didn't we find each other forty years ago?"

Susan looked at Charles again and saw tears welling in his eyes.

"We weren't Christians when we were young," he continued, "so we didn't seek God's will for our lives then."

He took her hands in his. "We can't get back that past… and… we don't know what the future holds… not next year, not next month."

Susan started crying softly as Charles brushed away his own tears.

"Sure, we might have money problems someday, but today… on this day, I have enough money for this, and I wanted to honor you with something special, something *extraordinary*… something we could make a memory of… together."

Susan slid closer to Charles and hugged him. Charles put his arms around her and she rested her head on his shoulder.

"Oh, Charles… I understand now… I think. You just… you're so much more than…" *more than I ever dreamed* "…than I ever expected."

"You're certainly more than I ever expected, and I've been thanking God for you since we first met. 'To him who is able to do more than all we ask or imagine, according to his power… to him be the glory!'"

Susan looked up, "Is that…"

"From Ephesians. Chapter three, I think."

More than all we ask or imagine… thank you, Lord. She gave Charles a stronger hug. *Thank you so much!*

They broke off the hug, and Charles stood up and helped Susan to her feet. "C'mon, let's make a memory!"

We just did, my beloved. We just did...

He ushered her toward the captain's seat. "You take the helm first."

She looked surprised but took the seat. "You want me to drive first?"

"Sure! There's nothing to it. I'll guide you every step of the way."

Just like when you taught me to waltz? A pleasant shiver went through Susan at the memory.

"See this switch?" Charles pointed. "I turned it on a few minutes ago. It's the power ventilation, and by now it should have removed any stray fumes from the gas tank and engine compartment, so we're ready to crank the engine. Turn the key just like you're starting a car motor."

Susan cranked it and smiled at the easy success.

"Okay, it'll be very easy getting away from the dock. Since we're pointed out, we don't have to back up. When we get back, I'll back it in, if you don't mind."

"Oh, no, by all means, you do any backing required!" she said happily.

"Okay, just let it idle while I cast off the spring lines. That means untying the ropes that hold it to the dock."

Susan nodded and Charles took in the bow and stern lines before sitting down beside Susan in the "companion's seat."

"We'll just leave the fenders hanging," Charles commented.

"The..."

"Fenders are the bumpers on the sides of the boat that keep the hull from hitting the dock. They'll be fine where they are." He elaborated as he started pointing out the controls. "Now, there's no gear shift and no brake pedal. All you have to deal with is the steering wheel and the throttle... these handles."

"These?" Susan asked for confirmation.

"Yep. Push them forward to go faster, and pull them back to slow down or stop. Just go real slow until we get out of the slip... that's this area between the walkways on each side. Then turn left and speed up a little, but not too much until we get into the main channel... Go ahead and ease the throttles forward."

Spring lines, bumpers, throttles... were you in the Navy or something? There's so much we don't know about each other. Forty years' worth. But, at least we know each other now, and we've started learning about each other. Susan smiled as she cast a glance at Charles and moved the handles up ever so slightly.

Charles rested his right arm over Susan's shoulder.

Mmm, I like this... and driving the boat too! She noted that the boat was only inching forward and moved the throttle handles forward just a little more.

The big cruiser exited the slip and Susan turned the wheel, feeling the boat respond quickly. She straightened it up and they were headed for the channel.

"Excellent," Charles complimented.

"I can speed up a little now?"

"Yes, indeed. We don't want to go super-fast while we're near the dock partly to avoid the chance of a collision with another boat, but mainly to avoid making waves big enough to rock the other boats against the dock. That would make the bumpers wear out unnecessarily."

"Okay, got it."

"Start easing her left as we approach that point, and when we pass it, make a full left turn into the center of the channel."

'Her...' I forgot, boats take feminine pronouns. She nodded. "Uh-huh, got it."

"Turning left will have us headed West, and downstream toward the dam. That way, when we're coming back to the marina as the sun is going down, the sun will be behind us instead of in our eyes."

Boy, you really do think of everything.

Susan completed the left turn into the channel and straightened her course to keep the boat centered. She looked at Charles and beamed. "How's this?"

"Perfect... Although that's a completely inadequate adjective concerning you..."

"Aww, thank you," she replied. "Uh... did you say this is when we could go faster?"

Charles leaned over and whispered in her ear, "No speed limit here. Let 'er rip!"

Should I throw the throttle all the way up? Probably not. I need to get used to things first.

Susan started pushing the throttle up more and more as the *River Rider* surged ahead.

Wow, it's pushing us back in the seat! Oo... better ease the wheel left a little bit.

"Perfect... again. Now we have a long straight shot coming up. That's it..." He leaned in again, "Go to full throttle now, let's see what this baby can do."

Full throttle? That means all the way forward. Should I... well, like the man said, let'r rip.

Susan rammed the throttles all the way forward in one quick push, and she and Charles were pressed hard into the backs of their seats by the acceleration.

"Hoo-wee!" Susan shouted over the roar of the engine. "Wow!"

"Yee-ha!" Charles added above the din and patted Susan's shoulder.

"Wow, it feels like we're flying!" Susan yelled.

"It sure does!"

As the force of acceleration leveled off, Susan gave the steering wheel a gentle turn to the left, and then back to the right, and the changes in direction pushed their bodies into each other as the boat tilted from side to side.

Ooo... I definitely like that!

"By the way..." Charles started, but was interrupted by Susan jerking the wheel hard left. The boat responded by tilting to a very steep angle, making them feel like they could fall, almost into the water.

"Oh, help! Charles! We're heading right for the shore!"

Charles reached up and coaxed her to turning the wheel into a gentler turn, as he reached around her and reduced the throttle. They completed a full circle, straightening out their direction to their original course at the end of the turn.

"I should have warned you sooner about turning real sharply when we're going real fast... at least now you see why." He leaned over and kissed Susan on the cheek.

Her heart was pounding as Susan pulled the throttles all the way back and the boat rapidly slowed down. "You should drive this thing."

"Why? That was my fault, I didn't warn you about that soon enough."

"Charles, I almost turned the boat over... and probably would have gotten us killed," she said while getting up.

Charles held her hand to keep her from walking away from the command seat. "First of all, despite how dangerous it felt, this boat is designed so that it can't turn over even at full speed and the sharpest possible turn. Second, the boat was turning sharply enough that we couldn't have run aground. And, like I said, it was my fault for not warning you about sharp turns at high speeds."

Susan looked doubtful.

"You had a little fright, but we weren't in any real danger," Charles continued. "So, now you know either not to do that, or if you decide to do it on purpose, you know what to expect."

"There's no way I'm going to do that again!"

"Okay, but you can still drive the boat. Just don't do that one maneuver," Charles said as he tugged on her hand to encourage her to resume her position behind the wheel.

Susan resisted the tug and got a pained expression on her face. "Uh... well, now that I've stood up... I'm sorry, but I need to go back to the marina to use the bathroom."

"Oh, you can use the head below," Charles said.

What? Is that some sort of crude joke? 'Cause I don't get it, nor do I want to, nor...

"'Head' is the word for bathroom on a boat or ship, and 'below' means downstairs."

Oh. "Oh...! There's a downstairs?!"

"Yeah, I thought you heard Sam say there was a stateroom and head below," Charles said as he got up and unlatched the sliding hatch-door in the center console.

"Wow, I guess I missed that."

Charles slid the door open and stood aside. "I can't go down to look over it with you right now, since we're not anchored or docked."

She peered down the dark steps. "Oh, okay."

"So if you don't mind, I'll keep going toward the dam. The water will be at its widest down there."

"Is it safe to get near the dam?" Susan asked.

"Completely. They'll have barriers to keep small boats away from the dangerous areas, and buoy markers further out from there."

Susan smiled and climbed down the ladder. Her eyes adjusted quickly, and she found a light switch. She started to look around for the bathroom, but her breath was taken away by the interior of the stateroom. *Oh, my! A big bed... don't you get any ideas from that, Charles...* She went over and sat on the edge and bounced, which reminded her of her need for a bathroom. *Desk area, kitchen... including a refrigerator...! And where's the bathroom?*

She opened a compartment door and peered in. *Ah! Very tiny, but very clean.*

After finishing in the bathroom, Susan took another few minutes to look around the stateroom. *Wow, this is so... elegant, so cozy.*

She ran a hand over the bed spread. *If we were already*

married... oh, but we can't be down here at the same time... no, I guess we could, we'd just have to anchor the boat first.

Susan didn't notice her breath quickening. *Oh, well, we're not married... yet.*

She started back up the steps to the cockpit, casting one more look back.

"Find it okay?" Charles inquired.

"Yes, thank you," she replied with a smile. "I had no idea that a boat this size could be so... elaborate."

"Cruisers are little homes away from home. You can make long trips on them, if you can afford the fuel for a long trip... want to drive again?" Charles inquired.

"No, thanks." Susan replied as she sat down on the companion seat. *This is nice. Must be designed for husband and wife, since it's so small your bodies have to be in contact...*

"You sure this isn't a fell-off-the-horse-get-right-back-on situation?" Charles asked.

She laughed, "No, I'm fine, I just don't want to drive right now."

"'Because you only did a sharp turn, you weren't even fishtailing."

"What's fishtailing?" Susan asked naively.

Charles squinted his eyes, "I'm soo glad you asked..."

"Oh, now Charles, don't..."

Charles gunned the engines, and moments later started rocking the steering wheel hard from one side to the other.

Susan grabbed Charles and held on tightly as her eyes opened wide and she looked at him with surprise. At a mid-point between turning, she leapt up, grabbed the top of the windshield frame, and yelled at the top of her lungs, "Woooo-Hooooooo!"

She looked down at Charles and grinned, and saw that he had a big smile of his own.

He began to slow down and keep a straight course as they approached another bend in the river. "You want to try that on the next straightaway?"

She sat back down, still grinning. "No, thanks. That was a lot of fun, but I'd like to just sit and talk while you drive, if you don't mind."

"That would be wonderful."

She snuggled up close and put her head on his shoulder, breathing the river air deeply and enjoying the view. "Charles... tell me more about yourself."

"Well," he smiled mischievously, "I know karate..."

"Oh!"

"Jujitsu..."

Well, I guess that helps you stay healthy...

"And several other Japanese words."

It took only a moment for the last statement to sink in, and then Susan drove her shoulder playfully into Charles' side as he laughed. "Oh, you... I'm serious. We get along great, but like you said, we missed knowing each other the past forty years, so we don't know each other's histories. And I want us to."

Charles nodded. "I know, but I don't want either one of us to get anxious about learning everything there is to know about our pasts as fast as possible. I want us to enjoy the journey of learning about each other."

He shifted in his seat so he could shift his gaze between Susan and the area in front of the boat and put his left arm over Susan's shoulder. "So... something about me... something serious. Okay, I've been married twice before."

He studied Susan's face to see her reaction, but she just nodded.

"My first wife Jennifer killed herself. My boys were both out of the house by then, and they blamed me for her death. I suspect she became depressed as a side effect of some medicine she was taking, but I can't be sure. Anyway, I guess it was at least partly my fault because I didn't notice how bad it was. And that was because I was spending most of my time at work, as usual. She was a good wife and mother, but I was a lousy father and husband."

"Is this too hard for you talk about?" Susan asked.

"No, I'm okay... but thanks for asking," Charles replied. "Less than a year after Jennifer died, I met another woman and remarried. Laura. That made my boys angry, too. They said it was disrespectful to Jennifer to get married again so soon. That was the objection they raised, but they also asked how long I had known Laura... and I guessed they were wondering if she and I had been an item before Jennifer died. We weren't, and I tried to make that clear to them, but I don't think they trust my word at all, so... I guess they still have doubts about that. In fact, as sad as it makes me to think they could, they may wonder if I killed Jennifer and made it look like suicide, so I could be with Laura."

Wow. No wonder they're so mad at you.

"They may not even know that I really loved Jen. I hardly ever did anything to show love to her or the boys except try to earn more money for them..."

That's still an improvement over Marty.

They were quiet for a few moments and Charles steered the boat through another bend in the river.

"What happened with your second wife?" Susan asked.

"Laura... I wish I knew. She divorced me after two or three years... about three. At the time we got married, I thought I was in love with her, but in hindsight, I think I mostly just wanted someone to have sex with again."

Charles looked sharply at Susan. "That's *not* what's driving my relationship with you. I wasn't a Christian back then, and I was very selfish, or at least self-centered." He looked at her as if looking for trust.

"I believe you, Charles," Susan reassured him, then looked up at him.

"Do you want to know about me?" she asked meekly. *That was dumb. I meant...*

"I want to know everything about you. But if there are things you're not comfortable sharing, I'll do my best to try to wait until you become comfortable with whatever that is. Even if that means never."

She shook her head. "I really don't have any secrets, and... I'm glad you want to know about me... I've only been married once, but I had sex with several guys before that. Back in high school and college." Now it was her turn to look at him for a sign of acceptance. *Oh, Charles... please tell me you still love me! Please tell me my slutty youth won't kill our friendship... our relationship.*

Charles looked down at her and held her gaze, then leaned in close and used a stage whisper to be heard over the engines, "If you were only half as beautiful then as you are now, it would seem impossible to have been otherwise."

What...?! 'If I were...?!' Wow, can you compliment a girl, or what! She skootched around in her seat so that she was facing him head-on. "Will you... forgive me? For..."

Charles pulled the throttles all the way back without looking and let the boat slow to a drift as he turned to face Susan and hold her hands. "Susan, we both made mistakes before we were Christians. Plenty after, too, but hopefully not quite as bad. I also had a few relationships I regret before I got married. Let's just acknowledge our mistakes and trust God that he's forgiven us for our sins. And let's concentrate on living the way he wants us to live today!"

Susan lunged forward and hugged him. *Oh, dear God... a gorgeous hunk of man who loves you as much as I do, and isn't afraid to bring you into normal conversations! And he doesn't hold my awful past against me! Thank you! Oh, dear God, thank you!*

She ended the hug and sat back, gazing at the man before her. *Ask me! Please, ask me! I want to marry you, Charles Parker! I want to marry you and get you into bed! I want to dance with you naked! I want to fall asleep with you in my arms! I...*

"Susan...?"

"Yes?!"

Charles' eyes twitched as he appeared to search for the right words. His brow furrowed. "Uh... I, uh..."

Yes...?! Yes...?!

"I'm sorry, but now *I* need to use the bathroom."

Susan just stared for an awkward moment before hurrying to get up and let him past. "Oh... uh... okay." *Boy, I thought... I guess I just hoped...*

"That's the dam up there. You can drive around if you want to, or just let it drift. And just yell down if you have any questions... okay?"

"Uh... sure."

Charles quickly disappeared below, and Susan looked around blankly.

Father, what... what will it take to get him to propose? He said he wants us to enjoy the journey of getting to know each other. How long will that take? This is so intense... I don't know how long I can handle this. Would... would it be okay if I propose to Charles? Is he afraid to ask because of what I said at the concert about just being friends? I thought I made it clear that's no longer the case. Oh, God... what should I do? I wasn't imagining all his compliments, and I just asked him to tell me something about himself... he's the one who chose to tell me about his previous marriages.

A few minutes later Susan heard the toilet flush, and a minute or so after that, Charles came back up and looked around.

"Just letting her drift, eh?" Charles asked rhetorically. "What do you say we drop anchor, put on some music, and talk back here where we have more room?" He nodded to the curved, white leather bench seats behind the captain's chair and companion seat.

"Sure... you'll have to do the anchoring, though. I have no idea how to do that."

Susan eyed the bench seats as they traded places. *Plenty of room for snuggling and cuddling, but I don't think I can handle that.*

"Hmm. Not much current or wind... and remarkably few other

boats about for a Saturday." Charles flipped a switch on the console to activate the windlass and lower the anchor. "We have plenty of room in all directions, so I'm just going to drop anchor and let it set itself."

Susan idly stepped over to the bench seat and sat down, but didn't relax. *Should I pick up on our last conversation? Ask him about anchors? Start a new topic?*

Charles plugged in an mp3 player to the ship's sound system, turned it on, and adjusted the volume low enough not to interfere with a quiet conversation.

Susan looked away as Charles sat down next to her. *Please don't kiss me. I'll catch on fire if we kiss right now.*

"What happened to your marriage?"

Oh, thank you, God! That topic will turn my motor off. Susan glanced at Charles before looking off into the distance.

"I met Marty in college. Marty Towns. I started dating him just because I thought he was good looking. A couple of months later I found out I was pregnant... and I decided I wanted to keep the baby."

Should I tell him it was because I didn't want to have a third abortion? "Anyway, Marty bounced back and forth between being supportive and being angry. Come to think of it, that's Marty in a nutshell: bouncing back and forth. We got married and I finished my degree before Steve was born. Marty dropped out of college to work, but he never really found a job he wanted to stick with. I..." Susan paused in mid-sentence. *Oh, no...!*

Charles' arm was on the back of the seat and he had just reached out and stroked Susan's hair.

"I'm sorry, I didn't mean to distract you," he offered.

What in the world would you have done if you had meant to distract me?! "That's okay. I mean... it is distracting... I like it... but, uh..."

"I apologize," he said after quickly retracting his arm a bit. "I'll keep my paws off."

Oooh, Charles, I wish you could put your paws all over me... I...

"You were saying Marty never found a job to stick with."

"Oh, uh, yeah... Marty. He was out of work a lot of the time, so I supported us financially. Marty... he cheated on me twice. At least twice, that I know of. Even then, I didn't want to end our marriage for the kids' sake. Then, two days before my thirty-seventh birthday, Marty left and never came back. Steve was only thirteen years old, and Stephanie was twelve. He didn't even tell them good-bye. Or me. We had a fight that morning... we had a lot of fights... and when I got home, most of his clothes were gone. I was crazy with worry for days, then weeks, but I never heard directly from him. A few weeks later, I tried to use a credit card and it was declined. It turned out he had maxed out our credit cards and taken all the money in our bank accounts. The bank said I should talk to a lawyer. The bank man seemed sympathetic... well, technically, he only implied I should talk to a lawyer, but I did. And the lawyer said the only way to protect myself and the kids financially was to divorce Marty. It was a divorce in-absentia since I didn't know where he was. That whole time was a nightmare, although Marty never showed up to contest anything, so I guess it could have been worse. Except for the kids. Steve kind of withdrew into himself for a while, then got into sports. He joined the Army right after high school, and... he was killed a few years later in Afghanistan."

Susan bit on finger for a moment before going on. "Stephanie, my daughter... Stephanie just never understood. She was always angry and rebellious after Marty left. She blamed me for Marty not being there, and she ran away with some boy right in the middle of her senior year of high school. She'd come by once in a while, or at least call... up until I had to tell her about Steve's death. She blamed me for that too, and I haven't heard from her since. I've been praying for her every day, but I'm not even sure she's alive."

Susan teared up as she turned to look at Charles and was surprised that he had moved closer. Now he put his arm over her shoulder and took one of her hands in his free hand.

"Heavenly Father," he began as they both closed their eyes, "we lift up Stephanie to you. Wherever she is, she's not beyond your ability to reach her. I ask you to reach her heart, Lord, and melt the hardness there with your indescribable love. Healing her wounds are beyond our abilities, but we ask you to intervene, we ask you to heal her. Protect her, Lord. Deliver her. Give her the ability to love her mother again."

"Oh, God!" Susan turned and buried her face in Charles shoulder and cried passionately, sobs racking her body. "Oh, God, *please!*"

Charles hugged her tight. "Father, I want to ask you to heal Susan's heart also, but I think the way to do that is by healing Stephanie. Lord, break the bonds that hold Stephanie in darkness. Set her free. Give her your life... let her come to know your love."

Susan continued to cry for long minutes, and Charles just held her, patiently waiting.

Just as she was about cried out, a small jolt shook the boat and she looked up with concern.

"It's okay, the anchor just set. That means it lodged into the lake bottom. It must have been skimming until just now," Charles explained.

"Is it safe?"

"It's fine. There still aren't any other boats to worry about, and we're a long way from shore and the dam."

Susan started brushing away her tears, and got some tissues out of her beach bag and blew her nose before reclining against Charles. He wrapped his arms around her as they looked out over the water.

"What about your sons, Charles? Shall we pray for them now?"

When he didn't answer right away, she turned enough to look at him.

"I find it strange, Susan. I pray for them every day, but I seem to have more faith while praying for other people than I do praying for my own children."

"Oh, I understand, I do! I can have lots of faith to pray for other people, but when it comes to Stephanie, it's like all I can do is plead for God to have mercy."

He nodded. "Yeah, it's just like that."

She snuggled down against Charles and began to pray, "God... I don't know William or..."

"Robert."

"Or Robert, but I know you know everything about them. You know every disappointment, every heartbreak, every doubt, every pain. Lord..." Susan's voice trailed off as she turned her hands palms-up, "...nothing is too hard for you, nothing. No matter how deep their pain, no matter how strong their anger, you can overcome it all. I ask you to break the hardness in their hearts with your love, and heal their grief. Bind their wounds and show them your awesome power to save, to make them your sons."

"Oh, God, yes, yes!" Charles agreed fervently. "Amen. Amen! Thank you, Lord!"

Susan and Charles just sat there in each other arms, listening to the instrumental music, small waves lapping the side of the boat, and faint sounds from shore drifting in and out.

"I'm starting to get hungry," Susan finally said.

"Hmm. Still a little early for our dinner reservations. How about if we split one of those sandwiches you brought to tide us over."

Susan laughed as she sat up and started searching through her bag. "Tide us over? Are you making nautical puns?"

Charles laughed too. "No, not intentionally. That was a good catch. Ooo, and no, that wasn't a fishing pun, just an observation regarding your wits."

Susan stood up to stretch and Charles joined her as they shared a peanut butter and jelly sandwich.

"If I had had my wits about me when we got on board, I would've put our sodas in the refrigerator downstairs."

"You didn't even know that area was down there yet," Charles corrected.

"Ah, so much for my vaunted wits!" Susan laughed.

"Your wits are still reliable, as evidenced by your instant observation that my amendment to your former observation could impugn the integrity of your wits!" Charles rejoined with a flourish.

"Oh, my, Charles! That was hard to keep up with! Say it again."

Charles laughed, "Not a chance. I've already forgotten most of it, and I'm not even sure I understood it while I was saying it."

Susan's attention was caught by a new song beginning on the stereo. "That sounds like waltz music, Mr. Parker."

"So it is, mademoiselle. Would you care to dance?" Charles asked, pronouncing the "a" in dance with an overly sophisticated "ah" sound.

"I would," Susan accepted, stepping into Charles' arms in the center of the cockpit.

Charles moved the last few bites of his sandwich to his left hand, and Susan moved hers to her right hand, and instead of holding hands, they just touched their wrists together.

"Think you remember, or would you like me to go over the steps again?"

"I'm ready, sir. Lead on."

Charles listened to key into the rhythm and started off. They did the "box" steps forward and back, slowly turning, making use of every bit of the small cockpit floor.

Oh, Charles, you're as hard as a rock down there, Susan observed to herself, as her emotions began to challenge her reason for control of her will. *Your chest, moving against mine… feels… so amazingly good.*

They continued to move their bodies together in harmony, finishing their sandwiches, and feeling warmer despite the breeze picking up.

What was it you said…? I'm burned into your heart. You feel like I'm part of you… like we were always supposed to be? Mmmm…

Charles' right hand slid from the center of Susan's back to the small of her back and pressed her lightly toward him.

Uuunng. She pressed her waist more tightly against his, and their steps became shorter.

The waltz came to an end as Susan slowly looked up, and Charles met her with a full-on kiss. Their feet stopped moving as the music shifted to another song and played on.

Susan slipped both arms around Charles and hugged him, subconsciously sliding her hips up and down against the front of his pants.

Charles' tongue entered her mouth and she groaned as she used her own tongue to toy with his, then suck gently on it. A moment later, Susan used her tongue to push his tongue back into his mouth, and then pushed her own tongue as deeply as it would go into his mouth, as Charles' right hand slipped further down and squeezed.

Uuunng... ohhh... Susan moaned without care as she became acutely aware of the protrusion in his pants moving against her, and she was powerless to resist its appeal. "Oh, Charles... take me! Take me downstairs..."

"We... can't..." he managed to say.

Ohhh... "I want you, Charles. I *need* you, right now!" She parted and pulled him toward the hatch to the stateroom, and he started to follow, then pulled her to a stop.

Susan panted lightly as she looked at Charles with hunger, noting his heaving chest, his whole body inclined toward her as he stared at her.

"No..." he croaked.

"No? No...?! You can't say no!" *I felt you pushing against me as hard as I was pushing against you!* She pointed to the bulge in his pants and said with some anger, "You want this as much as I do, Charles!"

He stood, wavering.

Susan's tone tuned to pleading. "Please, Charles! Please! I need you!"

Still holding one of her hands, he sank to his knees. "Susan..." his voice trailed off.

Get up! I can't drag you down there! You put your hands all over me and got me hot, now you've got to do your duty! Susan's voice changed again, this time to a commanding tone. "Charles. Get up, and come down there with me, right now!"

A tear rolled down his face as he strained to speak, clearly this time. "No."

Susan stared for a moment longer, then stormed down the steps alone. "Arrrrgh! I can't believe this! What's wrong with you?!" *What's wrong with me?! Is the thought of going to bed with me that repugnant?!* She started opening and slamming cabinet doors and throwing small items around.

"Charles Parker, take me home!" she yelled toward the hatch. "No! Take me back to the marina; I'll take a cab home! I'll... *I don't have enough money for a cab...* I'll hitchhike home! I'll..."

She picked up a throw pillow and launched it through the hatch. "Ohh, you impossible man!" The pillow sailed unimpeded over the transom and into the water.

"You can't just toy with a woman's affections! You can't... you can't just turn on her motor and... and not..." *drive her,* she finished silently.

She opened a cabinet and found a cooking pot and hurled it through the hatch just as Charles peered in and it caught him right at the hairline with a loud clang. Charles stumbled backward and fell as blood started pouring out of the gash.

"Charles!" Susan screamed. She rushed up the steps and tripped over the pot, falling on top of Charles' legs with her head coming down hard on his crotch.

"Oowwww!" Charles yelled and bent his knees up toward his chest, trapping Susan's head.

"Oh, Charles! I'm so sorry! Please don't be hurt...!" she cried as she untangled herself.

Susan scrambled up and gasped in shock at the profuse bleeding. "Charles, you're bleeding!"

"Uuunh," was his only reply.

"We've got to get you to a hospital! Do cell phones work out here? No, they can't come out here anyway! We've got to get the boat back! But first we need to do first aid! Uh, we apply direct pressure, I think, to stop the bleeding." She grabbed one of Charles' hands and put it on the cut.

"You've got to hold this Charles, so I can drive the boat back to the dock. Can you do that? Can you hold this?"

"Susan..."

"And for a head wound, we uh... raise the feet." She noted that his knees were still bent up toward his chest. "Okay, we've got that covered."

Susan jumped behind the wheel and put her hand on the

throttles.

"Susan!"

"Yes, darling?" she called back anxiously.

"The anchor's down."

"Oh…! Oh, Charles, how do I get the anchor up? Is there an axe I can use to just cut it loose?"

Charles laughed and rolled over onto his side. "No, hon, there's no axe… and you don't have to rush. Head wounds always bleed a lot to start with, but something like this should be easy to stop the bleeding. I'm going to be fine."

He laughed again. "Although it may be a bit longer before I'm able to stand up again."

Susan went back to his side and knelt down. "Oh, Charles, I'm so sorry! Will you forgive me? I… I don't know what came over me! I… I've never acted like that before, I promise! That's not like me at all! In all my fights with Marty, I never threw anything, not ever. I'm so sorry, Charles, will you forgive me?"

"Susan, of course I forgive for. I love you. Nothing will ever change that."

Susan looked away. "I'm so ashamed of myself. I can't believe I acted that way. I don't understand. I was like a wild woman. I can't even blame my period, or menopause. I'm definitely past my periods and I think I'm past menopause, too, though I miss having it to blame for mood swings."

"Susan…" Charles called, and Susan turned back toward him.

He motioned with a finger for her to come closer, and she leaned in.

"Yes, Charles?"

"Being a wild woman has a certain attractive aspect to it," he said grinning.

"Oh, don't you start getting me stirred up, again. You… maybe you don't understand what a powerful impact your words…" *and your body* "… have on me."

"Well, your impact on me is obvious."

Susan frowned until she realized he was exercising his dry sense of humor again, and they both burst into laughter. "Oh, Charles… I wish I had never made that particular kind of impact."

"Well, help me up, and down into the cabin… to look for a first aid kit, mind you. And nothing else."

Oh, Charles… I'm so sorry! Susan started helping Charles get up on his feet, though he couldn't straighten up completely.

You're still hurt! All because I wanted to have sex so badly... I was ready to sacrifice all my beliefs just to satisfy my lust. Oh, God, I didn't realize I was that low. I'm so sorry. Please help me to do better. Help me not to want sex unless and until we get married.

Susan got Charles to the edge of the bed, and he rolled over into a semi-fetal position with a groan.

"Oh, Charles, is it still that bad?"

"Well, I... it... was, uh... fully... uh, well, let's just say it was the worst possible time for a head-butt in that area."

"Ohhh, Charles...! Is there anything I can do?" *Other than taking your bloody clothes off, which would be a decidedly dangerous thing to do right now...*

"Just look for a first aid kit, please, for bandages... for my head. The... my, uh... that is, as far as walking normally, I just need a little more time, I think."

Susan rushed through the cabin searching for a first aid kit. *I don't suppose kissing your balls to make them feel better would be a welcome offer... Susan...! Dear God, please help me keep my mind clean! Please... Oh...!"*

She spotted a white box with a red cross on the front and unstrapped it from its mount. "Here it is!"

She brought it to him, and they looked through the contents. Susan picked up a large roll bandage.

"I could wrap this around your head..."

Charles winced. "And look like I was returning home from war? Help me to the bathroom, and let me get a close look at this. I think I'd like to go with the smallest bandage possible, not the largest."

He hobbled to the bathroom and washed a lot of the blood off his face.

He still can't stand up straight, and it's all my fault!

"It's not too bad. I can use a butterfly bandage to hold it together." Charles used some scissors from the kit to start shaping a band aid into a butterfly by cutting away from the center area to make it a thin strip while leaving the larger sticky areas on each end.

Despite his cheerfulness, Susan walked over and sat down dejectedly on the edge of the bed. *I can't believe I acted that way. I would have dragged him down here if I could have. Even prostitutes don't behave that badly. Oh, God! I was worse than a prostitute! I don't even deserve...*

"I'll need to cut away a little bit of hair so the bandage can stick, but hey, that'll grow back in no time!"

Oooh... God, I'm so sorry. I can't seem to control myself, so... doesn't that mean I should get married? I would have said yes if he had asked me, but... why didn't he? Does he want me or not?

Susan looked toward the bathroom. *It's apparent I can't control myself. I don't know how he's able to, and I don't understand why he wants to, for crying out loud. What kind of a man turns down sex with a woman he thinks is pretty, who wants to have sex with him? What kind of a man turns down sex at all...?*

Her eyebrows went up as a thought struck her. *A man with Godly character, obviously...*

A frown crept back onto her face. *Even though I've been a Christian much longer than him, he's a much better Christian than I am. Well, even if he has self-control, I obviously don't, and I can't handle the pressure... I just hit him in the head with a pot, for crying out loud! So... what are the options? Either he has to ask me to marry him, or I have to ask him, or... we have to stop seeing each other. Any other options...? I don't think so. But how long should I wait for him to ask me? What if he never does? So, then, I should ask him. But what if I ask him and he says no...?! Oh, Lord, why would a Godly man want to marry a woman who just acted like I did?*

Charles walked back in still a little bent at the waist, and buttoning his shirt, which he had washed in the sink with little improvement. "You look so serious... you know I'm not, uh, permanently damaged, right? Another half hour or so and I'll be as, uh... capable as I ever was."

Capable? To have sex? I don't understand you, talking like you want to have sex, but refusing to even when I begged you for it. Susan looked away. *Oooh, God, I was begging a man to have sex with me, and we're not even married!*

"Talk to me Susan," Charles pleaded, "what's wrong?"

"What's wrong...? What's wrong?! I... I lost my temper so badly I actually hurt you, and it could have been a lot worse. As far as you know, I may lose my temper like that all the time. And I wanted to have sex so badly, I might've raped you if I could have. And I thought I was a Christian."

"Being a Christian doesn't turn off a person's sex drive." Charles reached out to put a comforting hand to Susan's shoulder, but stopped, sitting down instead, with plenty of room between them. "A little while ago I had more will-power than you did. That doesn't mean I always will. Next time, you might be the strongest."

Next time? How long do you think I can go on like this? What can I say? Marry me now so I can satisfy my sex drive? Or leave me alone to my old sexless life even though I love you so much?

"I'm sorry I made you angry," Charles said quietly.

Susan looked down and shook her head. "You have nothing to apologize for. I shouldn't have gotten angry. And I shouldn't have asked you to have sex with me." *I shouldn't have wanted to have sex with you.*

"Well, we were both... aroused, and that's behind us now."

Susan started to smile as she turned to look at Charles, and then looked distressed. "Not for your head and ruined clothes."

Charles smiled warmly now. "Those are insignificant. My head will heal, and my clothes can be replaced... minor, temporary setbacks."

Susan sighed. *At least I didn't see you while your shirt was off. Well, maybe you're right... maybe my will power is strong enough to control myself now.*

"Well, how about if we head back toward the marina now? They should be expecting us soon," Charles suggested as he reached over and put a hand on Susan's back and brushed it up and down once.

Susan looked away and gasped quietly as her body responded with instant arousal. *Oh, dear, God. I... I...*

Charles didn't seem to notice as he got up, walked to the steps up to the cockpit and looked back. "Coming?"

Cumming? Susan echoed to herself.

Charles' expression turned to one of concern and he started to walk back toward Susan.

"No, Charles... if you don't mind, I'd like to stay down here by myself for a few minutes... to pray." *That's a lie. I don't really want to pray, I just want to find an off switch on my awful libido.*

Charles stopped and nodded with a smile again. "Okay, Susan. I'll get us headed back and you come up as soon as you're ready. Okay?"

Susan smiled and nodded and Charles went up the steps. As soon as he was completely around the corner of the hatch, she grabbed the remaining throw pillow, hugged it to her chest and curled up on the bed. *Oh, God, pleeaase help me! One stinking touch and I'm on fire...!*

Her breathing became rapid and deep as she bit the edge of the pillow and screamed into it. Her leg muscles tightened and she bucked her hips as she grunted, with the pillow still muffling her. She rolled face down and put the pillow between her thighs, squeezing it hard as she screamed again, into the mattress.

Any sounds that weren't absorbed by the pillow and mattress were drowned out by the boat engines and the sound of water against the hull.

Sometime after Charles has raised anchor and started the boat back toward the marina, Susan came up on deck, her face flushed. Instead of sitting next to Charles, she stood next to the seat and leaned against it, leaving plenty of room between them.

"Feeling better?" Charles inquired with a smile.

Susan nodded as she looked all around at the scenery, "Not good, but better, yes."

"Anything I can do for you?"

Susan just shook her head in response. *We've already established that you're not going to do what my body is craving for.*

He increased the speed until the engines were going all-out, and Susan held onto the top of the windshield again.

"Getting hungry?" he asked.

Susan sighed. *There you go again. Yes, I'm hungry... for you.*

She noticed some faint stomach-related hunger pangs, then looked at Charles' shirt, still damp, badly wrinkled, *...probably from twisting it to get the water out after rinsing it...* and still with large, obvious stains. "Yes, but... we can eat out another time. You can just take me home tonight." *Did that sound like invitation for sex at my house...? Did I want it to?*

Charles looked deflated, then furrowed his brow. "I, uh, already have reservations at the marina... and it is the closest place to eat. And you just said you're hungry..."

"Yes, but, did you forget about your clothes?"

He glanced down. "Oh. That bad? Well, I can wear my windbreaker, zipped up. Would that be okay? It's probably semi-casual, and they're used to boaters, of course."

"Are you sure you want to? I don't mind, but..."

"Oh, no, I don't mind either! And I'd rather eat soon, if you don't mind."

She nodded, "Okay, if you're sure."

Susan noticed Charles smiling broadly.

Wish you had been that hungry for me... No! No, I don't! Lord, I need more help to keep my thoughts pure, and my body... tame. Dear God, can I not keep my mind off sex for five minutes?

The rest of the trip back was uneventful, with no touching and lots of small talk. Charles parked the boat back in the slip as the sun was setting and showed Susan how to lash the spring lines. After putting on his windbreaker, they took their things up to the office. Charles was walking normally again, and they turned in the keys and life jackets.

Charles told Sam that he'd gotten a cut on his head without giving any details, and asked them to charge any extra cleaning costs to his credit card. Sam agreed, and Susan and Charles walked over to the restaurant in the fading glow of twilight.

"Are you sure you want to do this?" Susan asked with concern. "They probably wouldn't mind cancelling the reservation under the circumstances."

"Oh, no! I mean... yes, I'm sure I want to do this." Charles said but then stopped abruptly and glanced down again. "Oh, I'm sorry, Susan. I should have realized you'd rather not be accompanied by someone in such a state..."

"What?! You think I..." Susan grabbed Charles' arm and hooked her own arm in it. "Charles Parker, I am proud to be with you," she said, and they finished the walk arm-in-arm.

Charles zipped his jacket all the way up as he held the front door for Susan.

"Ah, welcome to The Point Marina Restaurant, Mr. Parker," the maître d' said briskly as they entered. "My name is Jefferson. Just Jefferson. And this is Juliette, our lovely hostess. Everything is ready just as you requested, Mr. Parker, and the band has been practicing all afternoon. And Sam called from the marina and explained about your clothes. If you like, sir, we have some spare clothes we keep for vacationers who sometimes come a bit unprepared and want to dress up a little. I believe we have some things that will do very well for you, and we have a changing room, if you'd like to try them on."

"Well, yes, that would be very nice, thank you. Susan... if you won't mind if I excuse myself for a few minutes?" Charles asked.

"Oh, no, Charles," Susan replied happily, "that's fine!"

Jefferson leaned over to Charles and lowered his voice, but Susan still heard him say, "And your package arrived about an hour ago."

Jefferson led Charles off to the changing room, and Juliette ushered Susan toward the back.

Band practicing... package arrived...? Charles has been busy planning again...

"Miss Susan, is it? Right this way, please, we have a very nice table set up for you on the patio. I'll bring Mr. Parker out as soon as he's changed."

I wouldn't change a thing about him, Susan thought lightly as she followed Juliette to the table, already set with a silk tablecloth, linen napkins, fine china, lead crystal water glasses, and ornate silverware.

"Is this table acceptable?" Juliette asked. "The tiki torches keep the bugs away in addition to providing romantic lighting."

"Yes, this is very nice, thank you. It's a beautiful view." *Romantic lighting... that didn't use to sound like a risky thing.*

"Your waiter will be right out with some appetizers," Juliette said as she helped Susan with her chair, then excused herself.

Well, this really is nice. I'm surprised no one else is out here... the weather's perfect. And it's no wonder Charles wanted to come so badly, he must have planned out the whole thing... and he's really good at planning. And that package... I wonder what that is? And the band practicing? I'll bet he asked them to play a waltz tonight. Susan put her elbows on the table, put her chin on top of her folded hands, and sighed. *Charles, I don't want to disappoint you, but I'm afraid to dance with you... even at arm's length. You're simply too attractive for me to... control myself. Which brings me back to my earlier quandary... should I ask you to marry me? Well, I can't imagine a nicer setting... but will that offend you? What if you say no? What do I do then? Oh, God... what would I do if Charles says he won't marry me?! How can I go back to who I was before I met him?*

Susan got up and walked over to a railing, looking out over the lake, as the waiter put a bread basket on the table and left.

A few minutes later, Charles came out in pleated khaki pants only a little too long, and white shirt that was a little too large, and a dark blue sport coat.

"Nice view," Charles said.

Susan turned, smiled, and sighed. "Oh, Charles, aren't the reflections of the lights on the lake beautiful?"

"Yes, those too," he smiled back.

"Oh, Charles... thank you. And you look great!"

"Thank you, ma'am," he responded. "Are we ready to dine?"

"Yes, let's."

Charles helped her with her chair and seated himself across from her as the waiter appeared and stood by the door, holding what appeared to be menus.

"How does salmon sound?" Charles asked.

"Fine, if they have it."

Charles looked at the waiter and nodded. The waiter opened the door, and two additional staff came out with their meals.

Susan, with raised eyebrows, said, "Well, isn't that handy? They just happened to have two salmon dinners ready…"

"Yes, how about that?"

The beautifully arranged plates were placed in front of Susan and Charles, and Susan looked at him.

"And if I hadn't been in the mood for salmon?"

The extra staff retired inside as the waiter poured wine.

"Then we would have looked at the menus, you would have picked whatever you wanted, we'd have waited for it to be cooked, and you'd have never known about the salmon."

The waiter retired as Susan stared at Charles and grinned, then started drumming the fingers of one hand on the table.

"A preplanned meal that had to be paid for even if not used…" Susan pointed out, "…a mysterious package… a band that's been 'practicing all afternoon'…"

"I may have gone a little overboard."

"Well, at least I didn't push you there."

"Huh?" Charles tilted his head for a moment, then started to laugh.

Susan joined in his laughter, but his increased until he was howling and tears streamed down his face.

Well, that joke worked out well… would this be a good time to propose, once you calm down, but while you're still in a good mood? She nervously toyed with her napkin. *Will you say yes? You said you wanted to make some memories today… Uh, oh… I think your wound needs a little attention… and you probably didn't mean for our memories to include a scar on your head…*

"Perfect," he finally gasped, "that joke was absolutely perfect! Oh, Susan, that was hilarious!"

Susan moved from her chair to a chair next to him and used her napkin to dab up a drop of blood forming on the cut on his head, as he studied her face.

"What are you grinning about?" Charles asked.

Susan laughed, "Well… I think we succeeded in making a memory."

Charles laughed heartily again, then calmed down to a warm smile. "We certainly did make some memories today. Though I had something quite different in mind."

"Oh? What did you have in mind?"

Charles slipped out of his chair, pushed it aside, and got down on one knee as he pulled a small ring box out of his jacket pocket and opened it facing her. "I love you with all my heart, Susan…" he said very nervously. "Will you marry me?"

Really?! You really want me? Tears clouded her vision as Susan gasped, then got down on her knees to hug him around the neck as tears streamed down her face once again. "Oh, Charles, Charles, I love you. I love you so much! I was praying you'd ask me. I was begging God for you to ask me!"

"Is that a yes, then?" Charles said in between kisses.

"Yes! Yes, I will marry you… anywhere, anytime… and the sooner the better! Very soon! Very, very soon!"

Susan removed the ring from the box, and Charles slipped it on her finger. A one-carat diamond was surrounded by a heart shape of tiny diamonds.

"It fits perfectly!" Susan said blissfully.

They stood up and hugged cozily.

"Are you serious about the very, very soon part?' Charles asked. "Because I seriously don't think I can keep my hands off you much longer."

"I don't want you to!" Susan blurted. "Let's set a record, Charles! What's the fastest we can possibly get married?" Susan asked.

"Are you serious? You don't want time to invite friends and make plans to…"

"Serious. No friends. No plans. Just fast…." Susan interrupted. "You saw what I was like on that boat. I want to get your pants off so bad I can…" *oops, "taste it" might have the wrong connotation…* "Charles… I've never been this horny before. I… oh, I'm sorry. Marty and I used to use that kind of language. What's a more polite word? Aroused? Excited?"

"Horny's fine. That is, the language is fine. I'm used to that kind of language, too. As for being horny, that will only be okay if we can wait until we're officially married. Let's see, we'll need a license, we'll need a minister, and witnesses. Oh, are blood tests required in Tennessee?"

"They didn't used to be. I don't know about now. My pastor will know, though, he does weddings all the time," Susan replied.

"Great, we can ask him first thing in the morning! Now, what else? We'll have to wait for the license office to open on Monday, but if they don't have a waiting period…"

"Then we could get married the day after tomorrow!" Susan

exclaimed.

"Yeah, that's the best case, but…"

"Yee-ha!!" Susan yelled before smothering Charles with kisses again.

After he got his lips loose for a moment, he commented, "You're a woo-hoo girl *and* a yee-ha girl? You're just full of delightful surprises!"

"Not as many surprises as you. But you just wait till I get your clothes off in two days, mister!"

"Oh, Susan…"

"What?! What's wrong?" Susan asked.

"Your last comment will make it twice as hard for me to wait."

'Twice as hard?' "Oh, Charles…" She said and kissed him again, pressing herself against the bulge in his crotch. *Does that mean you don't want to wait? Does your ring on my finger mean we can go ahead? I don't think I can get pregnant… no, definitely not, it's been years since I had a period…*

Charles ended their kiss and pulled away. "Two days never seemed so far away," he said. "But…"

He took Susan's hand and led her back to her seat, then sat down.

"Susan, it's really important to me that we not have sex until after we're married. Is that okay?"

Oh, Father… that's good, I know, but… it's impossible! "Charles… I don't know why, but… I've never wanted anything so… urgently as I want you. I get calmed down a little bit and I think I'm going to be okay, and then something insignificant sets me off again. I want to have sex with you so much it almost hurts."

Charles sat back in his chair. "I didn't realize this was so hard on you."

She fidgeted with her fork. "Why is waiting so important to you?"

"Well, I didn't wait before my first two marriages, and they… weren't exactly perfect. I guess I thought since we're both Christians now, I'd really like us to start our marriage right, in every way possible."

Susan gulped. *You're right, of course. But I don't want you to be. I want you inside me… tonight! But I also want to honor you, and this is important to you. And… I'm sad to think I thought of this last, but I want to honor God, too.* "Charles…"

"Yes, my darling?"

"If you want me to wait... for sex... if I can, it will have to be with your help," Susan pleaded.

"What can I do to help?" Charles asked.

The memories of their activities over the last few days that stirred her up flashed through her mind. "No hugging... no kissing... no dancing..."

"Okay, for your sake, until we get married, we won't do any of those things," Charles assured her.

"And don't rub your hand on my back," she added.

Charles cocked his head and furrowed his brow.

"On the boat," she said.

Charles frowned.

"When we were sitting on the bed."

No sign of recognition from Charles.

"You put your hand lightly on my back, to console me, I suspect, and you moved it up, then down, exactly once." Susan elaborated.

Charles shook his head. "I'm sorry, I don't remember that."

Susan sighed heavily. "Charles, that touch... overwhelmed me. And you didn't even notice."

Susan lowered her voice and leaned forward. "Do you see how hard this is going to be? If you have any little slip-ups, just as small a thing as that, I'm going to rip your freaking clothes off and impale myself on you."

Charles stared in surprise or shock, Susan couldn't tell which.

I can't believe I just said that! But... I'm glad I did. If you can't handle that, better to find out right now. I'll give you the ring back and I'll never want to see you again. No! I don't mean that! Oh, God, why doesn't he say something?

Susan dropped her head and closed her eyes. *My Lord, I'm so sorry. Please forgive me, Lord! I don't even recognize myself anymore! I don't know what to do. Please forgive me for my carnal desires!*

"Susan?" a sweet voice drifted into her consciousness and she looked up.

Charles was looking at her intently. "Susan... tomorrow we'll talk to your pastor. If he says there's any reason we can't get married in Knoxville on Monday morning, we'll go to the airport straight from Church and fly to Las Vegas and go straight to a wedding chapel."

Susan looked at him with great appreciation as she nodded. "Okay, then."

They spent several more moments just looking into each other's eyes.

"Oh, I almost forgot. I have an engagement gift for you." He started reaching into a pants pocket.

Interesting that you have it down there where you've also got a wedding present for me. Susan gave her head a shake. "What? What is it?"

"Well, it's an engagement gift because you said yes. Otherwise it would have just been a present for no reason." He pulled her keys out of his pocket and gave them to her. "Your car's working."

"Wha... my car?!" Her face lit up. "What...? How could you do that? They said it would take a week!"

"They didn't know what they were talking about, as I suspected. Or worse, they may have been trying to knowingly cheat you," he replied, and then grinned again. "You don't know what kind of work I've done for a living do you?"

"Um, no, come to think of it, that's one of the many things we haven't talked about yet. Why...? Oh, something to do with cars?"

He laughed.

Oh, I love to hear you laugh!

"Yeah, something... since high school," he said. "Started learning how to work on them then and stayed with it. I'm a pretty good mechanic, truth be told."

"Oh, well you ought to be able to find a good job quickly, then. Good mechanics are hard to find," she said.

"It can be hard to find competent mechanics, and it can be hard to find honest mechanics," he said as Jefferson came out on the patio, followed by the waiter. "And it's especially hard to find mechanics that are competent and honest."

"Is everything alright with the meal, Mr. Parker?" Jefferson asked with concern. "If not, we'll..."

Susan and Charles laughed as Charles stood up and patted him on the back. "Actually, Jefferson, we haven't even tasted it yet. I was too busy proposing, and Susan has blessed me by saying yes!"

Jefferson clapped his hands in delight and the waiter smiled with relief.

"That's wonderful news, Mr. Parker, wonderful news! And when you do get ready to eat, we can warm up your food, or prepare you new meals, whatever you wish."

"Susan?" Charles asked.

Susan took a bite of her salmon, and nodded as she swallowed.

"Yes, it would be nice to warm this up a bit."

The waiter quickly removed the plates and took them inside.

"Would you like us to move the band out here, Mr. Parker," Jefferson asked, "or perhaps just open some of the windows to let more of the music out here?"

"No thank you, Jefferson," Charles replied. "We've decided we won't be dancing tonight after all. But whatever you usually pay the band, double it tonight and charge it to me. Give them my thanks, and tell them we'll be back, so make sure they keep practicing some three-quarter time songs."

Jefferson bowed politely. "Yes, sir, Mr. Parker. That's very generous of you sir. I'm sure they'll appreciate that very much!"

Susan looked shocked.

"Now if you don't mind, I think we'd like to be alone again."

"Yes, sir! And our heartfelt congratulations to you both!" Jefferson said as he made a rapid retreat.

"Charles…!" Susan exclaimed quietly. "You…"

"How about if we stretch our legs while we wait for dinner again?" Charles asked.

Are you crazy? Paying the band like that? We may need that money to pay for plane tickets!

Susan got up without speaking and started walking with him toward the fence. *Do you have an uncontrollable urge to spend? Is that your kryptonite?* "Charles, I know this is a very special occasion, but paying the band double when you're out of work? Buying a huge diamond ring? You may have some money from selling your house, dear, but you've got to be more careful with your savings."

She frowned. "And another thing… they offered to move the band outside just for us. And Jefferson seems to be treating us like royalty. Do you have any idea why?"

"Well, yes, probably. I paid a lot extra to reserve the entire patio tonight, and that might have given them the impression that I'm a wealthy customer."

"Oh, Charles! Well, what's done is done, and you certainly made this an extraordinary day, an unbelievable day, stock full of memories, but from now on, no pretending to be rich, okay?"

Charles nodded. "Okay, no pretending to be rich."

"Good," Susan said, "I feel a little guilty bringing it up after you've proposed, but the sooner you find out, the better. My finances are in bad shape, Charles. I inherited my house, but Marty talked me into taking out a mortgage on it, and now I'm not sure I'm going to be able to make the payments. If something doesn't change, I may lose the house."

"I see," said Charles, "Well, I'm glad you told me now. And I have something I need to tell you, and I feel a little guilty about for not telling you before asking you to marry me."

The waiter returned with the dinner and Susan and Charles paused their conversation as they returned to the table. When he removed the covers and they each tasted the food, Susan smiled and nodded, and Charles thanked him and dismissed him. They both started eating with relish.

"Okay... so what's your big secret?" Susan asked.

Charles replied between bites, "Have you ever heard of Parker Automotive Centers?"

Susan shook her head. *'Parker' automotive?*

"There aren't any in Tennessee, not yet, anyway, but there are sixty-three, with most of them in Pennsylvania, Maryland, Virginia, and North Carolina. I'm Parker."

Susan stopped chewing and looked quizzical.

"I built the first one, I turned it into a franchise, and I'm still the largest shareholder. When I said I was out of work, that was technically true, but misleading. I'm sort of semi-retired."

Susan's eyebrows went higher and higher. *Largest shareholder... sixty-three stores... semi-retired...?*

"My interest in the company is probably worth at least eighteen million dollars," Charles concluded.

Susan dropped her fork onto the table. "That word... between 'eighteen' and 'dollars'..."

Charles was wolfing down more salmon and replied with his mouth full, "Million."

"Million," Susan repeated.

Charles nodded.

Susan's mind raced. "...You wanted to ask me to marry you and get my answer before I knew you were rich."

Charles nodded as he chewed, looking carefully at Susan.

Susan nodded slowly as her mind whirled. *...a beautiful woman... must have been fighting men off left and right... your smile makes my heart beat faster... I love being in your presence... God changed me, Susan... I have become in his eyes like someone bringing contentment... burned into my heart... you're part of me... like you were always meant to be... you're part of me... delicious tinge of green... carried up the stairs to a bedroom... they should* *marry... dancing while the world fades away...*

"Susan...? Are you okay?" Charles asked again.

Hmm? I feel a little faint, but that's better than being uncontrollably horny. "Yes, Charles, if I'm not dreaming, I'm okay."

"You are a dream, but you're not dreaming, sweetheart."

Sweetheart! I'm his sweetheart! I'd better not be dreaming!

An hour and a half later, after finishing dinner, taking a short moonlight stroll, and driving home, Charles pulled his car into Susan's driveway. He put it in park but left the engine running and they looked at each other happily, but wearily.

Charles glanced at the clock. "It's only ten-thirty. Feels a lot later than that."

"It's all the excitement today..." Susan commented. "You look exhausted. Are you sure you're okay to drive the rest of the way home?"

"Uh-huh," Charles replied. "You look like you're a little on the sleepy side yourself."

"Thank God for that. I don't know how I'd get any sleep tonight if I weren't exhausted from all the stimulation."

Susan started to lean toward Charles.

"No kissing," Charles recited.

"No kissing," Susan confirmed, leaning back. "And no hugging."

"And no dancing."

Susan laughed, "Definitely need a rule against dancing in the car."

"I love you, Susan."

"I love you, Charles."

"What time shall I pick you up for Church in the morning?"

"Umm..." Susan struggled to think it out. "Nine-thirty? I like to get there early."

"I will be here will bells on at nine-thirty."

Susan opened the car door and got out, then leaned over. "I love you."

"I love you."

"In two days, I'm going to give you a much better idea of how much I love you," Susan said.

"A day and a half!" Charles corrected.

"Mmm... Good night, my love."

"Sweet dreams, precious one!"

Susan walked slowly to her front door, looking over her

shoulder several times. She unlocked the front door, stood in the doorway and waved goodnight to Charles. He waved back, and she closed the door and locked it, listening through the door to the sound of his car driving off. She leaned against it and sighed contentedly as her thumb played with her new ring. *Oh, sweet Jesus... Lover of my soul... oh, wow... boy, have you surprised me! I never even imagined that you had anything this wonderful planned for me. Charles is so perfect for me! Thank you so much, Lord! Thank you so much!*

Chapter Seven

Susan kicked off her shoes and started to walk toward the kitchen and realized the house was darker than usual. *Huh. No light coming from the streetlights through the picture window. I guess Charles closed the curtains and I didn't notice.*

I wonder why he'd close them? She thought as she felt her way to the archway to the living room, found the lamp switch on the wall, and flipped it on.

"Hello, *Mrs. Towns*," said a harsh male voice.

Susan sucked in her breath sharply, dropped her things, and stepped back, away from the man standing in her living room. *Marty?! No, not Marty… and someone else on the couch!*

"Allow me to introduce myself. I'm Billy…" growled the man who appeared to be in his twenties, dressed in an old pullover shirt, old jeans, and sneakers. "…the closest thing to a son-in-law you'll ever have."

Son-in-law?! Susan looked again at the figure on the couch, a woman with spiky hair and heavy makeup, wearing a revealing paisley tank top showing off exaggerated breasts, and yellow hot pants. "S–Stephanie?!"

Stephanie looked away from her mother with a practiced air of disregard.

"Stephanie!" Susan cried as she rushed to the couch. "Oh, Stephanie, thank God you're okay!"

Susan tried to hug her, but Stephanie tried to shrug her off.

"Hello, Mom," she said flatly.

"Oh, Stephanie, how have you been? Where have you been? I'm so, so very happy to see you again! How long can you stay, honey?"

"Have you heard from Dad?" Stephanie asked, ignoring her mother's questions.

Susan shook her head sadly, "No, honey, I still haven't, even after all this time."

Stephanie pointed at the ring on Susan's finger and looked furious, "What xx-xx-xx is that, Mom…?!"

"I… I've met a man, sweetheart," Susan said as gently as she could. "He's…"

"Hey, xx-xx-xx, forget the family crap," Billy demanded. "We didn't come to Marble City for that xx-xx-xx, we have business to discuss."

Susan cast a sharp glance at Billy then turned back to Stephanie and put a hand on her shoulder. "Stephanie, baby, are you okay?"

"xx-xx-xx, Mom," Stephanie mumbled.

"Hey!" Billy shouted, "I'm the xx-xx-xx you need to be paying attention to, xx-xx-xx...! You owe me ten grand, and I'm here to collect! With interest!"

"What...? What are you talking about? I've never even met you before!" Susan replied.

"Your 'baby' is my porn star, honey, and she's had a boob job you must have noticed."

Porn star? Boob job? Susan glanced again at Stephanie's chest. *Oh, Lord, no...!*

"Top notch work, and I paid for that. Now you're gonna pay me back, *Mom...!*"

Billy grabbed Stephanie by the arm and put her in an arm chair, remaining between her and Susan. "How much you got in checking and savings accounts, xx-xx-xx?"

Susan's mind reeled as she tried to look around Billy to see her daughter, and Billy struck Susan hard across the face, knocking her back.

"Billy, don't! Please!" Stephanie cried.

"Shut-up, xx-xx-xx, or I'll xx-xx-xx you right in front of your mother! Then I'll xx-xx-xx her in front of you!"

Stephanie cowered and turned her head away, as Susan recovered from the blow and sat up again.

Billy leaned over to get right in Susan's face. "Answer my question, xx-xx-xx, how much you got?!"

How can I get this animal away from Stephanie? How can I help her...? Stall for time until I think of something... "Uh, no savings... I don't have any savings... and I have about two hundred dollars in my checking account," Susan stammered. "You can have it all."

"Xx-xx-xx! That's xx-xx-xx!" he said as he went over to Susan's bag on the floor.

Oh, God, please help us! Make this man leave Stephanie alone! Lord, now that she's alive, save her now!

Billy rummaged through Susan's things until he found her checkbook and flipped to the last entry. He threw it across the room, cursed again, and started pacing.

He paused and looked piercingly at Susan. "Nah... too old to farm out with your xx-xx-xx daughter," he muttered.

"Hey," he said as he slapped a hand against the doorframe leading to the dining room. "You own this place, or rent? Don't lie to me, or I'll stay here and go through all your papers till I find out for sure!"

Oh, Lord, the sooner he leaves, the better... "I own it," Susan answered. "But it's mortgaged."

"Hm, mortgaged, huh? You got a second mortgage on it, or a line of credit?"

Susan shook her head.

"What's this house worth, and how much you owe on it?" Billy demanded, pacing again.

Play along, Susan, there's no point in not telling him. "Uh... according to the tax assessment, it's worth about a hundred and fifteen thousand dollars, but I owe almost forty thousand on it, and..."

Billy smacked a fist into a palm. "Jackpot! That's what I'm talking about! That's like... over fifty thousand dollars equity!"

Over seventy five, you moron... "Well, it doesn't really matter, they..."

Billy stalked over to Susan and got in her face. "Oh, it matters, all right. You're gonna get that money for me, sweetheart. You're gonna get it with a second mortgage..." he stepped back over to Stephanie, "if you care about your daughter."

He squeezed one of Stephanie's nipples hard, then twisted it, and Stephanie screwed her eyes shut and winced in pain, but choked back her cries. Susan jumped up and lunged to get his hand off her, but Billy back-handed Susan in the face and knocked her to the floor, though he did let go of Stephanie.

Billy pulled out a large knife and kneeled over Susan.

"Billy, no!" Stephanie cried out.

Billy turned in an instant and waved the knife in front of Stephanie. "Shut up, Steph, and don't press your luck! You xx-xx-xx! You know better than to back-talk me!"

Stephanie cowered, but pleaded, "But please don't hurt my Momma, Billy. I'll do anything you want if you just don't hurt her."

"You xx-xx-xx! You'll do anything I want no matter what I do, and you'll ask for more! Right, xx-xx-xx?"

Stephanie nodded while looking at the floor, "Yes, Billy, I'll do anything you want."

Billy turned back to Susan, pushed her down and put a knee in her stomach, waving the knife in her face. "But your xx-xx-xx mother needs to learn I'm the boss, and I don't take no lip... you listening, xx-xx-xx?!"

Susan nodded. *God, we need you now! Right now! Send Charles back! Yes, Lord, send Charles!*

"Your xx-xx-xx daughter is one xx-xx-xx porn star, but that's not where the real money is. We're gonna start our own web site, get our own cameras and xx-xx-xx, but that takes a lot of money, and you're going to get it for us, you xx-xx-xx." Billy pushed his knee down harder, and Susan cried out. "How long does it take to get a second mortgage, xx-xx-xx?"

He lifted his knee enough to let Susan catch her breath and reply.

"I started to tell you, they won't give me a second mortgage because I don't earn enough money now," Susan explained, looking at Stephanie apologetically.

"You're lying!" Billy yelled.

"I lost my old job, and now I'm just a waitress... I mean barista, at a coffee shop. I get paid less than minimum wage, and I only work part-time!"

Billy just knelt there with one knee still on Susan's stomach as he thought.

"And besides that, I'm already behind on the first mortgage..." Susan added.

"Well, you really xx-xx-xx, you xx-xx-xx." Billy jammed his knee hard into Susan before he got up and towered over her as she gasped. *God, help! Help us!*

"So, you've got two choices..." Billy lectured, "Either you figure out some way to get that second loan, or you sell this tiny xx-xx-xx to get the equity. Yeah, get the loan, or sell it. I don't care which, but you get us our money, you understand? And get it quick, if you care about this xx-xx-xx over here."

Billy grabbed Stephanie's hair and pushed her face into his crotch. "You wanna show your Momma what we do for fun and money, xx-xx-xx?"

Susan turned her face away.

"Don't like to watch it in-person, Mom? I can take care of that." He let Stephanie go and reached into a pocket, pulling out a computer flash-drive, and tossing it on the coffee table. "Here you go, *Mom*... here's a video of your precious little xx-xx-xx, hard at work!"

"Bil..." Stephanie started to object, but quickly turned away when Billy gave her a hard look.

"Just giving your Momma a little extra incentive, you xx-xx-xx, so she'll have the motivation she needs to get the money for us," Billy said to her, then turned to Susan as she got up and sat back on the sofa. "You know what your little girl's porn-name is?"

Stephanie turned away and seemed to shrink into her chair.

Lord... please... save my daughter... even if he kills me... even if she never loves me... please save her from this man and every man like him.

"Slamantha Rock. Like it? I came up with that. That's what you call marketing. She's already got some fans, too. Guys who pay to watch her xx-xx-xx a whole room full of guys, and they all slam her. Get it? Slamantha? It don't matter she's so drunk she don't know what xx-xx-xx she's doin' or who she's doin' it to."

Billy turned back to Stephanie. "Go out to the car, Slam-baby, and wait for me."

Stephanie stood up and started to leave, then paused. "Momma..."

No! "Don't go, Stephanie! Stay here! I'll take care of you!" Susan pleaded.

Billy laughed derisively. "You think she's gonna do what you say when I'm telling her something different? Xx-xx-xx! Hey, xx-xx-xx, on your way out, show your Momma how you wiggle your butt when you walk and make those boys xx-xx-xx."

Stephanie covered her face and ran to the door, slamming it behind her.

"Stephanie...!" Susan cried after her, as Billy got in Susan's face again, still waving the knife.

"Now I know this mortgage and house-selling stuff dutn't happen overnight, so I'm gonna give you two weeks, then I'm gonna call you... yeah, I got your phone number from that xx-xx-xx daughter of yours. So if it takes longer than two weeks, that's okay... *if* you can convince me you'll have it soon after that... You know why?"

Billy put the tip of his knife between Susan's breasts and pressed it hard enough to puncture her blouse and draw blood. "Because if you don't, I'm gonna cut your little girl's heart out and send it to you in a box. Got it?!"

Susan stared in shock as he started walking toward the door and putting the knife away.

He paused at the door. "And don't call the police. I'll be

watching you every once in a while, and I'll know if you get the police involved. And if that happens…"

Billy's eyes narrowed. "I'll put her body in a freezer, and I'll cut off another part and send it to you every once in a while, just to remind you of how stupid you were… Or here's an idea… I'll kidnap you, and the only thing I'll feed you is hamburger. And you'll never know which hamburgers have some of your xx-xx-xx girl's body mixed in with the cow meat. That oughta give you some motivation over the next two weeks!"

Billy laughed and slammed the door behind him.

Crying and praying, Susan tried to get up, but hurt too much. She crawled over to her purse, got her cell phone, and struggled through blinding tears to find Charles' last call to call him back.

He answered almost right away, sounding tired but happy, "Hi'ya, beautiful, couldn't wait till morning to talk again?"

Susan tried to speak, but nothing came out.

"Susan?"

"Ch… Charles…" she choked.

Charles suddenly sounded fully alert. "Susan? Honey, what's wrong…?"

"Can you… I…" Susan started, but couldn't finish a sentence.

Charles waited a moment to give her time, but she just cried. "Susan, are you still at home?"

Amid the sobs, Susan managed to answer, "Yes."

"Are you okay?!"

"No…"

"Do you need an ambulance?"

"No," she stammered.

"Are you sure?! Do you need the police?"

"No!" she said emphatically. "No police!"

"Okay, okay, honey. I'll be there in five minutes. Will you be okay that long? Is that okay?"

"…Yes…please…"

Minutes later Charles' car screeched to a halt in Susan's driveway and he ran inside, where he found her lying on the floor, crying, bruised, and cut. "Dear God, Susan!"

He fell to his knees by her and started trying to get out his cell phone. "I'm calling an ambulance!"

"No, Charles, you can't," she said in between sobs, "the hospital will call the police."

"Well that's…"

"No! Help me up and let me explain before you doing anything else. Promise me!"

"But, Susan…!"

"I'm okay enough to tell you what happened. Now promise me you won't do anything else until I do…"

He reluctantly promised, and helped her to the kitchen table. She cried and spoke in fits and starts, but he got the gist of the story in little pieces as he assessed her physical condition.

He unbuttoned the top three buttons on her blouse to get at her cut and discovered it was minor enough to just put on some antiseptic she had in her medicine cabinet and cover it with a band aid. After he applied the band aid, she buttoned her blouse up again.

He put ice in a washcloth for her to hold against her face, but even after that, Charles remained angry, perhaps because of the continuing reminders of the blood stain on her blouse and the broken dining room window Billy had come in through.

When she had calmed down some, from exhaustion as much as anything, he took out his cell phone again. "Honey, we have to call the police. They…"

"Charles, no!" Susan said emphatically. "He said he'd kill her, and I really think he's evil enough to do it. Promise me you won't call them!"

"All right, I'll promise I won't call them right now, but we have to keep considering that option," Charles said.

"No, Charles, he said he had a way of knowing if I called the police. I can't take that chance. Promise me…! Please, Charles!"

He still kept his cell phone out. "Listen, Susan, I'm not going to call the police right now, but I'm going to call someone else, okay?"

"Who?"

"I'm going to call Nathaniel. He works for me, kind of like a personal assistant, as well as managing my company's finances. He knows a private detective, and I've met him before. He seems to be very good. This Billy guy won't have any way of knowing that we've called Nathaniel or the P.I.… okay?"

Susan hesitated.

"We need help, Susan. Professional help. It's either a private investigator or the police."

Susan slowly nodded, and Charles hit the speed dial. Susan put her head down on the table top and listened.

"Nat? I have an emergency. I want you to call Mike right away…

yeah, Mike Samuelson. Give him my cell phone number and have him call me right away. Not any of the guys who work for him, I want Mike... Okay, great. Next item. On Monday I want you to set it up so I can get fifty thousand dollars cash in small bills from a bank here in Knoxville anytime day or night. Wait, make it a hundred and fifty thousand, just in case... Well, no, not ransom, it's extortion... No, not me, it's Susan. Yeah, she said yes... Thanks, Nat, I was going to call you tomorrow, rather than call this late... Anyway, Susan has a daughter with a boyfriend who threatened her life tonight... a real bad character. Yeah, I'm sure... No, no, it's not like that. You'll understand when I tell you more about it, but that needs to be later... Yeah, thanks. I'll be waiting for Mike's call... that's the most urgent issue."

Charles got up and paced anxiously, looking frequently at Susan. "I can't believe I didn't notice his car outside!" Charles finally blurted out. "And I can't believe I didn't escort you into the house!"

Susan didn't respond.

A few minutes later Charles' phone rang and he answered immediately. "Mike...? Thanks for calling so quickly. Listen, there's a guy who's made lethal threats against my fiancée Susan and her daughter Stephanie. I want you to put a team together and find the guy, and I want round-the-clock bodyguards protecting Susan until you find him. Here's a catch: the daughter's with the bad guy, it's her boyfriend... Yeah, I know. I'd like you to come down here and supervise from here. Can you clear your calendar for that...? Yeah, I understand, that's acceptable... Yes, we'll do that... not a problem, Nat will take care of that... Okay, excellent... Yes, give my number to him and have him call me before he comes to the door... Yeah, okay... Yeah, here's the address..."

Charles finished giving Mike the information he needed and sat down beside Susan again.

Susan didn't stir, but her eyes were open, and Charles spoke gently. "Susan, we'll do everything possible to find Stephanie and get the creep locked up. Mike will be here tomorrow, but he knows a P.I. here in Knoxville, and he'll be coming over right away. I've actually met the guy before."

Charles reached out to put a hand on her back, but caught himself.

Susan raised her head up. "You've only been in town a few weeks, but you already happened to meet a private detective?"

"No... I didn't just happen to. I hired him. Through Nat, and probably through Mike," Charles said. "Remember the day I met you, when I waited in front of the coffee shop until you got off work?"

"Yes…"

"I had this guy watching the back alley, just in case you went out that way," he explained. "I didn't think you would, but I didn't want to take any chances."

"Wow," Susan said quietly. *That's impressive. Or intimidating. Or something.*

"I was head-over-heels for you the first moment I saw you. I had to make sure I could find you again."

She smiled, but it faded quickly as she put her head back down and closed her eyes.

"Susan, I'm not going to leave your side until they have a 24-hour-a-day guard protecting you."

A tear rolled across the bridge of her nose and dropped onto the table. "If I hadn't met you this past week… I… I don't know what I would have done tonight."

Charles was pacing again when his cell phone rang again. "Yes…? Hi, Frank… Yeah, okay. I see… then just knock on the door when you get through… okay, see you then. And Frank…? Thanks."

Susan sat up and looked at Charles.

"That was Frank Montgomery," he explained, "the local private detective. He's getting two other guys to help him check out the neighborhood… uh, Susan, how much do you want me to explain? If you'd rather…"

"I'd like to know everything, Charles," Susan said. "Please don't try to keep anything from me to try to protect my feelings."

Charles paused, then nodded. "Okay, then. They're going to start outside the neighborhood and work their way to us in case Billy is around here watching to see if the police show up. That will take a while, but if he's around here, they'll catch him."

Susan nodded thoughtfully. "That's smart. I wouldn't have thought of that."

Two hours later there was a knock at the door. Charles went to the door followed by Susan, and he let Frank in.

"Hey, Frank," Charles said. "Frank, this is Susan. Susan, this is Frank."

Frank shook hands with both of them. "Sorry to meet you under these circumstances, ma'am."

"So I take it you didn't find Billy around here," Charles observed.

"No. No one's watching this house except us now. I've been talking to Mike on the phone… he's driving down now… and he wanted me to have two guys watching the front and back of the house for now, and four more stationed further out as forward observation posts… to give the house-sitters early warning of anyone suspicious." Frank shifted his weight to one leg.

"Come into the living room, Frank, and have a seat," Susan said.

They all went into the living room, where the drapes were still closed. Frank sat in an arm chair while Charles and Susan sat close together on the sofa.

"So, I understand that your daughter, Stephanie, is with the man making the threats, Billy, and that she's with him by her choice?" Frank asked.

Charles deferred to Susan, and she nodded. "Yes," she said, "but… he was very domineering. The way she acted… it was like he's got her brainwashed or something."

Frank nodded. "So we need to provide protection to you, Susan, and at the same time, we need to make sure Billy doesn't know we're involved, since he'd probably think we're cops. We also need to find both Billy and Stephanie, and have Billy arrested."

Susan and Charles both nodded.

"Well, we can definitely protect you. We can probably do it without anyone knowing, but that takes more people than protecting you in an obvious manner."

"Do it the best way, whatever it costs," Charles said.

Frank nodded. "Yes, sir, Mike tells me you can afford it, but I want to make sure you understand there are no guarantees."

"Yes, I know something bad could happen no matter what we do," Charles replied, "but if something else does happen, I don't want it to be because we did something stupid or we didn't do enough."

"All right, well, maximum protection means you, Susan, don't leave the house, and we keep two trained men in here at all times. Keeping them hidden means we only change shifts at night. We'll also have groceries and anything else you need delivered at night.

"Finding them as quickly as possible means we need to track every lead we can find as quickly as possible, and that means if we have a lot of leads, we'll need a lot of foot soldiers… And until we find them, we'll have to keep a watch in case Billy comes around here to try to see if you've called the cops. That's pretty easy in the wee hours of the night, but it's really tough during other times because of all the normal traffic. One option there is to set up video surveillance in case we miss his car when it comes though, we might be able to get the tag number later off the video."

"Do it," Charles said without hesitation.

"All right," Frank agreed, pulling out a notebook and getting ready to write. "Now starts the hard part for you, Susan. I need to interview you about everything that happened, in painful detail, and that's not all. I may need to go over some things with you several times. And then when Mike gets here, he's going to need to do the whole process all over again. Any detail could be critical, so don't leave anything out that you can remember. Judging from the bruises on your face, all this could be a very painful process for you. Do you think you're up to it?"

Susan was looking at Frank, but she reached over and took hold of Charles' hand and held it tight. "I don't care about me, I just want to find Stephanie and get her away from Billy."

"All right, then. Why don't you just start at the top for me," Frank asked, and they started the long process.

About two thirty in the morning, Frank was fingering Billy's flash drive as he finally finished his questions and prepared to leave.

"Okay, folks, I've got a lot of work to do getting security set up. Finding Billy and Stephanie..." Frank shook his head. "That could be tough, depending on what we can find on this video thing. We don't have much else to go on, but we'll start trying to find Stephanie's old friends and see if we can find out how she met him, but that's an old trail since she moved out so long ago. Mike expects to get here around seven, so I'll come back then and give you an update."

Charles saw him out and locked the door behind him. As he came back toward the living room, he saw Susan stand, then get weak-kneed. He rushed to her and took her arm.

"Come on, Susan, you need to lie down and try to get some sleep."

She sighed as he led her to the bedroom and sat her on the edge of the bed.

Susan just sat listlessly as Charles just stood there for a moment.

"Do you, uh, want me to help you get your clothes off...?

She barely glanced up at him before lying down, facing away from him as she said, "No, thank you."

Charles watched her for a minute, then looked around and walked over to the closet and opened it. He found a blanket, took it out, spread it over Susan, and turned off the light. He stood in the door for a while before closing it.

Tired... so tired... Susan's eyes slowly drifted closed as her conscious thoughts quickly faded into mist. *That's odd... there's blood on my shirt... because there's a cut on my chest... Charles wants to see it... wants to see my chest... I'm glad... I'll pull my top off... oh, where's my bra...? Where did the blood go...? I guess my shirt soaked it up... You can touch them now Charles... that's it... reach out... closer... c'mon, Charles... get closer, not further away... Charles, the boat's drifting away from you... get back in the boat...! Charles, how do I make the boat come back to you...? Stephanie, do you know how to steer the boat...? Stephanie, why are you looking at me like that...? Don't push me out... Stephanie...! Help...! I'm too far from shore... I can't swim that far...!*

Susan barely began to wake and turned over to look at her bedside clock, glowing in red digits. *Six twenty-six. Huh. What is... I'm in my clothes... Stephanie's in trouble... Billy... Billy's got Stephanie... someone, the detective is coming over at seven... ouch, my face is throbbing...*

She got up and went to the bathroom, undressing as she went. *Lord, find Stephanie, and deliver her from evil.*

Susan got a shower, which her band-aid survived, then put on her favorite jeans and a soft brown pullover top with a V-neck and short sleeves, and she felt comfortable... safe. She added a thin gold necklace with a green opal pendant, but skipped the matching earrings.

She put on her tennis shoes and headed for the kitchen, and as she opened the bedroom door, she saw Charles lying on the hallway floor, gasped and staggered back. *Oh, God, no... NO!*

Susan's mind panicked as she simultaneously started to scream and noticed a dim snoring. She held a hand to her heart as the panic slowly faded and she realized he was sleeping on the floor... to guard her, she surmised.

She sank down to her knees beside him and gently stroked his hair, then his face. *Oh, Charles, my darling... sleeping on the hard floor just to keep me safe.*

Should I wake you up, or let you sleep? Hmm, your body could use the sleep, but if I let you sleep 'til later you might feel like you failed in your protector role. I wish I could lie down beside you. But those men will be here soon. "Charles? Charles, darling?"

Charles woke with a start, and looked around with a puzzled

expression.

"You're at my house, darling. You went to sleep on my hallway floor, just outside my bedroom door."

"Oh. Yeah," he said as he rose up on his elbows. "How are you feeling?"

"Tired. Worried. How about you?"

"What time is it?" Charles asked in reply.

"Almost seven."

"Uuhhh," Charles groaned, getting up. "Mike should be here soon."

"Let's get some coffee, then I'll cook us some breakfast."

As Susan started making coffee, Charles sat down at the table and started examining Susan's Bible. He found a Church bulletin in it and looked it over.

"Hey, Susan?"

"Yes?"

"Remember what I said about needing professional help?"

"Vaguely," she replied.

"Well, we've got professional investigators helping us... I think we should get professional Christians, too."

"What do you mean?"

"I mean your pastor, and any prayer groups in your Church," Charles said.

"That's a great idea, Charles."

"His phone number's listed here. Any objection to me calling him now?" Charles asked.

"You think it might be too early?"

"Seven A.M. Sunday morning. If he's not already up, he'd probably be getting up soon," he said.

Just then Charles' cell phone rang and he answered right away. "Hey... Good... Okay, see you in a minute."

He hung up and addressed Susan, "That was Mike. He's been down the street for a while, talking to Frank. He'll be here in just a minute."

"Okay. I'm making plenty of coffee."

There was a knock at the door and Charles let in Mike, Frank, and a bodyguard named Shad. Introductions were made all around, and Mike interviewed Susan all over again at the kitchen table, with Frank sitting in. Shad looked around the house before rearranging the living room furniture and stationing himself where he could sit and see through the crack in the drapes.

As soon as Charles saw that Susan was holding up to the interview, he stepped into the kitchen and made a phone call.

Mike's interview only took a half hour, and he and Frank got up to leave again, while Shad planned to stay until relieved that night.

"Susan, don't get mad at me," Charles pled, "but now that Mike and Frank know everything, I want to get their professional opinion on whether or not we should call the police. Is that okay?"

"Sure," she replied. "That is, asking them their opinion. I'd like to hear it before I decide whether or not I agree."

"Well," Mike said, "Stephanie's with him at least semi-voluntarily, so the FBI's not an option. The only reasons to call the police are to get their detectives to research a case, to arrest someone, or to put out a warrant for someone's arrest. We don't need an arrest or a warrant since we don't have him or know where he is. We're going to be able to dedicate a lot of man-power to researching the case, as opposed to them putting one or two detectives on it, detectives who have a bunch of other cases to work in addition to yours. They also have mug-shot books, but mug-shot books are strictly local, and Billy's statement about coming to Marble City means they're not in Knoxville, and we don't know which locality's mug-shots to look at. All of which means my advice is to wait. Let us call in the police once we find or capture the guy."

"What about them being able to trace phone calls?" Charles asked.

Mike smiled and held up his cell phone. "If he calls Susan's phone, that phone will automatically record the number he's calling from. As soon as we get that, we can find the address the phone is registered to as quickly as the police."

"But if Billy calls from a cell phone, you can't triangulate his location while he's on the phone," Charles objected.

"Normally, only the FBI can do that on live calls, but we can get it just like they can after the call is over." Frank said. "The phone records will have the tower information we need."

"And besides," Mike added, "he's not likely to stay on the phone long enough for anyone to get to him while he's still on."

Charles shoulders dropped a bit, and Susan noticed.

"Okay, then," Charles said, "no police for now."

Susan stepped next to Charles and put her arm in his and leaned lightly against him.

"Oh… you need to know some of our plans that you may have a role in," Mike remembered. "If Billy shows up with Stephanie, Shad or whoever's on duty will unlock the back door for us and then he'll hide elsewhere in the house. The rest of us will surround the house and the inside bodyguard will tell us when to come in. What we need you to do, if you can, is to get them separated. Ideally, get Billy sitting in a chair by himself. Once we have separation, we'll come in and capture him. Then we call the police to take over.

"If Billy shows up without Stephanie," Mike continued, "Susan and Charles, your job is to agree to anything he says and let him leave. The only reason we'll intervene is to save your lives, if it comes to that. While he's in your house, we'll attach a GPS transmitter to his car and we'll follow him until he leads us to Stephanie. Think you can do that?"

Susan and Charles looked at each other and then assured them they would.

"Another thing," Frank said, "who else knows about this?"

Susan looked at Charles and she shook her head.

"Nat, of course," Charles said. "I called him, and he called Mike."

"Call him and tell him not to tell anyone else unless we say so," Frank urged.

"Got that covered already, Frank," Mike said.

"Oh, and the pastor of Susan's Church," Charles added. "I called him while Susan was going over it again for Mike. He, uh, was planning on telling a prayer group."

Frank frowned.

Mike patted Frank on the back and ushered him toward the door. "Think of it as air-cover, Frank."

Mike opened the door and stepped out. "Whose car?"

"Oh, that's mine," said Charles.

"Give me the keys, we'll move it for you," said Frank.

Charles fished his keys out of his pocket, removed his apartment key, and handed them over without a word.

"You have a car in the garage, Susan?" asked Mike again.

"Yes," Susan replied. *A working one, thanks to Charles.*

"Okay," Mike said, "We'll move that tonight. We'll relocate your car for a while and that will let us load and unload where your neighbors can't see us. Okay?"

"Sure," Susan said.

"Best to stay away from the windows," Mike concluded.

"Got it," Charles agreed.

Well, if I'm going to be a prisoner, thought Susan, *I can't think of a better place…*

Chapter Eight

Shad didn't want breakfast, and didn't want to be disturbed, so Susan and Charles spent most of the next few hours sitting around the dining room table, talking quietly.

"Did you tell Henry we're engaged?" Susan queried after a silent spell.

"Who...? Oh, your pastor. Yes, I did." Charles looked at Susan nervously. "I hope that was okay."

"Yes, of course," Susan nodded and started a smile that turned into a wince from the pain. "It did occur to me, though, it might seem strange to some people that I jumped from no boyfriend and zero dates to engaged and about to get married from only one Sunday to the next."

"Hm. Does that bother you?"

"Well... it does seem like it might be a little embarrassing to introduce you for the first time as my fiancé already. You know, to people who have known me a long time." Susan paused and looked at Charles. "Oops."

"Oops, what?"

"We were planning to ask Henry today about marriage requirements..." Susan said.

"Yeah..." Charles said, too tired to pick up on Susan's train of thought.

"We were going to get married tomorrow if Tennessee law allows it, and get married in Las Vegas today if they didn't."

Charles looked distraught, but was speechless.

"What are we going to do now?" Susan asked.

Charles lowered his head to the tabletop with a soft "thunk." "Mmm... we can't leave the house, for Stephanie's sake. Not until they catch Billy."

"I can't, but they said you can," Susan corrected him.

"It could take days to catch Billy," Charles went on. "Ooo, you said Billy said he'd call back in two weeks... what if they can't find him before that?"

"Oh, and my job... I'm supposed to work tomorrow."

"Mm. I'll go over there this afternoon and tell that kid that, uh...

you've been hurt and have to stay at home for a couple of weeks," Charles suggested.

Susan sighed. "He'll probably love the excuse to fire me."

"Oh, remind me and I'll have Nat pay off your mortgage," Charles said. "You don't have to worry about that."

"Charles...! I... I guess we haven't talked about finances, but I didn't... I don't want to..."

Charles put up a hand to stop her. "You told Frank you told Billy you owe about forty grand. Is that amount right?"

"Yes, but I didn't..."

He held up his hand again. "I know you love this house, and I want you to own it free and clear again. No arguments."

"But that's too much!"

Charles smiled while shaking his head in mock disappointment. "You obviously don't understand the whole 'no arguments' thing... Susan, my car cost more than the balance on your mortgage. You're going to have to adjust your financial thinking a bit."

A lot, apparently... no debt on my house... no mortgage? Wow.

"Oh, and... Henry...? Henry said to tell you not to worry about the nursery this morning," Charles remembered. "What did he mean by that?"

"Oh." Susan said somberly. "Well, you may as well find out now. I'm 'the nursery lady' at my Church."

"I need more coffee," Charles said, and got up to meander into the kitchen.

"Doesn't that bother you?" Susan asked, turning to face him in the kitchen.

"Uh... well... why would it bother me if you take care of the plants?" Charles asked.

"What...?"

"What?"

"You said... oh, wait... you think nursery means working with plants?" Susan asked.

"Yeah, what else would it mean?"

"Urg. Men!" Susan said, getting up and heading for the kitchen. "How about nursery as in nursery school, or nursery rhymes?"

Charles looked puzzled.

"Babies, Charles! I take care of the babies at Church!" Susan exclaimed in disbelief at his failure to catch on.

Charles scrunched his face and rubbed his forehead. "Whose babies?!"

"Everyone's babies! It's the Church nursery! I take care of the babies so the parents can attend the worship service without having to worry about their babies needing bottles and getting diapers changed."

"Oh." Charles said sheepishly. "I, uh... I wasn't familiar with that..."

"Honestly! Men. Well, maybe that shouldn't be a surprise. It's the most taken-for-granted Church ministry there is. To lots of the folks there, I'm not a person with a real life, I'm just 'the nursery lady.'"

Susan refilled Charles' coffee cup and watched him add a half-packet of artificial sweetener and a spoonful of non-dairy creamer.

"Well, I guess it doesn't bother you," Susan noted with a smile.

Charles sighed and smiled. "That's one of the benefits of male obliviousness. Less stuff to bother us."

Susan put an arm around Charles and embraced him, rubbing her bruised face lightly on his chest. *Rich, good-looking, Christian, loving, sexy, and with a sense of humor, too. All these years, and now I get the cream of the crop. Or do I...? What if something goes horribly wrong?* "Maybe... maybe they'll find Billy today. Maybe with him in jail, Stephanie will be willing to come home. The way she looked at me right before she ran out... I've never seen her look that way before. She's had lots of pain, but this was the first time she didn't have enough anger to cover it up."

"God must be working in her life somehow," Charles said. "He has a plan for her life, too."

Oh, dear Father, when is her plan going to get better? Susan looked up. "Would you mind if she lived with us, if she wanted to?"

"Of course not," he assured her.

"Would you... uh, you said you want to pay off the mortgage on this house, but... I guess you'll want to find a bigger house for us to live in?"

"I'd rather not," he said.

"Wh... what?"

"If it's all right with you, I'd like us to live here." Charles put his coffee cup down and put his arms around her. "It's more than big enough. And my boys don't want me near them, anyway."

Susan put her coffee cup down and put both arms around him. He leaned his head gently on hers.

"No," he went on, "those things are true, but those aren't the main thing. The main thing is that this is more than a house, it's your home. It's been your home most of your life, and it was your parents' home, and your children's home. I'm honored... I'm humbled... that you want to share your whole life with me, including your home."

Oh, God, if I just knew that Stephanie would be okay, I could die happy right now.

"Hey, Mr. P.," Shad called out.

Susan and Charles broke their hug and hurried to the doorway to the living room.

"Is it Billy?!" Charles asked.

"No, no. I just need to hit the can." Shad said. "Mind taking over for a few?"

"Oh, sure," Charles said.

"Don't touch the curtains," Shad explained, "but keep a lookout through the crack in it and holler at me if anyone parks in your driveway, in the yard, or in the street in front of this house or the houses on either side."

"Oh, okay," Charles agreed as he sat in the chair.

"The bathroom is the first door on the right down the hallway, Shad," Susan said. "The lock on the door doesn't work, but since there's just us here, there's no one to walk in on you."

After lunch, which included Shad eating at his watch post at the window, Charles used some cardboard and packing tape to temporarily close the hole in the window that Billy had broken while Susan worked on a grocery list. A little later they both heard when Shad answered his cell phone.

"Yeah, I see it," he said into the phone's headpiece. "Mr. P.! Mrs. P! C'mere, quick!"

Susan and Charles rushed into the living room.

"Don't get close enough to the curtain to touch it, but look through the crack and tell me if you recognize the car that just pulled up or the guy in it."

Charles let Susan get the closest position to the window.

"That's Henry Walker, my pastor!" Susan said.

"You get that?" Shad said into the phone as he relaxed. "It's the Parker's preacher."

Susan noticed with surprise that Shad was holding a gun as he re-holstered it.

Susan headed for the door, followed by Charles.

"Hey, Mr. P.," Shad called out. "Frank says make it quick, and from now on, any visitors need to get cleared first."

"Oh, right." Charles replied.

Susan opened the door just as Henry was about to knock.

"Hello, Henry," Susan said with a weak smile, "Come in, please!"

Henry stepped inside, carrying some books and papers. He was shocked at the bruises on Susan's face, which were only partially camouflaged by the makeup she had applied that morning.

"Susan... those are awful looking bruises! I'm so sorry."

"They don't hurt too much," she said, turning to Charles. "Henry, I'd like you to meet Charles Parker. Charles, this is Henry Walker."

"Pleasure to meet you, Henry."

"I'm glad to meet you, too, Charles, though I wish it were under better circumstances."

"And that big guy over there is Shad," Susan added. "He's a bodyguard."

Henry raised his eyebrows. "Oh, uh, hi, there. Nice to meet you." Shad nodded and looked back out the window.

"Uh, Henry," Charles said, "we appreciate you coming over, but... we're afraid Billy... that's the guy who beat up Susan and Stephanie... we're afraid he might come back to check up on us, to try to see if we've called the police."

"Oh..." Henry said, looking back pointlessly at the closed door.

"And well, if he sees your car out there..." Charles hinted.

"Oh!" said Henry. "Well, I'll only stay a minute then. I wanted to come by and see if you need anything... but you can tell me that over the phone. You have my number. And I wanted to pray with you... and we can do that over the phone, too. There was one other reason I came by, though."

He turned to Susan. "Charles told me this morning that the two of you are engaged."

"Yes," said Susan, taking Charles' arm while simultaneously displaying her ring. "He asked me last night, and I said yes. That was before..."

"Before this Billy character showed up," Henry finished for her. He pointed at the cut and band aid on Charles' head, "Looks like you got hurt, too."

"Oh... it's a long story," Charles said.

"Yes, well, I want to hear all about your engagement, and anything about Billy that you'd like to share, but we'll save that for later." He handed his books and papers to Susan. "I want to leave these with you though. We can go over them together later, but it's all premarital counseling material. I'm just loaning you the books. In my experience, older couples… no offense… often want to get married right away, but it's just as important for them to make sure they're ready for marriage as it is for a young couple. The sheet on top gives you a guideline for going through the material."

Henry put his hand on the doorknob and started to open it. "Again, nice to meet you, Charles, and I'll look forward to getting to know you better. If Susan agreed to marry you, you must be a very fine man. We think very highly of Susan at Bethel Bible Church."

Susan was looking at the sheet on top. "Oh, well, thank you very much, Henry, but I really don't think we'll need these."

"Then you'll probably be surprised at how much they'll help. And, I hate to say this and rush off, that makes it kind of sound like an ultimatum, and I don't want it to. But if you're thinking of asking me to perform your wedding, it's my policy not to marry anyone who hasn't completed the premarital counseling material."

"Oh," said Susan. "Okay. Well, we do want you to perform the ceremony, right, Charles?"

"Uh, yes, right," Charles confirmed quickly.

"Okay, then, go ahead and get started on it, and we'll talk later over the phone." Henry said as he left, closing the door behind him. He hurried to his car and drove away quickly.

Susan and Charles looked at the armful of material, then at each other, and started walking back to the dining room.

"Wow, what is all that stuff?" Charles asked.

Susan handed him the top sheet.

"Children and Parenting," Charles read off. "Well, we can skip that. We're too old to have any more children."

"Well, maybe there's something in there about dealing with grown children," Susan suggested.

"We can look and see, but I'll bet it's focused on whether or not to have children, how many children to have, stuff like that."

Susan set the stack down on the table and started looking through it as they sat down.

"Conflict Resolution," Charles read and raised an eyebrow toward Susan.

Anything in there about throwing pots? "I recognize that gleam in your eyes, Charles Parker. Please don't make me laugh, it might hurt my face."

"Okay," Charles acquiesced before reading on. "Communication… sounds lame. Expectations in Marriage… sounds obvious. Faith… that's definitely something I hope we enjoy exploring together."

"Mm-hmm," Susan agreed.

"Finances." Charles went on. "We don't have to worry about that. Leisure Activities... that sounds fun. Marriage Roles... I prefer marriage biscuits, myself."

"Mmfph!" Susan tried to stifle a laugh.

"Sorry. Marriage Roles... sounds trivial. Personality... that sounds fun. Anything that helps me get to know you better, I'm all for. And lastly, Sexual Compatibility... and we can definitely skip that."

"We could probably write that chapter," Susan said.

"Yes, but I think we should conduct lots and lots of research."

"Mmfph!"

Chapter Nine

Susan put down one of Henry's papers and yawned, which caused Charles to yawn.

She folded her hands on the table and carefully laid her head down on them. "So, the books are just for reference. All we have to do is the questionnaires."

"Uh-huh," Charles said as he laid his head down.

Poor Charles. So tired. I guess it's not my fault... but I feel guilty anyway.

They looked at each other and Susan slipped one hand over to Charles and stroked his face.

"Well, in a minute," Charles said lethargically, "let's finish the grocery list, and figure out what we're going to do about your job. Are you scheduled to work tomorrow?

"Mm-hmm," Susan assented. "I'm supposed to be there at seven tomorrow morning." *Tomorrow morning... tomorrow morning... oh, yeah...* "Speaking of tomorrow morning..."

"Mm. You thinking about our wedding plans? That is, our former wedding plans?"

"Yes... I... I wasn't expecting..." *Well of course I wasn't expecting a murderous brute to show up with Stephanie. That's a dumb thing to...*

Charles opened his eyes and patted Susan's hand. "You hadn't heard from Stephanie in a long time, but now your concern for her is at an all-time high."

Susan nodded sorrowfully with her head still on the table and winced when it stressed her cheek.

"Careful, sweetheart." Charles said. "Yeah, this business with Billy kinda puts the brakes on everything else."

Susan sat up and stroked Charles' hair. "Would you like us to go ahead and get married, Charles? Maybe Henry could get the license for us and conduct the service over the phone."

Charles sat up and looked tenderly at her. "I'll do anything you want, Susan, but my preference would be not to have anything sad tugging at us on our wedding night. I can wait, under the circumstances. My heart is pretty full just knowing you love me enough to want to marry me."

Susan lowered her voice and glanced toward the living room door, then leaned close to Charles to whisper. "But do you need sexual relief? That was quite a boner you had yesterday."

Charles got red in the face and stammered quietly, "Uh, no, that's okay... I'm, uh... We don't need to rush just on that account."

Uh-oh. Was I too... something? Susan kept whispering, "Was my question too forward? Too personal?" *You said my old language was okay...*

"No, no, that's okay," Charles said, pulling some of Henry's study material closer. "But anyway, Henry wants us to do all these questionnaires before he'll marry us, so that will take some time..."

Yes... more time... "Oh, I looked over the book on children and parenting, and it looks like there're some things in it that might help us, even though our kids are grown."

"Really?" Charles said, "Anything that would help me there would be great. I feel like I'm about as bad as I can get in that department."

Susan gave Charles' hand a pat. "We'll read through it together and see what we can learn."

She picked up another book, then put it aside as the last book in the stack caught her eye. "Oh, my!"

Susan showed him the cover.

"'Grandma's Sex Handbook'," Charles read quietly, and with a smirk. "Does it say whether or not I get to look at your bloomers?"

Susan stifled another laugh and winced, then started reading the back cover. "Looks a little more modern than that... covers pornography, masturbation... wow, it's got a chapter called 'Sex Fantasy Cookbook.'"

Charles furrowed his brow. "Why would your pastor give us a book like that?"

"Loan it to us, he said, not give it to us. Maybe he didn't know it was in the stack," Susan suggested as she put it down and put another book on top of it.

"Okay, then, my next question is what's he doing with it in the first place?" Charles asked.

"Well, since pastors have children, it's possible they may sometimes have sex," Susan said, poking him gently in the ribs. *Maybe there's a side of Henry most people don't know.*

"Yeah, but 'sex fantasy cookbook'? C'mon..."

"Come to think of it," Susan said, "judging from the Church sex scandals that seem to appear in the news on an almost regular basis, I guess pastors get as tempted as anyone else."

"Uh," Charles replied and got up to stretch, looking at his cell phone in the process. "Hey, uh, Susan...? I'm starting to feel pretty grungy. I need to get my cell phone charger, and I'd like to get a shower, shave, brush my teeth, and get some of my own clothes..."

Oh, right, those are from the restaurant. I wonder how much they charged you for them? She looked at his face. *Mmm, you look good with a little bristle.*

"What I'd like to do is go over to my apartment and get my things," Charles said, "then come straight back and take a shower over here instead of at my place. That will get me back here the fastest, and I really don't want to be away from here any longer than necessary. Is that okay with you?"

She nodded, "You know, with a bodyguard here, you don't have to stay here tonight."

"I wouldn't be able to sleep anywhere else," Charles objected. "In one of the other bedrooms, I mean. Although... would it bother you if I slept on one of the other beds?"

"Oh, no, that's okay." *Stephanie's old room looks too feminine for you...*

"You can stay in Steve's old room," Susan continued, "first door on the left in the hall." *Unless... no, Susan, he's made it very clear he doesn't want to have sex until we're married.*

"You sure? Has that room been used since Steve left?"

Susan shook her head. "Steve's room isn't a shrine, Charles. It would have bothered me if it hadn't been so long since he was killed, but it has. Been a long time, that is... it won't bother me for you to sleep there."

Especially since it's you, and not some stranger, she thought, getting up and looking at Shad, still sitting at his post.

"Okay, then." he accepted. "Well, I'll call Mike and arrange a ride."

Susan went to the bathroom while he called.

"They haven't moved your car yet," Charles told her when she returned, "so Mike said I should take that, and I'll meet them when I come back to hand it off."

"Oh, okay," she said as she got her car keys out for him. *What a relief to have my car running again...* "Say, you didn't tell me what was wrong with it."

"Solenoid switch on the starter motor. Cost about twelve bucks for a new one. Plus cab fare to and from the parts store."

Susan gasped. "Twelve dollars?! And those other people were going to charge me over a thousand dollars! And not only did you fix it for twelve dollars, you fixed it in just a few hours!"

Charles nodded. "I'm ninety-nine percent sure they were trying to cheat you. Unfortunately, that happens a lot. In fact, that's a big reason Parker Automotive is so successful, because we combine honesty with competence and fair prices. Your car needs some other work, mainly a valve-job, but the switch was the only thing keeping it from running, and that's all I could manage at the time. That was a very busy afternoon though. I had to get your ring, too. And I was sooo nervous. I was terrified you'd say no."

"Really?" *You were scared?!* "I was starting to panic that you wouldn't ask me!"

"Really…? Wow…" Charles mused. "Say, do you like the ring, because…"

Susan's tired eyes lit up as she held the ring to her chest and looked down to admire it. "Oh, Charles, I *love* the ring. I absolutely love it!"

"Oh, I'm so glad. I didn't like any of the ones they had in your size…"

How could you know my ring size? Just by looking…?

"…so I picked one that had to be resized, and they had to call in someone to do that. And I had them drive it out to the restaurant."

"How did…" *Wait!* Susan gasped again. "The ring! You didn't have it when we were on the boat!" *That's why you didn't propose on the boat! You were waiting for the ring!*

Charles shook his head. "No, but I sure was glad they got it to the restaurant in time. And that I got the size right."

She held up her hand and wiggled the ring. "Well, you guessed perfectly. It's a perfect fit."

"Well, it wasn't a complete guess."

Susan cocked her head. *No…?*

"I hope this doesn't make you mad, but I snuck into your room and looked through your things until I found your ring box."

What?! Charles… that's… that's…

"That's how I got your size. I thought it was justifiable at the time, but just now as I started to tell you, I started feeling guilty. I apologize if I was out of line."

Hmm. 'Charles the Planner.' That's just your nature isn't it? You think out everything in advance. And you planned the whole day to surprise me with your proposal.

Susan walked up to Charles and gave him a full-body hug. "I forgive you, my love. But next time…"

She broke the hug and held Charles at arm's length. "Charles, you felt guilty before you told me, and thought I might get mad, but you told me anyway."

"Yeah…"

Wow. Susan hugged him again. "I'm wondering if you couldn't write a chapter on communication, too."

He stroked her hair. "Susan, I want to share my life with you. All of it, the good and the bad."

Oh, yes… our two lives, becoming one… Susan started running her hands up and down Charles' back, and he began to reciprocate.

Mmm… Charles, I might not object if you were a little more bad…

Charles broke their hug. "Well, uh… I'd better… get going." He started edging toward the door to the garage.

Susan watched him leaving and a horrible thought struck her. "Oh, Charles! What if Billy's out there watching where the detectives can't see him, and he follows you?"

Charles looked thoughtful for a moment. "Well, I've got my cell phone. I can call Mike and they can come get him. After I tear him limb from limb."

"Charles!" Susan said anxiously, "Please don't say that. Stay away from him. Let those men you hired take care of Billy."

Charles looked at her but didn't reply.

"Please? If you must go, be watchful, and don't take any chances."

"I'll keep my eyes peeled," he said and closed the door behind him.

Charles! I have a feeling I didn't change your mind… Lord, please protect him! Don't let him get hurt while trying to protect me and Stephanie!

When she heard the car start up, Susan walked through the living room toward the front door to watch him leave through the window next to the door. She glanced at Shad sitting motionless. *How can he do that, hour after hour? Still just sitting there like a statue, staring through the curtain.*

After Charles drove away, she wandered back into the living room. *He's sitting in Momma's chair,* Susan observed of Shad. *No one ever sat in it because that straight back makes it so uncomfortable.*

Maybe he likes it that way. Momma only liked it because she thought it was so pretty.

"Would you like something to drink, Shad?"

Shad removed an ear bud from one ear. "What's that?

"Oh, I didn't realize you were listening to something."

Shad turned his head and pointed to his other ear. "Cell phone." He held up the loose ear bud on the end of a wire. "Music. Helps me stay focused."

Susan nodded. "Oh. Well, would you like something to drink? Iced tea, perhaps?"

"Yes, ma'am, that'd be nice," he said as he replaced the music ear bud and turned his attention back to the window.

Hmm. Not much for chit-chat, are you? Susan thought as she went to the kitchen for his tea.

When Susan returned and handed the tea to Shad, he said, "Thanks, Mrs. P.," he said while continuing to look out the window.

"You're welcome, but I'm not Mrs. P. yet."

Shad removed the ear bud again. "What?"

"Oh. Mr. Parker and I are engaged, we're not married yet. We just got engaged last night."

"Oh," Shad acknowledged, and looked out the window again.

"You can call me Susan."

"Ok, Susan," he said while keeping his eyes trained outside and once again replacing his music ear bud.

Susan sighed. *I guess I should leave you alone, huh? But I don't see how you can sit there hour after hour and then turn down a chance for a conversation.*

She slowly walked back into the dining room and started to read one of Henry's questionnaires, but instead started praying that Billy wouldn't see or follow Charles.

"Susan, Mr. P's back," Shad called from the living room a half hour later.

"Okay, thanks!" Susan shouted as she ran to the garage. *Thank you, Lord! Thank you, thank you, thank you!*

A stranger parked the car in the garage, and as soon as she saw the garage door close through the kitchen-garage door's window, Susan hurried around to the passenger side and opened the door for Charles.

"No changes here?" he asked as he got out.

Susan gave him a bear-hug. "No, nothing. Uneventful trip?"

"Pretty much," he said, and Susan thought he sounded disappointed.

She ended the hug and Charles collected his things and put them in the kitchen and returned to lock the big garage door after the driver had backed her car out. Once it was closed, Susan walked up to him and hugged him again.

"I thought hugging was off our menu," Charles commented.

Susan stepped back but held his hands as she nodded toward the living room. "I guess it kind of feels like we have a chaperone. That seems to help me…" she lowered her voice to a whisper, "…not get too worked up."

"In that case…" Charles pulled her to him again, and as they hugged, he ran his hand up and down her back.

"Mmmm."

"This okay, under the circumstances?" he asked.

"Mmmmm."

"I love you so much," he said tenderly.

Susan's shoulders relaxed, followed by the rest of her body, and she felt Charles begin to relax. *I guess we were pretty tense after last night, and too little sleep.*

Finally, Charles kissed her head and broke their embrace. "Mind if we go inside and sit down?"

"No. Besides, Shad may start to worry about us."

"Not now I'm not." Shad said from the doorway.

Susan and Charles went back inside sheepishly, and as Shad resumed his perch in the living room, Charles took his things to his room, followed by Susan.

Susan walked around the room looking at Steve's old things while Charles opened the suitcase, removed his phone charger and plugged it into an outlet near the door.

Charles straightened up and the pair just looked at each other wearily across the bed.

You've moved into my house. Is this just temporary? How long will it be before they catch Billy? When will we get married?

"Well, uh, I guess I'll get that shower."

Susan nodded and Charles picked out some clothes and his toiletries bag and went across the hall and closed the door.

The relief at having Charles back safe and sound allowed Susan's mind to begin relaxing some, and she noticed feeling very tired as she walked back toward the dining room. *Oh, better tell Shad not to use that bathroom.*

She went into the living room, and signaled Shad that she had something to tell him. After he removed the ear bud, she said, "Charles is taking a shower in the closest bathroom. If you need…"

"I'm good," Shad said and replaced the ear bud as he stood up and stretched while still looking out the window.

Must have an awfully big bladder, Susan thought as she went back to the dining room table and sat down. She touched her cheeks to test them. *Ow…! Still pretty sore. May get worse over the next day or two.*

A few minutes later Susan heard the shower start. *I should be cleaning or something. Wash a load of clothes… no, not while he's getting a shower. Well, I'll just go see how many dirty clothes are in the hamper.*

She walked down the hallway and slowed down as she passed the bathroom door. She stopped and turned around, noting that although she could see into the living room, she couldn't see Shad at his position next to the window. *If I can't see him from here, he can't see me here.*

The shower was still running and she leaned close, putting a hand on the door. *He's in there. Naked. In my house. The lock is broken. What would he think if I walked in? I could say I couldn't wait to use the toilet… no, he knows I have the other one. He'd probably get angry. But he might not. Maybe he'd be glad. Maybe he'd haul me into the shower with him and take my clothes off. We could soap each other up, and hug, and rub…*

Susan stepped back from the door. *Oh, no!*

She hurried to her bedroom and quietly shut the door. *I can't believe that! My daughter's life is in danger, there's a strange man in my living room, and I'm lusting over the… the man I'm going to marry.*

She looked at her ring and sat down on the bed. *Dear Father in heaven, how can I be so carnal? I… I just don't understand why my sex drive has gone into overload. I've gone for twenty years without wanting sex, why now? Why so… urgently? Has my heart been full of evil all that time, and falling in love has finally let me see it? That doesn't seem right. Lord, I've been asking you for help, and frankly, I haven't seen much. Are you still there? Do you still care? Why did you let Stephanie go away with Billy? Why didn't you keep her here and change her heart?*

Rolling over, she pulled a pillow into her chest and hugged it as her mind replayed her thoughts outside the bathroom door. *Well,*

Lord, I don't know if it's an improvement or not, but that time I wasn't so much hungry to have him inside me as just to be with him. I think I would have been happy just to have been in his arms. Is that better than lust? Is it any different?

Susan sighed, and used her top hand to stroke the pillow. *I guess I'm not a very good Christian, Lord, and I sure don't understand what's going on, but it sure seems like a mess, other than meeting Charles and us falling in love with each other. But I'd give him up for Stephanie's sake, Lord.*

An idea hit Susan, and the pain of it took her breath away. *Lord! Is that it? Do I have to give up Charles for Stephanie's sake? To prove to her that I love her? Is that why our marriage plans fell apart? Is that why you brought him into my life, so I can have something big to sacrifice for her? Something she could understand?*

Another unwelcome idea hit her. *Oh, God, please don't take Charles' life! Let me give him up without him dying, Lord, please!! If someone has to give up their life in this mess, please let it be me! Yes, wouldn't that work, Lord? Could Stephanie find out that I gave up my life for her? Would that soften her heart toward you, to see that kind of love...? If so... why didn't you just let Billy kill me last night...?*

Oh... what would that do to Charles? Lord, can Charles handle it if I die? Would that break his heart? Does that mean... oh, God... would it be easier on him if he died instead of me? Oh... God, that's... too much to ask!

Oh, Lord... I just said something was too much to ask. Susan cried into her pillow. *I'm sorry, Lord... I... I'm willing to accept whatever pain you want me to endure. I trust your infinite wisdom... and I give you my desires... all of them. I put my love for Charles and my love for Stephanie in your hands. I'm afraid, Lord, of losing one of them, or...* she sucked in her breath... *or both of them. I'm much more afraid of that than I am of dying, Lord, but I'll trust you... no matter how bad things get. You're my God, and I'm your servant... by your grace, Lord, I'm your daughter. I am your daughter... and I ask you to use me any way you wish...*

Susan used a corner of the pillow to dab at her tears as she wept and prayed, but in a few minutes she fell asleep.

An urgent knock at the door was followed by its opening, and a fully-clothed Charles rushed in excitedly with still-damp hair. "Susan! I just heard from Mike! They have a lead from the video!"

Susan startled awake and rolled back toward the door, then sat up and swept her hair out of her face. "What...?"

Charles knelt down and put his hands on her knees as he repeated the news. "Mike's guys found a lead in the video, and now they know the people who produced it and where it was made, and they're talking to the owner of that company at home now!"

"Uh... okay... but how does that... what about Stephanie...?"

"Well, Mike didn't say, exactly," Charles replied, "but maybe the producer guy knows where they are. If Stephanie is an actress in his movies, surely he knows how to get in touch with her..."

Susan felt a drop forming in her nose and scooted over to pull a tissue from a box on her bedside table and blow her nose.

Just then she heard a buzzing, and Charles answered his cell phone.

"Yes...?" Charles said into the phone. "Yes... okay... okay... what happens after that...?"

"What is it, Charles?" Susan pleaded. "What did they find out?"

"Uh-huh... uh-huh..." Charles held up a finger to ask Susan to wait. "Okay... okay... alright, then, thanks for the update, Mike. Mike...? Thank you, thank you very much!"

Charles closed his phone and sat on the bed beside Susan, who grabbed his hand.

"The man who produced the movie had a phone number for Billy. It's a cell phone number, and the address isn't public, but they have a way to get it anyway."

"Oh!" said Susan, "Are they on their way to get him?!"

"Well, they just got the phone number," Charles explained, "It'll take a little while to get the address, but remember, that's just the address that the bill goes to. Billy may not live there. And even when they find Billy, Stephanie may not be there."

"Oh, Charles! Finding Stephanie is the main thing!"

"Mike knows that," Charles reassured her. "They won't move in on Billy until they know where Stephanie is, and they're sure they can keep her from becoming a hostage."

Susan leaned into Charles and laid her face gently against his chest. "Oh, Charles... oh, Charles!" she cried.

He put an arm around her and stroked her hair as he prayed for her, for Stephanie, and for the men tracking her down, and Susan added more prayers of her own.

A few minutes later, Charles finally let go. "Are you okay for now, sweetheart?"

Susan looked up into his eyes and nodded.

"Well, uh, I should probably call... Andy, is it...? Your store manager, and tell him you won't be in for a while. If we wait, we might forget it altogether."

She nodded and started to get up, "Oh, yes, I have his cell phone number in my purse for calling when the store's closed. Oh, wait..." she glanced at the bedside clock, "the store's still open, so you can just call the store."

"Uh, do you have that number?" Charles asked.

"Yeah, it's in my purse too. C'mon," she said as she started toward the door.

Charles paused a moment to look around the room. "This is a very nice room," he commented.

"Thank you," Susan replied automatically as she entered the hallway and headed for the dining room with Charles a few steps behind.

After getting off the phone with Andy, Charles walked from the dining room to the kitchen, where Susan was pondering their next meal.

"He just said, 'okay' and left it at that," Charles said.

Susan sighed. "He didn't ask how I was hurt or anything?" *He's probably just glad to be rid of me for a while.*

"No," he replied. "Don't worry, Susan. You said yourself it's just a temporary job. If he lets you go, you can take your time finding a new job. In fact... that's something else we need to talk about. I have some ideas in that area."

"Oh? If you're thinking of offering me a job, I don't think I'd care to be executive assistant to an unemployed motorhead."

"Motorhead?! I haven't heard that term in years!" Charles laughed. "But seriously, I've been trying to figure out what to do with my assets. I don't want my boys fighting over it after I'm gone. In fact, I want to give away most of it while I'm still alive, and that actually turns out to be hard to do in a responsible manner. I could really use some help."

Susan stared at him. "Giving away money is hard...? I'm sorry, I don't see how it could be."

"I can explain, but could we talk about it while we eat? I'm getting hungry."

"Sure. Me too. But do you mind if I don't cook a big meal? I'm not sure I have enough energy for that right now."

"Ah," said Charles and led Susan by the hand to a seat at the dining room table. "How about if I fix us some exquisite peanut butter and jelly sandwiches while you rest?"

Susan laughed, then winced and held a hand to her cheek. "Okay, Merrill, the exquisite peanut butter is in the ornate oak cabinet to the left of the fridge."

Charles bowed deeply and swept off into the kitchen and started the meal.

"Mr. P!" Shad called out.

Charles and Susan both hurried to the living room door.

"Change of watch," Shad announced. New guys comin' in. Didn't want them to startle you."

"Oh, okay, thanks," Charles replied.

So you startled us to prevent someone else from startling us? Susan laughed to herself.

A couple of minutes later, they heard a car parking and Shad joined Charles and Susan at the inside door to the garage. Shad opened it right as a very tired-looking Frank and a smaller man got out, closed the big outer door and came in.

"Charles, Susan, this is Brian Milner, another snipe," Frank said.

Snipe? Susan wondered.

They shook hands as Shad left without another word, and then Brian went through the house as Frank talked to them.

"We're only going to have one guy in here tonight, because we were able to get Brian." Frank told them. "He's as good as Shad, and that's as good as they get. Of course, Brian won't be completely alone; we have a solid team on the outside, too."

"Where's Mike?" Charles asked at the same time Susan asked, "What's a snipe?"

"Sniper," Frank responded to Susan first. "Mike said..."

"A sniper? With rifles and everything? I thought you were private investigators." Susan asked with surprise and glanced at Charles, who didn't seem to notice.

"We are. We're licensed private investigators, and when that work is slow, we're also bodyguards or mercenaries."

"Mercenaries?!" Susan exclaimed.

Charles put a hand on Susan's shoulder and started to talk, but Frank went on.

"Ma'am, snipers like Shad and Brian are highly trained to lie in waiting for hours, then act without hesitation when appropriate. And that's exactly what we need to keep you as safe as humanly possible."

Susan looked a bit stunned, and Frank turned to Charles. "Mike asked me to pass the word to you since I was just about to see you anyway. He just got to the stakeout at the address that goes with

Billy's phone. It's in Maryville, about 15 miles south of here. Nobody's in there right now, but someone's been there recently, so whoever lives there may come back tonight."

"What if Billy sees them?" Susan worried.

"He won't," Frank said flatly. "Until they get right in his face."

And what is that a euphemism for? Oh, Lord, I don't know and I don't care, just protect Stephanie. From Billy, and these men, and... from anything else that could harm her.

Charles gave Susan a shoulder-hug and said to Frank, "Shouldn't we get over there now, in case they find Stephanie?"

"No offense, but you're not trained in surveillance, and we can't risk them spotting you. And we don't know for sure who lives there. Could be Billy's mother or something. Best wait 'till we know for sure what we've got."

Oh... Susan wavered on her feet slightly. *Lord, Lord, what should we do...?*

Charles said something else, but Susan missed it. He looked closely at her and asked, "Susan, are you okay?"

"Uh... I'm a little dizzy. Lack of sleep, I guess."

Charles walked her back to the dining room table followed by Frank, and held a chair for Susan as she sat down. "You just sit and rest. I'll fix us something to eat. Frank, you hungry?"

"No, thanks," Frank replied. "I ate a while ago, and I've got to brief some new outside guys. I'll see myself out after I talk to Brian again."

"Okay, thanks, Frank. Oh, you know, this broken window is a weakness that..."

"The back of the house is being watched as closely as the front," Frank said without emotion.

"Oh, okay. Good to know."

Charles walked into the kitchen as Frank went into the living room and Susan idly picked up the sex advice book.

Charles finished the sandwiches and brought them and some drinks to the table, where Susan was now reading wearily but with interest.

"More waiting," Charles mumbled, "with no idea how long we'll be waiting. " He picked up one of the worksheets, looked it over, and asked Susan, "Where could I find a pen or pencil?"

Susan pushed her purse across the table toward Charles. "In here," she said with her nose still in the book.

"You don't mind if I go plowing through your private things?

Susan put the book down and looked directly into Charles' eyes for a moment, then smiled and waved her engagement ring in front of him. "Charles, we're going to be married." *Oh, wow, despite everything, that sure does sound good.* "Everything I have is yours, my love. My heart, my body, and whatever junk happens to be in my purse."

Charles laughed. "Okay, then. I like that... and you have to feel free to go into my wallet or anything else I have. Deal?"

"Sold." *Lock, stock, and barrel,* she thought as she started reading and eating again.

Charles got out a pen and started completing a questionnaire. When he finished it, he quickly picked up the Love Languages book Henry had loaned them to study the meaning of the results.

"Wow! This is powerful!" Charles said, then grabbed the worksheet and flipped to the second copy of the questionnaire.

"Susan, you have to take this test!" he said as he held out the papers and pen to Susan.

Susan reluctantly put her book down and took the material. "How long will it take?"

"Just a few minutes," Charles answered, "but it's amazing how insightful this is! Make sure you don't look at my answers and don't look in the book until you finish the questions."

"Okay, but then I want to get back to my book." *Love languages, huh?*

Charles paced as Susan completed the Love Languages questionnaire, then eagerly sat back down.

"Okay, now we score it and find out what your love language is." Charles said, pausing to explain before scoring Susan's paper. "This is so powerful! My dominant love language is 'acts of service' and that explains so much about me. I may have been a bad father, but I wasn't unloving, like I thought, it's just that doing things for people is *how* I show love! It's so clear now, but I never, ever had a clue until now."

Charles rapidly scored Susan's paper as she considered what he had just said.

Acts of service, huh? Is that why you like doing things for me? Making sandwiches, taking me out on boats, teaching me to dance? Maybe I'm like that too... no... maybe not.

Susan picked up the Love Languages book and started flipping through it, finding and scanning a list of the five "languages."

Charles excitedly finished the scoring and looked up the results.

"Your primary love language is... 'words of affirmation!'" he announced.

Susan furrowed her brow. *Words of affirmation... but what does that mean?*

Charles reached over and helped her find a page in the book that summarized the Words Of Affirmation love language, and they read it together.

"Wow. That makes so much sense!" Susan exclaimed. "That's me! That's really me! That's why... Oh...!" *Oh... no...! Marty!*

Susan looked horrified and got up and walked over to the dining room window, followed closely by Charles.

Oh, dear Father in heaven... that's why I was so... unhappy, no... miserable. I was miserable with Marty.

Charles put an arm over her shoulder, but didn't say anything.

Marty never gave me any words of affirmation. No wonder I never really felt loved by him. Oh, I wonder what his... Oh, God... no!! Oh, no, no, no!! Marty's love language had to have been physical touch, and that's why he wanted sex so often... and when I turned him down all those times, it must have been to him like I was shouting 'I don't love you' or something! All our fights, our broken marriage, oh, God...!! The damage to Steve and Stephanie's lives... it... was my fault! It was all my fault!!!

Susan grabbed Charles, hugged him, buried her bruised face into his shoulder despite the pain, and cried intensely. *Oh, God! Father in heaven, all those years I thought Marty was a terrible man, and instead it was my fault! I didn't understand how he felt love, how he showed it, and how he needed me to touch him to show him love in a way he could understand it! Oh, God, I've ruined my life! I've ruined Marty's life! Oh, God, no...! I ruined Steve and Stephanie's lives!!*

Susan sank to her knees, and Charles sat down beside her, and put an arm over her shoulder again.

"Pretty powerful, huh?" he said quietly.

Susan just sobbed.

"Thinking of past relationships?" Charles asked.

Susan looked up through blurry eyes. "How... how did you know?"

"I've been doing the same thing. And I can't imagine much else making you cry so hard." He dug into a pocket and handed her a tissue.

Susan sighed. "Do you always carry tissues, or do you just know ahead of time when I'm going to cry?"

"I was carrying that for me," Charles said. "I've been much more emotional since I became a Christian, and especially this past week... since we met."

"My people perish..." Susan mused out loud.

"What?"

"It says in the Bible somewhere, 'my people perish from a lack of knowledge...' a lack of knowledge about how we communicate love, in this case."

"Huh," Charles replied, stroking her hair.

Susan let her shoulders relax, and then without thought, she relaxed completely and melted into Charles' lap, putting one arm around him. *Oh, we can't touch like this, or we'll have a... what did the sex book call it... a sexual meltdown.*

Despite the thought, she made no attempt to move. *We need to get married right away, so we can have sex, despite what's going on with Stephanie and Bil... no... Stephanie has to come first, especially now that I know how badly I've let her down... oh, Lord, what is Stephanie's love language? I... I don't even know my own daughter's love language! Oh, God, No wonder she hates me! I must have been mistreating her as badly as I did Marty!*

Susan sucked in her breath. *Marty! Lord... did... do you... is this why Charles and I haven't been able to follow through on our wedding plans? Are you going to bring Marty back to me, now that I know about different love languages?*

Susan felt nauseous, and started to get up. "I'm sorry. I feel like I might throw up."

"Oh," Charles said as he helped her up, and tried to guide her to a chair.

Instead of taking the chair, Susan headed for the kitchen and got out the trash can. *Oh, God... do I have to... I mean, do you want me to marry Marty again instead of Charles?!*

Once she had the trash can out, Charles leaned her against the kitchen counter. "Are you okay to stand up a minute by yourself?"

"Yes," she said weakly. *Probably. Maybe.*

Charles rushed back to the table, and fetched a chair.

Although if I have to marry Marty again, I'd rather just crawl into the trash can. Oh...! Lord, I'm sorry! I want to do whatever you want me to, I just... oh, God, I'm just so tired... I don't know what to think.

Susan sat leaning over the trash can for a minute, before finally sitting up and leaning back in the chair.

"The nausea seems to have passed," she said.

"You've been through too much lately. I think you need to go to bed."

"It's only…" Susan looked at the clock on the stove, "…about eight thirty."

"Well, as little sleep as you got last night," Charles suggested, "I wouldn't be surprised if you could sleep twelve hours straight."

"Uhm. You may be right. What about you?" Susan queried.

"I'm really tired, too. Guess I'll also go to bed now."

Charles helped Susan walk to the master bedroom, and she noted the silent Brian in the living room as they passed that door.

Oh, should I ask Charles to read about sexual meltdowns? Susan wondered as they passed the kitchen table. *No, tomorrow will be soon enough.*

Susan leaned heavily on him as they walked down the hallway to her bedroom, and he helped her to the edge of the bed without turning on the light. Relaxed and sleepy, she turned to thank him and say goodnight, but didn't completely let go, and instead turned into a face-to-face full-body hug.

She lifted her face and he leaned in and kissed her, deeply, passionately. *Oh… that feels sooo good. You're such a good kisser… so soft, so warm, so…*

She became slightly more alert as she noticed a not altogether unfamiliar pressure from his crotch. *Oh, no. Yes, but no. Oh, how I'd like to fall asleep with you inside me. Holding me…*

Charles slipped one of his hands further down from the small of her back, and the sensual shock brought her fully awake and she broke off the kiss and the hug.

"Charles, we can't."

Charles pulled her close again by force and closed his eyes. "Yes, we can."

"Charles, no! We're going to wait, remember? You decided we should wait until after we're married, and you were right."

"No. I was wrong." His hands were caressing her back, and down to her buttocks. "I can't wait any more."

Susan put her hands on his chest and to push him away, but his embrace was too strong. "No, Charles. We have to stop!"

He didn't. He tried to kiss her, still with his eyes closed, and he started slowly thrusting his hips forward and back against her.

Susan turned her head away to avoid his kiss, but he just started kissing her neck.

Oh, God, help me! How can I...? "Charles! Listen to me! That man is in the living room! We can't have sex tonight, there's someone else in the house!"

"I don't care," he moaned.

"Well *I* care!" Susan said and pushed, again without success. *If we're going to have sex, we're at least going to have the door closed.*

The thought that he might force her onto the bed with the door still open galvanized her into action. She started to bring her knee up hard into his crotch, but her mind flashed back to the boat when she severely hurt his testicles, and she couldn't bear to hurt him like that again.

Charles' hands were pawing at her clothes, as if to get them off, without thinking about how, and one of his hands groped one of Susan's breasts.

Unnhg! Oh, that feels sooo hot! I can't take much more!

Susan leaned away from him as much as possible and slapped Charles' face lightly. "Charles!"

Charles just grunted.

She slapped him again, harder, and spoke more sharply. "Charles! Snap out of it!"

She slapped him a third time. "Charles! Stop this. This is *not* going to happen, do you hear me?"

Charles opened his eyes, and appeared confused at first, and then shocked. He let her go and stepped back. "Susan...! Oh, Susan...! I..."

He took two more steps back and his expression turned to fright. "I'm sorry! I... I'm so sorry! I..."

His appearance changed again from fright to heart-rending sorrow as he said, "I'm so sorry!" one more time before hurrying out and closing the door firmly behind himself.

Susan had been so compelled by his apparent regret that she'd taken a step toward him just as he turned to leave, and she was left alone now, standing in the quiet darkness, in the middle of her bedroom floor. Down the hall she heard his bedroom door close.

Susan stood there for a full minute, not knowing what to do or even think. Finally she backed up and sat on the edge of the bed.

God... I... I'm just going to go to sleep. We can talk tomorrow. Please take care of everything until then... She pulled off her top and wondered what she could do with it without walking to the hamper, and finally just tossed it on the floor. She looked at it for a moment, considering whether or not to pick it up, and finally decided to leave it there. She kicked off her shoes and pulled off her jeans and just threw them idly toward the shirt and shoes. The movement reminded her of her necklace, and she took it off and laid it on her bedside table.

Do I need to set the alarm? Uhh... let's see... I'm not going to work tomorrow... nowhere else I have to be by any certain time... so no, no alarm.

Lethargically, she pulled back the cover and crawled into bed, without changing into her night bra.

"Father, more than anything, please, please help Stephanie. Amen."

Chapter Ten

...Charles... Marty... one of you has to get out of my bed... I'm not going to have sex with both of you... no, I can't be married to both of you... Charles, this is our honeymoon, make Marty go away... what do you mean our divorce wasn't legal... well, you have an army of mercenaries, use them to make it legal... Marty, make sure you put the toilet seat back down... I'm going back to sleep... you guys work it out and one of you can have sex with me while I'm sleeping... just don't wake me up... no... don't wake me up... let me sleep... pleease, let me sleep...

"Susan! Susan, wake up, honey!"

"Leave me alone."

"Susan, they found Stephanie and Billy!" Charles insisted. "Wake up, they found Stephanie!"

"Stephanie...?" Susan murmured, as the jumble of ethereal dreams evaporated from her mind. "Stephanie! Is she okay?"

Susan threw back the covers and started to climb out of bed, realized the light was on and she was undressed, and quickly covered up as Charles turned away.

"She's okay, but they want us to come down there right away. I'll go if you don't feel up to it."

"Of course I'm up to it. But why don't they just arrest him and bring Stephanie home?"

Charles shoulders sagged. "She... doesn't want to come home, Susan."

He looked over his shoulder and saw that she was covered, so he turned around and studied her face. "I'm sorry, but... well, we need to go down there and talk to her."

"You can explain the rest on the way there," Susan said. "Go start the car, and I'll be there in two minutes! Close the door behind you."

Charles hurried out and Susan threw back the covers again as the door was shutting. She threw on her top, started pulling on her jeans, and grabbed her shoes as she buttoned the jeans and headed out.

As she got to the end of the hallway, she found Charles and Brian waiting in the foyer.

"They're driving," Charles explained.

"Package is ready," Brian said into his cell phone's headset, then opened the front door.

Another man was standing right outside, looking away from the house, and a black Chevy Suburban was waiting in the driveway. Charles took Susan's arm as they went to the big car.

"Good thing they're driving," Charles said. "I'm not sure I could manage it."

Susan looked up at him. *Wow. I wonder if I look that tired? Probably...*

"It's about eleven thirty," he said, and Susan just nodded.

They got in the back seat, and a driver was already behind the wheel. Brian got in the front passenger seat, and once his door shut, the car hurried out of the driveway and down the street, with another car of guardians right behind them.

"Guess you might want to explain all this to your neighbors later," Charles noted.

"I don't know any of the neighbors anymore," Susan said. "When I was growing up, every family knew everyone else, but now the other houses are rentals, and people come and go all the time without ever getting to know one another."

"Come to think of it, I don't have many real friends left at Church, either. None that're close, since Brigitte moved away."

Charles put an arm around her. "I guess we were both ready for a new best friend."

"Mmm," Susan acknowledged distractedly. *Please don't start getting chummy right now...*

Charles removed his arm to crane his head and look back, then asked Brian, "Is everyone coming with us?"

"No," Brian said. "We've still got people there to watch the front and back of the house. Probably not necessary, but this way we're not taking any chances."

"Good," Charles pronounced.

"Charles, what else do you know about what's going on?" Susan asked. "When you woke me up, did you say Stephanie didn't want to come home? If they put Billy in jail, couldn't she just stay wherever she is? Wouldn't we all be safer just by putting him in jail?"

Charles rubbed his face wearily. "Well, Mike says there's a couple of problems. One is if Billy were to get out on bail until his trial. He'd be a threat to you and Stephanie if that happened."

"Oh," Susan said. "So if Stephanie won't come home, it would be harder to keep her safe?"

Charles looked at Susan carefully. "Or impossible."

Susan looked perplexed. "Even with all these men?"

"Well, they can't live there, and stay between her and him. Billy could hurt her anytime the two of them were in their house together."

"Oh," Susan said despondently.

A moment later, Susan turned to Charles. "You said there were a couple of problems. What was the other one?"

Charles looked out his window and paused before finally turning back to her and replying. "Mike said... he said Stephanie threatened to kill herself if they put Billy in jail."

"What...?!" Susan exclaimed. "Why...? After what that brute did to her... why would she act like that?" Susan moaned as her mind replayed how Stephanie consistently complied with Billy's demands in their living room, despite the pain he inflicted on them.

"I wondered the same thing. Mike said it might be some kind of Stockholm syndrome kind of thing. Where a hostage or abused person becomes emotionally dependent on their kidnapper... or whatever... the bad guy."

"Oh, yeah, maybe so," Susan sighed, "What can we do...?"

"I don't know. I'm so tired, I'm not thinking straight." Charles rubbed his face with both hands and shook his head. "I'm sorry, Susan, I don't know what to do."

Oh, God, I don't know what to do either. This is beyond me. It's even beyond Charles, and even all the men Charles hired. Please help us, please guide us. Help us protect Stephanie. Please don't let that monster hurt her anymore.

Susan looked out the window at the passing lights as the car raced south on highway 129. She leaned over onto Charles' shoulder and winced as her face touched him, then readjusted her position to keep her face free, and her eyes closed as she relaxed against him. *Please, Lord... we need you...*

Charles leaned his head back and closed his eyes.

A few minutes later, Brian was rousing them as the car came to a halt in front of some small apartments in a run-down neighborhood.

Brian and the driver got out and stood guard as Mike walked up and got in the front passenger seat, and turned to face them.

"Hey, Charles... Susan. That's their apartment... ground floor, trash can by the door. I've got guys in there sitting on them, Billy's disarmed, and Stephanie's safe for now."

"What're our options?" Charles asked.

"Did you tell Susan everything?"

"Yes."

"Well, then," Mike continued, "one option is we call the police and have Billy arrested. There's no way to forecast whether or not he'd get out on bail, and if he does, we can't protect Stephanie from him as long as she chooses to live with him."

Mike looked at Susan. "That means he could kill her if he wanted to, and the best we could do would be to catch him afterward."

Lord... no... you have to help us...!

Mike paused before going on, "Another option is to leave them alone, if you're willing not to press charges against him for assault and terroristic threats. We have the same problem that if she still wants to live with him, he could kill her and we wouldn't be able to prevent it."

Susan started fighting tears. *God, there has to be some way! There has to be some way to protect Stephanie!*

No one spoke for a long moment.

"Any other options?" Charles asked.

"One," Mike said. "Let's go for a walk Charles. Just you and I."

Mike started to get out, but Charles stayed put.

"Mike, anything you have to tell me, you can tell Susan."

"I could, but I won't," Mike said. "I'll only tell you, and you need to hear it. What you tell Susan after that is up to you."

Charles and Susan looked at each other, as Mike got out and closed his door.

"Is that okay with you, honey?" Charles asked.

"I can't imagine what he wants to tell you that he can't tell me." Susan said. "What could be worse than Billy murdering my daughter? But you go ahead. You can always tell me later, and whatever it is, it'd be better for one of us to know it, rather than neither one of us."

Charles nodded, squeezed her hand, and got out.

Several bodyguards stayed around Susan, as Mike and Charles walked aimlessly down the sidewalk with a bodyguard trailing some distance behind.

Oh, God, my precious daughter is right inside that house! Oh, Lord, touch her heart! Heal her so she wants to come home... wants to get away from Billy forever...

She continued praying until Charles finally returned and sat in the back of the car with her, and she broke down and started crying. She hugged him, and cried into his shoulder, as he put a comforting arm around her.

"Charles, oh, Charles, is there nothing we can do to save her? I'll do anything! I'll do anything in the world to save her!"

Charles didn't speak for a long time, then gently pushed Susan upright and shifted in his seat to get ready to get out again. "Okay, Susan," Charles said with great emotion. "I'm going to take care of this the best way I can."

He opened the door, and Susan stopped him. "What do you mean? What are you going to do?"

"I can't tell you, Susan. Not ever."

She latched onto his arm and held tight. "Charles, don't you do anything without telling me first."

Charles waited at the open car door, and when Susan continued to hold him, he finally closed the door again.

"Susan… they're pretty sure Billy has killed two previous girlfriends."

Susan gasped in horror. *Oh, dear God in heaven, no…!*

"Are… are you sure you want me to go on?"

Susan's eyes were wide in fear as she nodded.

"They don't have enough evidence to get him convicted for that, and they don't think it's likely they'll ever be able to. He made a series of porn videos with each of them, with the videos getting worse and worse, from porn to group sex, to bondage… and ending with…" Charles' voice trailed off.

"With what?" Susan asked insistently.

"With 'snuff' movies," he said. "That's…"

Oh, God, no…!

"…that's a movie where they kill a person. Or… at least appear to, as far as the audience can tell. Mike says it's possible to make a movie like that where the person only appears to die, and they're really fine. But… some people really do kill other people when making those movies."

Charles took a deep breath and let it out. "The thing with those other girls Billy worked with… Mike and the guys have been pursuing every lead, not only to find Billy and Susan, but to get as much evidence as possible to hold against him in court. And those other girls… since they appeared in those snuff movies… no one's ever seen them since. They come from, uh, really lousy homes, but they tracked down some of their family members, and they haven't seen them since either. Mike said they don't appear to know about the snuff movies and his men didn't have the heart to tell them."

"Oh, no, Charles, no! How is that possible? How could such an evil man exist? How could my precious little girl be involved with a fiend like that?"

Charles waited for Susan to finish before continuing. "Susan, if we leave Billy alone, he's likely to kill Stephanie."

Susan was quiet, but tears were coming so fast that Charles was just a blur.

"If we have him arrested and he gets out on bail, he's very likely to kill her." Once again, Charles paused before going on, "In both cases, he may decide that if she's dead, she won't be able to testify against him."

Susan lunged into Charles and sobbed.

"There's one other option," Charles said. "The only other option."

What other option could there be...? Susan wondered as she wept.

"Mike offered to kill Billy."

What...? What did you say? Susan's crying subsided somewhat.

"Now. Tonight." Charles said as he continued to hold Susan.

"Did... you say..."

"I said Mike's offered to kill Billy, right now, as soon as I tell him." Charles said. "Not for money. Just because he's convinced that Billy deserves to die and because it's the only way to make sure he can't murder any more innocent women."

Susan sat back and wiped her eyes and nose on her shirt.

"And we would take Stephanie by force to a mental institution and have her committed until she's out of danger of committing suicide."

"Charles, you're talking about murder!"

"I'm talking about executing a murderer in order to prevent him from murdering again."

Susan was stunned into silence.

"If there's another way to protect Stephanie, I don't know what it is," Charles went on. "When you said you'd do anything for her... I was going to... make the decision on my own... to spare you the pain and guilt. And now I wish I had. I wish I'd told him to go ahead without telling you. I'm sorry..."

Susan shook her head. "Charles... I can't believe it..."

"Can you think of a better alternative?" Charles asked. "For the life of me, I can't."

"But Charles... we're Christians...! We... we can't... ask a man to kill another man..."

"We can if it's to preserve justice." Charles cupped a hand under Susan's chin and looked in her eyes. "If we don't let Mike kill Billy now, and Billy later kills Stephanie, maybe as soon as we leave, how will you feel then, about having let him live?"

Susan sucked in her breath. *I can't... believe this... God of Abraham, help us! Deliver us from evil!*

Charles let go of Susan's chin and held her hand. "When you marry me, Stephanie will become my daughter. I'm going to do this to protect her, Susan. I'm going to do it."

Charles opened the door and got out.

God...! Please...! Don't let Charles do this! This isn't your way! Please, show us your way!

In an instant, Susan decided to run after him to try to stop him, but Charles was still standing just outside the door. He got back in and closed the door.

"Did you tell Mike to go ahead?" Susan asked in a panic.

"No," Charles shook his head. "First, we haven't talked to Stephanie. Maybe you can change her mind. I pray you can. But if not, I've got a couple of other ideas... though one's still dangerous for Stephanie, so..."

"What're you thinking?"

"Well... maybe we can make sure Billy has the right incentive to make sure he won't hurt Stephanie, even if he wants to..." Charles mused out loud. "But let's try talking to Stephanie first. Come on!"

He got out with Susan right behind, and they held hands as they walked toward the house, with Mike joining them.

Dear Father, please help us! Please change Stephanie's mind!

"We want to talk to them, Mike. We'll keep... other options... off the table for a little while."

"I don't see how that will do any good, Charles," Mike said, "but I guess it won't hurt."

They entered the tiny living room, and found Stephanie sitting on a worn-out couch, leaning back, with Billy next to her sitting upright and tense. Three men guarded them, two with handguns out. There was a not-very-subtle odor of alcohol, and an empty liquor bottle on the floor.

Susan looked at Stephanie carefully and saw several bruises. She wanted to rush over and hug her, but didn't want to interfere with the men guarding Billy, so she took the only open chair, while Charles stood in the center of the room.

"Who the xx-xx-xx are you?" Billy demanded.

Charles ignored Billy, and after looking over the scene, he focused his attention on Stephanie. "Hello, Stephanie, my name is Charles. I'm your mother's fiancé, which means I'll be your stepfather soon, and I want you to know I care a great deal about you, just because you're Susan's daughter."

Stephanie just scowled at him.

"I'm going to have these men take Billy outside so your mother and I can talk to you alone."

"Like xx-xx-xx you are," snarled Billy. "Tell 'em Steph."

Stephanie looked like she was trying to figure out what to say, and Charles continued to ignore Billy. "They won't take him to jail, not yet, anyway. We'll give you a chance to talk, but alone, without Billy able to hear."

"You xx-xx-xx! Stephie, it's a trick. Once they get us apart, they'll take me to jail. You know it, it's a trick!"

Charles turned slowly to Billy and said through clenched teeth, "I'm not asking, I'm telling. You'll be carried out by force if necessary." He nodded to Mike, who nodded to his men.

Billy continued to put on a tough-guy act, but went outside with the men without a fight. Mike and Frank stayed in the room.

"I'm staying with Billy, Momma," Stephanie said sullenly to her mother. "and I want you and this creep to leave him alone. If you put him in jail, I'll kill my xx-xx-xx self just to hurt you."

"Stephanie... why...?" her mother pled. "Why do you hate me that much? Don't..."

"Oh, don't pretend you don't know. The same reason it's always been, you ran daddy off. And if that's not bad enough, now you're marrying this gigolo, or sugar-daddy, or whatever he is. I want to stay with Billy, and if killing myself is the only thing I've got to bargain with, that's what I'll use. And I mean it, 'cause I don't have anything else to live for."

"But Stephanie, you..." Susan started.

"Just shut xx-xx-xx up, Momma, and get xx-xx-xx out of my house! Leave us alone!" Stephanie turned away and stared at the door.

Oh, God... her heart is so hard... can anything ever melt it...?

"Stephanie," Charles said, "do you know what happened to Billy's old girlfriends?"

"Yeah, he told me about them. They retired."

"Retired...?" Charles looked around the room. "How? Do you think they made more money than Billy did? Do you make more money than Billy does? Do you think they're living the 'good life' in

Miami condos after a few years with Billy?"

Stephanie looked away. "Mm - maybe."

"Stephanie, no one has seen or heard from those girls since they were last with Billy. Not even their families."

"Families are xx-xx-xx," Stephanie snapped.

Susan closed her eyes tight and squeezed one hand with the other. *Oh, Lord, forgive me for everything I did wrong to Stephanie! Don't hold my failures against her!* She opened her eyes, but felt like crying.

Charles sighed. "Stephanie, after you left your Mom's house, do you know why Billy stayed behind a few minutes...? He told your mother if she didn't come up with the money he was demanding that he'd kill you."

Stephanie looked surprised for a moment, but she quickly adjusted. "That was just to get Mom to get the money. He didn't mean it."

Charles shook his head wearily. "Are you aware that Billy has made snuff movies?"

"That was just pretend," Stephanie said. "I know all about that. That's part of the, uh, long-term marketing plan."

Charles thought for a moment before asking, "Does the long-term marketing plan include the star of the movie disappearing from the face of the Earth after a very realistic death-scene? Where's the long-term value in that?"

"I... I don't know. Ask Billy... he's the one who deals with all that."

"Stephanie, I don't know how else to say this..." Charles continued, "we're afraid Billy will kill you. He might have been planning to kill you from the beginning..."

"That's a xx-xx-xx lie!"

"...that might be his real 'long-term' plan. But now that he knows we can have him arrested, if we don't arrest him tonight, he could decide to kill you to make sure you can't testify against him."

"He wouldn't do that! Billy loves me! And I'll never testify against him!" She shot a hateful look toward her mother. "Not about anything!"

"Stephanie, if we leave you here with him, you'll be risking your life," Charles went on. "The only way he can be sure you won't testify is for him to kill you. And if he's already killed those other girls..."

"I don't care!" Stephanie screamed. "I don't xx-xx-xx care! I don't care if Billy kills me! And if you take him away from me, I'll xx-xx-xx kill my xx-xx-xx self! Either way, at least I'd be out of this xx-xx-xx excuse for a life!"

Susan felt drained, and near hopeless. *Father... I'm so empty... I have nothing but apologies and prayers, and that doesn't seem to be enough. What can I do...?*

Susan noticed that Charles was looking at her. *I have nothing to offer Charles... my precious, only daughter, and I have nothing else to offer her... and it's not enough.* She looked at Charles sadly and shook her head.

"Mike, I'd like to talk to Billy alone," Charles said.

Mike went to the door and started to open it, and Charles added, "Completely alone. Just me... Susan, I'd like you to wait outside with everyone else."

"Charles, that's a really bad idea," Mike said.

"I figured you'd see it that way. I'd like you stay here for a minute before they bring Billy in."

"Charles, I think you should listen to Mike," Susan said. "I don't want you taking any chances with Billy. I..."

Charles interrupted. "Susan, please trust me."

"Why, Charles, what do you have in mind?"

"Well, those other ideas I mentioned. I want to try one of them." Charles helped her up as Frank started to escort Stephanie to the door.

"Charles, please be careful," Susan pleaded.

Charles gave her a shoulder hug. "Just trust me."

As Susan walked out behind Frank, she noticed him cast a skeptical look toward Mike, which kept her worrying. *God, please keep a big angel in there with him, and keep him safe. Please, please, please... if anyone has to get hurt again, let it be me.*

Some of the men put Stephanie in the back of a car and guarded both sides, and Frank asked Susan if she'd like to sit down in that car or another. Afraid of further antagonizing Stephanie if she sat in the same car, she chose to pace and pray outside.

A minute or two later, Mike came out, stationed some men around the house, and sent Billy in. Then Mike moved to the front of the house so he could see in the front window.

For a while, Susan prayed anxiously while pacing near the front door, but finally sat down on the single step. *God, I feel like Peter must have felt when Jesus was praying in the garden... I should be praying too, but I'm just soo tired... I need to be praying for Charles, but I'm so tired I can hardly think... I'm afraid I could fall asleep...*

oh, no…! If I fall asleep, I'll fall over, and the bodyguards will think I'm hurt, and they'll take their attention off Charles!

She struggled to her feet and leaned against the side of the house, but it didn't help relieve her weariness.

Finally, Charles signaled Mike through the window, and Mike came around and went in, with Frank and Susan right behind him.

Charles looked at Mike and shook his head, "Take him out, please, and give me a minute to talk to Susan. Then we'll want to talk to Stephanie again."

Once Charles and Susan were alone, he sat down with her on the couch. "I, uh… the best I could do, was, uh… I got Billy to agree to let Stephanie call you every day. And I told him that I'm going to keep these men watching him every day and every night. He, uh… offered to leave Stephanie alone, completely alone… kick her out, move away without telling her where he was going… if I paid him a lot of money.

"Oh… was that one of your ideas?"

"No, it was Billy's, and I thought about it… and you know I don't care about the money, but I decided that we can't do that. He can't be trusted, and he could take the money and pop up later and try to snatch Stephanie. Or kill us all, or anything. The point is, it just seemed out of the question to give him any money."

"Okay, Charles."

"So, what I told him is that if he lets Stephanie call you every single day, then we won't have him arrested, but he has to make sure Stephanie calls, or we'll have him thrown in jail despite Stephanie's threats to kill herself. And he's not allowed to hit her or hurt her in any way. Plus he's not allowed to let her act in any more movies…"

"Oh. Well, what if… uh… I'm sorry, whatever I was thinking… I lost my train of thought."

"Well, what I really have in mind is two things. First, if Stephanie doesn't call, I'll have these guys break in on them as soon as they can be sure they can do it without giving Billy a final chance to hurt her, and we'll have her committed until she's not suicidal, or she's de-Stockholm-syndromed, or whatever… until she's not emotionally dependent on this maniac."

"I'm hoping that won't be necessary though. I'm hoping that not allowing her to make porn movies might make Billy think of her as a useless mouth to feed, and he'll want to talk her into leaving him so he can find another girl to act in his porn movies. Then, if he kicks Stephanie out, maybe she'll be willing to come home. We can cross that bridge when we come to it, but anywhere is better than with Billy."

Susan nodded.

"We won't leave Billy to molest and possibly kill another girl, of course. Once Billy has kicked Stephanie out, we'll have him arrested and prosecuted to the fullest extent of the law. And in the meantime, I'll keep these guys working to see if they can find more evidence against him from those snuff movies."

"Second, when we get Stephanie alone in here, we give her a code-word. If she ever decides she wants to leave Billy but she's afraid he won't let her, she can use the code-word on one of her daily calls to you. If she gives you the code-word, we'll send in the troops to get her out and arrest Billy."

Wow. We're both so tired I can hardly remember my name, but you still thought of all that?

"And we'll still have Mike's third option… if we decide that's the best thing to do."

Susan shook her head. "I don't like that. I don't think that sounds like something God would want us to do, but we can talk about it when we've had some time to sleep and… can think clearly."

"Okay," Charles agreed. "What about a code-word? It needs to be a word that won't arouse Billy's suspicion, but not a word that Stephanie might use without thinking in a normal conversation. Not that she's likely to chat much…"

"Oh, Charles, I have no idea…"

"Well, I was thinking, was one of those dolls or stuffed animals in her room a favorite? With a name? That might work…"

"Oh… how about a favorite CD? She had a favorite CD by Robin somebody. It had a song called… 'Show me love' and she played it so many times, she wore it out. We got her a second copy to listen to, but she kept the first one as a keepsake. It's still in her room."

"That ought to work. She could tell you she'd like to pick it up the next time she comes over or something like that."

"Okay. Uh, I guess we'll need to see if that's okay with her."

"Considering her attitude right now, I don't think anything'll be okay with her. We'll just tell her what it is."

"Yeah, you're probably right."

Charles called Mike in and explained everything to him, and then he had Stephanie brought in.

Stephanie objected at first, but agreed to call Susan every day when she was convinced it was the only way to keep Billy out of jail.

Once that was accomplished, an exhausted Susan and Charles climbed back into the big black car. Mike gave instructions to a contingent of men that were staying behind and then took the front passenger seat.

Susan stared at the house as the car pulled away, and put a hand on the car window. *Father... heavenly father... please, please take care of my little girl. Please don't let him hurt her. Please help her!*

"Charles," Mike said, "under the current circumstances, I don't think either one of you should continue to stay at Susan's house. Stephanie knows to call Susan's cell phone, so she can be anywhere. Billy's still a threat, and if he should lose our men, he knows where Susan's house is. I'd like to relocate the two of you."

Susan looked at Charles, who had never looked so fatigued.

"Uh... well..." Charles mumbled.

"I'd like to put you in a hotel suite, with more limited access that we can easily control."

"Uh, okay, Mike. Is that okay with you, Susan?"

"I guess so... but we'll need to go home first. I'll need to pack some things. How long will be gone for...? Staying in a hotel, I mean."

"I'm taking you straight to a hotel, Susan," Mike said. "You get some rest, and we'll take care of your clothes and everything else. Okay?"

"O-okay."

Mike started quietly making phone calls, and Charles and Susan passed out in the back seat.

Sometime later, Susan had vague impressions of getting into an elevator and of walking down a hallway. Someone was half holding her up, but she thought she heard Charles behind her...

Chapter Eleven

"Uhhh..." Susan moaned. *Something's not right... my pillow. Doesn't feel like my pillow.*

With her eyes still closed, she stretched an arm across the covers. *Hmm... stiff. The sheets are too stiff...*

"Ungh..." she uttered as she struggled to open her eyes and rise up on her elbows.

"Good morning, Susan," a strange voice said. "Don't be alarmed. My name's Lisa, and I work for Mike on special occasions. Would you like some light?"

Who...? Mike... oh, the private investigator guy... "Uh, yes, please."

Susan heard a curtain being pulled open a bit, and felt the warmth of bright light filling the room. She put a hand over her eyes and squinted.

"Too much?"

"No... no. I'll get used to it in a minute. Where are we? What's going on? How's Stephanie?"

"This is the Knoxville Plaza hotel. We brought you up here last night. Or early this morning, rather. I can check with Mike for an update on Stephanie, but the last I heard, their house was all quiet."

"Uh, what time is it?" Susan asked, just barely getting her eyes to stay open.

"It's a little after Noon."

Susan gasped and started to look around for her clothes. "Noon?! Oh, no...!"

Lisa came over toward the bed. "Why, what's wrong? Are you late for something?"

Susan's mind raced, but came up with nothing. "Uh... well... I guess not. I... I just usually don't sleep in late. I guess I feel a little out of control."

"I understand. Well, you were really out-of-it last night, and from what I've heard, you haven't had much sleep lately. Maybe you needed to sleep in this time."

Susan nodded. "Yeah, I guess so."

"I helped you out of your clothes last night," Lisa said as she walked to the bathroom, "I'm a nurse, so I'm used to it. I left your underthings on, since I didn't know what you usually wear to sleep, if anything. I hope you weren't too uncomfortable."

"Uh, no." *How embarrassing!*

Lisa came back carrying a plush bathrobe and put it on the bed. "After you got to sleep I went to your house and packed some things for you. I put a change of clothes in the bathroom for you, but the rest are in the parlor. I didn't want to risk disturbing you by putting them away until after you woke up. I'll put them up while you're getting a shower. Or would you like to eat first?"

"Wait… the what?"

" 'What' regarding which part?"

"The, uh, parlor…? I thought you said we were in a hotel."

"Yes… the Knoxville Plaza. This is the presidential suite, on the twelfth floor. Just outside the door is a parlor room, and across the parlor is Mr. Parker's bedroom."

"Oh!" *Oh, my!* "And how is Cha… Mr. Parker?"

"I'll go check."

"No!" *No way I want you going into his bedroom!* "I mean, that won't be necessary."

Lisa looked a little puzzled, but didn't say anything. She pointed to Susan's cell phone on the bedside table, plugged into its charger. "Well, I just stayed to answer your cell phone if it rang before you woke up and to help you figure out where you were when you did wake up, so I'll just get your things from the other room, and I'll take off after I put them away. Unless you need me for anything else, or if you'd rather put your things away yourself."

Put my things away for me…? Well, I'm no invalid, I can take care of myself. And Charles. "Well, uh… I'm sorry, what was your name again?"

"Lisa. I'm a registered nurse, but I like doing a little work for Mike now and then just to do something different."

Well, that sounds different all right. "Thanks. Well, if you don't mind, Lisa, I'll take care of things myself, now." *Are you a James Bond type of playgirl, just looking for fun?*

"Okay," Lisa said with a smile. "Well, if you need me for anything else, Mike knows how to reach me."

Hmm… are you wearing a wedding ring? I can't see…

Lisa left the room and closed the door behind her.

And don't stop by Charles' room on your way out! Ooo…! Susan jumped out of bed and put on the robe as she hurried to the door to make sure Lisa didn't run into any hindrances on her way out.

She opened the door and strode into the parlor a couple of steps before she realized that there were several strange men scattered around the room.

Everyone stopped talking and looked at Susan, and she froze for a moment, before excusing herself and hurrying back into her room. She closed the door and leaned against it as her mind sped from one thought to the next.

Oh, my! Why were they looking at me like that? That's a huge room. And... I thought Charles would be alone... was Charles one of the men? No... he must still be asleep... I guess. Oh, those must have been my clothes piled up on those chairs. And there were some boxes. Lisa was talking to one of the men. Did I recognize any of them? And what did Lisa say about eating? I'm hungry.

Sheepishly, Susan opened the door and poked her head out. "Uh... Lisa, uh, I can call room service... right?"

Lisa broke away from the men she had been talking to and walked a few steps back toward Susan.

Aha, a wedding ring.

"Sure, but is there something I can help you with?" Lisa replied.

"No, no thank you. I'm just going to call down for something to eat."

"Okay," Lisa said, "But there's a big basket of fruit, if you'd like some of that while you're waiting."

"Oh, that sounds good!"

Lisa walked over and picked up a basket Susan hadn't noticed before, and carried it into Susan's room.

"Wow, that's huge."

"I'll just put it on the table over here..." Lisa offered, but Susan stopped her.

"Oh, no, just let me pick a couple of things, and you can take it back out there, if you don't mind, so those men can have the rest."

Lisa laughed, "I don't think these guys are big into fruit, but okay."

Susan picked a banana, a pear, and one strawberry, and Lisa left her alone again.

Susan leaned against the closed door once again and surveyed the room as she slipped the pear into a pocket of the robe and ate the strawberry. *Wow, this is... really nice. Very fancy. Very elegant private sitting area. Well, don't get used to it, Susan. This is just temporary. Charles likes our house just fine... Is he used to living like this? Will he really be happy living in my small... whatever's-opposite-of-fancy kind of house?*

Susan peeled her banana a little and started to take a bite as her mind flashed to memories of oral sex with Marty, and then imagined oral sex with Charles. *Oh, no...! I can't put up with lustful thoughts every time I have a stinking banana! What am I going to do...? Lord...*

Susan broke off a bit of banana and started eating, and laughed to herself. *Sorry, guys.*

Her mild mirth quickly turned sour, however, as sexual thoughts continued to plague her. *Where's my Bible... Oh, I wonder if Lisa's still here...?*

Susan opened the door and poked her head out again, and saw that Lisa was indeed still there. Lisa noticed and came over.

"Uh, Lisa... I guess we're not supposed to leave the suite, huh?"

"Well, in case Billy has someone out looking for you that our guys miss, Mike wants you to stay in the hotel. But they have a pool and fitness room. And of course you can come out here..."

"Oh, well, I haven't gotten dressed yet. But, well, would you mind going back to my house and getting my Bible for me? It's..."

"It's right here," Lisa said, finding a box labeled 'kitchen table' and handing it to Susan.

Susan was taken back a bit. "That... that was very considerate of you, Lisa."

"Well, I tried to think of what I would want if I were in your shoes." Lisa went back for another small box.

The golden rule? And you would have wanted your Bible?! Oh... I feel ashamed of myself for feeling jealous about you... and all night you were doing everything you could to help me.

"Cosmetics," Lisa said as she handed the second box to Susan.

How thoughtful! Susan almost choked up as she thanked Lisa and closed the door again. She sighed heavily and got out her Bible.

Well, the lustful thoughts are gone for now. I guess I'll get a shower, then get dressed. Then I'll study until Charles gets up. I wonder what time Stephanie will call? What if she doesn't call...? Oh... then all sorts of things happen again. Well, as long as Stephanie's safe, that's the main thing. But I'd better take the phone into the bathroom while I get my shower. And I have to pee!

Susan unplugged her phone, made sure it wasn't on vibrate, and went into the bathroom where she was stunned by the ornate fixtures. She took the pear out of her pocket and put it on the counter next to the phone, then hung up the robe and looked over the clothes Lisa had picked out for her. *Wow, nice taste.*

Despite several very large mirrors, Susan didn't notice her face until she spotted a close-up mirror hinged to a wall and glanced into it. She gasped as her jaw dropped. *My face! It looks awful! And that's even with some of my makeup still on! Oh, no... I wonder what I looked like last night?!*

She touched a cheek lightly, then harder until it stung. *It'll take an awfully thick coat of concealer to cover this up. This looks really bad! Well, I'll deal with that after a shower, and I can take stock au naturel.*

She found a toilet and bidet in a little alcove and peeled off her panties, then removed her bra while she waited for her bladder to empty.

Done with that, she looked around the bathroom more carefully. *Oh, my, look at all these full-length mirrors! A big shower... oh, with showerheads on both sides! Cool! And a sunken garden tub, how beautiful! I wonder how they did that? Does it stick out in the room below? Oh, it's a Jacuzzi tub! Wow!*

Susan sighed again, a weary-but-contented sigh this time. *Well, just a quick shower right now. I want to see Charles as soon as I can. But I sure will look forward to using that tub!*

Her mind flashed to a thought of Charles in the tub and she was sitting on his lap with him deep inside her. *Susan! C'mon! Think about whatever is pure, whatever is true, whatever is holy... what's that verse? I should look that up...*

Susan started the shower water, using both heads, and found a switch for a shower stall light, which was somewhat subdued. She noticed her own shampoo, conditioner, and razor on a recessed shelf in the shower. *Oh, how thoughtful of Lisa...! Like Charles' constant thoughtfulness... wow, he was so good last night... coming up with all those ideas, despite being so tired... Charles the planner. My Charles... Lisa, he's too old for you, and I wouldn't give him up even if he wasn't!*

She tested the water temperature and got in, luxuriating in the water from both sides. *Hmm. The showerheads are fancy, too. What do they do?*

Susan experimented with the showerheads and found a setting that had a powerful pulsating stream in the center, surrounded by many fine jets that cycled through a variety of pulses. She put the second showerhead on the same setting and started washing her hair.

Hmm, the main jet is almost like getting a massage... but those little jets are starting to make my breasts a little sensitive. I'll just point it a little lower, and... uunnghhh! Susan bent over in surprise at the sudden wave of pleasure she felt when the main stream hit her pubic area.

Aaahhh! In her bent over position, the powerful stream behind her was directed right between her legs. Susan slapped at the handle in front and got the water off, turned around and got the second one off and collapsed onto the floor with shampoo still in her hair.

"Uuhhh..." *Am I...? I am, I'm panting. I can't believe it! Two stinking seconds of stimulation and I'm panting like a dog in heat. How is that even possible? I'm an old woman!*

Susan looked down and noticed her nipples. *Look at that. They're standing out like when I last nursed... Stephanie. Oh...! God! How can I be horny when my daughter's life is in danger! Lord, I'm just not worth anything! I can't seem to keep my stinking mind clean no matter what I do! I've asked you to help me, and I'm having more trouble than ever! Are you even listening to me?!*

Susan sucked in her breath. *Oh, God... are you listening to me? Am I so bad you don't even listen to me anymore? Is that why you haven't helped Stephanie yet? Am I really worse than a prostitute like I thought the other day? But you even love prostitutes. Can't you love me, too? At least I haven't dragged Charles into the gutter... yet... although no thanks to me, that was his doing. Except for... when was that... just yesterday? Last night. It was just last night! I was the one who saved us last night... doesn't that count for something with you...? Lord, say something! How come I'm always the one doing all the talking in this relationship?! How come... ah, your 'still, small voice...' Do I not hear you because I talk too much? God, I don't know how you put up with me!*

Just then Susan's phone rang, and she jumped up and fumbled with the shower door to get to it quickly. *Is that Stephanie?! Or, Charles is awake and checking on me? Did he hear me fall in the shower? I didn't think I made that much noise. Oh, I hope Lisa doesn't come to check on me!!*

Susan grabbed her phone and snapped it open. "Hello?"

"Hello, Momma?"

"Yes, Stephanie! Honey, how are you?!"

"xx-xx-xx!" Stephanie cursed and hung up.

Susan sighed sadly as she stared at the phone, and slowly closed it. *At least you're alive. Thank God, at least you're still alive.*

Susan rubbed the back of her forehead with the back of a wrist to prevent suds from running down into her eyes, then made sure the bathroom door was locked and she went back to the shower. She used only one showerhead and changed the setting to a plain one, and the water swept away her silent tears. *Lord, please... if you're helping Stephanie, please keep helping her, and if you're not, please do! Well, that sounds pretty lame, I guess, but honestly, if you've been helping her, I can't see how. And please help me be quiet enough to hear your voice. Help me 'be still, and know that you are God.' And use me any way you see fit, if I'm worth using for anything at all.*

After carefully washing, Susan started to shave her legs, but stopped. *I hate stubbly legs, but do I have an ulterior motive? Am I worried about what Charles will think when he looks at them if I don't shave?*

She inhaled sharply. *Or am I worried about what he'll think if we become intimate and my legs aren't shaved? But even if we avoid sex, we've gotten awfully close several times. Did he feel my legs when we were on the boat? How long had it been since I had shaved then? Mm... I shaved Friday night, after dancing on the Star of Knoxville. Did he feel my legs while we were dancing? That dress only came down to my knees... but, no... he was wearing slacks, and his hands never got down there. He wouldn't be able to feel stubble through his pants legs would he? Even if not, he could see them! And I didn't wear hose! Let's see... before Friday night, I shaved the day before my first day at the Coffy Corner, which was Tuesday, so I shaved last Monday. Ooo, five days since I had shaved. Oh, noo... I hope he doesn't think I don't care!*

Susan soaped her legs and started shaving. *Well, God, it's not like I'm doing it just for him. I've been shaving even though I haven't been married, so I do it just because I like it, not to be sexy...*

She closed her eyes, lowered her head and leaned forward until she was leaning against the shower wall. *Okay, I admit it, I want to look sexy for Charles. And feel sexy for him? Well, I suppose if I'm honest, part of me doesn't want us to have sex, but part of me does. And if we were to have sex, I would definitely like to feel sexy to him, but...*

She sighed. *But I do it all the time anyway, Lord, so I shouldn't stop just because... I mean, gross, I don't want to let the hair on my legs just keep growing!*

Susan stood up and just stayed in the cascading water for a minute. *"f they cannot control themselves, they should marry."*

Charles, I think I need to ask you to sacrifice your preference to wait to get married until everything's okay. If you were serious about being willing to compromise on that for my sake... because I'm back to get-married-quick or stay away from you. It could be weeks, or months, before anything changes with Stephanie.

Plus, the sooner we go ahead and get married, the sooner I can quit worrying about Marty coming back or something horrible happening to keep us from ever getting married.

She set her mind to talk to Charles about immediate wedding plans again as soon as they could have a private conversation, and she finished shaving, dried off, and got dressed.

Lisa had picked one of Susan's favorite tops, a thick, bright white mid-sleeve number with a creamy-soft texture. Complementing that was one of her favorite skirts in several contrasting shades of brown, ankle-length with two pleats in front and two in back, a scalloped waistline, and a flattering embroidered design around the top third.

Susan stepped between two full-length mirrors to observe the overall effect, but her attention was captured by the bruises on her face. "Wow. I'm surprised it doesn't hurt worse than it does."

She fetched the cosmetics box Lisa had packed for her and emptied it onto the bathroom counter. *She must have gotten everything I had.*

She picked out the concealer and started applying it while looking in the hinged magnifying mirror. *I like to avoid heavy makeup when I'm wearing this top, but it can't be helped this time...*

Once she finished, she was surprised by the result. *Wow. That works a lot better than I expected. As long as none of it gets wiped off, you could hardly tell I have any bruising at all... I wonder how long it takes for bruises this bad to fade away? Marty bruised me plenty of times, but not this badly, and not on the face. Well, rarely on the face...*

She left the bathroom still in her bare feet and looked for shoes. Only the tennis shoes she was wearing the night before were evident, and they weren't suitable, so she went barefoot, hoping to find that a Lisa had packed a box of shoes.

Susan went into the parlor, and three men were still there. When Susan entered, they all stopped talking and stared at her.

"Is, uh, Charles up?" Susan inquired.

"No ma'am. Not yet," one of the men said. "But that's not a surprise considering how little sleep he'd had. They're setting up some surveillance equipment in another room, and we were gonna stay in here until Mr. Parker got up, but we can leave now if you'd like us to."

The man speaking got up as if to prove the sincerity of his offer, but the other two kept their seats.

"Oh, no... that's not necessary," Susan replied. "I'll just get my things and read in my room until Charles gets up. But thanks for offering."

Sure enough, one of the boxes was labeled "shoes" and Susan made a few trips to move all the boxes and clothes into her room and put them away. Next she got out the rest of the material from the "kitchen table" box and put it on the table in her sitting area with her Bible.

She got her pear and picked up Grandma's Sex Handbook, sitting down with it and curling up in a big overstuffed chair with the light from the window coming over her shoulder. *I wonder what else these ladies have to say? They sure nailed it on the sexual-meltdown issue, and the other topics definitely look interesting. Surprising... but interesting.*

She laughed to herself. *When I first saw the title, I thought it'd be too lame to be interesting, but after looking at the table of contents, I wonder if it's too wild...*

Susan picked up where she had left off, and an hour had passed before she stopped again.

Having a wife who wants to have sex with him, as opposed to just being willing... like I was with Marty most of the time... will meet his emotional needs like nothing else, eh? Well, Charles, I'm getting hornier every day, so the sooner I can "meet your emotional needs" the better I'll like it...

Susan jumped up and ran to the door, still barefoot. *Charles! You must be up by now! Can we get alone to talk about getting married?!*

Remembering her embarrassing entrance and retreat earlier that morning, she slowed down enough to avoid running into the other room.

Opening the door, she casually stepped forward and scanned the room. Only one man was still there, in the kitchenette, facing away from her.

That gray hair... "Charles!"

Charles turned around with a big smile, and when he saw her, he dropped the coffee cup he was holding. He ignored it as it hit, broke, and splashed, opting to stare at Susan instead. "Holy smokes!"

Susan giggled as she ran over to him and gave him a bear hug, being careful to avoid stepping on the shards of the cup or smudging her face. "Holy smokes? I haven't heard that expression since I was a little girl!"

She stepped well back from the broken pieces and spun slowly on a heel. "Do you like this outfit?"

"I... I..."

Susan basked in his obvious admiration as she set about cleaning up the spilled coffee and broken cup. She poured two new cups, added sweetener and creamer to hers and checked the empty packet on the counter. *Hmm... 'toasted maple' flavor. Weird. But an exotic flavor probably means he wants it black.*

She handed it to him, led him to the table and sat down with him, and all the while he stared slack-jawed at her.

"Silly boy," she teased. "You're going to have trouble drinking your coffee if you don't close your mouth."

"Coffee...? Who cares?"

Susan grinned happily and patted Charles' closest hand. "Listen, honey, I wanted to talk to you about something. Remember when you said you'd do anything I'd like, but you'd prefer to wait to get married until nothing bad would be bothering us on our honeymoon?"

Charles gave his head a shake, then his broad smile faded away. "Oh, yeah... bad things... I, uh, I've been thinking since I got up..."

You want to go ahead and get married too?! That's won...

"I think I made a big mistake last night."

Susan did a double-take, and her smile faded rapidly. *Mistake...?* "Last night...?" *Oh, when you tried to push me onto the bed...*

"I think we should take Mike up on his offer, and pray it's not too late."

Mike...? Susan looked quizzically at Charles. "What offer...?"

"To kill Billy... surely you couldn't have forgotten that."

Susan was startled. "Oh, Charles...! Why would you think we should do that? We prayed for an alternative, and God gave you one. A good one!"

Stephanie's cursing on the phone came into her mind. "As good as we could hope for, under the circumstances. Even though Stephanie seemed as far away as ever when she called."

"Stephanie called?! When?!"

"Oh... about an hour ago, while you were still asleep..."

"Oh, thank God!!" he gushed. "I woke up with a nightmare that Billy had killed her. Oh, honey, I think he's just a thoroughly evil person. Or demon-possessed or something. I tried to tell him about God's love and mercy last night, and he was just stone-cold silent. He didn't even argue, he just stared at me like he'd like to cut my throat."

"But you said you told him Stephanie can't make any more movies. That way Billy will push her away instead of us taking her away from him... if it works."

"If it works. If he doesn't kill her first."

"But he knows those men are watching him. He wouldn't hurt her again if he thought he'd get caught. Right?" she asked hopefully.

"I think he's evil enough to do anything. Absolutely anything. Reasoning and incentives may be useless with him."

Oh, God, what should we do?! I thought it was all worked out. I thought you gave us the answer last night. "But Charles, the Bible says not to kill."

"It says not to murder, but it also says we're to defend the innocent. Stephanie can't protect herself from Billy, and he may have already killed two other young women."

Oh, Father... what's your plan for Stephanie? What should we do...?

"What did Stephanie say when she called?"

"Sh-she just cussed me out and hung up," Susan said sadly. "I guess it was too much to hope that showing how concerned we are for her would soften her heart."

"Well, it still could. Maybe it will just take time."

I hope so... But should we take her away from Billy by force, to get her away from his influence? "Charles... what if we have the men get Stephanie, and we'll have her committed, and have them arrest Billy. Even if he doesn't stay in jail for a really long time, maybe it would be enough for her to start becoming independent. To start getting weaned off her emotional dependence on him."

Charles thought for a moment. "Well, okay, maybe that's the best thing to do. Should we call Mike right away, or dare we risk waiting a little longer to think about it?"

Susan looked plainly worried but responded, "Let's wait a little longer. She's already called today, so he apparently didn't object to that."

Charles nodded. "Yeah... that's a positive sign."

He sipped his coffee, looked at Susan, and furrowed his brow. "Was that... that wasn't what you wanted to talk about. You were happy. Glowing, in fact... and my worries burst your bubble. What were you so happy about? What did you want to talk about?"

Susan angled her head and looked lovingly at him, but hesitated before finally answering. "Well, I was thinking it might be a long time before anything changes with Stephanie. And if that's the case, I was thinking I'd like us to go ahead and get married. As soon as we could, but without leaving town for a honeymoon. We could go on a honeymoon later, but in the meantime..."

Charles held her in his gaze as he stood and took her hands, and she stood up next to him. "Yes," he said simply.

That's a tear in your eye. "I know you said you'd rather wait until..."

"Forget that. I want you. I want you more than I've ever wanted anything in life, no matter what. I want you in my arms without any reservations or restraints. I want you in my bed. I want you in my soul. I want you forever, and I want you now."

Susan could hardly believe her ears, and played his profession of love over and over in her mind. They hugged and kissed, lost to time, and she wished the moment would never end.

Oh, it would be perfect to make love together for the first time right now. We'll wait, to honor God, but oh... I've never felt so close to another person... so intimate. If I never feel this good again, at least this once... I feel like Eve with my Adam, all alone in our garden.

When they finally quit kissing, Susan rested her head gently against him, and he stroked her hair with one hand, while his other arm embraced her. Time still seemed to stand still for her, as she felt his heart beating, felt his warmth, and luxuriated in his caresses.

"There's no telling when anything will happen with Stephanie if we stick with the current plan. Mike wants us to stay in the hotel until we're sure Billy's not a threat to you. That means we can focus on knocking out Henry's questionnaires," Charles finally ventured.

"Mmm."

"Maybe we could finish today."

"Mmm."

"Maybe Henry could get a license for us and come over tomorrow."

Making tomorrow night our wedding night...! Susan slowly peeled herself away from Charles and grinned.

Charles raised his eyebrows expectantly.

"I'll get the questionnaires!" Susan said.

"I'll call Henry!" Charles replied.

Susan took off to her bedroom like she was set off by a starters' pistol while Charles dug out his phone.

"Hey, honey, I'm going to call Mike first and let him know that Stephanie called you, and I'll ask him if he sees any problem with Henry coming over here to marry us!"

"Okay," Susan agreed as she hurried back with her Bible and all of Henry's materials. She got started on the financial questionnaire as Charles was talking to Mike.

"Mike said congratulations and there shouldn't be any risk in Henry coming over here, since they know Billy's not following him. And if someone else was following Henry, they wouldn't know who he came here to see."

"Yeah, that makes sense," Susan concurred.

"Let's see…" Charles mumbled. "I've got Henry's phone number in my list of calls I made yesterday…"

"Hello… Henry? Charles Parker… Yes… she's feeling better after a good night's sleep, and she's looking gorgeous. We found Stephanie and Billy… no, not yet, we decided to hold off on that… Stephanie has promised to call Susan every day as a condition of us not having Billy arrested… yeah… uh-huh… Well, that's actually the main thing we wanted to talk to you about. We're staying at the Knoxville Plaza downtown for a little while for security reasons, separate rooms, and well, we've been working on your questionnaires, and we'd like to get married as soon as possible… yes, we expect to be finished going over all of them together by tomorrow morning… uh-huh… uh-huh… Okay, we'd really appreciate that… listen, can you get a wedding license for us, or do we have to appear in person for that…? Uh-huh… uh-huh… yes, we can get those… uh-huh… uh-huh… okay… about ten tomorrow morning, then…? Okay, great! Thanks, see you then!"

Susan looked up.

"He can get the license for us, no blood test required, but he'll need our social security numbers, my driver's license, and he'll need copies of our divorce decrees. I can get Nat to fax a copy of mine. Do you have a copy at home?"

Susan looked pained. "Uh… probably?"

"Do you remember the name of the lawyer who handled it for you? Maybe we can get a copy from him."

"Wait, I think I know right where it is, but… maybe I can get Lisa to get it for me."

"Oh, the girl that was helping you last night?"

Susan laughed, "Apparently. I don't remember that part of last night. But she was here this morning, too."

Charles called Nat and arranged for his divorce records, got Lisa's number from Mike, and called her, getting Susan to describe to Lisa where to look for her records. Then they ordered a meal from room service, and when he was done with all the calls he dug into the questionnaires with Susan.

The afternoon wore into evening, and they had room service bring dinner so they could keep working. They finished both the questionnaires and had discussions on the issues of finances, parenting, conflict resolution, communication, marital expectations, and marriage roles. Since they had already done the love-languages, all they had left to do was leisure activities, personality, and sexual compatibility.

They decided that since they had slept so late, they might have a hard time getting to bed at a normal hour, so they decided to take a break and watch some TV together, then complete the leisure and personality tasks before bed, leaving the sex questionnaire for tomorrow morning, so as not to stir up any extra emotions in that area when they were getting tired and ready for bed.

They sat on opposite sides of the sofa in front of the big TV to avoid cuddling and whatever else that would temp them to do, but Susan found it impossible to keep her mind on the TV, so they soon got back to the questionnaires.

At around midnight, they were done with their planned tasks, and went out on the balcony to look at the lights of Knoxville.

"Too bad we can't see much of the river because of those other tall buildings. It's so close," Charles commented.

"Yeah... or the SunSphere," added Susan.

"The what?"

"The SunSphere," she repeated. "The tower with the big round ball on top."

"Oh, yeah, I've seen that. I didn't know what it was."

"It was built for the 1982 World's Fair. It's got an observation deck up near the top. Would you like to go up there?"

"Now?" he asked, surprised.

"No, of course not, we're supposed to stay in the hotel. But we could go some other time. I like it best at sunset, and it's free. And there's also a restaurant up there. And a bar and grill on another level, but I've only been to the observation deck."

"Well, sure, that sounds great. But for now we should probably get to bed," Charles said somewhat sadly. "Beds, that is. For one more night?"

"Yes, and no more hugging tonight, or you won't be able to pry me loose."

Charles smiled.

They went inside and paused next to each other, and Charles started to take Susan's hand.

"Uh-uh," she said, pulling her hands out of his reach. "I'm hot enough right now that just holding hands could start a meltdown."

"A meltdown, huh?"

"Oh, you didn't read about that. It's in Grandma's book," Susan said as she stepped over to the table and picked up the book. "It describes sexual meltdowns, and it explains the, uh, temptations we've been having perfectly."

"Oh, really? Grandma knows something about that, huh?"

"Oh, Grandma knows a lot of things about sex. I'm not half-way through, and I've already learned a lot. And the next chapter is supposed to explain the difference between sexual fantasy and lust. I'm really looking forward to reading about that."

"Hm. Yeah, that sounds interesting, all right. I might like to take a look at it before we give it back to Henry. Uh... if you don't mind."

"Why, Charles, you naughty boy, wanting to read about sex," Susan said, whispering the last word.

"You just wait one more day, and I'll be doing a lot more than reading about it."

"Mmm! That sounds delightful."

Charles took a step forward, but Susan took a step back. Then she kept going, backing toward her bedroom door while keeping her gaze on Charles. She got to the door and paused.

Charles sighed. "You're *so* beautiful!"

Susan's smile lit up, and Charles took another step toward her. Susan used her free hand to reach behind her without looking, found the doorknob, opened the door, and stepped back into it.

"Tomorrow... you can unwrap me," she said before going all the way into her room and softly closing the door.

Should I lock the door? No... I should trust him... but I can't even completely trust myself... and last night, his desire was ready to "overwhelm his reason" so... just to be on the safe side...

Susan turned the lock, and then got ready for bed with great contentment, even though it hurt getting the makeup off her face. She put the sex book on her bedside table and set the alarm clock for seven, planning to read awhile, but once she got under the covers, she felt tired enough that she thought she could sleep, so she turned off the light and snuggled down.

"You're so beautiful" you said... and the way you look at me proves you really think so... ..."I want you"... "I want you more than anything else I've ever wanted... I want you in my arms... in my bed... in my soul"... ooo... you want me forever... and you want me now... well, you have me, all of me, forever and ever... what was that you said after you taught me to dance... the first time we kissed...? "You're like a part of me that's been missing my whole life, and now that you're in my arms, I don't ever want to let you go"... mmm... then don't, my love, don't ever let me go... I'm "burned into your heart"... and you're burned into mine... ..."I feel like you're part of me... like you were always... always... supposed to be"... ...just a few more hours... ...and I will be...

Chapter Twelve

Charles, I'm in the river! Help! Charles...! Oh, good, you see me. Charles... don't leave me! The water's pulling me down! Were you planning this? You're leaving me on purpose? ...because you know as soon as I go under I'll turn into a butterfly? Oh, I've never been a butterfly before... oh, there's my house! ...and there I am in bed, but, I don't have a water bed... and it's leaking... I've got to abandon ship... I've got to get out of bed, before it sinks!

Susan woke up quickly and the nightmare faded to the realization that her sheets were completely soaked with sweat. "Whhaat?"

Throwing off the covers, she climbed out of bed and turned on the bedside lamp. *Four AM! The sheets...*

She felt the bed, then pulled up the bottom sheet and felt under it. *Arrg... even the mattress is soaked. And I'm still burning up... Lord, I thought all this was behind me! It's been so long since I've had a hot flash this bad... What will Charles think...? Charles... how is your otherwise remarkable patience when you've woken out of a good sleep? Oh... did you get to sleep last night before they found Stephanie? Probably... so even when really tired, your patience is amazing.*

She started to pull the sheets off, and stopped. *This is a hotel, silly... I'll have to wait for the hotel staff to wash them... Well, I could probably get them to bring dry sheets now, but with the mattress wet, it won't help... well, at least this bed is so big I can just sleep on the other side once I quit sweating and get a shower. I won't have to sleep on the sofa like I do at home.*

Turning on more lights, Susan went to the door, unlocked it, and peeked out just in case Charles was up, but the parlor was dark and quiet, and his door was closed. She went to the bathroom and drank a couple of small glasses of tap water. *There are things that make you lose your patience, though, like with Andy. What caused that? Andy was giving me grief... so was your anger just to protect me, even though I was a stranger at that point? Or maybe it's injustice that gets a rise out of you? Or... could be lots of other things, I guess. I'll try to pay more attention to that.*

She took the refilled glass to the table, along with her book. *Hmm... what's next? "Fantasy vs. Lust," huh? Okay, Grandma, what's up with that?*

By the time she finished the chapter, she had finally finished sweating, and was starting to get cold, so she started a warm shower. *Wow, so sexual thoughts, even wild ones, aren't necessarily lust. Boy, I wish I had known that a lot sooner. I guess my recent sex fantasies don't mean I'm an evil reprobate after all. Although I'm still not comfortable with them. Well, if Grandma's right, then it would even be okay for me to enjoy them. Hmm... I don't know if I'll ever be able to do that... but honestly, it sure sounds like it could be fun...*

Susan bathed in a sleepy daze, shut the water off, and reached for a towel. *Hey! I washed all over and didn't get out of control! Cool! Thank you, Lord!*

As she dried off she tried to focus her mind on the day ahead. *My wedding day! Today, in just a few hours, Charles and I will be husband and wife! Then I'm going to take him into his room and hump him like a rabbit, and then just lie naked in his arms. I wish I knew how big his cock is. I hope it's not as small as Marty's. Guess I'll find out soon... but what if something goes wrong?! Oh, Lord, please don't let anything go wrong! What could go wrong? Maybe Henry won't be satisfied with our homework...? Will Stephanie be okay? I wish I could tell her... Oh! When will Charles tell his sons? He doesn't want to make them even angrier...*

Oh, no... what if I tell Stephanie and she wants to come and bring Billy?! And how am I even going to be able to tell you, Stephanie? You won't even talk to me now... and how should I try to sound when you call? Loving... firm... worried...? Well, no matter what I do, you're going to be mad that I'm not marrying Marty again.

Susan gasped. *The divorce papers! What if we can't get both sets of divorce papers?! Well, that just means a delay, I guess... we'd still be able to get married as soon as we get them... but dear Father in heaven, I don't want to wait anymore! Please, please, I can't rely on controlling myself anymore, and honestly, I don't even want to! Please, God, please... no more waiting!*

Hey, I'll tell you what, God, I'll sell you all my fears, cheap! Oh... you already bought them, didn't you...Well, I could use a little help transferring ownership, then.

She finished drying off, hung up the towel, and put on the plush robe. *Oh, I sure like this robe... oh no! What will I wear? Ohhh! That outfit I wore yesterday would have been nice, if I'm not going to have a white dress. Now what am I going to do...?*

She went into her bedroom and glanced at the clock again. *Ten 'til six. And Charles and I didn't agree on what time to get up. Phooey. Well, I'll look through the clothes Lisa brought over, but I don't remember seeing anything nice enough that I'd want to get married in it... Well, let's just start with... oh, no!! Panties and bras! I don't own a single negligee anymore... I don't have any lingerie at all!*

Picking through a drawer of her underclothes, she started to throw a handful of them onto the bed in despair, and stopped when she saw the cover thrown back and remembered how wet it was. *Oh, nooo... I wish I had Brigitte to help me... Arhh, I have no bridesmaid...! Brigitte, why did you have to move away and leave me all alone...? Just because your husband was offered a job across the country didn't mean y'all had to take it. I haven't had a good friend since you left!*

Susan started crying softly and sat on the edge of the bed. Just then she heard a soft knock at the door. She inhaled suddenly. *It's not locked!*

"Don't come in!" *Oh, what if he only heard 'come in'?!* She ran to the door to lock it, but then decided just to stand behind it and keep him from pushing it completely open. When he didn't, she opened it a crack and peered around.

"I hope I didn't wake you," Charles said.

"No, no... I, uh... I've been up for a while."

"Me, too. Want to get breakfast?"

"Yeah. Yes, that sounds good. Let me get some clothes on."

"Okay, I'll wait out here."

She shut the door and locked it. *He's wearing jeans and a pullover. He's got more muscles than I realized. And I don't think I've seen him in jeans before. Wonder what he looks like in those from the back...? Well, Lisa brought me a pair of jeans, I'll wear those for now and change later... but what I'll change into, I have no idea...*

Top... top... top... She picked a pale yellow short-sleeve cotton button-up, put her cell phone in her pants pocket, then grabbed a pair of socks and her tennis shoes. *I'll put these on out there...*

Susan joined Charles in the parlor and sat in an upholstered chair to dress her feet. "Do you know if the restaurant is open this early?"

Charles came over and sat nearby. "Have you been crying?"

Susan moved more slowly, but kept working on her feet. "Well... a little bit... But not because we're getting married! I still want to!" *Desperately!*

She sat up and looked at his eyes. "Do you still want to?"

"Oh, yes, my love, with all my heart. But what's bothering you?"

She looked down. "Well, I guess I'm scared... of a lot of things... that something will go wrong even now, and stop us from getting married. And I...I'm... I don't have anything nice to wear, and I so want to look nice for you today."

"What's wrong with what you have on now?"

"Now?!" She looked at him in disbelief. "Charles Parker, I am *not* getting married in a pair of blue jeans!"

"Oh, okay," he acquiesced. "What about that outfit you had on yesterday? You almost put me into cardiac arrest with that."

"Charles, honestly!" she protested again, but her eyes were smiling this time. "I can't wear the same outfit two days in a row."

"Well, it's not like you were tearing apart a car engine in it. You didn't really get it dirty or sweaty..."

"Arrg. Men!" she said while finishing her shoes. "So, what about that restaurant?"

"Well, it opens at six, but, uh... how's your face feeling?"

Susan sucked in her breath again. *Oh, no! I forgot about the bruises, and I'm not wearing any makeup!* "How bad do I look?"

"*You* don't look bad, but the bruises look pretty nasty."

Susan ran to her bathroom mirror, with Charles close behind.

"Oh, no! It's worse than yesterday! I look... I look horrible! All this dark blue and purple! Oh, Charles...! I don't want to look like this on our wedding day!"

Charles hesitated before asking, "Do you want to wait, then?"

"No...! No, I don't want to wait a minute longer than necessary, but... I don't want to get married with a bag over my head, either!" She looked at Charles with distress. "What am I going to do?"

Charles stepped forward and held her. "Susan, you can put on whatever you covered it up with yesterday or stay just as you are. Your spirit radiates through your smile and through your body, and it isn't affected by some fleeting changes of color."

"You... you really don't think I look hideous?"

He cupped her head in his hands and leaned in ever so gently and kissed her all over her face, and she felt the brush of his eyelashes. "You, my soul mate, are the most beautiful woman on the face of the earth."

Your soul mate...! beautiful... no, not just beautiful... "most beautiful"... oh, my... I'm getting hot again... is it another hot flash, or is it your hot body? Susan pulled him tightly to her and lifted her face and found his lips waiting. *This is me-wanting-you heat... Light me up, fire-boy...*

They continued to kiss and wriggle their bodies against each other until they were grinding pelvises, and Susan lifted one leg high and wrapped it around him with her knee at his waist and her heel digging into his butt.

After a moment of that, Charles slowly pushed her back. "Unngh..."

They were both breathing heavily.

"How can you turn me on like that so quickly?" Charles asked.

"Me?! You're the one doing it to me!" *Well, at least you proved my bruises aren't a big turn-off for you.*

"Come on," he motioned. "Let's go down to breakfast."

"Like this?" she pointed to her face.

"So what? Let's not worry about what other people might think. Let's just enjoy each other's company for a meal and ignore the rest of the world. Can you be that... unself-conscious?"

"Unselfconscious? Is that a real word?"

Charles smiled. "I don't really know. But you know what I mean. Can you eat downstairs and not be bothered by what a few strangers might think if they see your bruises?"

"Hmm... maybe I can just not think about it..." *If I've got your handsome face to look at... and your crotch to think about...* "Yeah, I think I can."

"Okay, then, let's go," he said and started back toward the parlor. "With other people around, we won't be tempted to rip each other's clothes off."

Ooo, that is a nice view, Susan thought as she followed him. "Less likely to, anyway..."

Charles froze in his tracks and Susan almost walked into his back.

"What is it?" Susan asked.

Charles turned slowly. "You just suggested you might rip my clothes off even with other people around."

"Well, I wasn't serious, of course."

"Maybe not, but do you know how hot that sounds to a man who's been making out with a hot chick while wearing tight jeans?"

I'm a "hot chick?!" Oh, boy, are you pushing me over the edge. Or... were you trying to hint?* "Well... you want me to take those troublesome jeans off for you?"

"Susan! Please…! We're trying to get out of the suite… you know, to try to preserve ourselves for a few more hours…? Have mercy!"

Guess not. A few more hours, then… a few more hours… "Okay, Charles. I'm sorry. I'll tone down the sex talk. Until after the ceremony." She walked past him into the parlor toward the suite door.

"Oh, just a second," Charles said. "I'm supposed to let the bodyguards know before we leave the room." He looked up a phone number and made the call.

"Five minutes. We need to give them five minutes to… check things out or something."

He took a casual step toward her, and Susan stepped away.

"Unh-uh. Don't you touch me if you want us to keep our clothes on. And you'd better not compliment me anymore either."

"Are you serious?"

"Oh, yes. Yes, sir."

Charles meandered over to the balcony window and looked out over the city, while Susan pretended to look around in the kitchenette.

God, I don't know why you chose to bring a man into my life after all these years, but since you did… precious heavenly Father, thank you for this one!!

Charles looked at her from across the room. "Gee, Susan, not even Jennifer ever got me this worked up, and our relationship started off based on sex."

"Oh…?" *Cool! I get you more excited than your first wife!* "It's been the same for me, Charles. But then, we've been violating Grandma's two rules for abstinence every day."

"What? What rules?"

"Not to touch and not to be alone together… Being alone with someone you're physically attracted to and touching them is like putting a match to gasoline."

"Well, we're adults, not kids…"

"Adults with strong, unsatisfied sex drives."

"Hm," Charles nodded. "I guess age doesn't override that factor."

"I'd say we've been proving that point."

Charles grinned. "Maybe we should get married."

"Tell you what, if you marry me today, I'll throw in free sex for life at no extra charge!"

"Sold!" Charles proclaimed.

They laughed across the room and their merriment turned to

inward thoughts as they continued to slowly pace around.

If Henry gets here at ten and has everything he needs... we can have a really short ceremony, hint as strongly as necessary for him to leave soon after... so we could be married and alone by... ten thirty? Less than five hours from now?! Darn it... if only I had the right clothes for the ceremony... and after... We'll need to use the bed in Charles' room since mine will still be wet... I wonder what your bathroom is like, Charles... does it have a Jacuzzi? Can we have sex in it? I wonder how big your cock is... uh-oh, there goes my... oh, wait... Grandma said thinking about sex isn't the same as lust... so... it's okay for me to think about your cock, since we're about to be married... oh, my... and the two will become one flesh... my body will belong to you... and your cock will belong to me... oh, my... I wish I could feel it now... with no clothes between us, that is... I wonder if we can have sex like in some of those drawings... are you strong enough to hold me while you're standing with my legs wrapped around your waist and let me ride you that way... ooo! In that fancy shower...! Rrrr...!

Charles' phone finally rang, and as he fished it out of his pocket and answered it, Susan found herself staring at the front of his pants. *Those are too tight to get his cock out through the zipper, I'll bet. I'll need to at least get them off his hips. I wonder if...*

"That was them," Charles said as he walked toward the door. "It's okay."

Susan reached the door first and opened it, finding it blocked by a huge bodyguard. Susan raised her head, and it seemed like he just kept going up and up.

"I'm Truck," he said in a deep, rumbling voice. "You do what I tell you if you want me to keep you safe. Okay?"

Susan nodded and Charles said okay.

Is there anybody who wouldn't do what you told them to?

They waited for the elevator, and Charles started to reach for Susan's hand but stopped himself. The elevator door opened and Susan got on followed by Charles. Truck got on after them, dipping his head to get in, bouncing the elevator with each step, and he almost filled the doorway.

Susan reached for Charles' hand, but stopped herself.

"Food," said Charles.

"Yep. Just food," said Susan.

Ding... ding... ding... the elevator sounded off as it passed each floor, then stopped on the ninth.

"Next car, please," Truck said to whoever was waiting there. Whoever it was didn't object.

Ding... ding...

Mmm... alone in your bedroom... I grab your shirt and yank it to both sides, and your shirt shreds and comes off... then I lick your nipple while I ease a hand into your waistband...

Charles cast a sideways glance at Susan, and she glanced back. She turned and smiled, and he turned and grinned. He slowly extended one finger toward her exposed arm, and she took a step to the side but could go no further. He reached farther until he touched her, and then slowly slid just the tip of his finger down her arm.

Susan turned straight ahead, closed her eyes, shivered, and sighed. *Mmmm...*

She looked at Charles and warned, "Remember what I said about clothes... in front of other people?"

He snatched his hand back and looked straight ahead. "Food."

"Just food, and you'd better behave," Susan said.

The elevator stopped on the ground floor and Truck looked around before he let Susan and Charles get out.

"Food and witty banter?" Charles asked.

"Depends on the topics."

"Yeah, I'm wondering if leaving a certain questionnaire for last was a good idea."

Truck escorted them to a booth in a back corner and left them alone.

A waitress appeared almost immediately and gave them each a menu. "Would you folks like some coffee?"

"Yes, please," said Susan and asked for non-dairy creamer also.

"Yes, make it two, thanks," Charles added.

I wonder what you'll add to your coffee this time? Susan wondered as the waitress disappeared.

"She seemed rather nervous," Charles observed quietly. "Maybe she knows we have bodyguards and she thinks we're celebrities."

"Mm. More likely my face scared her," Susan said. *Oop, don't focus on that while I'm out in public with no makeup.*

"Mm. Guess that could be. Does it bother you?"

"Does what bother me?" Susan said with a wink that caused her to wince, and Charles smiled in response. *Think about something else. Like his denim jeans that don't provide much room for expansion of his assets. I know that's tough on your balls when you get horny with tight pants on. Hey, you got to bed as late as I did, why did you wake up so early? Not for the same reason I did, that's for sure.*

Charles yawned, and Susan followed suit.

"Listen, I have a confession of sorts," Susan said while she toyed with the menu.

"Okay, what?"

"Well, I woke up early because I was having a hot flash."

"That's not a confession. Telling me you robbed a bank is a confession."

"Well... whatever it is, does it bother you? It means I may occasionally soak the bed and even the mattress with sweat."

"Okay."

"Okay? Just, okay... like it's nothing?"

"Well, it won't bother me except in how it bothers you. As for me, I don't care if we have to move to the floor, a pull-out sofa, or a hotel room, we'll deal with it."

Maybe I should try to indicate that, hopefully, I'm through most of it... "I thought I was over it, but obviously I'm not. Maybe it won't last much longer, though."

"Okay," Charles said and yawned again, followed by Susan.

Stop yawning!

"Jennifer went through that. Laura was already done with it by the time we got married."

"Oh." *That's good. So you know what you're getting into. Hey, wait a minute...* "Uh, Charles, how old are you?"

"I'm sixty one. How old are you?"

Sixty-one! Sixty-one? "I'm, uh, fifty-six." *You're five years older than me!*

"Oh," Charles said. "You look younger than that."

They saw the waitress approaching and paused their conversation.

I look younger than that?! So you're a December old man looking for a May girl? You're already five years older than me! When you were a senior in high school, I was only thirteen! And what do you think now that you know I'm older than you thought? You and your wish-we-had-known-each-other-forty-years-ago!

"Ready to order?" the waitress asked as she put the coffee down.

Charles looked expectantly at Susan.

"Uh, sorry, I'm not ready yet," Susan answered and focused on the menu.

"Why not try ordering off-menu?" Charles asked Susan.

"Off-menu? What's that?"

"Forget the menu and just tell her what you'd like."

Where'd you learn that, at the old folks' home? Susan sighed with exasperation and turned to the waitress. "Do you have grits?"

"Oh, yes, ma'am."

"Okay, how about grits, scrambled eggs, bacon, whole wheat toast, grape jelly, and orange juice?"

The waitress said, "Yes, ma'am," again as she quickly wrote it down.

"Grits, huh? Okay, make it two again, please."

"Yes, sir," the waitress said and hurried away.

"Is something wrong?" Charles asked.

Yes, but... I don't want to tell you what it is. Well, how seriously does this bother me...? You're five years older, for crying out loud!

"Okay, something's bothering you. What is it? Did you want more time to study the menu?"

Susan looked at him like it was a silly question. "No... it's just that I'm... you're... you're older than me." *Ooh... that sounds so petty saying it out loud. Now you'll probably tell me that one of us has to be older than the other. Or get frustrated, or...*

"How long has it been since you were born again?"

"What? Uh..." *I was forty-five years old, so that makes it...* "eleven years."

"And I was born again about a year ago. Since we become 'new creatures' in Christ, that means you're ten years older than me, and I'm just a baby in Christ. So you're robbing the cradle."

That's not... that's... that's...

"That would be a much better confession than menopause," Charles added with a smile.

Five... ten... but that's not... well, if God planned for us to be together, but now, not forty years ago, maybe it's not important as long as... Susan closed her eyes and remembered flashes of the dream she had from early childhood well into adulthood, about a handsome stranger who alone discovered the secret to her heart. Then she remembered getting out of the cab at the end of their first date, how she had been terrified to ask him what color her eyes were, and how he said her secret out loud, *"Dark brown with a delicious tinge of green around the outside edge."* *So. You know my secret, Charles Parker. In all my life, you're the only man who ever did. And all the rest of my life has been a miserable disaster. Are you the man God made for me, but for now, not forty years ago?*

A handsome man, who for some inexplicable reason truly loves me for who I am, and despite my considerable shortcomings... a man who finds me sexually attractive... a man who kisses like Casanova... a man who taught me... me!... to dance... do I care that you're slightly older than I thought?

She opened her eyes, and Charles was studying her, but not saying a word. "A baby in Christ, eh...?" *Well, that package in your pants is a lot more mature than that. And I want it. And all the rest that goes with it. And you want me.* "What do you say we apply some sort of logarithmic scale, split the difference, and consider ourselves equal?"

"Well... I don't know anything about logamathingies, but I've been considering us equals since we first met."

"Okay, well, I guess I'm still adjusting to that in some ways. But I'm sure now the age thing won't bother me. So, I guess I'm getting on the same page as you. We'll be equals." *Wow, that sounds... perfect!*

"Except in the knees."

"What?"

"Except in the knees."

"I heard what you said, but I don't know what you mean."

"I mean I get weak in the knees when you're around."

Mmm... I like having that kind of impact on you. Hmm... Susan smiled mischievously and put the toe of one shoe lightly against his groin. "For the sake of your knees, then, maybe I'll just have to keep you off your feet..." *Oh, no, I really wanted to try the sex-while-standing thing! I hope your weak-knees comment was just rhetorical.*

Charles laughed and fixed his coffee.

Hm... a half-packet of artificial sweetener and a spoonful of non-dairy creamer again. That must be his standard when it's not a specialty coffee.

"Are you hungry?" Charles asked.

"Yes. But..."

"Well if you don't behave yourself," he continued, "I may send you to bed without your breakfast, young lady."

"Oookay..." Susan said with a laugh while putting her foot back down. *A play on words about sex and about me being younger than you, huh? I guess you're confident the difference in ages isn't a problem.*

But about the other part... "Sending me to bed... would that be alone, or with company?"

"You were teasing me with your foot, and I was teasing you with my words, but Lord willing, I'm never sending you to bed alone again."

Really? Oh, duh, if we get married this morning or this afternoon...

"Hey, I was wondering," Charles asked, "Would you like to get married up in the SunSphere? If it's available?"

"Oo, wow. That's an interesting idea. But Mike doesn't want us to leave the hotel."

"Well, I've been thinking about that. I doubt Billy has hundreds of minions out gunning for us, and I'm sure Mike's team can protect us just fine for an excursion now and then."

Susan nodded thoughtfully. *That sure is a spectacular view.*

"So, would you like to get married there? If it's available?"

"Maybe! Let me think about it for a little while."

"Okay, but if you want to, then the sooner you decide, the better, so we can make arrangements."

Just then Charles got a phone call. "I think that's Henry's number," he said.

"Hello...? Yes, good morning, Henry. Are you... uh-huh... I see... well, how... uh-huh... okay... all right, we'll see you then. Thanks. Bye."

Charles hung up and looked at Susan. "Henry's going to be late. He thinks it might be close to Noon before he can make it over."

"Oh, okay. Well, we can wait that long. Oh! And I just remembered, do you want to call your boys and let them know?"

"I thought about that, too," he said, "and I don't think so. I mean, yeah, I'd love to, but it would end with yelling, and I just don't want to deal with that on the day we're getting married. I'll..."

Charles' phone rang again and he took the call. "Hello...? Yes, sure, just a second," he said and handed the phone to Susan. "It's Lisa."

"Hello, Lisa."

"Hi Susan... didn't you tell me your legal papers were in a box in your pantry?"

"Yes, in a shoebox up on the top shelf."

"In the closet pantry, by the door to the garage?"

"Yes, that's it..."

"Well, I've looked all through this pantry, and I can't find a shoebox at all. I've looked in every other box in here, and none of them has legal papers of any kind."

The waitress arrived with their meals and started placing them on the table.

"I... I don't understand. I thought that's where it was... nobody else would have... oh! Stephanie and Billy were in my house alone the other night, they might have been looking around for anything valuable... maybe he took it!"

"Oh, well, do you..."

"Wait, I just remembered, he didn't have it when he left. He would have had to have taken it out to his car before I got home, and that doesn't seem likely."

"Well, if he found it, and didn't take it..."

Charles nodded approval to the waitress and she disappeared once again.

"Maybe he threw it away?" Susan surmised.

"I'm already looking through your kitchen trash can. Has it been emptied since Billy was here?"

"Mmm, no... That was only Saturday night. No, it hasn't been emptied since then."

"Well, I'm down to the bottom, and I don't see it. I'll keep looking in the rest of the house, but if you come up with any more ideas about where it might be, call me right away, okay?"

"Okay. And if you find it, please call me and let me know!"

"Okay, Susan, I will. Bye."

"Bye."

Susan slowly handed the phone back to Charles with a very distressed look. "She can't find the shoebox where my legal papers are. I don't understand it. They were right there in that closet pantry..."

She looked at Charles in alarm, "We can't get married without that divorce paper! I should go over there and help look!"

"Hold on... I was thinking about that last night, and we have other options. Do you remember your lawyer's name?"

Susan frowned a moment as she struggled to remember. "Noo..." she said plaintively. "I never used him for anything else. And that was such a stressful time. I have no idea what his name was!"

"That's okay... your divorce will have been filed with the court, as a public record. We can get a copy from there. Although it might take a while..."

"How long is 'a while'?"

"That depends on how close you can remember the dates."

"Without my copy of the divorce... I can figure out the year, and the approximate month…"

"Mm," Charles considered. "That could be a lot of records to look through. It might take a few days."

Susan looked crestfallen.

"But maybe we can get a bunch of people searching the records, and that will speed things up," Charles said. "In the meantime, let's eat. I have a vague recollection that grits aren't very appetizing when they're cold."

"Yes, that's true," Susan agreed, and they started eating.

So if we have to wait a few more days… that gives us more time for my face to heal some, and the cut on Charles' head… time to get a dress from home… ooo, time to arrange for a photographer! I want at least a few pictures… Oh! I don't have a single picture of Charles yet, and he doesn't have one of me… oh, great… I don't have any recent ones, and now I look like an ad for a zombie movie…

So waiting has advantages, but… "if you can't control yourself, you should marry"… and controlling myself is definitely not working.

"Charles…" Susan said more quietly between bites, "you said you wanted to wait until we're officially married before we have sex, and I know Grandma agrees with that, but why? I mean, why is it so important to you?"

Charles took a moment to reply. "You feel like it would be okay, because we're already engaged, and our marriage is imminent?"

"Well, yeah… I mean, suppose we get married on… say Friday, but have sex tonight. By this time next week, what's the difference? The intention is to have sex with the person who's going to be your spouse." *Oo, that was the same reasoning I used in college, and how many different guys did I have sex with without getting married? But this is different… I never got engaged to those guys first, and Charles and I are just days away from being legally married…*

"Well, first of all, the Bible's very clear that God doesn't want us to do that, so that should trump everything else even if we don't have any other reasons."

But it's so hard to wait!

"But I can think of another reason. Suppose we were to have sex tonight, planning to get married on Friday. What happens if I were to die before then?"

Oh, don't talk like that! That's practically impossible, anyway.

"Or suppose you were to change your mind?"

"Oh, that would never happen!"

"Last Wednesday, you were pretty confident that you wouldn't ever want to be more than friends with me. Yet we got engaged, what... three days later?"

"That's different!"

"Yes, it's different, but my point is that things can change. Something could happen that would prevent us from getting married. Then that point you raised about it being irrelevant a week from now no longer holds. We would have had sex without ever having gotten married, and we'd have no excuse."

Susan let her head sink and closed her eyes. *Oh, God! I thought... I asked you, Lord, but... here we go again, with the wedding getting further away instead of closer, and more talk about what could go wrong... and Charles didn't even mention Marty... ohh... Oh, God, please don't let Marty come back now, not now!*

"Even for Stephanie's sake?" came into Susan's mind. *What? For Stephanie's sake? Let Marty come back now? Oh, God, are you telling me that Stephanie needs him, and that I need to accept him again for her sake? Do you mean I can't marry Charles? Did you bring Charles into my life just to test me, and we're not going to be married after all? Oh, Father, that's too much to bear!*

"God is faithful. He will not let you be tempted beyond what you can bear." *Oh, Lord, I remember that passage, but it says you'll provide a way out... where's my way out?!*

"Not my will but yours," Susan heard in her mind, and sighed heavily. She leaned her head far back and rested it on the back of the booth. *Oh, Lord... am I surrendered to your will? I haven't asked myself that about Charles. It seems like such a whirlwind, and it seemed... well, everything just seemed so much like your will, I guess I've taken that for granted. But maybe you just sent Charles to help with Stephanie. And if Stephanie needs Marty now... even if that means me marrying Marty again... well, God, I think that would be the biggest sacrifice I've ever made. Yeah, I know, it wouldn't compare with the sacrifice you made for us, but it still looms pretty large to me right now.*

Susan sighed again, and a tear ran down her cheek. *Well, Lord, you are my Lord, and I'm willing to submit to your will. No matter what. I was serious when I gave you my life years ago, and I'm grateful for your Life, and I'm not going to try to take back control now. I'm yours. I give you my life, my will... Lord, I give you my daughter, my ex-husband... I guess you could've changed him by now, huh...? And I give you Charles, and my love for him. Your will be done, in my life, and in every life I touch from now on.*

Susan took a deep breath and let it out slowly as she opened her eyes. Charles' head was bowed, and she reached over and put a hand on one of his.

Charles kept his head down a little longer and then looked up at her. "You were praying?"

"Yes," she said. "You?"

"Uh-huh."

They just looked at each other a moment before Charles asked, "You okay?"

"Yeah, Susan said. "Scared, but okay."

"Guess I'm a little scared, too," Charles admitted.

"Scared, or you have doubts about wanting to marry me?"

"Oh, no," Charles said adamantly. "Changing my mind about wanting to marry you would require an act of God as big as creating heaven and Earth. No, I've just been afraid that… that maybe it wasn't God's will."

You've had doubts about that too?! Is that a sign? Are we both sensing that God doesn't really want us to get married? Susan moved a finger back and forth against his finger as she continued to hold his hand. "And what do you think now?"

Charles turned his hand in hers so that he gripped her hand firmly, and he took a deep breath. "I think… I believe… that God made us for each other, and that he wants us to spend the rest of our lives together."

Oh, Charles, you do? You really do?

"I don't know the future, but I believe he wants us to experience it with each other."

I want that more than anything! Well, more than anything except Stephanie's well-being…

"How about you? Do you have any doubts about wanting to marry me?"

"None," Susan said, and Charles looked visibly relieved. "None about my desire to marry you. I… I've been uncertain whether or not God had something else in mind."

"And now?" Charles asked.

"I'm still scared, that your love is too good to be true. That something will go wrong, and we won't be able to get married, and that will prove that our getting married wasn't God's will."

"Oh…" Charles started, "well, then, would you like us to postpone…"

"No!" Susan said sharply. "I… I want to be willing to accept whatever God has planned for me and for you. No, not just want, I *am* willing to accept his will, no matter what it is. But I'm not sure what that is, so I guess... I kind of figure if we actually get married, then that will be proof that it was His will, and if He has something else in mind, then something will happen to stop us. I guess... that was one reason I was anxious to hurry... to get married before something could stop us."

Charles nodded slowly.

Susan shook her head firmly. "That was a fear I've given to God, so it no longer counts. But I still have a reason to want to get married as quickly as possible. A much, much stronger reason."

Charles looked at her questioningly.

"I want you in my bed. And if that takes too much longer... I may turn into a rapist."

Charles let go of Susan's hand and pulled back. "You won't have to," he said softly, before continuing in a normal voice. "Let's finish up our cold breakfast and go back upstairs and knock out that last questionnaire. We know we've got to get that done. Then we'll take things one at a time and, Lord willing, we'll get married just as soon as possible. How's that sound?"

Susan nodded. "Okay, lets," Susan said with a smile.

Charles smiled warmly and they finished their meal quickly, billing it to their room. They got up and Truck materialized from somewhere.

How does a guy that big manage to be inconspicuous...? Susan wondered. *The same way a shoebox hides itself, I guess...*

"Well, this is a lot of questions," Charles said after they got back to their suite and started carefully reading the sex compatibility questionnaire. "How about if we go through it verbally instead of writing our answers down separately? That ought to be a lot faster."

"Okay. Well, we've already told each other about our previous marriages... as to why ours will be successful when the others weren't, it's because we're Christians now, and we really love each other."

"Agreed. And we can skip the whole family-planning bunch."

They covered the sexual history questions and got started on the sexual preferences items, making rapid progress until they came to the issue of oral sex.

"Okay, how do you feel about giving and receiving oral sex?" Charles asked.

Do we have to talk about that? For the first time, Susan blushed and had trouble answering. "Well, uh, the truth is I really didn't like it much. No, that's not the truth... the truth is, I hated it."

Charles looked shocked. "You *hated* it? Why? And which one... both?"

"Both? Oh... well, with me and Marty... I mean Marty and I, there wasn't any giving and receiving, it was just Marty taking."

"Taking? I don't understand. How do you 'take' oral sex?"

Susan looked away in embarrassment. "Well, after a few years of marriage, I guess I just didn't want sex as often as Marty did. And now that I know about love-languages, I'm pretty sure Marty's love language was touch. But I didn't know that, so I guess I really let him down. So, it's my fault, I guess, but when he started getting more and more... forceful... we started having oral sex. He'd jam himself into my mouth, and he'd hold my head and force it in. I gagged and choked, but he didn't care. Most of the time I was afraid I'd pass out from lack of air, and I was seriously afraid that he'd keep going even after I passed out, and I'd suffocate. Sometimes I wondered what would happen to the kids after I was dead."

Susan just sat there, still looking away, and waited for Charles to say something. *He's awfully quiet... I guess he's feeling sorry for me... or worse, he's disappointed that I don't want him jamming himself into my mouth... Why doesn't he say something?*

She turned her head and glanced and Charles and was taken aback by his fierce look. *Oh, no! What did I say wrong? Why are you mad at me? What did I do wrong?!*

"Susan, I'm afraid I don't have a very Godly frame of mind right now..." Charles said through clenched teeth.

Susan's eyes started to water. *Oh, no, what have I done?! Oh, Charles, if it's that important to you, you can do it... you can do whatever you want to with me... I'll do my best for you... I'll try not to...*

"If he was here right now, I think I'd beat him within an inch of his life."

...he? Marty...? "You... you're angry at Marty, not me?"

Charles looked shocked. "What?! Of course I'm angry at him! Why would I be..."

Charles caught himself, lowered his voice and knelt by Susan. "Darling, of course I'm not angry at you! I'm angry at the poor excuse of a husband you used to have! Billy is one nasty guy, but Marty was your husband... he was supposed to love you and honor you! And instead he physically abused you! Oh, no, my precious darling, I'm not angry at you!"

Susan sniffed and wiped her eyes against her shirt. "Well... if you want to, you can do that to me..."

"What?! Don't talk like that Susan! I'll never force you to do anything! I... well, I like receiving oral sex, but that's not like what Marty was doing... if you want to give me oral sex, that means you putting your mouth on me, and only as far as you're comfortable with. You can suck on it, and use your tongue to tickle it, things like that... and... well, I can coach you... if you want to learn what makes me feel good..."

Susan smiled through tears and nodded. "I... I'd like to learn, if you think you can teach me." *I didn't think I'd ever be able to learn how to dance, but you taught me to waltz. You're such a patient teacher...* "I'd love to learn how to make you feel good that way. Do you think you'd like me to tickle it with my tongue... and things?"

"Well, yes, I'd like that very much. My first wife Jennifer used to do that for me, and I really liked it very much."

Oh, well I want to do it, too, then! Better than Jennifer did!

Charles sighed. "Laura, however, she didn't care for that at all. There were a lot of kinds of sex that Jennifer liked that Laura didn't. In fact, Laura didn't really seem to like sex much at all... after we got married, anyway. I certainly thought she liked it before we got married."

"Oh, Charles, I'm not like Laura! I'll want to have sex with you for the rest of our lives! And I'll try to learn any oral sex things you want me to try." *Tickling you with my tongue sounds easy enough.*

"Well, thanks, Susan," Charles said, getting back into his chair. "That's very sweet of you. But actually, I'm much more looking forward to learning your preferences for how I give you oral sex."

"What? Oh! You mean cunnilingus? I read about that in Grandma's book. Have, uh... have you ever done that?

"Oh, yeah!" Charles said eagerly. "Licking Jennifer's clit was the single most enjoyable part of sex for me. Unfortunately, Laura didn't like that either. But she didn't..."

"Wait..." Susan interrupted.

Charles paused and gave Susan his full attention.

"What you said... Did you say that, uh... licking your wife's clitoris was your favorite part of sex?"

"Yes, why?"

"You don't mean you liked it better than humping her."

"I most certainly do."

Okay, what am I missing? You can't mean what it sounds like you mean. Susan started to scrunch her face but was stopped by the pain, then shook her head. "Are you telling me if you had a choice and you could either lick her or hump her, you'd rather have licked her?"

"Absolutely," he said. "Well, most of the time."

Susan eyes grew wide in disbelief. "Charles! I… I don't see how that's possible. I thought men… I thought all men cared about was…relieving themselves."

They stared at one another for a moment.

"Well, I don't know how I could prove it to you, but I don't think I'm all that unusual. I think your husband and the other boys you knew in college were just selfish."

You really want to… lick me down there? You like that better than humping?! "Well… if it's that important to you, I'm willing to let you try."

Charles looked puzzled. "I beg your pardon?"

"About what?"

"You're willing to let me try?"

"Yes, honey, if you want to, I'll let you… try licking me… down there."

Charles scratched his head, then rubbed his chin. "You don't mean… you couldn't… nahh…"

"Well, you said you liked doing that to Jennifer, so I just thought you might want to try doing that to me."

"Well, of course I would! I just told you it's my favorite thing to do. But… well, you seem rather indifferent about it."

"Well, I guess I am. But if Jennifer liked it, maybe I will, too."

Charles raised his eyebrows and stared at her, then frowned. "For goodness sakes, Susan, it's not like there's that much difference in how guys do it, is there? Do you think I won't be able to do it as well as Marty did for some reason?"

"Oh, Marty never did that."

"What…?! What?!!!" Charles jumped out of his chair and failed the air. "Your lousy, no-good, rotten ex-husband never, ever gave you head?! He never licked your clit?! Are you serious?!"

Wow, now where's that anger coming from? And who's it directed at? "You're angry at him again, not me, right?"

"You're dam—oh, sorry… yes! Yes, I'm angry at him, I'm very angry! How long were you married?!" Charles asked stridently.

What does that have to do with anything? "Uh... about fifteen years... but..."

"Fifteen years! If your ex-husband was here, I'd have a serious problem not punching him in the nose!" Charles pounded a fist into his other palm.

Boy, you really don't like Marty, do... hey, why are you looking at me like that?

All of a sudden Charles dropped his arms to his sides and looked thoughtful. He walked slowly in a circle around the table and Susan, keeping his eyes on Susan.

Oh, dear, is this good or bad? What are you thinking? Is it about me or Marty?

"Susan, dear... if he never licked your clit... are you one of those rare women who can have an orgasm just by vaginal intercourse?" He sat back down as he finished the question.

Oh, no. I guess we have to talk about that, too. "Uh... well..." Susan looked away again. "I was reading about that in the sex book, and the way it describes it... I, uh..."

Charles' eyebrows went up.

"Well, I guess, maybe I've uh... never had one..." Susan voice trailed off and ended in a whisper.

"You've never had an orgasm?!" Charles exclaimed too loudly.

Susan cringed and involuntarily glanced around to ensure that no one else had come in to hear. *Could anyone hear that from the hallway? I hope not!* "Shhh! Charles, not so loud."

"How... how can that be? Don't you masturbate?"

"No, of course not!" Susan blushed beet red on the parts of her face that weren't bruised, and the bruised areas tingled. She spoke rapidly from nervousness, "Well... when I was a teenager... in high school... I did a few times... with my hairbrush. With the handle, I mean, not the bristles, of course. Although they were very soft bristles.

She glanced up and saw Charles grinning. "Oh, this is so embarrassing!

Is that enough? Can we change the subject now? Susan looked off into the distance, "I wish I still had that hairbrush... it was my favorite."

Charles snickered.

What's so funny about...? "No...! Not because of that... I liked it because if felt good!"

Charles started laughing.

"Ohh you… in my hair, it felt good in my hair! Really!"

"I'm sure it did!" Charles said through his laughter.

Quit laughing! You know what I meant. "Well, it was a great hair brush. In fact, I only got rid of it because I wore it out."

Charles howled and slapped the table.

"From brushing! I wore it out from brushing, not from… ohhhh…!" Susan dropped her head into her hands to hide her face, but recoiled from the pain from the bruises, and then lowered her head slowly and rested her forehead against the tabletop.

Charles was laughing uncontrollably as she rocked her head slightly from side to side. *Even with the hairbrush, it didn't seem to match how the book describes an orgasm. Now I'm fifty-six years old… and I've never… done that?! I've been so horny lately I could've humped a doorknob in the bathroom, yet I may never have had an orgasm? How messed up is that?! Is there something wrong with me? Or was Charles right… were the men I've been with just too selfish?*

Susan got up and whapped Charles lightly with a book from the table. "Okay, now that I have thoroughly humiliated myself in front of you, I will reluctantly admit that there may have been a minor element of humor in how I… expressed myself. But if you can get a hold of yourself, I have a serious question for you."

Charles tried to stop laughing as Susan's phone rang, and then he immediately sobered up and watched her closely.

Susan quickly got her phone out of her pocket and glanced at it before answering. "It's Stephanie already!" *Oh, God… please… help me handle it if she just cusses me out and hangs up again…*

"Hello?"

"Hey, Momma," Stephanie said flatly.

"Hey, darling, are you all right?"

"Yes, Momma, I'm fine. I'm always fine, and I don't need you butting in."

What do I say now? How do I convince you that you really do need help? Do I remind you what Billy did the other night? No, that will…

"Listen, Momma, who's this guy you're gonna marry?"

Susan looked hopefully at Charles. *She's talking to me! She's actually talking to me!* "Well, his name is Charles Parker, and he's a very nice man. He…"

"He's obviously some kind of rich big-shot, right?"

"Well… I hadn't thought of him like that, but I guess he is, kind-of."

"Well, what are you going to do with your house?"

"My house? We're going to live there…"

"Not if he's rich, Momma. He's not gonna want to live in your little house. He'll want you to move in with him."

"Oh, no… he and I have already talked about that, sweetheart, and he doesn't want to live in a big house anymore. It will just be the two of us, and we won't need a lot of room. Oh, but you're welcome to move back into your old room, and stay there as long as you want! You can move back home as soon as you want to!"

"Momma, he… wouldn't you rather live in a big mansion? I mean, if he can afford it, why not? Besides, even if he moves in with you, he won't be happy in a tiny little house for very long."

"Well, Charles isn't like most people. He loves God with all his heart, and his biggest desire for his money is trying to find out what God wants him to do with it."

"What?"

Susan heard some rumbling on Stephanie's end, and wondered if she was talking to Billy.

"Listen, honey, we… Charles and I… we're going to go ahead and get married. And you're welcome to come. But…"

"Can Billy come?" Stephanie asked.

Oh, no! I was hoping you wouldn't ask that! "Stephanie, I love you, but after what Billy did and said the other night… no, he may not come."

There was more rustling on Stephanie's end of the line.

"What if Billy and I got married?"

"What…?! Oh, Stephanie, no!"

"What if he apologized for the other night?"

"Stephanie…! What he did went far beyond an apology, he…"

"Well so much for your xx-xx-xx religion, then, huh?" Stephanie said harshly.

"Stephanie, he threatened to kill us both! And I believe he meant it! Honey, please…"

"Just xx-xx-xx forget it!" Stephanie snapped and hung up.

Oh, God, no! Please don't let that monster talk her into marrying him!

Susan hung up and dropped the phone back into her pocket as she walked into the kitchenette and leaned on the counter.

Charles followed her and lightly caressed her hair and shoulder with one hand.

Susan spoke without looking at him. "It seems Billy's now trying to figure out a way to use Stephanie to get money out of you as well as me…"

Susan and Charles both sighed.

"I'm sorry, honey," said Charles. "But I guess it shouldn't have been a surprise."

Susan nodded slowly.

"But hey," Charles said, "if his attempts to try to get money keeps him from hurting her, that's a good thing."

"Until he figures out it's not going to work."

"Maybe our guys will have enough evidence against him to put him away for a long time by then."

Susan nodded a little more energetically and managed a smile. "Yeah, that could be. If we can string him along? Do you think we should invite him to the wedding?"

"No way. Absolutely not. Just because I didn't break his neck the night before last, it doesn't mean I won't if I get in the same room with him again."

You have so much passion… yet you're usually so self-controlled and clear-thinking… "Okay… good. I don't want him here either. Maybe I can offer little hints of some kind to Stephanie that she'll pass along and keep him thinking he has a chance of getting money from us. She was asking about my house… maybe you and I could periodically discuss living somewhere else, and then I could hint to Stephanie that maybe she could have the house if we do."

"Mm… I don't like that, it's deceptive."

"Yes, but you were ready to…" Susan lowered her voice. "You know… option three…?"

"Yeah… I guess your idea's a lot better than that one." Charles admitted. "Okay, we can try it."

Susan started back toward the table, and then suggested, "Let's go out on the balcony. I like the view from up here during the daytime, too."

"Okay," he said, following her out. "Say, what was the serious question you wanted to ask me before Stephanie called?"

Susan didn't answer right away and Charles just waited. *How do I bring this up? Just a few hours before we're to be married? What if…*

While she looked out over the city, Susan asked quietly, "Do you think there's something wrong me? If not… why haven't I ever had an orgasm?"

"Well," Charles answered softly, "it's possible you could have a physical problem. And if so, we'll find out and deal with it as best we can... The way Marty abused you, and as selfish as he was, you may have simply had a hard time relaxing enough to have one. And if that's the case, I actually find that pretty exciting."

"What? Why...?"

"Because I was already looking forward to giving you lots and lots of orgasms," explained Charles, "but this means I can help you learn how to have your very first one! Wow, what an honor, what a blessing to me!"

"To you?"

"Oh, yes, Susan, yes! I really, really want to give you that gift, over and over! As many times as possible in however many years God gives us together. And to help you experience your first one, well, that's a priceless treasure!"

Oh, my...! "Do... do you really think you might could teach me?" *I wonder what it's like?!*

"Well, it was a long time ago, but I still remember that Jennifer had some trouble becoming comfortable having orgasms," Charles said, "But she did, and year after year, it just got better and better for both of us."

"Really?" Susan asked hopefully.

"Yes," he affirmed, "and maybe you only need a little help learning to relax under the ministrations of a talented tongue. And Susan, I have a very talented tongue."

Ohh, my... that's good, I guess, but what if you don't like the way I smell down there? I know I can hump you, and I can let you hump me, but you like licking a woman best. That's your favorite kind of sex, and I've never done that before! What if I disappoint you?!

Charles turned her toward him. "Are you starting to worry about it?"

There you go reading my mind again... how do you do that?!

"Don't. Don't even think about it, if that makes it easier for you." He drew her into his arms. "Remember when I taught you to dance?"

"Oh, yes...!"

Charles started waltzing with Susan on the balcony, without any music, and they moved fluidly together.

I could almost melt... oh, Charles, you're already part of me... and I want you so badly...

"As soon as we're married," he whispered into her ear, "I'm going to teach you how to feel better than you've ever felt before."

"Ohhh..." Susan murmured. *Unngh... I don't know how I could feel much better than I do right now...*

Charles' phone rang, and they stopped dancing while he got it out and answered. "Hello?"

"Just a sec…" he said, then handed the phone to Susan. "It's Lisa, again."

"Hello…?" Susan said anxiously.

"Susan, it's Lisa. I found it!"

"What?! Really?! You found it?! Oh, thank God! And thank you, Lisa! Thank you, thank you, thank you! Where was it?!"

"It was on the top shelf of the closet in the bedroom closest to the living room," Lisa explained.

"Steve's room…? Why would…? Oh, no! Now I remember! I moved it there years ago, because Marty used to know where it was in the kitchen, and I was afraid he'd come back and take it. But… that was so long ago… I… I guess I haven't looked at any of those papers in all that time…"

"Well, I'm on my way to your location now, document in hand."

"Oh, Lisa… oh…" Susan's eyes were watering. "I can't tell you how much this means to me. Oh, Lisa, this is an answer to prayer!" *A begging, pleading prayer, as usual.* "Thank you so much!"

"You're welcome, Susan. I'm glad I could help! I'll see you in a few minutes."

"Okay, Lisa, thanks again…! Bye…"

"Bye."

Charles was beaming. "She found it, huh?"

Susan gave him a bear hug. "I don't care about anything else, not bridesmaids, not photos, not anything except hearing 'I now pronounce you husband and wife' and getting your clothes off!" *I feel that lovely bulge, down there, Charles, and I want it! I want to feel you inside me!!*

"After Henry leaves…" Charles added.

"If he leaves fast enough…" she replied.

"Wow… well, listen, this means we can have the ceremony as soon as he gets here, *if* we finish that sex questionnaire."

He started pulling her back to the table, and then she ran ahead of him and started looking it over again.

"Charles… If I talk about the rest of these questions, or I listen to you talk about them… I think I'll explode."

"I, uh, 'feel your pain.' Well, we both read them all. Are there any more specific questions you want me to answer before the wedding?"

"No," Susan shook her head. *What about those other things*

196

Jennifer liked? "Wait! Yes. Uh…"

Your love language is acts-of-service, so I want to be at least as good as she was at doing the things you like, so… "Um… the things you mentioned that Jennifer liked that Laura didn't… well, never mind what Jennifer liked, exactly, what did you like? Other than…" she lowered her voice, "licking her…" then raised her voice back to normal, "what were your favorite things that she did for you?"

"Oh, well, there were three things that, well, I didn't realize how much I missed them until I married Laura and found out she didn't like to do those things…"

Oh, wonderful! I'll do those things better than both your other wives! I'll make you so…

"That was deep-throat, anal sex, and sex in public."

Susan was stunned. *D-deep-thr… a-a-anal… in-in p-public?? Ooooh…* She sank into a chair with her head spinning. *Y-you want… you l-like… you, she… all those things…*

"Are you okay, honey? You don't look so well."

"I, uh, I…" *Maybe your cock is smaller than Marty's? Tiny, maybe? Oh, no…! If you're tiny, I'll be disappointed, and if you're big, I'll disappoint you!*

"Are you worried about the ways I just mention I used to have sex with Jennifer? I was just trying to answer your question honestly. You don't have to do those things. She was different from you, and we can enjoy each other in different ways."

Different. As in not-as-good.

Charles stood next to Susan and put a hand on her shoulder. "Hey, don't worry… please. Jennifer was just… well, pretty uninhibited. I'm not asking you to be like her in any way. I love you the way you are!"

She lowered her head and hid her face with her hands. *Yeah, the way I am: sexually inferior. Incapable of having an orgasm. The essence of inhibited. Unable to give you your favorite kinds of sex. You married Laura and she didn't like them and you were disappointed. You just said so. We're getting married in a few hours, and I'm going to disappoint you even worse than Laura did!*

"Honey… I didn't mean to upset you…"

She turned away and sobbed. *Oh, God! I… I wanted so much to be good in bed for Charles, and now… I can't do any of his favorite things, and, and, he doesn't even want to do it at home!*

"No…! Honey, don't cry! Oh…!" Charles went around to her other side and got down on his knees, but she turned in the other direction.

This is horrible! How can I marry you knowing that I'll disappoint you every time we have sex? Every time you even think about sex! I-I can't do that to you! I love you, and it will break my heart every day to think of how badly I'm letting you down! Just like I let Marty down! No, even worse! Oh, God, I'll disappoint Charles even more than I disappointed Marty! At least Marty never wanted anal sex and sex in public! At least... or... or... was that why Marty cheated on me? Those other women Marty had sex with... it was because I was so bad in bed? Oh, God! I feel so... useless... I'm worthless...

"Susan..."

Oh, Father, make him go away! Make him leave me alone! I wish I had never met him, that I hadn't fallen in love with him! I can't marry him knowing I'll ruin his life!

Charles grabbed Susan's legs and pulled her body around. "Susan! Stop! Honey, you're torturing me! Why are you so upset?"

She looked through blurry eyes and lightly pounded her fists on his shoulders. "Humping is the only kind of sex I'm good at! I-I may not be able to have an orgasm, and I can't do those other things! All I can do is humping! And I'm probably not even very good at that!!"

"Is that all that's bothering you? For goodness sakes, honey, the way you were crying, I thought it was something serious."

"What? It... it is serious! I wanted to be the best lover you ever had! And instead I'll be the worst! Every day you wake up, you'll regret having married me!"

"What?! Susan! How could you even think such a thing! It's not true! That's not true at all! Susan, I love you! If all we ever do in bed is hump, then I'll praise God for that blessing! And when we get older... much, much older, if we can't do even do that, then I'll praise God for the blessing of just holding you in my arms! And if I get to the point where I can't hold you, I'll praise God for the blessing of being able to look at you! And if I lose my eyesight, I'll praise God just for the blessing of hearing your voice!

"But, but... you said..."

"I've said many things, but the most important... the only important thing I've said is that I love you, Susan! I love you with all my heart! You make me happy just by being in the same room as me. And when I see you smile, it makes me want to hug the whole world! If we can have sex, great, if not, still great. Although considering how tempted we've been lately, I'd bet we'll be able to hump each other till we can't walk straight.

Susan sniffled. "Y-you really think so?"

Charles stood up, picking up Susan in his arms and cradling her as he did so, and strode to her bedroom door. He whispered in her ear, "In a few hours, you're going to be my wife, and I'm going to be happier than I've ever been in my life. And I'm going to carry you across this threshold," he said as he stomped his feet, "and I'm going to hump you until one of us begs the other to stop. Any bets on who wears out first?"

"And... do you really think you'll be satisfied, with just humping?"

"I promise."

Oh, God... God, what a relief. Please let it be true! I'd do almost anything rather than disappoint him! "Well, okay... You'll really break my heart if you're wrong, but I'm going to trust you. And we'll need to use your bed, 'cause mine's wet from sweat this morning."

Charles marched her across to his bedroom door. "Okay, I'll carry you across this threshold."

"Okay, it's a deal. And to answer your last question..." Susan sniffled again and put both her arms around his neck and whispered in his ear, "you."

"Me, what?"

She nuzzled his ear with her lips, "You're going to wear out first. Forget walking straight, cowboy, I'm going to ride you till you can't even stand up... Hey! What's that?!"

Charles was using the fingers of the hand under Susan's upper body to stroke the base of her breast. "Just gettin' a head start, cowgirl. I reckon I'm gon' need it." He kept his fingers going.

"No fair! And you... you... mmm..." Susan started breathing heavier. "You'd better... uuuungh..."

Charles' phone rang again. "That's Nat's ring tone. It could be about my divorce papers..." Charles set Susan down on her feet and removed his hands completely.

Nat... that's your assistant. Lord, please don't let there be a problem with his divorce papers!

"Hey, Nat, good morning...! What...? Are you serious?"
He's smiling... that's good...

"Fantastic! Thanks, Nat, thanks!" Charles concluded and hung up.

"What is it?!" Susan asked impatiently.

"Nat's here! He and his wife Darlene drove down all the way from Pennsylvania last night! They're on their way up with Mike and

Frank!"

Alarm flooded Susan thoughts. "My face!" she exclaimed, running to her room. *How much concealer do I have left? I used an awful lot of it yesterday... how well will it do now...?*

"Hey, wait!" Charles called out. "I thought you weren't going to worry about the bruises..."

Susan stopped at the door to her bedroom. "Oh, Charles, that was just for breakfast, among strangers, not for our wedding among friends!"

"But... wouldn't our friends be more understanding than strangers?"

"Maybe, but I care more about what our friends think than what strangers think, and besides, I want to look as nice as possible for our wedding."

"Oh... okay..."

"Listen, I don't know how much good it will do, but I want to try to make myself look as good as possible. You... you don't mind do you?"

"Oh, no! Of course not. I just don't want you to feel bad because of something you had no control over. In fact, those bruises are a badge of honor you acquired while defending your daughter."

A badge of honor...?! Huh, I hadn't thought of it that way. But still... "Well, I'm glad you feel that way about it, but I'm equally glad you don't mind me trying to cover them up. You didn't seem to mind when I covered them up yesterday." *The way you couldn't take your eyes off of me...*

"Oh, no! No, no, I don't mind a bit!"

"Okay... I just hope I have enough concealer left. I could use industrial-strength makeup today."

"How about Bondo?"

"What's bondo?"

"Uh... never mind," Charles said nervously. "Sorry, that was a bad attempt at car-mechanic humor. It's a compound that... never mind."

"Oh, Charles, you can't start something like that and then ask me to forget it. Now explain it to me quickly before they get here."

"Uh, well... it was a reflexive insider's joke. The idea is that Bondo can be used to fix any problem at all. The more inappropriate the problem is, the funnier it's supposed to be to suggest it. And this was totally inappropriate."

"Oh," Susan said as she started to close her bedroom door, then paused. "Then in that case, it must have been very funny, right?" she said, and winked as she blew him a kiss and closed the door.

Well, if all I can do to satisfy you sexually is hump you, I'm at least going to hump you hard and long. God, please, please, let it be enough! Please don't let me be a disappointment to him like Laura was! I wonder how tight I am down there? Maybe Lisa would be willing to get me some lubricant. I've been... unusually, uh, damp, down there lately, but it might not last, and I really want to outlast Charles...

Susan went directly to her bathroom and looked at the stick of concealer. *Not as much left as what I used yesterday. I wonder...*

She went to the hotel phone and called the hotel shop, and it took the clerk several minutes of searching to conclude that concealer wasn't on the list of items they kept in stock. The clerk suggested that Susan try the concierge, and Susan was looking for that extension when her door opened and an older woman entered.

"Hi, Susan, I'm... gracious, those bruises really are bad... I'm sorry, dear, I'm Darlene, Nathaniel's wife. I didn't mean to embarrass you, but Charles said you were concerned about your facial bruises and I thought I'd see if I could help."

Do you have a gallon of paint in your purse? "Well, my concealer is better than I expected, but I don't have enough left to cover all this, and besides..."

"Well, I have an almost new tube with me," Darlene said as she reached into her pocketbook. She pulled it out and said in a stage whisper, "Age spots, you know. I may not be able to get rid of them, but that doesn't mean I can't hide them."

Susan smiled, and Darlene put a dab of the cream on her finger and spread it on Susan's face.

"Well, this covers it up completely, and there's more than enough here."

"Really?" Susan squealed, and ran to the bathroom to check it in the mirror as Darlene followed. *That is pretty good!*

"The color's a little off for you," Darlene observed, "but if you have some face powder that fits your complexion, then..."

"Oh, I do! And you're right, this does cover it up completely!"

Susan let Darlene apply the concealer as they chatted.

"So, Nat tells me he's never seen Charles this excited."

"Oh?" *That's a good sign...* "How long have they known each other?"

"Over forty years now."

Forty years? That means… he knew Charles when he got married to Jennifer and Laura… and he's more excited now than he was then? Maybe the sex thing really isn't as big a problem as I feared.

"Nathaniel was one of Charles' first employees. It could have been a little awkward for Nat, being older than Charles, and Charles being so young when he was starting his business, but it was the only job Nat could find at the time, and it turned out Charles was a great boss. Now Nat's kind of the boss. He used to look forward to retiring, but now that he's old enough for that, Charles pretty much lets Nat run the whole company and Nat's never been happier."

"They must get along well, huh?"

"Oh, they've been best friends ever since that first year. Charles wasn't a Christian most of that time, but Nat was always witnessing to him. When Laura left him, that hurt Charles real bad, and he came over to our house a lot. About a year ago, he gave his life to Christ, and he's been kind of at loose ends as to how to spend the rest of his life, wanting to work for God somehow."

Charles wants to work for God?

"So, he's been going to missions conferences and financially supporting more and more missionaries, but he's always wanting to do more."

Oh, yeah, giving money. He told me he wanted help with that.

"What about Jennifer? Did they get along well? Why do you think she killed herself?"

"Well, they got along part of the time, and part of the time they'd fight like cats and dogs. Charles doesn't seem to be able to see it, but I'm convinced Jennifer was an alcoholic. Menopause seemed to hit her pretty hard, and she started taking a lot of prescription drugs for it. Charles always thought she killed herself because she was depressed and he didn't notice, but I think it was mostly the combination of pills and booze."

"Oh… wow." *I'd say, "that's too bad," but the truth is, if she hadn't died, he'd still be married to her, and then he wouldn't have married Laura and been hurt by her, and given his life to God, and then he wouldn't have been available for me now. Well, maybe something else would have happened… only God knows what else could have been, I guess.*

"There was one thing that Jennifer always bragged about, though, and I guess you'll find out for yourself pretty soon, if you haven't already. Well, she didn't really intend to brag, she just talked about her sex life with Charles."

"Oh, no! Charles and I haven't... we haven't been intimate yet. We've been waiting."

"Well, you're in for a real treat, my girl," Darlene said with a wink. "What Jennifer said was so unusual to all the other ladies, everyone else kind of took it as bragging."

Yeah, I already know, she was really good at...

"Jennifer used to tell about how good Charles was in bed, and it used to drive the other women crazy."

Huh? She bragged about Charles being good at sex, not herself? But Charles said...

"All done with this. Now where's the powder?" Darlene asked.

Susan picked it out and handed it to her, and Darlene started gently applying it on top of the concealer. *Oh, I get it... maybe... his "talented tongue"?*

"Most of the women in our circle of friends from the company and the neighborhood wouldn't talk about sex as freely as Jennifer would, and most of their husbands probably didn't measure up very well in comparison."

Oh, so it was his size she bragged about?!

"Oh, she'd talk about the things he'd do with his tongue, and the other women would be green with envy."

So it was his tongue. Did she ever say anything about his size...?

"I never told anyone, but I was never envious, because Nat was really good in that department, himself, so I had nothing to be envious about. But I didn't tell the other women, because I didn't want them lusting over Nat the way they lusted over Charles."

"Wow." *My Charles? He... he had all those women lusting for him, and now... he chooses me? Charles chooses me? Out of all the women he could have...*

Just then Lisa peeked in. "You ladies need any assistance?"

"Oh, Lisa! You must have been searching the house from top to bottom to have found that box." *Even plowing through my garbage.* Darlene stepped aside and Susan gave her a big hug, being careful not to smudge her makeup.

"Darlene, this is Lisa. Lisa, Darlene," Susan said after the hug. "Darlene is Nat's wife, and Lisa is a registered nurse, and she found my old divorce papers for me! Well, uh, that's an old story... that was a long time ago. The divorce, I mean."

Lisa gave Susan a careful look-over. "Well, your makeup is great. I don't think anyone who hasn't seen you without it will have any idea that you have bruises."

Susan looked in the magnifying mirror and smiled, "I think you're right! Now I'm back to wishing we could have some pictures taken."

"Oh, Nat brought his camera, and he takes great pictures."

"Really?" Susan squealed again. "You know, I don't have a single picture of Charles, yet. And he doesn't have one of me, either."

"Well, why don't we get Nat to fix that right now?" Darlene asked and led them toward the parlor.

As soon as Susan came out of the bathroom, she heard an unexpected sound from the bed area and discovered a maid using a blow dryer on the uncovered mattress.

"Oh, no… this is so embarrassing," Susan said as she hurried over to the maid. "I'm sorry, I hope I didn't ruin it. I had a hot flash this morning… I didn't spill anything on it…"

"Is okay," the maid said with a smile, over the roar of the machine. "Is happens all the time."

"Don't worry," Darlene said, "it probably does happen quite a bit when they have women guests in the right age range."

"Yeah, but I thought I was over it. And I… well, never mind."

"Now, Susan," Darlene encouraged her as they stepped away from the loud dryer, "you can ask me anything you want to, and I've already been through that, obviously."

"And you won't shock me with anything, believe me," Lisa added. "I worked in an ER for a while."

Well… I guess… "Well, I… here I am still going through menopause, and, uh, lately my sex drive has been working overtime, and I thought… that, uh, menopause was supposed to make a woman's sex drive get weaker…"

"That's true for most women," Lisa interrupted, "but not all of them. Some women's libidos get stronger during and after menopause."

Oh? What do you think, God, can I use a medical excuse for being so horny lately?

"In fact, some women's libidos get so strong after menopause they have a problem with hypersexuality, although that's very rare."

Oh, Lord, please spare me from that. What I've been going through is just right for after I'm married again.

"And of course, emotions can be like a roller coaster during menopause," Darlene pointed out.

Oh, duh… I had forgotten that. Well, maybe that's at least partly why I've been crying so much lately. But... "Well, I started having hot flashes years ago, and I never had any problem with my, uh, libido before, so..."

"Were you dating during that time?" Lisa asked.

"No... I hadn't been dating in many years until I met Charles."

"And your libido increased after you started dating?"

"Well, yes..." Susan replied.

"Well, there you go," Lisa declared. "You're one of the few women whose libido increases during menopause, but yours didn't kick in until your romantic emotions became active."

"Oh, yeah, I guess that makes sense," Susan said thoughtfully.

Darlene leaned in just a little toward Susan but still said loud enough for Lisa to hear, "And after your wedding today, you won't need to keep those desires reined in."

Yeah, well, I hope so, but I really don't want to talk about that with anyone but Charles, no offense...

"Well, let's go let you meet my Nat and get him to take some pictures," Darlene said, and they all adjourned to the parlor.

Charles spotted Susan and hurried over, dragging Nat along.

Susan turned her face to both sides for Charles to see. "Well, what do you think?"

"Oh, honey, you're gorgeous, with or without covering up the bruises. Listen, honey, I want you to meet Nat, my right-hand man, trusted confidant, and the man who makes Parker Auto a big success while I take all the credit! Susan, this is Nat! Nat, this is Susan!"

"I'm very pleased to meet you, Nat," Susan said brightly.

There was a twinkle in Nat's eye as they shook hands. "Well, Susan, I must say I've been looking forward to meeting you. You must be very special the way you've captured Charles' attention."

"Well, thank you," she said, taking Charles' arm. "He certainly has captured my attention!" *And a whole lot more...*

"Well, Charles here has been a workaholic every day I've known him, until last Wednesday. Until that day, not one day went by that Charles wasn't looking over my shoulder and steering the business. He was supposed to have retired and left me to run it, but that only reduced his involvement a little bit. But do you know how many times he's called me about company business since last Wednesday? Not once! Not one single time! Let me tell you, Susan, that's a minor miracle!"

"Honey," Darlene intervened, "they don't have any pictures of each other yet. How would you like to fix that for them?"

"Oh, sure," Nat said enthusiastically, and he got busy with his camera taking pictures of Susan and Charles together, each of them alone, and a variety of group photos, getting Lisa to take pictures that included Nat.

As the photo session was winding down, Charles sidled up to Susan and Lisa as several conversations continued. "Listen, honey, I meant to talk to you at breakfast about what we'd wear today. Would you and Lisa like to go shopping for a wedding dress?"

"Oh, Charles, that would be wonderful! Not the delay, but... it's only a couple of hours, and... I guess it seems silly to you, but I'd really like to dress up for our wedding."

"It doesn't seem silly at all. I just thought you looked so hot in that outfit you wore yesterday..."

Oh, Charles, you make me feel so loved... "And would it be okay if Darlene came with us...?" Susan turned to Darlene, "If you'd like to."

"Oh, I'd love to," Darlene said eagerly.

"Oh, and Charles...?" Susan leaned in closer and lowered her voice. "Would it be okay if I bought some lingerie?"

"Oh, yes, absolutely, honey," Charles agreed with a gleam in his eyes.

"Well, it will be awhile before the shops open, so we'll..."

"I can take you to a lingerie shop that opens at nine and a wedding dress store that opens at ten," Frank said.

Conversation abruptly stopped and more than one pair of eyebrows were raised.

"I've got sharp hearing, a good memory, and a daughter getting married next month," Frank explained, followed by laughing and teasing.

Charles got out a credit card and gave it to Susan. "If you have any trouble using this, just have them call my cell phone."

"Oh, thank you so much, Charles!"

"Well, I admit to selfish motives, especially regarding the lingerie," Charles said. "And that reminds me, I have a dark suit, but would you rather I get a tux?"

A suit would be fine, but what would you prefer? And will you tell me what you'd really like, without just trying to please me? "Will you be just as happy in your suit, or would you rather have a tuxedo?"

"It makes no difference to me, sweetheart, so whatever you prefer."

You're rich enough that you could own a tuxedo if you wanted one. I'll be you'd be more comfortable in your suit... She put her arm in his and smiled, "Your suit."

A flash went off as Nat took a candid picture of the happy couple.

"Are you sure?"

"Completely."

"Oh, and what about the SunSphere?" Charles asked.

"Oh... I hadn't thought any more about it..."

"Very popular place for weddings," Frank piped up. "And very easy to secure."

It's a spectacular view... and a great place for praying... "Is that okay with you, Charles?"

"You bet it is! But remember, we're not sure it's available yet. I'll find out while you're shopping."

Susan gave him a big peck on the cheek as Mike made a phone call to arrange security for the shopping trip, and contingency plans for using the SunSphere.

"Oh, I almost forgot," Charles said, "I've got a guy from the jewelry store coming by with wedding bands. They already know your ring size. He's supposed to be here around nine."

Susan looked at a clock. "Well, that's in about fifteen minutes, so I guess we'll wait until after that to go clothes shopping."

Charles looked studious for a moment and then suggested, "Why don't you go on? I'll get him to wait here until you get back."

"Oh, hon, he won't want to wait that long."

"I'll make sure he won't mind. And the sooner you get going, the sooner you'll be back."

Susan laughed. "Bribery, again, huh? Well, we're going to have to curtail that habit!"

"That's no habit," Nat said, "That's Charles being in love. Am I right?"

"Well, we'll wait for the rings" Susan asserted, "and then we'll go shopping. Okay, dear?"

Charles nodded and started to answer, but his attention was diverted by Mike tapping on his shoulder, and he turned to talk to him.

I wonder how much a wedding dress costs these days? And how much it would cost to rent the SunSphere? Charles is already spending a fortune to protect me and Stephanie. So, in a sense, a wedding dress and the SunSphere would be relatively minor costs compared to all that. And it is a one-time thing.

Charles and Mike got Susan's attention.

"Honey," Charles said, "do you know some folks from your Church named Pendleton and…" He looked at Mike.

"Stroud," Mike said.

"Yes, there're two families by that name at Bethel," Susan affirmed. "Why?"

"Well, Henry told them about us getting married, and I guess they thought he was inviting them, 'cause they're here. Well, downstairs. That's okay with you?"

"Oh! Sure! But… it's the middle of a work day, how… well, that's really a nice surprise. Hey, did you pay them to come, or something?"

"What?! No, absolutely not. They did that on their own. For you, obviously."

Really? Wow…

Mike piped up again. "And a guy from the jewelry store is here, too."

Charles' phone rang, and he took it out and looked at the incoming number. "It's Henry," he said. "Hey, Henry, everything okay…? Really? Fantastic…! Okay, thanks!"

"Henry's here, with the license!" Charles announced, "He's parking now!"

"That's wonderful!" *Oh, everything is coming together perfectly! Everyone can shuttle over to the SunSphere while Lisa and Darlene help me get a dress and lingerie. Charles and I will both have friends in attendance. We'll have rings, pictures… Oh, Lord… thank you so much… thank you…*

"Oh, Lisa…" Susan called out. "Where's Lisa? Oh, Lisa, where's the document you brought from my house?"

"I gave it to Charles."

Susan worked her way back to Charles, and asked, "Charles, do you have both the legal documents?" *Everything else is flexible except those…*

"No, I've got yours, but Nat… Nat, you got a copy of my divorce decree to Henry, right?

"Faxed it to him last night, and talked to him to confirm he got it." Nat fished a folded paper from his inside jacket pocket. "But I've got another copy right here, if needed."

So it's really going to happen? I'm really going to marry Charles, and Marty isn't going to ruin everything at the last minute? Oh, Father, I'm sorry… I don't mean to backtrack right after I said I'd do anything you wanted me to, even… even if it means Marty again.

208

But the truth is, Lord... oh, God... Tears started welling up in Susan's eyes. *Oh, no... this is the wrong time to start crying, I don't want my makeup to...*

Charles slipped a tissue into Susan's hand.

There... did you see that, God? How could I not be head-over-heels in love with that man? She dabbed her eyes as Lisa put an arm around her.

God... the truth is... I'll do anything you want, but what I want, if it matters, is Charles. Lord, I'm so in love with him... I'd really rather die than have to deal with losing him and having to let Marty back into my life. But your will be done, Father. Above all else, I trust you, and I'll go through whatever you want me to.

Susan lost track of all the comings and goings with bodyguards at the door and service staff bringing food and drinks, Henry and his wife Sandy arriving with one of the deacons from Church, followed by David and Patricia Pendleton, and Ed and Donna Stroud.

Got to get away from here and finish getting ready, she thought as everyone stopped her to talk to share their good wishes.

Sometime during the greetings, Susan and Charles picked wedding bands with an entourage of well-wishers looking on and chatting, and then Susan was pulled away into several more congratulatory conversations and questions about how they met and fell in love.

Okay... let's get this show on the road... where's Mike? Is he ready for us to go get a dress?

When she spotted Mike, she also noticed Charles talking to Nat, who was putting away a cell phone, and Charles turned and started looking around. Susan waved, and he spotted her and started walking toward her as Susan heard her cell phone ring and started fishing it out of her jeans.

Stephanie already called this morning... but what if she's calling to give me the rescue code? What was it? Oh, about her CD. She looked at the phone number and furrowed her brow. *I don't recognize the number. Who... Marty? Oh, God... oh, Father... if it's Marty... why now, Lord...? Why couldn't...*

"Who is it?" Charles asked as he got close to her.

"I... I don't know," Susan said with a frightened look.

They were a few steps from his bedroom, and he quickly took her in and closed the door as she answered with great apprehension. "Hello...? This is Susan... Oh, Mr. Burton...!"

"It's the owner of the Coffy Corner!" she whispered to Charles.

"That's very thoughtful of you... and now that you've called I realize I should have called you, and I apologize for not doing that... well, yes... I-I got beaten up, actually... no, well, almost... well, I'm feeling pretty good now, actually, but most of my face is a dark blue or black... yes... uh-huh... well, there is another problem. The man who beat me up also threatened to kill me and my daughter, and... yes... we did, and... uh-huh... well, we're hoping for a resolution like that soon... well, thank you Mr. Burton... okay, Bill, then... that's very considerate of you, Bill... okay... okay, I will, and thanks again. I really appreciate that. Okay, bye."

Susan looked up at Charles. "Bill Burton... he said not to worry. Just let him know when I'm ready to come back to work." *Just a normal call...*

"Well, that's good," Charles said as Susan leaned into him. "And a relief. I was afraid..."

"Yeah..." Susan mumbled in agreement, "me too."

Susan plopped down on the closest chair, keeping the phone in her hand. "Would you mind getting me something to drink, please?"

"Wine, a soft drink, or... coffee, or..."

Would wine calm my nerves, or make them worse? Definitely no more caffeine. "Just water, I think."

Charles rushed off to get her water and Susan stared at her phone before looking up. *Oh, Father... please, no more... no more phone calls today...* The idea of turning her phone off briefly crossed her mind. *No, have to keep it on in case Stephanie calls again.*

Susan slipped her phone back into her pocket and walked back into the parlor. *Stephanie, I wish you could be here and be happy for me. I wish you were happy. Safe, and happy.*

Charles brought her glass of water and handed it to her with a kiss on her forehead.

"Thank you," she said, starting to feel a little fatigue.

"Well, I was going to tell you, we got the SunSphere. We can have a room there any time from now until five, but the more time we give them, the more likely they'll be able to get some staff in there to get it cleaned up and looking nice."

Susan nodded as she took another drink. *Okay... lingerie, wedding dress, SunSphere... and no Marty. Everything's set. Right? No more surprises? Or false alarms?*

Nat walked up and asked, "Everything okay?"

"Susan's boss called to check on her," Charles explained. "She didn't recognize his number, and it gave us a little worry there for a minute."

"Oh, okay," Nat said.

He and Charles started to talk about something Susan didn't follow, and she left them and went to the kitchenette to put her glass in the sink. *And if the phone rings again? If Stephanie calls with the code word? We'll drop everything to take care of her, of course, and we'll get back to this whenever we can... if we can... if one of us doesn't get killed or hurt... if Marty doesn't show up... if, if, if... ooooh!*

Someone gave Susan a shoulder hug and said something to her, but she missed whatever it was they said. She just nodded and they moved along.

The longer we take to shop, the longer we take to get to the SunSphere, and the greater the chance of something going wrong. Which means the sooner we have the ceremony, the more likely we are to actually get married... and the only reason left to delay it now is for a dress, some sexy bedclothes, and a location with a view...? Well... this suite is on the twelfth floor... there's a nice enough view from here... and I can get lingerie later. So how much do I want to risk just to get a one-time dress...? As opposed to a life-long husband...? No risk. I want no risk...

"Charles!" Susan called out and started looking for him again. He was just a few steps away and came right over.

"Hey, hon, they're ready for you to go shopping whenever you are."

"Charles, let's forget all that. You and I are here, Henry's here with the license, and we even have a lot of our friends gathered around. Let's do it now."

He looked puzzled for a moment. "You want to skip the dress, and the SunSphere?

"Right here, right now!" Susan said decisively.

Charles took a step back and looked at her with open admiration. "Right here, right now."

"Yes. No more waiting, no more delays." *And no more risks. No more worries about what could go wrong.*

Charles' smile grew into a grin and he started to shout, but caught himself and thought for a moment. "We're wearing jeans."

"Forget what I said about that, I don't care what we're wearing. I don't want to wait anymore."

Charles hesitated before replying, "If we didn't have anything else to wear, I'd have no problem getting married in jeans. But you have a really nice outfit that no one here has seen you in except some bodyguards, and when I look at our wedding pictures in the years to come, I'd really like to see you in that outfit."

You really like that, huh?...and I really liked the way you looked at me in it. "Okay, Charles, give me five minutes to change, and let's get married forever."

"And while you're changing, I'll put on my suit?"

Oh, yeah, if I'm not wearing jeans, I don't want you wearing them either... Susan smiled broadly and nodded, "Alright, suit-up, my Prince!"

Charles whooped, then stood up on a coffee table as all attention centered on him. "Folks, I have an announcement!"

Bold and passionate... that could be good in a husband...

"Susan and I have decided that since we have everything we need to get married right here, including all of you as witnesses, we're going to go ahead right now. We're going to change clothes real quick, and Nat, would you help Henry figure out where everyone needs to stand?"

That's my take-charge planner.

Charles climbed down leaned in to whisper in Susan's ear. "I love you. And I'm going to marry you and spend the rest of my life proving it."

Ooo, well, I... Susan started to lean up for a kiss, but Charles was already hurrying through the crowd to his room.

Susan ran after him and caught him at the door to his bedroom and hugged him so she could whisper close enough for him to hear. "Charles... I want to tell you... I love you more than any man I've ever known. You're the most loving man, the handsomest, and the kindest I've ever known. And you get me more excited than I think I've ever been. My love language is words, but words fail me. I love you more than I can say..."

She let go of him and leaned back, looking into his face. He moved his hands to her shoulders and blinked to fight tears.

"I hope we have many years during which I can try to show you how much I love you..." Charles whispered back.

Nat broke them up and escorted Charles into his room as Lisa appeared at her elbow.

"Want some company while you change?" Lisa asked.

Susan smiled, grabbed Lisa's hand, and drug her along. *Yes! You can help keep me from panicking...*

Susan closed her bedroom door and explained, "Thanks, Lisa.

You can help me focus on getting dressed instead of obsessing over what could go wrong at the last minute. Or last second... Okay, see, that's what I mean. Anyway, Charles wants me to wear the clothes you picked out for me yesterday, and I said okay since hardly anybody saw me in them except Charles. And oh, my... did Charles like the way I looked in it."

"It is a really nice outfit," Lisa concurred.

"You showed really good taste picking it out for me yesterday."

"Well, you're the one who bought them, so it's really your good sense of taste."

"Well, thanks," Susan said as she removed her yellow shirt and picked up the white pullover. "Can you help me get this on without getting makeup on it?"

"Sure," Lisa said, giving Susan two extra hands to keep the material well away from her face.

"Oh, Lisa, you should have seen him when he first saw me in it. He actually dropped his coffee cup, and just stared at me."

Lisa laughed, "Well, that's definitely making a good impression."

Susan took the skirt and ran into the bathroom to put it on. As she took off her jeans, she took out her phone and put it on the counter. *Okay, Charles, I like it when you stare at me, but try not to break any dishes this time. Let's see, how long since I shaved my legs? Yesterday morning... that's probably better than freshly shaved, anyway.*

Susan ran a hand lightly up her calf. *Yeah, that's good. Feels smooth, and definitely not scratchy. As good as it's going to get for our first time together.*

She smoothed the skirt, picked up her phone, dropped it into her pocket, and looked in the mirror. *Okay, that's good. Now which shoes?*

Her mind worked on recalling all the shoes Lisa had brought over as she went to look them over. *Flats or heels? Well, my only pair of heels are too dark, so flats again. Besides, I wouldn't want to risk stumbling...*

Lisa smiled as Susan reappeared. "Well, I can see why Charles dropped his coffee. That outfit is perfect for you."

"Really? You think so?"

"You could have a modeling career based on that one ensemble."

"Well, thanks. Now which of these shoes do you think will go best with it?"

There was a knock at the door and Darlene let herself in. "Just wanted to make sure the maid finished making the bed. This room has a king-size bed and the other room has two queen beds, so you'll probably want to use this room for your wedding night."

Ooo... my wedding night! Tonight! Right here in this room! Oh, my! Charles is going to be in this very bed! With me! Naked! And touching!

Sandy came in next and admired Susan's outfit as Susan and Lisa agreed on a pair of dark-brown open-toed sandals with delicately thin straps and Susan sat down to put them on.

"As soon as you finish that, Susan," Darlene asked, "how about if we touch up the face powder? I think the concealer's still fine."

"Okay, thanks!"

"Susan, honey," Sandy imposed, "could I interrupt first just long enough to get you to sign the marriage license?"

"Oh, sure!" Susan agreed, using the pen Sandy brought. *I'm signing my marriage license! Oh God of grace, I'm signing my license to marry Charles!!*

"Henry already got Charles to sign it," Sandy explained, "and it'll be official when Henry signs it right after the ceremony."

"Oh, okay," Susan said, handing back the pen and paper, and held her head still as Darlene dealt with the face powder.

"One more thing," Sandy said, "have you thought about what kind of service you want? We could..."

That's easy... "The shortest possible, Sandy," Susan replied. *Oops. Does that sound like we're hurrying just so we can have sex soon...?* "We, uh, just want to hurry in case my daughter Stephanie should call with an emergency."

"Okay," Sandy nodded. "Well, would you like Henry to use the traditional vows and all you and Charles have to do is say, 'I do?'"

"Oh, yes, that sounds perfect!" *And short.*

"Okay, I'll let Henry know, and he can tell Charles. Now you ladies wait in here until everyone else is ready, so Susan can make an entrance after everyone else is in place."

"Okay, thanks, Sandy!" *How about that?! I get to make "an entrance!"*

"One of you other ladies let me know when Susan's ready."

"Will do," Lisa agreed, as Sandy closed the door behind her.

"Well, your makeup's done," Darlene declared, and gave Susan's hair a few brush strokes.

"Dressed, makeup... anything else?" Lisa asked.

Anything else? Don't ask me! Yeah, I'm dressed... got shoes on… face is as good as it's going to get…

Darlene reached out and took Lisa and Susan's hands and said, "Let's pray."

Susan nodded eagerly. *Oh, yes, yes, let's do!*

"Lord," Lisa began, "we thank you for allowing us to have husbands to share our lives, and we ask you to bless Charles and Susan and let each of them share in the bounty of your harvest."

Harvest…?

"And let each of them give to each other something they've never had before."

I'm not sure I understand…

"Heavenly Father," Darlene picked up, "thank you for creating Charles and Susan for each other, and for bringing them together in your time…"

Now that I understand!

"We ask you to bless their marriage, and let them serve you with all their hearts. We ask you to protect them, Lord. Keep them safe, physically and emotionally. And Father, I ask you to use their marriage to bless Susan's daughter and Charles' sons and show them your love through Charles and Susan's love for each other and through their faithfulness to you."

Use our marriage to bless our children? Lord, the most important blessing we want for them is to truly know you…! Uh… I guess it's my turn to pray? "Lord…" *Lord, I don't know what to ask for! I, I… uh…* "Lord, help! Help me not fall apart. Help nothing to go wrong. If this is your will, please don't let…" *Marty…* "anything… go wrong."

"Amen," Darlene and Lisa said and squeezed Susan's hands before gathering by the door.

Lisa poked her head out and told Sandy that Susan was ready, and Sandy said they were ready for Susan's entrance.

This is it! If nothing goes wrong, this… this is it. I'm going marry Charles. Charles and I are going to marry each other. Married. To a Christian man. What will that be like? I have no idea what I'm in for, do I? And I guess he doesn't either. But you know, don't you, God? And you'll take care of us. Susan felt the phone in her pocket to reassure herself that it was there. *I'm still here for you, Stephanie, whenever you need me.*

Susan took a deep breath and nodded to Lisa, who opened the door and stood aside. Susan came out into the parlor, and everyone's attention was instantly drawn to the bride, and there was a collective murmur of awe.

Wow, I guess everyone likes the way I look in this. I should try to figure out which characteristics make it so special, Susan thought as she clasped her hands in front and slightly tilted her head down in modesty. Her excitement, however, caused her to bounce on her toes as she looked around the room.

The wall in front of the balcony was glass all the way across, from floor to ceiling. The heavy drapes were pulled all the way back, and the sheers were all the way closed, and they rustled under the flow from the air conditioning vent. The effect created a beautiful, perfectly lit white panel, and Henry stood in the center, with Charles on the right, Nat to his right, and all the guests standing in the center of the room, with a path from her to Charles.

It didn't dawn on Susan that much of the furniture had been removed in the few minutes she had been ensconced in her room, nor did she notice the flashes from someone else using Nat's camera, as her attention was focused on Charles.

Charles… my precious Charles! Look at the way you're looking at me! My handsome rogue… you and you alone hold the secret to my heart! My hero, and very, very soon… my lover. Hold me in your arms again, and never let me go… sweep me up the stairs to your bed…

"You can go up there now," whispered Lisa from just behind.

"Oh… yes!" Susan grinned and bounced on her toes again as she started toward the front. *I wish I had something to hold to keep my hands occup…*

"Flowers!" Susan said excitedly, and stopped to glance around the room. She ran to a nearby vase and pulled out the flowers, and started shaking the water off the stems.

Lisa was instantly by her side. "Let me fix this for you," she said and rushed them into the kitchenette, with Susan and Darlene close behind. In moments, she used a knife to cut the stems shorter and started a cut on a dish towel. She ripped a strip off the towel and quickly tied it in a bow around the stems and handed the bouquet to Susan.

Susan slowly turned to face Charles, and as she looked at him, her smile grew wider and wider. And as Susan's smile grew, so did Charles.'

"You can go up there now," whispered Lisa from just behind again.

"Oh… yes!" Susan said, and started forward. *Let's see, wedding march... step, pause, other foot, pause... step, pause... oh, this is taking too long!* she thought, and ran in little short steps up to the front, and stopped just a foot in front of Charles, and the two just gazed into each other's eyes.

"Um, Susan..." Henry said quietly. "Susan..."

Sandy stepped forward and took Susan's elbow, guiding her a few steps to the left. "Susan, honey, stand over here, so everyone else can see you."

Susan was compliant, but she didn't take her eyes off Charles, and Lisa and Darlene stood just to her side.

Satisfied, Henry looked up with a big smile. "Okay, you folks all know why we're here, and we're going to skip a lot of the usual talk about marriage, and get right to the heart of the matter, so please bow your heads and let's pray."

Please, Father, no more interruptions unless it's for Stephanie's sake!

"Heavenly Father, we thank you for the love you showed us by dying on the cross to take away our sins to restore us to a loving relationship with you, and we thank you for giving Charles and Susan a love for each other in addition to their love for you. Now we ask you to bless this union, and what you have joined together, let no one put asunder. We ask this in Jesus' name. Amen."

A chorus of other amen's followed, and Henry continued.

Susan's breathing was getting faster, and her pulse was quickening. *'Bless this union'... is it really going to happen? Are we really about to get married? Nothing's going to go wrong?*

"Do you, Charles, take Susan to be your lawfully wedded wife, to have and to hold, from this day forward, for better or for worse, for richer or for poorer, in sickness and in health, to love and to cherish, until death do you part?"

"I do! Praise God, I do, with all my heart!"

Now Susan's heart was pounding heavily. *Half-way there... oh, God... just one more vow... just one more minute!*

"Do you, Susan..."

"I do!"

There was gentle laughter as Henry asked Susan to wait 'til he finished.

"Do you, Susan, take Charles to be your lawfully wedded husband, to have and to hold, from this day forward, for better or for worse, for richer or for poorer, in sickness and in health, to love and to cherish, until death do you part?"

"Oh, I do! Yes! Yes, I do!"

"Then I now pronounce you husband and wife. You may kiss the bride!"

Really? Really?!

The small crowd broke into uproarious cheers and applause, and it rolled on and on as Charles and Susan just looked into each other's eyes and held each other's hands.

"Husband and wife?" "Husband and wife?!" Really? We really did it? It really happened? We're really married?!

Susan lunged into Charles arms and the two embraced as she kissed him passionately, mindless of her makeup or anyone else in the room. *We're married! We're really married! Praise God in heaven, we're really married! Nothing went wrong! Marty didn't ruin everything. Billy didn't ruin everything. Nobody ruined everything. Nothing ruined anything! It was... perfect! Absolutely perfect!*

Susan sighed with complete contentment in Charles' arms as they finally broke off their kiss and started a whirlwind of hugs and words of congratulations, but Susan never let go of Charles' arm.

I am my beloved's, and he is mine, mine, mine... all mine!

Champagne glasses were passed around and there were several toasts. David Pendleton still had Nat's camera taking candid photos, and Sandy Walker herded the small wedding party together for a few formal shots.

Uh-oh, how's my makeup holding up? "Do I need to touch up my makeup, Charles?" Susan asked.

"You're so beautiful... you're radiant... if there's a flaw, I can't see it."

But your jacket... "Well, some of my makeup's on the front of your jacket."

"What jacket?" Charles teased.

We're about to have wedding pictures being taken, and I want... Susan grabbed Sandy. "Sandy, how's my makeup?"

"It could use a little touching up. I'll..."

"I'll take care of it," Darlene said, with tools in hand.

Oh, Darlene, I don't know what I would have done without you and Lisa.

As soon as Darlene finished the repairs, the group pictures were taken, and shortly after that some of the men carried furniture back in from Charles' bedroom, and Nat climbed up on the coffee table Charles had used for his announcement.

"Folks! Folks, if you have anything else to say to Charles and

Susan, get it said now, because we're moving downstairs to a reception, and the newlyweds are staying here. So, everyone go down to the first floor, and someone there will direct you to the room."

Susan watched Darlene help her husband ease down from the makeshift podium, as a last wave of well-wishing swamped the happy couple.

How sweet! What great role models!

A little while later, Nat and Darlene were the last to leave, and Susan and Charles said goodbye to them at the door.

"Thank you so much for coming Nat, and taking care of everything," Charles said with a bear hug.

"Your very welcome, brother, you know that."

Darlene hugged Susan and Charles as Nat held the door for her, and after they left Charles locked the door.

Thank you, and lock the door. Lock everyone else out, and lock us in. Just you and I. All alone, with no restrictions.

Charles turned and looked at Susan, and she hugged him again.

Nothing between us. Oops... nothing except a thick coat of paint that keeps coming off on your jacket. "I hope you don't mind my spoiling your coat," Susan said, sighing happily.

Charles ignored the question and sighed as he leaned against the door, pulling Susan with him. "I believe, Mrs. Parker, that you have been making a variety of physical threats."

Mrs. Parker...! Oh, my... I'm Mrs. Parker... "Those were not threats, Mr. Parker. Those were promises!"

Charles picked Susan up and cradled her in his arms again, and she put her arms around his neck as he carried her to her bedroom. Their bedroom.

Chapter Thirteen

Oh, no! thought Susan as Charles carried her, *I didn't get any lubricant! Ohh, I don't want to get sore and have to ask you to stop. Well, maybe it won't be a problem for a while. Lord, please help me not get too dry... oh... how will we have sex for the first time? I'll bet you did it missionary style the first time with your first two wives. How can I make this time more special than those times?*

Charles stopped close to the edge of the bed and set Susan on her feet with her arms still around his neck and his hands on her waist. Their lips met and they caressed each other, while their tongues began to explore.

Ooo, you're such a good kisser, Charles. I wonder what it will be like when you kiss me down there? Oh, I hope you can teach me to kiss your cock the way you want me to, without... uh-oh... I guess I'm about to finally get to find out how big it is. And if it's tiny, maybe I can learn to do that deep-throat thing, as long as it doesn't go too far back. But then... Susan sighed, *if it's tiny, I won't get much out of sex. Well, I'd rather make you happy than...*

Charles broke off the kiss and whispered, "May I start undressing you?"

"Rrrr, yes," Susan said, tingling with excitement. "Oh, let's try to be careful taking my top off so we don't get my makeup on it." *If it's not too late. Oh! My makeup! I'm wearing too much...*

Charles began lifting Susan's blouse from the hem up, and Susan pulled her arms out of the sleeves, then they both used both hands to pull it over her head while keeping it away from her face.

It's just a plain bra, but it does lift and separate my old boobs pretty well. Ooo, he's looking down at them... in fact, he's staring at them. Susan took a half step back and asked, "Well, what do you think?

She smiled at his silent but obvious admiration. "Would you like..."

Charles dropped to his knees as he pulled and slid her bra up over her breasts and put his mouth lightly on one while using both his hands to gently caress them.

"Ohhh! Mmm..." *I guess you would...* she commented to herself as she reached behind, unclasped the bra, pulled it off, and let it fall to the floor. *Okay, if you get to unwrap your present, I get to unwrap mine...*

Susan started to work Charles' suit jacket off his shoulders and noticed the makeup stains again. *Oh, I sure hope that comes out. I wonder...* "Charles, would you rather make love to me with all this makeup on and get it all over you and the bed, or would you rather I get it off and you have to look at my bruises again?"

Charles wrapped his arms around Susan's rear and stood up, lifting her high into the air.

"Oh!" she giggled. "Charles!" *You're so strong!*

Somehow Charles managed to keep her up with one arm at a time as he worked his jacket off and let it drop. "What would you prefer, my darling? You're equally gorgeous with or without the makeup."

"You don't have a preference?" Susan persisted.

"I do, but all I really care about is pleasing you!"

"If you wish to please me, then, tell me your preference."

"I'd prefer to get rid of the makeup. It's artificial, and all I want is you..." he set her down again and cupped her face with his hands, "you..." he leaned in until his lips barely touched hers, "you," he finished with a whisper and started kissing her again.

She felt her breasts pressed into his shirt. *Nothing between us now but this...*

Susan started to unbutton one of his shirt buttons as they continued to kiss, but then stilled her hands. *I'm probably not strong enough... and I probably shouldn't even if I could... still, if ever there was a time for it...* she slipped all her fingers into the front of his shirt between two of the buttons and stopped kissing to get a quick deep breath.

"Yahhh!" she yelled as she yanked to each side with all the strength she could muster. Every button except the bottom button popped off as the shirt parted and exposed Charles' chest.

No t-shirt! Susan glanced up at Charles, who appeared to be happily astonished, and then back down at the shirt, and the last button still buttoned.

She took another deep breath, got good holds, and snapped her hands to the side again. "He-yahh!" she shouted as the last button gave way and she pulled his shirt all the way off and tossed it on the floor.

She looked up at Charles in delight, *I can't believe that worked!*

I really did it! I...

Charles grabbed Susan and pulled her tightly to him and leaned back, pulling her off her feet, and he stepped away from the bed and swung around and around. "Susan, you wild woman! You should come with a warning label!"

Oh, Charles! This feels so good! Oh, yes!

He slowed down and stopped, letting her toes just bear some weight. "We belong to each other now," he said softly.

"And I'm bone of your bone, and flesh of your flesh."

"Wow, that sounds erotic!"

"Erotic...? That's from Genesis. Adam said something like that after God created Eve."

"Yeah? Well, I'll bet they had sex right after he said that..." Charles' hands felt around the waist of Susan's skirt until he found the seam and fumbled with the fastener.

Susan helped and Charles sank to his knees as he lowered the skirt to the floor and held it as she stepped out of it and then he tossed it aside.

Oo, how sweaty have I gotten in the excitement? I hope...

Still on his knees, Charles' hands had found their places on Susan's waist and he leaned in very close and drew in a long, deep breath and held it.

Oh, Charles, what...

Charles started exhaling slowly, moaning warmly and turning his head to rest the side of his face against her. "You smell..."

Susan held her breath in a sudden panic.

"...absolutely delicious!"

Delicious? Delicious?! I loved it when you said my eyes are delicious, but how could...

Charles now pulled her panties down in one quick maneuver, and drew in another long, deep breath.

You can't really...

"Oh, Susan, I want to taste you so badly!"

Taste me?! "Oh, Charles, I don't think I'm ready for that!" *and I don't know how I can ever get ready for that...*

Charles rose to his feet. "Well, how about if..."

"Hey, you just unwrapped your wedding present, now I get to finish unwrapping mine!"

Charles smiled and waited for Susan to act.

Great, I get to postpone that moment of reckoning, but now I have to face which one of us is going to be disappointed because of your size...

Susan got down on her knees and very slowly started unbuckling his belt, removing it from all the belt loops one at a time. *The first time I get to take your pants off. The first time I get to touch you. The first time I get to see you...*

She tossed the belt away and unbuttoned the single button on his waistband, then very slowly unzipped it. *Wow, you've got a really big bulge in here, mister. But that could just be due to being hard, and pulling on the material, not from being big.*

Susan's finger took hold of the waist on either side and started working the pants down off Charles' hips. *Briefs, not boxers. I wonder if...*

Holy cow, Charles, what have you got in there? Your briefs are busting at the seams.

Now Susan hurried to help him step out of his pants. She took a deep breath and held it as she quickly pulled his shorts down, and was startled when his package sprang up and hit her in the face.

"Oww!" Susan exclaimed and put a hand up to her bruised and now stinging face.

"Oh, Susan, I'm sorry," Charles said and started to get down on his knees with her. "I..."

"No! Don't move!"

"But I hurt you! I didn't mean to..."

Charles kept talking but Susan missed it all and forgot all about the sting. *Charles... you're... huge! You... you're enormous... you're...*

Susan gasped sharply. In a flash, Susan recalled a childish idea she had gotten shortly after she first began thinking about boys in a sexual way. "You're not Charles... you're Adam!"

"What?!"

"Oh, honey! I... I'll explain in a minute. But, Charles..." Susan's face was still right in front of him, and she left his shorts at his knees as her hands moved to his erection without conscious thought. She touched it lightly with just her fingertips, and it began to throb in response.

"Ooooh," Charles moaned, as the shorts fell down around his feet. "Oh, Susan... ooooh..."

Susan jumped up and hugged Charles tightly, feeling his cock pressed between them. "Charles, I never dreamed a man could be as big as you are!"

Charles' eyebrows went up.

"Well, okay, I dreamed it, but I didn't think it was real!" Susan moved slightly from side to side to feel it, and she grinned like a Cheshire cat. "That thing is gigantic. I don't know how you keep it so well hidden!"

Charles looked somewhere between relieved and worried. "So, you like it? It's not too big, I hope…"

"Oh, Charles, I always wanted a big one… but honestly, this is… this is really big. Let's try it! Let me try it on for size!" *Oh, my, now I really wish I had some lubricant.*

"Uh… what was that about me being Adam… was that an old boyfriend of yours?"

Susan laughed, "Oh, no, Charles! None of my… no one I ever… I've never seen anyone as big as you are. Oh, but I'm not explaining it… I meant Adam as in Adam and Eve. You're the Adam of my dreams from when I was a teenager. And into my twenties, too, I guess."

"You fantasized about Adam? So you pretended to be Eve…"

Susan laughed again, "No, not exactly. It's sillier than that."

Susan turned her head and rested it against him, as she continued to rock slightly from side to side, savoring the feeling of him pressed into her abdomen. "I had this crazy idea that Adam, the first man, had the largest penis ever, and with every generation, they got smaller and smaller. I did dream about it sometimes, but I didn't, uh, fantasize, exactly. Oh, but when I finally actually had sex with several different boys, I guess that kind of reinforced the idea. Because they were smaller than I had hoped for."

She shook her head a little without lifting it away from Charles. "And my husband Marty was the smallest of all. Anyway, I eventually quit dreaming about that, and I had forgotten all about it until just a moment ago."

"Do you think I might be too big for you…?"

It's time to find out, but you wanted me to get the makeup off… "Give me a few minutes to wash my face, and…"

Charles grabbed Susan around the waist and lifted her up, until his cock was between her legs, pointing almost straight up. "We've waited long enough," he said as he slowly began lowering her.

"Oh, Charles!" *You're going to do it right now, standing up! Lord, help me make it special!* Susan first tried to wiggle a little to help aim it into her, but there wasn't enough room. She parted her legs a bit and then realized since her feet were off the ground there was no reason to let them dangle, so she wrapped her legs around

Charles' waist.

Susan felt the tip at her entrance and burned with desire to feel more. Without thinking, she reached down and pulled her cheeks apart as she took a deep breath and closed her eyes. *Oh... it's starting to go in! It's sliding easily... but it's tight! Oh, more, Charles, more!* "Oooo, Charles," she almost growled.

"Uuuunh..." was Charles' only reply.

It's not too wide...! Is it too long...? It... oooh... uuunh... it feels... so... "Aaaaah!" Susan cried out, as tears started to rapidly form and fall.

"Unh... unh... are you okay...?" Charles grunted. "Do you need to..."

"More!" Susan cried as she pushed down against him, "I want all of you...! Uuuuh..."

She settled down on him as far she could go, just as she felt the tip pushing against her on the inside. "Uuh... don't... move..."

"Are you okay?" Charles asked again, straining in guttural tones.

Susan nodded, "Not okay... better than okay... so much better... try not to move... I want... to burn this into my memory... uuh... uuh... Charles... uuuungh..."

Susan opened her eyes, then pushed herself up just a bit and then carefully lowered herself again.

"Uungh," they grunted in unison.

"I feel you... all the way inside me..." Susan said.

"It doesn't hurt?" Charles managed to ask.

"No... not exactly... no, it doesn't hurt, it feels... strange... I've never felt anything like this before... it's like a little tender, or something... that deep part of me isn't used to being touched..."

Breathing shallow and rapidly, Susan pushed herself up again, slightly higher this time.

"Uungh... oh, Susan... you..."

Instead of easing herself back down, Susan let herself fall back onto Charles as far as she could go. "Uuh! Uuh..." Susan moaned, "Aaaahhh, uungh."

"Did... that... hurt you...?"

"I don't... think so..."

"Do you need to quit, or change position?"

"No!" Susan said, shaking her head fervently. "I'm not used to it, but... oh, Charles, I want to get used to it. It feels..." *What's the word? How can I describe this? I'm all the way down on you, and the tip is just pushing against me. Full? I feel full inside? Yes, but it's more than that... it just feels... right. No, more than right...* "Perfect...! That's how it feels! That's really how it feels, Charles, it feels perfect! Like that's how it was always supposed to feel!"

"Are you serious? You're not just trying to flatter me?"

"Oh, Charles, no! I've never meant anything more in my life," Susan said as she started wriggling her hips to see what sensations that would create.

"Uuungh... oh, Susan, Susan... wow, that feels soo good!"

"Oh, you like that, do you?" She teased and wriggled more energetically.

"Uungh..." he grunted in response, and then started to bounce slightly by bending and straightening his knees.

"Oh, Charles... uuuungh... oh, that feels *really* good!" *You're really strong to... oh, no, I'm going to wear you out, you're doing all the work, and I'm so heavy!* "Are you getting tired? I don't mind if you need to put me down..."

"Never!"

Never put me down?! Susan giggled. *My big he-man. Oh, ooooh, yeah... my big fill-me-up he-man!*

Susan noticed Charles was leaning his head down to kiss her as they gently bounced, and started to lean her head back to meet his. "Oh!" *My makeup!*

"What's wrong?" Charles asked as he stopped bouncing.

"Oh, no, it's nothing," Susan assured him. "I just realized that I didn't get my face clean before we had sex for the first time, and I wanted..."

"Well, technically, we're still having sex for the first time," Charles noted.

"Yes, but I still have all this makeup on."

Charles grinned.

"Charles Parker, you have a very mischievous look. What are you thinking?"

Charles turned and started walking toward the bathroom, using his hands to adjust how much of her weight they bore in time with his gait to have her bouncing lightly again.

"Oh, Charles! Wow, what a ride!"

"You like this suspension system?"

"What?"

"Suspension system. Like in a car. What makes a car's ride feel smooth or firm."

"Oh, like shock absorbers?"

"Yes, exactly! Shock absorbers, struts, leaf springs... Well, you just married a motorhead so I'm afraid you may have to put up with a lot of automotive metaphors."

A smart motorhead who knows what 'metaphor' means, and who built a big successful company from scratch...

Charles stopped in the bathroom next to a towel rack.

"Well, I'll gladly put up with your car metaphors if you'll keep my motor running like this."

"Oh, wow, a metaphor that works for cars and sex! You can work for me anytime, Mrs. Parker."

Mmm, Mrs. Parker! "I'm going to spend the rest of my life working *on* you, Mr. Parker." And with that, Susan started shifting to ride up and down on him a little bit.

"Uuungh... oh... Suuusaaannn..."

Susan kept it up. "I want you to remember this, Charles. I know you must be getting tired, but I'm going to make it as hard as possible for you to put me down."

"It's... already... as... hard... as... possible..."

Susan laughed so hard she had to stop riding him, and he caught his breath.

"Okay, cowboy, put me down, and I'll get cleaned up."

"Unh-uh," Charles said without letting her go. "Grab a washcloth."

You want me to wash my face while I'm still hanging on your hook? She slowly reached for a cloth. *That will be a little awkward, but okay...*

As soon as she had the cloth, Charles turned and stepped over to the shower, reached in and turned on the water, then stepped to the other end, and reached in to turn the water on at that end also.

"Isn't this a great shower, Charles? Water on both sides, and the showerheads have all sorts of different options for water streams."

"Yeah, that's cool. The design, that it. I hope warm water is okay with you?"

"Oh, yes. Ready to put me down now?"

"Nope."

"Aren't you getting tired yet? I'm not exactly as light as a feather..."

Charles reached a hand in to check the water temperature, and then slid the door all the way open so he could get in with Susan still mounted on him.

"Is the temperature okay?" he asked, ignoring her question.

"Very nice…"

"Then wash your face, and you'll have your makeup off during the first time we ever had sex."

"Oh, Charles…! That's so considerate!" *And I'm not getting any lighter… get busy, Susan, so he can put you down as soon as possible!*

It took several minutes of soaping, scrubbing, and repeating to get the thick coat of concealer off since her face was still sore and she couldn't scrub as hard as she would have liked to, but she finally completed the job.

"Okay, I'm finished!" Susan said happily. "So we've had sex for our very first time, and with me having no makeup on!"

She turned her face from side to side for him to view the results. "What do you think?"

Charles studied her face for a moment with a glowing smile. "You're utterly gorgeous!" he pronounced and then leaned forward to eagerly kiss her.

Mmm… guess I'm willing to settle for "gorgeous"…

Susan felt Charles' tongue entering her mouth deeply, and she reveled in combined sensations.

Without a conscious decision, Susan started sucking on Charles' tongue.

"MMMMmmmmmm…" Charles moaned into Susan's mouth and started bouncing her again, more forcefully than before.

Ooo, you like that, don't you big boy? Emphasis on big, Susan laughed to herself.

He turned and put Susan's back against the long wall between the showerheads.

Oo! That's cold! Oh, well, it's okay already now.

Charles broke the kiss and gasped, "Would it be okay if I finished, for the first time, inside you?"

"Oh! Oh, Charles, I would love that! But aren't you too tired by now… to keep holding me up, I mean?"

"Not if you don't mind leaning against the wall like this."

"This is fine with me, I…"

Charles backed out of Susan some and then thrust into her.

"Oh!" Susan exclaimed.

"Too hard?" Charles asked worriedly.

"No, that was… oh!" she said as he thrust again. "Oh, Charles, you… oh! That feels really… oh! Uuungh… oh… uuh… uungh… uungh…"

Susan closed her eyes as she concentrated on the sensation of

Charles filling her, withdrawing, and filling her again.

Uuuuuuungh... oooohhh... oh, yeahhh... faster... yeah, faster... oh, would you like me to talk to you to help you finish like Marty used to like? "Ooh, yeah... yeah... do it... do it... oh, yes, Charles, do it to me... your huge cock feels sooo good... you fill me up... you're mine, now! Your cock is mine! Give it to me! Give it to me! I want you inside me forever!"

Charles howled as he climaxed on one last thrust and shook violently as he held her tightly. "Suuusssaaannn...!"

Yes! Oh, yes! Susan thought as she closed her eyes and relished the moment. *Oh, Charles, I love you so much! Thank you, Lord! Thank you for letting me satisfy Charles, and thank you for giving us a really special first time! The very first time I made you cum. We're married, and you came inside me! Oh, Charles... yes, yes, yes!*

She opened her eyes again as he pulled her away from the wall and hugged her so tightly she found it hard to breath for a few moments. His breath was heaving as he started to come down from the rush of orgasm, and he lowered himself unsteadily to his knees, sat back on his heels, and then rocked backward, without letting go of Susan. They ended up with him lying face up on the floor of the shower, with Susan on top, and a semi-rigid Charles still inside her, with him gasping and panting.

"Oh, WOW! Oh, Charles! That was so... perfect! That was incredible! That was the most amazing sex I've ever had! That was better than anything I've ever dreamed it could be! That was beautiful! That was magnificent!"

Just then Susan noticed that the shower water was hitting Charles in the face, and she sat up, still mounted on him, and tried to hold her hands so they protected his face from the streams of water. *What a man! Look at that heaving chest... and I can still feel you inside me, even though you must be soft by now. The man of my dreams, the man who discovered the secret of my eyes. Discovered...? You knew it the first day we met. You hadn't even had time to study me much...* "Charles... when did you first notice that my eyes have a hint of green around them?"

"The first time I saw your face," he said, still trying to catch his breath.

The first time...?! No one, not one single person, ever noticed before. Was it God that made you notice?

"I would have stared if it wouldn't have been impolite."

But... why? There must have...

"You're the most beautiful woman I've ever met."

Susan lowered one hand to playfully slap Charles' chest before putting it back up to guard his face again. "Oh, Charles, now you're just trying to flatter me. Not that I'm objecting."

Charles raised his head off the shower floor and shook it, "No, I'm being truthful and serious."

He rose up until they were almost nose-to-nose, and they put their arms around each other.

"Susan, when I saw you behind the counter, you practically glowed. I don't know what it was... it certainly wasn't because you were happy with that little manager being so rough on you. But your eyes drew me like a magnet. And when you smiled at me, I thought I'd melt. Your face, your magnificent hair..."

I thought my hair was worn-out looking.

"I know it seems crazy, but I wanted to come around the counter and hug you..." Charles continued, "I've never had such a deep longing to... know someone... to get to know them... to be part of their life... to have them be part of my life..."

"Not even Jennifer?"

Charles shook his head thoughtfully. "I thought I loved Jennifer, but that was before I was a Christian. Looking back, I didn't know what real love was back then. We got along well most of the time, but... well, I kind of hate to say it, but my interest in Jennifer was based on me wanting her to meet my needs. I obviously met some of her needs in return, but my focus was on my satisfaction. I don't think I was capable of being unselfish."

Is that how I was with Marty?

Without thinking, Charles had slowly moved his hands around until they were holding Susan's sides, and his thumbs were now slowly moving back and forth at the base of Susan's breasts.

Mmm... that feels soo good...

"I admit that even after becoming a Christian, and asking God to be Lord of my life, I can still be selfish. But the difference is that now, I'm not completely selfish. And when I met you... my overwhelming desire wasn't about my satisfaction... it was a desire to give myself to you."

To give yourself to me...? Not because I deserved you, but because... our heavenly Father gives good gifts to his children? Susan cupped her hands around Charles' face. "I think God gave us to each other..."

"Amen to that," Charles said, and started to get up while still holding Susan in position, and Susan wrapped her legs around his waist again as if it were a natural thing to do.

Susan laughed. "Charles, what are you doing? You can't carry me around on you like this forever!"

"No, but I can carry you to bed."

"But... we need to dry off..."

Charles turned off the water at both ends, opened the sliding door, and started toward the bed, dripping wet. "We can dry off on the bed, but I'm anxious to taste you, and see how you like my tongue."

Ohh, noo...

"You look worried again," Charles said. "I promise to go slow and be gentle. And since you've never had an orgasm before, it's okay if it takes you awhile to get used to me putting my mouth on you."

Charles paused in the bedroom. "It took Jennifer weeks to get comfortable enough with my tongue between her legs before she could relax enough to climax that way. And she was already used to orgasms from using her fingers to masturbate. So don't feel like you have to perform, or meet some expectation of mine. My tongue is all about making *you* feel as good as possible."

Susan didn't look or feel much relieved as Charles shifted his hands under her rear end.

"Since we're still wet, how about we go over to my room for now, and we'll come back here to sleep tonight, and this mattress will still be dry."

"Oh, okay..."

As they entered the parlor, Susan's eyes got wide in fright and she turned away from the window and pressed tightly against Charles' chest. "Charles! The window's open!"

Charles stopped. "Yeah, some wedding guests went out on the balcony to enjoy the view. So?"

"Don't stop! Run! Or put me down!"

Susan dropped her legs, but they just dangled, as Charles held her firmly, still ensconced inside her.

And just as quickly, she wrapped them around him again. "No, don't put me down! Take me back and let me get a robe on!"

"What? Why?"

"Someone will see us! I'm not a... a... an exhibitionist, and I hope you aren't either!" *Although now I'm wondering what that "public sex" business meant...*

"Susan, look out the window."

"No... take me back, please!"

"Susan, trust me. Just look out the window."

If looking out the window will get you to take me back... Susan turned her head enough to barely see the window.

"What do you see out the window?" he asked.

"What...? Uh... the sky..."

"And what else?" he persisted.

"Uh... that's all."

"No people. No one can see you. We're on the twelfth floor, and no one can see us."

Susan turned her head slowly until she was looking fully at the window. "Well... I guess you're right... but it makes me uncomfortable. It's a big window."

Charles laughed and started walking toward the window.

"What are you doing?!" Susan exclaimed.

"Proving a point. Which may increase your discomfort for a moment, but it may permanently increase your level of comfort."

"No! Take me away from the window."

Charles stopped again. "Now what can you see outside the window?"

"I don't want to look!"

"It's safe to look, I promise. Will you trust me?"

Oh, that's not fair! Asking me to trust you! She glanced out and hid her face again.

"Now," Charles explained, "from here we can just barely see any buildings, way in the distance, just barely above the edge of the balcony outside. Which means even if someone way out there had a powerful telescope, they'd only be able to see our heads. They wouldn't even be able to see our necks, so they wouldn't know if we have clothes on or not. See?"

Susan wiggled her head in a little shake. "No. That may be logical, but my emotions won't let me be logical!"

"Oh. I'm sorry. I didn't think about that," Charles said, and headed back toward his bedroom. "Will you forgive me?"

"Yes, I forgive you. And I apologize for not being logical."

Charles laughed, and leaned over to give her a peck of a kiss on her forehead. "No apology's necessary for that, my darling wife. You're plenty logical, and I like your emotions just the way they are."

They walked a few steps in silence, and Susan noticed she was still feeling his fullness inside her. "I'm amazed that you've been able to stay inside me all this time after you came."

Charles laughed again, "Well, you've had a lot to do with that!"

He got to the bed, and lifted her off and set her down on the edge of it, and Susan felt a sense of loss as he came out of her. "Ohh... I was really enjoying feeling you inside me for so long." *But I guess I can't keep you there forever, huh?*

Charles climbed into the middle of the bed and turned her to face him. They sat with their legs folded and he took her hands in his, but Susan couldn't take her eyes off his crotch.

Look at that! You're still hard! And still huge!

"Susan, that was a dream come true for me. I... I can't tell you how much that experience meant to me."

"What...?" *Your dream?* "What was? What part?" Susan asked eagerly.

"Walking around with me inside you."

Susan's excitement sank. "Oh, I thought maybe it was the first time for something, and..."

"It was!" Charles said happily. "As long as I can remember, I've always wanted to have sex while standing, while walking around, like we just did! I think you're perfect for me!"

But surely you've done that before...

Charles looked sad as he recalled, "Jennifer was, uh... that is... my cock was too long for her to do that."

He tenderly caressed Susan's cheek. "There were a lot of positions... and things... she and I couldn't do because of that. And Laura... well, I guess I was too long for her, too."

Susan's excitement bounced right back. *So there may be a lot of things I can do to satisfy you even better than your first two wives?!* Susan thrust her fists into the air, "Yahoo!"

Charles' eyes smiled, but he looked puzzled. "Yahoo?"

"So, you never got to walk around like that with anyone before?" Susan asked for confirmation. "Ever?"

"No, not ever. Not with anyone. But I always wanted to. And I've imagined it a lot... maybe because I never actually got to."

"Until now...?! Until our wedding day! Until the first time you and I had sex together!"

"Yeah, that's..."

"Yee-ha!" Susan shouted. "Woo-hoo! Praise God! Thank you, Lord! Thank you!"

Charles laughed, "I thought I was the one being thankful for this. Why are you so excited?"

"Because I asked God... no, I begged God... to let our first time be special, really special. And... wow! I had no idea that it could be that special! You always wanted to have sex the way, but you never could before, and we did it that way our very first time!"

Susan lunged forward, pushed Charles onto his back and straddled him. "And you are soo amazing! I've never had sex like that before, and I loved it! I loved when you walked around with me inside you. You feel sooo good inside me. I've always wanted to feel full inside, and I never, ever, have before. But you fill me up!"

Hey, we've each given the other something we never had before, just like Lisa prayed!

Susan reached a hand down between them and took hold of him and guided him back into her. "Aaaahhhh… Charles… you're so perfect for me…"

"Oh, Susan, you're perfect for me. I love you so very much!"

Susan started slowly rocking forward and back, just a little. "And I had no idea you're so strong. You were able to carry me for so long!"

"Well, I was getting pretty tired at one point, but I got a second wind when you started sucking on my tongue. Wow! That was hot! And then when you talked while I was… while we were…"

"Humping?"

"Yeah… wow that was *really* hot! I had no idea how energizing, how erotic it could be to… for you to talk sexy while we were… humping."

Susan grinned, as she rocked a little further and started rotating her hips a little. "You mean like when I tell you I love feeling your giant cock inside me?"

"Ooohh… yeah… ooohhh…"

What else can I say? I don't want to sound like a slut… "I *love* having your cock in my hot little love hole. I can feel you all the way up inside me, and it makes me feel full. It satisfies me like nothing else, ever…"

Charles closed his eyes, and was groaning loudly, thrusting his hips up in time with Susan's rocking. Susan started increasing her speed, and soon both of them were panting.

Got to keep talking… push him over the edge… "Oh, Charles…" Susan said as she rocked as hard as she could, at the same time trying to tighten her vaginal muscles as much as she could each time she came up and release them as she slammed down. "I've wanted you… all my life. I didn't know it until now… but it was you… I've always wanted inside me."

Charles roared as he climaxed again, bucking forcefully into her with abandon.

Yes…!!! Susan beamed with delight, and kept pumping until she knew Charles was starting to wind down, then she rapidly slowed down to a slow, very gentle rocking.

Charles continued to twitch and moan long after the main event. "How in the hell… uh-oh… I'm sorry… sometimes my pre-Christian language…"

"That's okay," Susan said, still gently rocking. "What were you going to ask me?"

Charles finally managed to open his eyes again. "How… how in the world did you do that…?"

You know what I did, you were part of it, so what do you mean? "How did I do what? I don't understand. I know you've had plenty of orgasms before."

"Not like that!" Charles said emphatically, raising his head and grabbing Susan's arms. "The way you were moving… I never… I didn't even know it was possible… whatever you did…" He let his head and arms drop.

Susan furrowed her brow. "You mean the rocking, the tilting, or the tightening?"

"Yes!" Charles shouted. "All of it. I want you to explain it to me! But not right now, I need to rest a little bit first."

Your first two wives didn't do that…? It seems so natural, I thought all women did those things…

He closed his eyes again and his body relaxed in to the mattress. "I can't… concentrate right now…"

Susan continued to wonder what it was he didn't understand. "Charles, are you telling me that Jennifer never did it like that?"

"Never," Charles answered in a fading voice. "Not even close. We did it often, but… Susan… I have never felt that good in my entire life. I didn't even know it was possible."

Susan finally stopped rocking. "Are you serious?!" *Did I just hear what I thought I just heard? Did I… Oh, Father, did I just give Charles the best orgasm he's ever had? Could I…*

"And you cheated…" Charles said faintly.

"What? What do you mean I cheated?"

"It was your turn for me to make you feel good…"

Tears filled Susan's eyes as he fell asleep and she slowly rolled off her now sleeping husband and softly stroked his hair. *You felt a little cheated because you think you didn't get to make me feel good? Oh, my most precious, darling husband… you'll never know… how incredibly wonderful you've made me feel!*

Chapter Fourteen

Heavenly Father, I know I didn't do anything to deserve your love, or any of your blessings, but you've given me so much, just because you love me. I used to dream about having a man who... no... I think I used to dream about having this man love me. And I guess I thought that dreams were always better than reality. But Father, this man, the man you brought into my life less than a week ago... he's so much more than I ever dared imagine. He's so much more... soo much more! Thank you, Father. Thank you! Thank you so much! Thank you, Lord! Thank you!

A growing awareness of dampness between her legs and a fullness in her bladder interrupted Susan's worship, and she slipped off the bed and squeezed her thighs together as she hurried to the bathroom that adjoined this bedroom.

Ohh... it's running down my legs... it's going to get on the carpet... oh, who cares! "I've never felt that good in my entire life," he said! I made Charles... have the best orgasm he ever had?

Susan reached the toilet, sat down, and spread her legs, letting gravity help the semen flow out of her. *I'm his third wife, and his first wife did all kinds of sexy things with him, but I made him feel better than she ever did?! Praise GOD, I won't be a disappointment to him!!*

Susan kicked her heels out and pummeled the air with her fists. *Oh, yes, yes, YES! Oh, God, thank you! Thank you so much!*

While her bladder was draining she started using toilet paper to wipe her legs dry. *Hey, and I wore him out! He fell asleep... because I wore him out with the best sex he ever had! Woo-hooo!*

Oh, God... oh, God... what amazing gifts you've given me today! Just being married to Charles is... Susan felt an almost overpowering desire to run back to Charles and give him a bear hug, even at the expense of waking him, but was stuck where she was until her bladder was empty. She got a handful of toilet paper to be ready to start wiping off as soon as she could.

The toilet seat... it was already down. He's had to have used this toilet to pee... oh, I guess the last time he used it he had to sit down. She sighed as she remembered dancing through her house and confessing that she wanted Charles so much she wouldn't even care if he left the toilet seat up. *But if I ask him, I'll bet he'll be willing to try to remember to put it down. I'm sure of it. I'm sure of him. I've known him less than a week, but it feels like we've known each other all our lives.*

When Susan finished on the toilet, she decided her urge to hug him could wait until he woke on his own. She shut the bathroom door and turned on the light and put the lid down on the toilet before flushing, to try to keep the noise from waking him. *Hmm... I'm a little sore inside, but not too bad... just like Grandma Brenda... the, what was it, the "low-libido" soccer mom...? Obviously the Grandma I'm most like...*

She stepped side to side, focusing on the soreness. *Yeah, I can see how Brenda could kind of enjoy this kind of soreness.*

Leaving the bathroom, she felt damp spots under her bare feet. *Should I try to find all the spots on the carpet and dry them?*

She looked around the floor. *I can't see them, so I'm not going to worry about it. Much.*

A few steps took her back to the edge of the bed, and Susan just stood there, admiring the view of her husband. *Ha! I wore you out! With sex! Woo-hooo! I may be a little sore, but I knocked you out, Champ!* Susan silently performed a little victory dance, though her eyes kept returning to study Charles' body.

Looks like you might leave a trail of drops to the bathroom, too... She went back to the bathroom and got a hand towel for Charles to dry off with when he woke up, and laid it on him. She felt a slight chill, and then pulled the top cover off the other queen bed in the room and spread that on top of him.

Huh. I've been standing here and walking around naked, and the bedroom door's been open this whole time. Oh, my! It was open while we were humping, and my boobs were bouncing all over the place. But... no one was around who could see us... so it didn't matter. I guess that's what Charles meant about being out in the other room. I guess it makes sense, what he was saying about that... but I'm just not that... whatever that is.

Susan walked to the bedroom door and closed it enough so that she could just stick her head out and look around the quiet room, before closing it completely. The drapes were drawn in this bedroom, but enough light leaked through that she could still make out Charles' form under the cover.

Susan remembered the dance steps Charles taught her and slowly stepped through them, hands in the air and playing a waltz in her mind. She giggled to herself as danced, *I'm stark naked, and I'm dancing!*

She imagined Charles in her arms, then she imagined Charles naked in her arms, and then imagined him inside her as they danced. *Oh, God... what a wonderful gift sex is. I do so love to feel Charles inside me. I love to make him feel good that way, and to feel his body go out of control with pleasure. Thank you for that, Lord! Thank you for giving me that pleasure, and thank you for letting me give Charles that pleasure.*

After a few minutes, Susan stopped dancing and went back to the bed. She quietly propped two pillows up against the headboard, climbed in and sat up with her legs under the top cover next to Charles. For a couple of minutes she just enjoyed watching in wonder as his chest rose and fell in the dim light.

God, how does destiny work? If we had been Christians when we were young, would we have met sooner? Or would we have been single until now, waiting on you to bring us together...? But it was Charles' trying to reconcile with his son from another marriage that brought us together. Oh, and losing my job! If I hadn't lost my job, would you have provided another way for us to meet...? Well, no matter what the answers are to those questions, I thank you for bringing Charles and I together now.

A song started pushing its way into Susan's mind, and she raised her hands in worship as she began recalling the lyrics and singing to herself,

> *"Even we who call His name so often miss the treasure;*
> *Still the voice of wisdom cries to those who will be stirred,*
> *sounding in the silence of dishonest weight and measure; Once*
> *again the common drum is heard, beating out the question*
> *only honest and courageous hearts will answer: Do you know*
> *Him? This is your destiny... when you obey Him, there is an*
> *open door. Do you believe... and will you love Him? This is*
> *your destiny... when you obey Him, there is an open door to*
> *your unspoken dreams."*

"I love the sound of your voice," Charles murmured, his eyes still closed.

In a flash, Susan realized she had started singing softly aloud at some point. She scooted down in the bed until she was even with him. "I'm sorry, darling, I didn't mean to wake you."

"I didn't mean to fall asleep. Is it night time already?"

"Oh, no, it just that the drapes are closed."

"Oh. What was that song you were singing?"

"That's called Destiny, by Twila Paris."

"Sing the whole thing for me."

"I don't know all the words, but I have it on a CD at home."

"Okay, sing anything for me."

"Oh, you... my voice isn't that nice."

"I *love* listening to you sing."

"Well, I..."

"Oh!" Charles cried and threw the cover off and jumped out of bed. "It's my turn!"

"Your turn for wh..."

Charles forcefully scooped Susan up. "This bed's wet, so I'm taking you to the big one."

Maybe I didn't wear him out as much as I thought... Yet...

He had no trouble getting his bedroom door open despite carrying her.

"Charles, the window's still open!"

"Uh-huh, and I'm hurrying, so people won't have time to form a line to watch me carry you through the room."

Susan slapped him playfully. "Women aren't required to be logical. That's the law."

"Yes, ma'am," Charles said as he placed her high in the king-sized bed, then kneeled by her legs and gently started pulling her ankles apart.

Ohh... I hope that's because you want to hump some more...

He kept moving her legs wider and wider apart, then got between them and wiggled down the bed until his head was near her crotch and he slowly took a deep breath and held it.

Oh, noo... "Charles, I need a shower..."

He moaned with satisfaction as he exhaled. "You just had one," he said as he stroked the inside of her thighs.

Mmm... that feels good, but... "I need another one if..." Susan gasped as Charles nuzzled her pubic hair with his nose.

He slipped one arm under each of her thighs and wrapped his arms around them. "Too late, now, Sweety. And my, you do smell sweet!

Sweet? I must smell awful! I... "Oh...! Charles, be... Oh...! Now, Charles, remember I might not be able to... Oh...!"

Charles rose up a bit on his elbows. "Susan, I'm going to go very slow, and if you can't have an orgasm for some reason, that's okay.

But *your* pussy is now *my* pussy, and no matter how long it takes, you're going to have to get used to my face being down here, and my tongue caressing you."

Ohh... I was afraid of that... Susan was almost panting from a mixture of fear and the sensual touching Charles had already begun. Her mind raced between objections, pleas, and worries of disappointing or discouraging him. Unable to focus on a single thing to say, she said nothing, and Charles devoted himself to tenderly touching her everywhere he could reach with his hands and tongue from the position he was in, quickly backing off whenever she gasped or flinched.

After what seemed like a very long time to Susan, she pleaded, "Charles, that's enough for now, please!"

"Okay, darling," Charles said happily enough. "You made some great progress!"

"Y-you think so?" *'Cause I didn't think...*

"Did you notice your hands were clenching the sheets when I started? You were very tense all over."

"Oh... I'm sorry, I just..."

"But you were pretty relaxed when I stopped."

Susan thought about that for a moment. "Huh. I guess I was, at that. I was still very nervous, but you're right, I was a lot more relaxed, at least physically, and it did feel really nice."

"It'll get better and better," he said confidently. "But are you nervous about what I might do next time?"

"Uh, yeah, I think so."

"That's reasonable. It'll take time to get used to the idea, and the sensations. Like learning to drive a car... you're hypersensitive and nervous to start with, but with enough practice, you eventually start getting used to it!"

Errg... I guess that means I'm in for a lot more "practice"...

Susan sighed, and Charles moved up in the bed and hugged her. "Do you trust me, darling?"

"I'm trying to, Charles, but I'm sorry, I can't help being so nervous..."

"That's okay, honey. But I didn't hurt you this time, did I?"

"No..."

"And I promise I won't hurt you next time, either. In fact, I promise never to hurt you. But by God's grace, sooner or later, your nervousness about having my tongue down there will fade and turn into a pleasure so wonderful you may not be able to imagine right now."

Hmm... "Well, I was pretty skeptical about you being able to teach me to dance, and I was really nervous about that, too... *Wow, if this works out that well... then it would be worth the nervousness for a little while.*

Charles released Susan from his hug and started to get up. "I've got to pee," he apologized.

"Well, you... my phone!" Susan also jumped out of bed and grabbed her skirt off the floor and took out her phone.

Charles froze while she checked for missed calls, and they both breathed a sigh of relief when she found none.

Charles then ran to the toilet. "We need to be more careful about keeping your phone close at hand," he called out loud enough for her to hear from the bed.

Susan followed him as far as the bathroom door, where she could hear him well, but not see into the little alcove that housed the toilet.

"And we need to make sure the battery's always got a charge," he added.

"Yeah," Susan agreed, looking at the phone. "It's got four bumps, so the battery's full."

"Great," he said a little more quietly. "You getting hungry?"

"Yeah. You want me to order room service?"

"I have another idea. How about a picnic?"

"Oh, okay," Susan said. "Sure." *But the bodyguards will need time to get prepared... I wonder how long it will be before we can actually start eating?*

Susan returned to the bedroom and started picking up clothes, and paused when she picked up her panties. *I don't want to wear these again, and I don't want to put on clean ones until I've had a real shower...*

Charles returned and Susan said, "I'm going to need to get another shower before we go out. To get clean this time," she finished with a laugh.

"Who said anything about going out?" Charles asked.

"You said..."

"Shhh!" Charles shushed, with a finger over his lips. He took her hand and led her to the door to the parlor, got down on his knees, and pulled her down.

"What are you doing?" Susan asked with a puzzled smile.

"Oh, I love your smile so much!" Charles said, but then opened the door and started crawling across the floor, pulling Susan with him. He let her go so he could go faster, but she continued to follow on all fours.

From her position behind him, she couldn't help but stare at the appendage swinging between his legs. *Are you trying to show me you want to have sex again? You're obviously not aroused... at the moment... and I was hoping you were hungry for food...*

Charles started pulling cushions off the sofa and chairs, moving the coffee table, and arranging the cushions in the middle of the floor.

Although if I keep looking at that pendulum, what I'm hungry for could certainly change... maybe that's what you have in mind...

Charles took Susan's hand and pulled her onto the cushions, then fetched the fruit basket and put it beside her. "Our love lunch!"

"Okay... but..."

He started crawling away again, and commented, "This is too slow." He got up and raced into his former bedroom. "And too hard on my knees."

He came back with the clock radio from his bedside table, plugged it in, and worked the dial. After a few moments, he found a station playing classical music. "Is this okay? It reminds me of our first date!"

"Sure..." Susan agreed. She expected Charles to join her on the cushions, but he raced back to his old room.

A moment later, he came running through the parlor and threw an armful of pillows directly at her. Susan put her arms up to protect her face, and when she looked up, Charles was gone. A moment after that, he reappeared from her room with all the pillows from the king size bed. He dropped them and flopped down beside her.

"Hand me an apple, please?" he asked.

A picnic... in the living room... in the nude... She picked out two apples and handed him one.

"So, being down here on the floor like this, the curtains being open don't bother you too much?"

"I guess not. But I hope you're not just trying to get me adjusted by degrees to the point where I won't mind having sex in public, because that's never gonna..."

"Well, 'public' doesn't mean with anyone else actually watching, but no, this is just this, just for now. And for our memories, forever."

Satisfied, Susan leaned back on some pillows and started to relax as she ate her apple, listened to the music, and looked at her "Adam."

Charles laid propped up on his side, facing Susan. "Thank you," he said quietly.

"For what, specifically?"

"For marrying me. For loving me. For giving me the best sex of my life. For loving me."

"You said 'loving me' twice."

"I appreciate that twice as much."

Susan turned on her side to put them face-to-face. "Charles... why do you love me?"

Charles was thoughtful for a moment before answering. "Well, you're very beautiful, but I don't love you because you're beautiful. You're also very smart, too, but I don't love you because you're smart. And you're *really* great at sex, but I loved you before I knew that."

"Then why *do* you love me?"

"Because God put you in my heart."

Oh, God... what kind of man have you given me? He's perfect... he's so perfect for me...

"From the first moment I saw your smile, somehow, inside, I just knew I wanted to spend the rest of my life with you. That was mixed in with my expectation that you were a Christian, and I think it was God's spirit shining in you that made me think that."

"So it was love at first sight for you. And it took me a little longer."

"Not too long... what's today... the seventh day... we got married the seventh day after we met. That's pretty fast," he said. "...Any regrets?"

"Yes," Susan replied and waited while Charles' eyebrows rose. "That we waited so long!"

They both laughed merrily, and as they laughed they began caressing each other.

"The best sex of your life?" Susan asked. "Really?"

"Oh, honey, yes," Charles said emphatically. "First you rode me while I walked around and let me finish in you like that for the first time. Oh, wow, what a dream-come-true first time! And then, well, you made me feel so good in the other bed, I couldn't even figure out what all you were doing. I... I just can't even begin to describe how good that felt."

"But what about the deep-throat and anal sex Jennifer used to give you. And sex in public..." *I wouldn't have done that even before I was a Christian.* "You said you used to like that a lot."

"Well, yeah, I liked it. I mean, I always liked sex no matter how we did it. And those things were fun, and provided some nice variety. But as far as mind-bending intensity, Susan, you broke the world record a little while ago!"

Susan put her apple down and snuggled close enough to Charles to kiss him, as she reveled in his praise. He put his own apple down and put both his hands to work caressing her, and soon Susan pulled him inside her again. *Oh, yes! What an incredible feeling! Even without humping hard, I can feel you so deep inside!*

They were still on their sides facing each other when Susan started trying to rock her hips again.

"Ungh... no... honey, don't do that right now..."

Susan felt a shock of disappointment. "But... I thought you really liked it when..."

"I did. I do... but if you do that again, you're going to get me off, and then I'll go limp, and I'd rather just stay inside you for a while first. We can do more later, if you don't mind. Is that okay?"

You just want to stay inside me awhile? You don't want to build up and have your fun and be done with it? "Yes, that's okay." *That's more than okay. With Marty, that would have been a miracle.*

For over an hour, they listened to the music, lying entwined in varying positions, sometimes having intercourse, sometimes not, but almost constantly caressing each other.

At one point Charles was spooning Susan and entered her from behind, then picked up his apple and started eating again.

"Are you eating?"

"Yeah. My apple."

"But... we're having sex!"

"Yeah, so?"

"So... you" *can't... well, obviously you can, but...*

He swallowed a bite and waited before taking another. "It doesn't bother you, does it?"

"Uh, well... I never... uh..." *I can't think of one single wrong with it. But it just seems so... inconsiderate? No... inappropriate? Yeah, that's it, but why?*

"You want me to quit eating, or quit screwing you, or what?"

Well, I want to keep feeling you inside me. But I'm also getting really hungry... Susan reached over and picked up her apple and took a bite. *I'm chewing an apple, and Charles is screwing me. Huh.*

Susan heard Charles take another bite. *Charles is eating an apple while he's humping me...*

She tried to turn her head enough to look at Charles, but it was a strain. "I want to turn over."

"Okay," he replied.

Susan flipped to her other side, once again facing Charles. She quickly reinserted him, and he started slowly moving in and out in short strokes.

He took another bite of apple, and Susan did likewise.

Hmm... we're having sex, and eating at the same time. How come Marty and I never did that? Well, for one thing, Marty never wanted to take it slow like this.

Susan started to take another bite, but Charles prevented her by putting his apple up close to her mouth, and she took a bite out of his apple. She started chewing and watched Charles carefully. When she saw him swallow, she held up her apple for him to take a bite.

Oh, my... this is starting to feel... strange... like hyper-erotic...? Yeah, definitely.

She swallowed and Charles held up his apple while she took another big bite. *Uuum... you're putting something in both ends of me... filling me... at both ends...*

Susan's breathing was coming more rapidly, and she stared into Charles' eyes as she chewed. *You're staring at my boobs. And you look like you like them.* As he finished a slow, short thrust into her, she tightened her vaginal muscles.

Charles' eyes widened, and he took in a sharp breath.

Okay, that got the reaction I was hoping for.

After he pulled back, she relaxed her muscles for his thrust back in, and then she tightened them again while he pulled back.

Charles shuddered and moaned as Susan continued the pattern. Susan swallowed the bite she had been chewing, and Charles looked like he had a little difficulty getting his apple to her mouth for her next bite, but he did.

They were both breathing faster when she gave him another bite, and Charles growled and rolled her onto her back and thrust hard and deep.

Uuh... that was too deep... no, it wasn't. I won't let it be. He likes me to be able to take him deep, and I'm going to be like Grandma Brenda and just bear up under it. Oh, I forgot to tighten that time. Got to concentrate... but want to keep eating... whoever would have thought that eating while having sex could be so sexy? Come, on baby, push that tree trunk into me again!

He pushed in again and Susan tightened, and Charles closed his eyes and growled again as he pulled back against her grip.

Charles shifted, and Susan felt pressure from her bladder. *Uh-oh...*

Charles pushed hard into her again.

"Charles... I'm sorry to interrupt, but I need to pee before we get going hot and heavy again."

"Uhhh."

Uh-oh, did I wait too late? Do you need me to stick with it until you finish?

Charles rolled off, and Susan jumped up and hurried to the bathroom.

She sat down on the toilet and immediately started peeing. She felt the relief, but her sexual excitement was calming down as her bladder emptied.

Suddenly she gasped. *The toilet seat! It's down. And Charles was the last one to use it. Was he...? He was, I could tell from the sound he made, he was standing up, which means... he put the seat down! After he peed, he put the seat down!*

She ripped a strip of paper off, wiped quickly and ran back to the parlor as fast as she could.

Charles was standing in front of their cushions and pillows and Susan noted he still had a full erection just before she ran into him and knocked him back onto the cushions.

She started to put him inside her, but then started rolling them over. "I want you on top!"

In hardly more than the blink of an eye, he was on top of her, in her, and pumping away.

"Uuungh..." Susan grunted, using her hands to try to pull him as deep as possible. She wrapped her legs around him and pulled her heels into his buttocks to spur him in, and Charles responded by increasing his speed and force. He felt so good to her that she was having trouble concentrating enough to time her muscle control, but after a half-minute, she started getting the rhythm. When she did, Charles turned into an animal, thrusting wildly and groaning without restraint.

"Aaahhh... ohh, Charles... yes... yes...! Take me... take my pussy... ram it into me... aaahhh... Chaarrles... my pussy is your pussy, Charles... hump it... hump me... my hot lover... do it! Do it to me...! I want you... I want you ... I want you...!

Charles screamed incoherent guttural cries as his back arched and he climaxed deep inside her, and she screamed in unison.

"Charles...! Yes...! Yes!!! Oh, Charles! Oh, my love, my husband!

Oh, yes…!"

Charles' back remained arched as his hips bucked involuntarily and he groaned fiercely. At last, his groans diminished as he began to fight to catch his breath.

Instead of collapsing on top of her, Charles leaned down and dug his hands under her, spread his legs out, planted his feet, and started pulling her up.

They were both panting as Susan felt him slide out of her as he stood up, picked her up off the floor, and held her in a bear hug. She kissed him over and over, on his face, his neck, and his shoulders. When he showed no signs of putting her down, she wrapped her legs around his waist to make it easier for him to bear her weight and try to keep the semen from leaking, and she continued to kiss him.

Charles walked and turned, almost dancing. "Aaahhh… Sussaann… oh, Susan… oh, Susan… ooohhh… ooohhh… I want you in my arms forever… ohh, Sussaann…"

Susan pulled his head toward her own until her lips finally met his, and she kissed him passionately. They broke the kiss to gasp for breath, and a moment later were kissing again.

"Marry me, Susan, please marry me!"

"Oh, yes, my love! I will marry you! My husband… I will marry you over and over! I love you with all my heart!"

"God's never blessed a man as much as he's blessed me, by giving me your heart!"

"Oh, Charles, the blessing is mine!"

He leaned his head back to look into Susan's eyes. "Oh, my darling! I never understood before… that two people can become one person! I… I never gave myself completely to anyone before. I tried, but I was too selfish, I couldn't do it. But in Christ I can. And you have my heart, all of it. I belong to you, Susan. All of me."

"And I belong to you, my love. With all my heart and all my soul, I belong to you forever!"

After several more minutes of carrying Susan and spinning around, Charles carried her back to their make-shift pallet. They laid down without ever letting go of each other, and they kissed on and off, very tenderly.

"I love the feel of my breasts pressed against your chest," Susan whispered. "I love to feel your hands moving against my skin… and if we could never have sex again, I will never forget how wonderful it felt to have you inside me."

"Oh, Susan, I love every part of your body… but more than that,

I love the fact that you want me... that you enjoy feeling me inside you..."

"Mmmm..." Susan murmured happily. "We certainly have made some good memories today."

"Today, and this past week. So intense... so rich... so much to treasure. It almost feels like we've caught up for not meeting each other until now."

"What's your favorite memory so far?" Susan asked quietly, with her mouth right to his ear, and then she started nibbling on it.

"Mmm... awfully tough to choose just one... but I'd say the hour or so we just spent together here... the part before you seduced me into a climax again."

Susan pulled her head back so she could look at Charles' face again. "Really? The slow part? Not one of the hot times?"

"No, definitely not. Oh, those were great, but definitely not as good as just being inside you for a long time. And if I had to choose between those hot times and the night I taught you to dance on the paddleboat, I'd take that night on the boat."

"But... why? It sure seemed like you got a lot more pleasure out the hot times."

"Well, those were certainly more intense physical sensations. But... even though I'm not as selfish as I was before I became a Christian, me having an orgasm seems like it's too much about me. About me feeling good. The hour listening to the radio, I felt like that was more about making *us* feel good. And the night I taught you to dance..."

"What?" Susan barely managed to ask, prompting Charles to continue.

"It was the first time we held each other," he said. "It was the first time we kissed. It was when we started to become part of each other..."

Susan wiped her eyes, leaned in close to Charles again, and sighed deeply. *I never would have believed it. If anyone had tried to tell me there was a man in the world like Charles, I never would have believed it.*

"What about you? What's your favorite memory so far?"

"Oh, my... you've given me so many... so very many! You've made me feel pretty... for the first time in many, many years. You shocked me, and I mean, really, really shocked me, when you told me that you saw that my eyes have a tinge of green around the outside edge. You encouraged me at a time when it seemed like my entire life was in ruins. You've given me courage to try things, like dancing. You actually taught me to dance, and... made me feel... sensual again, when I thought I never would..."

Not just sensual again...more sensual than ever before. And I don't think I've ever been naked this long before, either. And it doesn't even bother me!

"But a favorite thing?" she continued. *How about all the things you've said to me?* Susan started crying freely, still locked in their embrace. "You've told me so many things," she sobbed, "so very many things... that make me feel loved!"

Charles kissed her forehead and moved one of his hands up to stroke her hair.

After crying for a few minutes, Susan said, "No matter how long we live, Charles, I'll never be able to do anything for you as great as what you've done for me. The way you've made me feel so loved."

"Oh... I don't know about that..."

Susan felt a drop fall on her face, and she looked up and saw that Charles was quietly crying.

"Peace," he said. "You've given me peace. For the first time in my life. I just now realized it. The reason our quiet, intimate hour here listening to the radio is my favorite thing, is because it's the first time in my adult life that I've been at peace. That I've felt like I'm where I'm supposed to be, with the person I'm supposed to be with."

Susan was now crying again with Charles.

"Even after I became a Christian," Charles managed to explain, "I felt a pressure of some kind... I had to be doing something. But no matter what I did, it was never enough. I think that actually got a little worse after I gave my life to God, because I was so grateful for his love, I wanted to do things... something, for him. You know, as a way of showing my appreciation... I've heard sermons about God's grace. I read about it in the Bible. I know the greatest act of grace was when Jesus died to atone for my sins, and I understood that, at least a little bit. But not until now was I able to see it so clearly. Now I can see it physically."

Susan sniffed and furrowed her brow. "Physically?"

"You, Susan. There's no way in hell... oh... shoot, there I go again, just when I was being so spiritual."

"Okay, forget that," Susan said impatiently. "What were you going to say?"

"There's no way in the whole wide world that I deserve your love." Charles explained. "Yet you love me. I want your love. I crave your love. But I could never in a thousand lifetimes do enough to *deserve* your love. The fact that you're in my arms… is a physical example of God's grace."

"Oh, Charles… Charles… I see that, now that you've explained it. Except I see it from the other side. I don't deserve your love, either. God gave us to each other. Not because either of us is deserving, but because God has given us each other as a gift by his grace!"

"Wow…" Charles intoned.

"Wow," Susan echoed. *God's grace… extends to every aspect of life. Even sex.*

"Hey, I've got an idea!" Charles said, and starting shifting.

"What?" Susan inquired as she took a cue from Charles to roll onto her back.

"You know how erotic it turned out to be to eat while having sex?"

"Yeah…" she replied. *Which implies it was a new thing for you, too.*

"Well," Charles said as he grabbed a banana, put it in her hand, and started scooting down toward Susan's feet, "you eat another piece of fruit while I play with you again."

"Oh, no… let's not do that again so soon!"

"Too late!" Charles said as he got comfortable and started stroking a hand up and down Susan's thigh.

She sighed with minor exasperation and then tried another tactic. "I'm starting to get hungry for real. How about if we go downstairs to the restaurant?"

"After I finish down here," Charles insisted. "Tell you what. We'll make this a short session. I'll quit as soon as you finish the banana. It'll take a while to order the food and get it cooked, so the banana will help hold you till then, and I'll get to enjoy browsing in your garden again for a few minutes."

Browsing in my garden, huh…? "Alright, but I'm going to have a pear instead."

"Okay," Charles replied.

Too much recent trouble with bananas and wild sexual thoughts. But at least I can eat this pear in a couple minutes, and keep your "browsing" time down.

Susan started eating the pear as rapidly as she could without making it obvious that she was hurrying. *Mmm… I feel your breath down there. It's warm. I didn't notice that last time, but I must have missed it, because you couldn't have held your breath for thirty minutes, or however long it was. And I do like your touching me everywhere except the most sensitive areas.*

She sucked in her breath. *Like that... okay, you backed off... hmm... I might could get to the point where I could like the way you brush your fingers or nose in my pubic hair... ooo, yeah... that must be your tongue in that seam between my thighs and my... private part. Just don't touch the private part. Now that's curious... just a little while ago, you were jamming that big tree trunk of yours in and out of my hole, and I was loving it. Why does it bother me so much to have your face down there and using your hands and tongue to do less than that? Is it because your hands and tongue are using a lighter touch? Well, I don't think I want you to...*

Susan sucked in her breath again and held it. *Ooo... that's too sensitive... back off... back off... you're not backing off... I'm going to have to disappoint your by asking you to stop... wait... maybe I can just finish the pear real quick, and I can get you to stop without disappointing you...*

She took two big bites of pear and chewed quickly, as her breathing was speeding up. *Ooo... easy, there, Mr. tongue... oh, that's... too much...*

Susan swallowed before she had chewed thoroughly and took two more bites. *Maybe if I concentrate on your hand moving up and down my leg... oh, yeah, now that's a nice thing to concentrate on... ooo, I'm glad I shaved my legs yesterday... feels pretty smooth to your touch, at least it feels that way to me... I hope it feels that way to... YOU...! Oh, my! What was that?! Lord, have mercy! Focus, Susan, focus on the hands, not the tongue. Focus on his hand, sliding lightly up my shin... on the back of my knee... up the top of my thigh... and down... down the inside of my thigh again, back towards my knee... then back down my shin... oh, you're doing it different... you're massaging the bottom of my foot... ooo... that feels really good... really, really...*

"Charles!"

"Mm?"

"Did you... did you just put your tongue inside me?"

"Mm-hm."

Doesn't it taste awful? Doesn't it smell... what did you say? No... you're not talking... you're... moaning? As if you like it? As if you like tasting me? Even after we've had sex, and I've been sweaty, and I haven't had a shower? Are you crazy...? What was that Darlene said...? Jennifer was crazy about your tongue? All the other women

251

were lusting after you because of... because of what you're doing to me right now... and you said... most of the time, you'd rather do this than hump? Well, that was before you knew how good I am at humping... still though... you liked it better than humping Jennifer, and she did all those extra sex things with you. That's got to mean you really like this an awful lot... and it's you who's been eager for it... you pressuring me into it... why would you do that if you didn't like it? Maybe you really don't mind the taste and the smell. Maybe... maybe you actually... like the taste... wow... is that possible? Could you like the way I taste? Is that why you're moaning with your tongue moving around down there? Maybe you... well, you actually told me you like the way I smell, didn't you, and I have no reason to think you'd lie about it. Is it like flowers for you? Do you like to smell me the way I like to smell flowers? Is that why you called it my garden? Ooo, there it goes inside me again... that's not so bad... it's little... and it doesn't go in very far, but it's... warm... and wet... and it moves differently... it wiggles, sort of... oh, you took it out... are you going to put it back...?

Charles raised his head up. "How are you doing with that pear? You finished?"

The pear! I forgot! Oh, shoot! "Uh, almost done," she said and took a bite.

"Okay, well let me know when you're through."

"Okay," she said with her mouth full. *Aahh... yeah... that feels... pretty good... what are you doing...? Moving your tongue up and down again, instead of in and out... you tried doing that some earlier today, but it was too intense... why does it feel so much better now...?*

She swallowed a bite and slowly took another. *I don't have to hurry, do I? You didn't ask me to hurry... am I getting used to this... am I getting so that I can tolerate it... am I getting so that... I like it...? Oh, my, can I imagine if Marty had ever tried this? Impossible... it never even entered his mind to do something just to make me... feel good...? Yes...! It does... it feels good... it feels warm... it feels soothing... it's so intimate... my husband loves me... and has his head between my legs... using his tongue to make me feel good... and it's... starting to feel reeal good...*

Susan swallowed, but put off taking another bite. *Hey, if Marty's love language was touch, why didn't he ever try to make me feel good? Because he was too selfish? Or maybe he thought humping me was all I needed? I wonder just how long Charles can keep this up?*

How long would you want to? How long would I want you to? How do you decide when to stop if I don't ask you to? When would...

"YOW!" Susan yelled and sat up in a panic. "Stop! What... what was that...?!"

"I tried to be very gentle. That was your clitoris, and it's the first time I've touched it with my tongue. I'm sorry, I honestly didn't think I could hurt you by touching you that way, or of course, I wouldn't have. I don't know what to say, other than apologize."

Oh, God... please don't let me disappoint Charles. Especially not today, not after everything else has been so perfect. Don't let me spoil today for him. "It's okay, Charles. It... it didn't hurt, exactly... it's more like it, uh, startled me."

"It sounded more like I hurt you."

"No... it was... it was really intense, and I wasn't expecting it."

"Are you sure?"

"Do it again." *What?! Why did I say that?! Am I crazy?*

"Are you really sure? Because..."

"Yes, I'm sure." *I'm sure I'm crazy.* "Do it again, please. Gently!"

Charles lowered his head and Susan took a deep breath.

Oh, I'm tensing up all over, just like earlier today. Will that make it worse? Will... Oh! There's his tongue down near my hole again... okay, he's moving it up... should I try to relax... make myself relax...? As she felt him getting close, Susan out her breath and inhaled again quickly. *Here it comes... here it comes... ooo... that's it...! Easy... easy... easy...!*

Susan blew her breath out and panted. *Try not to move, Susan! He's holding his tongue still, just barely touching it... easy... don't start shaking... easy... ooo!*

She felt him remove his tongue, and felt a big sense of relief.

"How was that?" Charles asked.

You look like a little puppy dog... a worried little puppy, and I have to tell you if you did good or bad... "It was okay."

"Really?" Charles brightened visibly.

"Yes. It was a little intense, and I was a lot scared, but I was expecting it that time, and... it was okay."

"Oh, what a relief!" he said as he crawled back up to put them face-to-face again. "I want so much to make you feel good, and when you yelled a minute ago... I was really afraid I had scared you too much to let me try it again."

Susan smiled. "I'm glad you tried it again. And... thank you... for being so patient with me."

"I'll be as patient as it takes, Susan. But... you've now let me touch you in a way no one else has ever done before."

He gave Susan a tender hug, and she savored feeling her breasts pressing into his bare chest once more. *"You've let me touch you in a way no one else has ever done before." Oh... Charles...*

"I hope you'll learn to tolerate that more and more, and then come to enjoy it," he whispered, "But whatever happens, I'll always treasure the last few minutes."

Susan leaned forward and kissed her husband lovingly. *So will I, my love, so will I.* "Maybe I'll be able to enjoy it someday as much as you want me to. But in the meantime, are you getting hungry?"

"Starving... for food this time!"

"Okay, how about this?" Susan said. "Let's tell Mike we want to eat dinner in the restaurant, call in our order, and get showered while they're cooking it!"

"Okay! I'll call Mike while you order the food."

With both calls taken care of, they started both showerheads and stepped in when the water was warm enough. They started to soap up and Susan sighed.

"What's the matter? You want to postpone dinner so we can play in here for a while?"

"No... I have to pee again already, and now I'm all wet."

"Just pee here in the shower."

"Men! The shower isn't for peeing, that's what the toilet's for!"

"Both drains go to the same place..."

"That doesn't matter..."

"Plus, I want you to pee in here, so I can watch."

Susan looked mildly shocked. "You want... to watch me pee?!"

"Yeah!" he replied enthusiastically.

"It's a good thing I didn't know you had that kind of... interest... when you first asked me out, or we'd have never had a first date."

"Hey, when I say I love everything about you, I mean *everything*."

"But that's gross!"

"No it's not. C'mon, Laura wouldn't even shower with me, so I haven't seen a woman pee since Jennifer."

Ooo... did you know you were pushing my button when you said that? Making me compete with your first wife? "Rrrr," Susan growled at Charles as she spread her legs as wide as she could, and tried to relax enough to let the flow start.

When it started, it began to spray all over. "See? Women can't aim like guys can."

"Well, you can do better than that. Pull your lips apart."

"What?!"

"Pull your pussy lips apart. Here…" Charles got down on his knees and gently pulled her lips apart, and the flow of urine turned into a stream… right onto Charles.

See what happens when you do gross things, you get it all over you… hey… you were right!

"See? Just pull them apart a little bit, and the lips don't misdirect it all over the place. I'm surprised you didn't know that."

"I'm surprised you did."

"Okay, you take over," Charles said, as he stood up and turned around under his showerhead.

You're just going rinse it off? I'd have to use soap for an hour.

Susan looked at Charles' back, and then down at her private area. When he had let go, the stream changed a little bit, and now her lips were interfering more and more. *I don't believe I'm doing this…*

She reached down and pulled them apart again, and the flow became a stream once again. She let go with one hand, and saw that the stream started pointing to one side. Curious, she put that hand back, and used both hands to pull from side to side. *How do you like that? I can aim! Maybe not as much as a man, but at least a little bit.*

Charles turned back to face Susan, and she slapped his chest.

"Huh. What was that for?"

"For being right, when I didn't want you to be."

He smiled. "You're most welcome!"

Just as she finished peeing, she said, "Oh, shoot. I forgot to do my Kegel exercises."

"Your what?"

"My Kegel exercises… Are you not familiar with them?"

"No, uhn-uh. What is it… strength training… aerobics…?"

"Sex," she said simply.

"What?"

"It's how women train for sex."

"What? I've never heard of women training for sex. Are you serious?"

Susan laughed, "Yes, I'm serious. And yes, some women learn to control their vaginal muscles."

"Is *that* what you were doing to me?!"

She laughed again. "Part of it… but I thought I was doing it *with* you. I'm pretty sure I recall you having an active role."

"What else?" Charles asked with wide eyes.

"Well… the time when I was on top…"

"Yes, that time! What all were you doing to… with me…?"

Uh-oh… Susan thought as she noticed the beginnings of an upward movement from just below Charles' waist. "Well, I was rocking… forward and back, you know, my body was moving closer to your head and then closer to your feet, making you go in and out of me."

"Mmmm…!"

Look at that thing grow… "Then I started tilting my hips back and forth," Susan said as she demonstrated.

"Oh… wow…!" he exclaimed, his eyes locked on her hips.

"And then I started tightening and loosening my vaginal muscles. The vagina is mostly muscles, you know."

"Oh, I do now! Boy, do I know now!" Charles embraced her, with his full erection pressed into her abdomen.

Susan sighed silently. *If we keep having sex, we'll never get to eat a real meal again…*

"Honey…?" he prompted.

"Yes, darling…?" *Yes, it's okay. I've got enough strength to do you again.*

"Would you mind if we wait 'till after dinner to have sex again…? I'm really hungry."

Susan looked at his face in surprise. *Well, that's a first! You've got a full hard-on, and you want to wait?* "Well, you're full of surprises. No, I don't mind waiting."

"You're disappointed. I can wait to eat. I don't…"

"No! No, really, I don't mind waiting. I'm getting really hungry too."

"Are you sure?"

"Oh, yes, definitely sure. C'mon, let's finish washing off and go eat. We've already ordered, so it should be ready soon, and the bodyguards are expecting us." *You're the one who'll have a hard time getting dressed, but you're worried I'm so horny I can't wait? Hmm. Was Jennifer like that?*

They both washed quickly as Susan sighed to herself again. *Am I still competing with a dead woman? Hmm… I could offer to help him get his pants on, and make sure he doesn't… but I'm so hungry… Maybe he won't think any less of me for not wanting sex as often as Jennifer if I keep satisfying him better than she used to. I hope telling him my techniques won't spoil their effect…*

Chapter Fifteen

"What about this mess?" Susan asked as they walked through the parlor toward the front door, referring to the cushions and pillows on the parlor floor.

"I'll pick it all up when we get back from lunch," Charles offered. "Got your cell phone?"

"Oh, yes," Susan confirmed, patting her jeans pocket. *Stephanie already called today, but she could call us anytime to ask us to come rescue her. Lord... please don't let that be a useless hope...*

They had both agreed on jeans, and Susan was wearing a dark blue button-up blouse, hoping that would provide less contrast to her makeup-less face, and Charles had chosen a tight-fitting white pullover.

Charles started to open the door to the hallway, and Susan froze, staring at the eyepiece in the center of the door.

"What's wrong, hon?" Charles asked, then noticed what she was staring at. "Oh, don't worry. See the button?

He pushed the button in and released it. "No one can see in or out unless the button is pushed in."

"Oh!" *So you already thought of that. But...* "What about the noise we've been making?"

"Not a problem," Charles continued as he opened the door and held it for her, "the bodyguards aren't stationed right outside the door anymore, so they can't hear anything. There're in a room down the hall."

Is there anything you don't think of? Susan walked out and turned right into the mountainous Truck.

"Not anymore," Truck rumbled. "Since so many people know you're here now, Mike put us back on the door."

"Oh," Charles acknowledged with chagrin.

So... could we be heard through that door? How embarrassing would that be? Susan took Charles' hand as they walked down the hallway behind Truck.

Truck spoke into a cell phone's wireless headset. "Package coming down."

"And after you eat," Truck said loudly enough to be heard

without turning around, "Mike wants to talk to you about moving to another location... that we can keep a secret, hopefully."

Oops... well, it's worth it... it's not like we'll be getting married every day, and it was so wonderful to have friends here...

Once again, Truck made sure the elevator car was empty, ushered Susan and Charles in, and got in behind them.

"Uh... Truck... could you hear us from out in the hallway?" Charles asked into Truck's back.

Oh, no! Don't ask him! I'd rather not know than...

"I'm not paid to hear anything like that," Truck said.

"Like that?" That means you really did hear...! Doesn't it...?

"Which is a good thing, considering how much there was not to hear," Truck added.

Oh no...! Susan sank her head against Charles.

"Uh, thanks..." Charles managed to say, "for uh, 'not hearing' anything."

"Hey, you don't need to worry about me. I'm not paid to talk about what I don't hear, either."

Ohhh... Charles... we have to be more quiet from now on!

They got off the elevator and were shown to the same booth they had at breakfast, as it was the most isolated, while Susan carefully avoided looking at Truck until he disappeared again. Their previously-ordered meals were brought quickly, Charles having a well-done steak and Susan having salmon.

Charles reached across the table and took Susan's hand. They bowed their heads and closed their eyes as Charles began to pray, "Lord, we can't thank you enough for the blessings you've given us..."

Susan kept her head bowed, but looked up at Charles. *I never saw Charles in a shirt that tight-fitting before. He's got some good-looking muscles. If I had known that before, that would've made it even harder for me to wait to have sex, I'll bet.*

"Amen," Charles concluded.

Oh, no! He was praying and I was thinking about sex! Lord, I'm sorry, I... "What are you grinning about?" Susan asked.

"We're married!" Charles replied grinning even more. "I can't get over it!"

Susan smiled as they both began to eat, and her mind wandered back to that morning. *We ate breakfast at this same table, and we were single then. Now we're married to each other! And we've had our first sex. Definitely the best sex I've ever had. And Charles said it was the best he's ever felt in his whole life. Wow! I really did that! Oh, thank you God, thank you so much!*

And Charles' love language is acts of service, so he may see my hard work at humping as an act of... uh-oh... I was going to try to learn to deep throat him, but that was before I knew he was so huge. There's no way I can do that. How am I going to be able to tell him? And anal sex would be even worse! And there's no way I can have sex in public, either, so... if he really misses those things from when Jennifer did them... hey, how could she do that stuff?! Well, maybe she was an exhibitionist, and that would explain the public-sex part, but how could any woman get a cock that big all the way in their mouth or up their butt? It's way too big! Could Charles have been exaggerating? Imagining it? Maybe he's bigger than he used to be? None of that seems likely... so... I just don't get it. Well, all I can do is hump him, so thank God he really likes how well I can do that. I'm going to start practicing my Kegel exercises every single time I pee so I can make my vaginal muscles as strong as possible. Oh, Lord, please help me keep Charles enjoying sex with me so he never regrets marrying me, or wishing Jennifer was still alive... Oh, I almost forgot... I can swirl my hips around in a circle. Marty used to like that, I bet Charles will, too.

Marty! Praise God, Charles and I are married, and Marty can never mess that up! Oh, God! Thank you, thank you, thank you! Oh, Lord, thank you! Oh-oh... is that okay, Lord, for me to be so happy that I'll never have to be married to Marty again?

"Susan, what's wrong?"

Susan looked at Charles and realized her vision was clouded by tears. "Oh, I'm sorry. I... I..."

She started to cover her face with her hands, and then quickly scooted out of her seat and scooted in beside Charles. "Put your arm around me," she begged as she buried her face in his chest.

"Honey, what is it? Why are you upset?"

"I'm upset because I'm so happy..."

Neither of them said anything, but Charles stroked his hand up and down Susan's back and kissed her hair.

"Uh, darling... I don't quite understand what you meant," Charles said quietly.

"Oh. Well... I don't think I've ever been this happy."

"Well, isn't that a good thing?"

"But I don't deserve to be. Stephanie is in just as much danger as she was before. And... and I feel guilty about... about being so happy that God let me marry you, and didn't make me marry Marty

259

again…"

Charles continued to stroke Susan's back, and after a minute he used his free hand to start eating again as Susan rested again him.

I hope you don't think I'm being silly. Come to think of it though, maybe I am being silly. I've been on an emotional roller-coaster ever since I lost my job, and especially the last few days. What with… Hey… Susan looked up. "Are you eating?"

"Uh, yeah," Charles replied sheepishly. "I was trying to think of something comforting to say, but I wasn't coming up with anything, and, uh… well, I'm *really* hungry, and this food is really good, so I thought I'd eat while I figured out what to say… Are you mad?"

Am I mad? You're comfortable with me… even when I'm silly. "No, Charles," she said as she planted a kiss on his cheek.

She giggled. "I think I'm insanely happy."

Charles hugged her, took another bite, and started moving his hand up and down her back again.

Susan looked down at his crotch. *So big. Wonderful for me, but too big for me to do the extra things you like. Hey, wait a minute…*

Susan abruptly sat up.

Charles reached over and pulled Susan's plate in front of her. "Eat," he said. "I plan to make you need your energy."

I knew I was forgetting something! You said your favorite kind of sex is licking your wife! Not all the rest of those things…

Susan took a big bite of her fish and started chewing quickly, glancing at Charles, then off into space. *Now I know I can hump you better than anyone else you've ever had, and if I can let you lick me as much as you want… that would give you your favorite kind of sex and a huge bonus. Maybe you won't miss those other kinds if I keep your mind on the things I can do! If… if I can get used to your tongue.*

She took another big bite. *I have to. It's your favorite thing. I'll do it no matter what it takes.*

Her chewing slowed down. *Well, is all I have to do is to lie there and let you lick me?*

Susan looked around. *It's around one thirty or two o'clock. Not many people around, and the background music is loud enough to drown out our talk if we're not too loud…* "Charles…" Susan whispered.

"Yes, honey?" Charles answered despite his mouth being full.

"What is it about licking pussies that you like so much? I know you said it was your favorite thing, but you didn't explain why."

Charles thought for a moment as he swallowed what he was chewing and then looked intently at Susan. "Well, I've enjoyed doing that with you so far, but I haven't really succeeded… I want you to have orgasms, if you can. And if you can, then I should be able to help you have them by licking you."

"But… if I have an orgasm, that doesn't satisfy your sex drive."

"No, but it satisfies something even more important to me."

What…?!

"There's nothing more satisfying tha…" Charles paused. "Well, let's just wait and…"

"Charles!" Susan leaned in to whisper emphatically. "What were you going to say? Tell me!"

Charles furrowed his brow. "Well, I don't want to pressure you…"

"Charles, we're married now. It's the first time either of us has been married since we became Christians, and I want you to be able to share any thoughts you have with me. The more intimate they are, the better."

"Even if they hurt your feelings?"

Susan thought that over before replying. "Yes, Charles, even then. I want to know everything you feel. Everything you believe. And I want you to keep sharing your past experiences with me, even if it's hard for me."

Charles nodded slowly. He put his fork down and turned more toward Susan, putting both arms around her. He closed his eyes and whispered into her ear. "Well, it took quite some time for Jennifer to get used to my tongue enough to have an orgasm that way, but once she did, it became her favorite way. The reason I liked it so much… it's just such an amazing thing… a way I can… could, do something that made her feel so good. I could caress her all over and end up rubbing my tongue on her clit and I could literally feel her whole body responding, first with a wonderful pleasure, but building up, not just constant. Building up and up, and I could feel her body changing and reacting the whole time. And I'd hear her, too. After a while, she'd feel so good, she'd let herself go over the edge into an orgasm, with all the typical things that means… waves of pleasure that overwhelm the brain, throbbing, muscles contracting all over, moaning out of control. It was something she loved, something deeply intimate that I could give her, something she wouldn't let anyone else in the whole world give her. I mean, I gave her lots of gifts over the years… you know, flowers, jewelry, things like that. But I'd enjoy giving her one orgasm more than all the material gifts put together. And we struggled a lot financially in the early years of growing my company, and I couldn't afford to give her a lot of things, but I could always give her myself in bed, and my tongue is the way I could best give her orgasms. She usually seemed to like it when I fu... humped her, but humping made *me* feel really good. Licking her was something I did just to make *her* feel good, so... I guess licking her made me feel like I was really doing something nice for her."

That acts-of-service thing again. You need to do something to show your love. And that was the way you liked to show Jennifer. That and the whole work-hard, earn-lots-of-money thing.

"Okay, I told you what I was thinking and I didn't hold anything back. But I'm worried now that you'll feel too much pressure to let me do that to you."

"Shut up and kiss me," Susan replied.

Charles looked surprised, but obliged with a long, deep, passionate kiss.

Oh, God, I can't believe what a wonderful man you've given me to. Oh, Charles, you're such a good kisser. Confident that it would be completely hidden from anyone else by the table, Susan moved a hand to his crotch and gently rubbed her hand over it. *Not too much while he's wearing these tight jeans... don't want to hurt him since he's got so little room to expand in there... and he's got so much to start with...*

Susan broke the kiss and cupped Charles' face in her hands. *I don't know if I can take it, but I so much want to make you happy, whatever that takes.* "I want your tongue on me again," she whispered. "You're so patient, and gentle, and loving, and kind. And I think I was starting to enjoy it the last time you were doing it."

"Do you want to finish eating?"

Susan struggled with the question. *I'm getting really horny, and I could feel you are too, but I'm also still hungry for food. And this is really good.* "How about if we finish our food, and then you can have me for dessert?"

"Okay," Charles said gladly as he forked up a bite of salmon and fed it to Susan. "But I thought you'd be concerned about what the other people in the restaurant would think."

Susan almost choked on her food as her eyes got as big as saucers.

"Just kidding!" Charles teased, "Just kidding!"

Oh, you jokester... you almost got me with that one.

"That's not the kind of thing I meant when I said Jennifer and I used to have public sex."

"Well... I didn't think so, but I wasn't sure what you did mean."

"That's something else we have to look forward to discussing," Charles said merrily before winking and taking another bite.

That sounds ominous, but... you've been saying you won't make me do anything I don't want to do. But public sex? Does everyone have something crazy about them? Is this your crazy thing? Maybe God gave me to you to restrain you from that particular craziness. But... what do you mean...? "Tell me now," Susan pleaded.

Charles looked like he had been waiting for her to say something. "Well, there's two different things that can mean... for me, anyway. Neither of them means actually being seen by other people, but one of them is where you can easily pretend that other people might catch you. That can add a little excitement... make things a little more fun. Like... what Jennifer and I used to do, is have sex somewhere outside the house. And not in a hotel room. We had sex in a car, for instance, when no one could see in through the windows. And on camping trips..."

"Oh, inside a tent?"

"Well, yes, we did have sex inside camping tents, but we also had sex a few times completely outdoors. In densely wooded places where we were sure no one could see us. That kind of overlaps with the second idea... being outdoors, but not pretending someone else might see us. Instead we pretended a kind of Garden-of-Eden, just-the-two-of-us alone in the world kind of fantasy."

Susan screwed up her face.

"Doesn't sound appealing to you?"

"No..." Susan whined. "I'm afraid I'd be too worried somebody might actually see us, no matter how careful we were."

"Then don't worry about it. If *you* don't like it, then *we* don't like it."

"Say that again?" Susan requested.

"If *you* don't like something, then *we* don't like it," Charles repeated.

"If *you* don't like it, then *we* don't like it," Susan repeated after him. "What a wonderful thing to say."

"God's made us one person now," Charles said. "We're a team."

Susan hugged him and growled. "You're making me hungry for our dessert." *I got the best team. I got the sexiest man. I got the most loving man. I got a real man of God.*

They both went back to their meals, as Susan thought to herself, *I used to fantasize about sex when I was young, about a guy just like Charles. Warm and loving, hung like a horse…*

She glanced at his crotch again and felt a familiar stirring within her getting stronger. Her mind pictured Charles sweeping the dishes off the table and throwing her onto the table, ripping her clothes off and humping her while other patrons in the restaurant looked shocked and fled the room. *Do it to me, Charles, fill my body with your body.* Then she pictured them in the woods, with Charles roaring like a lion as came inside her, and she felt a warmness spread throughout her body.

Oh, my! I… Susan giggled to herself. *I used to have sexual fantasies about a man like Charles, but now that I have the real thing, I'm still fantasizing! Or fantasizing again, I guess. I don't think I've had any sexual fantasies for years.*

She leaned against Charles as she ate. *You've woken up my sex appetite Charles. Boy, have you! I think I'm ready for another "ride" in the shower.*

"Hey, I just thought of something," Susan said quietly. "You said you get weak in the knees when I'm around, but your knees were awfully strong in the shower."

Charles swallowed and leaned close to her ear. "That's the difference between being *near* you and being *in* you."

"Oh! Is that it?!" Susan said, laughing.

"When I'm near you, I'm weak-kneed. When I'm in you, I feel stronger than ever."

And when you're in me, I feel more complete than ever…

They finally finished lunch and discreetly caressed each other behind Truck's back in the elevator. Truck pointed out that Mike wanted to talk to him, but Charles asked him to pass Mike the word that he'd call him later.

Once they were inside their suite's parlor they locked the door and Susan started to take off Charles' shirt, but he ran over to the curtains, running right over the cushions and pillows.

"What are you doing?" Susan called after him.

"Closing them. I don't want anything bothering your mind while I 'eat' my dessert."

"Oh, my!" Susan responded.

"Yes, *your…*" Charles laughed as he ran back to her and they raced to undress each other.

"We're worse than teenagers," Susan laughed as they hugged,

kissed, and caressed.

"Much worse," Charles concurred. "If I had married you instead of Jennifer when I was young, I'd have never built my own business."

"Why?" Susan asked, perplexed. "What do you mean?"

"I mean I could never have been away from the house long enough," Charles said as he lifted Susan way up. "And by away from the house, I mean out of the bedroom."

Susan wrapped her legs lightly around him.

As Charles lowered Susan onto himself, he added, "And by out of the bedroom, I mean I could never have been outside of your body long enough to hold a job, let alone run a business."

Susan reveled in silent joy as Charles carried her to the king-size bed and placed her in it.

Charles grabbed the bedside clock and turned it to face Susan. "Two-twenty-three," he announced. "I'm now going to eat my dessert, and I'm going to make it last as long as possible, okay?"

"As long as possible? Why?"

"Well, I want to see how long you can stand it. And I just want to relax and enjoy tasting you without worrying about having to quit soon. Okay?"

"Well, I'll try, but…"

Charles got beside her on his knees facing her feet and reached out to spread her legs.

"Remember, Charles, I still need you to be patient with me."

"Oh, I intend to be very, very patient," he said as he lowered his mouth to her crotch and started caressing her pubic hair with one of his hands.

Susan's breath was coming faster and faster as she tried to forestall a sense of panic. Charles slowly moved one of his legs across Susan's body so that he ended up with his cock nestled between her breasts and his head still over her crotch.

Oh, now that feels good with your cock between my… Oh! There goes your tongue! Maybe if I concentrate on my breathing like I did when I was having babies…

Susan's mind, however, began to recall a little earlier, when Charles shushed her and got down on his hands and knees to go out into the parlor and make the bed of cushions and pillows where they had their picnic. *Hmm. We didn't have much food, but we had lots of sex. So it was a sex picnic! Lots of long, slow, quiet sex. Wow, that was… really good. What a great idea to have long, slow sex! What a precious time that was. And we ate food while we humped! Who knew*

*that could be so fun! Hey, we must have dripped all over the pillows
and cushions, and I didn't even care. I didn't even notice! Wow.*

*And you ended up with your tongue on me then, too. And it was
so much nicer than the first time. But you didn't do anything
different, I don't think, so I guess I just got used to it that much. And
now you're "browsing in my garden" again. This feels... much better...
because you're facing the other direction? Nah... Am I just getting
used to it? Mm... maybe. Maybe because I'm less self-conscious. I
really believe now that you like to do this. That you like... how I
smell and how I taste. Wow, did God make you for me, or what?! And
maybe I'm able to relax more. Oh, yeah, I'm much more relaxed.
And... I like this! Oh, I do, I do, I really like this! And, you're
moaning! You're licking me and moaning again while you do it!*

Charles shifted more weight to his knees and started slowly
inching his cock up and down between Susan's breasts. His seminal
fluid was leaking onto her chest, allowing it to slide freely.

*Oh, yes, that feels very good. The way your waist is caressing my
boobs is so... so incredibly... good... feeling your rock-hard tree
trunk between them is so... so... I'm not going to have enough
adjectives, here, am I?*

*Uhng... oh, Charles... I think I'm starting a hot flash...
uhnngg... uuhhh... oh, but don't stop. Your tongue feels so good. It's
almost as good as... Oh, no! No... I couldn't possibly like this better
than feeling you inside me. But... uhnng... this is so... so...*

Susan's legs tensed, then relaxed, then tensed and relaxed again.
Oh... oh... uuhhhnn... She began to twist subtly beneath Charles'
heavy body. *It's... intense... but in a good way... a very... soothing...
kind of way... a warm way...*

"Uuhhhmmm..." Susan moaned aloud. "Ohhh... mmmm... oh,
Charles... Chaarrrllles... oh... oh... oh..."

Susan began panting and twisting more. *I don't know if I can
take much... more... of this... I want to make Charles happy... and
it's been so nice... but it's... too much...*

"Ohh! Charles!" *Stop! Stop now! Do less, or do nothing! I don't
want to ask you to stop, but I can't help it...*

"OOOOhhhhh... CHARrrlles...! Oohhh!" *Ung! Unhg! Ungh!
What was that... Charles said... about letting go...? "Jennifer felt so
good, after a while, she'd let herself go over the edge..." Oh, God, I
can't take this anymore... help me! Oh, God, help me...*

Charles was rocking his torso forcefully back and forth on top of
Susan as his tongue kept going and he put his hands under Susan's

butt cheeks and squeezed hard.

Susan screamed incoherently and without restraint as her body overrode conscious decisions. She felt a wave of intense pleasure flooding her body, and was vaguely aware that her body was repeatedly arching, hammering up against Charles. Wave after wave of ecstasy caused her to continue screaming as she writhed violently.

Her body shuddered and went limp except for desperate, involuntary gasping for air. A moment later, more convulsions racked her body as yet another wave of white-hot pleasure hit her and she screamed again.

Again, Susan shuddered and went limp, still gasping for each breath of air. Less intense tremors continued off and on as Susan gasped, panted, and she began to regain her reasoning.

Charles was no longer using his tongue on her, and he felt very heavy on top of her. His whole body was also limp and he was panting as heavily as she was. *Could... breathe... easier... without... you on... top...* she thought, too tired to vocalize the words.

She pushed gently at Charles' body, and he flinched, and then slowly slid off to Susan's left side, but holding her very tightly. *Much... better... to breathe...*

Susan continued to pant as she lifted a hand and put it down on Charles' side. *What... what... was that...? What... how... did that... how in the world...*

Susan put her other hand on her chest as she continued to pant. *Chest... heaving... huh... so wet... didn't think we were sweating that much...* Susan struggled to lift her head to see if she was bleeding from her chest somewhere.

No blood... is this... it's sticky... did Charles...?

Susan slowly scooted a little toward the edge of the bed, rested a minute, scooted the rest of the way, then rested again at the edge. Then she slowly stood up, still panting heavily. Her legs were wobbly and she stepped over to the end table and held onto the lamp.

Her thinking still fuzzy, she looked at Charles. *Eyes closed. But he's breathing. He's okay. He's tired.*

Her attention shifted to the wetness running down her abdomen, and she looked at it again. *Cum. Charles came on me. Did he knock me out? Did... Oh, MY! NO! I was awake. I was screaming... I was... I had... an orgasm? Was that an orgasm?*

Susan's legs started wobbling more. *Was that...? It was! It had to be! It was just like it was described in the book. I had... but how...*

Susan looked at the semen again, and then at Charles, just as he opened his eyes.

Charles crawled over to the edge of the bed with great effort, and sat up on the edge, pulling Susan to him. He held her for a moment, and then they both fell backward onto the bed.

For a long time, they just held each other and panted until they both began to get their breathing back under control. They crawled further onto the bed so that their legs were also up on it.

"You... you're the sexist woman ever born. I've never... no one has ever..." Charles groaned. "You said I was your Adam. Well, that makes you Eve... and you're the best sex partner God ever made."

Oh, Charles...! Oh, my love... Susan moved her hand and took hold of Charles' hand. "Oh, Charles... we did it! You gave me my first orgasm! The first one in my whole life, and you did it. I doubt anyone else could have. It had to be you. Only you."

"And on our honeymoon. Wow. It took weeks for Jennifer to... oh, and wow, Susan, I don't think Jennifer was ever so... she... you... you were so wild..."

I had a better orgasm than Jennifer? That's another point for me! Susan laughed. "Hey, did you know you came on me?"

"Did I know?! Did I know...?! Oh, I knew, all right! Susan, you've given me four orgasms today. I expected to have one, maybe two since we were starting so early in the day. And each one... each one was better than any I can ever remember from before we got married. I wouldn't have even thought I was capable of that, but you... you're like the key to my lock. You're the perfect combination to rock my body off its hinges."

Susan giggled. "You're mixing metaphors. And I think you're the key and I'm the lock. You put a key inside the lock, right?"

Charles smiled. "After what you've done to me today, it's a wonder I'm able to do anything other than drool."

Susan laughed, and then got serious. "So, is that what you were talking about? Is that what you used to like to do with Jennifer?"

"Mmm... yes and no. Yes, that's what I used to do with Jennifer and that's what I was referring to as my favorite kind of sexual activity. No, because... because... you're so... you're..."

"What?! What?!" Susan urged him to complete his thoughts.

"It's like Jennifer was an amateur, and you're an expert."

Susan eyes lit up. She sat up.

"There's never been another woman even half as good at sex as you are," Charles added earnestly.

Susan launched herself at Charles, landing on top of him, and they rolled over. They rolled a little too far, and they tottered on the foot of the bed before rolling onto the floor. They managed to get enough hands and feet down first to avoid injury, and they laughed and kissed and hugged.

They finally got to their feet and Susan giggled.

"What?" Charles asked. "Did I do something funny?"

"You called me an expert at sex," Susan replied.

"Yeah, so?"

Susan laughed. "I'm glad you didn't call me a professional!"

Charles laughed enthusiastically until Susan grabbed him in a waltzing stance and looked into his eyes. Instead of starting to dance, he pulled her running into the parlor and turned on the radio and they both listened just long enough to recognize that the classical number that was playing wasn't very suitable for waltzing.

"Let put up the cushions and pillows while we wait for a better song!" Susan said as she set about the task and Charles joined in. "Make sure you look for wet spots."

Charles pointed to Susan's stomach, and she laughed. She pointed back. "Well, half of it's on you!"

Susan paused for a moment.

"Whatcha thinkin?" Charles inquired as he checked another pillow.

"How I've changed. How you've changed me. How different I am with you. I'm waltzing around... not literally, at the moment, not yet... but I'm waltzing around stark naked, and I'm not even self-conscious about it. I've even got cum drying all over me, and... it not only doesn't bother me... I'm happy! I'm a happy, sex-crazed Eve, on her star-struck honeymoon with her passionate, tender Adam with the world's largest..." she lowered her voice, "cock."

Charles dropped the pillow and took her into his arms. A waltz began on the radio, and they started dancing as if they were born in step with each other.

"It's probably not the world's biggest," Charles noted.

"Hmm..." Susan smiled. "You, Charles, have the world's most perfect cock for Mrs. Susan Parker."

Charles swung through a few steps a little ahead of the music and surprised her with a seductive dip. "Custom made, specifically for Mrs. Susan Parker's perfect pussy."

Susan giggled. "And my chest, apparently."

"And your perfect chest," Charles added as he lifted her back up and started dancing again.

You like my breasts, too? Oh... that makes me so happy... or even happier, I guess I should say...

Charles stopped dancing, and leaned in to kiss Susan, but they were right in front of the seam in the curtains, and Susan abruptly turned and poked her head through them, holding them closed below her face and wiggling her rear end.

"What are you doing?" Charles asked.

"I'm looking at the entire city of Knoxville while I'm naked!"

Charles stood behind her and reached around. He grabbed the edges of the curtains at her waist level and jerked them up and to the side, then jerked them back down.

Susan squealed as she turned around to face Charles, "What did you do that for?!"

"I thought I'd tease you back and give myself a secret to hold over you."

"What secret?"

"That you, my darling, have flashed the entire city of Knoxville."

"You're going to pay for that, my husband."

"I'm looking forward to making many payments on an installment plan with the highest interest rates, oh most beautiful one," he said as he held her tight and kissed her.

Oh most beautiful one? Oh... my...

Charles froze.

"What is it?" Susan asked.

"Your phone!" Charles said, rushing to the bedroom. "Even with the door open, we might not hear it over the radio."

He fetched both their phones and put them down on the coffee table. "And that reminds me, I was wondering... what if Stephanie can't pay her phone bill? How about if we offer to put her phone on our account. Oh, and we can merge our bank accounts, yours and mine, if that's okay with you."

"Oh... sure, I guess so," Susan answered, having resumed the cushion and pillow cleanup. *Back to reality, and what Charles was saying about God's grace. I certainly don't deserve Charles, or even Stephanie. Charles just showed more concern for Stephanie than I had. And after I had already forgotten my phone once today. I should have learned my lesson, but I was too distracted by... my sexy new husband... You hear that God? It's the man's fault!*

Susan laughed to herself as she continued her mental play on the words in Genesis. *It's Adam's fault! And it's your fault, for giving me the man! Oh, but what a man you gave me...! Oh, but Paul warned Timothy about men who took control over "weak-willed women, who were loaded down with sins and swayed by evil desires..." Oh, Lord, that's not me is it? Because I've been so horny with my new husband I've forgotten the danger my daughter is in? And the danger Charles and I may be in, because of her boyfriend? That awful Billy? Billy... have we prayed, really prayed for him? Should we...? All I've cared about is Stephanie, but... I guess you care about everyone, right, Lord? Even the worst of us?*

"Whatcha thinkin now?" Charles asked.

"Oh," Susan reacted, realizing she had just been standing there holding a pillow. She looked around and noticed that Charles had finished putting everything else away. "Would you be willing to pray with me for Billy?"

Charles gave a little nod. "Of course."

"I've just... I feel like we should have been praying for him, too," Susan explained, "and... well, I think we should now."

"Okay," Charles nodded.

They sat on the sofa and began praying quietly, but became more and more earnest as they got into it. After a while, they both felt prayed-out, and sat back on the sofa.

"Wow," Susan said. "I'm sitting on the sofa naked. In the living room. I don't think I've ever been naked in a living room before. Before today, I mean." An image of the room full of wedding guests just a few hours ago flashed through her mind.

Charles pointed toward the place on the floor where their pallet had been. "You were definitely very naked on the living room floor."

Susan threw an elbow lightly into Charles' side.

"Very naked, and very beautiful. Naked, beautiful, and... delicious," Charles added as he turned and began to caress Susan's breasts.

"All right lover-boy," she said, getting up and picking up their phones, "how about we go wash your stuff off of us?"

"That, or we could put more of it on us," Charles suggested as he rose and followed her into the bedroom.

"More?!"

"Well, I don't know if I could put out any more stuff today, but if it's possible, you're the one who could get it out of me."

"Charles Parker... hey," Susan interrupted her own train of thought on the way to the shower. "I know! Let's shower off real quick and then try out the Jacuzzi!"

Charles laughed. "Well, we can try, but so far we haven't

mastered the real-quick aspect of showering."

"That was all your fault. I was just telling God a little while ago, that me being so distracted was all your fault."

"Me?! You're the one who did all the wild... hey... I was just wondering... do you have any *more* wild sexual tricks up your, uh, sleeve?"

"Up my sleeve?"

"Your, uh, metaphorical sleeve," he elaborated.

Well, I haven't swirled my hips while I'm riding him yet...

"Yeah, I have one more little trick. But you'll have to wait..."

Charles snuck a hand between her legs and teased her. "Oh, yeah?"

"Woo-ooo!" Susan squealed again, trying to twist away from his hand. "Be-have yourself!"

Charles laughed, "We're married! This is behaving myself!"

A half-hour later, Charles and Susan were relaxing in the Jacuzzi, still naked, with a half-empty bottle of wine.

"This should be ground-hog day," Charles commented.

"What do you mean? Oh, like in the movie?"

"Yeah. There's no way this day could have been better. It's been perfect. If we were going to do one day over and over, this should be it."

"Says the man who's had four orgasms today," Susan teased. "So far."

"So far? Oh, girl, are you trying to go after my life insurance? And look who's talking... says the woman who had her first orgasm at, what, fifty-six years old, and it was so big it set of seismic monitors in China?"

"Oh, no! I wonder if Truck heard us again?"

"Truck? Honey, the kitchen staff heard you on the first floor. I've never heard anyone scream that loud before."

Susan covered her face with both hands. "I can never leave this room again!"

"Oh, that reminds me, I need to call Mike about us moving tomorrow." Charles picked up his cell phone and called Mike.

"Hey, Mike, sorry to... oh, sure... thanks... yeah, that'll be fine." Charles laughed. "Mike, we won't care where we are... yeah... oh? Okay, thanks, I'll tell her... yeah, see you in the morning."

"You'll tell her what?" Susan asked.

"Lisa and Darlene left a box for you. Truck has it outside in the hallway whenever you want to..."

Susan jumped up and started toweling off.

"...get it." Charles finished with a laugh. "What's in it?"

"I don't know, they didn't tell me they were going to drop anything off. That's why I have to hurry! If I knew what it was, I probably wouldn't mind waiting, but not knowing will drive me nuts."

Charles started to get up.

"You can stay here," Susan said, putting on a plush suite robe. "I'll be right back with it."

"Okay," Charles said agreeably.

A minute later, Susan came skipping back into the bathroom. "Lingerie!" She announced. "And a card. Lisa, Darlene, and Sandy went shopping for me. Lisa said she got my sizes off my clothes."

The top was already off as she set the box down near the tub and picked up a bustier on top and held it up to model it.

"Uhn-uh!" Charles objected, "Take off the robe and stop spoiling my view!"

Susan smiled and hung up the robe and held up the bustier in front of her again.

Charles' eyes grew wider, he gave a low whistle, and those weren't his only physical reactions.

"Oh, you like this, I see," she said as she swiveled side to side a bit.

She put the bustier down and picked up the next item. "A swimsuit! You know, I don't think I even owned a swimsuit anymore. You think they'll have a pool wherever we're going tomorrow?"

"Gatlinburg," Charles replied. "Surely they will."

Susan got out another item and was puzzled a moment. "What is..." she started to ask, then gasped. "Is this a..."

"Bikini," Charles confirmed.

"But... but..."

"'Butt' is right, that's a thong bottom," Charles finished for her.

Susan looked shocked. "I can't wear this!"

Charles looked unperturbed. "You could in private. Like now," he said with a smile.

Susan looked unconvinced. "Well, I'm surprised at Lisa. I would have thought she'd realize I have more conservative tastes."

Charles raised his eyebrows. "Uh, honey, I don't know Lisa or Sandy, but I know Darlene pretty well, and I'd bet anything that it was Darlene who picked out the bikini for you."

Susan's jaw dropped. "Darlene! Are you serious?!" She looked at the skimpy cloth in disbelief.

"I haven't seen her in anything like that, mind you, but from what Nat's told me in the past, Darlene is quite the daredevil in the bedroom or anywhere that's private enough."

"But… this is supposed to be a swimsuit!"

"They have a swimming pool in their back yard. And a privacy fence. Nat once told me that she'd swim nude back there except that her thong suit gets him more excited than her just being nude. She wears it for him."

Susan stared at Charles. "Are you saying… would you like *me* to wear something like this?"

"Well, yeah… especially if you're going to get back in the Jacuzzi and snuggle…"

Well, just in a private situation like this… I guess it's okay… Susan looked it over again. "I think it's too small, though."

"I bet it will stretch."

"It'd have to stretch an awful lot."

Charles shrugged.

You're acting as if you don't care, leaving it up to me, but your lower half clearly says otherwise. Susan started walking away, carrying the suit.

"Hey, where are you going?"

"I'm going to try it on," Susan answered.

"Well, why do you have to leave to try it on?"

"Because… I don't know, I just do." Susan looked over her shoulder and Charles was staring after her. *With all the sex we've had today, and you're still excited about me trying to put on a piece of cloth that hardly covers anything. I don't see what the fascination is.*

Susan stepped into the shower stall, out of Charles' sight, and put on the suit. It stretched enough, and wasn't too tight, but the top barely covered her areolas, and very little of her pubic hair was covered by the thong. She stuck her head out of the shower stall and saw that Charles had turned around in the tub so that he was facing her direction. He looked intent.

"Stay there," Susan requested. "I'll be a few more minutes."

"What? No! That's not fair! Why?!"

"I just will, that's all," Susan said. She pulled off the thong, started one of the shower heads and started shaving. *Oh, I hate shaving down here. It will bother me for days when it starts getting stubbly, and it will be itchy for a long time after that. If I had scissors, I'd try just cutting it real short, but I doubt there's a pair anywhere around here.*

She finished up and pulled on the thong again. *Oh, I feel so... embarrassed... I've never worn anything like this...*

Susan poked her head out of the shower, and Charles was still anxiously waiting. "Are you ready?"

"Yes, yes! Please...!"

Susan opened the shower door wide, glanced out one more time and took a deep breath before stepping out and facing Charles. Her head was tilted down in demur insecurity.

Charles' mouth fell open as he stared at her.

"Do... you like it?" Susan asked with great apprehension.

Charles slowly rose until he was standing, and his cock was pointing almost straight up, throbbing with his heartbeat. "Susan... Susan...!"

Wow, you really are excited. You really like the way I look. I mean, you physically *like the way I look...*

Susan was caught by surprise as Charles let out a roar and surged out of the Jacuzzi, ran to her, and took her in his arms. He carried her back to the tub and climbed in, and they had passionate sex yet again. With her suit still on, Charles pulled the stretchy thong off to the side to gain access to her, and pulled aside what passed for the top's tiny cups to put his mouth on her breasts while they humped.

A few minutes later Charles had yet another orgasm, and even after he was too soft to stay inside her, they cuddled and petted each other intimately, occasionally changing positions. After a while he began to get hard again, which didn't go unnoticed.

"So, you do like this suit on me?" she teased.

Charles growled in response and eased into her again, and they both just relaxed in their embrace.

Well, if Darlene gets this kind of reaction out of Nat, I can see why she'd want to wear something like this for him. She adjusted the top to cover her nipples again, since Charles seemed to be through sucking on them for a while, and then pressed herself against his chest again.

Charles responded with more kissing, gentle, tender, and sensuous.

All that time I spent worrying about whether or not I'd be good enough in bed... she giggled to herself *...or wherever... Oh, Lord, thank you! Thank you for letting me be good at sex for Charles...*

"The best sex partner God ever made," he said! And... thank you for...

letting me... you know... feel so good myself. Oh, God, and thank you that my first time was with Charles, on the day we got married. Thank you for making Charles for me, and making me for him. Oh, Lord, he's such perfect man. For me... he's so perfect.

Chapter Sixteen

Susan and Charles eventually got out of the Jacuzzi and took their cell phones with them to the bedroom, and Charles relaxed on the bed as Susan looked through the other lingerie. Susan was still wearing her bikini, and Charles was still in the buff.

Susan cast a glance as surreptitiously as possible at Charles' crotch. *I think you're as big when you're limp as Marty was when he was hard... Ooo... focus on the clothes, Susan, focus on the clothes...*

She held up a lacy white teddy with red and purple ribbons and a split-crotch. *Uh... thinking about these clothes isn't going to help me avoid getting all worked up again...*

Susan next held up a fish-net body stocking. *Wow. This got his eyebrows raised and some signs of life from his pecker. Guess I'll wear this tomorrow. I can't expect Charles to be able to stay hard indefinitely, but he sure has surprised me so far...*

Lastly she held up a matching lace bra and panty set, and she showed Charles that the panty had a split-crotch.

"They sure did give you a lot of things," Charles observed. "I'll bet most of them came from Darlene. She'd be likely to go overboard in that area. Not that I'm complaining, mind you!"

"Me either. But you have to wait to see me wearing them. No more than one per day, to make the fun last as long as possible."

"Sounds great to me!" Charles readily agreed.

"Hey... there's something else at the bottom..." she said as she picked up a bottle. "Oh, lubricant! I'll bet that was from Darlene also. She'd know that older women can... what...? It says it's flavored. Why would..."

Susan sucked in her breath and clutched the bottle to her as Charles laughed.

"Well, honey," Charles ventured, "that can work several ways, on me or you, wherever a tongue might go."

Charles started moving across the bed toward Susan. "Are you ready for me to..."

"No!" Susan almost shouted. "I mean, I did like it. Oh, I can't describe how much I liked it. But I... I don't think I could handle that again so soon." *Just because you can do it... five times today... so far... good heavens... it doesn't mean I can...* "I think I need more time than you do, to... you know, recover." *A lot more time.*

"That doesn't surprise me. You may be different from Jennifer in this regard, but she usually liked it best about 3 or 4 days apart. And you shouldn't expect every orgasm you have to be as intense as the one you had today. For one thing, you weren't used to it, and for another thing, you had a whole lot of sexual tension building up over the last few days."

Oh, boy, did I! Susan thought, as she remembered how wild she was on the cabin cruiser. She nodded and picked up the last item in the box, another bottle. "I'm glad you understand, and don't mind..."

She frowned as she read the label. "Numbing agent... why would anyone want a numbing agent to have sex. I thought everything was about making things more stimulating, not less."

"Uh, well, we don't have to use that," Charles said. "Don't worry about it."

Susan studied Charles a moment. "There you go again. You're not telling me something."

Charles sighed. "Any chance you'd just take my word for it, to just forget about that?"

"But Charles... of course, I trust you, but I don't understand. Why would you not want to tell me whatever it is you're thinking?"

"Because I'm worried that it'll make you worry. Or something."

Susan looked askance. "Okay, now you *have* to explain it to me," she insisted.

Charles gave a weak smile and nodded. "Yeah, you need to understand things. I'm starting to get that. I have a tendency to want to hide things to try to protect you from them, but you do better when everything is out in the open, even if it scares you."

He scooted to the edge of the bed and Susan offered him the bottle, but he declined with a shake of his head. "I recognize the bottle. Same kind Jennifer used to have. It's for oral sex. For numbing the back of the throat."

It took just a moment longer for the significance to sink into Susan's mind. "Oh! Oh, my! Oh... Charles..."

Susan sank onto the edge of the bed beside him. "Charles, I'd rather do anything than disappoint you, but... Charles... your cock is huge! I mean, I love it, I love how big it is, and how wonderful it feels inside me, but... it's much, much bigger than my throat. And even more bigger than my... well, 'more bigger' doesn't sound right, but..." She lowered her voice. "You're way too big for my butt hole, too."

"Hey, see all that frowning you're doing?" Charles said. "That's what I didn't want. Honey, we don't ever have to do those things. And I promise I won't be disappointed... I wouldn't have been disappointed about that, because I actually kind of expected that you might not be interested in those things. After Laura, I figured that maybe Jennifer had just been really unusual. So I never expected you to do those things."

Yeah, but how could...

Charles laughed. "And that's before I found out you're a world-class sexual athlete with your own special treats... hey, what about that other trick you said you have..."

Oh... "Well, don't expect too much. You may not get as much out of it as the other things."

"Well, what is it?" Charles begged.

"You'll have to wait," Susan said firmly.

"Ohhh...!" Charles wailed impatiently, then stopped abruptly. "Hey, what are you thinking? You've got that puzzled look again."

"Well... oh, now I'm afraid to tell you something I'm thinking. I don't want to get your hopes up for something I can't deliver." *Okay, you're just waiting for me to explain. I didn't let you out of telling me, so I guess I have to treat you the same way...* "Well, I was just wondering how Jennifer could do those things. Maybe she was different from me... but I don't see how her throat or butt-hole could have been big enough for your... Adam-sized cock."

"Oh, well, I never considered that before," Charles replied thoughtfully. "As far as I know, she just took a long time working at it and finally got comfortable with them both. I probably pressured her into anal sex, and I know she didn't like it for a long time, but she'd let me do it once in a while, and eventually it got to where she didn't seem to mind it. As far as oral sex, she never could take me in very far until after she started using that numbing stuff, and even then, it was a long time before she got used to it. Once she got used to that, though, she seemed to really enjoy it, as long as I didn't get carried away and I let her control it."

Susan looked at the bottle in her hands. "This stuff won't make my throat any bigger though."

Charles lifted it away from her and tossed it into the box. "Let's get something straight. I didn't want to marry Jennifer again. I want you. Even if we could never have sex again in any way, shape, or form, I would still want to spend the rest of my life with you."

They embraced, and Susan felt warm where her breasts pressed into him. *"Even if we couldn't have sex again, you'd still want to spend the rest of your life with me!" Oh, Charles... you're so... loving... and understanding... so considerate...*

"I do hope we can always at least hug," Charles said.

"I second the motion," Susan agreed. *Although I hope we can always do a lot more than that.*

"Hey," said Charles, "Want to watch a movie? With this huge TV, it'd be almost like being in a private theater."

"Very private," Susan said as she gently fondled her husband. "We wouldn't even have to wear clothes." *Listen to me, I'm not even horny any more, but I'm still talking like a sex-crazed maniac.*

"Suits me," Charles agreed. "Or rather, unsuits us. De-suits us? Non-suits? Well, that didn't work. I was trying to make a joke about us being in our birthday suits."

"Maybe you should stick to car jokes," Susan said with a grin.

"Hmph," Charles huffed. "Okay, then, how about a drive-in movie, and we'll neck in the back seat? We'll have to use your car, since mine doesn't have a back seat... and we'll have to be real quiet so the bodyguards in the front seat don't hear us."

"Oh, Charles! Don't tease me about how loud we've been... I'm already embarrassed enough about that." Susan put her hands up to hide her face, and the tenderness reminded her of her bruises. *Oh, and I'd rather not leave the hotel without putting on a ton of makeup again.*

"I see... so as long as we're quiet, you don't mind having sex in front of the guards?" he replied with a wink. "I think I'll get a soda. You want one?"

"Sure. Uh, that 'sure' was for the soda, not on the sex in front of other people... just to be clear."

"Got it. No sex in front of other people," Charles said as he looked at the choices in the little mini-bar. "Only behind other people."

Susan grabbed the closest pillow and threw it at him.

"Why don't you see what movies are on pay-per-view?" Charles suggested.

Susan turned her attention to the TV remote and started looking at the upcoming free movies. "What kind of movie?"

"Well, since it's our honeymoon, how about a romantic comedy of some kind?"

"Okay," she agreed as she searched.

"Popcorn?"

"Yes, that sounds good," she agreed. *A movie, popcorn...* "Hey, do they have any chocolate in there?"

"Mmm... yeah, several candy bars. What's your favorite kind?"

"I don't really have a favorite candy bar. Just pick one for me," Susan said as she continued scanning the movie list. "Do you have a favorite kind of candy bar?"

"Nah. Not really."

"Oh, 'Pretty Woman' is coming on regular TV in... about thirty minutes. Want to watch that again?"

"Again?" Charles looked puzzled. "Honey, we've never seen any movie together. Too short of a courtship..."

"Well, I didn't mean see it again together. Well, that is... I mean... you know what I mean, we'll be together and we'll each see it again."

"You'll see it again, maybe. I'll just see it."

"You mean you've never seen 'Pretty Woman'?"

"Unh-uh," Charles affirmed.

Susan stared at him. "The most famous romantic comedy of all time? You've never seen it?"

"I've never been much a TV or movie person. Too busy."

"Well, I'm going to call the newspaper. They'll want to know that the last person in the world not to see 'Pretty Woman' is about to see it."

"Uh-huh. Make sure they spell my name right."

"Oh, and 'You've Got Mail' is coming on after that," Susan stated, looking at Charles carefully to see his reaction.

"'You've Got Mail,'" he reiterated. "A modern remake of 'The Shop Around The Corner.'"

"So you've seen that one, huh?" she asked.

"Nope. Heard about it though. I think I saw the original on TV when I was a kid."

"Wow. Maybe it would be faster if you just tell me which movies you *have* seen before."

"'Ground Hog Day,' 'Shop Around The Corner'... 'The Jungle Book'... 'Cool Hand Luke'..."

"'Cool Hand Luke'?" Susan prompted with a puzzled expression.

"Paul Newman? George Kennedy? Paul's character, Luke Jackson, a war hero, can't adapt to normal life, and struggles in a chain-gang prison system?"

"A prison movie? Blah."

"It's not a prison movie, it's a character movie with a chain-gang setting," Charles corrected. "Oh, and I used to watch 'Man From U.N.C.L.E.' on TV."

"Oh, I *loved* that show. Actually, I loved Illya Kuryakin. No, I loved David McCallum, who played Illya." Susan sighed wistfully as she continued to look at the on-screen movie guide.

"I thought it might have been Mr. Waverly that did it for you, since you obviously like older men."

Susan laughed as she tossed the remote onto the bed, took her soda from Charles, put it down, and hugged him. "I think there was a little more than a five-year age difference between me and Mr. Waverly. And I only liked David McCallum because you and I hadn't met yet. I only ever liked anyone else because you and I hadn't met yet."

"You like a hint of danger in your men, though?" Charles suggested. "I could tell you I'm actually a retired spy, and my automotive company was just a front."

"Oh, I already know about your secretive past," Susan said, "and I've already discovered your biggest secret."

"Oh, you have, have you? And what might that be?"

Susan looked up at Charles and brought her lips close to his as she cupped one hand around his privates and softly squeezed. "To keep something this big so well hidden, you're obviously a master spy. And I'm going to seduce you into telling me all your spy secrets, no matter how many years and no matter how much bedroom activity it takes."

"Oh, wow. Well, you're off to a great start. You and your irresistible smile," he said as he closed the gap between their lips.

Oh... "irresistible smile"... I reeeally like that... Susan thought as she put her hands behind his neck and laced her fingers. *You're such a great kisser...*

Their tongues played with each other and Susan poked hers further into Charles' mouth and was startled when he gently sucked on it as he teased it with his tongue.

Oh, my... that's... erotic. That could get me horny again if I weren't already so satisfied. I wonder...

Susan withdrew her tongue, and as she hoped, Charles pushed his tongue a little into her mouth, and she began to suck on it as he had done to her. Charles moaned in response.

Ooo, that's different... hearing, or rather hearing and feeling Charles moan while he's in my mouth... and is... oh, my goodness, he is! He's getting hard again!

Charles broke their kiss. "Hey, honey, I'd like to do some more of that," he nodded down toward his lower extremities, "I guess it's obvious to you when I find something arousing like that... but I need to use the bathroom."

"Oh, okay, sure," Susan said and let him go.

"I, uh, I'll be a few minutes this time," he called after himself.

"Okay," she called after him.

Hmm... Susan picked up the pillow she had thrown at him and put it back on the bed. *Let's see, the chairs in here don't recline, so we could lie on the bed as we watch... I'll get the pillows from the other beds so we'll have more propping up choices.*

I'll have to make sure I remember that trick of sucking on his tongue. That certainly got a rise out of him, even after all he's already done today, she thought as she went into the other bedroom to gather the pillows. *Hmm... a big reaction to having part of him in my mouth...*

Susan sighed. *Well, I can't get his whole package in my mouth, but I can get the head in and touch those two spots the book says are most sensitive. I hope he doesn't get too excited from that though, I hated the taste of cum when Marty used to force me that way. Hey, wasn't there something in Grandma's Handbook about that...?*

She put the extra pillows on the bed and got the handbook as she waited for Charles and flipped to the table of contents. *Yeah... there it is, under Great Sex, Devoted Sex, Deep-Throating. Oh, Lord, please... I can give Charles devoted sex without deep-throating him, can't I? Guess I need to read the whole chapter, but I just want to see this part for now... it's only a couple of pages...*

Susan read through the material quickly, but it did nothing to reassure her. *I don't get it... They talk like any woman can deep-throat any man if they just practice long enough and overcome their gag reflex. And I'm definitely not one of the women without a gag reflex, but they don't talk about a man with a tree-trunk thick cock. That thing would make it impossible to breathe... oh, but they imply that's normal... that's why the woman should be in control during... Hey...! When Marty used to force himself into my mouth... there were times when I couldn't breathe. My memory was focused on all the awful gagging and choking... but there were also the parts when I couldn't breathe... that's why I thought he was going to kill me that way...*

Susan began to weep quietly. *But... if he was in so far that I couldn't breathe... then was I deep-throating him...? He was much shorter than Charles, and not as thick... at least if my memory isn't letting me down completely, but it's been... coming up on twenty years... but that was always so awful... terrifying... Oh, Charles, I hope you really meant it when you said you won't mind if I don't do that... well, I'm sure you meant it... but what if... what if you change your mind? What if your desire for that goes up? Oh... you liked me sucking on your tongue so much! That might... that might make you want deep-throat sex more! Oh, Lord, help! I'm afraid! Even after all his reassurances... after all, he's all about acts-of-service, and...*

"Hey, pretty woman, reading some more about sex before the movie?" Charles had walked up behind her and was standing right next to her.

Susan snapped the book shut in embarrassment. "You startled me..."

"Oh, sorry. Didn't mean to," he apologized as he turned and headed toward the microwave. "Anyway, it's time to get ready for the movie. I'll pop the popcorn."

Oh, I hope you didn't notice what I was reading and think I want to try that! Oohh... now I feel guilty for not even wanting to try it.

Susan sighed as they got settled on the bed and snuggled as they ate the popcorn. They occasionally discussed parts of the movie, mostly during the commercials, which for the most part consisted of Susan explaining things and expressing her opinion.

Hmm... I wonder how well I would have survived as a prostitute? Not well, I'll bet. If I hadn't been a Christian and I had tried it after I lost my job... fifty-six years old... gray hair... Charles may admire me, but that doesn't mean anyone else would have...

They watched the scene where Edward and Vivian negotiate a fee for Vivian's services for the week, and Susan looked brightly at Charles. "How much would you have paid me?" *...okay, so I'm brazenly fishing for a compliment... you'd better say you'd pay a lot, Charles...*

"All my heart," Charles responded with a penetrating gaze.

"Oh, wow... you're *good...*!" Susan enthused. "They should have gotten you for Edward's role."

"Only if you played Vivian."

Susan smiled and settled back down against him.

Charles discovered that the TV system would allow them to pause, and after Pretty Woman ended with Edward "rescuing" Vivian on the fire escape, Charles paused it as soon as the credits started rolling.

"Bathroom break," Susan said as she kissed Charles' chest and got up.

"Want to get dinner before we watch 'You've Got Mail'? Charles inquired.

Susan paused before turning into the bathroom. "Sure, that sounds good. Downstairs, or room-service?"

"Well, how about…"

"Ooo! How would you like pizza?" Susan asked.

Charles nodded as he got up and stretched. "That'd be nice. I rarely eat it anymore… I try to avoid cheese as one of the ways I try to keep my belly at bay, but on few special occasions, I still like it as much as ever. And this is the most special occasion imaginable… what would you like on it?"

"Pepperoni, hamburger, and pineapple. I know most people don't like pineapple, so we could get a half-and-half so you can have whatever you like."

"I can handle pineapple. Want anything else?"

"Another soda, please, caffeine-free, diet," Susan said as she disappeared into the bathroom. *Ooo… Kegel exercises…* she remembered, and once she started peeing, she used her muscles to force it to stop, despite how awkward it felt at first. Once it was stopped, she relaxed the muscles to let it start flowing again, and then stopped it again. By the time she finished, she had regained easy control over those muscles and felt comfortable with it again after so many years of not doing those exercises.

When she came back, Charles was dressed in his jeans and pullover again.

"Got to answer the door when they bring the pizza," Charles explained, "but you can stay in here so you don't have to get dressed."

"Ah, well, if you're planning to keep me barefoot and pregnant, I can think of a problem with that."

"Okay, fine. I'll let you wear shoes sometimes."

Susan laughed, "I think I'm really going to like your sense of humor, Mr. Parker."

"Put that in writing," Charles responded.

Charles excused himself to pee, and Susan laid back down on the bed, sweeping her arms and legs slowly back and forth, luxuriating in the moment.

My knight on a white horse said I'm the best sex partner God ever made! And he said there's never been another woman as good at sex as me... ooo, and he said my chest is perfect! Her mind recalled Charles' patient and tender suckling on her breasts, and how he had stroked and massaged them at times. *Mmm... so happy... and it's all happened so fast, it's hard to believe how God has poured out his blessings on me...*

But God, I want you to bless Stephanie... I'd give up everything, even Charles, for her sake. I have you, Lord, and so does Charles, but she doesn't. She needs you to touch her heart, and heal her hurts... Susan continued to pray for Stephanie until Charles returned, and then she started to get up. "If you don't mind, I think I'll get dressed for a while. I've never been naked, or as-good-as-naked, this long before, and I'm starting to get a little uncomfortable with it."

"No, I don't mind. Well, I'll only mind a little bit," he corrected himself with a smile.

Okay, I'll put my jeans on again, but should I change into regular underwear, or keep the bikini on underneath? I'll bet this thong would feel weird under jeans, so I'll go for the regular things. I suppose I might as well change in here... you've already seen everyth... seen...? You've done a lot more than see everything... boy, have you done more... "Oh, are you going to start reading Grandma's Sex Handbook?" Susan asked as she took fresh panties and a bra from the chest of drawers and started changing.

"Just looking at the table of contents again right now," Charles replied as he turned his attention to Susan dressing, "but yeah, it looks like it has some very interesting topics."

Boy, it feels so strange to be clean-shaven down here. Maybe I should keep shaving it every few days for a while to postpone the itchy phase of it growing back. Susan paused as she looked at Charles studying the book. *I wonder... I'll bet he'll read the chapter on Wild Sex first...* "Which chapter looks most interesting to you?" she asked as she resumed dressing.

"Fantasy vs. Lust," Charles replied, looking in the book again. "I guess I never thought there was a difference, but judging by the inclusion of a Sex Fantasy Cookbook, I'm guessing the author concludes there's a major difference."

"Yeah, I used to have the same idea, and I read that chapter. It made me realize I had too many unsubstantiated assumptions."

"'Unsubstantiated assumptions'? I hope your vocabulary isn't always going to make me feel inferior."

Susan walked over to Charles with her shirt still unbuttoned and hugged him. "Your vocabulary is perfect, Charles. But you surprised me. I thought you might go for the Wild Sex chapter first."

"That was a very close second," Charles laughed.

Susan ended his laughter by imposing her mouth upon his.

Mmm... maybe we could read that chapter out loud to each other... or maybe I should make sure I read it first, to try to maintain my status as a "sex expert" in your mind.

There was a loud knock at the door, and Charles went to get the pizza while Susan moved the table and chairs so they could sit at the table and easily watch the movie.

The pizza arrived and had already been paid for and inspected by the bodyguards.

"There's a slice missing already," Charles said as he brought it to their table. "They said it was a 'poison detection test'" he added with a smile.

"Oh. Should we order some for them? I don't imagine one slice went very far among those guys. What was the guy's name who... Truck. I'll bet Truck could eat several large pizzas by himself."

"Nah... they take care of themselves. I think that was just a way of saying they trust us."

Susan looked puzzled.

"You know... a kind of teasing among friends. A way to build rapport between them and us."

"Ah," Susan nodded and took a slice out. "Well, if they'd really done a poison test, they would have kept us from getting any of it."

It was Charles' turn to look puzzled.

"For the fat in the cheese, and what it will do to our arteries."

"Ah, I see!" Charles laughed as he hit play on the remote.

"We won't have it very often," Susan said but I'm glad you didn't mind having it with me tonight."

After they finished their meal, they laid down on the bed in their clothes and snuggled as the movie played on.

More than half way through the movie, Susan noticed Charles' head take a dip and bounce back. *Oh, he looks so sleepy. Come to think of it, I'm surprised I'm not more sleepy.* "Honey, would you like to turn this off and go to sleep?" *Ooo, going to sleep together for the first time... together in bed...!*

Charles looked at the clock. "Eight-thirty. We got up awfully early, and didn't sleep well last night... but if I go to bed this early, I'm afraid I'll wake up too early tomorrow."

Hmm... if he wants to stay awake longer... and he needs a little help... Susan picked up the remote and paused the movie. "Let's take off our clothes so we're ready bed."

"Okay..." Charles agreed sluggishly.

"Do you usually wear anything when you sleep?"

"My underwear. Underpants, that is, not t-shirts. How about you?"

"I usually wear whatever panties I've been wearing all day, and I put on a special bra that's comfortable for sleeping in. But how about if we sleep naked tonight?"

"I'd like that, but any special reason?"

"It's our first night together, and I don't want anything between us."

"Okay, sounds good to me."

I can't believe I really shaved down here, Susan mused as she removed her panties. *Makes me feel like a college girl going to the beach or something...*

They got back in bed after undressing and Susan rearranged her pillows a bit and ended up with her head in Charles' lap.

"Okay, turn it back on," Susan said. *And I'll bet I can help you stay awake now,* she thought as she reached out and started caressing his cock.

"Oh, hey! Hey, that's gonna make it awfully hard to watch the movie."

"Try," Susan said, without moving. "I'll go easy on you."

"Mmm..." Charles murmured as the movie played again.

Charles became harder and harder as Susan idly let her fingers explore him, and she very lightly ran her fingertips up and down. When he was fully erect, the head almost reached to her mouth.

So... you said you'd like your thing inside my mouth, even if it was only the tip of it. And since your love language is "acts of service" that would be a good way to show you my love, and help you stay awake. Hmm... I never did this with Marty except when he was shoving it in... I wonder how far I can get it in without gagging? I'll put it in as far as I comfortably can and put my finger where my lips get to, then take my mouth off and look. I wonder if I can get half of it in?

"Oh, hey, now! Oh! Ooohhh...! Susan... oohhh..."

She pulled her mouth off and looked where her finger marked her progress. *Oh, shoot, not even half way! Aw, shoot! Hey, listen to him... he's panting, just from a few seconds of that...* "Are you going to be able to watch the movie this way? Will it help you stay awake?"

"What movie?" Charles asked, opening his eyes.

"Too much? You want me to go back to just my fingers?"

"Uh... well... I don't think I'll be able to concentrate on the movie if you keep doing that."

"Okay, so I'll quit and just use my hands. Will that help you stay awake...? And let you concentrate on the movie?"

"Yeah, I think so," Charles said.

He sounded disappointed...

Charles rewound the movie a bit and started it playing again. Susan kept her fingers moving, and Charles stayed fully awake.

After Joe and Kathleen met in the park as NY152 and Shopgirl, a sniffling Susan looked up to find Charles brushing away a few tears himself. "Uh-oh... did my big manly-man get some dust in his eyes?"

"Alright, now, if you're going to tease me like that, I'm going to make you watch Brian's Song with me."

"Brian's Song? That doesn't sound very macho..."

"Brian's song is a movie, another one I've seen, about a friendship between two professional football players, one of whom dies of cancer. Every guy cries when he watches that movie."

Huh. That sounds like it might be interesting.

Charles started getting up and Susan moved off of him. "I've got to pee again," he explained.

"Okay, honey."

Susan watched Charles disappear around the corner into the bathroom and she jumped up and ran to the box of lingerie and started looking through it, getting more and more frustrated. *Where's that throat spray?! I know Charles threw it in here.*

She huffed and started pulling out each item one at a time and shaking it to make sure it wasn't tangled up in it.

Charles came walking back around the corner and they both froze for a moment, then tried to act normal.

"Uh... looking for something to wear tonight after all?"

Susan bit her lip and hesitated. "Well, I didn't want you to know because I didn't want to get your hopes up, but I was looking for the throat spray. And I can't find it. Didn't you throw it back in the box?"

Charles looked sheepish. "Yeahhh... I did... but then when you were in the bathroom earlier, I got it out and threw it away."

Susan tilted her head. *Why would you... You did that to help me avoid feeling bad about it, didn't you...?* She put the lingerie back, stood up straight, and walked over to Charles to hug him. "You're the most thoughtful, loving, considerate man I've ever met."

"Mmm... well, I don't know about that, but I'm sure I'm the happiest man you've ever met."

"Oh, Charles... I love you..."

"I love you with all my heart, Susan."

They kissed and caressed each other while they continued to stand.

He's all about acts of service, and he threw that away as an act of service to show his love for me, so I wouldn't feel pressured to do something I have some bad memories associated with. What a special man! Now I want to do an act of service to show him how much I love him... "I have a question for you, darling..."

"What is it?" Charles asked as he stroked her hair.

"Which trash can did you put it in?"

"Oh, no. Let's forget about that and..."

Susan broke away and ran to the closest trash can and ransacked it.

"Susan... forget that!" Charles protested, but Susan noticed a huge grin on his face while he said it.

That's exactly what I thought. It doesn't really matter what "that" is, what matters is I'm doing *something just for you...* A broad smile spread across Susan's face and she ran toward the bathroom to look in the trash can there.

She thought Charles might try to stop her, and they could play-wrestle, but he just stood there and let her rush past, grinning all the while.

"It's in the trash can in the kitchenette. I figured you'd be too likely to spot it by accident in one of these trash cans."

Susan turned in mid-stride and headed for the kitchenette in the parlor, and this time Charles did try to stop her, reaching out to grab her arm.

"It's probably all yucky, so..."

"I'll wash it off," she replied as she pulled away and ran into the parlor with Charles following at a slower pace.

She found the spray, rinsed it off, and quickly sprayed it into her mouth. Her eyes grew large. "Wow... that's... hey, will this make it hard to talk? Or make my whole jaw numb, like coming home from the dentist's office?"

"Uh... I don't think so. I never used it myself. Guys don't have the same issue since girls don't poke out as far as we do."

Susan nodded while focusing primarily on the changing sensations in her tongue and in the back of her mouth.

"Jennifer never seemed to have problems like that, though."

Susan looked at the label on the bottle. "It doesn't say how long it takes to take full effect. Do you know?"

"Umm…" Charles furrowed his brow, struggling to remember. "Just a few minutes, I think."

"Well," Susan said while walking back toward the bedroom with the spray bottle in one hand and Charles' hand in her other, "let's go get in bed. I want to see if this stuff makes any difference in how far I can get you into my mouth."

Once in the bedroom again, Susan excused herself to go pee, and when she came back, Charles was in bed and looking very sleepy again. *Oh, shoot… I wanted to see if this stuff actually works, but he looks like he's too tired…*

Charles looked up, smiled, and opened his arms wide. Susan smiled back and crawled into bed and into Charles' arms.

"Kiss me," Susan commanded, and Charles complied. *Hmm… feels odd with this spray in my mouth.*

She broke off their kiss and started moving down.

"Susan, please don't feel like you have to…" Charles sucked in his breath as Susan put him in her mouth again. "Ooohhh…"

Let's see… I can try sucking…

"Uuhhmmm…"

Oh, good, you like that… wow, you're getting hard fast… you really like that. Now what else did the book say…? Move my tongue around…

"Oooo… unnghhh…"

Okay, check. You like that too. Now… ooo, Charles, easy there… I don't mind if you move a little bit, but please don't start thrusting too far… Okay, now… let's see how far I can get you in… mmphf… got my finger in place…

Susan removed her mouth and looked at where her finger marked her progress. *Over half-way! That stuff really did help, at least a little bit. And it doesn't taste bad or make my mouth feel too weird… Wow, listen to that, Charles is panting…* Susan put her mouth on him again. *He's panting just from that little bit of oral sex? Maybe he likes it more than he was telling me. Or maybe he just didn't remember well after years without it… I've got an idea…*

Susan took her mouth off again and moved to the foot of the bed.

"Listen… Susan… just because I'm hard, it doesn't mean I can have another orgasm. I've already more today that I would have thought possible..."

"Okay, honey. But as long as you don't mind me experimenting a little bit, I'm having fun."

"Oka..AYyeee..." Charles yelped as Susan's mouth interrupted his thoughts.

This time when she put her mouth back on him, she tilted her head so she could watch his face at the same time. *Wow, look at that... eyes closed, mouth open... he looks like he's half-way to heaven... okay, Susan, do something more... I'll move my tongue again... oh, yeah... listen to him groan... oop, there goes his thrusting again... not too much, now, Charles... I'll bet you aren't even aware of what you're doing, are you? Hey... I think this position is a little easier on me than the other one...*

When Charles' thrust was as far forward as it would go, Susan pushed her head down and marked her progress with a finger again and pulled off to see where her finger was. *That felt very deep to me... all the way to the back of my mouth, I think... wow! Look at that! I had this monster three quarters of the way in!!* She looked up at Charles with a happy grin.

Charles was panting still harder, and Susan felt his cock throbbing.

Uh-oh... what do I do now? Do I keep going with my mouth, or mount him, or let him mount me... he said he was too tired to cum again, so how should we finish what I've started...? "Do you want me to do that some more?" Susan asked tentatively.

"Y-yeah!" Charles gasped. "Please...! More...!"

Susan watched Charles' face carefully as she slowly lowered her mouth onto him once again. Charles moaned and groaned loudly, and his eyes closed as his head tilted back.

My goodness, he really likes this, but if he can't cum, I can't do this all night. How do I turn him off? Maybe I'll get on top of him again. Watching him get so excited is starting to make me horny all over again. Except... I'm really kind of sore down there...

Charles' hips started moving again and his groaning changed, becoming deeper, more guttural.

Well, I'll keep going with this for now... got to keep alternating... suck for a moment, then move my tongue... then go down deeper for a moment... then...

Susan noticed Charles' panting was turning to gasping and wondered how much longer they could keep going like this when his groans turned a struggling cry. His back arched, which rotated his hips and pulled him away from the back of her mouth just a little bit. She felt him convulse and then felt him begin to cum in her mouth.

The hot, salty taste made her slightly nauseous, but she kept her mouth on him. *Oh, no! What do I do now?! I-I guess it's okay to swallow, but yuck! I want to spit it out, but I don't want to ruin the moment for him, either! Oh, Lord... help me...*

Susan squeezed her eyes shut and forced a swallow down, fighting an urge to vomit, but she succeeded, and Charles rose up and cried out again as she swallowed.

Almost immediately after swallowing, she removed her mouth, wanting to find a towel to wipe out her mouth, and Charles collapsed back onto the bed. Semen continued to ooze from the tip, and Susan laid his cock down carefully on his abdomen.

I'm going to eat a few bites of pizza and see if that gets rid of the nasty aftertaste. And I'm going to get another soda from the minibar. I don't care how much they cost.

"You... amazing..." Charles gasped with his eyes still closed.

Susan took a bite of pizza and smiled as she chewed. *Sore or not, I wouldn't mind getting another ride, if you can get "up" for it again...*

She swallowed. "You want to wait a little while and try for one more?"

"Susan... Parker..." he panted, "you've worn me out. I don't think I could move anymore no matter what I wanted."

Oh, well, we've got all day again tomorrow. I guess I can wait. And I know I'm going to enjoy falling asleep beside you... hmm... I wonder... "Charles... have we broken your record for most orgasms in one day?"

"Broke... that... record... early this afternoon," Charles barely uttered.

"And we broke my record, too, with my very first orgasm," Susan added with great satisfaction. "I never knew it could be that wonderful."

She took another bite of pizza. *I think this will take care of the taste. I don't need a soft drink after all.*

Susan watched as Charles' breathing began to slow into a steady rhythm. "We don't need to set the alarm clock, do we?"

Charles didn't react at all.

"Charles...?"

Susan swallowed her last bite as she put the rest of the slice back in the box, and was surprised by a sudden realization. *Charles! I did it!*

I wore you out! With sex! I literally wore you out with sex! You said you're too tired to move anymore!

Susan danced around the room. *Oh, praise God! I broke your record, Charles...! I gave you an incredible six orgasms in one day! On our wedding day! And you said I'm an expert at sex compared to your first wife! And you said there's never been another woman even half as good as me at sex!*

Oh, God! Oh, Father! Thank you! Thank you so much for letting me do something wonderful, something really special for Charles! With *Charles...! Oh, God...!*

Susan stood at the foot of the bed and gazed her new husband, now sleeping quietly. She lowered herself to her knees and bowed her head, thanking God over and over, with grateful tears dropping onto the sheets.

I thought I was an old woman. An old, gray-haired, washed-out, jobless has-been... or even worse, a never-was... I never really succeeded with my first husband or my children... and now, Lord, you've given me a man who really loves me... I don't know how, or why, but he does... and he's perfect for me... Oh, Lord, I can't live my life over again and make things up to Marty or Steve, but it's not too late for Stephanie... is it? If you could give her just a little bit of the joy you've given me... if you could touch her heart, and show her how much you love her... it was your love that changed my life, and I know it can change hers too, if she'll let you... Lord, please do something, anything, to open her heart to you... if you can use my life Lord, do it! This one week with Charles was enough for me. This one day was more than I could have ever asked for. So if you can help Stephanie by taking my life, somehow, I'm ready Lord... I know Charles would miss me, but you've given him some wonderful memories to treasure, and Stephanie has nothing...

When Susan felt like she had nothing left to pray for a while, she got up and watched Charles for a minute, then struggled to roll Charles over onto his side while pulling the cover and all the pillows but one out from under him, then straighten the cover out on top of him. She made sure her cell phone was on her bedside table and took one more long look at Charles, giving another sigh of thanks to God before turning off the light, climbing under the covers and cuddling up into a spooning position.

Mmm... wow... I married Charles today... I married him, and I humped him until he couldn't hump any more... six times...! Well, including that last time with my mouth... how about that...? I got him off with just my mouth, and without him jamming it down my throat so I couldn't breathe... and that ride... oh, wow, what a ride...! And he got me off, too... for the first time in my life, I had an honest-to-goodness orgasm... wow, was that good!

Susan slipped one arm all the way over Charles and felt his chest expand and contract. *Oh, God... what a blessing sex can be... how wonderful for us to be able to share our lives this way...*

Susan's thoughts began to fade, and drift into an old dream... once again she was in a ballroom and an amazingly handsome man strode up to her. This time she could clearly see the face of the man as he took her in his arms and swept her around the room. Their feet marched through intricate steps and all the other dancers moved to the walls and all eyes were on them. As the music faded, Charles dipped her low, with this mouth right next to her ear. "I love you with all my heart..." he whispered, "and I belong to you, and to you alone. And you..." he said as he raised her up again, "belong to me. You're mine. All of your heart and all of your body belongs to me." The crowd had disappeared as he lifted her into his arms and strode up the stairs two at a time. All of a sudden they were in his bedroom and he threw both of them toward the bed. Susan landed first, on her back, with no clothes, and as she watched him sailing through the air toward her, she spread her legs for him. As he landed on top of her, she felt him fill her. The feeling of fullness radiated through her body as they kissed, and their bodies merged into each other from the waist down. Her body was now part of his body, and always would be...

Chapter Seventeen

Susan was in deep sleep when her phone began to ring, and she struggled to wake up. *Phone… could be Stephanie!* She reached for her phone without opening her eyes.

What time is it? She flipped the phone open as she quickly became more alert. "Hello?"

"Momma, what have you done with Billy?!" Stephanie asked harshly.

"What…? What do you mean…? Stephanie, what's wrong?"

"You know what's wrong! You… you had Billy arrested, didn't you? I've been calling like you said, and you had him arrested anyway!"

"No, honey, I didn't. I don't know who arrested him…"

"Then how did you know he's been arrested?" Stephanie shouted.

"You just told me, sweetheart. I've been asleep. I didn't do anything." *Oh, Lord, did you do it? Did you get Billy arrested?*

It was a few moments before Stephanie responded, "Momma, you swear you didn't have Billy arrested?"

"Yes, honey, I promise."

"xx-xx-xx!" Stephanie cursed as she started crying. "That xx-xx-xx! And you don't know where he is? I thought you said those people were going to be watching us!"

"Well, yeah, I thought so. But just watching, honey, unless they saw him start to hurt you. Did he hurt you again?"

"No," Stephanie sobbed. "Then why don't you know where he is?"

"Well, uh… let me see if I can find out…" Susan covered the phone. "Charles? Are you awake?"

"I think so," Charles replied sluggishly. "What's up?"

"Stephanie's on the phone, and she says Billy's missing. She wants…"

Charles jumped up and fumbled to turn on his bedside lamp.

"…to know if we know where Billy is."

Charles grabbed his phone and hit a speed dial number. "We'd better know. That's why I have a private army on the payroll."

"Hold on, honey," Susan said into the phone. "Charles is checking."

"He's in bed with you?"

"Yes, honey, we just got married. I wish..."

"Just xx-xx-xx, Momma, and tell me where Billy is!"

"Mike?" Charles said into his phone. "Charles. Do you know where Billy is? Stephanie's on the phone with Susan right now and she says she doesn't know..."

"Just a second, Stephanie," Susan said into the phone, "Charles is talking to someone now."

"Uh-huh..." Charles responded to his phone again. "Huh... really...? Hold on a second."

He turned to Susan, who covered her phone.

"Mike says Billy's been sitting alone in his car in a grocery store parking lot, for over an hour, and appears to be pretty upset. Mike's called in all his guys, just in case he gets violent again."

Susan caught her breath sharply. *Oh, Father, please, please protect Stephanie!* "What do I..."

Charles held up a finger to ask Susan to wait a minute as he listened to his phone again for a moment, then continued his explanation to Susan, "Mike says they have one guy still at their house guarding Stephanie, and two guys watching Billy. Mike is almost to their house, and Frank and two more guys are on their way there."

"What should I tell Stephanie?" Susan asked, "Should I try to warn her? She's very upset."

"Mm... hold on," Charles to Stephanie. "Mike, what should we tell Stephanie? She's upset and... uh-huh... okay."

Turning to Susan again, Charles said, "He'd like you to tell her as little as possible. Billy's started driving again, and it looks like he's going to turn toward their house."

Oh, no... I have to tell her something! No matter how bad he is, Stephanie's worried about him. But what if he's gone crazy mad again? How do I warn her? She won't believe anything I tell her... "Stephanie, honey," she said into the phone again, "They have been watching Billy, and... they said he's behaving... oddly."

"What the xx-xx-xx do you mean, 'oddly'? Where is he? What's he doing? Who's with him?!"

"He... he's alone, I think, and he's just been sitting in a parking lot." *I hope that's not...*

"What the xx-xx-xx do you mean, he's just been sitting in a parking lot?! For how long?"

Charles addressed Susan again, "Mike says Billy's definitely headed in the direction of their house, but he's driving normally, not in a hurry."

"Stephanie, honey," *How do I warn you?* "They say he's on his way back to your house. Stephanie, they said he looked like he was real upset in the parking lot. Oh, Stephanie, please don't let him hurt you anymore."

For the next few minutes, Charles stayed on the phone with Mike, Susan stayed on the phone with Stephanie, and Stephanie was crying and cursing, while Susan tried to talk her into leaving the house with the bodyguards.

At one point while Stephanie was ranting, Susan asked Charles, "What's going on now?"

"Not sure," Charles replied. "Mike's spending most of his time talking to his guys, not me, and I can only hear his side of it."

"What? No!" Charles suddenly said into his phone, "Of course not!"

Susan looked at Charles with questioning eyes, but he was focused on the phone.

"No, I have no idea who it could be. You sure it's not one of your guys…? Uh-huh…"

"Charles, what is it?" Susan implored.

"Somebody parked right in front of their apartment but didn't get out. They slunk down like they don't want to be seen."

"Who is it?" Susan pressed.

"They don't know," Charles explained. "Mike asked me if I had hired another investigator, but I didn't." Charles became attentive to his phone again.

"Mike is just down the street from their apartment now," Charles narrated, "and Billy's just a block away…"

Oh, Lord, please protect Stephanie! This is the last chance for her to get away! "Stephanie, please," Susan pleaded, "Billy's almost home. Please go stay with the bodyguards outside until…"

"xx-xx-xx, Momma," Stephanie yelled again, "I'm not gonna leave Billy! Not now or ever! Just xx-xx-xx and leave us alone!" The line went dead.

"Stephanie…?! Stephanie?!" Susan cried and turned to Charles. "I think she hung up!"

"Billy just parked his car," Charles replied. "Mike and his guys are there, honey, and he says they're going to talk to Billy before they let him go in the apartment. *If* they let him go in."

Oh, thank God! That will give Stephanie more time…

"What was that...?! Mike?! Mike...?! Mike!!" Charles unexpectedly shouted into the phone. He held it in front of him for a moment.

"What is it?!" Susan asked in alarm.

Charles just stared straight ahead for a long moment. He slowly put his phone down and turned fully toward Susan, and looked like he might be fighting tears.

"Charles! What is it?! What happened?!"

Charles tried to put his arms around her, but she resisted, imploring him to explain what he had heard.

"Please, Charles, tell me what happened!"

"Right before the line went dead... I heard..." Charles forcefully pulled Susan against him and put an arm around her. "I think... I heard gunshots..."

"Oh, God, no!!" Susan wailed. "No, no, no...!!"

She closed her eyes and felt the room spinning. *Oh, God... oh, God... no... please, no... not Stephanie! Not my little girl... oh, Savior!! Oh, Father, if she's still alive, please keep her alive! Oh, God, don't let my baby girl die without knowing and loving you! Please, God! Please love my little girl!*

"We should get dressed and go down there," Charles said, "however things turn out."

"Oh, Charles..." Susan cried, then grabbed his arm. "Why aren't you calling Mike back? Maybe it..."

"I think it's important not to interrupt him right now. I'm so sorry, honey, but I'm sure he'll call back as soon as he can... Maybe everything will be okay... but whatever happened, we need to go down there..." Charles voice trailed off.

Despite her tears, Susan rolled over to the other side of the bed, got up, and started throwing on clothes.

Charles put on his undershorts, pants, and slipped on a pair of shoes without bothering with socks. He grabbed his shirt and started walking to the parlor. "I'm going to see who's in the hall and tell them we need them to take us down there. We don't have a car here."

Susan put on panties and pants and fumbled with her bra, struggling with the idea of leaving it, but unable to make herself do so. Once she had it on, she quickly put on a pink button-up shirt, grabbed her sandals and carried them as she headed after Charles.

Charles was at the door talking to a guard Susan hadn't seen before.

"Then get out of my way," Charles was ordering. "We'll take a taxi if we have to."

The bodyguard shrugged. "My job is to keep you alive, sir, and the best way to do that is to keep you here. But if you're going anyway, we'll take you in an armored Suburban."

The car was waiting out front as soon as they got downstairs. Unlike their previous trip to Maryville, the driver wasn't hurrying.

Susan was cuddled into Charles and they were quietly praying when the bodyguard pressed a finger against his earpiece for a moment, then turned around a bit and interrupted.

"Mr. Parker, Mike asked me to give you an update. He can't do it himself right now. Stephanie is okay. She hasn't been hurt at all…"

Susan broke down and sobbed, the intense relief causing her body to shake as Charles continued to hold her. "Oh, God…! Oh, God, thank you!" she exclaimed before burying her face against Charles. *Oh, thank you, Lord! Oh, God, you took care of my baby! Oh, Lord…!*

After Susan's crying quieted down a little, the bodyguard continued, "There's more… the guy Billy… he was shot, and he's being taken to the hospital in an ambulance." He hesitated before adding, "Doesn't look like he'll make it."

Oh, God… I don't know whether to thank you for that or not! I know I shouldn't be happy if Billy dies, but… I am, even if I shouldn't be.

Susan's thoughts and emotions were in turmoil for the rest of the trip, and she was still very anxious to see Stephanie and see for herself that she was okay.

Oh, Lord… Stephanie… she's going to be so upset, and probably blame me… no matter how awful Billy was, she seemed to love him, or at least want him… and she's probably going to think it's my fault, that I've taken him away from her… and with this on top of me divorcing her father, she may… she may never even want to talk to me again… oh, Lord… oh, Lord… is there anything I can do? Is there anything I can do to show Stephanie that I love her…?

As the car finally turned a corner and approached Stephanie's apartment, the night was lit by the strobing lights of several police cars, and neighbors stood in little clusters on the sidewalks, in various states of dress.

"Any chance I can convince you to wait in the car until we…" the bodyguard began.

"No," Charles answered succinctly, prompting a sigh from the front seat.

"I've got to find Stephanie…" Susan said in anguish.

As soon as the car stopped, as close as they could get, Charles got out and Susan got out behind him. Charles started to put his arm over Susan's shoulder, but she ran toward the apartment, and Charles ran after her, followed by the bodyguard and driver.

"Whoa!" a police officer demanded, getting in Susan's path. "Sorry, ma'am, but you can't..."

"That's my daughter's apartment, officer!" Susan explained quickly. "Please! I need to see her!"

"Not just yet," the officer said as he put his arm out to restrain her as Charles and the other men caught up. Charles took his place beside Susan.

"And you are?" the officer inquired of Charles.

"Uh, Stephanie's father," Charles answered.

"And these other guys?" he persisted.

"Samuelson Security," one of the men offered.

"Just a minute," the officer demanded, then shined his flashlight on Susan's face and examined it carefully. "You need a doctor, ma'am?"

"No. No, sir," Susan said, putting a hand over her bruises in embarrassment.

"That's from several days ago, officer," Charles explained.

"Uh-huh, okay," the patrolman said as he nodded and then keyed up his radio. "Sergeant, we've got the girl's parents out here, and two more from the security company."

"More of them? xx-xx-xx. Just have 'em wait out there," a voice came back over the radio. "I'll come out and talk to 'em in a little while. And sit on 'em... make sure none of 'em leave."

"You heard him," the patrolman said. "They'll get to you after a while."

Susan's shoulders sagged, "But officer, my daughter needs me!"

"She's upset, ma'am, and drunk as a skunk, but other than that, she's fine. I talked with her myself when I first got here," the officer said kindly. "You can wait in the back seat of my cruiser if you'd like, ma'am."

Susan leaned heavily against Charles and nodded to the officer, who walked them over to his car and opened the back door. Instead of sitting, Susan just stood in the door with Charles hugging her for a while.

"Oh, I'll call Nat and tell him what's going on," Charles said, getting out his cell phone.

The police officer interrupted, "Sorry, sir, you're not allowed to talk to anyone until after the detectives get through talking to you."

"Officer," Charles said politely but firmly, "I don't want to make your job harder, but unless I'm under arrest, you can't tell me whether or not I may call anyone."

The two men stared at each other for a moment, and then the policeman reluctantly withdrew his objection, and Charles gave Nat a quick update while Susan sat on the police car's back seat and leaned her head back and closed her eyes.

Oh, Lord... she started to pray, and the next thing she knew Charles was gently waking her.

"Honey, we have to go back to our car. We need to go to the police station, and you'll need to tell the detectives about Sunday morning."

"What...? What about Sunday morning? Where's Stephanie?!" she asked, jumping up. "Can I talk to her now?"

"I'm sorry, Susan," Charles said, putting an arm around her, "but they won't let us talk to her until after they talk to each of us alone."

A police detective standing next to Charles spoke up. "We need you to tell us what happened when Billy broke into your house, Mrs. Parker."

"Oh... that," Susan said. "Can't that wait until after I see Stephanie?"

"No, ma'am. We have to talk to her alone some more, and we need to talk to you alone and get your story before we can let you talk to her."

Charles walked Susan back to their car, and Susan looked over her shoulder toward the apartment.

"They've already taken Stephanie to the police station, honey," Charles said.

"And you didn't wake me up?!" Susan asked with alarm.

"Honey, I tried to," Charles said, "but they weren't going to let you talk to her anyway."

"How long ago was that?"

"Uh... about fifteen, maybe twenty minutes ago."

Susan sighed in resignation and got into the car. Minutes after she did, she was asleep again, leaning against Charles.

Once at the police station, she drank some coffee and told two detectives everything that had happened since Saturday night. It didn't come up that she had only met Charles about a week ago, but retelling all the events of the last few days seemed to compress time, and she felt embarrassed telling them that she got married so soon after learning how much danger Stephanie was in. She felt that she somehow should have done more to protect her, and should have placed her own desires on hold.

When the detectives finally finished interviewing her, they took their own photos of her bruises to go with the ones Mike's crew had taken Sunday morning, and then took her to a waiting area with a few well-worn upright chairs. A few minutes later, she spotted Charles coming toward her, walking wearily. Susan ran to him, and they hugged tightly as she started crying.

"When are they going to let me talk to Stephanie?" she wailed again. "If she's even willing to talk to me..."

"I don't know," Charles sighed. "C'mon, let's sit down."

They sat down and held each other while Susan tried to fight sleep, and that effort was helped by the chairs, in which she found it impossible to get comfortable.

An hour later, a casually dressed but very tired looking man approached them. "Mr. & Mrs. Parker?"

Charles merely nodded. They stayed seated and the stranger pulled up a chair and sat in it backwards, leaning on the backrest and facing them.

He looked at Susan's bruises and grimaced. "I'm Chief Detective Benson. I appreciate how patient you folks have been, but we've had a lot of work to do to figure out what all has been going on."

Benson shook his head. "And I'll tell you what, I've never seen evidence so well documented as these Samuelson guys have done. Detailed, complete... Of course I'm going to tell you that you should have contacted the police department in Knoxville Sunday morning, and you could have created a lot of problems for yourselves by not doing that, but the evidence those guys put together seems to cover just about everything. We still have a lot to do, though. With a homicide, we're going to be as thorough as possible."

"A homicide...?" Susan echoed quietly.

"Yes, ma'am. William Baker, better known as Billy, died on the way to the hospital. He was declared right after they got there."

Susan gripped Charles' arm. *Oh, Lord God, it's finally over... at least that awful nightmare is finally over...* "What about Stephanie? My daughter? When..."

"Well, you can see her soon, but, if I understand correctly, you haven't seen each other for years until this past Sunday morning?"

"Yes," Susan acknowledged sadly, and a wiped a tear with the back of her free hand.

"Well, ma'am, I don't know how to be tactful about this, so I'm just going to ask. Are you aware that she's an alcoholic?"

"What...?! Oh, no...!" Susan wailed. *She probably started drinking to be like her Daddy, and it got hold of her, just like it got hold of him...*

"I'm afraid so," the detective said. "There's no question about it, and she's coming down off a binge. She's starting to have withdrawal symptoms already, and it's going to get a lot worse."

Susan looked at Charles with deep worry. "What should we do? What can we do?"

Charles looked at Benson. "I've drunk enough beer in my life to float a ship, but I've rarely gotten drunk, and I quit on my own, so I really don't know what to do here. Can you recommend anything?"

The detective nodded. "Well, if she were my daughter, I'd get her into Cambridge Treatment Center, just north of Knoxville. It's a real nice place on an old plantation. Almost like a resort. I, uh, happen to know they have a very good detox program there, and if you can afford the Samuelson company, you can probably afford Cambridge."

Susan looked at Charles hopefully, but after he glanced at her, he looked back at Benson.

"Do you know if she's willing to go there?" Charles asked.

"Didn't ask, but I doubt she'd do it voluntarily. However, we can explain things in such a way as to... sort of encourage her to choose to go."

"What do you mean?" Susan asked.

Benson hesitated before explaining, "Well, we can tell her that no matter what, she's not going to get any alcohol for a long time. We need her as a material witness, and we can either keep her cooped up in a cheap motel room with round-the-clock police escorts, with no treatment for what will probably be very nasty withdrawal, or she can have a private room in a very nice treatment center and get medication to minimize the withdrawal. If we put it that way, she'll probably choose to get treated. Whether or not she goes back to alcohol later... well, frankly, the odds aren't good."

"Oh..." Susan moaned and looked at Charles again. *Lord, please, please help Stephanie. Make the most of this chance...*

"What do you need her as a material witness for, since Billy's dead?" Charles asked.

The detective looked puzzled. "Well... I thought you were aware that she was living with Billy, and working for him..."

"Yeah..." Charles said, "but if he's dead, isn't that the end of it?"

"No, I expect the D.A. will want her to testify in at least two trials."

"What?!" Charles exclaimed, "You mean you intend to prosecute my bodyguards?!"

"What? No, we..." Detective Benson stopped and cocked his head. "Wait... did you think your guys shot Billy?"

"Yeah, to protect Stephanie from him. I figured he pulled a knife or a gun, and they..."

"Oh, no, you've got it all wrong," Benson interrupted, as Mike Samuelson joined them. "I thought you knew this part. Billy was apparently working for a guy named Edmonds who was involved with organized crime... in the sex slave market, prostitution, porn films... and snuff films. One of Edmonds' goons shot Billy, and then," he nodded toward Mike, "your guys collared the goon right after that. And another one of your guys got the whole thing on his surveillance video camera. Slam-dunk case against that guy. We're going to have to do a lot more work to nail Edmonds, but we've got a really good shot at it, thanks to your team."

Susan and Charles looked at each other in amazement and at Mike with appreciation.

"Did you tell them what Billy said?" Mike asked Benson as he rubbed the stubble on his face.

"No... guess you didn't hear that either?" Benson asked the Parkers.

Charles looked at Susan, who gave her head a shake. "No, we didn't," Charles answered for both of them.

"Well," Mike said, "the hit-man only got off one shot, but it was to the chest. Stephanie was beside him right after he was hit. After we had the shooter secured Tony and I started to give Billy first aid, but there was no way he wasn't going to bleed-out. But he did have a minute or two before he lost consciousness, and..."

Mike paused and his voice cracked as he continued, "His last words were begging Stephanie to forgive him. He said you were right, Charles, and he said tonight, or last night now... he gave his life to God. Then he called Big Ed, the guy he was working for, and told him he was quitting. Then a little later he went home to Stephanie."

"'Big Ed' is Edmonds," Detective Benson interjected.

Susan felt dizzy, and stopped following the conversation as she held tightly to Charles and prayed. *He... Billy... gave his life to you, Lord...? Not Stephanie...? All these years I've been praying for*

Stephanie, who never hurt anybody, and, and you haven't done anything for her... and we pray one stinking time for Billy and you make him give you his life? God! Why?! Why?! Why not Stephanie first?! Or at least Stephanie at the same time! Dear God, why haven't you helped Stephanie love you?!

A policewoman was gently trying to get Susan's attention as the three men waited.

"Honey..." Charles said softly as he gave Susan a gentle shake.

"Mrs. Parker," the policewoman said, "your daughter's in the bathroom and would like to see you."

Susan jumped up and took a step, but started to lose her balance, and Charles jumped up and steadied her.

"I'm okay, I just stood up too fast," Susan apologized in parting.

Walking around a corner and down a hall the policewoman explained, "Your daughter's really upset about her boyfriend's death, of course, but she's also sick. She's been throwing up... and, well, ma'am, the way she smells, that's probably from drinking too much."

They got to the bathroom, and Susan followed the sound of crying to a stall in the otherwise empty bathroom. Stephanie was sitting on the floor with her head next to the toilet, and when Susan got down next to her, Stephanie threw her arms around her. Stephanie sobbed as Susan hugged her and cried in a mixture of sympathy, anxiety, and relief.

"Stephanie, I'm so sorry... I love you so much, and I'm so sorry..."

"Oh, Momma... he's gone... he left me just like Daddy did..."

"Oh, no, honey," Susan said as she stroked Stephanie's hair near her neck, avoiding the spikes on top. "He was taken away from you, but he didn't leave you. And... and Daddy... well, Daddy leaving was my fault... I... he and I, we...

"Every xx-xx-xx man I've ever had has left me, and I'm all alone again, Momma. I'm all alone."

"Oh, no, Stephanie, I'm here for you. I'm here. I won't leave you..."

Stephanie pushed back from her Mom. "xx-xx-xx, Mom, I know you... you try to care about me, but you can't... I need a *man*, Momma. Maybe Billy wasn't much, but he was mine, and he took care of me."

"Darling, if you'll give us a chance, Charles and I will take care of you. We..."

Stephanie sighed with exasperation. "He took care of me in bed,

Mother. I need a xx-xx-xx man in my bed!"

"Oh," was all Susan could think of in response.

To Susan's surprise, Stephanie's shoulders sagged and she leaned over and put her head in Susan's lap. Susan started stroking Stephanie's hair again and Stephanie started crying again.

Stephanie cursed again as she cried, not in anger, but in sorrow.

Oh, Lord, what can I do? What can I say? What can... Susan's prayer was interrupted by a new thought. *Lord, what if Stephanie's love language is touch? If I was right about that... that would explain why she missed Marty so much... he hugged her all the time, and I... well, I hardly ever did, even after he left us. And that could be why she chose to stay with Billy despite him being so bad, if he at least gave her the physical comfort she needs to feel loved. Is... is what I'm doing now... this should count, shouldn't it? It doesn't have to be sex, right? As much as she seems to have hated me, she just put her head in my lap... Lord, I can try to be conscientious about hugging her, but only if we're together. What happens now? If we stick her in a treatment center, I can't... well, maybe we could visit every day... or even more than once a day... Charles doesn't have to work, and I guess I don't either... if they allow visitors... and if Stephanie will go there... and if she...*

Stephanie rose up suddenly and threw up again into the toilet, heaving painfully.

Susan watched as Stephanie waited to see if another spasm would come, and then started to get up. "I'll be right back, Stephanie, I'm just going to get some damp paper towels."

Susan got the towels and set about cleaning Stephanie's face and clothes as well as she could. "Hey, at least with your hair in spikes, it stayed out of the way," she tried to say lightly as she sat back down on the floor.

"xx-xx-xx," Stephanie mumbled as she leaned against her mother.

Susan put an arm around her and leaned over and kissed her head in between some of the spikes.

"The first time I..." Stephanie started to say, but her voice trailed off.

Oh, Lord, it sounded like she was going to talk to me, share something with me. Please... please help us talk to each other... But talking's more my thing than hers... Susan thought and then started moving her hand tenderly up and down Stephanie's upper arm.

Stephanie lowered her head on to her mother's shoulder and

barely said aloud, "The first time I cut my hair short was because I kept getting vomit in it. I didn't even remember that until just a minute ago."

She did it, she told me something private about herself! Should I say something? Should I ask her more about it? I don't want to mess this up, Lord... tell me what to do! While she waited, listening for Stephanie or God to say something to her, she continued to caress Stephanie's arm.

"Momma..." Stephanie whispered.

"Yes, darling?" Susan said softly.

Stephanie paused a long time before continuing. "I need help."

Susan wanted to get excited, but tried to stay sedate for Stephanie's sake. "Charles and I will help you any way we can, Stephanie. Any way that... well, we have to believe it's really in your best interest."

"Yes ma'am," Stephanie said quietly.

'Yes ma'am'? ...! Stephanie hasn't said that since she was little... since Marty left... she hasn't said that since Marty left.

"I'm a drunk, Momma. Just like Daddy. I drink and drink until I pass out. And... when I'm drunk, I... I do things that... that you'll think are really bad."

"Do you know that I'll always love you, no matter what?"

Stephanie started crying again, a little harder. "Did you know we're being evicted?" she asked in a broken voice.

"No, honey, we didn't know that."

"That's why Billy was so freaked out. We got the notice last week..." Stephanie started sobbing and shaking and buried her face against Susan. "But you know what we did the last time Billy got some money? We spent most of the xx-xx-xx money on booze," she wailed.

Oh, Lord, please don't let me blow this... Susan decided to just stay quiet and let her cry.

"We knew the rent was due, but we spent what little money we had on booze instead..."

When Stephanie's sobs began to subside, Susan spoke gently. "Stephanie... the police want you to testify in court..."

"Yeah, they told me that," she said between sobs and nodded without lifting her head. "I hope that guy who killed Billy gets the electric chair."

"Well, honey, they don't want you to drink any more at least until after the trial... and that could be while, you know. That... that could be hard for you."

Stephanie sat up dejectedly, pulling away from Susan far enough that Susan had to put her arm down, but she put a hand on Stephanie's knee instead. "I can't do it Momma. I feel like I need to have a drink right now, and I... I know I won't be able to get by without it. I've tried... I can't count how many times, but I can't even go one day without it."

Stephanie looked off at the wall and slowly shook her head. "Whatever it takes, I haven't got it. I have to drink."

"Well," Susan ventured, "there are treatment centers that have medicine just for that."

Stephanie looked at her mother sharply and frowned. "I knew somebody who went to one of those places, and they said it was horrible. They were tied to a bed, and they had to pee in bed, and someone washed them off with a garden hose, and all sorts of terrible things."

"Oh, my," Susan said with concern. "Well... what if there was a nice place? Run by good doctors? And if they didn't do any of those things? Your..." Susan started to say, "your father and I" but caught herself, afraid that referring to Charles as her father might offend her. "What if Charles and I could visit you every day to make sure they weren't doing anything bad to you?"

Stephanie looked thoughtful for a minute. "Really...? Do you think... I mean, Momma, I don't have any money, and..."

"Oh, no, Stephanie, we'd pay for that. That's something that could really help you, and we'd be happy to pay for that!" *Uh-oh... I'm promising Charles' money without even discussing it with him first... but he's been nothing but caring and generous... and we're married now... I'd bet anything he'll want me to think of his money as belonging to both of us...*

"What if we go visit a place like that," Susan continued, "and... and if you decide you don't like it, you wouldn't have to stay."

Oh... Lord, I just ruled out forcing her into it. I can't go back on my word now... "And just like I told you before, you're welcome to come home again..."

Tears welled up in Stephanie's eyes, and as she tried to look at her mother, they began to fall. "Momma... how can you still love me...? I've..."

"Stephanie..." Susan started to say.

"And don't tell me it's just because you're my momma. I've known other girls whose mommas didn't care a xx-xx-xx about them. And they tried to be nice to their Mommas, and I... I... I've been really mean to you. I didn't know anything about men when Daddy left, and..." Stephanie choked up and fell silent.

Susan reached out, and gently pulled Stephanie to her. Stephanie was racked with sobs again, and Susan just held her. After a minute, Susan started rubbing a hand lightly up and down Stephanie's back.

After a few minutes, Stephanie spoke again without moving. "When Daddy left... I tried to convince myself it was your fault, and I focused all my anger on you. I'm so sorry, Momma, but... I talked myself into hating you... and the truth is... I..."

Stephanie began sobbing again, but continued to talk as best she could, "I really felt... deep down... I believed it was my fault. I thought you were jealous because Daddy loved me."

"Oh, no, honey! No...!" Susan said consolingly. Your Daddy did love you, and Steve, too! And I didn't mind him loving you, I... I just didn't feel like he loved me very much, and I... well, I used to think that everything was his fault, but now I know it was at least partly, if not mostly, my fault. I just... I didn't know how to love him enough, not the way he needed it. I didn't..."

"Did you hate Daddy because he drank?" Stephanie managed to ask.

"What...? Well... I-I don't think so. Well, I mean I don't think I ever hated him... I just hated how we used to argue... and I don't think he knew... how I needed to feel loved. I think you and your father show love through touching..."

"Well, of course," Stephanie said, calming down a little.

"Well, that's not the way I am, Stephanie. I need words. I mean, I like... you know, touching... but I need words much more than I need touching."

Stephanie pulled back and stopped crying, and looked at her mother carefully. "Are you serious?"

"Yes, honey. And I never understood your father's need to be shown love by touching, and I'm pretty sure he never understood my need to be shown love through words."

"xx-xx-xx!" Stephanie said in shock. "xx-xx-xx, xx-xx-xx...! I never... Momma, I never knew that either. I... Oh, xx-xx-xx!"

All of a sudden Stephanie launched herself into Susan's arms and hugged her as tight as she could, and cried harder than ever. "Oh, xx-xx-xx, Momma...! Oh, xx-xx-xx...!"

Susan was surprised and a little puzzled, but happy, and she hugged Stephanie right back.

"Oh, xx-xx-xx, Momma! All those years growing up… I remember now… you used to brag about me, and praise me, whether we were alone or with the family, or even around strangers. I remember one time at a restaurant, I was embarrassed because you were bragging about me to the waitress. But I thought you never loved me much because you didn't hug me as much as Daddy did… and all that time… you were loving me with words?! Oh, xx-xx-xx, Momma, I never knew… I never knew that…! Oh, Momma… Momma… can you ever forgive me? Oh, Momma, I'm so sorry!!"

Susan was shocked, stunned, and she was crying every bit as hard as Stephanie was.

When Susan could finally manage a few words, it was to tell Stephanie how sorry she was for misunderstanding her and her father, and for driving her father away, and to tell her how much she really does love her.

Their reconciliation was interrupted by Stephanie having to throw up again, but Susan didn't leave her side, and they continued to cry and apologize to each other.

Finally Stephanie said she felt like she wouldn't have to throw up anymore, at least for a while, and they helped each other up. There were several sinks side-by-side with a huge mirror behind them, and they washed their faces together.

Stephanie glanced at Susan's face, and then stared. "xx-xx-xx, Momma, I didn't realize how bad Billy hurt you. I'm so sorry…" she said, throwing her arms around her again.

"Well, it looks worse now, but it doesn't feel very bad anymore. It just stings a little if I touch it too hard… but what about you?" Susan asked, remembering how savagely Billy twisted her breast.

"Oh, I'm okay, Mom. I mean, Billy did hurt me sometimes, but mostly when he was upset and sober. He was nice when he was drunk, but when he was sober, that's when he'd sometimes get so angry he'd lose control. He actually talked worse than what he did, though… I guess you'd rather have it the other way around, though, huh?"

"Mm… well, your father…" Susan started, but stopped herself short.

"That's okay, Mom," Stephanie assured her. "You can talk about Dad with me. I know he had his own… problems."

Susan studied Stephanie's face, and decided to continue what she started to say, but watch Stephanie closely and stop if it started bothering her. "Well, your daddy never got really angry except when he was drunk. Toward the end of our marriage, though, he… he was drinking a lot…"

"Oh…" Stephanie said thoughtfully. "Maybe that's another way we were alike… xx-xx-xx, I wish I had a drink right now!"

Susan started to reply, but there was a knock on the bathroom door, and it cracked open.

"Susan," Charles voice called out, "You guys okay in here?"

"Yes, Charles," Susan called out. "It's okay, you can come in. There's no one else in here."

Charles pushed the door open and peered at them through eyelids so droopy he looked like he was squinting. "Anything I can do?"

Susan put her arm around Stephanie's shoulder, and Stephanie put an arm around Susan's waist. Charles' eyebrows went up, but his eyes were still slits.

"Charles," Susan asked, "would it be alright if we visited that treatment center we heard about? Stephanie would like to see it."

"Y-yeah, sure, of course!" he said with as much enthusiasm as he could muster at that hour of the morning, and he held the door wide open for them. "We've got a car ready whenever we are, and… uh, I'm guessing we could grab some breakfast on the way there, and they'd probably be open by the time we get there. Want to do that?"

Susan looked at Stephanie hopefully.

"Well," Stephanie said, "I'd rather drink my breakfast, actually, but I'll try to eat something."

They started to walk out past Charles, but Stephanie stopped and looked Charles over very carefully from head-to-toe. "xx-xx-xx, Mom, he's a good-looking guy…"

Suddenly Stephanie buried her face in her mother's shoulder and sobbed again. "Oh, Billy… Billy… I miss you so much…"

After a minute or two, Stephanie recovered her composure some and went back to a stall to use toilet paper to blow her nose and wipe her face. "Billy was pretty good looking, too, don't you think?"

Susan started to panic, trying to think of some way to agree, but the only images that came to her mind were the way he snarled at them on Sunday morning.

Fortunately, Stephanie didn't seem to require an answer as she put her arm around Susan again and leaned on her shoulder as they walked out.

They went out to the bodyguards' cars and Charles talked to Mike, who was also looking much worse for the wear.

They drove to a nearby fast-food restaurant, and two men took orders and went in to buy it all. They all ate in the cars, including the guards.

On the drive to the Cambridge Treatment Center, Stephanie sat in the middle and fell asleep leaning against Susan. Susan watched as Charles quickly fell asleep leaning against the far door. *Lord… thank you for your help so far, but please, please help us get Stephanie the help she needs to overcome her drinking… and help her love you… and… Lord…*

Susan awoke with a start and realized that Charles was trying to wake her and Stephanie.

"Girls…? We're here, and they're ready for us," Charles said again.

They got out, and Stephanie clung to Susan as they walked in.

Oh, no, I haven't had a chance to tell Charles I promised Stephanie we wouldn't force her to stay here… well, her biggest worry seemed to be about being tied down and things like that. If we can make sure they won't do anything like that, maybe she'll choose to stay. "Charles… Stephanie's concerned they might use rough treatment, and she heard some awful stories about other places… Can we make sure they won't do that here?"

"We most definitely can," Charles assured them. "And if you don't like this place for any reason, Stephanie, we'll find a better one."

"Thanks," managed a lethargic Stephanie.

They all met together with the Director, Dr. Nester, as well as another doctor, and two attendants, who explained the program and answered all their questions. Reassured that no harsh treatment was ever used at Cambridge, the doctor and an attendant showed Susan and Stephanie around the facility while Charles talked further with Dr. Nester.

After the walking tour, Susan and Stephanie rejoined Charles and Dr. Nester in the reception area.

"Well, Stephanie, what do you think?" asked Charles.

"Well, they have some beautiful gardens," Stephanie said, then hesitated. "The truth is, I'm scared xx-xx-xx. This all sounds good, and I guess it's as good as it gets, but…"

"If we're not the very best, we're very close to it," Dr. Nester said, "and we're always working hard to become even better."

"But what happens if I crap out here?" Stephanie said dejectedly. "What if I'm just a loser, and I'll always be a drunk?"

"Oh, honey," Susan began, "Don't think…"

"Stop, Mom. I don't need 'everything's going to be fine' right now, I need the straight xx-xx-xx."

"Well," the doctor replied, "our success rate for alcohol-dependency clients staying sober for the first six months after they leave is better than ninety percent."

Stephanie thought about that for a moment. "And after six months?"

"The success rate of patients at the three year mark is about seventy-five percent," Dr. Nester admitted. "But most of those in the twenty-five percent who relapse don't have a good family supporting them."

Stephanie thought again. "Seventy-five percent, huh? I guess that's better than a hundred percent chance of xx-xx-xx."

Stephanie looked up at Charles. "What about you? This place has got to cost a xx-xx-xx of money. How you gonna feel about it if you pay all this money and I foul up again after I get out?"

Charles put a hand lightly on her shoulder as he answered, "If you're willing to try this, your Mother and I don't mind paying. And if you need to come back over and over again, that's okay, too, as long as you get the best care available, and you still want it."

"xx-xx-xx," Stephanie said flatly. "xx-xx-xx."

"We can start right now, if you're willing, Stephanie," offered Dr. Nester.

Stephanie sank into a nearby chair and dropped her head. Susan took the chair on one side, and Charles took the chair on the other.

Stephanie was fighting tears again as she looked at her mother. "You promise me you'll come and visit me every day?"

"Yes, Stephanie, we promise. We'll be here every day."

"That will be a big help," the doctor said.

"And Stephanie…" Charles began, "they don't usually let patients leave during the early days of their treatment program, but I talked to them about… well, when… when they have the funeral for Billy, we can take you to that."

Stephanie lunged for her mother's embrace again and sobbed for a minute before wailing, "Billy…! Oh, Billy… he didn't have a family… all he had was me…! Nobody to… nobody will…"

"We'll take care of it," Charles said lovingly. "We'll make sure he has a very nice funeral."

Stephanie continued to sob, and Susan gingerly moved a hand up and down her back to comfort her.

"We can have an attendant go with you to the services, and they can administer a sedative, if necessary," the doctor said quietly.

When she was able to quit crying again, Stephanie agreed to begin treatment, and Charles left them to deal with some paperwork. He brought a couple of documents for Susan and Stephanie to sign, and they were all done.

Stephanie began crying again as they parted, and she and Susan told each other again how sorry they were for everything they had done wrong to each other over the years.

As Stephanie was finally being led away and Susan and Charles started to leave, Stephanie cried out, "Wait!" and ran after them.

Susan opened her arms to hug Stephanie again, but Stephanie threw herself into Charles' arms instead and gave him a bear hug.

"Thank you. For everything." Stephanie whispered before letting go and then hugging her mother again before running back to the attendant.

Susan and Charles just stood there this time and watched Stephanie walk away.

"Thank you so much, Charles," Susan said quietly. "I'll never have the words to say how much..."

"Not me," Charles interrupted as they began to walk back out to the car, each with one arm around the other's waist. "It's not me, it's God. This is all His doing... Oh, by the way, Mike's investigation confirms that Billy had no living family, so I'll have Nat find out what it takes for us to be able to legally make the funeral arrangements. And I doubt he had a last will and testament, so Stephanie probably won't be able to keep his car. If there's a loan against it, the bank will probably get that."

"Oh, I didn't think about all that. Thank you for dealing with all those things..." *And, Lord, please keep helping Stephanie. Help her overcome her addiction, her grief, and help her come to know you, and love you. Oh! Lord, I've been so focused on Stephanie all these years... but now I have two stepsons. They won't replace Steve, but now I have two sons, and they need your love. I've never even met them, but I need you to really put them on my heart, Lord, so I can pray for them as much as I pray for Stephanie. Lord, Charles is such a wonderful man, surely you can reach his sons like you're reaching Stephanie...*

A while later, Susan and Charles leaned heavily against each other in the elevator ride back up to their suite, and trudged down the hall behind their escort.

They got in the room and locked the door.

"It feels like a week since we've had any sleep," Susan said, walking slowly toward the bedroom.

"A week...?" Charles mumbled, following along. "A week... today's Wednesday now... Yeah, it is, today's Wednesday!"

I hope you're not going to make a wisecrack about it being hump-day and wanting to...

"It's our anniversary!"

Susan stared at him, not comprehending.

"Our one-week anniversary!" Charles announced. "Since we first met!"

"Oh! I'm sorry, Charles, I didn't know what you were talking about. I'm too tired to think very clearly right now."

"And today is our one-day wedding anniversary!"

"You haven't had any more sleep than I have, and you're being way too energetic." *And I hope you're not trying to hint you want sex right now, 'cause if you are, you may have to do it with me snoring... oh, well, guess I'd better find out...* "Charles, is that your way of asking for sex?"

"What? No..." he replied, his level of excitement fading rapidly. "No, if I wanted to ask you for sex, it would sound something like, 'Do you feel like having sex?'"

"Oh. Okay."

"And the truth is, I'm kind of sore," Charles said as he began to undress sluggishly. "I'm not used to as much... 'activity' as we had yesterday."

"Me either. And we haven't had much sleep," Susan agreed as she went to the drapes and readjusted them to get rid of a couple of cracks letting sunlight in. "That light's awfully bright."

"Yeah..." Charles responded. "Hey... you want to sleep naked again?"

"Yeah... we didn't really get to finish our first sleep together and wake up with time to snuggle. That okay with you?"

"Sure..." Charles agreed, pulling off his shorts.

Susan went to the edge of the bed and plopped down while she took off her clothes and Charles crawled under the covers.

He took a deep breath and let it out as he settled into his pillow, then moaned and propped up on his elbows. "Uh... should we get a wakeup call?"

"Uh... I don't know..."

"Well, Stephanie was up all night, too, so she probably won't wake up soon," Charles pointed out.

Susan had started to get under the covers, but paused halfway in. *Uh...*

"And the doctors will call us if Stephanie needs us," he added.

"Uh, yeah," Susan acquiesced, and finished getting into bed. "No wakeup call."

"Okay," Charles said, laying his head down again.

"We'll call them as soon as we wake up." *As soon as we wake up... I wonder how long we'll sleep...? It's already late in the day...*

Chapter Eighteen

Rather than waking up normally, Susan gained consciousness slowly. *Uhhh... where am I...? The wedding... Stephanie... was all that a dream...?* She didn't move or even open her eyes while she struggled to think.

Lying on her back facing straight up, she took a deep breath and exhaled slowly. *Why am I so tired...? Where was I before I laid down...?* When the answers didn't come, she slowly opened her eyes, and just stared at the ceiling, trying to figure out which ceiling it was.

I don't recognize this room. It's not my room. She rolled her head slightly to the side and saw a glimmer of light through the curtains, then remembered closing them, and then she noticed the large lump in the covers next to her. *Charles...! We are married... and this is where we... oh! Stephanie! All that ruckus with you and Billy and the hospital place... that was last night... and this morning... that was real, wasn't it...?*

Susan quietly moved the covers and slowly slid her legs over the side and sat up, causing her head to throb for a minute. *Oh, Lord, this feels worse than when Billy beat me up... What time is it, anyway?*

She held a hand to her head as she turned enough to read the red digits of a bedside clock. *Two seventeen... P.M.... afternoon... we went to sleep just before noon didn't we...? That's only a few hours of sleep, but we need to get back to the treatment center to see Stephanie.*

At her bladder's prompting, she got up and walked slowly toward the bathroom, feeling her way instead of turning on any lights. *Hot tub's down there, toilet's this way...* a scene from their recent hot tub activities flashed through her mind.

Good gracious, how many times did we have sex yesterday? It was all day long... we had sex for hours... literally... for hours! She furrowed her brow as she sat down on the toilet. *Dear Lord, I hope Charles isn't going to expect that all the time, or even most of the time. Oh, I hope you know what you're doing Lord ... I'm old, and Charles was like a stallion yesterday. He's old too, older than me, but I feel older... worn out... I don't think I can keep up with him. Well, I hope I'm not too big of a disappointment to him, but at least you had him here to help with Stephanie... thank you so much for that, Lord!*

She shuffled her feet back to the bed, and decided against snapping the lights on to avoid waking Charles abruptly, opting instead to lie down next to him to wake him gently. "Charles..." she said softly. "We need to go back to the treatment center now. Charles..."

He was lying on his side facing away from her, and she shook his shoulder, but he didn't respond. Suddenly she noticed how heavy her head felt, and she let it sag down to her pillow while shaking him again. "Charles..."

Hours later, Susan woke up with a start and quickly sat up, ignoring a flash of pain in her head. She put out a hand to her side and discovered Charles wasn't there at the same time she noticed the bedroom door was ajar. "Charles... Charles are you here!?"

"Yes, honey," he replied immediately from the living room.

She jumped up, still naked, and ran to the door and stood behind it. "Is anyone else here?" she asked, peering around the edge.

Charles was fully dressed, clean-shaven, and was standing alone on the other side of the room. "No, of course not, honey. I wouldn't have left the door open if there had been. I thought you might need a little light, and I was hoping to hear you when you woke up."

"Oh, yeah, okay." *Why didn't you wake me up?* She turned on the light switch and started to get dressed in a rush. "We're late to go back to the hospital. I'll hurry. Let's leave right away. I don't want Stephanie to feel alone."

"I just called the treatment center a few minutes ago, and they said she's still asleep. She was up all night too, remember."

"Oh. Oh, yeah." She slowed down a bit, but kept dressing, then paused. "Maybe I should get a shower first?"

"Sure, if you want to."

"No," she decided and started dressing again. "Let's go. Maybe we can be there when she wakes up. That'd be good."

"Okay," Charles agreed, "I'll tell the boys."

Oh, yeah, I forgot about our escorts. "How long do you suppose we'll need body guards?"

"I haven't really thought that out yet. I'll talk to Mike about it."

On the way back to the treatment center in the back of an armored Suburban again, Susan leaned against Charles and held his arm. *We've been gone from the hospital... treatment center, too long.*

Stephanie may have woken up since Charles called. "Did they say how long Stephanie will need to stay there?"

"I talked to the doctor about that, and it's usually weeks or months, but there's no way to guess until she's been there awhile. It depends on how dependent her body's become to alcohol. And her mind. How dependent she feels may be more important than how dependent her body is."

Susan nodded while still resting her head against him. "Well, God can heal her mind and body."

"Oh, I think I forgot to tell you, this a Christian place."

"Really?!"

"Yeah," Charles replied. "They have a full-time chaplain, who's also a doctor, but most of the other doctors and staff are Christians, and addressing faith is a big part of the overall treatment plan."

Well that's good news.

"Their success rate is much higher than State institutions that exclude faith-based treatment. It's a shame, but those public facilities refuse to adopt a Christian approach even though it's proven to work so much better."

"That's too bad. I'm sure glad this place exists, and that we can afford it." *Oh, thank you Lord! This sounds like just the right place for Stephanie!*

Charles yawned, and infected Susan with it, then continued, "The first few days could still be very hard, though. Maybe even the first few weeks."

"Oh? But they said they have medicine to help with the hard parts."

"They do. And the drugs make it eas*ier*, but not necessarily easy."

"Well, how bad can it get?"

Charles sighed heavily. "Okay, I'm not going to hold back to try to keep you from worrying. That's the way you'd like it, right?"

"Yes, Charles," she said, "and thank you for remembering."

"Okay, well… she may have hallucinations, and uh, delirium tremors… seizures… even a heart attack or stroke."

"What…?" *A heart attack?!* "Charles, they didn't say anything about things that bad!"

"Well, the doctor told me that stuff. While you and Stephanie were being shown around."

"But… that's too dangerous!"

"Well, yeah, it is dangerous, but it's actually less dangerous than if she continues to drink. And the dangers are far less here, because she'll be watched around the clock until the worst of it's over, and there's always at least one doctor there in case she needs one."

Susan frowned as she absent-mindedly bit her lip. *Well, Lord we still need your grace and mercy as much as ever.*

Susan's cell phone rang and she fished it out of her purse and answered anxiously, thinking it might be the treatment center. "Hello?"

"Hello, this is the police department, is this Steph's mother?"

"Yes, yes it is. Is there something wrong?" Susan covered the microphone and whispered to Charles, "The police department."

"No ma'am. We have Steph's phone, and we need to return it to her. This number was listed in the phone under Mom, so we thought you might be able to tell us where she is so we can return it."

"Oh, she's at the... just a minute," she turned to Charles, "What's the name of the treatment center again?"

"Umm, Cambridge Treatment Center."

"It's the Cambridge Treatment Center, just north of Knoxville. I'm afraid I don't know the address."

"That's okay, we can look it up. And what's your name, ma'am?"

"Susan Taggart. Oh, no, I just got married. My name is Susan Parker now," Susan corrected herself with a pang of guilt, looking over at Charles and smiling an apology for the error.

"Uh-huh. And your husband's first name?"

"It's Charles," Susan replied, "Charles Parker."

"Uh-huh, and what's your... just a minute..."

Susan heard some background noises while the caller was talking to someone else. "They have..." she started to tell Charles.

"Okay, ma'am, that's all we need. We'll get Steph's phone back to her real soon."

"Okay. Well, thank you very much."

"Don't mention it," the caller said before hanging up.

"The police found Stephanie's cell phone," Susan explained to Charles, "and they're going to bring it back to her, but he didn't say exactly when."

"They're going to send someone all the way from Maryville just for that?" Charles asked.

"I think that's what he said."

"Huh," Charles grunted as his stomach growled.

"Do we need to stop and eat?" Susan asked. *I hope not, but... when did we eat last...?*

He looked at her thoughtfully and said, "They have a cafeteria at the treatment center. We can eat after we see Stephanie."

Susan smiled inside and quickly agreed, putting her arm back through Charles' arm and snuggling up close. *Perfect. Thank you, Charles.*

When they got to Cambridge, Susan was impatient as they followed an attendant to Stephanie's room, which was guarded by two of Mike's men. Susan and Charles entered quietly and Susan was relieved that Stephanie was still sleeping. She hurried to her side and started to take her hand, but refrained out of concern that she might wake her.

Stephanie was hooked up to an I.V., heart monitoring equipment, and at least a couple of EEG monitoring wires were attached to her scalp. Susan just stood there watching Stephanie sleep as Charles came to her side and put an arm around her. She took a deep breath and let it out slowly. *Well, Lord, here she is. Out of harm's way, in a place made for healing. They can help with her mind and her body, Lord, but she needs you to give her eternal life and love. Please lift her spirit to you, embrace her, Lord, let your love draw her to you.*

It was a medium-intensive-care room with a single bed which Susan and Stephanie had seen on their tour, just across from a nurse's monitoring station, and next door to a larger medium-intensive-care suite with four beds. Stephanie's room had an extra-wide doorway and a curtain instead of a door, but it had a private bathroom. Completing the room were a closet, end table, two chairs, and a ledge wide enough to sit on under a window that went all the way across the outside wall. There wasn't a television set, as it was later explained that the noise from one might interfere with the nurses' ability to carefully monitor the patients.

There were a lot of trees and flowers outside, and many of the trees could easily be seen from the bed if the drapes were open, even when fully reclined. Currently, a set of heavy drapes covered half the window, and a set of sheer curtains covered the rest. The sun was setting outside, so most of the light in the room was from an indirect light fixture that provided subdued lighting.

Susan shifted her weight to one foot, and Charles got one of the chairs and moved it to where Susan was standing. Susan thanked him with a smile and sat down, then frowned. *I can't see her well from down here...* "Charles," she asked quietly, "Do you think they might have a stool or something? This chair puts me down too low, and I want her to be able to see me as soon as she wakes up."

"I'll find out," Charles whispered, and disappeared from the room.

Her hair spikes are all messed up. I wonder what she needs to take care of her hair like that? Susan stood up again and leaned on the bed rails. *I wonder how Stephanie would feel about me reading the Bible to her while she's recovering? I wish I had thought to bring my Bible with me. I'll definitely bring it the next time I come...*

Charles returned a little later with an old wooden stool. He moved the chair back to its original location and put the stool where Susan had been standing, topping it with a folded linen blanket to provide a cushion. He helped her up onto it and put his arm around her again as he stood beside her.

"We'll need to get her some cosmetics and toiletry items," Susan whispered as she kept looking at Stephanie.

Charles nodded and left the room again.

Probably some kind of gel for your hair, but we'll have to wait 'til you wake up to ask you what kind. We can guess at basics... oh, Lord, she's my own daughter, and I have no idea if she uses pads or tampons now...

Charles returned with something to write on, and they stood in a corner of the room while Susan told him what to put on the list. He helped Susan back onto the stool, gave the list to one of the bodyguards just outside the door, and then sat down in one of the chairs.

Minutes turned into a few uncomfortable hours in the small room, with occasional visits by nurses or aides, who brought coffee to Susan and Charles, but when Stephanie finally started stirring, Susan was right by her side.

"Hello, sweetie, Momma's right here," she said as she slid off the stool and took Stephanie's closest hand in both of hers.

Stephanie struggled to open her eyes and focus on Susan. "Momma?"

"Yes, honey, I'm right here." *And I'm going to be here as long as you need me.*

"Uhh... headache," Stephanie mumbled as her eyes closed again. "I need a drink."

"We can get you something for your headache, but honey, you're in a treatment center, remember?"

Stephanie's brow furrowed. "Is... is Billy dead? Was all that real?"

Oh, Lord, help me not mess this up... "Yes, honey, I'm sorry, but it was. You agreed to come to a treatment center, remember?"

Stephanie opened her eyes, looked around the room, and closed them again. "Yeah. I remember."

"They're going to help you get better," Susan said. *That sounds so lame, but I don't know what else to say...*

Stephanie moaned and twisted a little in the bed. "I feel like xx-xx-xx."

Oh, honey, I wish I could take your place for you...

Charles had stood up but stayed where he was, and now he stepped over to the bed and pressed the call button.

"Yes?" came a female voice over the speaker.

"Stephanie's awake," Charles said, "and she's not feeling very good."

"I'll be right there," the voice said.

Oh, why didn't I think of that...? Charles is action, and I'm... I'm just a talker. Stephanie needed something, and Charles had to think of what to do instead of me... Lord, help me help my little girl... my precious little girl...

Less than a minute later, a nurse appeared, checked Stephanie's vital signs, and questioned her about how she was feeling.

"I can give you one of two different medications to help you feel better," the nurse explained. "One will make you sleep and the other won't. If you're hungry, I can give you the non-drowsy medicine and get your supper, or you can wait for the medicine until after you eat and then take the sleepy kind. Or if you're not hungry..."

"Knock me out," Stephanie requested. "I'm not hungry for food and I feel like xx-xx-xx. I'd rather sleep."

"Okay," the nurse replied, "I'll be right back."

"Don't you think you ought to try to eat something, sweetheart?" Susan entreated.

"You eat," Stephanie replied curtly, without opening her eyes.

Oh, I knew it. I knew I was going to say something wrong. I don't know what to say right... Well, since Stephanie's love language is touch, I think, I'll try to concentrate on that instead of talking...
While she kept holding Stephanie's closest hand with one of her hands, Susan used the other to stroke the back of Stephanie's hand and wrist.

"I need a man, Momma," Susan recalled Stephanie telling her.

If only you had a good husband like Charles. Maybe he could help you better than I can...

The nurse returned, administered the medication through the I.V. tube, and explained that Stephanie would probably sleep for at least several hours.

Susan never let go of Stephanie's hand from the time she woke until she was sound asleep again. When she finally got up, she kissed Stephanie on the forehead and stroked her cheek. "I love you, Stephanie. God loves you, and so does Charles," she whispered softly.

Susan heard Charles' stomach growl from across the room and smiled as she walked over to him. *He sure has been patient. Not a word of complaint.*

Charles got up and met her in a corner of the room. "You hungry? We haven't eaten since breakfast."

"Yes, very. I was too nervous to eat before, but now I'm really hungry."

"You want to stay here and I'll bring you something, or do you want to join me in the cafeteria?"

"Probably sleep all night," the nurse said. Still... Susan thought while looking at Stephanie. "You wouldn't mind eating alone and bringing me something? I know I can't do anything for Stephanie by staying here, but... it's just that... she's been gone so long... I just want to stay and look at her."

Charles nodded, "I understand. I'll get something for both of us and bring it back. We can both eat in here."

Susan smiled and hugged him. *I wouldn't be surprised if you're the most thoughtful and understanding man in the whole world...*

"Any particular request?"

"No," Susan replied, "I don't think so. I don't know what they have, and I don't have a taste for anything in particular, so whatever looks good to you, just get enough for both of us."

"Okay," Charles agreed with a smile. "I'll be right back," he concluded and hurried from the room.

Susan stepped to the foot of the bed and teared-up as she prayed for Stephanie. After a few minutes, she sighed and sat down in the chair Charles had been sitting in. *I wonder if we could we stay here? Do they have portable cots or something like they do in some hospitals?*

She glanced around the room. *There's enough room in here for one cot, but not two. Maybe they have a bigger room available. Uh-oh... but if we stay here, or if just I stay here, Charles won't be able to have sex with me whenever he wants to. And judging by yesterday, he likes to have sex a lot...*

She thought about some of their activities from yesterday and realized she had a feeling of soreness somewhere inside and wondered if that was the same kind of soreness Grandma Brenda had referred to. *Well, that's not too bad. If it doesn't get any worse than that, that'll be easy to deal with. Shoot, I can just ignore that.*

Susan shook her head and silently chastised herself. *Here I am with my daughter in a hospital bed, and I'm thinking about sex. Lord... help me! Well... I have to think of Charles now, too. Right? And like the handbook says, I need to keep him sexually satisfied...* She remembered Charles passed out on the bed last night while she did a little victory dance and a subtle smile crept across her lips.

She shook her head again, stood up, and stepped over to the bed. *Well, there's a time and place for everything, and this is the time to take care of Stephanie. Besides, Charles said he doesn't normally need as much sex as he got yesterday. And hey! He wasn't getting any sex before that! Not since Laura divorced him a few years ago! Maybe he won't mind too much if we spend a lot of time with Stephanie. We can go back to the hotel to have sex every couple of days or so if he needs it...*

Susan idly walked around the bed and picked up the makeshift stool cushion that had fallen on the floor. *I asked for a stool. Charles not only found one, he got me a cushion to boot. God, what a loving man you've given me. If there's another good man... that would probably be the next best thing you could do for Stephanie. Even if Billy gave his life to you before he died, he was the worst possible kind of husband... or just boyfriend, I guess.* She put it back on the stool, sat down on it again, and just watched her precious daughter sleep until Charles returned.

When Charles returned, he was carrying a tray with two large sandwiches, two slices of chocolate cake, and two soft drinks. They sat in the two chairs and Charles rested the tray on one armrest from each chair.

"Sorry it took so long," Charles said in hushed tones, "It was after normal hours and I had to find a cashier. Not much of a selection, either."

"That's okay. This is fine," Susan said just before digging in.

"I started to get chips," Charles commented after eating a few bites, "but I thought they'd be too noisy, so I opted for the cake instead."

Susan nodded. "Great idea," she said, savoring the anticipation of biting into the cake. She took a deep breath and let it out before chewing again. Her shoulders relaxed and she leaned back against the chair, splitting her time watching Charles eat and Stephanie sleep.

Charles finished his sandwich a little before Susan, and Susan gave him the last couple of bites of hers. They polished off the cake, and kept the sodas while Charles took the tray and trash outside.

Thank you, Lord, for the cake. That was a nice treat. Which was because Charles was so thoughtful about making noise that might disturb Stephanie. Susan sighed happily as she stepped back over to the bed. *My darling Stephanie... you're here... we're together... even if you're sleeping. And you saw me here when you woke up. Oh, thank you Lord, for that. Please open Stephanie's heart to you. And Charles' boys, too...* she added as Charles came back in.

Susan's hands were on the bed rail as Charles came up behind her and put his arms around her, under her arms, lacing his fingers right under her breasts. She sighed again silently when he kissed the side of her neck. *Lord, please don't forget Charles' boys, either. They need you, too. I wish they had been able to come to our wedding. Oh, Lord, and please help them not resent me for marrying their father. Oh, my, Father, I have no idea how to be a good step-mother. I sure will need your help with that...*

They stood like until Susan noticed a growing pressure against her rear end. *Oh, no, you can't be getting horny now... this is a terrible time. I hate to put you off, but I want to stay here tonight. Stephanie may wake up when the medicine wears off, and I want to be here if she does. There's no doubting that bulge pushing against me, though. What do I do now, Lord? How long would it take to go back to the hotel, let Charles hump me, and then rush back here? Maybe he'd like to stay there and get some more sleep. He won't want to stay here all night. Oh, I haven't told him I'd like to stay... maybe he's expecting us to leave soon, to come back in the morning...*

Susan let go of the rail and turned, but Charles only loosened his arms enough for her to turn, keeping her in his embrace, and she rested her hands on his hips rather than let them dangle.

"Charles," she whispered, "I'd like to stay here tonight..." She was acutely aware of her breasts now pressing against his chest, and his bulge pushing into her from the front side now. *Oh, Lord, how do I...*

"Me too," Charles whispered back.

You do...? But... "But... you're all hard. Don't you need us to go back to the hotel for a few minutes?"

Charles chuckled. "Of course not. A man can have an erection without wanting to have sex."

What? Really...? Not based on life with Marty... "You... you really don't need to have sex?"

"Obviously, I'm physically aroused, but no, I don't need to have sex. Just holding you right now is all I need. And all I want."

Wow. Holy smokes. You're not only not Marty, you're like the anti-Marty. Susan moved her hands to his back and turned her head as she rested it against him. Instead of worrying about his erection, she began to relish it, subtlety moving against his body to let her feel it better.

"I love you so much, Susan."

She smiled and hugged him tighter. *Wow! This is so cool! Being able to cuddle without it turning into a big effort to get my husband off.* Her breathing started to get a little faster, and she noticed her breasts feeling warm and tingly. She drew in a deep breath as she closed her eyes and remembered their dancing on the boat. They began to sway, as if slow-dancing without their feet moving, and Susan day-dreamed of Charles sweeping her off her feet and carrying her up the stairs, only this time she felt his cock pressing up against her as he carried her.

All of a sudden Susan silently gasped in shock. *Oh, no! Now I'm getting horny! I've been practically grinding against your... forget practically, I was actually doing it! And right here in the...* Susan shot a glance at the closed curtain in the doorway, put both hands against his chest and shoved, which resulted in her pushing away from him while he stayed in place, since he was much heavier.

"Charles!" she exclaimed. Though still whispering, it was much louder than she had been.

Charles looked puzzled.

She motioned to him, and they stepped over to a corner of the room and she kept her hands off him. "Charles, I'm sorry, that was getting me all worked up, and we can't do that here. Stephanie could wake up, and a nurse or the bodyguards could come in at any minute..."

"Yeah, you're right, we need to calm down."

Her eyebrows went up. "You... does nothing ever get you upset?" As she said it, she remembered how upset he had gotten with Andy on the day they met. *You got upset when you were protecting me...*

"Darling, right now I'm just immensely satisfied."

Satisfied. Satisfied just to hold me in your arms... Susan started to open her mouth to reply but couldn't think of anything to say. *Yeah... that felt... very nice. But... I think maybe we shouldn't tease each other like that when we can't... Forget about me... you really don't feel compelled to have sex when you're hard...? I think it may take me awhile to get to where I can really believe that...*

She cast a glance at his crotch as surreptitiously as possible, and still felt extra warmth in her breasts and tingles from where he pressed into her own crotch. *Oh, Charles... that did feel soo good... but I really need to cool my jets so we can stay here.* She glanced at his pants again and walked into the bathroom. She spotted a towel, slashed water on her face, and grabbed the towel to dry off.

Charles stepped into the doorway as Susan was drying her face. "Oh, while I was getting supper, I asked a nurse if they had a roll-away bed or something, and she said they do. They should be bringing it in soon, I should think."

She turned to face him as she finished toweling off and dropped the towel on the sink's counter. *When you said you wanted to stay tonight, you weren't just saying what you thought I wanted to hear. You were already thinking about how we could arrange things...* "But... how big is it?" Susan asked. "There's not enough room in here for a bed big enough for two people. Unless... maybe they have a bigger room?"

"You're right about this room," Charles concurred, "but I'll sleep in one of the chairs. This is the biggest intensive care room they have, and she needs to stay here until she's out of danger from the physical withdrawal symptoms. By the way, they have a building fund to create a new wing where they plan to have a couple of executive suites. Maybe we could help with that."

Yeah, if we have any money left after paying for the private army. "No, you take the bed and I'll take the chair. I may not sleep much tonight anyway since I slept all day."

"Well then, let's wait and see which of us gets sleepy first. Maybe we can take turns taking cat naps."

Susan perked up. "That's a great idea!"

A folding bed was finally brought in and set up, and the night whiled away for Susan and Charles with quiet sitting and occasional whispering, hand-holding, cat-napping, and caring for Stephanie when she woke up once in the middle of the night. At one point,

Charles went for a walk to stretch his legs and came back with some magazines from a patient lounge, but it was difficult to read with the only light coming through the doorway curtain and the monitors around Stephanie's bed.

Chapter Nineteen

Around ten in the morning, Dr. Nester came by and asked Susan and Charles to join him just outside the room.

"I've looked over Stephanie's chart, and so far she's doing very well. Have either of you noticed any signs of hallucinations yet?"

"Hallucinations?" ask Susan, a little startled.

The doctor looked at her. "Did Mr. Parker not explain to you what we can expect over the next few days?"

"I probably forgot to tell her a lot of it, doctor," Charles admitted, "and Susan likes to know everything, even the bad parts, so if you wouldn't mind going over it again..."

Yes, please...

"I see. Well, it's been..." he looked at his watch, "about thirty-six hours since Stephanie last had a drink of alcohol, according to what she told us during her initial work-up. Visual hallucinations are fairly common in severe cases such as your daughter's. If they occur, they usually begin within the first two days, and can last for hours, days, or even a few weeks, but they're not dangerous as long as the patient has someone looking after them."

Susan nodded and nervously clasped her hands in front.

"We're much more concerned right now about any seizures or convulsions, which could begin any time in the first few days. In another day or two, she may get delirium tremens, commonly referred to as the D.T.'s. If she gets D.T.'s, the risk of seizures, strokes, and heart problems increases for a week or so, but sedation will dramatically decrease those risks. We have cardiologists and neurologists on call at all times, but the first week or so is the period of highest risk."

Charles put an arm around Susan's and gave her a gentle shoulder-hug as they continued to give the doctor their undivided attention.

"One of our goals is to minimize the stress of physical withdrawal, and for that we're giving her Thiamin and other vitamins and minerals and allowing her to spend a lot of time sedated. We don't want to keep her constantly sedated so we give her periodic doses and let her come out of it a little in between doses so we can monitor what her body's doing more accurately."

Despite her devotion, Susan was so tired she was beginning to find it difficult to concentrate on the doctor's explanation.

"She'll stay in this unit until her body's rid itself of physical dependency on alcohol, and then we'll wean her off of the sedatives as we begin intensive treatments for psychological withdrawal. Evidence indicates it's primarily the psychological dependency that causes most relapses, and that's where your participation in the recovery process will be the most important. For now, just spend time with her when she's awake if you can, and report any symptoms or problems to the nurses right away."

Susan and Charles nodded again.

Spend time with her while she's awake. Report symptoms. Got it.

"Do you have any questions?" Doctor Nester asked.

Susan took a deep breath and looked at Charles.

"Guess not, right now," Charles replied for both of them.

"Well, you can ask the nurses anything, and if they don't have the answer, they'll get someone who does."

After they thanked him and Dr. Nester left, Charles left to eat breakfast in the cafeteria while Susan napped again, and he brought her a breakfast that she ate while he napped again.

I sure wish I had thought to bring my Bible with me. I wonder... After looking carefully at Stephanie to make sure she was sound asleep, Susan stepped out to the nurse's station. "Excuse me, uh..." she glanced at the name tag, "Nancy... but I was wondering, do you know if there's a spare Bible in the chapel that I could borrow until..."

"Oh, you can borrow mine," Nancy replied cheerily, as she reached over for it.

"Oh, well, are you sure? But then I'd be keeping you from reading it..."

"Yes, absolutely. I have a New Testament and Psalms in my purse I can read if I get time for it."

"Well, okay. Thank you. Thank you very much. I'll be sure to bring mine the next time I come."

"You keep that one as long as you need it, Mrs. Parker, and if I'm not here when you want to return it, you can just put in on the desk here."

Susan went back into the room, checked on Stephanie and Charles, and then sat down to read and pray. *Not my translation, but it'll do. Oh, I see Nancy highlights and write notes in the margins like I do. Still though, I'd rather have my own notes... makes mine seem more like an old friend.* Despite her preferences, she found herself drawn to perusing Nancy's highlights and notes, which gave her a feeling that she and Nancy were kindred spirits.

After a while, she got up and stood by Stephanie's bed. *Oh, Stephanie, I wish you'd wake up and talk to me. I know you need to sleep a lot right now, but when we get past this, will you talk to me then, like you did that night at the police station? But you need touch, not talk... "I need a man, Momma,"* Susan recalled Stephanie saying.

She remembered how seriously Stephanie had looked at Charles the first time they met and said, "Xx-xx-xx, Mom, he's really good-looking..." An image flashed through her mind of Stephanie living at home with them and trying to seduce Charles. *Oh, no, Lord! How can I think such things?!*

Unwillingly, she remembered Billy talking about Stephanie having sex with lots of men. *She was a professional porn star...! Her appetite for sex, and her skills must be very strong if she... No, Lord, she's my daughter, and even if she's not born again, Charles is. Charles would be faithful to me...*

Her mind flashed to the look on Charles' face when he saw her in the bikini, and how he had charged out of the tub. *What if Stephanie dresses provocatively around the house? Will Charles be able to resist that? She's not related by blood. I wonder what Stephanie sleeps in?*

Next her thoughts jumped to the hallway bathroom in her house with the broken lock, and how she herself had stood outside the door, tempted to enter while Charles was showering, and then she pictured Stephanie standing there, turning the doorknob. *Oh, God, what is wrong with me? Why am I thinking these terrible things? Charles is a Godly man, and he'll be taking showers in our bathroom from now on, and we can get that lock fixed, and...*

Susan imagined Stephanie coming out of her old bedroom in a porn-worthy set of lacy panties and bra, casually strolling into the dining room for breakfast, and sashaying her hips when she Charles notice her. *"How in the hell..."* Susan remembered Charles saying, *"Oh, sorry about my pre-Christian language." Oh, Charles, if you can slip up in that...*

No! Dear God, I will not think such things! Oh, Lord, help me to think about things that are true, things that are noble and right, things that are pure and lovely, things that are excellent and praiseworthy!

Susan closed her eyes and raised her hands as she continued

praying, *Lord give me a clean heart and a pure mind. Don't let me be tempted by evil thoughts. Let your thoughts be my thoughts, Lord, let your ways be my ways.*

All of a sudden, a realization struck Susan: *Lord, Stephanie told me plainly that she needs a man. If touch is her love language, then she may need a man sooner rather than later. It doesn't matter how old we are, when we long for a man, it can be really hard on our hearts. It can cause terrible pain. She doesn't need that kind of complication, Lord! She needs to be born again, but she also needs a Godly man who can overlook her past and thinks she's beautiful no matter how she wears her hair. She needs to love you, Lord, but she also needs someone she can hold. Can you get her to go to my Church? Can you bring someone else there to meet her? Oh, Lord, we need you in so many ways!*

A beeping noise interrupted Susan, and a moment later Nancy entered.

"Stephanie just moved her arm and pinched off the I.V.," she explained as she moved Stephanie's arm back down to her side.

A moment later the beeping stopped and Nancy left as Charles started getting up.

That afternoon, both Susan and Charles had much longer naps, and twice Stephanie woke up, but didn't feel like talking much, though she ate and drank a little. The second time, she got up to use the bathroom, and after that Susan, Charles, and a nurse escorted her on a walk through the halls, with Stephanie pushing her wheeled I.V. stand ahead of her, and two bodyguards trailing behind them.

Late that afternoon, while Stephanie was sleeping and Susan and Charles were sitting in the chairs, Mike Samuelson came by and gestured from the doorway, indicating he wanted them to join him outside the room.

Uhhh... does he want me too? Susan struggled to her feet, and noticed that Charles looked a little stiff himself.

"Hey, Mike," Charles said with a somewhat dull tone of voice, "sorry I haven't called today. Guess I just plain forgot."

"That's okay. But there are some issues we need to discuss."

"Yeah, definitely," Charles agreed. "I guess you're winding things up?"

Susan noticed that Mike's face got a little cloudy in response to the question.

"Well, we can wrap it up if you want us to. It's certainly true that

Billy's no longer a threat, and he was the original reason you hired us."

"But there's some reason you think you should stay on?" Charles asked.

"Well," Mike continued, "doesn't it bother you how quickly Big Ed got a hit man to kill Billy? It appears Billy was killed less than an hour after he told Big Ed he was quitting."

What difference does that make? Susan pondered.

Charles' phone started vibrating, but he ignored it.

"That was really fast, and it indicates Big Ed has a big organization. And Big Ed must have wanted Billy killed to keep him from talking, so he must have figured Billy could have a significant amount of information about his operations."

Neither Susan nor Charles said anything, but Charles took out his phone, glanced at it, hit a button that made the vibrations stop, and put it back in his pocket.

Mike looked a little frustrated. "As far as Big Ed is concerned, Billy might have told anything or everything he knew to Stephanie."

It took only another moment for Susan to grasp the implication, and she gasped as she grabbed Charles' hand and clutched it. "So he might try to come after Stephanie?!" *Heavenly Father, I thought that was nightmare was over!*

Mike nodded. "That's a possibility you should consider... and that reminds me, Dennis was riding shotgun on your drive over here this morning, and he told me he overheard you got a phone call from a police department about returning Stephanie's phone."

The phone... "Yes..." Susan acknowledged.

"You know," Charles mentioned, "I kind of thought there was something strange about that, but..."

"Well, I checked with Detective Benson," Mike said, "and he did some checking, and he couldn't find anyone who knew anything about it. We're guessing that Stephanie left her phone in their apartment?"

Susan frowned and shrugged. *Who cares where they found it? We could have gotten her another one anyway...*

Charles looked at Susan and shook his head. "We have no idea."

Mike took a deep breath before going on. "Well, someone searched her apartment since the police left it, even though it was taped off as a crime scene."

Something clicked in Susan's mind. "Are you saying the police don't really have it?"

Panic made her instantly alert. "Are you saying that call may have been from Big Ed or his men?!"

Susan tightened her grip on Charles' hand like a vise, "Charles! I told them we're here! I told them our names!" *Oh, God, what have I done?!*

"Are your men..." Charles began.

"They're on high alert, and well prepared, but I'd recommend that we stay on, and that we make some changes."

"Of course, of course," Charles agreed without hesitation.

Oh, God... oh, God... Susan continued praying, *what have I done? I told a killer right where Stephanie is...!*

Mike got Stephanie's cell phone number from Susan and then explained, "If the case against Big Ed becomes a Federal case, Stephanie could probably get protection from the Marshals Service..." Mike explained. Getting no reaction to that, he continued, "But the big choice right now is whether you want Stephanie to stay here or not. This place is kind of isolated, which has advantages and disadvantages from a security standpoint. If Big Ed knows this address, we'd have to come up with some elaborate tricks to try to prevent them from following us to a new treatment center, and whatever we do might not work. So, we can try to move her somewhere else that might or might not be any better security-wise, or we can try to defend her right here."

Susan turned toward Charles and started crying into his shoulder. *Oh, God, lead us! Guide us! Help us! Protect Stephanie! What should we do?!*

"You also need to consider how much effort it would be to find another treatment center you like as well as this one," Mike said. "Oh, and Big Ed's people might also be able to follow us to a new hotel, but if Stephanie stays here, the current hotel is highly defensible, so you don't have to change hotels."

Charles took a deep breath and let it out slowly while he rubbed a temple. "So you don't think we need to move right this minute."

"No, and we'll need some time to prepare if you do decide we should move."

"How... how long do you think we could take to decide? Without adding to the danger," he added wearily.

"Well, we'll keep doing our best to protect you all here and at the Knoxville Plaza. Take as much time as you need to think it through, and if you decide you want us to move, we'll be ready."

"I... we... don't know of any other treatment centers, and this one seems to be really good," Charles said.

Susan stopped crying enough to voice a protest. "I don't think staying here's a very good idea. What about Dr. Nester? Maybe he could refer us to some other good ones."

Charles nodded. "Yeah. Yeah, I'll ask him about that."

Another man entered the intensive care suite and stood behind Mike.

"Oh, and one thing to set your expectations," Mike went on, "Whenever Stephanie gets moved to a private room, wherever it is, I want a man inside her room at all times. Another just outside the room, some roving men, and another room nearby as a command post, like we have now. But if you agree to having someone inside Stephanie's room, it will eliminate any family privacy there."

"Safety first," Charles said. "Safety comes before privacy. Do whatever it takes to protect Stephanie as well as humanly possible."

"We will, Charles," Mike said and started to leave.

The man behind Mike took a step forward and touched Mike's arm. Mike noticed, and introduced him.

"Oh, Charles, Susan, this is Dr. David Martin. He's the chaplain here."

Oh, no, I must look terrible, Susan fretted. Susan turned to face him, struggling with tears, and everyone shook hands as Charles pulled out a tissue and handed it to her.

"Mr. and Mrs. Parker, Mike told me a little about your predicament yesterday, and I've been praying for you. I'm also a licensed psychologist, and I'll be part of Stephanie's counseling team once she's ready for that step, and I'll be happy to speak with you or her or pray with you or her at any time. And also we have a small chapel with a private prayer room that you're welcome to use any time."

"Thank you…" Susan began, then hesitated.

"Just call me David."

"Okay," Susan agreed. "And just call us Charles and Susan. Stephanie and I saw the chapel… I guess it was yesterday."

"Do you know how to find it from here? Just turn left when you leave this suite, and it's down the hall on the left, just across from the entrance to the cafeteria."

"Yes, thanks, I remember," Susan replied. She was still gripping Charles' hand tightly, and she heard him sigh.

"How about show me where it is, honey?" asked Charles somberly.

"Well, I'm going to get back to work," Mike said, excusing himself. "I'll talk you later."

"I'll be happy to show you…" David began.

"Just… I'd like Susan to show me, if you don't mind," Charles interrupted.

"Oh, certainly. I'll see you another time then," David said. He turned to depart, then paused. "By the way, there's a lot of insulation in the walls of the prayer room. Someone could be quite loud and not disturb anyone outside."

I guess he wants us to know we can cry or whatever and not worry about it.

Susan and Charles watched him leave and Charles put an arm around Susan.

"Stephanie will probably sleep for at least a couple of hours," Charles said, his voice cracking. "Do you think… would you mind if both of us spend a little time in that prayer room?

Oh, Charles… Susan saw him raise his hand to his face to brush away tears, and a wave of concern for him washed over her. She nodded her assent, but instead of leading him there right away, she hugged him and he leaned heavily on her. *Oh, Lord… Charles' heart is as vulnerable as mine. We both need you Lord… and Stephanie! We all need you so much… How bad is it that I told someone where we are? You can protect us anywhere, from anyone, can't you? I know you can, but will you? You don't protect everyone from every harm all the time, and I don't know your will… Lord, I don't care what happens to me, but please take care of Stephanie. Bring her and Charles' boys to your salvation, and Lord…*

Quiet sobs shook them both.

Oh, Lord… please take care of Charles… in whatever way is best for him… he loves you with all his heart… please take care of him…

After a moment, she looked up and one of Charles' tears splashed on her cheek, mingling with her own. She took his hand, and started leading him toward the chapel, and in the hallway they walked with an arm around each other's waist.

They spent the better part of an hour in that prayer room, praying and crying out to God for grace and mercy, asking for guidance about what to do, and ended by giving him thanks for all he had already done for Stephanie, Billy, and themselves.

There was a tissue box in the prayer room, and the small trash can had almost filled up as Susan blew her nose again.

"I think… I feel…" Charles began, "I kind of have a sense that we should stay here. That this is where God wants us to be."

"I feel that way, too," Susan said. "It kind of doesn't make sense to me. My brain says that if Big Ed knows we're here, we should go somewhere else, but I do have strong feeling that we should stay anyway."

"Okay, then, we'll stay, at least for now. We can keep praying, and if we sense God telling us to move, then we can always move later."

"Yes," Susan agreed, "maybe God does want us to move, but not yet. It's just as important to do what God wants us to do *when* he wants us to, as opposed to just doing it whenever we first think of it."

Charles nodded as they both got up and headed back toward Stephanie's room.

"Who was that call from?" Susan asked.

"What call…?"

"When we were talking to Mike."

"Oh, I almost forgot," Charles said, fishing his phone out of his pocket. "It was Nat."

Charles called Nat back, and they paused just outside the intensive care suite. "It's about the funeral arrangements for Billy, Susan. I asked Nat to take of it, and he wants to talk to me about it. You go on in in case Stephanie wakes up early, and I'll tell you about it later. I'll stay out here to make sure Stephanie doesn't hear any of it…"

"Okay. You're right, she doesn't need any more stress right now than she's getting from the withdrawal symptoms."

Susan went into Stephanie's room and sat on the stool, which now had a regular cushion one of the nurses brought in. *That was very thoughtful of someone. More padding than the other one… and my rear end likes this one a lot better.*

When Charles came back in, he stood beside Susan and whispered, "Saturday at eleven A.M., if the staff thinks Stephanie can handle it then. Cemetery's in Knoxville."

Susan nodded and yawned. "Mind if I take the bed for a while?"

"Sure, go ahead."

Susan laid down face down and pulled a sheet over her shoulders. *Need to get back to regular hours… sleep at night… wish Charles was in bed with me…*

Around nine thirty that night, Susan was napping on the folding bed when Stephanie woke up.

"Susan? Susan, honey? Stephanie's awake," Susan heard Charles say, and realized he was gently shaking her.

Susan struggled to jump up as Charles went to the doorway and called a nurse. "What is it, honey," she asked when she heard Stephanie moaning.

"My stomach... I've got cramps..."

A nurse entered and Stephanie repeated her complaint.

"The doctor didn't say anything about cramps," Susan worried out loud. "Is this normal?"

"Well, it's not unusual. It could be from withdrawal, or it could be a reaction to the sedation medication. I'll call the doctor and ask if he wants to change the medication."

"Good," replied Charles. "Thank you."

Stephanie continued to moan and slowly writhe and Susan held her hand. "Hang in there, sweetie. It won't be too long. They just need to figure out what to do."

"How long have I been here? How am I doing? How much longer will I have to stay here?"

"You've been here a couple of days," Susan replied. "They're keeping you sedated most of the time to try to help you avoid a lot of the physical side effects of withdrawals... do you hurt anywhere other than your stomach?"

"Noooo, just my stomach..."

Lord, should we tell her about the funeral...? Well, I guess I'd want to be told... "Stephanie... a friend of Charles' has made arrangements for Billy's funeral..." Susan waited for a response, but Stephanie just groaned.

"Today is, uh, Thursday," Susan continued, "and the funeral will be Saturday. Is that okay with you?"

"I, I guess sooo..."

"Would you rather talk about this later?"

"Yeaahhh..."

A few minutes later, the nurse returned and said the doctor had made a prescription change, and she administered it through the I.V. tube. "You should start to feel better in just a minute or two," she said.

Very shortly after that, Stephanie's groaning and squirming began to subside. "Am I going to get to go to Billy's funeral?" she asked Susan as she started to look like she was going to nod off.

"Yes, honey. They're planning on burying him in Knoxville. Is that okay with you?"

"Where in Knoxville?"

Susan looked at Charles and he gestured to indicate he didn't know. "We're not sure yet, Stephanie. Do you want me to find out?"

"Doesn't... matter... as long as... as long as I'm... there..."

The nurse stayed until Stephanie was sound asleep again, and told Susan and Charles, "Dr. Nester wanted to make sure she gets a good night's sleep, and this medication should make sure she doesn't wake up again until morning. If one or both of you want to take a break and go home for a while, this might be a good time."

"Thank you, nurse," Charles said. "We'll talk it over."

Susan sat down in one of the chairs and Charles sat next to her. *I wonder if I look as tired as Charles does?* "Would you like us to go back to the hotel to get a good night's sleep, Charles?" she asked in hushed tones.

"Haven't really thought about it. What about you?"

"Well, I do need to get my Bible, and a change of clothes, but maybe your men could do that. I need to bathe, but I could wash off pretty well in the bathroom sink. What about sex? Do you need to go back so we can do that?"

"Well, we could do that in the bathroom, too," Charles suggested.

Susan looked at him like he was crazy. "We'd make too much noise!" she said, leaning in and lowering her voice even more. "Besides, if we were both in there that long with the door closed, the bodyguards and nurses would probably guess what we were doing!"

Charles seemed unconcerned by that thought.

Is that one of the kinds of things you meant by your semi-public sex? "Charles, I can't do that!"

"Okay. It was just a suggestion. Don't worry about it."

Now does he mean don't worry about having sex in the bathroom or don't worry about having sex at all? He must need sex, or he wouldn't have suggested doing it in the bathroom. Maybe that was just so we wouldn't have to leave here. Acts of service is how to show Charles love, and Grandma's handbook makes it pretty clear that wives need to keep their men sexually satisfied... "How about this? We'll go back to the hotel and have sex. I'll get a shower and come back. You stay there and sleep where you can stretch out well, and you can come back in the morning."

Charles was shaking his head when Susan was only half-way through. "Nope. I'm not leaving you. We'll just stay here... Make a list of what you want from the hotel, I'll do the same, and we'll get the guys to bring it all."

Shoot. There he goes doing his acts of service in order to show me his love. How do I out-act a man who thinks that way by nature? Susan leaned back in her seat. *How long has it been since we had sex? Tuesday evening… this is Thursday night, so two days. That's not too bad. Maybe he could wait longer. Oh, but how long will it be before we get another chance? How long are we going to stay with Stephanie around-the-clock? At least until she's out of intensive care.*

Charles yawned as Susan tried to go over in her mind what Dr. Nester had said about the side-effects and when they would happen. *Stephanie may get worse before she gets better…*

She glanced toward the bathroom. *If I don't want to let Charles screw me in there… ick… maybe we should do this while Stephanie's knocked out for the whole night. We can't be sure when we'll get to again.*

Susan leaned forward again. "Okay, how about this, Charles? We'll go back to the hotel, have sex, and we'll both get showers, change clothes and come back here right after that. How's that sound?"

"You sure?" Charles asked sleepily.

"Yes."

"Okay, I'll tell the guys to get ready."

As their two-car caravan left the treatment center, Charles was sitting right next to a rear door, as usual, and Susan was sitting mostly in the middle next to him. She unbuckled her belt, curled up her feet into the seat, and turned so that her body was facing the seatback while her head was in Charles' lap looking up at him. He put one hand on her waist and began to stroke her hair with his other hand as he closed his eyes. His head slowly leaned back, and Susan closed her eyes.

Mmm… that's nice… I hope you don't mind having sex like we're going to tonight, kind of on a schedule. Have to make the best of things, though, for Stephanie's sake… Susan's mind wondered until it went back to the night she and Stephanie were leaving the bathroom with Charles and her day-dreaming shifted to dreaming as she fell asleep.

Susan saw Stephanie putting her hands on Charles' chest as she spoke lustfully, *"Mmm… Momma, he's really hot…"* She looked on in horror as Stephanie stretched up and tilted her head back and Charles started leaning down to kiss her.

"No!" Susan shouted and started flailing to sit up.

"What?! What is it?!" Charles asked anxiously.

"What is it ma'am?" the shotgun-rider asked, equally anxiously.

"Uh... oh... I'm sorry... I just had a bad dream. I'm sorry. I didn't mean to panic everybody. I guess I just nodded off and had a little nightmare."

"After all you've been through, darling, it's no wonder," Charles said and everyone settled down a bit.

Yeah, but that's one dream I don't want to share with you, so I hope you won't ask about it. How can I change the subject...? Well, I'm sorry I startled everyone, but since we're all wide awake now, do you want to stop for something to eat, Charles?"

"Well..."

"Ma'am, that wouldn't be safe," said the bodyguard riding shotgun. "No unnecessary stops."

"Oh. Okay," Susan acquiesced.

"After you're in your hotel room," the bodyguard added, "we can bring you anything you want."

"Sorry, hon," Charles said.

"That's okay. Really."

When they arrived at the hotel, the guards told Susan and Charles to stay in their car, and the driver and shotgun rider stayed with them while the men from the other car went into the hotel.

A few minutes later, another black Suburban pulled up beside them. Susan noticed and tugged nervously on Charles' arm. "Charles..."

"They're with us, ma'am," said the driver as more men got out of the third car.

Ten minutes later Susan and Charles were escorted into the hotel, completely surrounded by Frank and several other guards.

Well, this is different... Susan thought. *Is it because Big Ed is a bigger threat than Billy was? Maybe because no matter how mean he was, Billy was just one guy, and Big Ed has a bunch of thugs working for him...?*

A man was holding an elevator open and Susan, Charles, Frank, and one of the men walked right into it. When the elevator door opened on their floor, Truck was in the hallway and led the way to their suite's door, where there was another man standing guard.

A thought struck Susan hard. "Charles...! All these men here. Is there anyone left back at the hospital... I mean the treatment center?!"

"Security is as tight as ever back there, Mrs. Parker," Frank said.

"Well, some of the men who were there are now here," said Charles with a serious look.

"Mike is back there supervising, Mr. Parker, and he has all the men he needs to guard your daughter. I'm supervising here, and we're well prepared to guard both locations."

"But…" Charles started to protest.

"The guys who've been out in the field investigating are taking a break from that to do bodyguard duty for now," Frank elaborated. "We need more men for transporting and clearing a location than we do to keep a location secure."

"Uh, okay. That makes sense," Charles acknowledged. "And as soon as we get back there, a lot of your men can get back to investigating?"

"Right."

Susan sighed as she and Charles entered their suite, locked the door, and headed for the bedroom with the king-size bed. *Shoot. That makes me want to hurry. I hope Charles won't mind being a little rushed… Well, shoot, that sounds bad… asking him to hurry might actually make it harder for him to hurry. I need to focus on making him feel good as fast as possible instead of asking him to hurry. Oh, shoot…* "Charles, I need to pee…"

"Okay. You use this bathroom, and I'll use the other. But I'm going to be a few minutes…"

"Oh, okay."

As Susan was leaving the bathroom a couple of minutes later, she noticed her reflection in one of the large mirrors. *Oh, no! I look hideous! My bruises are all purple and greenish and even some ugly yellow! I haven't been putting on makeup, my hair is unkempt, and when's the last time I brushed my teeth?! My breath must…*

Her toothbrush and paste were right in front of her and she grabbed them and started scrubbing, then gasped. *When's the last time I shaved?!*

She paused with the toothbrush in her mouth while she pulled up a pants leg and rubbed the stubble on her calf. *Oh, nooo! I don't want to scratch Charles, I don't want him to think I don't take care of myself. Oh, why didn't I shave my legs when I shaved my privates?! And how long's it been since I showered? After we last had sex? Then we were in the hot tub… that was… Tuesday night, so… two days ago. Oh, shoot, we'll need to shower after we have sex, but I don't want to shower twice if I can help it. But I don't want to stink when Charles gets close, either. And I've been off my usual diet… oh, Lord, please don't let me get gassy while we're having sex...*

As soon as she finished her teeth, Susan started putting on enough concealer to hide the bruises. *Well, Charles, I hope I don't stink so much that it puts you off, and I hope I can keep my legs out of the way so you don't notice I haven't shaved... Oh... what should I wear? I want to get you off quickly, so what's the hottest thing I have?*

She thought about all the lingerie the girls had gotten her and what Charles' reactions were when she modeled them for him. *Maybe that fish-net body sock...*

She went into the bedroom to look for the body stocking, intending to change in the bathroom, but then another thought struck her. *I'm going to get my Bible and put it by the door to make sure I don't forget it this time.*

Her Bible was on the same table as Grandma's Sex Handbook, and Susan paused at the table. *I'll have lots of reading time... but I don't want anyone but Charles to see me reading this... although... if I could borrow a post-it from the nurses, I only need to cover up the word "sex" on the cover, and it'd be fairly incognito...*

She scooped it up and put both books on the floor right by the bedroom door, making sure the Bible was on top. *If I have it with me, I might be able to read it without anyone noticing. If I don't have it, I can't. I can always keep it hidden if I want to...*

"Hey, sexy, ready to play?" Charles said as he was crossing the living room area.

"Oh, Charles...! No, I haven't changed yet!"

"I... I though the idea was to get naked..." he said, closing the bedroom door.

"Well... you liked having sex while I was wearing my bikini..."

"Oh, yeah!"

"Well, I thought you might like having sex while I'm wearing my fish-net, if it has a place for access. I was just about to check..."

"That certainly sounds nice, but I kind of thought you'd want us to hurry, so..."

Susan nodded, "Well, we don't have to set a record. I'm guessing it will take you ten or fifteen minutes, since you seem to last a long time..."

Charles looked confused.

"Did I say something wrong?" Susan worried.

"Uh, well... I figured I'd put my mouth on you for a half-hour or so, and that would get me aroused. Physically aroused, I mean. I'm looking forward to having sex with you, but I'm not hard yet."

A half an hour just to play with me...? "That's very thoughtful Charles, but I'm really not in the mood for myself tonight. I just want to satisfy you..."

Even as she was saying it, she remembered reading how important it is to most husbands to be able to satisfy their wives. *Oh, shoot. I'm messing this up already.*

"Are you sure...?" Charles asked.

"Oh, yes, Charles," she answered, putting her arms around him. *Oh, but we'll probably need lubricant. Is that still in the box...?*

"Well, if you're sure you can wait, it may help you have a bigger orgasm whenever I do play with you next time."

"That's fine." *Argh, why does that still scare me? He's been so gentle, and it really did feel better than any experience I've ever had...*

"I will need you to pump me up, though," Charles said.

"Pump you up?"

"Get me hard."

"Oh..." *You've been doing that without any special effort by me so far...*

"You could use your mouth, or..."

Susan snapped her fingers and pulled away a step. She looked mischievous at first, then frowned.

"What?"

"Well, I had an idea I thought you might like, but then..."

"What? Tell me," Charles pled.

Susan considered it for a moment, then took a deep breath. "I'm going to try something. I hope you don't hate it. If you do, you have to promise to tell me."

"I promise," Charles said without hesitation.

Susan took another deep breath. *Okay... here goes...* "Give me a dollar."

Charles looked puzzled, then started pulling out his wallet. "The minibar gets charged to the room. Everything gets changed to the room."

"Oh, trust me. This does definitely not get charged to the room."

He handed her the dollar.

"Okay, Charles, our sex book explains that fantasy and lust aren't the same thing, and that fantasy's okay for Christians as long as the sex is only between husband and wife."

Charles' brow was furrowed, apparently trying to figure out where her idea was headed.

"It said something like 'God gave us imagination, and it's okay to use our imaginations even while we're having sex.'"

"Okay... I'll buy that..."

She waved the dollar. "Yes, you just bought it. You bought my unrestricted services for the next... hour. Or however long it takes you to cum."

His face scrunched up for a moment, then his eyes got very wide. "You mean..."

"You just hired me to perform sex on you. Any way you want it. Just tell me what you want me to do."

Charles' jaw dropped, open-mouthed.

Susan became very meek, "Is this okay for us to pretend? I didn't think it would offend you..."

"Offend me? Susan, I'm the polar opposite of offended!" He picked her up and gave her a spin. "What a very erotic idea! I love it!"

"Really...?" *That's exactly the kind of reaction I was hoping for...*

He set her down. "Any way I want it?"

Susan nodded shyly. *And I hope you understand we still have the limits we've already discussed...*

Charles half-grinned, half-smirked, and walked over to a chair and sat down. Susan started to follow him, but he stopped her. "Nope. You stay there... and strip for me."

This time Susan's eyes went wide. "I... I don't know how to..."

Charles spoke softly. "Just role-play honey. Pretend I've really hired you, and you have to do whatever I ask to get paid. If you're not sure how, just do the best you can."

She blinked. *You know the only dancing I know is slow-dancing and the waltz you taught me...*

In a flash, she remembered a scene from a movie where Jamie Lee Curtis was in a similar situation, and began to strip very awkwardly. *Well, I can do at least that well, maybe... and this was my idea...* "Okay. My best won't be very good, but you're... the customer," she finished with hint of a smile.

Charles' smile was much more than a hint as he watched intently.

No music... Susan started unbuttoning her shirt at the top, working down, and noticed her hands shaking ever so slightly.

"Slower," Charles requested.

She slowed down, and when she got the last button undone, she started to pull it off her shoulders, but changed her mind. She turned her back to Charles, took a deep breath, and slowly pulled her shirt off one shoulder. *How's this...*

Susan glanced over her shoulder and Charles looked like he might start drooling. *Wow... I'm terrible at this, but you sure seem to like it...* She turned her bare shoulder slightly toward him, and pulled that side down a little more.

"Oh... yeah..." Charles said under his breath, but just loud enough for Susan to hear.

She twisted in the other direction and pulled the shirt off that shoulder even more slowly, then she pulled her shirt tail out. *Now what do I do...? Anything that gets more clothes off, I guess. Slowly. He seems to like it when I reveal just a little at a time...* She pulled her shirt tail up a little so he could see the small of her back and was rewarded with a moan from Charles.

Uh... let's see... Susan leaned forward slightly at the waist and wiggled her rear end slightly from side to side.

Charles moaned again.

Really...? You really like this that much...? How about this..." She tilted her pelvis forward and back the way she had when he had enjoyed it so much during sex, and he groaned louder.

Susan half-turned to look carefully at Charles and she giggled at how enthralled he was. She didn't think about how much time was passing as she very slowly removed her shirt the rest of the way, then her sandals, and then her pants, ending up facing him in bra and panties. *Well, you're certainly hard now, Mr. Parker. You're about to bust your britches!*

"Stop," Charles said firmly, but in a half-choked voice.

Susan started to worry that she wasn't doing something right before Charles continued.

"Please... put on a pair of high-heeled shoes...?" It wasn't really a question... he was begging.

"I-I've only got one pair..." *Well, dummy, he didn't ask you to wear two pairs...* she thought as she got them out and slipped them on.

While she was slipping them on, Charles got all his clothes off in record time and he met her at the end of the bed, his cock straight out but waving as he walked. *I'm going to have to remember how sexy you think high-heels are.*

"I need you right now," he said with intensity.

"Okay..." *And I should practice dancing in heels before we go dancing again...*

Charles positioned her and lowered her to the bed, face up, then immediately rushed to remove her panties. Next he grabbed her legs and pulled her butt to the edge of the bed.

Susan remembered the lubricant but before she could say anything he had completely impaled himself inside her and started humping as fast as he could. *Ow... well, I'm wet enough, but oww... too deep, too hard... OWWW...* "Charles..."

Charles had his hands on Susan's waist, using his arms to pull their bodies together with great force, but just then he began to howl and changed from rapid thrusts to thrust-pause, thrust-pause, and Susan saw his eyes roll back.

Oww... that hurt! That was fast, that was incredibly fast, but that hurt. Well, at least it's over...

Charles drew back and thrust into her again.

Ohh, owww... doggone it... owww...

Charles started gasping for breath, taking it in huge gulps.

Susan realized her legs were up in the air, and she lowered them until her feet reached the floor. *You're exhausted... I need to be ready in case you collapse on top of me... try not to hit me with your elbows...*

After a minute, Charles' breathing shifted to panting, and he opened his eyes. He straightened up and took Susan's hands as he slid out of her and pulled her to her feet, then embraced her.

Susan squeezed her thighs together. "I need to run to the bathroom..."

"But you just went..." Charles said between pants.

"I don't need to pee again... it's your cum... it's going to start running down my legs..."

"Oh! Okay..."

He let go, and Susan did a little running shuffle, trying to hurry without letting her thighs apart.

Man, that really hurt, Susan thought as she sat down on the toilet. *And it still hurts some... Boy, I'm glad it wasn't like that the first time we did it, or... hey... we had sex a bunch of times and only once did he pound me a little bit.*

She sighed quietly. *Guess I've got a lot to learn about how to have sex with Charles in ways that satisfy him without killing me. Hey... he didn't say anything about my face... did he not notice, or not want to say anything on purpose...? Huh... I think I need to pee again after all...*

Charles poked his head around the corner. "By the way, I only told the guys we were coming back to get showers and change clothes." He grinned. "If we hurry, they might not assume we also had sex…"

"What…? Oh! I didn't think about that! Okay, let's hurry, then!"

They showered quickly despite showering together, got dressed in fresh clothes and each gathered a spare set of clothes, some of their toiletries, and their Bibles. Susan also tucked their sex handbook into her spare clothes, and put it all in two plastic bags the hotel had in the closets for sending dirty clothes to their laundry service. Charles told the men they were ready to return to Cambridge, and then he sat on the sofa with Susan until the men were ready to take them.

"Susan…" Charles said quietly.

"Yes…?"

"Was I too rough?"

Well, I expect you to be honest with me, even if it hurts, so I guess I need to treat you the same way. "That was… a little past my limit, I think." *Oh, no… I wish I hadn't said that. I can't stand the idea of disappoint…*

"I thought that might be the case," he said. "I'm sorry, Susan. I'll try to be much more careful from now on."

"It's okay," she said, patting his hand. *Can't see it, but I'll bet I'm going to be bruised in there. That could make it even harder to have sex next time… but if we're at the hosp… treatment center for several days, maybe that'll be enough time for me to recover. As long as he doesn't pound me like that next time…*

"That wasn't a conscious decision on my part," Charles said. "I mean, it was, up to a point, but once I was inside you… I… I just really lost control. My body went on automatic pilot once I… once you were on the bed. I'm so sorry I hurt you."

Susan smiled softly, "You were kind of like a wild animal. But you weren't like that on our wedding day…"

"I need to make sure I'm never like that again."

Susan thought about that for a minute. "Maybe I just got you too excited, too fast."

Charles nodded with a gleam in his eyes. "I… you…" He shook his head.

As lousy a striptease as that was, I still turned you on so much you couldn't control yourself…? A half-smile, half-smirk began forming on Susan's lips. *You're really that attracted to me? I really have that much control over you… over your sex drive…?*

"Susan," Charles began, his gaze not meeting her eyes, "I

promise I'll do my best not to…"

"Stop," Susan said abruptly. She waited until Charles looked up at her.

"If you're about to promise to never having sex with me as rough as you did a little while ago…" She paused before continuing. "I don't think I want you to make that promise, Charles."

He tilted his head and raised his eyebrows.

Her half-smile grew to full strength. "Maybe… I think every once in a while… I might like to try to turn you into an animal again. Not often. Rarely, perhaps. But let's not rule it out."

Charles looked intently as Susan, smiled, and took her hands in his. "Susan, you sexy woman, you. You can do anything you want to me, any time, any place."

A loud knock on the door interrupted the conversation, and they stood up to leave the suite, but not before Charles picked Susan up off the floor in a bear hug.

"You are the most awesome woman ever," he whispered in her ear.

"Oh, Charles…" she whispered back. "I love you so much…"

"My Eve… my erotic, seductive, soul-mate…"

Oh… Susan felt her body become aroused almost instantly at his last words, enhanced by his body's warmth. "Oohhh… Charrllles…" *Yes, yes, yes… we are soul-mates, and I want to be your erotic seductress whenever you need me to… whenever you want me to be… oh, I love you so…*

They began to kiss, but another knock on the door prompted them to stop and gather their things to leave.

As Susan was walking arm in arm with Charles, she felt a little soreness with every step, but as she recalled how Charles charged at her from the Jacuzzi and how he had looked so lustfully at her while she stripped, she couldn't suppress a grin. *Oh, Lord, not only have you helped me not disappoint Charles… you've helped me really satisfy him. Thank you so much, Lord… and Lord… thank you for how good Charles makes me feel…*

After returning to the treatment center to find Stephanie still sound asleep, Charles called Susan's attention to the fact that one of the chairs had been replaced with a narrow recliner. With everything quiet, Susan and Charles spent the night alternating between reading and napping, and Charles insisted on Susan taking the folding bed.

Early that morning, Susan finished reading the sex handbook

and set it on the window ledge with a folded towel on top of it, just as Charles was waking up. *I'll sneak this back to the hotel the next time we go. I wonder when that will be? Maybe not for...*

"Momma...?"

"Yes, honey, I'm right here," Susan replied immediately.

"My mouth is dry. Could you get me a glass of water or something?"

"Of course, honey," Susan said as Charles refilled Stephanie's cup from a bedside pitcher. "Do you feel like sitting up? There's a bendy straw if you don't feel like it."

"Yeah. I'm tired of laying flat."

Lying flat. But I'm not going to start nagging you about grammar.

Stephanie worked the bed controls to raise the head until she was sitting up, then raised the part under her knees a little bit. Susan handed her the cup, and she sipped the water through a straw. *We really need to do something about your hair...*

"Thanks," she said, handing it back.

"Would you like anything else?" Susan asked.

"Breakfast should be here soon," Charles mentioned.

"Do you think you could eat something, Stephanie? You haven't eaten much the last couple of days."

"Yeah, I think so. I'm a little hungry. How long have I been in here?"

"Two days," Charles replied.

"Two days?" asked Stephanie with a scowl. "I thought you told me two days a couple of days ago."

Oh, please don't get into an argument. Especially over something as petty as that...

"Oh... uh, that was yesterday when we said that. Yesterday was Thursday, and you were here Wednesday and all day yesterday, so that's probably how we counted two days then. But you only checked in on Wednesday morning, so this morning it makes it about forty-eight hours. So today starts the third day."

"Xx-xx-xx. Time drags by when you're not drunk."

Susan gave Stephanie a look of sympathy and patted her closest hand. *Lord, please give Stephanie patience, and help her stick with this program all the way through.*

Charles yawned and stretched his arms as Susan started to climb up on the stool.

"You could put one of the rails down, Momma, and sit on the

edge of the bed."

Susan thrilled at the offer and took advantage of it, taking Stephanie's hand after she was seated.

At a knock on the doorway, they all turned to see Mike Samuelson enter, followed by Brian Milner.

"Hey, everybody's awake! How're you doing Stephanie?" Mike asked as Brian silently studied the room.

"Uhh... tired, hungry, irritable... and sore... probably from laying down so much."

"Mm. Sometimes progress causes problems," Mike said, "but you'll overcome them."

Stephanie merely grunted and Mike glanced at Charles, then back to Stephanie.

"Well, earlier your parents and I discussed that I'd like to have a guard in your room at all times once you're moved to a private room, but I've decided it'd be best to start that now."

"Oh?" Susan mumbled. *But you've got men right outside...*

"Has something changed?" Charles asked with obvious concern.

"No," Mike replied, "nothing we're aware of. I just reconsidered and think it would be best not to wait."

Everyone looked at Stephanie.

"I don't care," she said.

"It will mean less privacy," Mike pointed out.

"Xx-xx-xx, I don't have any privacy now. I don't guess I will until I get out of here. I don't even have a xx-xx-xx door."

"Okay, then..." Mike said.

"Breakfast is here," called a nurse from the doorway. "Do you think you feel like eating?"

"Yeah," Stephanie replied.

Susan got off the bed while the nurse brought in the tray and positioned the tray table over Stephanie's lap.

"Alright then," Mike said, "Brian here will take the first shift. Stephanie, this is Brian Milner. Brian, Stephanie."

Brian nodded and Stephanie blushed slightly and looked away. She started eating, but Susan noticed she frowned after she raised a hand to her head and felt her hair on the side away from Brian.

I'll really need to ask her what she wants to do with her hair, but I'll wait until things quieten down a bit, Susan thought as she stepped over to the window and began to open the curtains.

"Keep the curtains closed at all times," Brian said firmly.

Susan stopped and looked at him, but kept her hands on the

curtains.

When no one responded, Brian added, "We don't want anyone to be able to see in. You don't need to keep the heavy curtains closed, just the sheer ones."

"Okay," Charles agreed without complaint.

"But it's such a lovely view," Susan objected, "and the sunshine would..."

"Lots of places out there where a sniper could hide," Brian said without emotion.

"A sniper?!" Susan asked in alarm.

"It's just a possibility, Susan," Mike said, "but it's one we can eliminate just by making it too hard for them to see in."

Charles put an arm around her. "It'll be okay, honey. That's why we have Mike and his men. They're going to keep Stephanie safe. As long as it takes."

Susan took a deep breath and let it out slowly. *Stephanie's still in danger, I've put Charles and I in danger, Stephanie still doesn't know God's love, Charles' boys are still estranged... How did we manage to get married in the middle of all this...? The same way Charles met me in the first place... God's unending grace.*

"Well, I'm going to excuse myself for now, but I'll be right down the hall," Mike said.

"Speaking of 'as long as it takes,'" Stephanie said, "how long do I have to stay in here?"

Uh-oh, another chance where Stephanie could give up. Lord, how do we keep her willing to stay with it...?

"A few weeks," Charles said after an awkward silence.

Stephanie paused for a moment, then replied, "Oh, yeah. I think I remember them saying something like that when you brought me here... Didn't they say it might be months? Or did I imagine that?"

"Well," Susan began reluctantly, "it depends on how well you progress, Stephanie, but yes, it could be months." *Oh, please don't give up now...!*

Susan noticed Stephanie frown as she looked around the room. "Oh, but you won't be in this room the whole time! As soon as you're over the physical withdrawal symptoms in a few days, you'll move to one of those nice private rooms we saw."

Stephanie paused in thought again. "Okay. I don't remember the other room very well, but as long as it's better than this one. And you're still willing to pay for it," she said as she looked at Charles for the last comment.

Susan and Charles tried to make conversation with Stephanie while she ate breakfast, but Stephanie responded with little other than grunts and shrugs.

As soon as she was finished eating, Susan moved the tray table and sat on the edge of the bed again. "Honey, there's something we need to talk about... Do you remember that we told you yesterday that we're planning to have Billy's funeral tomorrow?"

Sorrow washed over Stephanie's face. "Yeah. I think so. Tomorrow, huh? You told me I can go, right?"

Susan nodded. "Yes, honey. Someone from the staff here will go with us to help take care of you."

Stephanie looked away and began crying. Her tears ran down her checks and she didn't bother wiping at them. After a few minutes, she sighed heavily and she blew her nose after Susan handed her some tissues. "My hair's a mess... I haven't been taking care of it since... And I haven't had a shower in... a while."

"One of the nurse's aides gave you a sponge bath yesterday and the day before. You slept right thought it," Susan told her.

"Oh," said Stephanie, slightly brighter, then sighed again.

Susan picked up her nearest hand and stroked the back of it. "How... how do you take care of your, uh... hair spikes? Is that what you call them?"

"Yeah. Billy suggested it. I mean, he didn't make me or anything. I thought it was a good idea, but... it makes a mess on the pillows, and it's hard to keep it looking good. And you can't wash it."

"What kind of gel do you use? We could get you some..."

"Gel doesn't work for big spikes. I use Elmer's glue. It works pretty well, but sweat messes it up, and... well, never mind."

"Well, do you want to wash it out?" Susan asked. "And start with a fresh coat of... glue?"

"It doesn't wash out easy. I tried once. It's supposed to dissolve in water, but when I tried it, it just sort of turned gooey."

"Just cut it off."

Susan turned to confirm that it was Brian who had made the suggestion. *Huh. First time I've seen him participate in a normal conversation, but... he's just staring at the doorway.*

"Do a Natalie Portman?" Stephanie asked with a ponderous look.

"Actually, I think Sigourney Weaver was the first actress to shave her head for a movie," her mother pointed out.

"Uh. I... I'd like to look nice for Billy's funeral, but... I guess that's not really an option."

Now what do I say to that? I can't lie, and your hair's pretty messed up...

No one said anything for a moment, then Stephanie looked at Brian. "How do you think I'd look bald?"

Brian glanced at her and immediately trained his eyes back on the doorway. He cleared his throat and said, "Nice."

"Some of those actresses who shaved their heads for movies kind of made it socially acceptable," Susan commented. *But I guess if you want your hair to be a sign of rebellion, you don't want it to be socially acceptable...*

"I could do it for you," said Brian without taking his eyes off the doorway. "One of the other guys can take my post for a few minutes while I shave it for you. I'm sure they'll have barber's shears and razors here since some people stay here a long time."

Susan tried to picture Stephanie with no hair and remembered when she was a baby. *It was a few weeks... or was it months, before you finally grew some pretty locks?*

Stephanie shifted in her bed to lie a little on one side. "Oh, really. Have you ever done that?"

"Sure. In the Special Forces, we have to take care of everything ourselves when we're out in the field for a long time, including haircuts. We all take turns, but we usually just cut it with shears, we don't usually shave it."

"You were in the Army...?" Stephanie asked, her voice trailing off.

Oh, dear. Lord please don't let her get despondent about Steve again on top of everything else.

"Twelve years. Got out to try to earn more money. A couple of years after that I started working for Mike. He was my commanding officer for a while in Afghanistan."

Susan held her breath for a moment while she waited to see Stephanie's reaction.

Brian kept his eyes on the doorway, but Stephanie's were now riveted on him.

"Y-you were... in Afghanistan?" Stephanie asked.

"Twice."

"Did... did you know someone names Steve Towns...?" Stephanie asked, and Susan shared Stephanie's heartache.

"Mmm... nope. Don't think so. My unit was very small and... our missions didn't give us a chance to meet many people in other units."

"Oh," Stephanie said with obvious disappointment. "What, um, kind of missions did you do...?"

"Uh... I'm sorry, I really can't go into any details. It was... field work... away from the main bases..."

Stephanie sighed and looked away. Her eyes teared a little and no one said anything for a few minutes.

"Well, xx-xx-xx, I guess I couldn't look any worse than I do now..." Stephanie finally said, then looked at Brian again. "You really think I'd look okay that way?"

Susan breathed a sigh of relief that Stephanie hadn't started obsessing about her brother's death.

"Wouldn't have said it otherwise. And there's another benefit in your case."

"Oh? What's that?"

"Sometimes in the Old Testament, when a person lost a loved one, they'd shave their head as a sign of grieving. Then as their hair slowly grew back, it was like beginning all over again. Some people have suggested it was very cathartic."

He knows the Bible? What's his name...? Brian?

"What's cathartic mean?" Stephanie asked.

"Healing. Therapeutic," Brian answered.

Hmm... I never knew that was why they shaved their heads back then...

Stephanie was quiet for a minute, then announced, "Do it."

"Are you sure you don't want more time to think about it?" Susan asked.

"Funeral's tomorrow, right, Mom?"

"Yes..."

"Well, I can't get the glue out or fix my hair nice before then. And... let's get it done now, so if the shaving makes it red or bumpy it'll have at least a little time to fade."

Well, if you're going to do it, I guess the sooner, the better...

Brian mumbled into a microphone, then said, "Danny will be here in a minute. I'll go find the stuff and be right back. I didn't think about shaving it causing it to get red, though. How about just a buzz cut?"

Stephanie thought about it and nodded. "Okay."

Danny relieved Brian, and Brian borrowed a pair of electric hair shears from the one-room barber shop they had in the building. They put an upright chair in the spacious bathroom and rolled in the portable I.V. with Stephanie. Brian made quick work of it, and in only a few minutes, all her hair was on the floor.

Every time he puts his hand on one of her shoulders, she looks like she's about to start purring. How could I have not noticed how important touch was to her when she was growing up?

Stephanie stood up and looked at herself in the mirror over the sink, and Brian looked at the reflection over her shoulder. Again, he casually placed a hand on one of her shoulders.

"Well, this was your idea," Stephanie said to Brian. "What do you think?"

Brian nodded. "I was right. You look good. Your hair must have grown out some since you put the glue in it, 'cause there's no glue left on your scalp." He paused before adding, "I think you look very nice this way."

Stephanie came out of the bathroom smiling.

Oh, Father! That's the first time I can remember Stephanie smiling since... since she was a teenager...? Since Marty left. I can't remember her smiling a single time after that. Not even on Christmas mornings...

"I think I'd like to go for a walk..." Stephanie said, but then one of her knees buckled a little.

Brian was right beside her and took her around the waist. "Maybe you better..."

Just then Stephanie started shaking all over.

"Nurse!" Shouted Susan, Charles, and Brian at almost the same time.

One of the nurses had been watching through the doorway, and was already calling out, "Put her on the bed!"

Brian easily lifted her weight onto the bed, and Susan and Charles tried to help him hold her arms and legs still.

The nurse rushed in with a syringe and injected it into the I.V. port closest to where it went into Stephanie's arm.

"Is this DT's, or a seizure, or what?" Charles asked.

"DT's," replied the nurse.

"It's xx-xx-xx scary," Stephanie managed to say.

They all continued to hold her, and in less than a minute, the shaking began to subside, and a couple of minutes after that, she was asleep.

"Should you call the doctor?" Charles asked.

"I'll do that as soon as I've checked her vitals, Mr. Parker. Everyone step back a little, please."

Dr. Nester came not long after, and two other doctors later in the day. Susan spent much of the day pacing and praying, while Charles occasionally left to bring them meals. Brian had relieved Danny after Stephanie went to sleep, and except for Brian being relieved occasionally for bathroom and meal breaks, he stayed rooted in the corner, either standing or sitting, but eyes always locked on the doorway.

From then until Saturday morning, whenever Stephanie started to come out from under the sedation, she was checked by a nurse and re-sedated.

Saturday morning, Dr. Nester came by about nine, checked over a still-sleeping Stephanie, and began talking to Susan and Charles. "Her latest medication should be wearing off soon, and I'm going to give her something else until after she gets back from the funeral so she can be conscious for it. She may not be able to remember it very well, though, so I suggest someone takes some photos for her to look at later."

Susan glanced at Charles. *That's good idea, but we don't have a camera here.*

"I plan to be her attending physician on the trip, and nurse Summers would also accompany us. She should have enough time to take some pictures, and I took the liberty of asking her yesterday to bring a camera this morning."

Susan lit up. "That's a wonder offer! Both for you to come with us, and for the camera. That was very thoughtful of you! Thank you so much!"

"Yes, thank you very much, doctor," Charles chimed in.

"You're very welcome," he replied, then looked at Stephanie. "She's at a critical juncture right now, and I'll feel more comfortable with the situation if I'm there myself."

Oh, it was the right thing to do to stay here, Lord! Stephanie will get to go to Billy's funeral like we promised, and the director of the whole place will be there to take care of her!

"So, what time are you planning to leave?" the doctor asked.

"Ten," Charles said. "The funeral's scheduled for eleven, but we're the only people going, so if we get there a little early or a little late, the funeral home will work around us. For security reasons, the only service will be inside the funeral home."

"Ah, good thinking," said Dr. Nester. "You can always take Stephanie to visit the grave site later. Unless..."

Charles shook his head and looked at Susan. "I forgot to tell you honey, Nat arranged for a burial plot instead of cremation. I hope that's…"

"That's fine," Susan replied, giving Charles a hug. "That's perfect." *A place to visit will be better for Stephanie than an urn in the house, where it won't remind her all the time…*

"We can remove Stephanie's I.V. tube here," the doctor said, lifting a twist joint in the tube. "She can do without it for a while, but we'll leave the catheter in her arm in case I need to administer something intravenously. Plus it will save having to re-stick her when she gets back."

By ten o'clock, Stephanie was awake and in a wheelchair, but groggy, as Mike explained the arrangements.

"Okay," Mike announced, "The funeral home is already secured and they're waiting for us. I'll be in the lead car, and Stephanie will be in car two with Susan and the doctor beside her. Car three is the limo from the funeral home. That's just a decoy, so there's only a driver in it, one of my guys. Right behind that, Charles, you and Frank will be in the back of car four. Car five will be trailing well behind, but they'll be in constant contact with me. Any questions?"

I sure wish we could ride in the limo so Charles could be with us. I guess it's my fault we can't, Susan thought sadly.

No one asked any questions, and the caravan packed up and made an uneventful trip.

There was somber music in the background until the funeral director gave a brief, generic speech about living and seasons that come to an end. Susan and Charles sat in folding chairs on either side of Stephanie's wheelchair, and afterward took her up to the open casket for a final good-bye. They helped her stand so she could see Billy, and she touched his hands and caressed his face while she sobbed.

On the way back to the Cambridge Treatment Center, Stephanie began to shake again, and Dr. Nester gave her more medication. A few minutes later, Stephanie was asleep, and two orderlies took her from the car to her room on a gurney.

Once she was settled back in her bed and sleeping peacefully, Dr. Nester left after telling Susan and Charles that he planned to keep her heavily sedated at least until tomorrow morning.

Susan flopped into the recliner and sighed. "I sure wish she hadn't had to go through that."

"Yeah, but she made it okay. And if Dr. Nester's right, it may all be a blur to her later anyway."

"Oh! Do you think the nurse remembered to take pictures?"

"She did," Charles assured her. "I noticed her taking one while Stephanie was standing at the casket."

Susan closed her eyes and tried to remember her mother's and father's funerals and was disappointed that they seemed to be a blur to her too, but she also took comfort that perhaps today wouldn't be too painful of a memory for Stephanie. *Lord, please heal Stephanie's grief as well as her body.*

"You hungry?" Charles asked.

"Huh? Oh, uh… yes, I guess so, now that you mention it."

"Stephanie won't be waking up soon. Want to go to the cafeteria with me?"

Ohh… I'd rather stay here, but I've given so little time to you lately… "Okay, but I need to pee first." Susan blushed as she realized that Brian had resumed his watch from the corner of the room, and he had been all but transparent to her.

Oh, that was embarrassing, Susan fretted as she used the toilet, remembering to do her Kegel exercises. *Saying that right in front of a stranger… oh, well, I guess it wasn't that bad. Oh! Can they hear my pee starting and stopping? The fan is on, and it's pretty loud. I think that probably drowns out my noise. And I don't make nearly as much noise as when Charles pees standing up. Charles… we got married… just four days ago. And it's been… uh, it's only been a day and a half since I let Charles have sex. He ought to be okay a little longer.*

Susan finished and touched up her makeup in the mirror. *Hmm, that sex book says most men relieve themselves a lot, every day sometimes, or even more than once a day! But that doesn't mean Charles does. Hm… he hasn't had a chance to do that while we've been here. Hey, I wonder if Marty did that…? If he did, I'm glad I didn't know. It would have made me feel like I wasn't good enough to satisfy him.*

Charles was waiting with a smile as she joined him to walk to the cafeteria. Susan paused at the doorway and gazed at Stephanie, then glanced at Brian before she turned and walked out. *How can he do that, just stare at the doorway for hours…?*

Charles took Susan's hand and put it in the crook of his arm.

Maybe I should ask if you need to go back to the hotel again. Even if you don't yet, you might appreciate me asking… "Charles…" she said quietly as they walked down the hall, "when do you think you'll need to go back to the hotel?"

"Hadn't thought about it. Did you forget something?"

"No, silly, I mean, when will you *need* to go back?" She looked at him and it was clear he didn't understand. "For relief. Like last time."

"Oh," Charles said. "Well… I was doing okay, uh, without relief, before we got married, so… uh, correction, I was doing well without relief before I met you."

Charles…! I wonder if that means you relieved yourself between when we met and when we got married. But if you did… you were thinking about me…?! It's so hard to believe you really had the hots for me. I guess you gave me plenty of evidence, but…

He stopped just outside the cafeteria and looked around before going on. "I don't expect we'll need to go back just for that. But I sure am looking forward to tasting you again, whenever that is."

Oh, my. Well, I'm not in any hurry for that… "Okay… if you're sure. And promise you'll tell me if that changes?"

"I promise," he said, and they went in.

"I sure am looking forward to tasting you again," she replayed in her mind while choosing her lunch. *Why is that so hard to believe…? Because it doesn't fit my experience with Marty? I was married to Marty for years… maybe it will just take a little longer before I can really get used to how different Charles is…*

Near the end of their meal, Charles said, "I think I ought to try calling Robert and tell him about us getting married. He's my youngest, and… I guess he doesn't hate me as much as William does. Robert can tell William."

You look so sad…

"I think I'll call from the prayer room," he continued. "I kind of hate using the room like a phone booth, but it's the only place I know around here where the guards… won't hear me…"

"Well, prayer is talking to God," Susan reasoned. "And you can talk to God before and after your call, so that kind of makes it right. And if you'd like me to be with you, I can pray the whole time you talk to him."

"I'd like that, but I thought you'd want to sit with Stephanie."

"Dr. Nester seemed sure that Stephanie won't wake up 'til tomorrow. But if you'd rather be alone…"

"If you really wouldn't mind, Susan, I'd really appreciate you praying for me while I call. I think the truth is, I've been putting it off because I'm scared to tell them. They were so angry with me about Laura…"

They went together, and when Charles finally called, Robert was the one who answered. Charles struggled, but got the news out, and it seemed to Susan that Robert must have just asked a few questions and not said much else.

"He said he hoped we'd be very happy together," Charles told Susan after he hung up. "He didn't sound angry. Or even hurt. Not even disappointed…"

Charles began to cry. "It was almost like telling a total stranger…"

Chapter Twenty

The following week felt more like a month. Susan and Charles went back to the hotel only twice for quick sex, showers, and fresh clothes, and then right back to keep their vigil over Stephanie. Though they had plenty of time to sleep, they never slept a whole night through, and as a result, they constantly felt less than fully refreshed. In between trips to the hotel, they occasionally washed off at the bathroom sink.

One bright spot for Susan was when a beautiful album of wedding photos was delivered from Nat and Darlene. She was surprised at how many wonderful shots had been taken, and very thankful for the permanent reminders of how many friends had helped to provide such a festive atmosphere for their very suddenly-announced wedding.

Otherwise, nurses bustled about on a regular basis, doctors came and went, and the Chaplain came by several times.

Stephanie was awake but groggy for several hours at a time, several times a day, and had simply shrugged when Susan asked to read to her from her Bible. She started with the entire Gospel of John, then Luke, then 1st Corinthians, Ephesians, and more, trying to discern the best selection each time by praying and trying to listen to God's Spirit. Stephanie never asked questions and never commented, but she never objected except when she wanted to go to sleep again.

Mike had someone pack Stephanie and Billy's possessions and store them in Susan's garage for the time being, and he informed Susan and Charles that Stephanie apparently didn't have much in the way of clothes in their apartment: a pair of jeans, a half-dozen shirts, one pair of high heels, and a handful of accessories.

Susan asked Mike to get a cloth tape measure, and he provided one the next day. She used it to get Stephanie's measurements and provide them to Lisa, who spent two days shopping, and several large boxes arrived a couple of days after that. The boxes were stored by the staff until Stephanie moved into her new room, since she was only wearing hospital gowns in this room.

In addition to worrying about Stephanie, Susan often fretted about whether she was giving Charles enough attention, but Charles kept reassuring her that he was okay. While Stephanie was sleeping, Susan had been reading in Charles' Bible instead of her own, and she enjoyed perusing the many passages he had underlined. Reading his favorite passages made her feel closer than ever to Charles, as if she were peeking into his mind and spirit. She was surprised and pleased to discover that Charles had been doing the same thing while reading in her Bible. She also couldn't help but notice that Charles read through Grandma's Sex Handbook, during the days, and without trying to hide the cover.

The bodyguards continued working twelve-hour shifts, and Brian was the inside-the-room man for every daytime shift, spending all those long hours staring at the doorway. Even with occasional breaks, it seemed like he was always there, just staring.

One day while Stephanie was sleeping and Charles had gone to the cafeteria, Susan sat close to Brian and turned toward him.

"Do you mind if I ask you something?" she asked under her breath.

"Go ahead," Brian replied quietly, without taking his eyes off the doorway.

"How can you do nothing but stare at the door for hours on end? And for day after day? I wouldn't have thought it was humanly possible until I saw you doing it."

Brian smiled. "It only looks like I'm doing nothing. I've had extensive training for this, and despite what it may look like, my mind stays busy."

Doing what? You...

"Plus, different people excel at different things. You know, like you were reading to Stephanie from Corinthians, God gives different kinds of gifts, different kinds of service. I tried out for sniper school in the Special Forces, and it turns out my gifts are very well suited to it. I was very good at it, and my ability to calm my mind and focus, observe, and analyze threats is the biggest reason why I was so good at it."

Wow. I never thought of fighting skills along with gifts of wisdom and healing and the rest, but I guess if God calls you to that line of work... "Oh, and you've been listening to us even if you haven't been looking at us..."

"Heard every word, Ma'am."

Hmm...

"And I pray a lot, Ma'am."

"Oh…?"

"I don't claim to be good at it, but I can claim to've logged a lot of hours making the effort. I don't get carried away with it when I'm on the line, I mean, when I'm working… I mean, you know, I don't let it distract me from my mission. But overall I do get a lot of praying in."

Amazing. How unexpected… "What do you pray about, Brian?"

"Since I started this job, mostly Stephanie."

What…?! Susan blinked, momentarily at a loss for thoughts as well as at a loss for words. *Lord… oh, Lord… your people show up in the most unexpected places, in the most unexpected forms… and here you've provided a guardian angel, or at least a… yes! A prayer warrior! How amazing you are Lord! How full of surprises! How much more do you do for us that we're never aware of…?!*

Just then Stephanie started waking up, and Susan kissed Brian on the cheek, gave him a shoulder-hug, and thanked him, all without him taking his eyes off the doorway.

Toward the end of the week, Stephanie was spending more and more time awake during the day, with increasing mental clarity, and that led to good news. Dr. Nester came by that Saturday morning, one week after Billy's funeral, and announced that Stephanie's physical withdrawal had progressed rapidly and if nothing changed over the weekend, he was planning on transferring her to a regular room the following Monday. At lunch, they celebrated by putting a candle on a slice of chocolate cake for Stephanie.

Nothing did change, and that Monday morning Stephanie got her I.V. removed and she was transferred to the largest private suite at Cambridge. And it had a normal door. It also had a spacious bathroom, a normal full-size bed, a bed-side table with lamp, a beautiful vanity with triple mirrors and adjustable lighting, a chest-of-drawers, walk-in closet, desk and chair, a small sofa, two upholstered chairs, a casual table, two floor lamps, and a wide-screen flat-panel television hanging on a wall. Across from the door, a large window with ledge ran the full width of the wall, just like in the intensive care room.

As they looked around the room, Susan immediately noticed an assortment of cosmetics and female personal-care items on the vanity, and more items in the bathroom, including a toothbrush still in its package. That discovery was followed by Stephanie finding that her chest of drawers and closet were full of the new clothes Lisa had selected.

Stephanie was beaming as she held up one outfit after another, with Susan and Charles both admiring and commenting. Stephanie glanced several times at Brian, whose eyes never left the now-closed door. She held up a light-blue dress with a hem just above her knees that Susan said brought out the color in her eyes, and she swirled around right in front of Brian as she held it up.

"Well, Brian, what do you think of this one?"

Brian looked at her from her feet to her eyes before answering, "Impressive."

Stephanie paused for a moment, then happily resumed examining the clothes. When she had seen them all, she chose the blue dress, stockings, and a cute pair of open-toed woven flats and eagerly took them into the bathroom to change out of her gown.

When she stepped out of the bathroom, Susan started to say, "You look beautiful," but she stopped when she realized that Stephanie looked sad and was slowly looking around the room again.

"What's wrong, honey?" Susan asked. *Oh! Touch...* She stepped over to her and put a comforting arm around her.

Stephanie didn't answer right away, and tears started forming. *Oh, Father, what's wrong now...? What can I do...?*

Charles spotted a tissue box on the vanity and handed her a couple of tissues.

"Momma..."

"What is it, Stephanie?"

"It's... too nice."

Susan furrowed her brow.

"I don't... this place..." She sighed.

"It's just... too much for me," she finished, the last two words barely audible.

Without thinking about it, Susan turned to face Stephanie and hugged her tight, and Stephanie started sobbing. *Oh, Stephanie... Father, please help me to say the right thing...!*

"I can't handle this, Momma... I can't... I'm going to let you down, and all this will be wasted... you should have just left me alone..."

"Stephanie, I love you, and I'm never going to leave you alone, not ever. I'll always love you, and..." Susan released her hug and leaned back, looking at Stephanie face-to-face. "Stephanie, how do you think all this came about? By accident? By chance? It's because God loves you..."

Stephanie shook her head. "No, Momma, you don't know what I've done. I've… I've done terrible things, horrible things… I… " She wiped at her tears, "God doesn't love me, because I don't deserve it…"

Lord, give me your words… she prayed, and an idea popped into her mind. "Stephanie, do you think I deserve God's love?"

Stephanie thought only a moment, then slowly nodded, tears still flowing down her cheeks, "Yeah…"

"Well, you're wrong. I don't deserve God's love, and no one else does either. He doesn't love us because we deserve it; he loves us because he chooses to. I may not have done the same wrong things you've done, but I've done some horrible things. I hurt you terribly, I hurt Steve, and I hurt Marty. God only knows how much, how deeply I hurt all of you, and if I hadn't, you might have had a much better life, and…" Susan started crying now, "and Steve might still be alive…"

Stephanie tried to look at her mother through her tears, and she put a hand on Susan's cheek. "No… Momma…"

Susan took a handful of tissues from Charles and led Stephanie over to the upholstered chairs. After Stephanie sat in one, Susan moved the table back, scooted the other chair over and sat down beside her.

"You see, Stephanie? None of us deserve God's love, not me, not anyone, but that doesn't stop him from loving us. That's the greatest miracle of all. God sent Jesus to atone for our sins on the cross… and he took our punishment… but he did that *while we were still sinners*. He doesn't love us because we love him; we love him because he loved us first. And that proves he loves everyone, not just people who are good enough somehow."

Stephanie helped herself to some tissues from the tissue box on the little table behind them and blew her nose as her crying began to subside. "I don't know, Momma… I've seen so many bad things. I don't think I can believe in God like you do. It doesn't make sense to me."

There was a loud knock and the door opened in. Dr. Martin the chaplain was there with another psychologist to explain Stephanie's counseling program, and although they offered to come back later, Stephanie asked them to stay because she was eager to hear what was ahead for her.

They explained that the counseling program was a comprehensive faith-based system that included patients learning about the five love languages and how that may have impacted them in the past and present, specifically in regard to dependency behaviors. The counselors planned to begin that afternoon with a private session, then a group therapy session where Stephanie would just be an observer, followed by another private session. Susan was pleased to hear that at some point, the counselors would like to have her and Charles participate in some sessions, and they explained that if Stephanie made plans to live at home with them when she got out, she would probably be able to leave the center sooner than if she wanted to live alone after being fully released.

Stephanie seemed impatient to get started, and agreed to everything, including the idea of moving in with her mother and step-father when the time came.

After the doctors left, Stephanie spoke up, "Uh, Mom…"

"Yes, darling?"

"Uh, I don't know how to say this politely… so I'm just gonna ask. Would you and… xx-xx-xx. What do I call you?" she asked, looking at Charles.

"Oh. Well, what would you like to call me?"

"Is it okay if I call you Charles?"

Charles glanced at Susan who winced inside but gave a little smile and nodded.

Better that than nothing, I guess, but it seems a little too intimate to me…

"Okay, sure," Charles told Stephanie.

"Okay, well… Mom, will you and Charles please move out of here? You've been here all day and all night, every day. Go somewhere else. And Brian, too. This is a nice room, and I'd like to have it mostly to myself if I'm going to be here a long time."

Susan felt like her heart stopped. *But… you need me here! We've got so much lost time to make up for! I want to tell you more about Jesus! I want to keep reading the Bible to you!*

"I can check with Mike," Brian said. "See how he wants to redeploy… uh, see where he wants to relocate us."

"Stephanie…" Susan said, distress written all over her face.

"Susan," Charles interrupted, "she's going to be busy here during the days. And she's going to need some time alone."

"But, Stephanie…"

"I'm not saying you can't come back, Momma. Just quit camping out here."

But I've missed you so much, for so long…

Charles put his arm around Susan as he addressed Stephanie

again, "How often do you think you'd feel comfortable with us coming back?"

"Uh… I haven't thought about it. How about… how about leave me alone tonight… that means the rest of today, and tomorrow morning, and… and you can call me at lunchtime tomorrow and talk about it then." Her tone brightened up a little, "Maybe visit an hour or so, every other night? Something like that?"

Nooo…! That's not enough… that's not nearly enough…

Charles gave Susan an extra squeeze, and Susan noticed Stephanie notice the squeeze.

"How about the weekends?" Charles asked hopefully. "You only have one session late on Saturday morning, and a Chapel service Sunday morning. How about if we spend all Saturday and Sunday afternoons and evenings with you?"

Stephanie nodded slowly. "Okay, we can try that. See how it goes."

A little later, Brian was re-stationed to what was now a two-man post just outside Stephanie's room as Susan fought tears while she and Charles gathered their things to leave.

"Can… can I leave my Bible with you, Stephanie?" Susan asked. "Charles and I can share his…"

"Okay, sure. But please don't ask me to promise to read it or anything. I don't want to make any promises at all. I just want to focus on whatever they're going to do to me here. I'm not sure I can stick it out, but I sure don't want anything extra hanging over my head."

Once their little caravan was ready to take them back to the hotel, they got in, and Susan's floodgates opened up. "Oh, Charles, it feels like I'm losing her all over again! Things were going so well…! It was the first time she ever let me try to explain Jesus' love to her, and then we got interrupted! And then she obviously didn't want to go back to that discussion…! Oh, Charles, I thought she was so close to giving her life to God…" She went through one tissue after another.

"That's in God's hands, honey. It always has been. She's heard a lot while you've been reading to her for the last week, and you got to share from your heart this morning, and she was open to it. And… and this is very important… by leaving when she asked you to, even though it was clear you didn't want to… you showed her your love. You not only told her about God's love today, you demonstrated it, and that's just as important, maybe more important."

Susan looked up at him. *Oh, Charles, you really think so? That makes a lot of sense... but... it just hurts so much...*

She pulled out another tissue and noticed the box. "You brought these...?"

Charles nodded.

"How did you know...?"

"Just thought you might need it."

Oh, God! Oh, God, what a man! How thoughtful, how considerate, and... as little time as we've known each other, he's already started getting to know me so well... Oh, God, thank you for Charles! Thank you, thank you... thank you with all my heart!

Ohh... but Lord... as grateful as I am... I still lift up Stephanie to you, she still needs you, Lord...

Susan had finished crying in the car, but when they finally got into their suite at the hotel and closed the door, she felt emotionally drained. *I sure hope Charles doesn't want to jump right into bed... or have sex... wherever...*

She dropped her purse on the kitchenette counter, sat down on a stool at the small breakfast bar, and sighed heavily.

"Any chance you're hungry?" Charles asked.

Susan looked up and raised her eyebrows. *For food, I hope... but...* "What did you have in mind?"

"Pizza?" he asked. "I know we had some recently, but it's relatively fast, and it's comfort food."

Mm... "Pizza and diet coke?"

Charles pulled out his cell phone and made a call.

Once the bodyguards delivered the pizza, with a slice missing again, Susan and Charles took off their shoes and laid down on the king-size bed without much discussion and found a romantic comedy that sounded interesting enough to both of them. Charles laid back, propped up on pillows, and Susan snuggled up close.

When the movie was over, Charles scooted down a little in the bed and they began kissing.

"Mmm..." Susan purred. *Can't see your crotch...* "Do you want to have sex?"

"Not right now, but I might get worked up if we keep making out. Would that be okay?"

"Sure..." she replied, and Charles began kissing her again. *Mmm, you're such a good kisser...*

He leaned over a little more and Susan put her hands up to caress his shoulders, and he put his hands on her sides.

Their tongues played, with his tongue caressing her lips, then exploring her tongue inside her mouth, then she used her tongue to explore his lips and tongue.

"Mmm…" she moaned as she felt both his thumbs moving gently back and forth at the base of her breasts. She pulled her mouth away long enough to say, "That feels nice…"

"What does?"

"Your thumbs…"

"My th… oh, I didn't realize I was doing that."

Wow… getting that intimate, turning my burners up to high, and you did it without even thinking about it…?

They kissed again, and Charles' hands began to explore further. They were both wearing button up shirts and jeans, and Charles pulled her shirttail out and put a hand under it, caressing her stomach, moving upward ever so slowly.

When he touched her bra, Susan's toes curled and she sucked in her breath. "MMmmm…" *Keep going… please keep going…*

He began gently squeezing one breast, and she began to unbutton her shirt. She pulled it open, and he leaned down to kiss her cleavage. She leaned forward enough to reach behind her, up under her shirt, and unhook her bra, then pulled her hands out, reached into each short sleeve and pulled the straps out and over her elbows. Finally she removed her bra from the front while her shirt was still on. *I wonder if that trick will impress you…?*

Charles kept kissing her, growing more passionate, and his hand now caressed her naked breasts. He began to rock his hips against her, then slid over a little to her side and began to reach under her waistband. Finding it too tight to get his hand in, he struggled to unfasten her belt and her pants' snap with one hand, finally getting them undone, and he slowly unzipped them.

He slid his hand between her pants and her panties, gently exploring and rubbing. *Ooo… my panties are damp… I hope you don't mind. And how long has it been since I shaved my legs? Too long, darn it…*

They continued to kiss, and after a minute, he withdrew his hand and began to slide it down inside her panties. Susan held her breath as she felt his fingers get closer and closer to her clit. She instinctively arched her back slightly and raised her hips, trying to get his fingers to her most sensitive spot. When his fingers finally touched her clitoral hood, she sucked in her breath and groaned into his mouth.

With his fingertip slowly moving back and forth, she began to rock her hips very slightly to magnify the effect.

Susan felt a wave swelling that she was powerless to stop. She pressed her lips harder to his while her back arched her breasts into his chest and his finger continued its rhythmic pressure. Her toes curled again, and her feet began to point straight out as the wave overtook her. Her head went back and broke the kiss as her body shook.

"Uh-uh-uhh-uhhhh... unghhh... uhhhh..."

While the crest was receding, she heard Charles asking, "Are you okay...?"

"Yes..." Susan managed to say. "That felt good..." *Wow, did it feel good... Why didn't Marty ever get me off? Did he know it was possible and he didn't care, or did he just not know...?*

Charles kissed her again for a moment, then stopped and began to take his shirt off. Just then a buzzing sound went off. He tried to reach in his pocket, but was having too much trouble in that position, so he rolled onto his back before he could get the phone out.

"Hello? Yes? Okay..."

"Is it the treatment center?" Susan asked in a hushed tone.

"Well, how about call Nat about that? Whatever he says is fine with me... Sure... Okay, thanks," he concluded and hung up. He dropped the phone over the edge of the bed onto the floor. "That was Mike. He just wanted to talk business."

Charles finished getting his shirt off, and Susan began to remove her pants. "Un-uh," he said to stop her. "I want to do that."

"Okay..." she said, and relaxed.

He removed his pants and shorts, moved to the foot of the bed, then slowly began to pull her pants off. *Wow, Charles, you have the patience of Job... I never realized how... stimulating it could be to do something as simple as taking off my pants so slowly...* When they were gone, he slowly repeated the process with her panties.

Susan smiled and spread her legs, waiting for him to mount her. *Please don't notice my scratchy legs... I don't want you to have to stop while I shave them again... hey...* "What are you doing?"

Instead of climbing on top of her, it was now clear he planned to settle down with his mouth between her legs. "Charles! No! You already made me feel good. Now it's your turn."

"Okay, and for my turn I want to taste you."

"But you already..." her words were choked off when his tongue touched her and her legs automatically tensed, held, then finally began to relax again.

"Charles..." she said, wriggling slightly beneath him, trying to escape his mouth.

"Ow!" he exclaimed when her pelvis jerked up against his mouth.

"Oh no! What did I do?" She tried to rise up on her elbows to see.

"Just bumped my lip a little I think. It's okay," he added and bent back down to his task.

Noo...

His tongue was now moving steadily up and down in long strokes, from the bottom of her vaginal lips to her clitoral hood. *Need... to stop you... but feels soo... goood... oh... Charles... it's not fair, it's your turn to cum... but... oh... it feels so good... I can't tell you to stop anymore... I don't want you to stop...*

Susan's breathing increased its pace and her hips began rocking again, in sync with Charles' tongue. She could sense a wave building again, and it seemed even more intense than last time. It was slower in coming, but it felt like far more power was building up. She raised her legs and they wavered in the air as her hips continued to move back and forth. Then her legs lowered until they rested on Charles' back, and she used her legs to push her hips up and down into Charles' face. His tongue was moving faster now as he inserted a finger into her and slowly moved it around. She felt the wave begin to wash over her as if in slow motion at first, as an incredible heat began to make her breasts tingle. She grabbed handfuls of bedcovers as the flood of endorphins took over her brain. She threw her head back and her chest up, every muscle locked and straining, as she sucked in a huge breath and held it. When her body could hold in the air no more, it exploded out of her and her body began a series of violent, but ecstatic convulsions while she gasped for breath.

Her head was spinning, and she heard groaning or growling. She was still gasping for air, and it took her a few moments to realize that half of the moans were hers, and the rest were Charles'. He was now on top of her, thrusting in and out, and she was rocking her hips, driving her pelvis into him as hard as she could. She seemed to float as he roared, his hands under her, lifting her. She was grunting, or he was, and one or both of them was still rocking their hips together.

The next thing she knew was the weight of his body covering hers, making it harder for her to gasp for breath. He seemed to have one elbow on the bed, making less pressure on her there, and she wiggled in that direction. Charles moved or slid a little to the other side, and she could breathe easier again. They both continued to pant rapidly.

That's odd... kind of... feels like... you're still inside me... can't tell how hard you are... but it's enough... to give me that full feeling... One of her arms was pinned to the bed by Charles' body, and she raised the other to stroke his arm. *Mmm... slick with sweat... so smooth... wow... who... knew... sex could be... so... so... so much like that...?*

She explored both their bodies with her free hand, and everywhere she touched was soaked with sweat. She relaxed her arm with her hand on his arm and she gently moved it back and forth.

I've gotten sweaty before... with Marty, just because sometimes it was so hard to get him to cum, but... why didn't someone tell me sex can let me feel like... like that...? Like men do...? Like Charles does...? She bit her lip. *This wasn't me giving Charles sex. And it wasn't Charles taking what he wanted from me... we had sex together... That's it! We had sex together! Wow... first Charles taught me to dance, and now he's teaching me how to have real sex... sharing all of ourselves with each other...!*

Tears of joy rolled down the sides of Susan's face, releasing all the tension and frustration from the days past. *Oh, Lord... I've never felt so whole, so complete... Charles... is part of me now... the two of us share one life, in you...*

When her breathing had recovered to just rapid, regular breaths, Susan's eyes opened and for some reason it surprised her that there was plenty of light in the room. She turned her head and tried to rise a bit to look at Charles. Perhaps because he felt her move, he opened his eyes.

His breathing, too, was recovering quickly now. "Now... do you see... why I like licking pussy so much...?"

You... you're used to that...? That's what you wanted all along? Susan's disappointment was almost palpable. "So, you're used to that, huh?" *All this time I've been subpar, and now I'm just getting up to average?!*

"Well, yes and no," he rolled more onto his side, sliding out of her and taking most of his weight off her, then propped up on one elbow. "Yes, I'm used to giving my wife an orgasm, well, my first wife, anyway, by licking her. But... no, because... because... you remember on our wedding day when you asked me what my favorite memory was…?"

Susan looked off as she tried, and then remembered. "Yes… you said…"

"Well, I have a new favorite," he interrupted.

Susan's eyebrows went up. *Could that mean… it must…* "Does that mean it was better than what you were used to… you know, before…?"

Charles began to tenderly massage Susan's closest breast with his free hand. "You mean was it just my favorite with you? Oh, no. And I didn't mean just my favorite just with you last time, either. I mean my favorite of all time. That was the most delightful, sensual experience I've ever had. And after breaking that record again and again on our wedding day, I honestly never thought we'd come close to breaking it again, but Susan! Susan…!"

Susan felt the tears forming once again. *You're going to think I cry all the time…*

"Susan, almost nothing makes me happier than giving my wife an orgasm. The better I make my wife feel, the better it makes me feel. The more sexually aroused I get, too. And you, Susan, you're just a beginner at this, but you just had, what appeared to me, anyway, the biggest orgasm I've ever seen. The loudest I've ever heard was on our wedding day, but this seemed to me to be the most powerful."

Susan grinned and giggled. "Really?"

Charles nodded, then his eyes got as big as saucers and he gasped.

"What is it?!" Susan asked anxiously.

"I just remembered something…!

"What? What?"

Charles sat up and sat cross-legged on the bed, pulling Susan up to a sitting position, with their shins touching. Susan glanced at the bedroom door and was relieved to see that it was fully closed, so it helped block any noise they made from reaching the hallway.

"Years ago, before I even got married, I heard some older men in a locker room bragging about their sexual accomplishments, and one of them bragged that he'd given a woman two orgasms in one night. He put it more crudely than that, and the other men obviously didn't believe him, but… that made a lasting impression on me, and after I got married, I wanted to reach that goal, but Jennifer never was able to do it. Once she had one orgasm, she… you know, she came down from it, and I couldn't get her worked up again. In fact, it seemed to bother her whenever I tried. But I wanted to so badly, I used to dream about it. It frustrated me for years, and then I guess I finally gave up on it and quit thinking about it."

Susan was listening, but thinking hard at the same time. "So... when we first started kissing, and you put your finger down there... I had an orgasm. And I know it was one, because it fit the description in the sex book, and I started to be like..." *What was her name...?* "Jennifer... I was satisfied. *Really* satisfied... so much that I didn't want you to play with me anymore, but you got your mouth down there before I realized what you were doing, and I tried to object, but before I could convince you, it started feeling so good I stopped wanting you to stop. Uh, did that make sense?"

"Yes! Exactly!! And you ended up having a second orgasm, right on the tail of the last one!! Right?"

"Oh, that was so much more than right, you stallion, you..."

Charles laughed, "Do you realize you *literally* made my dream come true?!"

"Well, I think it had more to do with you, than me..." Susan said.

Charles jumped out of bed and pulled Susan close to the edge.

She quickly squeezed her legs together. "Oh, no, I forgot! I've been dripping all over the bed!"

He pulled her up off the bed and into a hug. "Let it drip!"

She put her arms around his neck and laced her fingers and they gazed into each other's eyes.

Ooo, shoot. I can feel it leaking... I hate that...

"I wish we could stay like this half of forever," Charles whispered as he slowly turned them in place in a slow-dance without music.

Well, I can't interrupt our hug to wipe off after a comment like that... Susan closed her eyes and rested her head against Charles. "Mmm..." she murmured.

This is nice, but there's a drip running way down my thigh, and... your thigh keeps brushing again mine... hmm... you're not getting close enough to get it on you, though... "Let it drip," you said... but I just can't... "Charles...?"

"Mm?"

Susan looked up. "It's running down my leg."

Charles looked back with a smile while continuing their dance. "Mmm... now *that* is a very sexy thing to say..." and he closed his eyes and tilted his head down to touch hers.

What...? That... you think that's sexy...? Dripping feels very annoying to me... but you like it? You like knowing your semen's running down my leg? Huh. Well, I guess that means if I can choose not to let it bother me, I can give you happiness just by... Susan grinned to herself and gave Charles a squeeze. *"Let it drip,"* the man *said...*

Charles stopped turning and began rocking her from side to side. "I love you more than words can say..."

Mmm... I don't know... you've said a lot of very wonderful words... She opened her eyes. "You've told me in so many ways. You've shown me in so many ways..."

She lifted her head and Charles lowered his lips to hers, their tongues teasing each other again. When his tongue made its way into her mouth again, she began to suck on it, off and on, tickling the tip of his tongue with hers each time she sucked. She heard a low growl and smiled inside at her ability to make him feel good. A few moments later she wasn't too surprised to feel his cock grow stiff between them, and she stopped kissing to giggle, remembering how many times they'd had sex on their wedding day. "Well, I can tell someone's ready to go again..."

"Mm... but I'm not ready to break this spell," he said, then bent over and scooped her up, cradling her in his arms as he resumed turning and swaying.

Susan pulled his head down into a kiss. *Mmm... Do you realize your cock is poking up and caressing my butt... and I love it...*

"Say, I have an idea..." Charles dropped his arm from under Susan's legs and they fell toward the floor without reaching it while his other arm held her up. He put one hand under each of her arms and lifted her up.

You're so strong...

"Try to put me in you again."

"Okay!" Susan agreed as she moved her pelvis until she felt his tip at her entrance and then let herself down onto it. *That went in easy. Still pretty wet, I guess...*

"Now wrap your legs around my waist."

Susan complied. "Are you going to..."

Before she could finish asking if he was going to walk them around or into the shower, he sat on the edge of the bed. Charles was now sitting comfortably, and she was sitting comfortably in his lap, with him inside her, and her breasts pressed against his chest.

"Oh, Charrrlllesss... we're going to have to remember this little arrangement," she said as she began to kiss him again.

When they stopped kissing for a moment, Charles said, "If you don't mind, I'd rather not try to reach a climax again."

Susan looked very surprised. "You're hard. You're inside me." *And it feels very good...* "So... why don't you want to cum in me again?"

"Well, I read that sex book... and it said that tantric sex... I'm not sure I pronounced that right... is about delaying orgasm as long as possible to focus on enjoying the part before orgasm more. I think that's the basic idea, anyway. I certainly don't want to do that all the time, but right now... right now, nothing could be better than this."

"Oh, wow, Charles... now *that* is a sexy thing to say." *That time on the living room floor... and now this... I never knew sex could be this much fun... that it could be so emotionally satisfying.* Susan sighed blissfully.

And... I'm not objecting to the physical satisfaction, either, Susan thought as a mischievous grin appeared. "Can I try something else though? Without you moving?"

He cocked his head a little to one side, apparently having mild concern about her mysterious plan. "Okayyy..."

Okay, big boy... you try not to have another orgasm, and I'm going to try to make you have one... Susan grinned as she leaned back until only her nipples were still touching Charles' chest, then she moved a few inches left, paused, then right. *Oh, Charles... Oh, Lord... this feels incredible... Oh, God, you made us capable of this kind of pleasure...*

Susan began to groan loudly, "Ohhh... ohhh... Charrrlllesss... oh, God... this feels... sooo... incredible... so... erotic..."

In only seconds, Susan was panting. She paused the movement, trying to catch her breath, but felt compelled to move again. She eased her nipples down very, very slowly, then up. Her breath couldn't keep up, but she couldn't stop herself from doing it again. *There's... that feeling... coming... again... It can't be... just from this... can it...?* She looked at Charles wide-eyed, and he looked delightfully happy. She felt her vaginal muscles tighten without conscious effort, and it gave her a diffused sense of an impending wave of cataclysmic proportions. "Charles...?" she said in a tiny voice.

"Charles...?!" she pleaded. She felt her vagina clamp down on him like a vise and her legs tried to squeeze him in two. "Hold... meee...!" she shrieked as she threw her head back, then lost track of the world.

When she came to, she was lying on the bed and Charles was

sitting beside her, gently stroking her hair. He said something, but she didn't catch it. For what seemed like several minutes, she just lay there with Charles caressing her, and he didn't try to say anything else. She closed her eyes a few moments, and then opened them again.

"Charles..." *What have you done to me...? You've... you've turned me into... what...? A real woman? A real lover? A sex maniac?*

Charles smiled and raised her closest limp arm. "And still the champion...!" he quietly teased.

Susan blinked, and began to smile despite some confusion. *Did I hit my head? I've got a concussion? Delusions? How long have I been out...?* "Have I been dreaming...?"

"No, baby. You had a hat-trick!"

"A whaat?"

"Oh, that's a hockey term. Do you... never mind. It means three goals by a single player in a single game. And you, you stellar vixen you, have had three orgasms in less than an hour."

Susan's smile turned into a grin. *And... Jennifer... never even had two in a row...!*

"The people from the Guinness Book of Records and the people who monitor earthquakes have been calling constantly."

"They have? Wh... Oh, you!"

Charles laughed. "That last one really knocked you for a loop, huh?"

"Oh, Charles... that may have been the last one for today, but..." she pulled him down into a hug. "If you're willing to help me experience something like that again... I... I'd like that," she finished in a whisper.

He kissed her, then whispered back, "I'm not only willing, I'm eager, and I have a lot more tricks to try to help you feel good."

"Like what?"

"You sure you don't want me to save them as surprises?"

"No! Please, tell me now!"

"Okay, okay. Well, now you know how sensual your clitoris is, right?"

She nodded.

"And we've clearly established that your breasts can be very sensitive."

Susan shivered at the memory. "Oh, my... I never even imagined they could ever be *that* sensitive..."

"And your mouth, and... did you read in the book about your G-spot?"

"Oh, yeah... I guess that didn't really sink in at the time."

"Well, we have that to experiment with, plus a lot of other erogenous areas, like where your uterus comes into your vagina. And your A-spot at the back end of your pussy. Plus the little area between your vagina and your anus, and your anus itself."

Susan scowled a little bit. *I thought we talked about that...*

"I'm not talking about putting my cock in it, I'm just talking about just a lubricated fingertip. Pinkie fingertip," he added, holding a pinkie up to let her see the size.

She still frowned. *I still don't like...*

"And not to start with. Plus your neck, your feet, your inner thighs... We have a lot other things to try other than your anus... But if you'll trust me, someday when I think you're ready for it, when you're already highly aroused, I'll try stimulating it just a little bit. If you don't like it, we can quit any time. If you like it, then anything that works can go into my bag of tricks to help you have as many orgasms as you ever want."

Susan sighed and relaxed. "I'm sorry I got afraid again, Charles. You've given me every reason to trust you."

She shook her head. *I'm not going to cry again. I'm not.* "Charles, the first time we came back to the hotel from the treatment center, you told me I can do anything I want to you, any time, any place."

He nodded.

"I want to make that same promise to you... but I can't, not yet. I want to, I really do, and I hope I'm going to get to the place where I can. If you can be patient enough." She nuzzled his neck. "You know, this orgasm thing is still pretty new to me. A lot of sex things with you are new to me, but I'm learning..."

"Boy, I'll say..."

She smiled. "I am learning, but I think I still have a whole lot more to learn than what I've learned so far. And it'll take time to learn it all. Or most of it."

"And I don't care how long it takes," Charles replied, "or how much you learn, as long as we're both enjoying the journey together as much as we are now."

Susan grinned. "Enough talking. More kissing!"

Charles obliged, and Susan's mind wandered while they made out. *I don't think I've ever been so... sexual. Even in my teens and twenties when my hormones must have been at their peak. And for years my libido seemed dead and buried. Maybe I'm one of those women whose sex drive increases after menopause… but… it still seemed dead right up until I met Charles… Boy, it sure woke up then!*

Hmm… when Marty and I got married I was fairly… enthusiastic, and that did wear off after a while, so maybe I'm just going through a honeymoon effect. But so far this really doesn't feel like a short-term thing. Lord, it feels like you're actually changing me again… but do you really care about us enjoying sex?

Susan remembered some of the things she had read, especially about sexuality, even orgasms, being part of God's design, and one of God's many gifts to us. *Heavenly Father, I don't want to get all my rewards on earth, if I have any rewards at all… I want Charles and I to share them in heaven, with you… But Lord, if this is really your gift to us now… I can't thank you enough… sex with Charles is so far beyond anything I've ever imagined… "immeasurably more than all we ask or imagine…"*

When they were satisfied with their kissing and cuddling in bed for the time being, they agreed to a bathroom break, showers, and then a soak in the Jacuzzi again, but when Susan started to sit up, a pain in her pelvis caught her off-guard.

"What is it?" Charles asked with obvious concern.

Susan gently moved one leg, then the other, then bent a little at the waist, experimenting to find out which motions would have what effect on the soreness. "I… I guess I'm bruised in there again…"

"Oh, no… Susan, I…"

Susan gave him a smile that stopped his apology. "I think it was at as much my fault as yours this time, Charles."

She moved her hips a little more. "Maybe we can learn to be energetic in ways that won't cause you to hit the back of my pussy so hard…" she said, but then remembered how the pleasure she was experiencing compelled her to violently thrust her hips into him. *Whether we can or not… I honestly doubt I'll ever be able to give up those incredible feelings. I think you've started something I won't want to turn off…*

She eased off the bed and ended up walking to the bathroom slightly bent at the waist. *Hmm… definitely sore… quite sore… but… oh my goodness, there's something definitely erotic about it! It… it doesn't make me want to have sex again right this minute, but… it's definitely arousing… it sure is making me look forward to the next time we have sex… We'll need to be careful not to injure me worse, but Lord, this kind of feels good at the same time it feels uncomfortable. Is the discomfort just because I'm not used to it? Is this what Grandma Brenda was talking about...? I don't know if I can get used to this, but I'm beginning to think I'd like to!*

After using the toilet, Susan washed her face in the sink to get a good look at her facial bruises.

"Look, Charles, they're really fading fast now. Mostly what's left is yellowish, with just a little brown in a couple of spots."

Charles put a hand on her waist as he looked over her shoulder. "You're right, it's almost gone. But like I said, as long as you smile, no one will ever notice anything else anyway."

That comment resulted in a bigger smile, followed by another hug and kiss.

Susan and Charles cuddled while they showered, spent a half-hour in the Jacuzzi, and had supper brought up to their room, after which they ate at the dining room table. When their meal was over, they had decaf coffee in the living room while they watched another movie.

After the movie, they undressed each other completely, piled up their pillows against the bed's headboard and sat up snuggling in bed.

"Do you need to have sex again?" Susan asked.

"No, not if you don't need it. I don't know why, but I'm tired."

"Oh, no, I'm good. I'm more satisfied than I knew was possible... and I'm tired too."

They spent a few minutes praying out loud for Stephanie, William, and Robert, and thanking God for his limitless mercy and grace, then turned off the lights and settled down to sleep.

Mmm... so far every time we've gone to bed naked together, we've been woken up by a crisis of some kind and didn't get to wake up in each other's arms... Lord, I sure am looking forward to that... and I sure hope we don't have any more major problems...

As Susan began to drift off to sleep, she imagined that a forlorn Marty was watching them through a window, and that he was cold and hungry like the Poor Little Match Girl. He was dressed in rags, and Charles invited him in, which frightened Susan. Marty returned Charles' kindness by spitting on him, then taking a drink from a bottle wrapped in a brown paper bag. He kept drinking, becoming more and more angry, cursing and threatening them. It bothered Susan enough that it caused her to wake slightly and roll over, and as she did, her dreams faded away as she quickly fell into deep sleep.

Chapter Twenty One

Susan was standing in the back of the cabin cruiser in the middle of a lake, and Charles was looking at her with desire in his eyes. *You're attracted to me, and that gives me power over you...*

Charles got out of the driver's seat and took her roughly into his arms. "I want you, and I'm going to take you, right now."

"Very well, Charles, I shall let you have your way with me, but we have to go down into the boat's basement first."

"No," he said, and ripped the front of her shirt open.

Susan was startled. *I want you in me, but I must maintain control over you...* "Charles, we can't undress out here in the open..."

Now she was wearing only a string bikini with ties on each hip, behind her neck, and between her breasts. Charles pulled all of them at once and pulled the fabric away from her. She pressed herself against him to hide her body as well as she could, and he was naked and hard. "Charles, please, someone will see us!"

He ignored her pleas as he lifted her as high as his arms would reach and exposed her to the world before ceremoniously lowering her onto himself.

Oh, you feel so good, but I'm so embarrassed... she thought as she rocked her hips to increase the feeling of fullness.

The next moment, Susan was a concubine of King David's, after he had fled Jerusalem from his son Absalom's rebellion. She tied to move her hands and realized she was tied to a bed on a roof where Absalom was about to have sex with her for all Israel to see. Absalom towered over her, ripped away the only cloth that covered her, and he tilted the bed so that the entire crowd below could see between her legs.

Just then Charles appeared, and with an angry roar, he pushed Absalom off the roof to his death. He picked Susan up and laid her in her own bed and covered her with a satin sheet and bedspread. She moved her feet and felt the smooth material rise and fall.

Susan rolled from her side to her back and her hand touched something unfamiliar, prompting her to wake up. As her dreams flittered away, she moved her hand, touched something, then realized what she had touched was Charles. She moved her hand a little more and determined she was touching the small of his back.

Mmm... I'm in bed with my Charles... and we're married... She smiled, drew in a deep breath, and slowly let it out. *My husband... my precious Charles...*

And I don't think... she rocked her torso slightly and felt the sheet against her bare breasts, confirming that she wasn't wearing her usual night-bra, then she moved a hand to her waist to confirm that she wasn't wearing panties. *And Charles...?*

With her eyes still closed, Susan rolled onto her other side to face Charles and lightly ran her hand from his waist to his hips, then down his butt before her hand retraced its path and continued up to his shoulder. *Mmm... this is so nice...*

Charles slowly rolled over onto his back, fluffed the bedcovers, and took hold of her hand. "Good morning, gorgeous," he said warmly but sleepily.

"Gorgeous!" Not sweetheart, not honey, but "gorgeous!" Susan finally opened her eyes to discover Charles looking at her. "Good morning, handsome!"

Oh, I see we have a tent pole under the covers. I wonder if you're going to ask me if I feel like having sex, or just build up to it?

Charles turned on his side to face her and wiggled closer. He put out his arm and Susan wiggled closer and rested her head on his arm. Charles put his other arm over her and pulled her body into his own, moving his cock so that it was between their abdomens. Their foreheads touched, and then he slowly stoked his hand up and down her back.

Just build up to it, eh? That's fine with me, but I'm going to need some lubricant this time. Hm... should I get it now or wait? You're already hard, so... "Honey, I think I'm going to need lubricant before you come inside me."

"Oh?" Charles replied. "Okay. Well, if you want to have sex, do you mind if I pee first?"

"If *I* want to? You're the one who's raring to go."

"Me?" Charles asked with a puzzled look.

"Yes, silly. You can't exactly hide it..."

"Uh, honey, that's just because I have a full bladder."

Now Susan looked puzzled. "But... you're hard. That means you want to have sex."

Charles laughed. "No... and I'm puzzled. We've talked about the fact that a man can have an erection without wanting to have sex..."

"Oh… yeah… Guess I'm a little sleepy. I forgot you told me that at the hos… I mean, at the treatment center."

"Yeah, but surely Marty didn't want to have sex every time he got hard, right?"

"Oh, yes he did," Susan asserted. "He'd often want to when he wasn't hard, and he'd want me to get him hard, but anytime he got hard on his own, he wanted me to, uh… get him off."

"Huh. Well, not me."

Hmm… I think I like that a lot… instead of one aerobic, frenetic humping session after another, Charles' likes some opportunities for calm, peaceful intimacy … mmm… I definitely prefer this right now…

Susan reached between them and traced a finger over his cock, and she felt it twitch. *Uh-oh. Maybe you're just trying to delay your own satisfaction because you think I don't want to have sex right now…?* "You really don't need sex right now?"

"Don't need to, and don't care to if you don't need it," he said, shifting enough to kiss her.

Wow… this is so wonderful… you're hard… you're pressing into my stomach… I've offered to let you hump me… but you're satisfied just to snuggle and make out…? Yeehah!

They broke their kiss and Susan felt Charles' body relax as he sighed.

"That's a sigh of contentment, I hope?" she asked.

"If there's such a thing as extreme contentment, that's what I'm experiencing right now in your arms."

Susan felt a tingle all over, and she let herself relax completely, with her body conforming to his. "Extreme contentment… oh, Charles… I never knew I could be so happy…"

Later, as they ate a leisurely breakfast together, Susan started pondering how they'd spend their day, but she ruled out most of what she thought of because they had to stay in the hotel.

"Charles, what are we going to do today? Assuming we don't spend the whole day having sex, we can't go back to visit Stephanie yet, and we can't leave the hotel. I can spend some time reading my Bible… oops, reading your Bible, and praying, but I can't do that all day. And I hate the idea of watching TV all day…"

"Hmm…" Charles mused. "I hadn't thought about that. I've been neglecting overseeing Mike Samuelson's work and Parker Automotive, and I can spend some time getting back into that, but that won't take all day, either. There are some things I could do if we could leave, but you're right, we can't. And… honey, I hope you don't mind, but I'm kind of sore this morning. I thought it might feel better after I peed, but it doesn't. I think the tip of my cock might be a little bruised."

"Really? I guess I never thought about that possibility. About you getting bruised, I mean."

"We could get some board games…" Charles thought out loud.

"How are you spelling bored?" Susan asked, a twinkle in her eye.

"B O A… oh, I get it. Cute," he said with a smile.

"Well," Susan suggested, "you could see about getting a few games, maybe a deck of cards…Oh! What about the hotel pool, and the exercise room? Could we use those?"

"That's a great idea!" Charles replied. "I'll talk to Mike about it. Along with some cards and games…"

For the rest of that week, Charles made regular phone calls to more actively manage things, but overall it didn't consume much time. Susan called Stephanie at lunchtime on Tuesday, but couldn't keep her on the phone long. Stephanie agreed to their visiting her Wednesday night after supper, but other than that she asked them to wait for the weekend to return.

As a result, the week seemed to pass very slowly, with regular Bible reading and praying, with most of the prayers for Stephanie and Charles' sons, plus occasional sex, swimming, exercise, games, and television. Despite those activities, they still had cabin fever and felt bored much of the time.

The weekend finally came, and Susan and Charles anxiously waited to spend Saturday afternoon and evening with Stephanie.

When they finally got together with Stephanie, they had to exercise even more patience as Stephanie reluctantly gave out bits and pieces of her past week. Nonetheless, they were encouraged that while Stephanie wasn't exactly enthusiastic, at least she showed no signs of giving up.

Stephanie also let Susan read more to her from the Bible, and they played some three-handed games of Rummy for a while.

On the way back to the hotel suite for the night, Mike rode shotgun in the car with Susan and Charles in the back.

"Charles, Susan… I've got a concern I need to discuss with you."

"Sure, Mike, what is it?" Charles replied.

Mike seemed distinctly ill-at-ease. "Well… it's about Brian. He was on duty in the room with you guys today until shift change…"

"Yeah…" Charles said.

I didn't notice anything out of the ordinary, Susan thought.

"Well… Brian has insisted on working every single day shift so far on the team guarding Stephanie's room… These are twelve-hour shifts, so normally, I'd insist on a man taking some days off to rest, to be able to keep up his concentration, but Brian's fought me on that. Now, I've never known Brian to balk at anything I've ever asked him to do, so that was one unusual thing. As it happens, I believe Brian's as sharp as ever despite no breaks. He seems to thrive on this kind of work. But…"

"One unusual thing," you said. That implies there's at least one more…

"On Monday morning, Stephanie kicked us all out. You included… But at supper time, she pretty much demanded that the door be left open."

"Yeah, you told me about that," Charles commented.

Mike told you about it on Tuesday when you called him, and then you told me…

"Well, Wednesday, she said she wanted Brian back in the room…"

She must have been feeling lonely…

"Then on Thursday morning, she agreed to have the door closed again, with an inside man, like we wanted from the beginning…" Mike hesitated, but neither Susan nor Charles said anything, and he finally continued, "Well… with Brian in there every day… just the two of them, with the door closed… that is, when Stephanie wasn't in a therapy session somewhere else, well… I guess I started getting a little… concerned. I, uh, came up with excuses to make surprise visits, without them seeming like I was checking up on him, and he was rooted to his position, eyes on the door…"

"So…" Charles prompted.

"I can keep checking on them, but I want to ask the two of you straight-out if you're okay with Brian being in there every day. If you aren't, I'll order him on R&R or transfer him to another post."

Charles looked at Susan. "What do you think, hon?"

Brian is a prayer warrior… a real one… he knows the Bible pretty well, and seems to be mentally stable… even Mike seems to think that… plus, Stephanie and Brian must know anyone could walk in on them at any time… Well, we shouldn't "rely on our own understanding..." and the bottom line is what God wants...

Susan put a hand on Charles' arm and closed her eyes. *Lord...? What do you want...? Is it safe for Brian to stay with Stephanie all this time...? Is that your will? Is that what's best for Stephanie...?*

A paraphrase of a fragment of a Bible verse popped into Susan's mind. The memory of exactly where she had seen or heard it before was vague, but she felt a sense of power in it, *"I have made him a watchman for the house of Israel."*

Susan opened her eyes and looked at Charles, feeling a sense of peace in her heart. "It's okay. I trust him."

Charles looked back at Mike and concurred, "It's okay with us, Mike."

"Okay," Mike said. "I'm still going to keep close checks on them, and I'm going to yank him out of there at the first sign that he's losing his edge."

Mike spent the rest of trip reviewing the progress they'd been making on tracking down Big Ed and mapping out his operation, and giving them a general idea of what their upcoming plans and options were.

That Sunday morning seemed to pass quickly for Susan, beginning with sex, and with her having to insist that Charles wait longer before he used his mouth on her again.

They were back at Cambridge by noon to have lunch in the cafeteria with Stephanie as soon as the Chapel service was over. Susan had been disappointed that Stephanie didn't want her and Charles to attend the service with her, but she was delighted that it had been Stephanie's idea to have lunch together.

After lunch, they strolled back to Stephanie's room and played a game of monopoly, which Susan won. Stephanie felt tired after that and lay down to relax while Susan read to her from the book of Acts. Charles sat next to the window and listened along.

Around two-thirty, a smiling doctor entered the room and walked over to Stephanie, on the side of the bed closest to the door, opposite from where Susan and Charles were sitting.

He held up a plastic cup with a pill in it and a cup of water with a straw. "Well, hello there, I've got some medication for you. You're Steph Towns, right? Short for Stephanie, I'm guessing? I just need to confirm you're the right patient."

Stephanie nodded and sat up.

"Okay, great. If you don't think you can swallow this, I can give you an injection instead."

"I can swallow it," Stephanie said and reached out for the cup.

One moment, Brian Milner seemed to be relaxed, sitting on the window ledge, and in the next moment he jumped to the floor while whipping out a pistol with a silencer and pointing it at the doctor. "Don't move!"

The doctor dropped the cup of water onto the bed, but otherwise, he and everyone else froze as Brian yelled, "Truck! Tiger One!"

What...?! What's...

The door flew open and was filled by Truck, who was drawing a gun of his own. In a flash he trained it on the doctor, stepped inside, shut the door, leaned against it, touched a finger to his ear and started mumbling.

"Charles...!" Susan exclaimed as Charles jumped up at the same time Truck had come barreling in.

Charles quickly scooped up Stephanie and backed away from the bed, pushing Susan and her chair toward the window as he did so. Susan jumped to her feet and put her arms around Stephanie as Charles put her down and stood between them and the doctor.

"What the xx-xx-xx is this?!" the doctor snarled, though he still didn't move.

"You called her Steph," Brian said with a fierce, but calm tone of voice, "but you weren't sure her name was Stephanie. Stephanie is the name all the staff here calls her by, which means that's what's on all the records around here." Brian's gun didn't waver in the slightest.

"I just..." the doctor tried to interject.

"Then I realized the name pin on your coat doesn't have the name of this place like everyone else's."

The doctor started slowly lowering his right hand. "That's because..."

"If you move that hand one inch lower, I'll kill you. I can't afford to try to shoot you in the shoulder or leg 'cause it might go through you, through the wall, and hit someone else. That means it goes center-mass, buddy."

The doctor's eyes narrowed, but he raised his hand slightly.

"And when I trained my gun on you, any normal person would have reacted with fear. You had anger in your eyes. You were ready to fight. Still are."

"Okay... I surrender," the doctor said as he dropped the little medicine cup holding the pill and held his hands in front of his chest, then relaxed his shoulders as he took a step back. "I have a gun under my coat, right side. You can take it."

"So you can try hand-to-hand combat? Much as I'd enjoy that, we'll relieve you of your gun in a minute. Right now ease your hands to the top of your head. Then and only then, step back against the wall. Deviate, and I shoot."

The doctor's face morphed into an angry red, but he slowly obeyed.

Susan struggled to take in the events as she held tightly to Stephanie, but she began to pray silently but fervently.

Brian and Truck stood frozen with their guns pointed.

"Brian..." Stephanie said.

"Just stay still Stephanie," Brian said calmly, "our backup should be here any..."

"Truck, it's Whit!" came a voice through the door.

"Password," demanded Truck.

"Jupiter," came an immediate reply.

Truck eased away from the door, taking a step toward the doctor. Two more men entered with guns drawn, assessed the situation, and also trained their guns on the doctor.

"Said he's got a gun under his coat," Truck said. "Right side."

Truck eased closer and closer until the barrel of his silencer was against the doctor's temple, as one of the new men crouched low and duck-walked between Brian and the doctor, well below where Brian was aiming. Once on the other side, he removed the doctor's gun, then began a pat-down from top to bottom.

"Who do you work for?" demanded Brian.

The man shrugged, his anger fading away. "Myself."

"You were hired just for this, or do you work for Big Ed?"

"I'll trade what I know for a deal," he replied unemotionally.

After the pat-down, they stripped him on the spot in an exhaustive search and Susan turned her face away, but neither Charles nor Stephanie did.

"You were really going to murder an innocent girl?" Brian asked, still holding his gun on him.

"Innocent?" spat the man with derision, "She's a xx-xx-xx whore. She's nothing."

Susan hugged Stephanie tighter. "That's not true," she whispered in Stephanie's ear.

"She's something," Brian countered, "And you're a killer who's going to spend the rest of his life in jail."

They finally finished their search and handcuffed him behind his back before one of them pulled up his undershorts.

"Who the xx-xx-xx trained you people?" the man asked as he was led out of the room.

After he was gone, Brian and Truck re-holstered their guns, and Susan's breath began to slow back down.

"That was intense," Brian commented as another of Mike's men began the process of photographing, bagging and tagging the clothes, pill, and cups.

"He… he was going to poison me…?" Stephanie asked. "To keep me from testifying?"

"Looks like it," Brian agreed, looking into Stephanie's eyes. "I'll have to be gone for a few hours to take care of the legal work, but I'll be back."

Stephanie broke away from her mother and hugged him. "Brian… you saved my life," she said meekly.

"Yes, but only temporarily, Stephanie. You still need saving long-term." He gently eased her away and left.

Stephanie began crying, and Susan stepped over and hugged her again. "Don't you believe that man, Stephanie. God created you in His image, just like everyone else. And God loves you, just like Charles and I do. Nothing you've ever done or ever will do will change that."

Stephanie didn't reply, but she rested her head on her mother's shoulder until her crying began to subside, and then she sat in an upholstered chair and stared at the window curtain and Susan sat next to her and tried to comfort her. After a while, Stephanie stood and moved over to the center of the window, parting the sheer curtains enough to see out.

"Honey," Susan said with a mixture of compassion and concern, "you can't stand in front of the window with…"

"I don't care, Momma."

"But honey…"

"Besides they're not likely to have a- a sniper out there while they had… that man in here. But even if they do, I don't give a xx-xx-xx."

Susan stood next to her and put an arm around her waist. *Lord, what should I say…?*

"I'm thirty years old, Momma. Thirty. And I've ruined my life. I totally ruined it. The only thing wrong with what that man said was he left out I'm a drunk. I'm nothing but a drunk whore. I'm worthless.

I'm thirty years old, Momma, and I've wasted my entire life."

Susan wanted desperately to interrupt and tell her she was wrong, explain how she was wrong, but she had a stronger sense that she needed to let Stephanie say everything she was thinking, everything she was feeling.

"Did you know the Bible says that drunks won't go to heaven?" Stephanie asked.

Just then a Bible verse popped into Susan's mind. "Yes... but it also says that when anyone is in Christ, they're a new creation. It's not like they're just the old person fixed up a little bit. It says they're a new creation."

Stephanie seemed to seriously consider what her mother said before responding, "But Momma... I'm thirty. *Thirty*, and my whole life up until now has been garbage. Even if I can straighten out, I've wasted my entire life."

"I..." Susan began, then cut herself off.

"You what?" Stephanie asked after a few moments.

"I was about forty-five when I became a Christian..."

"Yeah, but you had a family. You had Dad, and me, and Steve. I've got xx-xx-xx."

Susan was at a loss for words, and turned her head to look for Charles to see if he could pitch in, but neither he nor anyone else was in the room, and the door was closed.

"Momma...?"

"Yes, darling...?"

"I don't want to hurt your feelings, I really don't. Not anymore. Especially right now... but... would you mind leaving me alone again...?"

Susan's face expressed shock and grief at the same time. *Alone...? Oh, Stephanie...! You need me... please let me be here for you...!*

"Please, Momma?"

"But, Stephanie... you shouldn't be alone now. You..."

"Actually, I was hoping you could get Chappy to come see me." *Chappy...?* "Who's Chappy?"

"Oh, that's my nickname for the chaplain. Dr. Martin."

Susan stood still, not knowing what to do or say.

"Please, Momma."

Susan's head was almost spinning. "If... if I leave... and get the chaplain... will you at least sit back down and let me close the curtains again?"

Stephanie closed the curtains herself and sat down, but then just stared at the closed curtains. "Momma... please ask Chappy to come see me, and then you and Charles go on home. I mean, to your hotel..."

Susan moved slowly toward the door, her heart breaking. *Oh, God... Father, Father... why are you letting her push me away again? She needs you... she needs me...*

Charles was just a few steps down the hall talking to Mike and spotted Susan as she came out of the room downcast and he rushed to her side. "Susan! What's wrong?! Is Stephanie alright?"

He started to open the door, but Susan put out her hand to stop him as she shook her head, then she pulled him into an embrace and cried. "She wants to talk to the chaplain... and she doesn't want us here... she-she asked us to leave... she even said please..."

Charles got a nurse to call the chaplain and he took Susan to the Chapel's prayer room, where they stayed until a police detective had to interview them and get statements from them. Afterward, they spent the better part of another hour in the prayer room until the Chaplain came by.

"Hey, folks. Mike told me you were here," the doctor said, poking his head in the door after a light knock. "Okay to come in? If you want more time to be alone, I can..."

"No, no, that's all right, David," Charles said.

He entered and sat across from then. "I got here a while ago and stayed with Stephanie while the police talked to her, then I talked to her privately after they left. Stephanie's fine physically, and she's fairly stable emotionally. She's in something of a spiritual crisis at the moment, but that's actually a good thing. A very good thing, because she's reacting to the events earlier today by evaluating her life. As recently as last week, she probably would have had an automatic reaction of wanting to turn to alcohol for comfort."

"But..." Susan began, "she really needs to give her life to God..."

"Yes," David replied, "she does. And she's already heard the Gospel presented clearly, more than once. She has the intellectual information she needs to give her life to Jesus, but as you know, it's not an intellectual decision, it's a spiritual one. It's a surrendering of our will to God's, and it requires a leap of faith. Some people make that leap only when they've come to the end of their rope, when they feel utterly hopeless or worthless. Other people make that leap under other circumstances. Right now, Stephanie doesn't feel like she's hopeless, and she may never feel that way because she has a very strong will. That doesn't make her any more or less likely to surrender her will to God, that's just part of how God made her."

"What can we do, David?" Charles asked.

"I expect this is very hard on you, but she's asked for time alone, and I think she needs that right now. She needs time to think about her life... what's it's been up until now, and what it can be. And she's strong-willed enough that if she comes up with any questions, or needs anything else, she'll ask. She has my cell phone number, she knows she can call me any time, day or night, and I'm sure she wouldn't hesitate to call you, if she needs you. The best thing you can do in the meantime is pray for her..."

David left after praying for Susan and Charles, and they waited in the prayer room while the security team got ready to transport them back to the hotel again.

They really tried to kill Stephanie... they really tried to kill her... "Charles... my faith is really weak right now... for that man to get so close to murdering my daughter, after all our prayers..."

"It's true he got close," Charles said, "frighteningly close... but God did protect her. And it's almost a miracle that that Brian figured out that doctor was a fake. With Brian working such long hours for so many days, to think that clearly after that guy had gotten past everyone else... it was almost like God put him there just for that."

That idea struck Susan. "Do you remember when you asked me if I thought it was okay for Brian to spend so much time in Stephanie's room?"

"Yeah."

"Well, I prayed, and I remembered a Bible verse that said that 'God made him a watchman over the house of Israel,' so that part makes sense to me... God put Brian here, and Brian did watch out for Stephanie, in fact, he saved her life... but... why didn't God do it better? Why did He let a killer get close enough to touch her? Why couldn't he have made that guy have a car wreck on his way here, or let one of the other men catch him before he got into Stephanie's room?"

Charles looked thoughtful a few moments before replying. "I don't know why he let things happen the way they did, honey. But that doesn't mean he didn't have a reason... A little while ago, I remembered a Bible verse, and I think maybe God was trying to tell me it applies to Stephanie..."

"Which one?"

"I think it's from Jeremiah, and it goes something like this, 'I know the plans I have for you. Plans not to harm you, but plans to give you hope and a future.'"

Susan felt a faint thrill as Charles quoted the verse and she leaned into his shoulder and cried again. She stopped quickly, though, and used some tissues to wipe her eyes and blow her nose again. "You must think I cry all the time. I seem to be worse than a leaky faucet lately…"

Charles chuckled. "It amazes me how well you've stood up to so much turmoil. You lost a long-term job and you were struggling financially before we met, we had a whirlwind romance… that was positive emotions, but they were some very powerful ones… you were attacked in your home and beaten and stabbed, by your daughter's boyfriend… and it was the first time you had seen your daughter in years… then we got married… and how we managed to get married in the midst of all this just blows my mind… then Billy got murdered and we got interrogated by the police… then Stephanie reconciled with you, at least a little bit, then she ended up here and went through alcohol withdrawal… then she asked you not to visit her here very often, and on top of all that, someone tries to poison her to death right in front of us…"

He took a deep breath and let it out while shaking his head. "I doubt anyone else could have handled things half as well as you have."

Oh, Charles… you're such a wonderful comfort to me…

Mike knocked on the door, and Susan and Charles were driven back to the hotel, where they spent a mostly-somber evening praying for Stephanie off and on. They both had trouble getting to sleep that night, and didn't get into deep sleep until well after midnight.

Susan and Charles got up just before eight in the morning and immediately spent some time praying for Stephanie again, then got showered and dressed. They were just sitting down to another room-service breakfast when Susan's phone rang, and she looked carefully at the incoming number before answering.

"It's the treatment center," Susan nervously told Charles as she hit the button to answer the call. "Hello?"

"Momma? Momma, I did it! I gave my life to Jesus, Momma!"

Susan was stunned for a moment, then jumped up.

Stephanie kept talking very rapidly, "…Brian told me something this morning that was like… a missing piece, and when he explained it to me, everything I've been hearing about Jesus finally made sense, about how he loves us, he really loves us, even... even though I've done so many bad things... and he changed me, Momma! Jesus has changed my life! Just like it says in the Bible!"

"Oh, praise God, Stephanie! Praise the Lord!" Susan shouted into the phone, thought it didn't slow Stephanie down.

Oh hallelujah! Oh, Father, praise your holy name! Susan wasn't able to follow everything Stephanie was saying but she certainly got the gist of it. Her heart felt like it might explode with joy, and she was crying and jumping and pacing about. She saw Charles looking at her with obvious hope, and she nodded vigorously and put her hand over the phone's microphone as she told Charles quickly and quietly, "She did it! She gave her heart to Jesus!"

"...He took out my heart of stone and gave me a heart of flesh..." Stephanie continued, "Oh, Momma...! I'm so happy... and I'm sad at the same time... I'm so sorry for all the pain I caused you, for so many years... I'm sorry I never loved you like I should have... but I was never full of God's love before, and now I am, and I do love you, Momma, I love you so much...!"

Charles picked Susan up and held her with one arm while he raised the other arm to heaven, praising God quietly, but earnestly.

"Oh, Stephanie, Stephanie!" Susan cried out, "Praise God! Oh, Stephanie! My precious Stephanie! I've prayed for you for so long... I've wanted you to know the joy and love that I found when I gave my life to Jesus!"

Susan and Stephanie repeatedly interrupted each other and sometimes talked at the same time while sharing their newfound joy, and Charles put Susan down and raced to the suite's outside door and practically shouted as he asked the guards to get ready to take them back to the Cambridge Treatment Center.

Susan wanted to keep talking to Stephanie on her cell phone until they arrived in person, but Stephanie begged off so she could share the good news with her nine A.M. therapy group.

Once Stephanie hung up, Susan let the phone drop to her side and she and Charles looked at each other a single moment before rushing to close the two-step gap between them and share a joyous embrace.

Charles praised God out loud, while Susan cried and silently gave thanks.

Oh, yes, Father! Oh heavenly Father! You gave your only Son to atone for our sins, and that love has finally won Stephanie's heart! Oh, God, you're so wonderful! And Charles...! Oh, God, this man you've given me... if it weren't for him... You gave Charles the wealth to protect Stephanie, and he didn't hesitate to use it all... oh, God... what an incredible man! Oh, Jesus, after all these years! Is it really true? You've replaced Stephanie's heart of stone, just like you replaced mine years ago? You put your Spirit in Stephanie, just like you put yourself in me, and in Charles... just like Ezekiel said thousands of years ago!

"Oh, Charles...! I need to call Pastor Walker!"

"And I need to call Nat! Oh, I'll call Mike first. He'll want the good news, and he might be wondering what's going on when he hears I asked the guys at the door to get us back there fast..."

Susan stopped dialing and took Charles' hand. "Sit down with me first."

Charles was puzzled, but sat down next to her at the dining table.

Susan took his hand again and bowed her head. "Lord, we do thank you for loving us so much, and for giving us your life... Charles and myself, and now Stephanie. Now we ask you again to call William and Robert to you, and pour your Spirit into them. 'Your loving kindness is better than life,' Lord... we know it first-hand, and we ask you to help Charles' sons come to know it first-hand too..."

When Susan stopped praying she waited to give Charles a chance to pray, but when he didn't, she opened her eyes. Tears were streaming from his eyes as he gazed upward. Susan slipped out of her chair, knelt beside him, slipped an arm around him, and prayed for him.

When Charles was done, they both stood up and hugged and his voice was broken, "Thank you for that, Susan. Thank you so much."

Oh, my darling, I know that ache so well... and we'll pray for your sons more than ever...

Susan and Charles made their phone calls, which were received with elation, and when they finally arrived at Cambridge, they rushed to Stephanie's room. Stephanie wasn't there at the moment, but Brian was, and he was grinning from ear-to-ear.

"Hey, Mr. and Mrs. Parker!"

"Hey, Brian, where's Stephanie?"

"She's in the chapel's prayer room right now. By herself. I think she just wanted to spend some time alone thanking God."

Wow, I didn't even know you could smile like that... but I guess if you love God, Stephanie giving her life to him is the best reason there is to smile...

"Uh, she's still being guarded, isn't she?" Charles asked.

"Oh, yes, sir! I'm not guarding her today, but she's being guarded, sir. I have the day off."

"Oh?" Charles replied. "Then why are you here...?"

"Well, sir, when I was guarding Stephanie, I couldn't talk to her. Not a real conversation, because that could have compromised my mission to protect her. I felt like God wanted me to take today off and talk to her between her therapy sessions, and Mike had been wanting me to take a day off anyway."

"Oh," Susan interposed, "Susan told me you told her something that made a big difference, but she didn't tell me what. Do you remember what it was?"

"Yes, ma'am. She had heard about Jesus dying on the cross to make up for our sins, and how we can be born again by faith in his sacrifice, not by good works, but I think she was hindered by seeing a big inconsistency in Christians. She saw a sincere faith in you, Mrs. Parker, but she knew a lot of other people who say they're Christians that she thinks are hypocrites. I shared with her that there are really two Christianities, and one is a just a cultural thing. People go to Church because their parents did, or they call themselves Christians just because most everyone else they know does. In America, anyway. But I explained that there's another Christianity that's made up of people who love God with all their hearts, and we've surrendered our lives to his will, and God transformed us somehow, and made us into less selfish people.

"Oh," Brian continued, "and I also explained that many bad things in life, like her Dad leaving or her brother dying, are often the opposite of what God wants. That they often happen because one or more people haven't surrendered to him and aren't following his will. She understood what I was trying to say, and that seemed to get those road blocks out of her way, and she prayed with me right here and gave her life to Jesus."

Susan leapt over to Brian and threw her arms around him. "Oh, Brian... thank you! Thank you so much...! Thank you for listening to God, and being obedient!"

She let go of him, and Charles put out his hand and gave Brian a hearty handshake, and before he let go completely, he hugged Brian too. "Thank you, son. We owe you more than we could ever repay you."

"Oh, no, sir... God blessed me by using me, and thanks to Jesus, the only thing any of us owes each other is 'a continuing debt to love each other.'"

"Oh, that's from the book of Romans!" Susan remarked.

"Yes, ma'am, thirteenth chapter."

"You seem to know the Bible pretty well, Brian," Charles observed.

"Well, I love to study God's word, sir, and when I'm on sniper or guard duty, it gives me a lot to think about, and that helps me pass the long hours."

A watchman… Stephanie's watchman… and you not only saved her life, you helped save her soul!

Dr. Martin entered as he knocked, and they greeted him enthusiastically. After the welcome, he began to review Stephanie's treatment plan in light of Stephanie's spiritual rebirth.

"True faith in Christ is an ideal outcome, of course," David explained, "and it dramatically increases Stephanie's chances of success in overcoming her alcohol addiction, but I want to emphasize that, barring a miracle, Stephanie will always be an alcoholic. It may be a genetic weakness or an acquired one, but you shouldn't expect her new life in Christ to affect that. Her faith will give her much greater strength to resist temptation, but that temptation will recur, and will need to be constantly guarded against and actively resisted."

"Will this change how long Stephanie needs to stay here?" Susan asked.

"It may or may not. We'll have to…" David began to reply, but Stephanie came in just then, and the conversation was lost in the ensuing celebration.

Susan and Stephanie rushed into each other's arms and cried for joy, but after a minute, Stephanie was sobbing and begging her mother to forgive her for all the pain she had caused. Susan did, and begged for her own forgiveness, which Stephanie was able to give without reservation.

Once Susan and Stephanie ended their hug, Stephanie hugged Charles, Dr. Martin, Brian, and the on-duty bodyguard in the room, thanking them profusely for taking care of her and helping her.

Stephanie was excused from her regular therapy sessions to spend the rest of the day with her parents, and no one objected that Brian stayed with them. After lunch, Mike surprised them with the news that he'd arranged for his men to secure the entire perimeter of the center's gardens, and Stephanie was allowed to stroll through them for the first time, still happily accompanied by her parents and

Brian.

All day, the four took turn telling stories about how they had come to give their lives to Jesus, and other spiritual events in their lives. That evening, a fellow patient who played the guitar began an impromptu worship service in the Chapel, and someone came by and invited Stephanie and her entourage.

It was late before Susan and Charles left to return to the hotel, and Susan was reluctant to go, but was finally convinced because Stephanie's therapy would resume its normal schedule in the morning, which meant that Stephanie needed to try to sleep. Unfortunately in Susan's view, that also meant she wouldn't be able to visit with Susan and Charles again until the late the next afternoon.

Tired out by the wonderful excitement of the day, Susan and Charles quickly went to bed, and Susan fell asleep while silently giving thanks to God for his bountiful mercy and grace.

Susan and Charles hadn't set a wakeup alarm, but they were woken early anyway by Charles' cell phone.

"Honey, that was Mike," Charles said after he hung up.

Susan was marginally awake, and Charles gently shook her.

"Hon, wake up… Mike wants us to go back to Cambridge now."

"Now…? But will Stephanie have time to…" She snapped awake as she sat up quickly. "Is Stephanie all right?! Is something…"

"Everything's fine. He didn't want to get into it over the phone, but he said it's important. His team's ready to take us back as soon as we can get ready."

Susan threw the cover back and sat up on the edge of the bed. "Well, why the mystery?"

"I don't know, honey, but I'm sure he has a good reason. And the sooner we get there…"

They skipped showering and got dressed quickly, with Susan applying a minimal amount of makeup. Once in the car, one of the men provided egg biscuits and coffee for them to eat on the way. Mike was in the lead car ahead of them, and the driver and other escort in their car wouldn't talk, so the reason for the trip remained a secret.

Once they arrived, Mike escorted them directly to Stephanie's room, where a pair of bodyguards flanked the outside of the Stephanie's door as usual, and Mike mentioned that Stephanie had been excused from her first therapy session of the day.

As they entered, Susan spotted several men standing in a corner of the room, and then Stephanie sitting in one of the chairs by the table, Brian sitting next to her. She also noticed Stephanie and Brian were holding hands. Brian jumped up and offered his seat to Susan, then stood behind Stephanie. Neither of them looked distressed, but Stephanie looked puzzled and Brian looked happy.

After Susan sat next to Stephanie, she noticed one of the men in the corner was Frank Montgomery, and then she recognized the detective from the Maryville police department. *Uh, oh… what's wrong now…?* Charles stood next to Susan and she reached up nervously to hold his closest hand.

"Okay, now what's this all about?" Charles asked firmly.

"You remember Chief Detective Benson?" Mike asked.

"Has there been a break in the case?" Charles asked. "You could have told us that over the phone."

"I'm afraid that's my fault," Benson replied, "I asked Mike to get you folks together so I could tell you something in person. In my line of work, it's rare I get to be the bearer of good news."

No one said anything, but everyone's attention was riveted on Benson.

"Well, I'll get right to it… First of all, Big Ed is dead." Benson paused a moment to let that sink in.

Susan, Charles, and Stephanie instantly became more alert, glancing at each other, and Susan squeezed Charles' hand as her mind raced, trying to figure out what the ramifications would be.

Benson continued, "That alone may mean that Stephanie, and you…" he nodded toward Susan and Charles, "are no longer in danger, since he's the one who hired De Luca. Horace De Luca… that's the hit man that tried to kill Stephanie the day before yesterday. Word of his arrest got out, and that really stirred things up. The FBI took over the case, and with him sure to go to prison for life, he took a deal to turn State's evidence, and go into the witness protection program."

"Does that mean they're not going to prosecute him?!" Charles asked with a scowl.

"I know you won't like that part, but De Luca's apparently done a lot of work for a lot of different mob bosses, so his testimony could hit them hard. At any rate, it's out of our hands."

"I want the names and contact information for everyone involved in that decision," Charles said, and no one missed his tone of smoldering anger.

"All, right. I'll get you the ones I know of," Benson said.

Everyone was quiet for a moment, and Susan noticed most of the men were looking at Charles.

Charles finally sighed and nodded, then asked, "So... who killed Big Ed? And why?"

"There was a shoot-out at his house last night," Benson said, "Several people were killed and several more wounded. A team was sent to kill Big Ed, probably to keep him from turning State's evidence against higher-ups, but they underestimated his gang, and they just about wiped each other out. Since Ed can't talk, that makes De Luca all the more valuable.

"We were ready to bust Big Ed and most of his men when the Feds took over, but they wanted to take things slower. Once we found out about the gunfight at Big Ed's, we went ahead and arrested the locals we have a case against, and we got them all. The ones that're still alive, anyway. The FBI will pursue the bigger fish based on De Luca... oh, and the lug that killed Billy is going to plead guilty to avoid the death penalty. He'll get life in prison, and Stephanie won't be needed to testify against him, either."

Charles sat down on the edge of Stephanie's bed, his emotions unclear.

"So... we're out of it now?" asked Susan with cautious optimism. "The investigation, the bodyguards, the threats... it's all over?"

"I believe so, yes," Benson confirmed. "We'll need Mike's men to testify in court about their investigations, but you and your family are out of it."

Susan began to get very excited and looked at Charles, who appeared to be deep in thought, then at Stephanie, who was frowning.

"Well, what if you're wrong?" Stephanie asked. "What if Big Ed put out a contract to kill me, and his death won't stop that?"

"There's nobody to make good on the payment, for one thing," Benson replied. "I don't think we missed anyone, but if we did, they'd be small fry, on the run. I really don't think there's anybody left to threaten you anymore."

Oh, Lord, is it true? Are we all safe now?

"That's easy for you to say, you're not the one they tried to kill," Stephanie retorted.

Detective Benson looked a little hurt. "Well, there's no guarantee, but that's my professional judgment."

Charles squared his shoulders and looked up. "We appreciate all your hard work, Chief Detective... you and your men. I hate to admit that someone's death comes as good news, but in this case, it certainly seems to be for us, and we appreciate you coming all the way up here to tell us about it. As for what dangers might remain, we're going to need some time to think about things, and we'll talk it over with Mike and his team before we drop our guard completely."

Everyone nodded or mumbled agreement.

Charles stood up again and there was a lot of hand-shaking as Benson and one of the other men left. Once they were gone, Charles asked Mike to explain his views on how Big Ed's death and the arrest of his gang affected their safety.

"Well, what Benson said agrees with our investigation. Stephanie isn't a witness against any of Big Ed's gang, and we don't know of anyone else who would want to harm Stephanie or you," Mike said as he nodded toward Susan and Charles. "I understand your concern, Stephanie, and we can't be a hundred percent certain, but I think this is as certain as we can ever be."

But is that enough? Lord, what do you say...? Stephanie's still worried, and...

"Mike, we need some time to get used to everything we've heard," Charles said. "You can go ahead and stop investigating, but I'd like you to keep all the bodyguards watching over us at least until tomorrow. Let us think it over today, sleep on it, and we'll talk about it tomorrow morning."

Charles looked at Susan and Stephanie before continuing, "Tentatively, I'm thinking we could drop the protection for Susan and myself, and we could move home, but we keep a team guarding Stephanie for a few more weeks... just in case..."

Susan was looking at Stephanie, and at Charles' last comment, Stephanie's frown was instantly replaced by a smile.

"I think that might be good," Stephanie said with a hint of eagerness she was apparently trying to hide.

Hmm... maybe you're not worried about bad guys as much as you'd just like a certain bodyguard to stick around...? Susan smiled and looked at Charles.

"That okay with you, Mike?" Charles asked.

"Absolutely," Mike agreed. "I'll tell Nat the particulars, and our investigation will be over as of now, except for court testimonies, but we'll stay in full-protection mode until you decide otherwise."

Stephanie needed to attend the rest of her therapy sessions for the day, so Susan and Charles were driven back to their hotel, and on the drive, Charles spent most of the time on the phone with Nat, though Charles was mostly listening.

All that horrible business is over now... Stephanie has given her life to you, Lord, and we can finally move home... Oh, thank you, Lord, thank you! Hmm... Charles will be in my old home as my husband for the first time... I hope he'll really be as comfortable there as he thinks he'll be... it's not big, and it's not luxurious, especially compared to what he's probably used to... hey, at least we won't have to keep our hands off of each other anymore at home... come to think of it, though, I haven't had sex in that house since Marty left me... and Marty and I never had sex anywhere but in bed... of course, we had kids in the house back then... Stephanie will probably move in with us toward the end of her treatment program, but Charles and I will be alone in the house until then... I wonder if he'll be as, uh, adventurous at home as he was in the hotel suite... I'm not sure if I want to have sex in my own living room... how would I feel about that later...? If friends come over to visit and I remember us having sex on the sofa the friends are sitting on...? She smiled to herself. *Hmph... maybe that wouldn't be so bad... a little secret just between Charles and me... Charles and I... a sex secret... Well, if we're going to try anything like that, it'll need to be before Stephanie moves home. I wonder how long she'll live with us? Until she gets married? Maybe she'll decide to go to college after all... oh, but maybe she'd want to start at the community college for a nursing or business degree or something, and live at home until she graduates... so it could be a long time...*

Susan laced her fingers in her lap and tightened her grip. *Lord... help me not be too jealous of Charles with Stephanie in the house... she loves you now, and Charles loves you, so they shouldn't be tempted by each other, right...? Except King David loved you with all his heart, and he still committed adultery with Bathsheba after seeing her bathing, and then he even committed murder to try to cover it up, so just because someone loves you doesn't mean they can't fall to temptation... Oh, Lord... it'll be okay to lay down some rules for Stephanie before she moves home, won't it...? I hope she won't want to rebel against them... just some simple rules to make sure she doesn't go from her bedroom to the hall bathroom half-dressed like she used to when she was young...*

Once again, Susan remembered the way Stephanie looked Charles over at the police station, and shivered. *Oh, Lord... what if she does it intentionally...? Maybe not consciously... but... Charles is a very handsome man... authoritative... rich... Lord, what woman*

*wouldn't want Charles...? Oh, Father, I don't want to be like this...
always worrying about other women trying to take Charles away
from me... especially Stephanie... oh, what if Brian... no, Brian
probably doesn't live around here, so he'll be gone as soon as
tomorrow if Charles doesn't keep some people to guard Stephanie, if
we can even afford to do that any longer... she sure seems smitten
with Brian, but that doesn't mean she's aware of it... Lord, please don't
let Brian leaving hurt Stephanie more than she can handle... and
maybe you could let her meet someone else at the treatment center,
someone who can share her struggle to resist alcohol from now on...
or let her meet someone at my Church...*

Once they were alone in their suite, Susan started making coffee
for them as she told Charles, "I didn't want to say anything in front of
the bodyguards, but I suspect the only reason Stephanie wants them
to stay is because she likes Brian."

"Oh? You don't think it could be fear in addition to interest in
Brian?" Charles asked as he sat down at the little breakfast bar.

"I guess it could be, but I suspect it's mostly Brian... She might
not even realize she's getting a crush on him."

"Well, it seems to be mutual."

"Oh...? Yeah, I think you might be right. Although Brian's
interest may just be that of a Christian wanting to share God's love."

"There's that," Charles agreed, "but I'm pretty sure he also has
romantic interest in Stephanie."

"Hmm... you haven't told me how much these men cost, but I
got the impression they're very expensive."

"They are, but they're worth every penny. Do you think anyone
else in the world would have caught on to that fake doctor like Brian
did?"

"Not many, if anyone. But do we want to pay expert-bodyguard
rates just so Stephanie can have a boyfriend close at hand?" *I'd
actually love to, but...*

"Forget the money. That boy saved Stephanie's life, and I'm
inclined to do anything at all for him."

"But wanting to is one thing, and being able to is something
else. How close are we to running out of your fortune?"

Charles grinned. "Well, that's something I didn't want to tell you
in front of the bodyguards. That call from Nat where I just said, 'uh-
huh' a lot? He knew we were in the car and I didn't want to talk, but
he gave me some pretty good news.

"By the way, Nat has a power-of-attorney for me, and when all this started, I just left all the finances to him. Mike's had eighteen to twenty people full-time working for us most of the time, either guarding or investigating, or both. Well, the total bill is right about at a million dollars."

Only a million? "So, it didn't take your whole fortune after all."

Charles' grin grew wider. "No... and Nat had more news about that. For one thing, Nat didn't sell any of my shares in the company, he just got a loan using some of my shares as collateral. Well, anyway, a few months ago, Nat hired some kind of whiz-kid named Paul to eventually take over as Chief Financial Officer when Nat retires. Well, Paul presented a plan to Nat to make Parker Automotive a public company and develop or acquire stores nationwide. He wants to come down and let Paul present his plan to us..."

To 'us'...? Susan savored the inclusion as she sat down on a stool beside him with two freshly poured cups of coffee.

Charles leaned in and lowered his voice conspiratorially, "If we do, the kid thinks my share of the company could be worth well over a hundred million dollars."

Susan's set the coffee mugs down hard as her eyes opened wide and her jaw dropped. "A... a..."

"Hundred million dollars. More, according to Paul."

"Charles...!" Susan exclaimed and they just looked at each other in astonishment. "You were already having trouble figuring out what to do with your wealth before, and now it turns out you may have three or four times as much?"

Charles nodded.

"Well... wow... during some of those long nights at the treatment center I thought about when you asked me to help figure out how God might want you to use your fortune, and I came up with an idea, but... hmm... come to think of it, I guess it would work just as well even for that much money."

"Really?" Charles asked eagerly. "What is it?"

"Well, I wasn't going to say anything because I thought we might end up broke, but basically the idea is to give endowments, rather than unrestricted cash. You could even fund the endowments directly with your stock, and allow the recipients to sell no more than a certain amount or percentage per year."

Charles took only a moment to consider the suggestion before enthusing, "Hey... that's not bad!"

"Suppose you know of a ministry that's worthy of support, but you're not confident they could wisely handle a million dollars in cash. If you give them a million dollar endowment that allows them to withdraw five percent per year, they'd get fifty thousand dollars a year, which is much easier to be responsible with. In the worst case, if the endowment never appreciated at all, it'd last twenty years. And if the endowment principal increases over time, it could last indefinitely, and the total they'd end up with would be much more than a million dollars."

"That's it!" Charles exclaimed. "You're a genius, Susan!"

"Well, thanks, but I'm not the first person to think of it. Lots of rich people have been doing that for a long time, I think."

"Well, Nat's pretty much a financial genius himself, but he never came up with this idea! You're incredible! Your idea's perfect! We can give my stock to... uh oh... I didn't tell you one thing yet... there's one hole in Nat's plan right now."

"What's that?" Susan asked.

"It'll require a whole lot of time on my part. It's out of the question right now, I know. We have to stay here while Stephanie's in treatment and to give her a stable home environment when she gets out. But to go public, at some point, I either have to get back into managing the company in a serious way... meaning spending most of my waking hours working, or..."

Susan tried to suppress a frown.

"We could bring on someone else to take over the company. I'd still have to work more than I'd like while they build up experience in managing and expanding the organization, but once they fully take the reins, I could just serve as Chairman of the Board."

Charles rested a hand on Susan's thigh. "That worries you, huh?"

"I'm not worried, exactly, but I really like spending all day with you. Every day. We don't know how long Stephanie will need or want to live with us, but once she moves out, I won't mind if you work long hours again, but... would you mind if I worked with you? I can do a lot of office work, and..."

Charles' grin bounced back. "Oh, baby, I love you so much! The truth is, I want to spend as little time with Parker Automotive as possible from now on. That was almost like another life. But if you don't mind working beside me, I could stand it long enough to train someone to take my place. That is, if it doesn't take too long to find the right person... I'd actually been looking for someone a long time, and had kind of given up."

"Maybe it just wasn't God's timing yet," Susan suggested. *Uh-*

oh... "Does that mean we'll need to move to Pennsylvania? Is that where you're from? You said that's where Nat and Darlene drove here from..."

"I don't know... about the need to move, that is. But yes, our headquarters is in Mechanicsburg, Pennsylvania."

"Mechanicsburg? Seriously?" Susan asked.

"Yeah, it's really a city named Mechanicsburg. It's where I grew up, and that's where I opened my first shop, so that's where our main office is. Maybe we could spend a week there, then a week here, until I can get out completely, and then we can stay here. Would you be okay with something like that?"

"Charles... I love my childhood home, but I'd give it up in a minute for you. Being with you is more important than any house, even mine. Tomorrow we can ask Stephanie how she might feel about living somewhere else, but I suspect she won't mind... Say, what about one of your boys taking over your company? That might..."

"I started talking to them about that when they were still in high school. They've got no interest in car mechanics or running a business. Not an automotive service business, anyway. William's a corporate lawyer, and Robert's an I.T. manager in Dallas."

"Mm. Okay, well what about Paul, who came up with the idea of going public?"

"Nat already covered that. Said he's brilliant on the financial side, but he's really limited to that..." Charles voice drifted off, then he reached out to take Susan's hands. "Let's pray about it."

"You know, that's something I love about you, Charles. You don't just say you're going to pray about something as a rhetorical remark, you actually mean it, and you don't put it off. Yes, let's pray!"

They began taking turns praying out loud about the future of their company and Charles' role in it, about where they would live, and then continued praying for Stephanie, for Charles' sons, and then for everyone who had been involved in rescuing and protecting Stephanie.

Once they finished praying, they began studying the Bible together until around lunchtime.

"What are you thinking, Susan?" Charles asked during a pause in their study. "You've got a far-away look in your beautiful eyes."

Susan smiled at the compliment, especially one from Charles about her eyes. "Just thinking about how nice it will be to be normal again... like being able to go out to eat anywhere we want, without having to wait for other people to get ready to take us."

"Well, I feel at peace about letting all the bodyguards go," Charles said. "How about you?"

"Yeah. I think so. Do you mean the men guarding Stephanie, too?"

"Yeah... I think Mike's right, there'll never be a guarantee, but it seems we're as safe now as we used to be. And Stephanie may actually be the safest she's been in a long time. I wouldn't mind the money if she needs bodyguards longer for her for feel safe, but if she just wants to keep Brian around, that doesn't seem right."

I just hope that doesn't hit her too hard... Susan nodded. "I agree. I'll be worried about Stephanie until we see how she reacts to Brian leaving, but I think you're right that it's time for us to let them all go."

Charles waited until Susan was looking directly at him before he spoke again, "So... we're ready for me to tell Mike? We don't want to wait 'til tomorrow and sleep on it like we said?"

Lord, we've been asking you to lead us and guide us, and you've certainly protected us... we feel like this is your will, and your timing, but if we're wrong, please let us know... Susan felt a strong sense of peace, and finally nodded.

"Okay, then," he said, pulling out his cell phone and dialing.

"Mike? Susan and I have talked it over and we've decided there's no point in waiting. You can go ahead and stop everything... yes, Stephanie, too."

"Oh, Charles..." Susan interrupted.

"Hold on a second, Mike. Yes, honey?"

"Most of them used to be in the military, right?"

"Yeah..."

"Well, when Steve was in the Army I learned they like to have lots of little ceremonies for promotions and changes-of-command and things like that. Maybe we ought to do something like that for these men."

"Hm. Good point," he replied and then spoke into the phone again. "Did you hear that, Mike...? Uh-huh... okay, that sounds good. What time...? Uh-huh... okay... say, what about our hotel bill? Do we need to... I see... okay, then... well, we'll see you tonight, then."

Charles hung up and looked at Susan again. "He said he'd tell all his men, but he'd let Stephanie's guards stay on duty until we get back to the treatment center. That way we can tell Stephanie before they just disappear without her knowing why."

"Oh, that was very considerate! I'm so glad he thought of that...

oh, but how will we get there? Where are our cars?"

"Mike said he'd have your wagon brought over since it has more room to take our things home than my car does, and they'll leave my car at our house."

"Our house..." I sure like the sound of that...

"Someone will come by to give us both sets of keys... Say, why do you have a station wagon? That's usually for big families, and you've been living on your own a long time."

Susan looked sheepish. "It was the cheapest car I could get at the time. I had a newer car, but after I lost my job at the dealership, I couldn't afford the payments, so I called a salesman I used to work with who found a job at another dealership, and traded down for a station wagon they took as a junker trade-in. It still ran, though, and George got them to buy my old car for what I owed on it, and they sold me the wagon for just a few hundred dollars."

"So it's not sentimental?"

"Not in the least," Susan replied definitely.

"Well, how about we go shopping for a new car for you sometime while Stephanie's having her morning therapy sessions?"

Hmm... "Do you think we really need two cars? If you..."

Charles smiled and kissed her. "You're right. I much prefer being in the same car with you at all times. My car's got enough room for groceries and a few suitcases for vacations. So if it's okay with you, after we use your car to move our stuff home, we'll give it to a charity that specializes in taking used-car donations."

"That's be fine!" Susan agreed, "I love your car!"

"Good. Well, how about lunch? Want to just go for a walk until we find a sandwich shop or something? No escorts, just us normal people?"

"That sounds great. Oh, when are we supposed to meet Mike and his men for an official farewell or whatever?"

"Tonight, after we leave the treatment center. He's going to try to find a place with a private meeting room that serves good steaks and alcohol. I got the impression most of his men will stay up late getting drunk tonight."

Susan frowned. "Well, I don't want to be responsible for that..."

"I think you misunderstand. We won't be hosting it. They haven't been drinking at all while they've been working for us, and they're going to celebrate now the way they usually do. We're just invited to come by and say good-bye."

"Oh." *Well, at least they weren't drinking on the job, I guess...*

"Mike also told me that Nat's taking care of the hotel bill, so we can check out whenever we want. We could take our stuff home right after lunch, and then go back to the treatment center. Or we could check out in the morning if you'd like to, since it's already past check-out time today."

"Well, since we're already going to have to pay for it, one more time in that Jacuzzi sure would be nice. Although another option is to go from here to the treatment center and then go home after the party tonight."

Charles frowned.

"You don't like that idea, Charles?"

"Well, I was hoping to avoid taking you home for the first time to a dark house. I thought it might remind you too much of that Saturday night Billy attacked you."

"Oh…" *That's very thoughtful.* "And it might be pretty late when we get done tonight. Although we don't have to get up early tomorrow."

"Say… would you like a welcome home party?"

Susan's eyebrows went up. *Hmm…!*

"We could stay here another day or two, on our own," Charles mused, "while we set up a party. You could have a house full of friends over when we go home."

"I think I'd like that…! Oh, wait… when could we have it? I want to spend every evening and weekend at the treatment center, and I doubt we'd be able to get many friends in the middle of the day on a weekday… okay, well, an awful lot of them showed up for our wedding, but that's far more special."

"I see what you mean…"

Susan hugged Charles from behind and ran her hands up and down his chest. "You are so amazingly thoughtful, Charles! You make me so happy… I think I want it to just be the two of us when we go home, and I'm going to start thinking about how I'm going to seduce you for the first time in our home…"

"Mmm… you're doing a pretty good job right now…"

There was a knock at the door and Charles looked over his shoulder at Susan and they both froze for a moment. Then Charles walked cautiously to the door and pushed the button to look out the peephole.

"One of the guards," he said, relaxing his shoulders and opening the door.

"Keys," the large man said gruffly, extending his hand.

"That was quick," Charles noted as the guard dropped the keys into his hand and then extended the large, flat box he held in his other hand.

"Pizza," said the guard simply.

"But we didn't..."

"Compliments of Samuelson Security."

Charles took the box as he said thanks, and the man turned and left. Charles stepped forward and looked into the hall, then came back in and closed and locked the door.

"No guards outside anymore," he said and took a deep breath and let it out. "I think I like that."

"I guess this was their idea of a going-away gift?" Susan suggested.

"I guess," he said, putting the box down on the counter. "But if you'd rather go out..."

"No, this is okay with me if it's okay with you."

Charles shrugged. "I really need to cut back on cheese again, but I wouldn't want to offend anyone," he concluded with a smile and opened the box. Charles' smile grew wider as he turned the open box for Susan to see it.

There was one slice missing.

Chapter Twenty Two

After their pizza lunch, a bellman used a cart to help Susan and Charles load most of their belongings into the station wagon, and they kept out one suitcase and the clothes they were planning to wear the next morning. They drove home and put the items on some shelves in the garage to save their official homecoming until the next morning, then parked the station wagon on the street where Charles' car had been. This would allow them to park the newer car in the garage when they came home tomorrow. Once done, Charles let Susan drive his car, soon to be their only car, back to Stephanie's treatment center.

They got back to Stephanie's room while she was in her last therapy session of the day, and Brian and another bodyguard were there.

"Hi, Brian," Susan said, "everything okay?"

"Yes, ma'am. Stephanie should be done for the day in a few minutes." Brian nodded toward the other man, who remained silent. "Bruce's on duty. I'm taking today off again."

"Have you heard from Mike this afternoon?" Charles asked.

"Yes, sir. He told us we're ending the protective detail after you tell Stephanie. She still doesn't know."

"Okay, good. We wanted to tell her ourselves."

"Yes, sir."

"So, where will you be going...?" Charles began to ask when a very chipper Stephanie entered.

Brian discreetly ignored the question as Susan and Stephanie hugged, and Stephanie began telling them about what she had learned throughout the day.

Once they were all comfortably seated, Susan broached the subject she was afraid to bring up. "Honey, Charles and I have spent all morning thinking and praying about the bodyguard service, and we've already concluded that we agree with Mr. Samuelson. We believe the threat really is gone, and we... we don't really need them to protect us anymore."

Susan watched the cheerfulness in Stephanie's face drain away as she spoke, replaced not by anger or fear, but by disappointment.

Stephanie slowly slumped back against her chair and nodded. "When... when do they leave...?" she asked flatly.

"Today, if it won't upset you too much. I think they're pretty much ready to go."

Stephanie looked up at Brian, who looked as solemn as she did.

"Is this going to upset you too much, Stephanie?" Susan asked.

Oh Lord, we still need you, every minute of every day. Please help us now...

It was a few moments before Stephanie replied to her mother, "I kind of figured... ah, never mind. I'll be okay... I guess it was kind of cool having my own bodyguards. It made me feel important."

"You are important..."

"Thanks, but that's not what I meant. It doesn't matter, I'll be okay."

"Are you sure?"

"Yeah..."

Charles stood up and stepped over to Bruce and shook his hand. "Thank you very much for taking care of our daughter."

"Glad we could do it," Bruce replied. He nodded to Brian and then excused himself.

Brian was standing by now, and Charles gave him a bear hug.

"Brian, you saved Stephanie's life," he said, choking up. "We can never, never repay you for that."

Susan was next to hug Brian, as she cried and tried to thank him.

A stoic Brian turned to face Stephanie, and held out a hand. She took it, just holding his hand and looking at his face for a moment before finally letting him pull her up from the chair. She hugged him for a full minute without crying or saying anything.

Charles hugged Susan while they watched.

Stephanie finally let go, and Brian stepped back. As he turned to leave, she ran back to him. "Oh, I almost forgot... I wrote you a note," she said as she pulled a folded sheet of paper from her jeans pocket. "Just in case."

"Don't read it now," Stephanie added.

Brian nodded, his eyes cloudy, and Stephanie threw her arms around him again. When she let go this time, she went quickly to the window and looked out. Brian watched her for a moment and left without another word.

"Stephanie..." Charles asked softly, "do you have Brian's phone number and email address?"

Stephanie just nodded, still looking out the window.

Touch… Stephanie's love language is touch, and she sure needs it now… Susan left Charles' embrace and stepped over to put an arm around her.

Stephanie turned into Susan's arms and began to cry, and then to sob. Charles left them alone, and for over an hour mother and daughter wept, and talked, and prayed.

Charles rejoined them when they were ready for supper, and the three of them ate quietly together in the cafeteria. After their meal, they went on a long walk in the garden, taking breaks to sit on the benches. When they went back inside, Stephanie asked her mother to read to her from the Gospel of John again while she laid down.

"Momma, would you or Charles mind calling Chappy and ask him if I can have something to help me sleep tonight?"

"I'll take care of it," Charles said.

Stephanie got dressed for bed, and it was less than fifteen minutes later that a nurse arrived with a sleeping pill. Susan and Charles stayed with her until she was sound asleep and quietly prayed for her again before leaving.

Charles called Mike to get directions to the restaurant where the farewell celebration was being held and entered it into the car's GPS, and he and Susan prayed for Stephanie most of the way there.

Mike's team members were finishing their meals and were already raucous by the time they arrived. Susan and Charles went around the room thanking them all and shaking hands.

"Where's Brian?" Charles asked over the din when they had gotten over to Mike.

"Oh, he came by to say goodbye, but he didn't stay. He doesn't ever drink alcohol, but I don't know why he didn't stay for the steak."

"Oh," Charles acknowledged.

As Susan and Charles were about to leave, Mike toasted them, Stephanie, and a successful mission, and Charles toasted them for a job well done.

Susan sighed deeply as Charles drove them back to the hotel. "Well, it really is over."

"Yeah… and we move home tomorrow morning."

That's right… I get to move back to my home again, and I get to welcome you into it as my husband for the first time…

"Are you looking forward to it?"

"Oh, yes! I sure am, Charles."

"Me, too, darling," he said as he reached over and stroked the top of Susan's nearest thigh a few times.

I wonder if you want to have sex tonight, in the morning, or wait until we get home tomorrow? I sure hope it's not all three, 'cause I really don't think I'm up for that. And I desperately need to shave my legs and... the other area... She reached down and scratched a shin to inconspicuously check for stubble. *Hmm... not awful, but bad enough for it to feel scratchy to you. Let's see, I did it last... Friday morning, and today's Tuesday night, so it's been four and a half days since I shaved. And it's been... two and a half days since we had sex. That's a long time for you, I think. I'm feeling so tired, though... I wonder if I could talk you into just using me tonight? Wow, that always used to bother me when Marty did that, and now I'm wanting it? My sex drive sure is... unpredictable...*

They were alone as the elevator started up to the top floor. Charles yawned, and Susan got caught by a ricochet yawn.

"Well, Mr. Parker... how would you like me served tonight?" *Oops, sounded a lot raunchier than I thought it would.*

Charles put an arm around her waist and yawned again as Susan tried to clarify. "What I meant was... well... every time we've had sex so far, we've really made love. And that's wonderful, but, just this time... I was thinking... would it bother you if I... just kind of lay there and let you hump me?"

Charles looked puzzled.

Shoot. I've disappointed you. I'm going to have to get myself psyched up to really participate...

"Um... do you want me to do that?" Charles asked quietly, "Or are you just offering to do that because you're tired but you want to, uh, satisfy me anyway?"

Oh, no... I really blew it. Well, I'll just be honest... "I'm sorry, Charles. I know you need relief more often than I do, and I want to do a good job of taking care of your sex drive..."

"But you're not really in the mood right now, are you?"

The elevator stopped on their floor, they got out, and Charles turned to face her.

Yep. Busted. "No, not really," she moped. "I'm sorr..."

"You're too tired to enjoy it yourself," Charles said, lowering his voice even further, "but you're willing to let me just... use your body to satisfy myself?"

"I'm s..."

"That's amazing," Charles said.

"What…?" Susan asked, arching her eyebrows.

They began to walk slowly down the hall, still talking barely above a whisper.

"Jennifer never did that. Laura…" he sighed heavily, "that's kind of the only way we had sex… but that was different. With her, it wasn't because she was too tired sometimes, it's like she just didn't care… that was very different from having a loving wife who's just tired. From Laura… it seemed like an imposition. But you just made it seem like a gift." He pulled her to him and kissed her briefly, but tenderly. "That really means a lot to me, Susan."

Susan beamed. *Really? So I did good after all?*

"It means an awful lot, but… as much as I appreciate you offering to do that for me," Charles said, "I'm pretty tired, honey. I think Stephanie's reaction to Brian leaving kind of exhausted my emotions."

"Really? You're right, I am tired. And probably for the same reason." *Hm… I wonder… does my offer to do an act-of-service for you mean as much as actually doing it…?*

"So we'll just go on to sleep, then?" Charles asked for confirmation. "We can play around in the morning if you want to. One last time in this fancy suite?"

"That sounds nice." *In the Jacuzzi again? I love that room…*

Charles took out the room key-card and opened the door. "And… maybe some other time… if you really wouldn't mind, I'd like to try the, uh, one-sided sex offer."

"Okay… so that means you actually like the idea?" *Shoot. I was game to try it tonight, but I don't know if I like having that hanging over my head…*

"It sounds very erotic, honey. I hope that doesn't bother you, and I certainly wouldn't want to do that often, but the thought of you offering your body to me for sex even when you're too tired… I can't describe how that makes me feel… Like you don't just love me, but you really want to give all of yourself to me… Ah, I don't know how to say it…"

Huh. I guess it really does mean a lot to you… "Well, how about we try it once, some other time, and let me see how well I like that before we consider again."

"Oh, okay. Sure."

Susan kept thinking about that as they got ready for bed. *Nuts. What if you like it but I don't…? Could I like it, or at least tolerate it more than once? Hmm… I used to despise Marty for doing that, but maybe that was because he just took what he wanted from me. When he was drunk, he didn't even ask, he just forced himself on me. But if I offer my body willingly to Charles, maybe that would make all the difference... I could just lie there and focus on how it feels to have him penetrating me over and over, without having to do any work. Huh. I think I actually might want to try that... well... once, at least.*

Soon they began to settle into bed with the lights off and said their good-nights.

Susan rolled over onto her side, facing Charles, who was laying on his back, and she snuggled up close, resting her head on his arm. *I hope Charles likes my little surprise when we get home tomorrow.*

Susan idly moved her top knee over his thigh. *Oh, I need to shower and shave first thing in the morning, before Charles starts getting frisky... Mmm... that sure is a nice shower they have here... I wonder if Charles will want to try showering together in my tub? It's not nearly as big... and it only has the one showerhead...* Susan put her hand on Charles' stomach and rubbed back and forth.

Lord, it's hard to believe how perfect Charles is for me... Have I told you "thank-you" lately? She slid her hand down to his penis and found it flaccid and half-tucked between his thighs. She gently pulled on it until it was resting on his abdomen, and she explored it lightly with her fingers. *It's amazing how drastically these things can change in size... and I sure do like the size and shape of this one, Lord...*

"Are you trying to get me aroused after all?" Charles asked groggily.

"No... I just wanted to enjoy touching you while I fall asleep. Is it too much?" Susan asked as she felt him begin to get bigger and harder.

"No, darling, just don't be surprised by my reaction down there. The physical reaction is kind of automatic, but I'm not getting emotionally aroused. Yet."

She stilled her hand but left it resting on top. *I can feel your heartbeat through your penis... I didn't know I could do that...* When she noticed him getting bigger still, she reluctantly removed her hand, kissed his chest, and rolled over to her other side.

"Your eyes are the most beautiful shade of brown, magnificently framed by a perfect tinge of green on the edge," Charles whispered into her ear on the dance floor. Susan felt his extraordinary muscles ripple through his tuxedo as he lifted her into his arms as if she were as light as a feather. *"I know your secret..."* he said, *"so you belong to*

me, and to me alone." "Yes, my love, I belong to you, body, soul, and spirit," she replied breathlessly. A flight of stairs flashed past and they were naked in the center of a four-poster bed, elegant linen and gauze shrouding them from the rest of the ornate room. Susan turned her face to gaze on him as she spread her legs apart and took a deep breath. "Come into me, my love. Thrust yourself inside me and melt your body into mine." She gasped as he filled her, taking over her body, irrevocably joining them in euphoric pleasure...

A harsh light snapped on overhead in her parents' old bedroom, blinding Susan for a moment, but she instantly recognized the voice. "Hey! Wake up and get those crappy clothes off!" She felt his hands ripping at her bra and panties, and she tried to close her legs and cover her breasts, but he was too strong. The stench of alcohol was overwhelming as he painfully forced her legs far apart and drove himself into her. She was dry and it felt like she was on fire where he touched her inside, causing her to cry out, which resulted in a hard slaps across her cheeks and breasts. "Shut up and act right!" he shouted as he slapped her again.

"Get off of her!" she heard a commanding voice say. She saw Charles coming to rescue her, but Marty swung his arm with something in his hand, and Charles collapsed into a heap on the floor. "Charles!" Susan screamed, flailing to get to him.

Susan dragged half the covers with her as she fought them to get off the bed, crying and screaming. She spread her hands across the carpet, trying desperately to find Charles.

"Susan! Susan, wake up! I'm right here, honey! Wake up!"

Susan came to in the darkness, and fought a moment until she knew it was Charles who was trying to hold her.

"Charles... are you all right?! Turn the light on!"

"Susan, what's wrong?" he asked as he found a lamp and turned it on, then rushed back to sit beside Susan and take her in his arms.

"Oh, Charles! It was just a nightmare... but it was horrible! I thought..."

"It's okay, honey, it's okay... you're safe. I'm with you, and Stephanie is safe in her room at the treatment center, and everything's fine..."

Susan sobbed, unable to talk.

"What was it honey? Was it about Billy? Was it..."

Susan shook her head, "I thought... I thought Marty had come back, and he hurt you..."

"Marty? Oh, no, honey... he's not here. He hasn't been here, and everything is okay."

Charles continued to console Susan until her crying subsided.

"You think you're okay, now?" asked Charles, rubbing a hand slowly up and down her back.

"I think so... but oh, that was so horrible. I don't think I've ever been so scared in my life," she said as she shivered.

"Come on, let's get you back into bed," Charles said, helping her up. "Unless you'd like to stay up a while. Would you like me to get your hotel robe?"

"What time is it?" and looked toward the clock.

"It's almost five in the morning."

"Uh. Five. Still too early to get up for the day. Do you think you could sleep some more?"

"Only if you do. You scared me pretty good there. You started screaming bloody murder and I didn't know what was going on. I thought maybe some of Big Ed's men broke in because the guards were finally gone."

"Well, let's lay back down and hold each other and see if we can sleep."

"Okay," Charles agreed.

"I tell you what," Susan said, "I'm going to crack the curtain if you don't mind, so we get a little light in here, but I'll turn off the lamp."

"Sounds good."

Once they were both in bed again, Charles prayed out loud, "Lord, I thank you for keeping up safe, and I ask you to help Susan not have any more nightmares, about anything."

"Amen," Susan prayed. *And help me not scare Charles any more.*

About 8:00 AM, Susan was woken out of a dream by Charles nibbling on her ear.

"Feeling better?" Charles asked when she finally opened her eyes.

"Yeah," Susan giggled.

"What's so funny?"

Susan laughed a little. "I was having some kind of crazy dream. Not a nightmare, though, thank the Lord," she said, then snickered.

"Well what was it?"

Susan burst out laughing until tears were streaming down her face. When she could catch her breath, she managed to explain, "You were on all fours, and I had a little stool and bucket... and I was milking you! I was milking your cock, but it was real milk coming out, and the bucket was almost full, and it spilled, and we were upset because we were planning on having it for breakfast!"

Susan continued to laugh, while Charles observed, "Yeah, that qualifies as pretty crazy. But at least you got a hoot out of it. Does that make up for the scare earlier this morning?"

"Oh... yeah... I don't even remember that well. I remember crying on the floor, and you holding me, but I don't remember the nightmare well at all."

"Well, that's good."

"Yeah, I guess so, but I rarely have dreams I can remember when I wake up. And I can't remember the last time I had a nightmare, it was so long ago. I wonder why this morning was so different?"

"I dunno. Maybe relief from stress has something to do with it? No more threats, no more bodyguards...?"

"Mm. Maybe. Hey, I'm hungry, what about you?"

"Starving!" Charles said, throwing the covers back and getting up. "What do you want, and where do you want it?"

Oh, that's a perfect opening for a sex joke... "This is our last morning here, how about room service one more time?"

"Okay... and how does French toast sound?"

"Delicious," agreed Susan. "With maple syrup, orange juice, and coffee?"

"Sold. And turkey-bacon?"

"Oh, good call."

Charles frowned. "And NO milk."

Susan laughed heartily, "Fine, you spoil-sport, no milk."

Charles ordered while Susan used the toilet, started water running in the Jacuzzi, and put on some makeup.

"Hey, I've got an idea," Charles said after getting off the phone. "Want to try eating in the Jacuzzi? It's got that little tray thing that goes all the way across."

"Huh. Okay, we can try it... Oh, nuts. I meant to shave before we got intimate again. Do you mind if I do that first?"

Charles got a gleam in his eyes. "May I do it?" he asked eagerly. "I'll finish dressing and open the door for the food, then we'll eat in the tub, and you let me shave you?"

"Hmm... well... okay, but turn-about is fair play. May I shave your face?"

"Oops. Didn't see that coming... Okay, deal. But you shave me first, okay?"

"Sure..." *And I'm predicting you wanted to shave me second because you want it to lead to sex. I'm on to you... and soon I'll be on you...*

They laughed and told each other stories from their youth as they ate, and then Susan did a meticulous job of shaving Charles' face. When it was Charles' turn to perform the shaving, Susan sat in one of the built-in seats such that she was able to raise one leg at a time completely out of the water and rest her heel on the edge.

"Mmm... it feels so good to have you touching my thighs, even if you're not trying to be erotic. I've never had anyone else shave me before..."

Charles laughed. "Come to think of it, no one's ever shaved me before, either."

Yea! Another first for me!

"I wouldn't object if you wanted to do it again sometime, as long as it's on the same terms."

"You naughty boy," Susan said with a smile that betrayed her mock disapproval.

"Not as naughty as I'm about to be," he said as he stood up and lifted Susan to sit on the edge of the tub.

"You're not going to shave that part!" Susan protested.

"I most certainly am. Check the fine-print in our contract."

Susan dipped a foot into the water and splashed at him. "Cheater. Maybe I should..." Her train of thought was broken as she gasped from his intimate contact.

"If you'll notice, I have a bunch of the plush towels behind you, so you can lean all the way back," Charles said.

"Oh..." Susan said as she took him up on the offer. "There you go again, Charles-the-planner, thinking about ways to make me... Oh...! Now Charles, you have to be very careful around the *tender* parts! Oh... that feels... very... nice..."

I can't believe how erotic it feels for Charles to shave me, when it feels so mundane when I do it myself. Oh... I almost forgot... he probably wants to get me excited, so I'll get wet enough for him to hump me. I had hoped we'd wait 'til we got home, but... this is our honeymoon suite, after all... once last time here seems... oh, Lord, that feels good...! You sure did design us with an incredible ability to feel... good. Well, if we're going to be honest... okay, if I'm going to be honest, this is way, way past merely feeling good. It's so sensual... my lover's touch... my precious husband...

Susan was totally unaware of when Charles finished shaving and began caressing her with his mouth. She closed her eyes and felt the pleasure building inexorably between her legs, and her breasts seemed to her to need something, some attention, some pressure. Her hands had been clenching the towels under her, and she moved one hand to a breast and grasped it, instantly ratcheting up the intensity of her pleasure. She began to writhe as Charles continued his ministrations without letup, and her other hand grasped her free breast. Without conscious thought, her hands squeezed her bosom tightly, and her body launched into a series of breathless spasms of incredible rapture. Her hands kneaded her breasts as the convulsions continued for long seconds, and her back arched high and her legs locked rigidly around Charles' head. In a moment, her body seemed to collapse, only to be caught in a second delirious wave of spasms.

Gulping mouthfuls of air, Susan panted as fast and deeply as her body was capable of, as her conscious mind began to develop rational thoughts again. *Charles... where... where's Charles... did you hump me... did you cum, too...? My feet are in the water... is your cum going to drip into the water... do you care... I hope not... 'cause I don't think I could move if my life depended on it...*

When her panting finally began to diminish, she realized Charles was lying next to her, on his side. She turned and smiled weakly.

"Now," Charles said lovingly, quietly, but with a firmness in his tone, "take me to your home. Take me to your bedroom... and it will become *our* home, and *our* bedroom, as we make love together there for the first time."

If I weren't a Christian, Charles Parker, I'd be tempted to worship you...

He lifted her mostly limp body and eased her back into one of the molded seats in the Jacuzzi and gently washed her face and shoulders, and then her hair.

As he rinsed the shampoo from her, she finally spoke in a whisper, "Oh... Charrrlles... you're... so... good... so sexy... so hot... so... sensuous... so captivating... this... was the... best ever... the shaving... the sex... the incredible bathing after... it was all... beyond imagining... oh, my lover... I'm yours... without reservation... *you... can screw me anytime, anywhere you want... any way you want... I'm yours... Oh, Father, in heaven... what a man you've given me... my very own "Adam"... and what an awesome gift marital love can be...*

"You really thought that was your best yet?" he asked softly.

"Oh, yesss!"

"Huh. You hardly made any noise at all that time..." he observed.

I wouldn't know, and I didn't care in the least... "That was... unbelievable..."

Finally she lifted her head up on her own and rested it against Charles' shoulder. "We're still going to need to rinse off in the shower, since I've been leaking cum into the water."

"Uh, not for my sake. I mean, I didn't cum."

"What?!" Susan exclaimed quietly.

"I hope you don't mind, but I didn't want to this time."

"But... why not...?" Susan asked in a tiny voice.

"I guess I should have asked you, but I kind of wanted to wait until we get home. I didn't think you'd mind."

Susan mind shifted from low gear to high. *You did all that, just for me? So patiently, so devotedly, and you were waiting to satisfy yourself until... until what you were talking about after I came, about me taking you home, taking you to my bedroom and making it ours, and you planned it that way all along?*

She tried to jump up, but Charles had to steady her. "Let's go!" she said emphatically. "Let's get a bunch of speeding tickets on the way home, if the cops can keep up with us!"

Charles grinning as he helped her out of the huge tub, "Okay, beautiful. Let's make tracks!"

"Oh! You have to take your clothes across to the other bedroom and dress over there!"

"But..."

"Don't argue, just do it! Hurry!" she said, pushing him on the butt.

"Okay, okay..."

Susan blew-dry her hair as quickly as she could and got her carefully chosen going-home clothes out of hiding. She began by putting on her new teddy, made mostly of white lace and trimmed with red and purple ribbons, tied into numerous dainty little bows. *I wish I could have worn that fish-net body stocking, but I couldn't have hidden it with it going all the way down to my fingers and toes... oh, my... I knew this teddy had a split-crotch, but I didn't realize it had these little overlaps that can spread apart to get to my nipples... maybe this is just as good as the fish-net anyway...*

Over her teddy, she slipped on the same ankle-length, brown-toned, pleated skirt she had worn on their wedding day, followed by the same blouse she had worn then. Next she slipped on her wedding-day pair of open-toed sandals, and checked the overall effect in one of the full length mirrors, and finally she applied a little makeup – just a normal amount, since the bruises were now almost imperceptible.

Susan stood just inside her closed bedroom door, nervously pressing the front of her skirt with her hands. *Charles probably finished getting ready way before I did, so he's probably waiting for me... I hope that doesn't bother him.* She opened the door and spotted Charles standing behind the breakfast bar as she stepped forward.

He looked up and looked as stunned as the first time he saw her in this outfit. "Holy smokes!" Charles said under his breath, but it was loud enough to warm Susan's heart, and she looked down demurely.

When he didn't move, she finally looked up to see him brushing back tears, and she launched herself across the room toward him.

"You're so incredibly beauti..." Charles managed to say before she fell into his arms and smothered him with kisses.

No broken cup this time, she laughed inside, *but that reaction was worth a fortune in cups... Lord, help me keep being pleasant for Charles to look at, as long as we live...*

All of a sudden, Charles lifted her into his arms and began to march across the room back to the bedroom.

"Charles! What are you doing?"

"I'm going to make love to you until one of us can't stand up."

"But... we were going home!"

Charles paused.

"C'mon, honey," Susan pled, "let's go to the car and go home. I want you inside me at home!"

"Wow. Say that again."

"I want you inside me at home, Charles!"

He spun on his heel and put Susan down as he was walking to the door. "You can say that as often as you want to," he said, and Susan giggled as they raced to the elevator.

As they approached their car, Charles asked, "Would you like to drive, darling?"

"Mm... no. You're taking me home for the first time as your wife, and I want you to do the driving."

Susan saw him start to reply, but she cut him off, "Yesterday doesn't count because we didn't go in the house. This is our homecoming."

"Yes, ma'am," a smiling Charles said as he opened the passenger door for her.

Susan inhaled the leather smell deeply as Charles got in and buckled up, and she scooted over toward him as far as her seatbelt would allow, then rested a hand on his thigh. *Mmm... I never imagined myself in a car anywhere nearly as luxurious as this... and to think it can be justified as a good investment... at least until we can give away the rest of Charles' money... our money, I guess... and it sure is fun to drive...*

Susan recalled her first time driving it alone, and the trips to the riverboat and the lake. *Hmm... we haven't danced in public yet as husband and wife... I wonder if Charles would like another ride on the riverboat... and this time if he gets all excited... okay, if we get all excited, we can go home and do something about it... Oh, yeah, and Charles can teach me to dance something besides the waltz...! Boy, we sure were lucky at how many waltzes that band played. Hey... that was an awful lot of waltzes...*

Susan eyes flared wider in recognition. *They played waltzes all night long except while we were eating! Or when you specifically asked them to play a slow-dance song. Hmm... 'Charles the planner'...* "Oh, Charrlless..." she said sweetly as she turned to look closely at him.

"Yes, honey?"

"That night on the riverboat when you taught me to dance. Did you happen to notice they kept playing waltzes as long as we stayed on the dance floor?"

Charles' face flushed noticeably red. "Uh, yeah. I did notice that."

She tilted her head down. "And did you have anything to do with that?"

"Uh, yeah... a little bit, maybe. Well, more than a little bit."

"I knew it!" Susan grinned with great satisfaction. "What did you do?"

"Well... I texted Nat, and he was going to make reservations for us, but they didn't sell enough tickets, so they were going to cancel the trip for that night. So I, uh, asked Nat to see if he could charter it."

"Charter...? As in rent the whole thing?!"

"Yeah," Charles replied sheepishly. "I thought it would be romantic..."

"But... the band... the caterers... all those people... did you hire them all?!"

"No... not all of them. Not exactly. The other guests on board were the people who run the business and friends of theirs. They just got a free ride and dinner."

"But... why? We could have gone somewhere else..."

"Well, this way I could make sure there were a lot of other people dancing. I thought it would help you not feel conspicuous while you were learning to dance if we were kind of lost in a crowd. That was part of the deal... they had to get enough people to go with us, and they had to keep the dance floor full."

"Charles! That must have cost a small fortune!"

"Actually, it wasn't very expensive at all. It's not like I was buying the boat... they would have sailed if I had just paid for the minimum fifteen couples. I paid extra for the meals for the additional people to fill up the boat, of course. And I paid them a bonus to let me choose the music. Considering what a wonderful night it was, it was worth a whole lot more..."

Susan looped her closest hand under Charles' arm and rested her head on his shoulder. "I want to go back there," she said softly.

"Now?"

"No, silly, not now. Right now I want to take you home and have outrageous sex with you. But one evening, after Stephanie gets out of treatment, I guess... and when we can sail without having to rent the whole boat... I want you to take me back there, and teach me to dance another kind of dance, and I want us to both get all horny and go home and make out like a couple of rabbits."

Charles sighed happily. "Yes, ma'am," he agreed.

As they pulled into the driveway, Charles stopped for a moment and reached in the glove box for the garage door remote. "You know, I thought to get this out of your old car, but I forgot to get new batteries..." He pushed the button and the door started opening.

"Yea!" Susan said, throwing her arms up like a football referee signaling a touchdown. *Mental note: Get some new batteries for that thing...*

Charles just sat for a moment, lovingly studying Susan's face, before finally easing the car forward. "Now don't you go running into the house. I want to carry you across the threshold of the front door."

"Oh, okay," Susan giddily agreed. "You know, this garage is the only one on this street that has a person-door going out to the front

428

yard in addition to the big garage door."

"Really? That's a nice touch," Charles said as he shifted the transmission into park, pressed the remote button to close the garage door, and turned off the engine. He unbuckled and started to reach for the door handle, but then stopped and leaned over to kiss Susan.

Susan kissed him back, and then he withdrew, but their lips were still almost touching. She could feel his breath mixing with her own, and she leaned her head forward and began to kiss him again. *Oh, you're such a good kisser... I love that about you...*

She felt him adjust his body to get more comfortable while maintaining the kiss, and she felt his hands embrace her sides as their tongues explored each other's mouths. His thumbs began to move slightly back and forth at the base of her breasts, and she felt a warmth begin to build. "Mmm..." she moaned as they continued to kiss. *Oohhh... you're soo good at turning on my motor...*

Charles stopped kissing her for a moment as he adjusted his body a little more, but kept his hands in place. When he did, Susan took the opportunity to murmur, "That feels good..."

Charles' lips made contact with hers, but he stopped and asked, "What does...?"

"Your thumbs..." she purred, and he began to kiss her even more passionately, and his hands began to explore further.

She felt one of his hands go under her blouse and noticed he quickly gasped as his hand made contact with her teddy. *Ah ha, you noticed the lacy material that's normally not there, so you know I'm wearing something sexy under there... but have you figured out what it is...?*

He worked his hand up and began to massage her breast, and she began to suck his tongue. Then she felt the hand under her shirt leave her breast and work its way down to her waistband, and she subconsciously began to lift her hips toward his hand.

When he had difficulty squeezing his hand under her skirt, she unzipped the side and immediately felt his fingers exploring her genitals, as if trying to map out what was where under the teddy. She felt his fingers come to rest just at the top of her cleft where her clitoris was, and he began a rhythmic stroking, while his palm applied pressure to her pubic mound. *Can you find the seam in the crotch...? I'd much rather feel your fingers directly against my skin... maybe I... Oh! Yes...! That's it...!*

Susan quit sucking on Charles tongue and now thrust her own deeply into his mouth. A shock flashed through her body as he sucked her tongue into his mouth and began sucking hard and soft, hard and soft. "Unngh," she moaned as a shiver ran through her and back arched and her head fell backward, pushing hard into the seat and breaking the kiss.

She shivered again as Charles asked, "Are you okay?"

"Yesss..." Susan said quietly and managed to nod.

"Was that an orgasm?" he asked.

"Oh, yes... my love... it wasn't earth-shaking this time, but it sure was *very* nice..." *And the first time I've ever cum in a car...*

"Ready to go inside and continue in the bedroom?" Susan asked, feeling a strong desire to feel him inside her now.

"Oh, yes!" Charles agreed enthusiastically.

He jumped out of the car and raced around to her side to open her door and she carefully adjusted her blouse and zipped up her skirt again before they walked out and to the front door. Susan got the house key out and handed it to Charles, who unlocked it and handed the key back to her.

"We need to get a copy of the key," Susan said, putting it back in her purse.

"Plenty of time for that later," Charles said as he lifted her into his arms and swung the door wide open.

Susan saw him close his eyes as he began to pray out loud, "Lord, by your grace, this is now our home, and we dedicate it and our shared life to you."

"Amen," agreed Susan, and Charles stepped over the threshold.

He continued to hold her as he stepped past the door, used a foot to push it closed, and leaned back against it. Only when they heard it latch did he put Susan down, and Susan reached around him in a bear hug.

Oh, I want you inside me, Charles... I wish you could stay inside me forever...

Charles sighed deeply, and half-whispered, "You know, I had in mind that this house would start to feel like my home after we had sex here, but it already feels that way."

Susan gave him an extra squeeze, then released her hug and began unbuttoning his shirt as fast as she could. "I hope you're not trying to back out of having sex with me!"

Charles laughed, "No, but if you're not really in the mood any more..."

"Oh, I'm in the mood, buddy-boy..." As soon as she finished unbuttoning his shirt, she pulled it off, threw it on the floor, and began working on his belt.

Charles pulled up on Susan's blouse and she quickly raised her arms to let him pull it right up and off, and she was delighted to hear him gasp.

It's the first time I've worn this for you... "Do you like it?"

He pushed her back slightly to take in the view, and he literally licked his lips as he gawked. The idea that he found her so attractive increased Susan's need to feel him inside her, and she bent down to pull down Charles' pants and underwear in one fell swoop. His cock sprang loose, but she ducked her head aside and it missed hitting her in the face as she got down on her knees and forcefully pulled his shoes off without untying them. She ripped his socks off, and he was completely nude before her, with his cock standing out proud and strong.

Susan started to jump up, but eyeing his package right in front of her face gave her another idea at the last moment, and instead, she rose more slowly and licked the entire underside of his cock as she rose.

"Uhhhhh..." Charles moaned and closed his eyes in response.

Susan slipped off her shoes, unzipped her skirt, and let it fall to the floor. Charles opened his eyes again, and she jumped up and wrapped her legs around his waist as her hands held onto his shoulders. "Pick me up a little and put me down on you," she said eagerly.

His hands were on her butt, supporting her weight, and she added, "Use your fingers if you can to pull the material apart."

"Uh..."

"It's a split-crotch. That's how you got your fingers inside it in the car."

"Oh...!"

Susan thrilled to see a shock of surprise and delight on Charles' face, and then he lifted her bottom and worked the opening apart. They moaned in unison as their bodies merged.

"Remember you said it was always a dream of yours to walk around with your wife riding you like I did in the hotel suite? Well, now I want you to fulfill that dream here, in *our* new home."

"Oh, Susan... Susan... thank you! Oh, I love you so much!" he said as he turned them in place, and she closed her eyes as he began to kiss her.

Susan's mind was focused on the strange, but wonderful sensations she felt from his penetration as he slowly walked through the house. He occasionally paused their kissing while still keeping his lips touching hers as he announced their progression through the living room, kitchen, dining room, hallway, and finally their bedroom.

Susan opened her eyes to discover they were standing at the foot of the bed, and said, "Okay, big boy, throw me on the bed, and then climb into me again."

Charles grinned as forcefully lifted her up and away, and Susan helped push off from him. She sailed through the air, landed in the middle of the bed, bounced, and scooted up a bit, followed quickly by Charles climbing right up and putting himself inside her again.

After he humped her a few minutes missionary-style, with Susan rocking her hips, she said, "Oh, now sit up like you did in the hotel once, with your knees under my thighs!"

Charles slid down a bit and tried to comply. "Like this?"

"Yes, perfect," Susan approved. "Now lean down and put your mouth on one of my nipples...?"

She parted one of the cups at the seam, exposing her breast to Charles' surprise, and he went right to work on it.

"Oh, yessss..."

Charles started speeding up, and Susan could tell he was getting close to cumming.

"Oh, wait! Let me get on top!" Susan implored.

It was obvious to her that he had a fair amount of difficulty in making himself stop at that point, even if for only a moment, but he did. They changed positions quickly, and Susan squatted over him, with her feet beside his hips. She began pumping her body rapidly up and down on him, and he immediately began to try to thrust up into her, and it only took a few tries for them to get in sync.

When she knew Charles was almost to the point of no return again, she called out loudly, "Okay, lover... here's my last surprise..." With that, she stopped pumping up and down and started swirling her hips in a circular motion.

Charles stared open-mouthed, and she only got to make a few complete circles before he began to roar, and his torso came way off the bed, lifting Susan with him. *Yes! I love making you so excited you cum inside me...!*

Charles' body lifted Susan so high she couldn't continue the swirling, but she thought to concentrate on flexing her vaginal muscles, which resulted in Charles' torso quivering while his head and arms writhed on the bed and his roar descended into a guttural, stuttered groan. It was several seconds before his body collapsed underneath her, and his body convulsed, calmed, and convulsed again. *This is the first time we've had sex in my home... our home... and the first time you've cum inside me on our bed...*

This time was his turn to gasp desperately for air.

Susan thought she felt him begin to soften inside her and she stayed on top, straddling his waist. She grinned as she watched his muscular chest heaving as a result of the pleasure she had provided. *In a few minutes, I'll get up and try to keep from leaking on the carpet while I go to the toilet... to let your precious semen leak out of me for the first time in our very own bathroom... Oh, Charles, I love you so...!*

When Charles' breathing finally began to slow toward a normal speed, she realized he'd fallen asleep. *Oh, I hope I can get up without waking you...*

She slowly eased off of him, which meant she couldn't prevent some leaking, but the crotch of her teddy closed a little and caught some of it. Once she was off the bed, though, she squeezed her thighs together and waddled into the bathroom to clean up. She decided to leave her teddy on until after Charles woke up to make sure he could see her in it again, even though the material in the crotch was going to stay damp. She forsook flushing the toilet to try to avoid waking him, and she went to the foot of the bed and just stood there admiring her husband.

Heavenly Father, this is such an amazing thing... what an incredible gift... to bind our hearts together, and give us a way to pleasure each other like this... You've given us your love and your life, and you've given us so much more...

Susan eased onto her knees and rested her elbows on the edge of the bed. *Lord, we haven't always known your love, or recognized your gifts, and now that we do, we realize that there are many people who still don't know you personally, and many who don't have the luxuries we have. Savior, you've put it in Charles' heart to try to use the wealth you've provided to us to help others, but we need your help to do that. There're many people who'd take too much and waste it, so we ask you to guide us and lead us, to give all this money away to the people you want it to go to, to be used to help those you want to help, in the way you want to help them. We'll mess it up, Lord, if you don't come through and help us do it right...*

Susan took a deep breath and let it out slowly. *Thank you, Lord, for always being with us, and for leading in your paths.*

She rose to her feet and started to get a robe to put on before leaving the bedroom, and then decided to get dressed, but as she considered what to wear, another thought occurred to her, and she tiptoed to the bedroom door and looked down the hallway. *I've never been naked in my house except in my bedroom or bathroom, but I went naked all over that hotel suite. I'm not completely naked in a teddy, but it sure feels… naughty.*

Susan stepped into the hallway and held her breath for a moment. When no sirens went off, she took another step, then another. She eased forward past the door to Stephanie's old bedroom, which was also hers when she was young, then the hallway bathroom, then Steve's old bedroom, and finally to the far end of the hallway that opened into the foyer on one side and her dining room on the other.

From there she could see into the living room just enough to see that the living room drapes were partly open. She covered her mouth in shock as she realized Charles had paraded her past that window while she was impaled on him and he was butt-naked. *Charles Parker! How could you?!*

As much as she wanted to blame Charles, she recalled how she had aggressively disrobed him and jumped onto him at the front door, just as she had carefully planned to do. *Oh, shoot! We didn't even lock the front door! Oh… in all my planning, I didn't even think about the door or the window. I guess Charles didn't either…*

Susan gasped quietly. *All the windows!* she thought as she glanced through the dining room and saw that the curtains in the dining room were also wide open.

Oh, no…! She squeezed her thighs together and pulled at the top of her teddy to make sure her nipples weren't exposed, then covered her face with her hands. *Oh, Lord… I'm not as good a planner as Charles is… why didn't you warn me…?*

Just then Susan remembered a passage from the Book of the prophet Isaiah, about how God asked him to walk naked in public for three years as a sign and a wonder against Egypt and Ethiopia. *But, Lord, that doesn't apply to me! I'm not a sign and a wonder!*

Almost as clearly as if it were audible, Susan heard in her mind, "You are to the husband I've given you."

Susan sank to her knees in confusion and astonishment. *Oh, Lord… I trust you with all my heart and soul, but I don't understand… You don't want to go around naked, do you…? Or do you just mean… that it's good to let Charles see me naked…? Well, I*

434

still have a hard time believing he can enjoy looking at me, but from the looks on his face, he sure does seem to... come to think of it, I've seen him look at me like that when I'm naked, wearing lingerie, or fully dressed...

She continued to sit on her heels, lifting her hands into the air, trying to listen to God. In the stillness, she realized that it was mid-to-late morning when she and Charles had marched through the house. *Huh... I don't know the neighbors, but I never see them out on the street during the day. And if the people across the street are at work, no one could have seen us from there... so... maybe... maybe no one saw us...?*

She crawled low to the floor into the living room and poked her nose above the window ledge. As she looked out, there were no cars across the street, and no cars at all on the street except her station wagon. She recalled that her mailman only came by late in the afternoons as she pulled on the drapes and got them completely shut.

Then she finally stood and walked to the edge of the door to the kitchen and looked in. The back yard was full of large, broad-leafed hardwood trees that blocked any backyard neighbors from seeing in except when the leaves were gone in the fall and winter. Susan crouched low anyway and went into the kitchen, reached up and pulled the curtains closed, then repeated the process for the dining room window and back door. Finally, she went down the hall, got on her hands and knees, and closed her kids' bedroom doors rather than go in to close those curtains.

I came by these windows just a few minutes ago, and I wasn't even caught up in sex... I guess I can't blame Charles for making the same mistake...

Then to her surprise, she realized the curtains were still open in the hallway bathroom, and possibly, probably, in her own bedroom. She closed the door to the hallway bathroom and crept back to her bedroom door. Sure enough, the curtains on both windows, one facing the side yard and one facing the back yard, were both wide open.

How could I have not realized that?! she thought as she crawled over and closed them. The curtain rings made some noise as they closed, and Charles began to stir after she closed the second one.

Susan stood up, noting there was still a fair amount of light penetrating the curtains and seeping around them.

"Susan?" Charles called out sleepily.

"Yes, Charles," she said as she laid down beside him. "I'm here."

And still wearing my teddy if you want to look at me in it...

He rolled onto his side to face her, and he stroked her hand as he breathed in deeply and slowly let it out. "It's nice to be home with you."

Oh, Charles... we are home. We're finally home.

After a half-hour of cuddling and postplay, Charles asked Susan if she might be getting hungry.

"Yeah, a little bit... " she replied, and then she sat bolt upright in bed. "Oh, no! My kitchen! The fridge is going to have a bunch of spoiled food..."

She started to get up and run to the kitchen, but stopped and remembered her state of dress. Then she remembered her circuit through the house closing all the doors or curtains. *So, Lord, you've made my body a sign and wonder to Charles? That seems like a crazy idea, but you're the boss, and I can't argue with the way he looks at me...*

She pulled Charles up and led him by the hand, still stark naked down the hall. He started to go into the foyer to get his clothes, but Susan pulled him into the dining room. "I closed all the curtains, so..."

"The curtains!" Charles exclaimed, fear registering in his eyes as he looked at Susan. "Oh, Susan! I didn't think about that! I'm so..."

She cut him off by pressing the front of her body against his and putting a finger over his lips. "I didn't either... but I feel sure no one saw us. At any rate, it's over, and all the curtains and drapes are closed now, so... I want you to sit down here while I take stock of my kitchen."

She could see him visibly calming down, as he nodded and pulled out a chair.

"You're sure?"

"Yes, my love," she said and kissed him after he sat down.

"Hey, there's a box of mail here. And the window's been fixed!" Charles observed. "Had to have been Mike's crew."

"That was very thoughtful of them," Susan said as she went into the kitchen and started feeling flustered because she hadn't prepared her kitchen for their homecoming. *I don't remember how much food we had before we left... and I'll bet everything in the fridge is spoiled.*

She looked in the refrigerator and found little in it, and most of what was there was just condiments and soft drinks that had little or no danger of spoiling. Puzzled, she glanced back at Charles and smiled. *Wow, look at that! A gorgeous nude man sitting at my dining room table! And I'm not the least bit embarrassed. And he's all mine...!*

She opened a couple of pantry doors, and saw much more food than she recalled having, including some canned Spam that she was pretty sure she hadn't bought. Racking her memory, she opened the freezer door and discovered it was full of frozen dinners and one container of chocolate ice cream that she was completely certain she never bought. *Lisa! It had to be Lisa! What a doll! And I'll be she threw out the old stuff I had in the fridge...*

She looked in the trash can under the sink, and it was lined with a brand new trash bag, and nothing in it. An almost empty box of trash can liners sat of top of a large new box of them. *That dear girl... she took such good care of me...* Her eyes teared a bit, but she didn't start crying as she had a hungry man to take care of, and she went about preparing some peas, beans, Spam, toast, and coffee. She reluctantly put on an apron while she cooked the Spam in case it splattered, but she took it off as soon as that was finished. She kept glancing back in admiration at her naked husband, who seemed happy just to watch her putter around in the kitchen.

"You okay?" she asked as she was finishing the cooking.

"Just amazed that God has blessed me so much."

"Ah... well, he gave you the ability to build a successful business for a reason..."

"Huh? Oh, I wasn't thinking about that..."

Then... you meant me...! A man worth tens of millions of dollars, many tens of millions, and he counts me as a blessing! Here in our simple home, while I prepare a simple meal... after a morning of loving sexual escapades...

As Susan brought the food to the table, Charles moved a chair so they could sit side-by-side while they ate, close enough so their sides were touched. And, when their hands weren't busy with the food, they were often busy touching each other.

It was easy for Susan to notice that Charles' cock was getting harder again, and she finally reached over and stroked it lightly. "Okay, so I can tell you're physically aroused, but I know now, at least with you, it doesn't necessarily mean you're emotionally aroused, so I guess I have to ask... Are you?"

"Are you kidding? Sitting here with no clothes on beside my sexy wife wearing nothing but this hot little lingerie? Oh, yes... I'm aroused in every way..." he said as he began kissing her and gently fondling her breasts.

Okay... I guess we're going to have sex again... I didn't expect that, but if he keeps this up, I'm definitely headed in the same direction...

Charles moved his chair a bit. "Will you get on my lap, and put me inside you again?"

Can't even wait 'til we finish eating, huh? "Okay... but how...?" She stood up and he moved her chair away, then turned his chair sideways. Following his lead, she straddled his lap, facing him, and inserted him through the opening in her teddy. She thrilled again, both at the delicious feeling of fullness and at the way he closed his eyes and moaned as she settled down on him.

Charles opened his eyes and smiled, then scooped up a forkful of peas from Susan's plate and fed it to her. Susan grinned and returned the favor.

This is incredible! We're having sex at the dining room table, while we eat! In the house I grew up in! I was a little girl, eating from a high-chair right here, and now... Oh! Susan was startled by Charles using one of his hands to caress her breast. She tossed her hair back as she moaned and her vaginal muscles involuntarily contracted.

"Uhmm..." Charles moaned.

"That was entirely your fault, Charles," Susan said as her breathing picked up pace.

"Okay," he said and dropped his hand.

"I didn't say you had to stop!" Susan objected.

He kissed her for a moment as he began to caress her again, and then he leaned back and handed her coffee to her.

Susan handed his coffee to him, and they sipped together. *I never even imagined a marriage could be this good... this loving... this tender... this intimate...*

Epilog

After their meal, Charles carried Susan to the living room sofa, where they continued to have sex, and they stayed on the sofa while they snuggled and kissed, even after Charles climaxed again. Susan realized how much she had changed lately when she noticed that instead of worrying about staining the sofa, she was already treasuring her memory of the first day they came home together and made love there.

Eventually they got up and gathered their clothes from the foyer and took them to the bedroom, then showered together and got dressed. Susan cleaned up from their lunch and Charles carried in the things from the hotel they had stored in the garage the day before. With plenty of time to spare before Stephanie would have time for them to visit, they took the station wagon to Charles' apartment and brought most of the rest of his belongings home.

That afternoon, they returned to the Cambridge Treatment Center, apprehensive about how Stephanie had been coping with the loss of Brian's companionship, and were caught off-guard by the fact that Brian was there with Stephanie. As Susan and Charles stood in the door, looking back and forth between them, Brian spoke up and told them that since Mike didn't have any other work for him right then, he went into business for himself, and Stephanie hired him for a dollar a week, on credit.

The four of them sat down and had a serious talk, and Brian and Stephanie explained that they just liked each other's company, and they wanted to date as soon as Stephanie's doctors allowed her to make day trips away from the center. Both Susan and Charles harbored some doubts, especially about the prospects of a young man who worked as an occasionally employed bodyguard, but decided to support their plans for the time being.

Charles called Mike Samuelson and had Brian put back on the payroll as Stephanie's sole bodyguard until further notice, and Brian sublet Charles' apartment.

The discussion of Brian's employment reminded Susan that she hadn't given the owner of the Coffy Corner an update since right after Billy attacked her. She felt remorseful for not thinking to call him sooner, but he was very understanding when she told him that things had much improved but she wouldn't be coming back to work there. She was sure Andy wouldn't be disappointed.

For the rest of that week, Charles spent most of the mornings trying to manage his business by phone and explaining it to Susan, and they made plans for Nat and his protégé Paul Nowakowski to come down and meet with them the next Monday morning to discuss their plans for going public. Charles and Susan gave the old station wagon to a charity, after deciding that if they later gave Stephanie a car, even a used one, it shouldn't be an old station wagon. Their evenings were spent visiting Stephanie and discussing how she'd begin to ease into a normal life outside the treatment center. Though it would probably be weeks before Stephanie could come home, Susan and Charles began consuming an old bottle of wine she had in her cupboard to make sure it was gone well before Stephanie finally arrived.

When the next Sunday came around, Susan took Charles to her Church for the first time, and they were welcomed with joyous celebration, for their marriage, their deliverance from evil, and especially for Stephanie's salvation.

Nat and Darlene got there that afternoon with Paul and all three were invited to come by the treatment center to meet Stephanie and Brian. The next day Paul presented his plans, followed by lengthy discussions about the options for limiting the amount of time Charles would have to be involved and for bringing in someone else to take Charles' place as head of the company. With Charles being very reluctant to work the extreme hours he had in his younger years, a lot hinged on their ability to find a suitable replacement, and they finally agreed that Nat would engage an executive search firm to help reach that goal.

The following week brought a minor milestone in Stephanie's recovery, which was the inclusion of Susan and Charles in two of her counseling sessions each week. Stephanie also began a physical exercise program that she hadn't looked forward to until Brian volunteered to be her exercise partner. By this time, Stephanie's hair had grown out about half an inch, and she frequently discussed what she might like to do with it when it got a little longer. It was also around this time that Susan noticed that the worst of Stephanie's bad language seemed to have disappeared.

A much larger milestone occurred on July 4th, a Saturday, in the form of Stephanie's first day-trip away from Cambridge, after fifty-three days in treatment. Susan had trouble sleeping the night before due to the excitement of Stephanie coming home, even if for only a day to start with. They planned to have a cook-out in their back yard, with celebratory cake and ice cream, and Charles had reservations for them to watch the Knoxville fireworks that night from the Star of Knoxville paddleboat.

Around nine that morning, Susan and Charles heard the sound of Brian's vehicle pull into their driveway, and they rushed out the front door to greet them. There were lots of hugs (just handshakes between the two men) and a few tears (just from the women), and one very big extra surprise for Charles. Brian's truck was an old step-side pickup truck that had been fixed up into a perfect show-truck that had won Brian a few awards, and much to Susan and Charles' amazement, Brian had done all of the restoration and modifications himself.

Susan took Stephanie into the house to her old room, and centered on the bed was Stephanie's old CD by Robin S. with its 'Show me love' song. Stephanie picked it up and hugged her Mom, saying that she finally found the love she had been looking for in Jesus. Susan offered to fix up the room any way Stephanie wanted it, but she said it was fine the way it was, and said she was very much looking forward to moving home as soon as her doctors allowed it.

When the girls went back to the front of the house, they discovered the boys were still out front, with Brian's hood up, talking enthusiastically about the modifications Brian had made. Susan and Stephanie thoroughly enjoyed standing on the front porch for a few minutes, each with an arm around the other's waist, watching their men talk.

The two couples drove separate vehicles to the pier that evening, and Charles excitedly told Susan all about Brian's prowess and passion with engines, transmissions, ignition systems, even body work and upholstery. Naturally, they were both excited about the possibility that Brian might be interested in working for Parker Automotive as a senior mechanic at the very least, and they dared to harbor hopes that he might be the perfect person to take over managing the entire company. One cloud in that picture was what the ramifications might be if Stephanie and Brian ended up parting ways on less than amicable terms.

They all had a delightful time on the boat that night, and not only did they get to watch the fireworks from a coveted spot, but Charles taught all three of them how to dance the Cha-cha. While dancing, Charles told Susan that since they were married now, the next time they went out dancing alone, he wanted to teach her to dance the foxtrot. He confided that the foxtrot involved a lot of full-body contact, which he looked forward to experiencing with her, but he wasn't comfortable with the idea of teaching that particular dance to Stephanie and Brian, and that's why he wanted to wait.

That night, Brian took Stephanie directly back to the treatment center after the boat ride, and after Susan and Charles got home, Susan got a very excited phone call from Stephanie, telling her all about Brian kissing her for the first time just before he saw her inside. Considering Stephanie's past, Susan was a bit surprised that Stephanie seemed as excited as high-school girl by that simple kiss.

The following week, Charles began discussing with Brian the possibility that Brian could work for Parker Automotive. Brian expressed interest, but had some reluctance and said he'd need to take some time to consider it.

The next weekend was marked by Stephanie's second day-trip, on Sunday, beginning by Stephanie and Brian joining Susan and Charles at Church. The Church held a pot-luck lunch afterward, and everyone made Stephanie and Brian feel welcome.

The third Saturday in July was Stephanie's birthday, and her third day trip, which was a day-long date with Brian. Susan reluctantly waited until the next day to throw her a birthday party at the treatment center, and was surprised to see that her now one-inch-long hair had been dyed... teal. As part of their date, Stephanie had gotten Brian to take her to get her hair done, with Brian paying for it, and afterward Brian taught Stephanie how to drive his stick-shift truck.

Around that time, Susan was woken by another nightmare about Marty returning and causing trouble. This time, once Charles had helped Susan calm down, he shared with her that after the last time, he had asked Mike Samuelson to see if he could find out where Marty was and what he was doing. He had hoped if Marty was happily married, it would help Susan not be afraid, and it might help Stephanie if he could arrange for him to see her again. Unfortunately, Mike had found out what became of Marty, but it was tragic news. Marty had been killed in a bar brawl in a little town just west of Knoxville not long after he had left Susan. With great concern for how it might affect Stephanie, they decided to share the information first with the Dr. Nester, and he concurred that it would be best to tell Stephanie while she was still in the treatment center. Not surprisingly, the news broke Stephanie's heart, but it didn't cause a setback in her recovery.

In fact, the milestones in Stephanie's treatment continued to tick by, saying goodbye to day trips and getting to spend all weekend, every weekend, at home. Not that they spent every minute in the house. Part of the time on those weekends they went out shopping, so Stephanie could have a nice selection of clothes that she got to choose for herself.

After a couple of regular weekends at home, they were extended to three-day weekends, only staying at the center from Mondays through Thursdays. These weekends often involved bicycling or canoeing trips to the Ijams Nature Center, or hikes in the nearby State parks, sometimes with Susan and Charles making it a foursome, and sometimes just Stephanie and Brian.

As part of her treatment, Stephanie began job hunting. At Susan's suggestion, she checked with the Coffy Corner, and discovered they were short-handed and would love to hire her.

After several extended weekends at home came a huge day: coming home to stay. Stephanie continued to participate in therapy and counseling, but as an outpatient with declining frequency. And as Stephanie's time at the treatment center went down, her hours at the Coffy Corner went up, topping out at thirty hours a week. Charles, with Susan's agreement, offered to buy her a used car, but Stephanie declined, saying she'd rather walk to work as long as that was possible. Often while Stephanie was at work, Susan and Charles would walk down to the shop to enjoy some coffee and watch their daughter working and laughing with the customers and other employees.

Susan struggled with feelings of jealously when Stephanie moved home and she couldn't refrain from asking her to dress modestly around Charles. Stephanie assured her mother that she'd behave herself as a Christian woman should, and Stephanie's growing relationship with Brian also went a long way to relieving Susan's anxiety. It also helped that Charles had fixed the lock on the hallway bathroom door shortly after they had moved home.

The transition of Stephanie moving home also impacted Brian. He had quickly become bothered by the idea that he was getting paid by Charles to guard Stephanie when he wasn't really guarding her, and had resigned from Samuelson Security, initially living off his savings. He and Charles discussed a number of options, and it was finally decided that he would begin a career with Parker Automotive. Charles would begin the process of finding a suitable location and opening a new Parker Automotive Center in Knoxville, and Brian would assist him. Brian would then manage that center for six months while Charles trained him and an assistant manager. In the six months after that, the assistant manager would take over as manager and Brian would take the lead to open a second center in Knoxville, assisted and guided by Charles. After that, if everything went well, they would all move to Pennsylvania and Charles, Nat, and Paul would begin training Brian to manage the entire company. If everything continued to go well, Susan and Charles would then move back to Knoxville to stay.

Beginning a couple of weeks after Stephanie moved home, she and Brian began to make occasional trips to find and visit with girls Stephanie had known in the porn industry in order to share the news of Jesus' love with them. The fact that Brian was with Stephanie on those trips helped Susan not be as anxious as she otherwise would have been, and she and Charles prayed earnestly for their safety and effectiveness.

Charles' birthday was the twentieth of August, which came on a Friday that year, and Charles took the opportunity to take Susan out and finally teach her how to dance the foxtrot. As a surprise, instead of going home afterward, he took her to a hotel for the night. He had been planning that for a while, and had discussed it with Stephanie well ahead of time, since it would be Stephanie's first night home alone. Unknown to Charles, Stephanie had spilled the beans to Susan, and Susan had discreetly hidden her fishnet body stocking in her purse. She had saved wearing it for the first time for a special occasion, and while Charles had intended to surprise her, it was Susan who won that game. Nevertheless, Susan ensured that Charles was a *very* satisfied loser.

Charles also failed with another ploy. While they were dancing the foxtrot for the first time, he asked Susan to pick east or west, without knowing why. She picked west and asked why, but Charles told her it was a secret, and it would be months before she found out. To his chagrin, Susan wheedled the secret out of him before they left the dance floor. He was planning a trip for their first anniversary next May, and it had come down to the Bahamas versus Hawaii, with Hawaii winning when she chose west. Susan was a very satisfied winner.

Brian's birthday fell on September 13th, and to celebrate he took Stephanie to dinner up in the Knoxville SunSphere. There he proposed, and Stephanie eagerly accepted.

That began a flurry of excited planning, and Susan was overjoyed that Stephanie involved her in all of it. Stephanie had trouble deciding between having the wedding at their Church, at the SunSphere, or at Ijams, but when Susan suggested the Knoxville Botanical Garden, Brian took her there to look it over and she fell in love with it. The Botanical Garden was available for the Saturday after Thanksgiving, with an outdoor area if the weather was nice enough and a small indoor area if it wasn't. Since that date would give Brian's family plenty of time to make travel arrangements, they booked it immediately.

Stephanie and Brian were now regular members of Bethel Bible Church, and they planned for Pastor Walker to officiate their wedding. While they first planned to have their wedding reception at the Church, they changed that to the SunSphere in order to accommodate friends who would appreciate having beer, wine, and dancing at the reception. As usual, Pastor Walker required them to go through his pre-marriage counseling program, with a schedule that would ensure they finished it before the wedding.

One morning after the engagement, as Susan, Charles, and Stephanie had breakfast together at home, Stephanie asked her mother if she knew what Brian's love language was. She didn't, and Stephanie leaned forward and informed her it was physical touch, the same as Stephanie's. *Husband and wife both with physical touch as their love languages... that should lead to some fireworks,* Susan thought at the time.

Then Stephanie asked Susan to be her matron-of-honor, and of course, Susan was thrilled. Then while Susan was still crying for joy over that, Stephanie asked Charles if he would give her away in the wedding ceremony. Charles got a little choked up and said he'd be honored to. Stephanie followed that up by asking him if it would be okay if she started calling him Dad instead of Charles, and the question obviously caught him by surprise. He could only nod a reply, and Stephanie jumped up from her chair and hugged him, while profusely thanking him for all he had done for her. Although Charles seemed very happy by Stephanie's gratitude, Stephanie picked up on a sadness in him.

After that breakfast, Charles excused himself to go sit in the back yard, and though he sat facing away from the house, it was obvious he was distraught. Susan explained to Stephanie for the first time about the estrangement between Charles and his sons, and the more Susan told her, the more questions she asked. Later, Stephanie apologized to Charles for never having thought about his family, and she asked him to tell her all about them.

Brian had made arrangements for himself and Stephanie to fly out to California to meet his parents, and with the agreement of the young couple and Brian's parents, Susan and Charles flew out to meet them two days later. By tradition, the bride's parents pay for the wedding and the wedding reception, and the groom's parents pay for the rehearsal dinner. The Milner's seemed fine with that, and it could only help that Stephanie and Brian planned for a very small wedding party consisting only of themselves, the pastor, the parents, including Susan as the matron-of-honor, and Brian's best man.

The reception however, was growing into a much larger affair. Everyone from Church was invited, as well as many people that Brian had served in the military with and those he had worked with, and a number of employees and regular customers from the Coffy Corner. Adding what Susan felt was a bit of a risk was the news that quite a few of Stephanie's old porn-industry friends had accepted invitations to the reception.

Charles had privately discussed with Susan his desire to treat Stephanie on an equal footing with his sons from a financial perspective. When they had gotten married, their wives' parents had paid for the weddings and receptions, and the rehearsal dinners hadn't been a financial imposition, so Charles and Jennifer had given each set of newlyweds a lavish honeymoon and enough money for a down payment on a house. Once they met the Milners, it was obvious that they were solidly middle class, and Charles was concerned about possibly making them look bad by out-giving them.

The Milners, however, seemed quite down-to-earth, and not bothered by the fact that the parents of their future daughter-in-law were far wealthier. The Milners took them all out to dinner at an inexpensive steak house, and when Charles cautiously got around to the subject of he and Susan giving Stephanie and Brian a honeymoon vacation and help with a down payment on a house, he was greatly relieved that the Milners weren't offended in the least.

A minor mystery developed for Susan and Charles in early October, when Stephanie told them she was going to be out of town for several days, but she didn't want to explain why or where she was going. She didn't ask to borrow their car, and she didn't take Brian's truck. Both Brian and Pastor Walker did their best to reassure Susan and Charles that they knew what she was doing and that it was worthwhile, whatever it was, but Susan still worried and wondered... what could she be doing that she could share with Brian and their pastor, but not with them? Did it have something to do with her reaching out to the kinds of girls she used to work with? Would she be tempted to start drinking again while she was on her own? Did it have something to do with their upcoming wedding? Was she working on a surprise present for someone? If so, it must be for their honeymoon, as no one else had birthdays or anniversaries for months to come.

Stephanie returned after three days and went about her business as usual for a while, still without giving any explanation for her short absence. The mystery deepened less than two weeks later, when Stephanie disappeared again, this time taking Brian's truck, with his permission. Again, she returned after three days, but with no explanations.

A few days after Stephanie's second return, she and Brian announced they were moving up their wedding date by three weeks to November 6th, and had already changed their major reservations. Susan asked Stephanie if she was pregnant, but Stephanie promised her that she and Brian were waiting until their wedding night to have sex for the first time. Stephanie hinted that she and Brian just didn't want to wait any longer than necessary.

The next evening, Stephanie and Brian joined Susan and Charles for dinner at home, and Stephanie told them about some of her recent efforts with some of the porn girls she had worked with, and then asked her mother and father what their plans were for Thanksgiving. Susan explained they were planning to stay home, and she'd like to prepare a fancy turkey dinner. They invited Stephanie and Brian to join them since they'd be home from their honeymoon by then, and the young couple readily accepted.

Susan thought Stephanie seemed relieved at the invitation and chided herself for not teaching Stephanie more about how to cook. However, that train of thought was lost when Stephanie told them she had told Andy and Mr. Burton that she couldn't work on Thanksgiving Day. They had both protested, citing the fact that she had already taken more than a few days off and she would be taking many more off for her wedding and honeymoon. Then Stephanie surprised her by asking Charles if she could learn to work with Brian in managing the new automotive center they planned to open in January.

Susan saw Charles look thoughtful, then start to smile and nod, and after glancing as Susan for approval, he said he'd be happy to give her a shot at it. Stephanie smiled as she thanked him and asked him if that was a firm enough offer that she could tell the Mr. Burton that her last day at the coffee shop before the wedding would be her final day working for them. Charles thought, smiled again, glanced at Susan again, and agreed.

Susan reflected on how Stephanie's natural assertiveness had been changing since she had surrendered her life to Jesus and going through alcoholism treatment... she was still assertive, but she was more thoughtful about it, and more willing to compromise. With those changes, she thought Stephanie might perfectly complement Brian in business management. Her train of thought was interrupted again when Stephanie asked if it would be okay if she invited other people over to share the Thanksgiving Day and the holiday meal with them.

Susan asked how many girls she was thinking about, and Stephanie told her she'd like to invite at least six people, and as many as ten.

Susan glanced at Charles as she briefly wondered about the wisdom of having a house full of porn actresses in her house with Charles and Brian being the only men there, then she asked Stephanie if it would be all girls, and Stephanie said it would probably be mixed. Brian was obviously trying to suppress a smile and let Stephanie answer all the questions, and eventually Susan and Charles agreed. When Susan and Charles discussed it after Stephanie and Brian had left, they both admitted they were a little disappointed that it wouldn't just be a family time, but that it would be a good thing to do to help Stephanie minister to a group of people who were trapped without God in the darkest aspects of society.

One morning shortly after that, at breakfast with Susan and Charles, Stephanie asked Charles if she could have four thousand dollars without explaining what she wanted it for. Both Charles and Susan asked a number of questions... was it for a car... was it for someone in trouble... was it for a present for Brian...? Stephanie answered a simple 'no' to most of their questions, but she steadfastly refused to tell them the purpose. She did explain that Brian knew what it was for, and that he was willing to give her the money, but she would prefer if Charles and Susan would give it to her since they could obviously afford it more easily than Brian could.

Susan and Charles were torn with the decision, and told Stephanie they'd like some time to think about it. That night they agreed that they would trust her if Brian confirmed he knew what it was for and approved. Brian did, and Charles had Nat transfer the money to Stephanie's checking account.

Nothing else mysterious happened as the wedding preparations escalated to a fever pitch the week before the wedding. The wedding rehearsal was over all too quickly, and the dinner was in a private room of a simple buffet-style restaurant. At the dinner, Brian rose and called for a sparkling-water toast to his lovely bride and then to both sets of parents.

The wedding day itself was a whirlwind for Susan, and the weather was perfect for an outdoor ceremony at the botanical gardens. Stephanie's hair was now about three inches long, with the bottom half a bright teal and the rest of it was her natural dark brown. Throughout the day, Stephanie seemed surprisingly calm, and a radiant smile never left her face.

Charles ensured that Susan had some tissues in her hands in addition to her flower bouquet, and she definitely needed them as Stephanie walked down the aisle on Charles' arm. The ceremony was delightfully festive, rather than too-serious, but that was nothing compared to the loud celebration at the SunSphere afterward.

By eight o'clock, they said their goodbye's and spent their wedding night in the same Knoxville Plaza suite Susan and Charles had stayed in for so long. The next morning, a limousine took them to the airport in Knoxville and they spent the rest of their honeymoon in the Caribbean.

~~~~~~~~~~~

"I love you, and nothing will ever change that," Charles whispered as he and Susan slow-danced in the small cockpit of the cabin cruiser, at anchor on the lake. They were both very aroused at a cool gust of wind blew over them. *I'm going to take you downstairs and we're going to rock this boat, and this time, I don't have to take "no" for an answer,* Susan thought as she snaked a hand between them and into Charles' shorts. She took hold and began to gently squeeze off and on.

"Come with me Charles," she said as she led the way to the stateroom with her hand still holding him. "This time, you're going to make love to me until one of us can't stand up."

Once there, Charles cupped her breasts and stroked them with his thumbs. "Susan, I'm going to make love to you until neither one of us can stand up..."

The next moment, Susan was rocking her hips slightly, confused that she couldn't feel Charles pressed against her. *Where are you...?*

Why is it getting colder...?

Susan tried not to wake up so she could hold onto her dream, but a chill in the bedroom and the covers off her shoulders prevented her from staying asleep. *Oh, fooey...*

She found the edge of the covers pulled them up under her chin. *The heater will probably kick on again soon...*

Realizing Charles was behind her, she scooted backwards until her bottom was pressing against his bottom. *Mmm... toasty warm... now, we were about to have sex on that boat again...*

Oh, wait... today is Thanksgiving Day, and it's extra special this year... we have so much to give thanks for... Stephanie giving her life to God, Charles and I meeting and getting married... hmm... Charles moved to Knoxville to try to reconcile with one of his sons when we met... strange how God can use something bad to do something good... and if we hadn't met, only God knows what would have happened with Stephanie... or with me... I may have tried to sell this house to try to protect her from Billy... and Charles wouldn't have been there to tell Billy about God that night... Charles has been like an answer to prayer... no, not like an answer, he's actually been an answer to many of my prayers... and he's given me more joy... and pleasure... than I knew was even possible... he even fulfilled my dream of a handsome man who discovered my secret... all that, and the son he came here to see left him here...

Susan turned around to get into a spooning position behind Charles, planning to press her chest against his back. *Oh, you like it better when I do this without a bra*, she thought as she stopped and removed it before snuggling up tight.

One thing that makes me so happy is that you're so very, very good at telling me loving things... like telling me I'm the best sex partner God ever made... which is kind of surprising since words of affection isn't really your love language. But you were doing that from the very first day we met, before we even knew anything about different love languages. Which is just more evidence of how perfect you are for me. Oh, thank you, Lord, for my wonderful Charles!

Hmm... this should be a day of celebration, but it may be sad for you if you focus on how your sons... Maybe having the house full of Stephanie's friends will help keep your mind off that. Or maybe we shouldn't be keeping our minds off them. Maybe we should be praying for them instead...

Heavenly Father, I ask you again, please do something with

Charles' sons. Help them see that their dad has changed, and he wants to make up for his failures when they were growing up... maybe we should have waited to get married and maybe they would have come to our wedding... but, Lord, it's too late for that now... so what can we do now? Lead us, and guide us, Lord. Tell us what to do... and whatever we do, we're going to need you to soften their hearts toward their father... and please show us if there's any way for us to help do that...

Hmm... what was that I was reading in Lamentations a few days ago...? "Because of your great love we're not consumed, for your compassions never fail. They're new every morning, and great is your faithfulness..." Oh, Lord, we need your compassion for Charles' sons... please help them...

"Mmm..." Charles moaned as he slowly rocked his torso against Susan's breasts. "I sure do like that."

He turned to face Susan and that caused the sheets to pull off her shoulders and she noticed the room was warming up.

"Do you want me to play with you?" Charles asked as he nuzzled her neck.

Stephanie said she'd be over early this morning, but she didn't say what time... "No, not right now. I'm really enjoying this, though. What about you?"

"No, I'm okay," Charles replied. "Maybe tonight?"

"Okay, and maybe I could feed you Susan a-la-carte for breakfast tomorrow?"

"Oh, in that case, let's skip sex tonight so I'll have a full appetite tomorrow morning. And let's make sure we close all the curtains before we go to bed tonight."

Susan giggled. "As you wish, kind sir..." Her memory replayed their homecoming and then as she studied his face again, she noticed the fading scar at his hairline. That triggered her memories of when they were on the boat the first weekend after they met. *"I love you,"* he said while he was recovering from her angry outburst. *"Nothing will ever change that."*

"Charles... what would you think about us spending our anniversary on that big boat on the lake again, instead of going to Hawaii?"

"I'd love that," he replied. "I think about our date on that cabin cruiser from time to time, and I'd sure like to, uh, try that again... with our magic marriage rings on this time."

"Magic marriage rings, huh?"

"Yeah, 'cause before we had them, we had to fight as hard as we could to resist our desires for sex, but with them, we get to have sex that magically keeps getting better and better!"

Susan felt for Charles' left hand under the covers and touched his ring as she remembered many of the things he said during their first week of marriage about how she had exceled at sex in many ways. "Has it really been getting better and better for you, Charles?"

"If you had asked me while we were staying in the hotel, I'd have said it wouldn't be possible, because that was so incredible. But week after week, I feel closer and closer to you... I feel like we're more and more intimate, and yes, you continue to amaze me with how much better sex keeps getting. Sometimes the intensity reaches higher peaks, sometimes our lovemaking seems to last longer and longer, and sometimes it seems like I can actually feel the bond between us growing stronger."

Wow... I have the best lover in the whole world... I know it's been getting better and better for me, but I didn't know it was for you, too. Maybe... maybe the fact that sex has kept getting better for me is part of the reason it's kept getting better for you. After all, you've told me several times how making me feel good is even more important to you than humping me...

Susan sighed contentedly and relaxed her body against Charles, and for a while, neither spoke while Susan basked in his warmth.

Once they got up and dressed, Susan began leisurely cooking breakfast for Charles and herself and Charles was making coffee when Stephanie and Brian arrived, carrying in several bags of groceries.

"Mom, you're cooking breakfast? I figured you'd have cereal or something with all the cooking we'll be doing today."

"Oh, this isn't much," Susan countered. "Just scrambled eggs and toast. Would y'all like me to make enough for y'all, too?"

"Oh, we've already had breakfast," Stephanie replied.

"What's with all the groceries? Did you invite more than the ten people you told me about?"

"Well, no extra people," Stephanie replied, "but they'll be here all day and, uh..."

"Well, you know, better to have leftovers than not enough," Brian interjected. "Hey, I'm going to move the car out of the garage and onto the street so I can bring in the folding tables and chairs if that's okay."

"Oh," Charles spoke up, "I'd rather you put my car in the front yard instead of on the street. I guess there'll be a lot of other cars, and, uh…"

"I know," Brian smiled, "You don't want to take a chance on getting any scratches."

Charles grinned and nodded. "How many cars do you expect?"

"Actually, I think everyone's coming in only two cars," Stephanie said.

"Really?" Charles responded. "That's a little surprising. These friends of yours must live all over the place, and there's plenty of street parking, so why car-pool?"

Stephanie glanced at the wall clock. "You'll see. Hey, Mom, you're going to show me how to cook a turkey, right? I got a twenty-two pound one, like you said, and it's thawed out, like you told me. Oh, and I also bought a canned ham. I'm hoping you can show me how to cook that too, since I don't know much about cooking meat. I know how to heat vegetables in a pot, and I can follow package directions for microwaves as good as anybody, but I've got a lot to learn about the meat side…"

Susan and Charles ate breakfast while Stephanie put the groceries away as best she could and Brian set up some tables and chairs in the garage, along with a couple of space heaters. Brian also brought a large folding table and a number of folding chairs into the dining room and leaned them against a wall for the time being.

Once breakfast was over, the boys sat at the table and talked business while the girls worked in the kitchen. Stephanie kept glancing at the clocks on the wall, the stove, and the microwave, and she started getting more antsy as time passed.

"My goodness, Stephanie, I think you're more excited about this than you were about your wedding," Susan commented, as Charles weaved through to refill his coffee cup.

"Yeah, well, I knew what I was getting myself into then," Stephanie said, half under her breath.

Susan stopped what she was doing to look carefully at Stephanie. "Uhm… what is it that has you worried?" worried Susan.

Stephanie glanced at the clock again. "I'm not worried, exactly… It's just… we haven't done anything like this before, you know…"

"Oh, don't fret, honey," Susan tried to reassure her. "Everything will be fine. There's plenty of food, and beverages… oh, are you worried they won't like it since we don't have beer or something?"

"No, no. I asked about that. That's cool."

"Hey," Charles said, having wandered over to the kitchen-garage door with his coffee, and looking through the window in the door. "These are kid's chairs out here. Some of your friends are bringing kids, huh?"

"Uh, yeah," Stephanie said as Brian called Charles back over to the dining room table.

"Oh, that explains the Kool-Aid," Susan said. "I guess I shouldn't be surprised about, uh, adult actresses having children."

"Well, that does happen, Mom..."

About a quarter past noon, Stephanie's cell phone beeped, and she took it out anxiously read a text message. She took a deep breath and let it out as she looked around. "Are we at a good place to pause for a while, Mom?"

"Well, we need to keep a close eye on the turkey now," Susan said. "We should check it every five minutes or so."

"Good enough. Come over here and sit down, Mom."

Brian stood up and joined Stephanie, putting his arm around her, while Susan sat beside Charles.

Oh, my! I wonder if they're going to tell us we're going to be grandparents...!

"Mom... Dad... I never said the people who are coming today are the people I used to work with. You assumed that, and I didn't say anything different. Well, I... I kind of encourage you to think that... But that text message I got a minute ago was from Robert. They're on their way from the airport, and they should be here in a few minutes..."

Robert...? Charles' Robert...?

Stephanie looked worried, Brian looked hopeful, and Charles looked confused for a moment before recognition set in.

"M-my... my... Robert...?" Charles strained to ask.

Stephanie nodded, and Charles clutched a fist to his chest. His faced flushed and his eyes watered. Susan took his free hand and held it tightly.

"Robert and Karen, and all four of their kids," Stephanie said softly. "The money you gave me a while back was for their airfare. And a hotel. They're staying in town until Sunday afternoon."

"Coming... here...?" Charles asked in near disbelief.

"Yes, sir," Brian answered. "Stephanie went out to see them, to talk to them face-to-face, to tell them about you. How God changed you, how you helped her, things like that..."

Charles looked at Susan in partial disbelief.

"I think I hear a car in the driveway," Brian said, and stepped over to the doorway. "It's them," he confirmed.

Tears were flowing down Charles face now, and the other three all helped him up and toward the front door, but he stopped as soon as he could see them through the living room's picture window.

"Dad," Stephanie said, "Robert's love language is words-of-affection."

A look of alarm struck Charles' face as he leaned heavily on Susan. "Oh, God! Oh, God, no! No wonder I hurt him so badly... he... he..."

"Dad... he understands now," Stephanie said as she hugged him from the side opposite Susan. "I told him all about the five love languages, and he knows that yours is acts-of-service. He knows now that you really did love him and you two just didn't understand how each other demonstrated your love. And... I think... he's been as upset about things as you've been."

Brian opened the front door wide open and waved.

Charles brushed at his eyes with his sleeves and walked to the front door with the girls' help, and then out onto the front porch.

Standing in front of a rented minivan and looking toward the house were Robert and Karen. Robert had one arm around Karen, who held a baby in her arms while two children stood shyly around them, and a younger one ran around in circles. Susan noticed they were casually dressed, and Robert was lean and handsome, like a younger version of Charles.

Robert stepped forward a pace, then two, then ran to his father. The men hugged and cried as they apologized to each other over and over again.

After a few awkward moments for the rest of them, Susan walked over to Karen, and Stephanie ran to catch up and introduce them. When Stephanie introduced the children to Susan, she introduced her as Grandma Susan.

Oh, my! I never thought about that! These are my grandchildren now...! I'm a grandmother already!

Brian joined them at the car, and eventually they all headed into the house. The men sat in the living room while Susan and Karen sat at the dining room table, and Stephanie minded the kitchen.

After some small talk, Susan broached a serious topic with more than a little nervousness. "Karen... Charles told me that the boys really resented his second wife Laura... and I... well, I'm worried about what they, and you, think of me..."

Karen nodded. "Well, honestly, when Mr. Parker called Bob a while back and told him he'd gotten married again, I don't think they thought much about you. I mean, you know, they didn't know anything about you. Mr. Parker said you were a wonderful woman, but he originally said the same thing about Laura."

Karen scowled as she mentioned Laura's name. "But once we met Stephanie, and she told us all about you, well… I think we're all are very happy for both of you."

"Really…? That kind of surprises me," Susan said. "It relieves me more than I can say, but I'm really kind of surprised."

"Oh…? You do know why we disliked Laura so much don't you?"

"Well, Charles…" Susan started to say.

"Oh, I guess Charles is the only side of the story you've heard," Karen interrupted, then looked toward Stephanie.

"I didn't tell them anything, Karen," Stephanie said from the kitchen.

"Uh, should I call you Susan, or what?" asked Karen.

"Susan's fine," Susan assured her.

Robert and Karen's oldest boy ran into the kitchen and asked Stephanie if she had any games, and said she thought there were some board games in her old closet, and she went with him to get them.

"Well… Susan… it was clear to everybody except Dad, uh, Mr. Parker, that Laura was nothing but a nasty little gold-digger. She was sweet as honey around him, but full of venom when he wasn't around. Until they got married, anyway. Then she treated him like a hired-hand. She wanted his money, and nothing else, but he just couldn't see it."

Well, that explains a lot… and maybe the fact that we live in a modest tract-home will help them realize I'm not after Charles' money.

"The boys tried over and over to talk sense into him, but the more they tried, the madder everybody got. I was surprised that things turned out as bad as they did, but I guess I shouldn't have been. When Stephanie came and explained that love-language stuff, it finally made sense why Dad and the boys had such a bad relationship. And that was before Laura. That business with her… well, Bob didn't like it, but Bill just couldn't take it anymore. I guess he felt like not talking to Dad at all was the only way to manage his own anger."

"Wow… but they aren't worried about me being a… gold-digger?"

"Oh, no. At first they just didn't care. They both decided they didn't care if they ever got an inheritance or anything else from their dad ever again, so if you took it all, it just didn't matter to them. But then Stephanie came and, well... we all felt like we got to know you pretty well. She told us all about her past, and how Dad met you and fell in love with you, while you thought he was poor and out-of-work, and how he hired a big company to protect all of you from a bunch of criminals. That made us all feel good... but for the boys... that stuff Stephanie told us about people having different love languages... well, I think that made all the difference in the world to them."

Susan nodded. *That makes so much sense... wait, she said "the boys"? If Stephanie talked to William, too...*

Karen lowered her voice to confide, "And I suspect learning about love languages may help Bill and Jenny's relationship immensely."

Stephanie was passing back through the dining room and Susan caught her attention. "You said ten people...?"

"Up to ten, Mom. As of yesterday, Bill wasn't sure if they were coming or not."

"Oh, Bob talked to him this morning," Karen offered. "He still wasn't sure then, but when Bob turned his phone on after we landed, he had a voice mail from Bill that they were on the way."

"Oh, that's wonderful!" exclaimed Susan quietly as she clapped her hands together. "Where are they coming from?"

Karen's face clouded over. "Uh... I don't know if..."

"Oh... I understand," Susan said. "It should be up to William to decide whether or not it's okay for Charles to know."

"Well, if Bill's coming, that's a good sign," commented Stephanie from the kitchen.

And with his wife and children too, apparently! My... grandchildren! I've gone from no grandchildren and no prospects to... six grandchildren all at once!

"Hey, Mom, can you come see if you think the turkey's done?"

"I'm not used to hearing them called Robert and William," Karen mentioned as both women joined Stephanie in the kitchen. "I think everyone but their dad calls them Bill and Bob..."

Hm... should I call them what everyone else does, or should I call them by the names Charles' calls them by? Susan wondered as she checked the big bird. *I can ask them what they'd prefer, and if they don't care, I think I'll do like Charles does...* "Yes, I think it's done, Stephanie. Just close the foil back up as well as you can to keep the moisture in, and put it back in the oven and turn the temperature setting to warm-only. It should keep until we're ready to eat. Oh, Karen, are y'all hungry?"

"Oh, no," Karen answered. "We lost an hour on the plane, and we had snacks on the plane. We can wait until Bill and Jenny get here."

The baby had woken up and was squirming more and more. "Well, I guess Joey here is ready for another meal," Karen corrected herself. "Should I go to one of the bedrooms to…"

"Oh, no!" Susan insisted, "You're welcome to breast feed anywhere you want in my house! If anyone doesn't like perfectly natural breast-feeding, they can be the ones to go somewhere else."

"Okay, thanks! That's the way Bob and I feel about it, too."

"Umm… Karen…" Stephanie said, "uh, would you mind showing me how you do that…?"

Susan cast a sharp glance at Stephanie, who noticed the look.

"No, Mom, I'm not pregnant," she said, then giggled. "Well, probably not… Not that I know of. But I've heard… some women have trouble breastfeeding, and I want to learn any tips I can for whenever my time does come…"

Oh, my! Susan smiled broadly as Stephanie sat next to Karen at the table, and Karen showed her how she held the baby and all the rest. *I guess I'd given up on Stephanie ever being a mother, but Lord, it looks like you've restored that, too!*

"Susan!" Charles voice called out a few minutes later from the living room. "It's William!"

Susan ran to him, and Stephanie excused herself to join the group in the living room.

They were all standing, looking out the window at an S.U.V. that had just parked behind Robert's rental car.

Susan stood beside Charles and put her arm around him and gently pulled. "Come, Charles. Introduce me to our son."

"Dad…" Stephanie said quietly, getting them to pause. "Bill's love language is quality-time."

Charles' head dropped, and no one else moved.

Oh, no… What should I do, Lord? Susan prayed.

"That's the… the worst possible… I was never there for him…" Charles whispered hoarsely.

"That's because you were busy doing your acts-of-service to provide for him," Stephanie said as she hugged him. "He didn't understand that then… but he does now."

They went outside and walked up to the car as William's wife

Julie and their daughter and son got out of the car and started to stretch. William sat still behind the wheel, looking straight ahead, until he was finally the last one to get out.

William was tall, with broad shoulders, a stern countenance, proud, and a little more formally dressed than anyone else. He was handsome in his way, but he didn't look as much like Charles in the face as Robert did. He simply stood beside the car as Charles and Susan approached.

"Hello, Dad," he said as he extended his arm for a handshake.

Charles took it and shook, and they dropped their arms to their sides.

"William... I can never apologize enough... but I'm so sorry... I never realized that I was hurting you so deeply by spending so much time at work..."

William nodded, then sniffed. It was the kind of sniff a man might make to try to avoid tears, not the kind that might reflect haughtiness. "I..." There was a long pause waiting for William.

He hung his head in the same way Charles had inside. "I... thought..." William paused again, and bit his lower lip. He took a deep breath and huffed it out, and still he struggled to talk.

Stephanie approached Julie and the kids and a little knot of people formed around her, leaving Charles and Susan alone with William.

"Growing up, I really thought..." he turned his head to the side and brushed at a tear. He looked at his father for a moment, then dropped his head again.

Stephanie was leading the other group to the house.

"I thought you didn't love me..." William said, barely audible.

Charles stepped up and put his hands on William's shoulders, tears streaming down Charles cheeks. "It's my fault, William, it's all my fault! I'm so sorry!"

William began to sob, and Charles closed the final gap to hug him. "Oh, son, I'm so sorry... I'm so, so sorry! I did love you, I always loved you, and I tried to show you in my own way... but I was too stupid to know you couldn't see love that way... I'm so sorry that I never showed you love the way you needed to see it..."

William pulled out a handkerchief and wiped his face and straightened up, and the men parted. William nodded again. "Yeah... Stephanie explained all that... but... it still hurts, Dad. It hurts bad. I always tried to ignore it, because it didn't hurt as much that way. But when Stephanie... well, it... it started hurting worse than ever..."

Because you weren't ignoring it anymore... Susan realized, *and because healing often causes pain...*

"What can I do, son? Is there anything I can do?"

"There you go, Dad. See? You're wanting to *do* something. I need *time.* I don't know how much, but perhaps a lot of time to... to assimilate this love-language business into my life."

"Can I... would it help... if I spent time with you? Just you and I? Or with you and your family?"

"Eventually, yes. I think so. But my feelings are really raw right now. I can't handle too much all at once, and this trip... this has me right at my limits, Dad."

"Okay, son. Okay. I'll put aside everything but family for you, any time you want me to, for as long as you want me to. Wherever you are, I'll come. We'll spend time any way you want to. Whatever you need. Whatever you want. You just tell me, okay?"

"Okay, Dad." William straightened up even more, throwing his shoulders back, and seemed to notice Susan for the first time. "So, I guess you're my new mom, huh? I guess you've deduced that I'm Bill Parker."

"Oh, I'm sorry..." Charles apologized.

"I'm very pleased to meet you," Susan said as they shook hands. "Would you prefer that I call you William, or Bill?"

"Oh, well, Dad's the only one who calls me William, but you're welcome to call me either one, I guess," he replied as they began to walk to the house.

"Well, since your father refers to you as William all the time, I think I'd like to do that, since you don't mind."

"Sounds fine."

Brian and Robert were standing just inside the living room, and Robert introduced Brian and William.

I'll bet they'll all want to talk in here, and I haven't met Julie or her kids yet... Susan rose up on her toes to kiss Charles' cheek and whisper "Happy Thanksgiving," as she started to head to the dining room.

Charles caught her and gave her a long hug, whispering back, "Oh, Susan..."

Oh, Charles... we've been blessed beyond measure...

She felt him start to release her, then squeeze her again before letting her go. "I'm going to go meet Julie. Why don't you stay in here with your boys?"

Charles nodded and brushed at his eyes.

Susan went into the dining room and Karen started to introduce Julie, but Susan begged for a delay. "Just a second," she said, grabbing a box of tissues.

"I want to give these to Charles and I'll be right back."

She delivered them as the men were taking seats, and Susan returned and met Julie, and a few minutes later she met their daughter and son when they went running through with the older two of Robert and Karen's children.

That seems familiar somehow... Déjà vu or something...?

The women sat at the dining room table and chatted happily about how nice it was to see Charles and his boys finally getting together without arguing, about raising families, events in the kids' lives, plans for the near future, and far future. Every few minutes one or more of the children would ask about eating, and their mothers kept putting them off.

Susan excused herself to use the bathroom, and she used the master bathroom to leave the hallway bathroom free for others. When she was done, just as she began to pass the doorway to Stephanie's old room, two boys came flying out and raced down the hallway. They were laughing and shouting, and had apparently not even noticed her. *That seems so familiar...*

Susan walked slowly down the hallway, then gasped as she remembered walking down that same hallway many years ago. *I must have been... less than ten years old... one of my uncles and aunts were here, and it was Thanksgiving... I don't even remember if it was Dad's brother or sister or Mom's, but they had a little baby... just a little older than Joey is, I think. It seems like they were poor, and Mom and Dad were helping them out, but I don't know what makes me think that.*

"Where's the bathroom?" one of the children asked Susan.

"It's right there, sweetie," Susan replied, pointing.

She walked a few more steps, and she could barely see a little bit of the living room and she could hear the chatter all over the house. *I remember... I stood right here, listening to Mom and Dad and whichever uncle and aunt they were, and I... I pictured... this... a house full of people, family... with kids running all over the place... was it a dream...? Probably not... I'm probably just pushing today back into old memory fragments... No! It was a dream... I went into the kitchen and told Mom I was going to have a lot of children someday, and they were all going to be in this house! Mom just patted me on the shoulder and said something about me getting married someday... but I told her that because I had that daydream...*

"You okay, Mom?" Brian asked, breaking her remembrances.

"Oh, yes, I'm fine, Brian," she said, and stood aside so Brian could go to the bathroom.

"You sure?"

"Yes, I was just... thinking... Oh, and I think the master bathroom is free..."

She returned to the table, and the conversations went on. *I was a child here. I bore two children and came back here to raise them. And now I have... three couples makes six children... and six grandchildren here in my house... together with the most wonderful husband in the world...*

"Grandma Susan, when are we gonna eat? One of the children asked plaintively, tugging on her skirt.

Susan noticed that she was getting quite hungry herself. *Well, I guess I'm the lady of the house, so maybe everyone else expects me to run the show. So...* "Well, are you girls getting hungry?"

Stephanie, Karen, and Julie were in general agreement, so Susan checked with the men, who also readily agreed, so the final preparations were made. Hands were washed and bathroom trips made as the extra table and chairs were set up in the dining room, leaving little room around them. Stephanie spread a large cloth she'd brought that covered both tables, making them almost look like a single table. By the time they were covered with food and place settings, it looked like it was ready for a magazine cover.

Charles sat at the head of the combined tables, farthest from the kitchen, and Susan sat at the end closest to the kitchen.

"Well, this is a beautiful meal," Charles said, "and if it's alright, rather than spend a lot of time talking while the food gets cold, how about if I lead us in a short prayer of thanks for the food and us all getting together. Then after the meal, let's go around the table and talk about things we're thankful for?"

Everyone agreed, and after Charles prayed, a clamor began as everyone talked and parents fixed plates of food for the kids, and the kids ran in and out from the garage. Susan had never managed such a large meal, but she instinctively ate quickly between jumping up over and over to refill serving bowls, the iced tea pitcher, quickly pop some more rolls into the oven, helping her grandchildren, and clearing the table and reloading it with desserts.

"May I start the 'official' giving of thanks?" Stephanie asked as the first slices of chocolate cake and pumpkin pie were being passed out, and she received enthusiastic encouragement, including Brian slipping his arm around her waist.

"I think a lot of us have a lot to be thankful for, but I think I've got everyone else beat. God delivered me from... well, my life was hellish. It was my fault... but my life was miserable because I was a miserable person... so the biggest thing God did for me wasn't rescuing me from my circumstances... it was rescuing me from myself. That was more than I'll ever deserve, but God gave me a whole lot more than that. He gave me my Mom back... no, scratch that, he gave me back to my Mom. Well, you know what I mean."

Susan got up to get a box of tissues, and cleared a space on the table to put them where everyone could reach them.

"And that was more than enough," Stephanie had continued, "but God gave me still more... I found out that my dad died years ago, but God gave me a new dad... a dad who..."

Stephanie choked up for a moment. "A dad who really showed me God's love. And *that* was more than enough, but again, God didn't stop there. I wanted to be friends with Brian because I missed my big brother so much. I wanted a friend, but I got so much more. Boy, did I get more," she said as she shoulder-hugged Brian.

Everyone clapped and cheered, and Brian went next, telling how he had waited for many years for God to bring him a woman who was perfect for him, and though it had often been painful to wait, it had also been well worth it.

William went next with two major highlights. First was Stephanie coming to visit and explaining how he and his dad had different love languages, and how that was responsible for their falling-out. The other thing was that he had been offered a senior partnership in his law firm. They had moved to Nashville, where he was to play a major role in managing the local office for two years, after which he would be promoted and move to the firm's headquarters in Atlanta. There was an awkward pause, and then he added that Charles and Susan would be welcome to come visit them sometime.

Charles and Susan both thanked him, and then Charles had to excuse himself for a few minutes.

When he returned to the table, Stephanie piped up, "Hey, if the rest of you don't mind waiting a little longer, there's some kinda big news I didn't tell you about yet. Dad's partner has hired a hotshot accountant who wants to take Dad's company public."

That statement launched a lot of congratulations and questions, and after a few minutes, Stephanie raised her voice over the din. "Hey, Dad, did you know that Bill's law firm handles initial public offerings?"

"No, I-I didn't know that…"

William looked half-sheepish, and half-hopeful, and Charles immediately said that he'd love to give the IPO legal work to him if he'd be interested. William was elated and began chattering about how that would make him a hero in his law firm, but his naturally reserved demeanor took over again quickly.

"One more thing, Dad," Stephanie said. "You and Mom have talked a lot about setting up a charitable foundation and funding a bunch of annuities and endowments, but that it's hard figuring out who to help and how much you should help each one. I think you should get Bill and Bob to help you decide those things."

Charles had wanted their involvement all along, of course, but it hadn't seemed possible until Stephanie had bridged the communication gaps between them. After that was discussed excitedly for a few minutes, Charles begged to postpone that topic until later so everyone else could share their thanksgivings. Everyone agreed and talked Charles into sharing next.

He used a few tissues himself as he talked of his confusion and pain in having thoroughly alienated his sons throughout their lifetimes, without understanding how it had come to that. Then God sent him an angel in the form of Susan, and it was through their pre-marriage counseling that he first learned about the different love languages, but he was afraid he found out far too late for it to do them any good. Charles went on to describe what a wonderful comfort and encouragement Susan was, and how perfectly he complemented her, and then he thanked Stephanie for being God's instrument of healing between himself and his sons.

Everyone at the table shed at least a few tears of happiness while Charles spoke.

Next Robert shared his joy in God's gift in the form of a brand new life in baby Joey, and he added how wonderful it was to find new life in his relationship with his father, thanks to Stephanie.

Karen and Julie took brief turns echoing their husbands, and then it was Susan's turn.

Her mind raced, trying to think of what to say first, and how to say it, but her love for words seemed to fail her as everyone else quietly waited. "Stephanie," she finally said. "God gave me my daughter back… and now we're sisters in Christ… and then…"

Susan looked at the new faces around the table. "And then he multiplied my blessings, with two more daughters and three more sons..."

Someone pulled a few tissues out of the box and passed them to her. She didn't notice who it was, because despite her tears, she was gazing steadily at the man at the far end of the table.

"Charles..." Susan whispered, "...the man I always longed for... my best friend ever... God gave me... the man of my dreams..."

Susan's six children all cheered and applauded, but Charles' loving face was all she noticed.

~~~~~~~~~~~~

That evening, Susan made a pot of decaf coffee while Charles and William waited for it with their coats on. William took the first cup, black, and took it out the back door while Susan added a half-packet of artificial sweetener and a spoonful of non-dairy creamer to a cup for Charles.

"Can you believe what Stephanie did for me?" Charles said quietly as he leaned lightly against Susan. "For us? Going and talking to William and Robert, and, and..." he choked up and couldn't continue.

"Do you realize what you've done for Stephanie?" Susan said.

"That was all God's doing. 'Every good and perfect gift is from above, coming down from the Father...'"

"Yes... every one," Susan agreed as she picked up her own cup and followed Charles to the dining room's back door. He buttoned up his coat and went out to sit next to William.

Now that's a wonderful thing to see. I guess it's the opposite of God's children 'perishing for lack of knowledge'... this is... what's the opposite of perishing... prospering? We're prospering because we've gained knowledge...

As Susan stood by the door watching them and cradling her coffee cup, Stephanie and Brian passed through the dining room as they went from the living room to the kitchen. They also poured cups of coffee, but temporarily ignored the coffee while they hugged and whispered.

Susan could hear Robert, Karen, and Julie talking in her living room, and children playing in the bedrooms.

That daydream of this house being filled with family... and my dream of a special man discovering my secret, as a sign that he was a man just for me... God was working in my life way back then... decades before I became a Christian. And that first night, when Charles dropped me off at home, and I asked him what color my eyes were... it seemed impossible for that old dream to be true... I had been resigned to life as it was for me then, and then this man came along and asked me for a date... and it was amazing how quickly my emotions went wild... Charles was figuratively sweeping me off my feet just as the man in my dream did it literally...

She saw William point at something and speak a few words, and Charles nodded in response.

If Charles hadn't noticed the faint green tinge on the edge of my eyes... I'd have told him I never wanted to see him again... I'd have hurt either way, but I know that's what I would have done after all the years of heartbreak I had with Marty... there's no way I would've risked falling for a man again if it hadn't been for that sign from my dream... and... if Charles hadn't noticed... Billy would have come that Saturday night anyway... and everything would be different... so different... Stephanie... Billy... Brian... William and Robert... we'd all be so much worse off... but we aren't... all because God led Charles to that little apartment over the coffee shop... all because Charles was doing his best to follow God's will... and because he noticed the green in my eyes...

Feedback...

Like this book? Tell us what your favorite passage is, and why, at www.InitmatePress.com/Contact.htm. Don't like it? Hate it? Feel free to tell us that, too.

If you want to encourage Georgia to write more novels like this one, a good way to encourage her is to post favorable reviews on Amazon, Barnes and Noble, or Facebook.

While you're at www.InitmatePress.com, you can submit your email address and we'll let you know when we publish new books.

You May Also Like...

For more information about alcohol and other addictions, see *Thorns in the Heart: A Christian's Guide to Dealing With Addiction*, by Dr. Steven Stiles, available on Amazon.com. (Not affiliated with Intimate Press.)

For more information about the 5 Love Languages, see www.5LoveLanguages.com (not affiliated with Intimate Press). Dr. Chapman's web site has free online assessments, descriptions of the different love languages, videos, and other valuable resources.

Grandma's Sex Handbook, a non-fiction work that in the words of one professional reviewer, "encourages women to accept and embrace their sexuality as God's natural design. It is well organized and extremely thorough, written in a conversational tone that puts readers at ease... a forthright and honest exploration of nearly every aspect of sexuality between couples..."

Forgotten Dreams is a Christian-oriented, sexually-explicit novel is based on the premise that there's a critical difference between sexual fantasy and lust, as described in *Grandma's Sex Handbook*, and the "Fantasy vs. Lust" chapter is available online for free at www.GrandmasSexHandbook.com.